The Court

The Court

Elizabeth Walker

GUILD PUBLISHING
LONDON · NEW YORK · SYDNEY · TORONTO

This edition published 1989 by
Guild Publishing
by arrangement with
Judy Piatkus (Publishers) Ltd

CN 2427

Printed and bound in Great Britain by
Mackays of Chatham PLC, Chatham, Kent

Chapter One

A soft breeze was rustling the grass. High up, almost out of sight, a hawk hung quivering in the air. So early in the morning the sun held little heat and Henry shivered. He flapped his long arms and said grumpily, 'I hope it's worth it. This was supposed to be a rest, not some sort of survival exercise.'

His wife shot him an anxious glance. 'Don't you like it? I thought you wanted to come.'

When he didn't reply Charlotte leaned back against the Land Rover, taking in the sheer beauty of the morning. The world seemed wider here somehow. The land stretched beyond the limits of her vision, the sky was vast, limitless. In the distance a flock of tiny birds seemed to be swimming across the grass, rising and falling in long, flowing waves of movement. As yet there was little colour. The sky was pale, the grass bleached to a sandy white, except in the purple shadows, untouched by dawn.

'If only it wasn't so bloody cold.' Henry flapped again, huddling into his Shetland wool jumper and stamping his feet.

'It's going to be much colder in the balloon,' said Charlotte. 'Shall I get your coat?'

'I wish you wouldn't fuss!' He reached into the Land Rover and picked up his jacket himself. 'I feel an absolute fool,' he grumbled. 'Tembo's in shorts and shirt.'

'I suppose they're used to it.' Charlotte shaded her eyes to see if the truck was coming. She was a tall woman, with a handsome high-boned face, her greying hair held back in a silk scarf.

Henry flapped his arms again. 'If anyone's used to cold, it ought to be us. The Hellyns have frozen to death in Yorkshire since time immemorial. But I wish the sun would get up.'

A plume of dust appeared on the far horizon. It was the truck, bearing the balloon, basket and gas cylinders. Tembo flashed his

1

brilliant smile and slid down from the bonnet of the Land Rover, his bare soles thudding into the dust. 'She comes now, Lord. She comes soon for us to fly.'

Henry grunted and as Tembo walked away, Charlotte said softly, 'What is the matter, darling? Are you feeling ill?'

'I shall be fine once we can do something. Everything takes so long in this bloody country.'

'I thought that was what you liked about it. The pace of life.'

He smiled, grudgingly. 'That was yesterday.'

The truck was followed by the Land Rover from a neighbouring game lodge, carrying a couple from Scotland and a German on his own. They were all festooned with cameras and Henry muttered, 'Oh, my God! The length and breadth of Kenya is filled with the sound of camera shutters, like a million machine guns.'

'Darling, please!' She shot him a pleading look. If Henry took it upon himself to behave badly, the day would be impossible.

As the newcomers approached she stepped forward rather regally, smiling, her hand outstretched. 'How do you do? I was so pleased to hear that someone else wanted to come on the trip.'

Tembo, with that infectious African enthusiasm, leaped in with introductions. 'Lord, Lady, this is Mr Mrs Harris, and Mr Herr Waldstrom. They is Lord and Lady these two. Very special. Lord and Lady Melville.'

Charlotte shook hands. 'Isn't it a lovely morning? We're staying with the Demouths, which is a little remote but very pleasant.'

'Oh. Yes. How do you do.' Mrs Harris seemed rather overcome, especially since Henry remained by the Land Rover, looking forbidding.

But at last it seemed that the balloon might be assembled. Half a dozen men had jumped down from the truck and were hauling out ropes and canisters with the familiarity of long practice. A black man in a crisp safari suit strode towards them, stepping in that liquid, jointless way that was so typically African. 'Aren't they an amazing people?' whispered Charlotte. 'I feel quite the white hunter.'

Henry grunted, and she glanced at him nervously. He sounded bored, but here, seeing this, it was impossible. If only they hadn't started so early; Henry was never at his best in the morning.

'We are almost ready,' said the African, speaking precise English. 'I am your pilot. Please make sure you all have sufficient clothing. It is most cold in a balloon.' He looked anxiously at Henry, still shivering by the car.

'We'll be fine,' said Henry, standing up straight and dropping his hands into his pockets. Involuntarily his shoulders hunched inwards.

2

'Feeling better, darling?' asked Charlotte.

'I wasn't aware that I was feeling ill.'

'The balloon, minutes before only a collapsed bladder, was swelling into a vast, blue and white globe. 'I really feel quite nervous,' said Mrs Harris, and the German, already taking photographs, remarked, 'It is indeed exciting, is it not? On this holiday I have taken more pictures than ever before. It is so wonderful. So much as I wished, and then more.'

'Yes, isn't it?' Charlotte beamed at him. 'I thought it might be dreadfully commercialised, and I can't bear that sort of thing. But with the country, and the animals, it can't be.' Henry came up behind her and she turned to him. 'We're so glad we came, aren't we, dear?'

He put his hands on her shoulders and forced a smile. 'Of course we are. I just wish we didn't have to get up at the crack of dawn every single morning.'

'We take a nap at lunchtine,' confided Mr Harris.

'Oh, he does that,' said Charlotte, laughing. 'But it doesn't make him any better-tempered at five o'clock next day somehow!'

Tembo came bounding towards them. 'Lord. Lady. Everyones. Balloon goes up now.'

'At last!' Henry visibly roused himself. He fastened the button of his jacket, rubbed his hands together and swept them all with a glare from his rather prominent blue eyes. 'Off we go, then. Give me your arm, Charlotte.'

With the air of one taking first position on a shoot, he led her to the balloon.

Henry stood against the wicker basket, watching the earth glide by beneath him. Everyone was entranced, and for once even the cameras were idle. There was only the silence and the wind, bringing the scent of trees and water. A clump of thick mopane scrub was away to his left, and as he watched a tiny, spike-horned antelope stepped out.

'Charlotte.' They were so close to the creature he felt he must whisper. 'Charlotte, look!'

She closed her hand on his arm and he knew she had seen. Silently the balloon drifted towards the scrub, coming lower and lower. They could see the twist on the horns, like barley sugar, the short rope of its tail. Suddenly he felt disorientated. How many times, how many hundred times, had he sat at his desk at The Court and seen that self-same head? It had just this air of bright curiosity, preserved since the very day his great-grandfather bagged it.

Then with a sudden roar the burner fired, and the antelope, leaping on pencil legs, careered back into the bushes.

3

'I am so sorry,' said the pilot, grinning. 'But I should not like to come down in such country. Most unpleasant. I trust you enjoyed the antelope.'

Henry glanced at him. Apparently Toto, the faithful native guide recorded so movingly in his ancestor's letters home, had turned into this educated know-all. What would the old boy say if he could see him now, the fifteenth Earl of Melville, poncing about in a balloon, snapping photographs instead of trophies? It made him smile.

They soared away again, high into a sky that was turning from palest blue into a saucer of deep, hot metal. Zebra ran beneath them – possibly scared by lion, it was hard to tell. The pilot apologised. It was not a good morning, they had seen little.

'But I think for us it is wonderful,' said the German, spreading wide his hands. 'To see the world, and such a world, like this!'

'I suppose it does have a certain aerial charm,' said Henry. He cleared his throat.

Although the sun was hot, he found he was still shivering. Despite himself it became a deep, racking tremor that he could not control. He closed his eyes, only for a second, and when he opened them again Charlotte's face was close to him suddenly, looking so much younger with her tan. He must have fallen. She seemed to be mouthing silently. He gripped on to the basket and tried to stand.

'Henry? Henry, what is it? Oh God, I knew he was ill.'

'It is the cold. I will come down at once, the truck will come to us.' The pilot pulled toggles, letting puffs of gas out of the balloon.

Henry, half-crouched against the side of the basket, said grimly: 'I should much prefer it if you didn't make a fuss. It's only a chill.'

They made an easy landing, settling on to the grass with the balloon descending on to them like popped bubblegum. Henry was helped out and sat on a dried hummock of earth, white-faced and bad-tempered. 'Will you please stop all this, Charlotte!' he kept urging. 'I'll be fine in a few minutes. It's nothing.'

The truck had seen them come down and was there in minutes, and only minutes later Tembo roared up in the Land Rover. Charlotte went up to him. 'He's ill, Tembo!' she burst out. 'Will you take us home, please?'

'There's nothing the matter with me,' snapped Henry.

Tembo looked from his white and drawn face to Charlotte's and said diplomatically, 'Anyhow, time to go back and see missus. Drink of whisky set us up, eh, Lord?'

Henry chuckled briefly. 'Best suggestion I've heard all morning.'

They were staying with Genevieve Demouth, on her sprawling farm on the edge of the game reserve. They had know her for ever, but this

4

was the first time they had been out. Until Henry's father died they'd been quite short of cash, but now he was gone at last and Henry had the title and the purse strings. It had been Henry's idea to visit, a celebration of long overdue independence. Genevieve and Henry had gone out together briefly, before either of them married. Then Henry met Charlotte and after a while Genevieve became engaged to Jan and came out to Kenya. She'd written frantic letters that first year, begging her friends to come and see her. Once she and Jan had come to England. Charlotte recalled a horrible wild party, with women running around naked and Henry always missing.

Genevieve was in her garden when the Land Rover drove up: a tall, plain woman in her fifties, with skin like leather. She came over at once.

'Good God, Tembo, what have you done to Lord Henry?'

'He sick, missus. They bring the balloon down quick.'

Henry struggled to get out. 'Complete fuss about nothing, as you can see, Genevieve. Got a bit of a tummy bug, that's all.'

'You do look a bit washy,' commented Genevieve.

'He looked terrible in the balloon,' said Charlotte.

'Probably a bug, as Henry says. Why don't you take him to lie down?'

Genevieve watched as Charlotte and Tembo helped Henry along the narrow path to the guest bungalow. They brushed against the bougainvillaea, and the scent hung on the warm air. Henry looked so old suddenly. And this was the man who had taken her virginity, seducing her in one of the bedrooms at a terrible debutante ball. She wondered if he remembered. But then, he was so good-looking and such a catch, he'd had dozens of girls. And out of them all, the beauties, the sirens, and the plain girls like her who would let him take them to bed, out of them all he had to choose Charlotte. Genevieve always wondered about it; although in those days Charlotte had been lovely, and there was money of course, not a fortune but enough. Nonetheless the match always did seem one-sided, Henry so forceful, so much in charge, and Charlotte becoming paler and paler by comparison.

Genevieve wrinkled her nose. Once she would have given anything to marry Henry, but now she thanked God for her deliverance. Not that life was easy. It was ten years since Jan died – ten years of heat, dust and little money. Her mind went to the shaded grave behind the orchard, and automatically she shook herself. She had three boys, three good strong boys, that she ruled and adored in equal quantity. It was enough.

*   *   *

5

In the evening Henry and Charlotte joined the family on the verandah before dinner. Giant moths beat their wings against the mosquito screens, and there was a deep bass accompaniment: the grunting of a family of warthogs that lived across the stream. All Genevieve's boys stood up as they entered, three blond shaggy heads just like Jan's.

'I hope you're feeling better, sir,' said Edward, the eldest at nineteen.

'I'm quite well, thank you,' said Henry, lowering himself rather stiffly into one of the long, padded chairs.

'Did you see much?' continued the boy. 'I've never been up in the balloon. It looks fantastic, but it costs a mint and we can't afford it. Too bad you were ill.'

'Yes.' Henry accepted a whisky from Tembo and closed his eyes for a second.

Genevieve said, 'Boys, take yourselves off somewhere, you can help in the kitchen. We want some peace and quiet.'

Obediently all three got up and went into the house. Edward caught her eye and grimaced, because he wanted to stay and talk. He was more than old enough, and yet there Ma went again, treating him like a child. He closed the door with a jerk.

'You amaze me, Genevieve,' said Henry. 'You've brought the boys up so well. I don't know where we went wrong.'

'I thought your twins were doing all right,' she said. 'Aren't they at university?'

Charlotte nodded. 'Oxford. The same degree, politics and economics. Their housemaster thought they ought to go together. Marcus is often — well, unsettled.'

With a snort, Henry said, 'Is that what you call it? My dear Genevieve, it is not unusual for Marcus to be found blind drunk at four in the morning outside the Oxford branch of Marks and Spencer.' Faint colour touched his cheeks and he leaned forward in animation. 'Drink, drugs, and for all I know thieving and women, that's what Marcus learns about at Oxford. He'll be lucky if he isn't sent down this term.'

'You know Angus won't let that happen.' A crease was forming between Charlotte's brows. This simmering worry about Marcus never improved when discussed.

He laughed briefly, a harsh chuckle. 'Genevieve, there has to be some advantage in having twins. When one behaves like a lunatic, the other can always take care of him. I suppose we should be grateful. And at least we have the girls.'

'Aren't they still at school?' asked Genevieve.

'Lisa is, yes,' said Henry. 'Mara's rather given it up. But she's an absolute gem, isn't she, darling?'

Charlotte looked glum. 'Yes.'

Henry grinned fondly. 'You should see her, Genevieve. Our pretty, gangly girl has become quite beautiful! A stunner, and I'm not the only one who thinks so. If The Court had a moat I'd fill it with crocodiles and chuck in the ranks of mooning lovers.'

Charlotte shifted restlessly in her chair. 'I do feel we should have sent her to Switzerland.' She rubbed at her forehead. Her nerves are showing, thought Genevieve.

Edward came in with a new bottle of whisky. 'I thought you might need this, Ma,' he said.

Henry almost choked on his drink. 'Can you believe it, Charlotte? They even bring us booze!'

'I can't bear children making a nuisance of themselves,' remarked Genevieve, glowering at her son. 'Off with you, Edward, Now, what are you two going to do tomorrow?'

Under Edward's aggrieved stare, Charlotte said quickly, 'Oh, I think we'll take it easy for a few days. I don't think Henry's quite up to scratch yet.'

'I'm as fit as a fiddle,' he declared, swallowing most of his drink. 'I'm here for a change of air, not to coddle myself in bed!'

The two women exchanged a glance. There was a pallor beneath his tan, he looked tired to the point of exhaustion.

Tembo appeared in the doorway, flashing his brilliant smile. 'Dinner is serving, missus,' he declared. Henry put down his drink and stood up, extending a hand to Charlotte to help her out of the long chair. It annoyed Genevieve. Charlotte was ineffectual and vague, she didn't deserve to have someone like Henry. She was devoted to him, of course, even when he was ill and bad-tempered. But that gesture, somehow intimate and caring, made Genevieve feel very alone. Just then Henry turned and extended his other hand to her, and suddenly she remembered that he had always been an unusually charming man.

'Come, my dear, we can't keep the young lions waiting,' he said, and ushered both women before him into the house.

Three weeks later Genevieve and Edward came to the airport to see them off. Charlotte was brown and well, but beside her Henry still looked pale and rather thin. 'You're not eating enough,' said Genevieve, giving him the critical appraisal that she usually reserved for a horse.

7

'Nonsense! I've eaten like a fighting cock. I don't know why we put up with Britain. We shall have to get ourselves a place out here, won't we darling?'

'What a lovely idea.' Charlotte reached up to kiss Edward on the cheek. With the enthusiastic friendliness that only an imminent parting can arouse, she said, 'You must let him come to us, Genevieve. Why not for Mara's ball? He'd love it.'

Edward's eyes flew to his mother's. She said, 'You'll be far too busy to be bothered with Edward. And he's too young to go jaunting off to Europe!'

'My dear, he is nineteen and a young man.' Henry rested a hand on Genevieve's shoulder. 'You send him. Do him the world of good.'

'And he could be really useful,' said Charlotte. 'It is Mara's season – he can take her round to parties and things. It's always nice to have an escort, and our boys won't oblige.'

'When has Mara ever lacked escorts?' demanded Henry. 'But we'll find something for him to do. Let the boy come, my dear, it's about time he saw the old country. We'll put him up in some draughty turret and he'll return to the farm reconciled forever to his lot. Best thing you could do for him.'

'Well ...' Genevieve was conscious of a great and shameful reluctance. She sent her boys off on safari without a qualm, but she felt instinctively that English society was far more dangerous. She forced herself to say, 'Edward would love it, I'm sure. Shall I write to you?'

'Yes, indeed,' said Charlotte, 'but make sure he comes in time for the ball. He mustn't miss that. Henry dear, they're calling our flight.'

They embraced and parted. Genevieve and Edward stood watching as Henry's tall figure moved slowly away, and Charlotte turned and waved.

Edward said, 'You won't let me go, will you?'

Genevieve, watching her friends pass from sight, said, 'What? Oh, yes, you can go. Yes. It's probably time you saw something of the world. Come along now.' Briskly she smoothed her greying hair, turned and marched towards the exit.

Chapter Two

Mara sat in the deep window embrasure, looking out at the rain. There was nothing else to look at. Occasionally a bird flew across the garden, or a cow in the park walked towards the lake, flicking a wet tail. But she knew that if she sat there forever there would be nothing of interest to see. Everything was tranquil; everything was green; and she was bored.

Today the statues looked dark and oily. Bought by the cartload by some previous earl who had grabbed everything Italian that was not tied down, they dominated the gardens like an odd tribe. Almost as soon as the old man, her grandfather, died her father had installed floodlighting, so that at night the gardens looked eerie and unreal. It was an act of defiance. The old earl had never liked the things.

How she wished her father was home, but he wasn't due back till the following afternoon. Without him the house seemed joyless somehow. He was the one who inspired things, who organised picnics and dances, and jokes. If Henry was here today they would go and have tea in Harrogate, or they could fish perhaps, for muddy tiddlers in the lake, which she was much too old for and never did when she was alone. If only he was here! She remembered all those days at school when she had longed to be home, to be in the midst of everything. And now she was home, and everything was somewhere else.

Suddenly something caught her interest: Lisa, enveloped in a long oilskin, walking her fat spaniel across the lawn. Irritation sparked within Mara, she knelt on the seat and rapped on the window glass.

'Lisa! Lisa! That's my oilskin!'

Her sister turned and looked up at the house. A small, pale, pointed face. Then she shrugged, pretending not to understand, and went on.

'Damn her!' All Mara's boredom flared into annoyance. She got up, swinging her long golden hair back from her face. Lisa was always borrowing her things, whether or not they fitted, with the sole point of infuriating her sister. And more often than not she succeeded. Sinking her hands into the pockets of her skirt, Mara went in search of someone to talk to.

Angus was in the library, working at one of the desks. She knew at once which twin it was, though she could hardly have explained how she differentiated. In looks they were identical, but everything about them was different. Marcus would never have worked in quite that calm way. He was always restless, on the verge of distraction.

'You don't have to work all this holiday, do you?'

Angus put down his pen. 'It's such a filthy day I thought I should get some done. What's the matter?'

Mara flung herself down in one of the worn leather chairs that hadn't been recovered since the library was revamped, two hundred years before. 'Lisa's borrowing my things again. My oilskin, and it's a foot too long! Why on earth does she do it?'

'Perhaps she couldn't find her own.'

Mara let out her breath in an angry sigh, swinging one long leg over the other. Angus felt sudden sympathy for Lisa. To be the runt of the litter, the pale, undersized copy, was hard indeed. Her attempts at rivalry, if that's what they were, seemed pathetic.

'You shouldn't take it so seriously,' he said.

'Shouldn't I? How would you feel if Marcus borrowed all your things, all the time? Except he does, of course.'

'Yes. But I know, it's different.'

She considered him for a second. Angus was always a peacemaker, he never wanted to get involved. 'Aren't you bored?' she demanded.

He grinned. 'Not terribly, no. But we could go for a ride.'

'It's raining. And Lisa's borrowed my oilskin.' But anything was better than stifling indoors. She got up. 'I'll find something, I suppose.'

She went up to her room to change and put up her hair. Doubling over before the mirror to do her ponytail, she viewed her bathroom door at an unusual angle. It was open. There, on the shelf, was the perfume bottle her father had given her before he went away. The cap was off. 'Lisa!' She straightened up, stormed to the bathroom and checked the evidence. Damn the girl!

As they walked across to the stables the rain began to fall in earnest. Mara and Angus sheltered in the coachhouse doorway, underneath a thick fringe of creeper. Water ran down in front of them like a frosted glass curtain and the stone drains, made in the shape of gargoyles and dragons, bubbled and overflowed.

10

'I just wish she wouldn't be so sneaky!' Mara complained.

'She isn't. She lets you know she's done it.'

Mara laughed. Her sister might drive her mad but they were still close. 'I suppose so.'

The rain hissed against the creeper and from the stables came the sounds of the boy tacking up. 'Where's Marcus?' asked Mara suddenly.

Her brother hit his riding whip against his boot. 'In his room. In the dark.'

'Still?'

Angus nodded. For a moment they stood in silence. Suddenly, as if he could bear no more of his thoughts, Angus strode out into the rain. 'Come on! It's only water.'

'You're mad,' said Mara, and winced at her own choice of words. But Angus seemed not to notice. He barged into the stable and demanded his horse.

Even the horses hated the rain. They crossed the park with hunched backs, tails clamped down tight. Water ran down Mara's neck, between the cleft of her breasts, off the hem of her too short oilskin and on to her saddle, leaving her sitting in a puddle. She pushed her mare up beside Angus's good black hunter.

'When I go to London, I shan't ever go out in the rain. I'll dance till dawn and stay in bed till lunchtime. I'll have fifty satin night-dresses and two dozen pairs of shoes.'

'And Father will be fool enough to buy them for you,' said Angus wryly.

'Why not? Now the old skinflint's gone, he can afford it.'

'I hope he can spare a few coppers for the house! It's falling about our ears.'

As if on command they each swung their horses round, and sat facing The Court. Dark, almost black in the rain, it filled the near horizon. Over the centuries it had grown and grown again, swelling from the medieval centre until it spanned the gardens that surrounded it like a huge mongrel dog.

'Don't you hate it?' said Mara. 'Other people have houses they can manage, that they can afford to heat. They don't have roofs that leak through two floors!'

'No.' The wind blew a squall of rain towards them, stinging their faces. 'I can't imagine life without it,' said Angus. 'The Hellyns without The Court. They'd be nothing.'

'They'd be warm and dry, that's for certain. If it rains on the night of my ball, people will have to dance in wellington boots! It ought to be pulled down.'

11

'Don't say you want to build a housing estate for the deserving poor!' mocked her brother.

She made a face at him, swinging her mare away across the grass. 'I'd prefer a house for us. With a decent hot water system and a sound roof!' They both knew she didn't mean it. The Court was part of them, part of their lives. None of them ever came back to it without a sense, almost, of relief.

Angus let go his hunter. The big horse stretched into a raking canter, outrunning the mare. They were headed for the moor, across the park and up through woodland tracks to the gate. It was quiet in the wood but when they stepped from the shelter of the trees the wind caught them, tearing like a dog at horse and rider alike. Angus glanced across at his sister. Her scarf was sodden with rain, her cheeks blotched and mottled. He wondered at her. Eyes as blue as corn-flowers, full lips the colour of plums. Even at her worst she was lovely enough to make the breath catch.

The Court had been built in a rich fold of land, formed by centuries of silt washed down from the moors by wind and weather. Of the estate, only Home Farm was prosperous, for the rest was hill country, fit only for sheep. The rocks gleamed black through the scrub grass and bracken, like the wet backs of seals. This was poor country, harsh country, where only the foxes lived well.

They made for Hell Rocks, a granite outcrop where nothing hellish had ever happened as far as anyone could tell. In the shelter they could dismount and regain their breath. The horses pulled at the yellowing grass between the boulders.

'Do you think Marcus will get his degree?'

Angus shrugged. Then he shook his head. 'He oughtn't to go back. He's at his worst there, I can't keep enough of an eye on him. He does what the others do, drinking, popping a pill or two. It's not good for him.'

'Have you spoken to Father?'

He looked his sister in the eye. 'Now what good would that do? He won't have Marcus see a doctor and that's that. Won't think about it. He just says he's got to pull himself together.'

Mara never could bear to hear Henry criticised. 'It's hard for him,' she defended. 'Marcus is the eldest, he's the heir.'

'I don't think that makes it any easier for me.'

She didn't want to talk like this. She sat down on a rock and took out an apple, biting into it with strong, white teeth.

'Did you bring me one?' demanded Angus.

'No.'

'Then give me half.'

12

Reluctantly she handed over the apple. He ate it though she was sure he wasn't hungry. 'You never fail to be selfish,' he said thoughtfully.

'I'm always letting people have things! I have to with Lisa around.'

'It doesn't seem to have cramped your style.'

Mara made a face and went to her horse, waiting for a leg-up. Angus tossed her into the saddle and remounted himself. Together they went out into the wind racing across the moor, the horses leaning against the gale. It was a relief to reach the shelter of the trees, where last autumn's leaves still lay thick and unrotted. It was quieter here, the trees soughing far above their heads. When they came out below the wood the rain had eased off. The valley was spread below them, washed as clean as the sky. Twin spirals of smoke rose up far to the left, the silver billows of a wood fire.

'Damn! The gypsies are back in Slates Lane.'

Angus didn't know what to do. They came every year and stayed for as long as anyone would let them. The old earl had been ruthless, moving them on within days, but Henry was more lenient. It might have been kindness; more likely that he was setting his own seal on things. His father had lived too long. Henry had been champing at the bit for years and would go against what had gone before just for the sake of it. If the decision were Angus's — and today it was — what would be right? However briefly they stayed they left behind pram wheels, half burned bonfires, broken fences and old tin cans. But when they moved with their coughing children and ragged grey washing, it was to live on a patch of mud next to a chemical works in Leeds.

'Leave it till tomorrow,' advised Mara. 'Father will be home.'

'He'll think I should have done something. Or that Marcus should.' They went on, more quickly now as the horses scented the stable and their riders tea and toast. Angus thought about Marcus, about his degree. If it hadn't been for Marcus he would have read law and not politics. He should have read law. He felt unsettled about everything. He felt that he hovered between events.

Suddenly Mara let out a cry. 'He's back! Look, he's back!'

There, on the gravel before the great oak door, was the Rolls-Royce. Henry was home.

That night they had a celebration dinner, in the formal dining-room. On this cool summer evening the chintz and yellow paint of the family room might have been more pleasant, but instead Curtiss set out the silver on the long oak table in the panelled dining hall, lit by antlered sconces and candelabra. But the fire redeemed it, big enough to roast

13

an ox, sending out a red glow that defeated the night. Still Henry shivered, hunched in his chair with his back to the blaze.

'How have you all been? This damned climate, I'd forgotten how dreadful it is. I told Genevieve we should buy somewhere in Kenya, and I think I ought to mean it.'

'You're just tired,' said Charlotte. 'It's been a long journey.'

'And we've all been bored to tears without you,' declared Mara.

Henry laughed. 'How you do flatter me, my darling!'

But he barely toyed with his food, pushing a few pieces of meat around his plate and instead drinking the wine. Angus chatted about the estate, about a problem with sheep scab on a neighbouring moor, a tenant with a complaint about ramblers. When Curtiss came to take away the plates, Henry said, 'What about you, Marcus? How have you been?'

'He's been very well,' said Angus quickly.

'Yes. He's been fine,' agreed Mara.

'I think I'd like to hear it from Marcus himself, if you don't mind. How's the work?'

Marcus looked down at his plate, flinching slightly as Curtiss moved to take it. 'I – er – I'm – I'm very well.'

'I don't think I asked that, did I? How is your work? Your degree?'

'I – I've done what I could. What I can. Haven't I done that, Angus?'

Henry threw down his napkin. 'Can't you at least answer a simple question without recourse to your brother? Can't you at least do that?'

'Henry –' Charlotte put out her hand to him. At the same moment Mara got up from her place in a flurry of satin. She sank down beside her father, her hand on his arm. 'Don't squabble on your first night back! Let's talk about parties, about my ball.'

Charlotte withdrew her hand. As always, when Mara demanded her father's attention she received it. And on this occasion Charlotte was glad.

'Is the world ready for you, my darling? Are you ready to be launched on all those unsuspecting young men?' Henry leaned back, enjoying himself.

'They'll be taken by storm,' declared his daughter, and they both laughed. It was a game they played, mocking their own charm and good looks, when there was nothing either of them took more seriously.

Lisa said, 'Curtiss is waiting to serve the puddings, Mara. Do sit down.'

'I'm not stopping you, am I, Curtiss?' said Mara.

'He can't get past you! Oh, do get up, Mara.'

But it was Henry who moved her, tapping her arm with his long brown fingers. Curtiss set down overcooked lemon meringue pie, fruit salad and the cheese board. Henry took a small square of camembert.

'Shall we dance after dinner?' said Mara. 'When we've finished this horrible pie. The cooking's getting worse, Mother. Since you've been away we've had underdone liver twice a week.'

'It doesn't seem too bad,' murmured Charlotte. She had no wish to dismiss a cook on her first day back. 'Why don't we dance? Would you like that, Henry?'

All at once he pushed back his chair. His face was drawn, white. 'Curtiss — I think I need your arm. Rather tired — go to my room.'

They all sat, rigid, until he was gone. Then Mara said in a high, tight voice 'He's ill. He isn't tired, he's terribly ill.'

And suddenly, without any warning, Marcus began to sob. No-one stopped him. It seemed entirely appropriate.

Chapter Three

Mara was trying on hats. It was an old game, played ever since they were old enough to go up into the attics and find the boxes, piled ten high on the worn floorboards. Once the old man had come out of his rooms and caught them, just when Marcus was being a cavalier, wearing a huge felt hat with bright red plumes.

'My God! D'you think I'm housing a bloody poofter?'

The saying had been incorporated into family lore. If the boys put on so much as a flowery tie someone would mimic the old man's guttural rage. 'My God! D'you think − ?' and the point was made.

Nowadays, with the old earl at long last dead, they could try on hats forever. Mara had brought a dozen or so downstairs, away from the drips, and kept them in one of the unused rooms. There were far too many of those at The Court, rooms for which there was neither usable furniture nor adequate heating. For this room though she had discovered a pier glass and a lumpy sofa. While she tried on hats, Marcus lay on the sofa and watched.

'Do you like this?' She tried on blue velvet, dipped forties-style over one eye.

'Too small. The straw's good. You should wear it for Ascot.'

'Good heavens, no! I'll have a new one. Like this though.' She put on the straw again, a wide cartwheel draped in tulle. She looked like an extravagant milkmaid, or an early female motorist. Mara smiled at her own gorgeous reflection.

There was rap at the window. 'Help! What's that?' She jumped behind the sofa.

'It's all right,' said Marcus. 'It isn't anything.'

'What do you mean − look! There's someone there!'

Marcus looked from her to the window. He laughed, and passed a hand across his eyes. 'So there is. You do see it too, don't you?'

'Don't start that again. Is it a burglar do you think? One doesn't expect them to knock somehow.'

The figure on the far side of the glass knocked again, loudly, and mouthed words. Mara went to the window, still wearing the hat. The glass distorted close images. It was two hundred years old and flawed. 'What do you want?' she yelled.

The figure, apparently a young man, yelled back, 'I've come to visit! For the ball!'

'Go away,' said Mara. 'You're three weeks too early.'

'But – I'm Edward Demouth! I'm expected.'

'Not at windows, you aren't! Go round through the kitchen garden, it's at the end of this wing. Go on !'

The face retreated. Mara stood at the window and watched him tramp back across the straggling lavender bushes to the path. 'I wonder how long he's been trying to get in,' she mused.

Marcus sat up, his hands clasped together in front of him. 'Don't go,' he whispered. 'Please don't! He's the devil!'

'Darling, of course he isn't! He's from Kenya.'

She felt helpless and bewildered. Before her eyes Marcus seemed to crumple. There was nothing to say, nothing to do. No amount of explanation helped. He began to mutter, twisting his hands together in ceaseless motion. She was conscious of an overpowering urge to escape.

'I'll go and see to him,' she said quickly. 'Lie down for a minute. Have a doze. Try on the hats.'

'Don't go, Mara! Please! Don't go!' Marcus's eyes burned with an agony of desperation. He got up, as if to hang on to her. Mara opened the door and fled.

She found Edward Demouth standing disconsolate between rows of basil and sage. At first she couldn't believe he was the person she had seen through the glass, he was so tall and brown, his hair bleached almost white. But when he saw her, he grinned with boyish relief. 'I thought you were never coming. I thought I'd imagined you.'

'Through the window you looked like a goblin. My brother thought you were one. I'm Mara, by the way.'

'I thought you must be. The raving beauty.'

She didn't know what to make of him. She stood back a little, twirling the long ends of the tulle bow on her hat. 'How old are you?' she asked curiously.

'Nineteen. Older than you, I think.'

'I'll be nineteen in three months.' To her own ears it sounded childish. But he kept on staring at her, his big brown hands fidgeting.

He was like a puppy, thought Mara. An adoring puppy. He should be her pet.

'Why don't you come and meet Mother?' she said, and led the way towards the kitchen, consciously letting her hips dip and sway. When she glanced back over her shoulder he was close behind, anxious, eager to please.

He hung back in the kitchen, staring at the long, black solid fuel range. 'The house is so big. All these stoves — it's like the middle ages.'

'The cooks often say so. They get tired of struggling with the ranges, and leave. I keep telling Father we should get electric or something.'

'I never saw such a big table in all my life.' He ran his hand wonderingly over the scrubbed pine board.

'Our formal dining table is longer than this. When it's extended.'

She lost patience with him. Taking guests round the house was something she always avoided. 'Look, are you coming? I want to introduce you to Mother.'

'Yes — yes. I'm sorry.' He kept close as she wound her way through passages and up stairs.

'I'm afraid my father's ill,' she said brightly. 'Nothing too serious. He picked up a virus of some sort in Kenya, and it's really pulled him down. So you won't be seeing him for a day or two, I'm afraid.'

'It's not malaria, is it? He should have taken the pills. Not that we get much up our way.'

'Well, you've got something,' said Mara curtly. 'He's been ill ever since he came home, he was in hospital last week for tests.'

Edward realised that sympathy was in order. 'I'm — I'm sorry to hear that,' he mumbled.

Mara relented and said more softly, 'So you should be.'

She opened the door to the sitting-room. 'Mother? Mother, Edward's here. I found him wandering around like a burglar.'

But Edward was standing stockstill in the doorway. The room was triangular, with the door at the point of the triangle. The entire opposite wall was made up of a series of French windows, leading out on to a terrace and beyond to the lake. Two chandeliers hung from a ceiling encrusted with plaster relief, picked out in blue and gold. And in the midst of all this magnificence sat Charlotte, embroidering some sort of wool cushion.

'Edward! How nice to see you.'

'Er — how do you do, Lady Melville?' They had been on first name terms in Kenya, but he knew instinctively it wouldn't do here. He had expected grandeur, even style, but this vast, crumbling palace amazed him. He felt hopelessly overwhelmed.

18

Mara said, 'He thinks Father's got malaria. He ought to be careful in case we give him death watch beetle in return, oughtn't he?'

'But your father hasn't got malaria, darling! It's a virus, that's all. I hope Mara hasn't upset you, Edward.'

Mara leaned one elbow against the mantel, the long line of her leg outlined against her skirt. Framed in the hat, she looked sweet yet infinitely seductive. 'She's been wonderful,' said Edward. 'Really kind.'

One of the French windows opened. Lisa came in, followed by her spaniel.

'Darling, the mud!' complained Charlotte, but the girl took no notice.

'What are you vamping for, Mara?' she asked. 'Is this a visitor or has the man come with the fish?'

'It's Edward Demouth,' said Charlotte, helplessly flapping her hands. 'Don't be rude, please, dear. Edward, this is Eloise — we call her Lisa.'

They stared at each other, the tall brown boy and the little mousy girl. Exactly Mara's type, thought Lisa, and discounted him. Not a patch on Mara, decided Edward, and did likewise. He found it hard to keep his eyes away from Mara, she drew his gaze in a way that was only half pleasant. And when he stopped looking at her she made sure that he began again.

'Has the doctor been?' asked Lisa.

'He rang. He's coming tomorrow.'

'Oh. Oh, I see.' She sat down on a lemon satin sofa. 'I thought we might find out something today.'

'He's better today,' said Charlotte. 'Eating very well, a sandwich at lunch. Have you lunched, Edward?'

He had not, but decided to lie. 'Yes. Yes, thank you.' The fat spaniel sat down at his side and began to chew at his shoe, though whether out of spite or boredom it was hard to tell. He couldn't decide if he should let it continue or not. In a household like this even the dog seemed worthy of respect. But then he saw Mara's face and felt a fool. He shook his foot half-heartedly.

'I'll show him his room,' said Mara, and drifted languidly to the door. Edward followed, almost falling over the dog, and in the corridor burst out: 'I've never seen anything like this! It's fantastic. Majestic.'

'It's only a house,' said Mara thinly. 'We didn't build it. Once people see the house they think differently of us, you know. They think we tell better jokes.'

She decided she was disappointed in him. As she led the way up the

19

staircase to the guest wing she took off the hat and let it swing by the ribbons from her fingers. Edward was to stay in one of the few rooms that had a ceiling that did not let in water, but had a turn of the century bathroom so far from the hot water tank that it only ever dribbled lukewarm. Usually Mara apologised, both for that and catching your feet in the threadbare carpets, but she decided not to bother. He wasn't worth it.

She stood aside to let him go into the room in front of her. He paused, looking disconsolate, and then saw his bags, which he had stashed behind a laurel bush in the garden. Unseen hands had brought them in, unpacked them, and laid out his pyjamas on the bed. Ma had bought those pyjamas, old man's stripes, and he cringed at what Mara must think. He wondered if he should tell her that at home he slept naked.

'Well, then, you're settled,' she said, wishing he looked a little less hangdog.

'Yes. Thank you.'

She was going to go, but on a sudden impulse turned. He was looking so dejected. Hadn't she meant to be kind to him? 'There's a party tomorrow night,' she said. 'Will you come? It'll mean staying over, but I'd like you to come with me.'

She watched the colour come and go in his face. Through the window he'd seemed confident, fun. Once away from The Court he might be again, she decided.

'Thanks very much. Thanks a lot,' he stammered. Mara smiled at him.

Chapter Four

Edward's room unnerved him. It seemed so shabby and neglected. He wondered if in putting him here they were dealing him some obscure insult. Ought he to have known Henry was ill? Should he have left the moment he discovered it? Perhaps the invitation to visit had been mere form, perhaps they hadn't intended him to come.

He was starving hungry, but no mention had been made of dinner. He sat on the edge of his bed and wondered what he should do. Outside his door there seemed to be dozens of people, only a few of which were family. At least at home you knew the black ones were staff. The butler, Curtiss, was stiffer and more intimidating than Lord Melville himself and the maids, if that's what they were, clumped past him in the passages as if he wasn't there. Chauffeurs, gardeners, maids — he hadn't expected this. The public face of England was of a country in which all that had been swept away, and yet here it was, thriving.

Half embarrassed at himself, he got out the note Ma had written before he went away. She was a dear old thing really, you knew where you stood with her. Or at least he had thought he did. He hadn't expected her to come over all sentimental. How lonely it made him feel. He had a moment's deep, fierce longing to be back on the verandah, tired after a hard day's work, surrounded by people that he knew.

Was he perhaps supposed to change for dinner? All he had was his father's old white dinner jacket, preserved for years against the ravages of damp in the rainy season and moth in the dry. He thought how much of a fool he would look if he went down in that and they were all in jeans. Surely it would be less embarrassing not to have changed. He couldn't decide, it was the devil and the deep blue sea.

There was a knock on the door and before he could answer, a tall, dark, thickset young man came in.

'Hello,' said Edward, wondering if he was some sort of servant. He was wearing a rough shirt and a knitted tie. He seemed on edge.

'How do you do?' said Edward, thrusting out his hand. When it wasn't taken he withdrew it, feeling stupid.

The man fixed him with a desperate stare. 'I'm Marcus Hellyn. You saw me.'

'Did I? I'm sorry, so many new faces − '

'What have you come here for? This country's dying, didn't you know that? Everything's falling apart. This house is crumbling.'

'Er − I was invited.'

'Bloody awful place. Nothing but gloom and rain.' He went to the window and looked out into the wet afternoon. 'Bloody charnel house, this is.'

Edward looked at him. He thought him very depressed. He said, 'I didn't know your father was ill. Of course I wouldn't have come. They didn't tell me, you see.'

'Well. They wouldn't.' Marcus wandered restlessly about the room, and picked up a photograph set out on the bureau. It was of Ma and the boys. Just to see him with it brought a wave of homesickness crashing on Edward's head.

'Don't touch that,' he said.

Marcus glanced at him and put the photograph down. 'I wish I lived there,' he said jerkily. 'I hate this house, I hate the way the trees crowd round. When there's no-one here, it's as if they're watching you.'

'I know what you mean,' said Edward. 'But then I'm used to things watching you. We live near the game reserve, we get leopards in the garden sometimes.'

'With us it's snooping kids from the village. Well, are you coming?'

'What for?'

'It's suppertime. Did you think we'd leave you here all night?'

'No, no − ' He wondered if it was stupid to raise the question of clothes. 'Can I come in jeans?' he asked.

'For tonight you can. Mother normally likes people to smarten up.'

'Should I put on a tie, do you think?'

'As you like.'

Marcus waited, walking noisily up and down, while Edward hunted around for a tie and put a hurried knot round his neck.

'God, but you're slow!' said Marcus and Edward followed him out while still unsure that the tie was on straight. He looked for a mirror in the hall, but there was none. The furnishings, lavish in the family rooms, dwindled to almost nothing in the guest wing. All that marked this high hallway was a giant chandelier, held on an iron chain, its crystals tinkling gently in an unseen breeze. Paint was peeling from the ornate plaster ceiling and they clattered down bald staircarpet held in place with tarnished brass rods of ancient design.

There were mouse droppings under his bath. He wondered if it would be unforgivable to mention it. The Hellyns intimidated him, even Charlotte, who lived in the shadow of her husband. And Marcus seemed so odd. He tried to make conversation. 'What part of the house are we in?'

'Still the Georgian wing.' Marcus sounded tense. 'Get Angus to show you the medieval part. It's thick with ghosts.'

The family were drinking sherry out of cut glass and waiting for them.

'We thought you were never coming,' said Mara. She had changed into pale pink silk that swirled and clung, although her mother and Lisa were in skirts and jumpers. Edward shook hands with Angus, neat in grey flannels and a sports jacket. It was a good, firm handshake, reassuringly solid.

'We thought you'd got lost,' said Charlotte, and Lisa remarked, 'After his treks across Kenya, I shouldn't have thought The Court would pose much of a problem.'

Edward swallowed. 'I think it's very confusing. I mean – where is the court? I mean, the courtyard.'

'That's in the old part,' said Angus. 'Obviously very little of the house is absolutely original, but the courtyard is.'

'Lisa can show you,' remarked Mara, making it clear that she would not.

Charlotte noticed that Curtiss was waiting. 'We are all here, Curtiss.'

The butler inclined from the waist. 'At your pleasure, my lady.'

The food was lacklustre, though Edward felt happier with some of it inside him. Everyone talked, about people he didn't know, things he didn't understand. Every now and then someone would ask him a question, just as he had filled his mouth with food. He got indigestion from swallowing half-chewed meat. At last he plucked up courage. 'About the party,' he ventured. 'Will a white dinner jacket do? Ma said – I mean, my mother suggested I should get a new one here. It's awfully old.'

'Was it your father's?' asked Marcus, leaning forward. ' I should wear it if I were you. Coats were made better in the old days.'

'Just make sure it's aired,' said Charlotte. 'Quite frankly, when Parliament is opened and all those robes come out of hibernation, I could suffocate in the smell of mothballs. Mara, dear, where are you going?'

Her daughter paused at the door. 'To see Father. Honestly, I can't eat burned potatoes. If that woman touches the food for the ball, I'll kill her.'

'It's all outside caterers. But Mara – Mara!'

The girl was gone. For a moment Charlotte looked almost distraught.

Angus said, 'Just let her go, Mother. It doesn't matter.'

I just wish she wouldn't bother Henry all the time. He isn't up to it.'

'I really don't know why you can't leave her alone.' Marcus was sitting tensely, eating nothing. 'That's you all the time, Mother, you can't ever let anyone lead their own life.'

'Oh, God,' said Lisa. 'Don't you start. Drink some wine.'

'No. I'm going for a walk.' Marcus got up and made for the door.

'Angus –' said Charlotte plaintively, but he continued to ply his knife and fork. 'Angus, please!' she said again.

He looked up. 'I'm not his keeper, Mother. If he wants to tramp round in the rain half the night, then he must. It's nothing to do with me.'

There was a silence. Edward said tentatively, 'Shall I –' but Lisa leaned over and put her hand on his arm. 'He'll be all right,' she murmured. 'He'll walk for hours. If he isn't in by midnight, Angus will look for him. It is all right, really.'

He felt uncomfortable, and guilty, as if he might be the cause of it all. The food was sour on his tongue, and now Mara was gone, the room seemed cheerless and cold.

They took coffee in the small drawing-room, with a wood fire crackling in the grate. Charlotte brought out some embroidery while Angus watched a documentary about South America on television. Halfway through, Lisa went off to study in her room.

'She has her A levels,' explained Charlotte. 'During the week she's at boarding school, but they do like to come home at weekends. Mara couldn't have cared less about exams but Lisa wants to go to university.'

Rain came down the chimney and hissed on the fire, sending puffs of smoke into the room. Charlotte said, 'Angus, I think I'll go up and sit with your father. Don't you think – Marcus –?'

Angus nodded. 'All right. This is just about over anyway. I don't suppose you want to come, do you?' He glanced at Edward, who got up at once.

The rain, so unlike that of Africa, fell with a gentle, endless murmur. Angus kitted them both out with boots and old macs, culled from a mountain of gear in what was called the dog room, although the only dog was Lisa's. From the piles of food bowls there must once have been dozens. Ancient hats mouldered on shelves next to stained glass flower vases and the tarnished silver ends of walking sticks. Such profusion was bewildering. The Court was steeped in times past, dwarfing the present in importance. Today was only of interest when turned into yesterday.

Edward felt better outside, with a cool breeze on his face and the smell of wet earth rising up around them. He tightened his grip on reality. Angus took a torch but decided not to use it. The moon peeped out now and then from behind the rainclouds; the night was a grey curtain. Edward said, 'Where is he, do you think? Why won't he come in?'

'Don't ask me,' said Angus stolidly. They walked on a little further, out across the damp grass of the lawns. Edward sensed Angus's bad temper. At last he remarked 'It isn't as if he isn't old enough to look after himself. I suppose your mother doesn't realise that.'

Angus grunted. 'You don't understand — no-one does really. He gets these moods, I can't explain it. Very gloomy, very depressed. They last weeks sometimes, and he does this sort of thing. Walking off, in the rain or the snow, anything. Then he gets better again. He'll be very wild, quite mad sometimes, doing things no-one in their right mind — and then this again.'

'Has he always been like that?' asked Edward. He felt nervous suddenly, nervous of the night, and Marcus.

'He was always excitable, the one with the wild ideas. Next to him I was dull, the one no-one noticed. For years and years people have liked him best. Now of course they don't like him at all.'

'Has a doctor seen him?'

'My father doesn't want all that. We hope he'll grow out of it. We hope I don't catch it.'

Angus looked at him in the dark, the whites of his eyes flashing.

'Poor old Edward! What a disaster we've plunged you into. No need to worry, old chap, he isn't mad, not as you think of it. Gets a bit unbalanced sometimes, that's all. He distresses himself. And us, of course.'

They walked on, making for the wood. Edward followed blindly through thick undergrowth, hearing pheasant murmur and squawk, too sleepy to run. They came out on to a vista cut through the trees, and at the end, looming black against the grey sky, was a crenellated summerhouse.

'The place is littered with this sort of thing,' remarked Angus. 'That's the Hellyns for you, build, build, build . . . never occurred to anyone to do any running repairs. Marcus! Marcus, are you there?'

His voice echoed against the stone. Edward felt fear creeping up the

25

back of his neck. He had felt less afraid out at night with lion. Ma always said he'd taken on board more of Africa than he knew, including the superstition. Suddenly he saw Marcus. He was sitting, head in hands, under a cracked gutter. Water was running continuously on to his hair.

'Oh, for Christ's sake!' said Angus. 'What are you doing now, trying to drown yourself?'

Marcus did not appear to hear him. Gently, with kind hands, Angus drew him to his feet. They could hear his teeth chattering.

'Here, put this on him.' Edward drew off his coat and held it out.

'You don't have to,' said Angus quietly.

'He'll be ill. Please.'

Edward was soaked by the time they reached the house, but Marcus was cold as death. Between them they steered him to his room and began to rub him down, throwing the sodden clothes into a heap on the floor. It was a room overflowing with clutter, a jumble of objects set down without any clear plan. Some drawings lay on a table: confused and unsettling images, half animal, half plant. Together they lifted Marcus on to his bed. He seemed passive, almost drugged. 'Is he all right?' asked Edward, looking into those cold, unseeing eyes. The room unnerved him, it was unpleasant, fantastic.

'He'll be fine tomorrow. He'll be better. Look, let's have a night-cap in front of the fire.'

Downstairs, Edward felt better. They put fresh wood on the embers and it blazed up cheerily. Angus poured them both a brandy. Drinking it, feeling it warm him through and through, the nightmare began to fade. The presence of Angus, so normal and sane, reassured him. Edward felt happy suddenly. He felt privileged to be allowed to know so much.

'Mara's so beautiful,' he heard himself saying.

Angus laughed. 'And doesn't she know it! Don't let her play with you, Edward. That's all it would be. You'd be her small amusement.'

Edward sipped at his brandy, letting the spirit burn his lips. He had travelled from Africa, but it might as well have been from another universe. He hadn't known a world like this existed.

Chapter Five

Mara loitered irritably about the hallway leading to her father's room. The doctor had arrived before ten, and it was past eleven now. She wanted to know if Henry would be up and about for her ball, because if not she wanted to put it off. Without him half the fun would be lost.

The door opened. Charlotte and the doctor came out together.

'At last,' said Mara. 'Can I go into him now? He will be up soon, won't he, doctor?'

'He's resting,' said the doctor firmly. 'I suggest you come back later, my dear.'

Mara paused. She saw that her mother's face was streaked with tears. The first cold fingers of apprehension stroked her heart. 'Mother?' she said cautiously.

Charlotte shook her head, wordless. 'I'll see myself out,' said the doctor. 'We'll talk again tomorrow, when you've had time to think.'

They said nothing while his footsteps still echoed on the stairs. Now and then Charlotte caught her breath on a sob. 'What is it?' said Mara slowly. 'What's the matter?'

Charlotte swallowed. 'It's cancer. He's going to die.'

The words seemed to mean nothing. They echoed in Mara's head, as if there was no brain that could understand them. This was the real world, real life, her father couldn't die!

'You didn't understand what he said. You're trying to frighten me.' She took a step backwards.

'As if the truth isn't frightening enough! Your father — has widespread cancer. They give him six months.'

Mara turned and ran, straight into her father's room. He lay in the high four poster bed, propped against banks of pillows. His skin, stretched tight over the long Hellyn nose that lived on only in Lisa, seemed to have turned yellow.

27

'Father! You don't know what they're saying!'

He turned his head as if he didn't want her there, didn't want her to see. He was crying.

The day passed — how did it pass? Lunch was served, Mara knew she must have eaten something. She felt distant from everything, from everyone around her. None of them knew what it meant. She was the only one that seemed surprised.

After the meal Angus followed her into the conservatory. It was a huge, Victorian construction, full of cracked glass that swayed and shuddered in every gale. A vine spread its branches against the roof. Only today did Mara realise that they looked like old, gnarled hands.

'You must have suspected,' said Angus.

'Don't tell me that you did! Don't tell me you even thought of it!'

'But I did. In all honesty, Mara, ever since he came home. He'd lost so much weight.'

She looked at him almost with loathing, as if to let the thought of disease enter his head was to encourage it. 'You're all just accepting it,' she said hysterically. 'Why isn't anyone trying to find a cure? We should go to faith healers. Anything!'

Her brother just stood, watching her, saying nothing. She felt a great need of comfort, a need that all her life had been satisfied by her father. What would she do when he was gone? What should she do now?

The door opened with a creak. It was Edward. 'I wondered — could I have a word, Angus? I thought perhaps I should go home.'

'Don't be ridiculous!' Angus went to him, gripping him by the shoulder. 'We can't all sit around moping month after month. With the right drugs, Father could be up and about in a few days. No, you stay and cheer us all up. You're taking Mara to a party tonight, aren't you?'

Edward glanced at Mara. Her face was completely white, with only her eyes blazing dark, hot blue. 'I don't suppose she wants to go.'

'Yes, I do,' said Mara. 'I can't bear to stay here, not tonight.'

'Good — good.' Angus's tone sounded inappropriately jovial. Mara turned and pushed past him, her heels hitting the flags in perfect rhythm, like hammerblows.

Because it was such a strange day, Lisa came and sat on Mara's bed while she changed for the party.

'I can't believe it,' said Lisa. 'It's only six months since grandfather died. And now Marcus will be the earl.'

Mara took out her favourite dress of black taffeta. Wordlessly she rejected it and looked for something else.

'Should I wear this?' A tube of grey silk, strapless and relieved by any sort of ornament.

'You could wear pink roses perhaps.' Lisa was always useful when it came to clothes, although she dressed others far more successfully than herself. She was too short, and she made almost no attempt at softening the angles of face and body. Where Mara was all curves, Lisa was nothing but straight lines. She sat impassively as her sister, wearing only panties, eased her heavy breasts into the dress. There was something luscious about Mara, like a peach holding rich juices within its downy skin.

'You should put your hair up,' advised Lisa. 'I'll do it, if you like.'

'Thanks.' It was a rare moment of truce. Mara sat before the mirror and watched her sister creating a perfect chignon out of her golden curls.

'It could be a terrible mistake.'

Lisa's face remained absorbed. 'Wear the diamond earrings,' she advised. 'And no other jewellery.'

Mara reached up and caught her wrist. 'But it could be! there might be some treatment that we don't know about. He doesn't look about to die – does he?'

Lisa swallowed. 'Yes,' she said. 'Actually, I think he does.'

Mara dug her nails viciously into her sister's skin. 'Bitch!' Lisa wrenched her hand away.

When she was ready, she went down to find her mother. Edward was there, resplendent in the white dinner jacket. At a distance it looked magnificent, but at close quarters there was a strange mottling of the cloth, as if old stains had never quite come out. The sight of Mara, the swelling curves of her body outlined against grey silk, caused him to flush scarlet.

'I thought I'd go and say goodbye to Father,' she said, holding out her shawl for Edward to drape across her shoulders.

'Not tonight please, dear.' For once Charlotte was decisive.

'He'll want to see me, Mother. He always does.' Mara started for the door, but Charlotte stopped her. 'He wants to see no-one. No-one except me. It's been such a shock, you see.'

'And what about us? Hasn't it been a shock for us? For me? I must see him.'

'Mara! I quite forbid you to disturb your father!'

Charlotte's pale eyes met Mara's deep blue ones. It was Mara who looked away. 'Come along, Edward,' she said tightly. 'We've a party to go to.'

In the Rolls she was absolutely silent. Constrained by the presence of the chauffeur, Edward tried a few desultory comments, to no avail. After ten minutes or so Mara sighed, reached into the door pocket and withdrew a silver flask. Edward watched in fascination as she drank, following every movement of her throat. When the tipped her head back her breasts rose up in her dress almost to the nipples.

'Here.' She held it out to him. In his head Edward heard Ma's voice, saying, 'Only fools take every drink that's offered.' But from Mara, he would take anything. He drank. It was some kind of sweet brandy, perhaps apricot. He stole a look at the chauffeur to see if he was watching, but he appeared not to be paying attention. Mara took the flask again, and he could not wait to put his lips where hers had been. He wondered what sort of a head he had for drink. Every sip made him long more and more to be alone with her.

The party was being held at a big country house famous for its formal yew hedges. To Edward's eye, conditioned by The Court, it seemed both small and somewhat manicured. They had come a long way and they were late. The party was in full swing. Through the lighted windows they could see a crush of people. No sooner had the car stopped than Mara was out, calling, 'Come along, Edward,' and taking long, confident strides up to the open door. He felt drunk, with the brandy, and the night, and Mara.

At the door a slim, quietly pretty girl welcomed them. 'This is Diandra,' explained Mara offhandedly. 'It's her party. We all go to each other's you see. Mother rang about Edward, didn't she? He's from Kenya.' She was off, leaving Edward to cope with Diandra's polite chat about home and family. He shifted from one foot to the other, wanting to follow Mara, to be close to her. At last he escaped. As he came up to her, he heard someone say, 'And how is your father, my dear? Better?' And Mara said, 'Much, thank you, He's fine.'

She seemed to know everybody. She drifted through the rooms, turning and greeting, and every head swivelled to watch her. He heard someone say: 'God! That is the most gorgeous thing I have seen in my entire life! What a fuckable piece of meat she is.' If he could have seen the man who spoke, he would have hit him.

A trio was grinding out dance music at one end of the room. Hurrying over the parquet, Edward caught Mara's arm. 'Why don't we dance?'

'What? Oh, later. Look, I don't want you following me. Go and find someone else to pester.'

'Oh, Mara, don't be horrid to him!' said a girl. 'He's lovely. Come and talk to me, Edward, you're the only person here with a decent tan. Does it go absolutely everywhere? And I mean − everywhere?' She linked her arm through his, letting her thigh press against him.

30

Without appalling rudeness Edward couldn't get away. He watched as Mara continued her saunter round the room, collecting a train of men wanting introductions. Someone gave her a glass of champagne.

'Do stop watching her,' said the girl. 'It isn't fair. You won't get a chance anyway. Mara can be very sophisticated.'

Reluctantly he pulled his eyes away. 'It's just − I'm supposed to be looking after her − '

'Well, you can look after me instead.' The girl managed to invest the words with gross indecency. He felt embarrassed and stupid. Behind him someone said, 'Who is that gorgeous boy Mara brought? He's so shy and sweet, I adore him!' And all her friends laughed.

He went to get a drink. Not five minutes after she had refused to dance with him Mara was dancing the quickstep, very close to a man with greying hair. She was laughing up into his face and he had the sharp, absorbed look of intense sexual excitement. Edward felt sick. The other girl was looking for him; he took his beer and moved away into a crowd of men. No-one spoke to him. He felt abandoned in a sea of indifference, at the edges of which lurked a land of lewd women.

The party was well alight, and soon the trio gave way to a disco. Diandra's parents circulated, nervously smiling at people they didn't know. Edward, who knew absolutely no-one, stood in a corner feeling lost. Diandra came up to him. 'I wish you'd dance with me,' she said. 'It's my party and no-one is.'

'Oh. I'm sorry − yes, of course.'

He put down his beer and took to the floor, jigging around to unfamiliar music. Gradually he began to dance properly, adopting the African movements with which he had grown up. Diandra said, 'Do you always dance like that? Everyone's watching.'

Edward looked round and saw that they were. He blushed scarlet. 'Do you mind if we stop?'

'Oh. All right.'

They went and sat down by an open window. Outside they could hear couples groping and the girls squealing. Diandra said, 'You're not having much fun, are you?'

'Yes, yes I am,' he lied. Then he said, 'It's just − are the girls really going to − you know? They all seem to want to.'

Diandra shrugged. She was softly pretty, with brown eyes and short brown hair. 'I don't know. They've got to make a hit, you see. It's the worst if you're not popular. It's best if the boys like you.'

'Won't they like them if they don't − '

'They might not. I mean, if you're not pretty and you're not clever, it isn't very easy. When there's someone like Mara here, who's going to notice them? She's my friend from school, but I'd much rather she

31

couldn't have come. She makes everyone else seem second best.'

'She's having a difficult time. Her father's dying.'

Diandra looked away. 'Oh. I didn't know. Is that why you're so worried about her?'

'Yes,' lied Edward. Suddenly he liked Diandra, he felt safe with her. 'Would you mind if we had another dance?'

In the early hours of the morning, with the records still playing and couples clinging together on the dancefloor, Edward went to find Mara. People strolled about amongst the yew hedges, and every now and then a girl rushed past, tear-stained and bedraggled. The assumed sophistication of the night before had shattered into weary vulnerability. For every embracing couple under a yew hedge there was someone being sick.

Diandra's parents were trying to persuade forlorn girls to go to bed and half-conscious young men to drink coffee. Nobody had seen Mara. Edward wandered down a path towards the stables, letting the noise of the party fade away into the night. His head was throbbing. He knew he was very drunk, but perhaps, like his father, he was carrying it well. Jan had been famous for it.

The stable yard was as neat and well-trimmed as the gardens. Edward thought how furious Diandra's father was going to be the next day when he surveyed the wrecked hedges and trampled flowerbeds, let alone the drinkstains and scratches in the house. It was very dark here, and from a box in the corner a horse snuffled curiously. Edward wandered around, knowing she could not be there, looking aimlessly into doors. Suddenly he heard her.

She was crying – harsh, racking sobs that seemed to be wrenched up from the very core of her being. In between each one she took dragging breaths, gathering air for the next giant sob. It wasn't grief, it could hardly be that. It was torment.

He fumbled for the light and switched it on. She was crouched on a hay bale, her lovely dress covered in straw, the pink roses dropping despondently downwards. Tendrils of hair had worked loose from her chignon and fell about her face. Her eyes were as swollen as if she had been in a fight. Her nose was running.

'Has someone hurt you? Has something happened?'

She shook her head. 'No. No. Oh, Edward, it's all so dreadful!'

He took her in his arms. It was the least he could do. He sat beside her on the bale and held her and comforted her. She used his handkerchief to mop up her face, still sobbing, still heartsick. Somehow he found himself kissing her.

It was delicious, inflaming, setting alight a fuse that ran straight from his tongue to his groin. Her mouth was wide open, hungrily licking him. He crushed her close, and the roses pricked them both, a delicious pain. Edward dragged them off her dress and Mara groaned. She pulled away.

Panting, beside himself, he watched the slow, deliberate release of her breasts. Against the silk they were white, shaped like perfect fruit from an all-white tree. Her nipples were dark, surrounded by a fine web of dark blonde hair. Like a supplicant at the feet of a goddess, Edward reached out his hands.

As he touched her she fell further and further back. He half lay across her body, fighting the urge to suck her. It seemed obscene, perverted. But he had no control over himself. His own hands, unbidden, were dragging her skirt to her waist. She watched him almost sleepily, her mouth slack with arousal. The blood was throbbing round his body, coming to a tight, hot volcano in his groin. He thought, 'When they hear of this they'll flay me.' But just the same, he unzipped his trousers.

His erection reared up. Mara let out a low giggle. 'God, but you're disgusting.' She reached up for her panties and pulled them to her knees. The hair between her legs was dark, wet blonde. He came down on to her urgently, desperately. He thought of a bull on a cow at home and his buttocks plunged aimlessly. He felt the place, he was sure of it, but it seemed closed to him. She let out a low, soft sigh. He had never been so hard, he was like steel. And the steel of him broke into her, parting soft flesh with no mind, no thought, only exquisite sensation, driving with hammer blows towards a shattering convulsion.

As he panted on her, Mara lay wide-eyed. She moved against him, once, twice, three times. She gave a long moan.

When she woke the next morning she was sticky between her legs. It was a mixture of blood and semen with a strange, fishy smell. She went quickly to the bathroom and washed it away. The whole scene replayed itself in her head, in colours of red and black. Suppose she was pregnant? She imagined all her friends mocking her.

She and two other girls were sharing a room. The others were hungover, and anxious in case they had made fools of themselves, doing things they wished they hadn't. But Mara had done nothing she hadn't wished to do. She wasn't sorry, even now. Her skin tingled, as if newly awakened to sensation, not all of it pleasant. How sore she was.

Going stiffly down to breakfast, the misery came back. It had lost none of its sting. She saw her father's face, turned against the pillow,

33

crying, and suddenly she had to stop and press both hands to her belly. It was like a physical pain.

'Mara? Are you all right?' Diandra was staring at her.

'Time of the month,' said Mara, and tried to smile.

Edward wasn't at breakfast, but neither were two-thirds of the guests. Only the stalwarts could face bacon and egg. Mara sat drinking black coffee, trying to still her shaking hands. Yesterday had been a nightmare, it couldn't be true. When she went home her mother would say, 'Darling, your father's much better! The doctor made a silly mistake.'

The car came for them just after eleven. By the time Edward appeared, green and ghastly, Mara had lost her temper with him. 'I've been waiting ages!' she declared. 'We've got to go, no-one wants to put up with people after a party. It isn't fair.'

'I'm sorry. I've said my goodbyes.' He got gingerly into the car. His head was splitting.

They hardly spoke for half an hour. Finally Edward said, 'About last night – I must apologise.'

'I dread to think what Father would say if he knew.'

'You're not telling him, are you?'

She cast him a look of scorn. 'Naturally not. You should count yourself lucky. The first man ever to screw Lady Mara Hellyn. I don't imagine you'll be the last.'

Edward flushed to the roots of his hair. 'Look,' he said finally. 'If there's any trouble –'

She raised her eyebrows. 'You mean if I'm pregnant? If I am, I'll get it seen to. And don't you dare think this means anything! I'm not going to think about it again, and neither should you.'

'That's ridiculous!' burst out Edward. 'You can't pretend it never happened!'

She stared at him. There were violet shadows under her eyes. 'Oh yes I can.'

Chapter Six

After so much rain, leaving the lawns sodden and the stone statues greasy with algae, there began to be a summer. In the mornings the air was cool and clear, hinting at heat to come. Bees bumped drunkenly into the windows, struggling back to the hive, overloaded with pollen. There was a new drug treatment for Henry, which left him quite free of pain.

Without a word exchanged between them, the family decided to pretend it had all been a horrible false alarm. Henry stayed in bed for much of the day, but he got up in the afternoons and sat on the terrace, reading. Charlotte and Mara sat with him, sipping lemonade and discussing the ball.

'The designer wants white satin drapes. I do hope Diandra didn't have them?'

'It was all rather plain actually, said Mara. 'Neat and suburban.'

Henry looked up from his book. 'Don't for God's sake do it by halves! I can't bear these budgeted affairs, sparkling wine and pretend caviare. Any booze that's left can be saved for her wedding.'

'Just so long as you don't save the caviare,' remarked Mara.

Henry snorted. 'I've never been to a do when there was the slightest morsel left over. We shall be left with sloppy salmon mousse and vol au vents for weeks, but not a pearl of caviare. Charlotte, I'm a little warm.'

His wife got up at once to take off one of his blankets. It was a glorious day, and on the grass Marcus, Angus and Edward could be seen playing croquet. It was difficult with only three, but Mara wouldn't play and Angus was formidable enough to challenge both the others. He played a vicious roquet. 'We ought to get a lawn properly laid,' remarked Henry. 'There used to be one for croquet, in my father's day. Why don't we do that?'

'What a lovely idea!' said Charlotte. That foolish doctor, she thought. Now Henry has his pills he's quite well, and soon he will be better.'

He went back to bed shortly after supper that evening. Everyone wanted to play cards, but again Mara wouldn't. It was Edward's fault. During the week, with Lisa still at school, she found herself paired automatically with him. He seemed to watch her all the time: sometimes he had the absolute gall to seem protective. He was the innocent colonial, she the sophisticate, and she had no intention of permitting him to turn the tables. Her period had come absolutely on time, and that was that as far as she was concerned. After her ball she would go to London, stay in the flat her father was renting for her and go to parties every night.

The gardens were soft in the twilight. Leaving the others in the lighted drawing-room, she slipped out of the French windows and walked towards the lake. To her fury, Edward followed her, trotting across the grass with long-legged ease.

'Would you like my jacket?' he asked. 'It's cool out here.'

'If I'd wanted a jacket I'd have brought one,' she snapped. 'Go away. I don't want you.'

'Are you afraid I'll try and make love to you again?'

She pulled back her hand and hit him, hard, across the face. It made a short, flat sound, like someone stamping. 'Why don't you go away?' hissed Mara, hating her voice for trembling. 'It was just once, that's all. I was unhappy. I thought my father was dying. And now he's better I don't want to think about that night at all, so why do you keep on reminding me?'

The slap had upset Mara far more than Edward. As the eldest of three boys he was used to physical assaults. He scratched his head. 'But – he's dying! Can't you see that?'

Mara laughed. 'Oh, dear me, hasn't anyone told you? He's on new drugs. He can get up, soon he'll be absolutely up and about.'

He caught her arm and spun her to face him. 'What he's on is morphine! He's doped to the eyeballs, that's why he gets out of bed. Don't you look at him? Don't you see what he looks like?'

In the dark his face was a white mask, his eyes pools of black. 'Why do you say these things to me?' she asked shrilly. 'Why do you hate me?'

'Mara – I love you. You know I do. I can't bear you to deceive yourself.'

She pulled away and went back to the house, running awkwardly in her heels. Even in tennis shoes she never ran well; her breasts were too heavy and she had wide hips that made her waist seem narrower than it was. Edward watched her bottom and felt helpless with desire. At

36

least, he thought, I'm not homesick any longer. He was sick for wanting Mara.

In her bedroom, Mara put on her dressing gown and paced up and down. She hated Edward. Tomorrow she would tell Father that he had tried to seduce her, and he'd be sent home in disgrace. He wanted her to be miserable, so she'd turn to him again. Of course Henry wasn't dying.

Unbidden came the picture of her father that night, picking at a slice of chicken. Against the light his hands were almost transparent. When he left the table Curtiss had to help him stand.

Mara clutched the fabric of her gown, pressing both fists hard into her belly. That was where grief began, that was where the knowledge of it lay. If she could crush that nerve centre she need not feel this pain.

If only Lisa were here. Charlotte she could never talk to, but sometimes she and Lisa understood each other. They gave her father pills to help him sleep, but Curtiss held those and he would never give her one. Her thoughts darted about, like bats around a chimney. She began to feel a gathering hysteria. She had to escape from herself, get out of herself.

Without any conscious decision she flung open the door and ran out into the hall, leaving the lights in her room blazing. To reach the guest wing she had to run up two flights of stairs and along the picture gallery. The eyes of a hundred dead men followed her progress, and no amount of mourning had kept one of them alive, or brought him back. It was the way of the world, the way of life and death, going on now as always before. Mara felt that she had stumbled across a fundamental secret, which made all happiness and all joy no more than childish fantasy.

She burst into Edward's room without knocking. He was awake, lying naked on top of the bed, leafing through a car magazine. When he saw her he put the magazine over his penis. And now that she confronted him, in the light, neither of them drunk, it seemed ridiculous. Yet she couldn't go back to that room and her thoughts, it was impossible.

'I'm on the pill,' she said jerkily. 'But I don't want you to think anything. I don't want to be alone tonight.'

Edward tried to swallow. 'Do you mean — do you want me to —'

She unfastened her dressing gown and held it wide. Beads of sweat glistened like diamonds on her breasts. 'I mean this.'

He clawed his way across the bed towards her. She was the creature of his dreams, of his wildest erotic imaginings. When his hand closed

37

on her breast she gave a cry of pain, but it was better, far better, than thinking. He couldn't wait. As soon as she was down on the bed he was on her, desperate as only a boy can be. Seconds later he was done.

Mara began to cry. 'You didn't do it right! It wasn't enough!'

'I'm sorry. God, I'm sorry.'

She ducked her head into him, making him aware of her. Her nipples were like grapes against his chest. She moved herself backwards and forwards, each breath causing friction between their two skins. He joined in, fanning the flame of his excitement. His thigh was between her legs; she started to rub herself on him with short, panting breaths. Her eyes were wide, unblinking. Her abandon embarrassed him. He wondered how she could do this and not be ashamed. He was hard again. He held himself up on his hands and went into her with the ease of a piston into the cylinder in one of the supercharged cars he had been reading about. 'Yes. Yes,' and she stared right at him, so he had to close his eyes to be away from her. She started to convulse around him. He couldn't believe that women should do this! He kept his eyes tight closed and worked himself in and out, in and out, and she put her arms round him and clawed his back. She gave a sort of wailing scream.

Ten minutes later she wriggled off the bed and picked up her dressing gown. 'You're not to think anything,' she said.

'I don't! I wouldn't!' He would agree with her forever if it meant more of this. She loves me, he thought exultantly. She won't admit it but she does.

She pulled her gown around her and knotted the cord firmly at her waist. 'You're not to come to me. If I come here, then I come. You mustn't ask me or anything. This might be the last time.'

Edward decided to risk a comment. 'It won't be. You liked it too much.'

Raising an eyebrow, Mara said thinly, 'That doesn't mean that I liked *you* all that much. Goodnight, Edward.'

Chapter Seven

Lisa stood in the centre of the ballroom, quite still. All around her people swirled, moving ladders, bowls of flowers, huge bolts of cloth that were being tied in vast white bows from window to window. The designer was creating a pink and white temple, made up of satin and roses, a romantic vision that the girls who came tonight would remember all their lives and speak of to their grandchildren. Lisa hated it.

She found it hard to understand why. It was Mara's ball, and the plain younger sister should expect to feel left out, but it wasn't that. It was vulgar, of course, and extravagant, but that was the designer's trademark and in the right setting she wouldn't have minded at all. That was it then – the setting. Dressing up the ballroom of The Court was like balancing the figurehead of a great wooden ship on the bar of a pub, and hanging frilly knickers on its nose. It was undignified, and it was wildly inappropriate.

She wandered around, watching as tacks were hammered into the panelling. This room was as ancient as it was huge, a long, high space in which blackened oak glowered from the walls and ages old plaster dust fell from the ceiling. The inner windows overlooked the court-yard, a space so large that two oak trees grew contentedly in the shelter of its walls. Some past earl had installed a fountain in the centre, a confection of marble dolphins and nymphs that had long since ceased to function. It was actually pornographic, since one of the dolphins was in the very act of impaling a nymph with its nose, but neither the dolphin nor the nymph looked anything other than pleased about it.

On the other side of the hall the windows commanded a view over the gardens and the lake, but all in all the room seemed dark and heavy. Ancient tapestry banners hung down from the great beams, too high for anyone to take down. The original structure was

39

medieval but had suffered a dozen changes since. Once it had been a library, once partitioned into three lesser rooms, twice it had been closed and abandoned. Now, and perhaps worst of all, it was being dressed up like a can-can dancer.

Charlotte came in and Lisa said at once, 'Mother, they're nailing this stuff on to the panelling. They must stop.'

'Oh dear.' Charlotte looked round, as if noticing for the first time what was going on. 'At least it hides the damp. And there's such a lot of woodworm, I don't suppose a few more holes will matter.'

'We ought not to let them do any damage,' said Lisa stubbornly. They stood together while the world bustled about them.

'Has the doctor been?' asked Lisa.

'Yes − he'll come again, he says. Your father does want to get up for the ball. He says Mara expects it.'

'I think it's mean and selfish of her,' said Lisa in a low voice. 'She knows he isn't up to it. But she must have everything her way, just like always. Why doesn't anyone stop her?'

'Well, dear −' Charlotte allowed her gaze to wander round the room, her brow furrowed slightly as someone dropped a hundred pink roses. 'I'm sure your father won't do anything he doesn't want.'

'Mara can make him do anything.'

'Yes.' For a moment Charlotte's face was grim. Then she said, 'I wouldn't let him come down if he wasn't so much better. And he'd hate to be left out. Don't make a fuss, dear, will you?'

Lisa felt helpless suddenly, without friends. Charlotte had never been close to any of her children, perhaps to her youngest least of all. Nanny had been their stalwart, so rigid and old-fashioned that a mere parent was excluded from everything except the occasional tea. They hadn't minded when they were small, they hadn't needed a mother. And then of course they went away to school and it seemed that was that. Fully fledged adults who had outgrown maternal need.

Except that Lisa, at least, hadn't. Sometimes she felt like a sweet pea plant waving tendrils as it looked for a stick to cling to. If she had had that stick all her life, would she now be strong and sure? She thought so. It was all her mother's fault, she decided, laying everything at Charlotte's door.

She went out into the gardens. It was a warm afternoon, overcast and dull. She looked up at the woods, thick and dense, much of the standing timber sold by her grandfather to be felled when it was ready. A man was riding down from it, his white jersey like a flag of surrender. Angus riding back towards the house.

She hurried across the grass to meet him. There was the smell of hot horseflesh, and Angus was glowering.

40

'What's the matter?'

He hit his whip against his boot. 'Nothing. Oh, the gypsies I suppose. They've been there weeks, so I decided it was time to give them the heave-ho. They barely speak recognisable English, but one of the lads had the gall to ask if I had the authority. I said yes, of course.'

'Except it should have been no.'

Angus grimaced. 'You do have such an uncompromising way of putting things, Lisa. I couldn't help thinking – wondering.'

She knew what he meant. If Henry died, *when* Henry died, what was to happen? Angus had his own life to lead, and here he was, without any clear plan. As a brother, and even more a twin, if Marcus was forced to carry a burden that could crush him, wasn't it Angus's duty to lend him his strength?

He looked across at the shambling giant that was The Court. 'If it were mine,' burst out Angus, 'then perhaps I shouldn't mind. But I'm damned if I'll be a bloody caretaker all my life.'

'Thank goodness the age of the usurper is done,' remarked his sister.

'Don't be rude,' he said.

Lisa flushed. 'I'm sorry. I didn't mean to be. Everyone's so horribly sensitive these days.'

'If you thought before you said things – or borrowed things,' he added meaningfully, 'you'd make yourself a lot less unhappy. This nag's getting cold. Go and make yourself useful somewhere.'

As he rode towards the stables, he wondered if he'd been a bit hard. Lisa was only just seventeen, at that gauche stage where you and the world seem completely out of step. It couldn't be easy for her – but it was no less hard for them all. Nonetheless he resolved to be more charitable.

Henry never felt easy with Marcus on his own. It was something he couldn't explain, perhaps some legacy from his own father who had never spoken to him if it could be avoided. Having twins of course was easier, there was never the awful embarrassment that accompanied talking individually. But sooner or later he had to talk, and he might as well get it over with.

'Sit down, my boy, sit down.' He waved a thin hand towards the bedside chair and Marcus sat, managing to convey restlessness.

'I hope you're well, sir,' he said jerkily.

'I think it's quite clear that I am not.'

'Yes. Sorry, sir.'

Marcus clasped his hands between his knees, pressing the palms together with subdued violence. Henry said, 'It's got to stop, you

41

know! Don't think I don't know what's been happening. I haven't told your mother, of course.' Marcus's dark eyes, that were identical to those of his brother and yet unimaginably different, fixed on his face. 'The drugs!' went on Henry. 'Do I have to spell everything out? There's always that sort of circle at college – I thought Angus would keep you out of it. The drinking's one thing, but you are my heir! Ordinarily –' he paused, and seemed to catch his breath – 'it wouldn't matter you see. But we can't know what's going to happen.'

His son was looking at the floor. 'I don't take anything,' he said in a low voice.

'This isn't any time for lies ! Are you addicted to the stuff?'

Marcus slowly shook his head.

Henry's fist clenched as if to strike at something, but then fell limply on to the bed. 'It's the voices,' whispered Marcus.

'Oh, for God's sake, let's have none of this! We all try things we shouldn't, we all do things we regret. I understand that. I know it can happen. But if you lay off the stuff and take regular food and exercise, and remember who you are, it'll be the end of the problem. Look at me.'

Marcus deliberately avoided his gaze. 'Perhaps I should see a doctor,' he said diffidently.

'Nonsense! I know my sons. If it's willpower that's needed, they've more than enough. You're a Hellyn, remember that.'

'I get these headaches,' said Marcus, and as his father sighed he burst out, 'I'll do my best, Father. I will try. But it isn't easy when they keep talking at you. Sometimes they never stop, they go on and on! I have to do things, you see. They – they make me.'

But Henry was tired, weary to the point of extinction. He had resolved, years ago, to be a better father than his own, but now he hadn't the strength. Instinctively he closed his ears to what his son was saying. 'You don't have to finish your degree,' he grunted. 'We'll get you away from the place, they won't follow you here. They're scum, you know that, don't you?'

'Yes. Yes.' He began reciting beneath his breath, a personal litany. 'I know what's real and I know what isn't, I know where they are, I don't have to go there. If they call me I won't go. Ever!'

'I knew – you'd see sense.'

His father's eyes closed and Marcus got up to go. He stood looking down at the grey face, bones so close to the skin that he almost thought he could see them. If there was no skin there would be bone, and beneath that veins and arteries ... His eyes were X-rays boring down, seeing everything. He saw his father's brain, pulsing with thought, and within it was a world of tunnels and giant spaces. He

42

saw it all, it was there for him to see, and the wonder of it held him quite still.

Curtiss came into the room. He saw Marcus frozen over his father, his hand raised and yet absolutely unmoving. For a second he wondered if he should strike him down, he'd always known the boy would go completely barmy some time. He cleared his throat. 'Well, sir. You'll be wanted downstairs, I dare say.'

Marcus turned, almost dreamily. 'He isn't asleep, you know. I can see his thoughts, like red and blue water.'

'You won't want to be disturbing him with things like that, sir.'

'No. I'll go downstairs.'

Marcus went out, but on his way down he stopped at the window and put his hands flat against the glass. His mood swung and hovered. He felt an odd sort of amusement, almost an elation. Was it drugs or drink or madness? He didn't understand himself, he didn't know why the world went on without seeming to understand or include him at all. Sometimes he felt that he alone could see what was really happening, and if that was a delusion then it was theirs, not his. But it hurt to be like this. If he could live in the simple way that others did there would be nothing to care for, nothing to suffer.

He banged his hand against the glass, harder and harder, until the pane creaked and almost broke. He closed his eyes on tears. They blamed him for being as he was, his father knew it as weakness and lack of courage. He felt, suddenly, the weight of guilt and confusion, and a voice, loud, shouted in his head: 'It's your fault! All your fault! You ought to be dead!'

Marcus turned and ran down the stairs, away from the voice, but it chased him, at times whispering and then shouting so loud it hurt.

'Is something the matter?'

Edward. Marcus stopped, breathing hard. The voice subsided to a whisper, a sibilant threat. He felt his nerves steadying.

'I'm all right,' he said gruffly.

'It's exciting, isn't it? Everything looks so magnificent.'

Banks of flowers, like exquisitely soft beds, filled every corner. Silver bowls overflowed with roses, and in the dining-room, on the white-swathed tables, there were garlands of blue and green. All the servants were dressed in their best: the footmen in green and gold livery that had been passed down through generations, Curtiss immaculate in crisp black and white. Even the maids, dumpy and middle-aged as they were, had pinned starched aprons to their black dresses and settled frilly caps on their hair. They looked contemptuously at the catering staff, who did not belong, and had no notion of how to behave at The Court. Curtiss watched them

43

constantly, certain that they were here to steal the silver.

'Do you often have parties like this?' Edward stood watching; it was like the mobilisation of some great and powerful army.

'No — no, not often. A lot of dinners and things, but nothing like this. The old man wouldn't spend the money. We haven't had a ball since I was a child. The servants love it, you know. When I'm the earl I shall hold parties once a week.'

He didn't seem to be joking, although otherwise it was both a tactless and childish remark. Edward glanced at him, feeling uncomfortable. There was something unsettling about Marcus, something horribly unpredictable. He was the person Edward least wanted to be with at The Court.

'I've got to go,' he said abruptly. 'I've got to find Mara.'

To his surprise, Marcus laughed, quite naturally. 'You shouldn't let her tease you,' he said. 'She always has people in love with her, it's the way she's made. You'll be all right till she gets bored.'

Edward's face was flaming. Did Marcus know she slept with him? 'It isn't like that — she's very kind to me.'

'Is she?' As Edward watched, the bright, humorous look faded. It was as if Marcus was listening to something. He looked unsure, anxious. Without a word more he turned and walked away.

Lisa changed early for the party. It was a dress of violet silk, and when she had chosen it she had thought it sophisticated and smart. Now, in the dim light of her bedroom, it seemed to leach the colour from her skin.

The maid said, 'Shall I put your hair up, Miss? Then you can wear your earrings.'

Lisa stared at herself in the mirror. There seemed no point in making an effort, knowing that Mara would extinguish her. 'Leave it down,' she said. 'You can go now, I'll see to everything.'

When the woman had gone she toyed for a moment or two with lipsticks and mascara, but in the end powdered her face into blankness. God forbid that she should be seen as pathetically trying to compete with her sister, she would rather not enter the lists at all.

As she prepared to go downstairs her spaniel wheezed and snuffled from under the bed, pressing himself into her skirt. 'Bad dog,' she said automatically. 'You shouldn't be in here. Come downstairs and I'll shut you in the dog room.'

The corridors were cold and she scurried downstairs. White-jacketed caterers were everywhere, and Curtiss was struggling to marshal them. 'Is everything all right?'

'Ah, Lady Eloise!' Curtiss always made a point of using her full

44

name, managing to convey his opinion that it should never have been corrupted. 'Lady Melville did say she would bring me the amended guest list, but so far I don't appear to have it.'

'Don't worry, I'll get it for you.' She flashed him a brief smile and hurried off to find her mother. Last minute additions and cancellations were inevitable and Curtiss liked to be aware of them. He prided himself on his ability to deter gatecrashers and in London he was invaluable, but at The Court? Lisa could hardly imagine anyone venturing out to the wilds of Yorkshire just to inveigle their way into Mara's ball, whatever its magnificence.

She found her mother in Henry's room. Charlotte was wearing pale blue silk, not new, and she did not look well in it. As the days passed she seemed to become more vague, her hair more wispy. But the Hellyn necklace was slung round her throat in an act of defiance, diamonds and sapphires trembling on wires.

'You look lovely, Mother,' said Lisa.

'Thank you, darling. This necklace always brings me out in a rash after an hour, but I felt I should wear it. Don't you think, Henry?'

'You look wonderful. As always.' Henry extended his hand. He was in evening dress, the clothes lying against the pillows as if there was barely a body within.

'Curtiss wants the guest list.'

'Good heavens, yes, I forgot. Look after your father, will you, dear? I'll be back to see him safely downstairs.' Charlotte rustled away, and Lisa noticed that her mother's bare elbow was smeared with some of Henry's medicine. A sense of an evening doomed came over her.

'How are you, Lisa? Not letting all this get you down?'

'She sat on the edge of the bed. 'A bit. You oughtn't to come down, you know.'

'Nonsense! I shall be fine. And Mara wants it, I couldn't spoil her ball.'

Jealousy, like hot green bile, bubbled up in her chest. She ducked her head. Outside she could hear Marcus calling to his brother as they set up the car parking signs.

Henry said, 'Now, Lisa, I want you to know that I'm relying on you. You're a good, hard-working girl. I want you to look after things.'

She felt like choking. 'What sort of things?'

'Now, how can I know that? It's for you to judge, my dear.'

She knew he meant when he was dead. If she was Mara, if it was Mara here now, he wouldn't be saying these things. He'd cuddle her, stroke her, tell her not to cry. Lisa couldn't cry, not one tear could

45

she shed. 'What's going to happen?' she asked thickly. 'Marcus is ill, he can't even finish his degree.'

For a moment Henry seemed roused to irritation. 'Marcus is not ill! As I've told your mother again and again, he's got himself into bad company. He's been running himself ragged at Oxford, all this drinking and partying. Once he settles down — well. There's always Angus.'

'Yes.'

He began to cough, muffling it against the pillow. Lisa held a water glass to his lips and after a moment he lay still.

'I'm going to miss you all,' he said softly.

And then she was crying, hot tears that coursed in rivers down her cheeks. She bent and threw her arms around his neck, hugging him tight. Her tears ran down inside his shirt, the collar gaped wide now that he was so thin. He patted her feebly. 'My good girl. My steady one.'

After a moment she pulled herself together, blowing her nose fiercely on a tissue. Her mother came in, looking flustered. 'Two whole boxes of glasses have gone missing,' she said distractedly. 'Nobody knows where they are. If we can't find them we'll have to let people use the Waterford. I'd rather they had paper cups.'

'They're in the dog room, I saw them,' said Lisa, and got up. 'Have you seen to the band, Mother?' They must have something to eat first.'

'Oh, good heavens, yes, we don't want them passing out from drinking on empty stomachs. But I daren't ask in the kitchen. Everything's so terribly muddled!' She put a hand to her head.

'I'll see to it.'

Lisa went downstairs. All around were last minute details needing attention, from the glasses, to the ice in the giant bowl of punch, to the Coalport tea service which should be discreetly set out for those older ladies who might prefer tea. The upheaval in the household was taking its toll. The elements that made up the ball had been assembled, but no-one had woven them into a pattern. She hurried about, moving from Curtiss to the musicians, to Cook and on into the ballroom. Edward was there, seemingly at a loss.

'Hello,' said Lisa. 'Your tie's crooked.' She reached up to straighten it.

'Oh. Thanks. He was sweating slightly, she could see it glistening on his neck. 'Don't you think the room's wonderful?' he said jerkily.

'No, I think it's in horrible taste. But everyone else will like it. Have you seen Mara?'

'No. No, I haven't.'

In fact they had just parted. He'd tried to kiss her and in a flash

46

she'd turned. 'Stop mauling me, damn you! Go away. Can't you make yourself useful?'

He wondered if she got some sort of pleasure from reviling him. If he could only be cool and distant, the piper instead of the fawning puppy, squirming as Mara played the tune. Suppose he was cold to her tonight, letting her see that she couldn't treat him like this? He had a brief but delicious fantasy of Mara begging, naked, for forgiveness.

At that precise moment the door opened and Mara came in. She had caught up her hair in a diamanté clip, letting spun-gold ringlets fall to her shoulders. Her dress was deep blue, edged with weighty silver embroidery, full-skirted, strapless and slightly old-fashioned. But it was a fashion that would always suit Mara, a Cinderella dress that on others would look outlandish.

She caught Edward's eye and smiled, amost apologetically. 'This is so tight I can hardly breathe.'

'It's worth it. You'll have a triumph.' Lisa's voice was cool, controlled.

'Why haven't you put your hair up, Lisa? You were going to wear it in a bun. And you should use some make-up. Shall I do it?'

'No thanks. I'll leave it like this.' Against Mara's brilliance no other sun could shine.

Lisa turned to look out of the window, where the creeper was two feet thick, down to the front door. They had prised it open for tonight, set the huge oak panels wide and it had groaned – squealed almost – like a creature wakened from sleep. 'People are coming,' she said. 'I'll get the band.'

'Oh God!' said Mara, and put her hand on Edward's arm. 'What's going to happen tonight? I shall be all right if – don't let me make a fool of myself.'

'I suppose you'd rather make a fool of me,' he said, and her head flicked towards him, startled.

'Are you going to be horrible?' she asked. 'I'd rather you weren't tonight. My father's coming down.'

She moved away from him and he felt familiar rage. When he treated her as she treated him, everything went wrong. He hadn't wanted to drive her away. It was his own fault. He was so solid and plodding and she as wilful and capricious as a fairy.

The band was striking up, light summery music as if to conjure up summer spirits and a warm fresh evening, but it was lost in the heavy air. Two or three photographers came in, festooned with equipment, ready to snap the arriving guests for posterity and the evening's antics for the Fleet Street rags. Lisa whispered to Curtiss, 'Make sure they go before eleven. We don't want anything embarrassing.'

Curtiss nodded. These events always got completely out of hand after midnight. He had the boat ready to fish out non-swimmers from the lake and the stable doors were locked to forestall any re-enactment of the ride from Aix to Ghent.

'They're bringing Father down,' said Mara, and her face lit up.

'Deb of the year, that one,' murmured a photographer. 'And her heart belongs to Daddy,' grinned another.

They watched as she bent over the long figure of her father. He was in a big leather wing chair, near a window, immaculate in crisp white shirt and dinner jacket. His legs were elegantly crossed to reveal shoes with silver buckles, and tartan socks, his lifelong affectation. An early guest came in, a brigadier escorting his daughter. He looked, looked again, and finally went across for a few words.

Afterwards he lifted a finger for Curtiss. 'For God's sake get me a stiff whisky! I didn't recognise him. And the Lord knows, we were at prep school together!'

Curtiss obliged, discreetly. The band swept into a waltz and Henry said to Charlotte, 'Get the children to dance, darling.' Marcus took Mara and Angus partnered Lisa. They swept round the empty floor, laughing to each other. 'Enchanting,' murmured the brigadier. At the end, Henry lifted his thin hands and clapped.

He was taken back to bed just before midnight, when the ballroom throbbed with people and heat, when the open windows could admit nothing more than leaden, oppressive air. Thunder was rumbling in the far hills, occasional silent flashes of lightning lit up the gardens.

Marcus stood on the stairs and looked out of a window. In the flashes of light the statues seemed to move, this way and that, waving arms they did not possess. He knew it wasn't real. Sometimes he hardly knew where his thoughts ended and reality began, but tonight wasn't that sort of time. How could it be when upstairs his father lay exhausted in bed, dragging air into his lungs desperately, hopelessly?

Angus came downstairs and stood beside him. 'The doctor's coming.'

'Is he dying?'

'I don't know. He doesn't seem able to breathe. I shouldn't have left Mother, but I can't − I can't watch.'

'I'll go.' Marcus turned from the window and went quickly up the stairs. He knew he should be there, it was his place.

Outside the door he hesitated, trying to steady himself. He could hear voices in the room, they echoed inside his head, each one going on and on and merging with the next. He let out a sob of pain, for himself. Why wouldn't it stop? He wanted to cry for his father but his damned head, the damned and damnable things in his head, wouldn't let him! His face was wet with sweat and when he turned the door handle his hands shook. Mara, Lisa and his mother all turned to look at him.

Charlotte was sitting by the bed, supporting Henry on a bank of pillows. She glanced up. 'Don't come in if you're feeling ill. We can't be bothered with you.' Henry's face was grey-blue, and his eyes stared unseeingly. He breathed in short, shallow pants.

Marcus said, 'I'm all right. I thought I should be here.'

Mara rose up in a rustle of taffeta. 'The doctor should be here. He's taking forever, I'll have him struck off! Doesn't he realise it's an emergency?'

'It's only ten minutes since we called,' said Lisa reasonably.

'But he should be here. Father needs oxygen. We should have it, now!'

Henry emitted a low groan. Charlotte said, 'It's all right, my darling. The doctor's coming, he knows it's an emergency.'

Lisa, her own heart shuddering in her chest, thought how calm her mother seemed. Knowing her, she wouldn't have thought she could cope with this, she was too fearful, too weak. But suddenly all that was gone. Amongst them all there was only compassion, for even their grief held back, waiting. They were all waiting.

Marcus went again to the window and looked out into the gardens. From here he could see people strolling about on the lawns, he wondered if the statues were amongst them. A sudden hiss and the rain started. Shrieks, screams, everyone began running back to the house. Two groups of young men were howling, attacking each other with curtain poles held like battering rams. Lightning lit them up like flame, their hair was plastered to their heads by a deluge of water. They dropped the poles and fled back to the house.

'I wish the doctor would come. He's worse, Mother! Mother, what can we do?'

'Sit down, darling. The doctor will come, there's nothing we can do.'

But Mara still stood by the bed, her fists clenched in the skirt of her lovely dress. Her father's breath was raking in his throat, his eyes were half turned up in his head. A pulse in his temple beat wildly, erratically. Mara started moaning like a child.

'Don't. Please don't.' Lisa stood beside her, arms around her waist.

The breathing changed, rattling in fluid, but the thunder crashed again, rolling round and round the towers of The Court like the roar of an angry bear. At it ceased, falling away into nothingness, Henry died.

49

Chapter Eight

They were in the dining-room. Marcus stood at the head of the long oak table, his hands against the wood. To his right sat his mother, to his left Angus and Lisa. Mara, unable to relax, stood tensely against the fireplace. No fire burned today. An arrangement of lilies filled the space, like the marble of a tomb.

Marcus cleared his throat. All morning he had been closeted with lawyers and accountants, trying to make sense of what at first seemed incomprehensible. It was as if his imaginings, kept battened close within him, had seeped out and tainted reality.

'There — it seems there are some problems,' he began huskily.

Mara snorted. Her face was white, her eyes violet shadowed. 'Surely not! Father's dead and buried, what could possibly be wrong?'

'Shut up, Mara,' said Angus tightly. 'Let him tell us.'

Almost jovially Marcus said, 'Actually, there isn't a lot to say. We're broke. According to the accountants, we've been living on borrowed time for at least a year, and probably more.'

Lisa said, 'Marcus, are you sure this isn't one of your silly ideas? I know Grandfather was as close-fisted as can be, but since he died we haven't had to economise! We were going to do the roof. Father was talking about buying a place in Kenya! There must be shares — and things —' she trailed off, looking towards her mother.

Charlotte sat quite still, her face like creased paper. All her children waited, expecting enlightenment. 'Mother?' said Angus at last.

'I — I'm not really sure I can help,' she said apologetically. 'When your grandfather died we had discussions with the accountants, naturally. I know your father felt they were being very gloomy — we were so tired, you see, of living on the old man's charity. You've no idea how it was, going cap in hand to ask for the school fees, or the rent for the London flat.'

'Of course we were extravagant,' she went on defiantly. 'We needed to be. The Kenya trip was wonderful – your father deserved it! And after all those years living cheek by jowl with his father, I deserved it too. We knew we'd have to tighten our belts eventually. We just didn't imagine – he should have had thirty more years! He should have been given a chance!'

The tears were brimming. Angus got up and put his hands on his mother's shoulders. 'Why don't you leave this to us?' he said gently. Charlotte nodded. Hardly an hour had gone by without tears since Henry died, even the doctor had suggested she go away. They were sending her to Scotland, to her sister, who lived in a cottage near the Spey, and she wanted to go, to be away from everything. They all waited, silent, while she walked unsteadily out of the room.

'So there you are,' said Marcus as the door closed. 'I haven't grasped it all, but what I do know is this: two lots of inheritance tax, farm incomes down, and the stock market on the floor. Father's been selling great chunks of stock lately. He had to. The upkeep of this place is crippling in staff costs alone.'

Mara came towards the table, her hands clasped in front of her. 'All right, so we're not rich. We don't have a lot of money. But we do have something, don't we?' She glared at her brother, as if this whole appalling nightmare was his personal responsibility.

'I don't know. I don't understand it all. There are some shares left, but we can't sell those apparently, they're held against taxes. And the farms and things – Father took out loans. None of it's straightforward.' He rubbed at the anxious furrows between his brows.

'Oh, for Christ's sake, can't someone sensible get involved in all this?' said Mara cruelly. 'He's been imagining doom and gloom for years, and now he wants us to believe it's come true.'

'I did sit in on the discussions, Mara,' said Angus mildly. 'If anything he's understating the case.'

Very softly, dreading the answer, Lisa said, 'What's going to happen then? To all of us?'

That, it seemed was the crux. 'In a few moments I'm going to see Curtiss,' said Marcus heavily. 'Everyone's going to be dismissed. Absolutely everyone. We'll do our best as regards pensions but there wasn't any fund or anything. Tomorrow's Friday. We shall pay the wages in the morning and expect everyone to leave.'

'Not the grooms, said Mara in amazement. 'There's a stable full of horses out there.'

Angus said harshly, 'We're selling them. Every last one's going to a dealer.'

51

'Angus, you can't!' wailed Lisa. 'What about the hunt? Father was Master, now it's Marcus or you!'

'If you give up all the horses, people will know what's happened,' agreed Mara. 'And we mustn't let it out! I can't bear people watching us, feeling sorry.'

'More like dunning us,' said Angus. 'You can't buy on account when you're broke.'

'There you are then! Keep the horses ... keep just two. We can look after two, can't we?'

Angus and Marcus looked at each other. They thought of the opening meet, always held at The Court; the Hunt Ball, for which they flung open the house. Even the puppy show was held on the lawn, and had been for generations. 'It's never wise to rush into things,' said Angus. Rigid with tension, his brother nodded.

A little victory won, Mara pushed ahead. She sat at the table, her long fingers pressed to her temples. 'We must sell things,' she said determinedly. 'The library chairs. The silver. What about the paintings – there must be something worth money?'

Marcus shook his head. 'The Hellyns have been through those once already, half of them are copies. Even Mother's jewels – the Hellyn necklace was sold to an Arab four years ago. But you're right, there are things we could sell. Suppose we do gut the place? Flog the hangings, pawn the silver? What's the point of it?'

'Because then we wouldn't be poor!' snapped Mara.

Marcus grimaced. 'I don't think we'd be very rich, either. We'd have something, I suppose. But it's The Court we have to think of! It isn't anything without things inside.'

'Can't we give it to the National Trust?' asked Lisa shrilly. 'They let you live in the house, you just have to put up with people tramping about.'

'Not visitors!' said Mara, horrified. 'The place would be unbearable! Anything but visitors!'

Angus sighed. 'The National Trust won't have it. Father tried. Apparently when you give them a house you have to give them a fortune to keep it up. Although why, if you've got a fortune, you should need to get rid of the house in the first place I don't know.'

Mara shook her head in bewilderment. 'This is absolutely ridiculous! I mean, we could sell the place. There's no point in being here now Father's gone.'

'Could we sell it?' said Angus. 'A place this size, in terrible condition, miles from anywhere? It's listed, so no-one can alter it to turn it into an hotel or offices. What could it be?'

'I don't know! There must be something!' Mara banged her fist on the table. 'We can't stay here and starve.'

'More like drown,' said Angus sardonically. 'The timbers have gone in the roof over the hall. If we want grants to do repairs we have to open the house. No contents, means no visitors, means no grant. One tumbledown house.'

'So what?' snapped Mara. 'Let the place fall down − at least we'd have the money. We should sell everything, every last teaspoon.'

'You sound like a scrap dealer,' said Angus contemptuously.

'Just plain selfish, if you ask me,' said Lisa.

'Except that you'd know more about plainness than I would, don't you think?' Mara's smile glittered. She looked wonderfully beautiful and cruel. And then, suddenly, she put her head in her hands and sobbed. The others watched her, patiently waiting for the paroxysm to cease. Since Henry's death, since the funeral, they hadn't understood any of her moods, but that she should have them, that they understood.

At last she stopped, drawing shuddering breaths. 'I'm sorry,' she whispered. 'I didn't mean any of that. It's just so dreadful. We're all in the middle of things ... my season, university, school. What are we going to do?' Wet strands of hair trailed across her eyes and she pushed at them with her palms.

Marcus said, 'I won't be going back. Obviously I've got to stay here now. Try and sort things out.'

'I shall go back,' said Angus, and his voice held a note of defiance. 'I've got to get a job. I need a good degree.'

No-one challenged him, and he was almost disappointed. He almost wanted to be made to change his mind.

'Which leaves us,' said Mara, meeting Lisa's eyes. 'We can't leave Marcus here all on his own. Can we?'

No-one, not even Marcus, could imagine him alone here. Someone had to stay. Mara looked at her sister. 'You could always do your A levels later,' she coaxed. 'I'll stay home next year, if nothing's changed. I might meet someone, a millionaire. That is best, isn't it?'

Angus said, 'Good God, you don't think we can pay for your flat and everything, do you? Haven't you understood a word of what's been said?'

'If we're keeping your horses, we can afford my season,' flared Mara. 'There must be something we can sell. And if there isn't, if you really are that mean. I'll sleep on someone's floor. But I won't stay here without Father. I simply won't!'

They all waited for Lisa. In a low voice, quite without expression, she said, 'I don't mind staying. I think it's what Father expected, actually. We'll manage all right, won't we, Marcus?'

53

He nodded. He was twisting his hands together. He hardly seemed to be listening.

'If you would like to say goodbye, my lady?' Curtiss stood in the doorway, looking oddly out of place in his trilby hat and overcoat. Charlotte's hands fluttered up and down. 'To everyone you mean?' She looked wildly around, because if Henry was here this wouldn't have happened, he wouldn't have permitted it.

'I'll go,' said Mara suddenly. She felt a deserter, leaving her post in the thick of the battle. Leaving the house. She had to do something.

The entire staff was lined up by the front door. In their outdoor clothes they were a motley collection of people: old faces that Mara had known forever, youthful under-grooms and under-gardeners that she barely recognised. So many of them. How in God's name was the place to keep going? she thought wildly. But she stood before them and made a brave little speech.

'I can hardly tell you how sad this makes us all,' she began. 'Some of you have been with us almost all my life. The house is being closed, and I can't tell you when it will open again. But it will open again, that I promise. And if you want them, there will be jobs waiting for you. Goodbye, and the very best of luck.'

An elderly housemaid started to sob. One of the men shouted, 'Three cheers for Lady Mara!' and they cheered, raggedly. Beginning at the far end of the line Mara shook hands with them all, and she thought, What did these people do here? All these hands, to service one huge house. No wonder they were ruined.

A coach was waiting to take them to the station, all except Curtiss. The chauffeur's last job was to drive him there in the Rolls, which was then to be delivered to the saleroom. Her father had loved that car, and so had the chauffeur. She half hoped he'd go away with it and keep it forever, like a pet. It was old and probably wouldn't sell. 'It's like a charabanc to Blackpool,' said Mara tensely. Curtiss said nothing. When she glanced at him she saw his face set against tears. 'Where will you go?' she asked.

He sighed, mastering himself. 'My sister in Bournemouth, for a holiday. Then London. Butlers are in great demand, I hear, on a temporary basis.'

'I might see you,' said Mara. 'You will come back, won't you? One day.'

'I shall advise the earl of my address,' muttered Curtiss. 'It's a bugger, that's what it is!'

Mara tried not to laugh. Suddenly everything seemed terribly hysterically funny. Last night she had wandered through the house, looking at things, trying to imagine what everything cost. She had no yardstick, she had scarcely bought more than a book for herself in all her life. Even her clothes went on the account. How many silver teaspoons went towards one flat? How much of a carpet bought food for a week ... were these things she should know? Did the housemaids know them? She turned and ran indoors, ran until she cannoned into Edward.

The laughter came out, a series of shrill giggles.

'Mara. Mara, stop it!'

'I don't think I can.' But she did. She stood while he held her arms, as if she might run away and do something stupid.

'I'm going in the morning,' he said.

'What, you as well? As Curtiss says, it's a bugger, that's what it is.' She started to giggle again, but checked herself. 'Are you going home?'

'Well – actually no. I thought I might go to London. Ma doesn't want me home for three months or so. I'd have gone before, but the funeral and so on – '

'Yes. We haven't exactly been ideal hosts.'

She threw back her head and looked at him. His hair was darker now that there was no sun to bleach it, and it needed cutting. She reached up to smooth his fringe aside. He said thickly, 'Come to my room, Mara. Please!'

'No.' Looking up into his face, she said, 'But I'll come to London with you. I haven't a bean, you'll have to get the flat. We'll live together.'

'Do you mean that? Really?' He thought she must be teasing.

'Of course I do.'

He thought, suddenly, 'She'll marry me.' Against all the odds, all probabilities, this gorgeous creature wanted him. He put his hand on her breast, feeling its weight through her blouse. He loved the softness, the solid boneless mass. 'Yes,' said Mara softly. 'In London we can do just as we like.'

They dined formally that evening, to please Charlotte. But she stayed in her room and they were left to themselves, eating a casserole left by Cook and cheese uneaten since the ball. No-one could find anything, and Angus had failed to light the fire. The house felt empty, unfamiliar. Lisa felt a start of surprise when she went to her bedroom and found the bed unmade since the morning.

'A terrible day,' said Mara, her fingers tight around the stem of her wineglass. 'The end of absolutely everything.'

'Only the past,' said Edward suddenly, loudly. 'Tomorrow is the start of the future. It can be a new beginning!'

Marcus laughed and sat up in his chair. 'He's right, you know. We've lived in the past for too long. It's up to us now. Up to each one of us to get free of this place and make something in life!'

They looked round the table at each other. They had so much on their side, youth, intelligence, beauty, each one in different measure. It seemed, suddenly, as if they were about to take a magic carpet ride, out across the world.

Chapter Nine

Edward and Mara took the train to London, and even the fare cost more than they expected. 'We'll economise,' said Mara airily. 'Mother thinks I'll be staying with Diandra, so we'll both stay there and save on the hotel. We'll have a place of our own in a week.'

It seemed eminently sensible, and they took a taxi from King's Cross to an exclusive block of flats in St John's Wood.

'We could get something here,' said Mara. 'There are always places going, the embassies move people in and out all the time.' She swept into the lobby, blinding the porter with a brilliant smile. 'The Honourable Diandra Venables, please. We're friends of hers, she isn't expecting us.'

The porter looked nonplussed. 'I'm sorry, miss. Miss Venables is away in Italy at present. With her family.

'Oh God!' Mara turned to Edward and pulled a dismal face. 'I'd forgotten. While we've been tied up at home everyone's gone abroad. Well, we'll just have to see if there's somewhere we can rent. Tell me – ' she turned to the porter ' – do you have a flat available? I'm Lady Mara Hellyn.'

'Mara – ' Edward tried to distract her, but without success.

The porter was murmuring, 'We do have a number of flats at this time of year,' and consulting a list, while Mara leaned over his shoulder and encouraged him. 'We must have two bathrooms,' she insisted, hurrying the porter's finger over some unsatisfactory abode. 'Does that have a verandah? How lovely.'

'Mara!' Edward was insistent, and pulled at her arm.

'Honestly, Edward! I'm trying to sort out somewhere for us to stay, what on earth is the matter?'

'I've got to talk to you. In private.'

'Oh, for God's sake.'

She stepped dramatically over to the elegant window, in which stood plants, a sculpture and a small notice informing anyone who was interested that the premises were directly wired to the police, 'What is it?' she demanded.

'I — I can't afford a flat here. I don't think I could even afford a cupboard.'

She didn't understand. 'Look, it's us that's flat broke. You've got the Kenyan coffee farm, remember? Dozens of blacks to do the work and a life of ease, except for shooting lions and things. You can always phone home and ask for more cash.'

Edward ran a hand through his shock of fair hair. 'It isn't like that any more! We have a good life on the farm, a very good life, but not like this! Ma does what she can — but I work on the farm, we all do. There isn't the money for expensive flats and — and all this!' He waved his arm at the polished marble, the unctuous porter, the glossy street beyond.

'How on earth did you make Father believe you were loaded then?'

'He didn't. I think you just assumed —'

'I see. So it's all my fault.'

She turned on her heel and went back to the porter. 'I'm so sorry, but my friend seems to feel we'd be happier taking something by the river. May I come back if we don't find something to suit? Thank you so much.'

Out on the street with all their baggage, Mara said, 'Since you are Mr rather small Moneybags, where do you suggest we go?'

Edward shrugged. 'I don't know. A flat agency or something?'

Mara let out her breath in a long sigh. 'Oh God! Very well, needs must when the devil drives. Let's see what they have to offer.'

Hours later they sat at a table outside a pub. Mara drank gin while Edward had beer. They had registered with three agencies and looked at a dozen flats, all of them vetoed by Mara on sight.

'You shouldn't be so concerned about being central,' said Edward.

'There isn't any point in being here if we're not. If people were back in town, we could stay with someone — it's just the time of year. Oh, if we'd been around four weeks ago we could have been invited on a yacht, anything! Would you like to be on a yacht?' She gazed at him dreamily.

He covered her hand with his own. 'What I'd like most is to be alone with you. Just the two of us, with no-one barging in all the time. Don't you want that?'

She didn't, particularly. In fact, now that they were together here she was doubting the wisdom of it all. Would they have to sleep together? It wasn't the sex she minded, more the thought of Edward's ever-present body, invading her privacy all through the night. 'Why don't we go to a hotel?' she said coaxingly.

'I think we'd better go and take the place up five flights.'

'It smells.'

'They all smell. So did the St John's Wood place.'

'But that was the smell of money,' said Mara and licked her lips. Edward laughed and so did she.

The flat was actually a large attic, with one part of it partitioned off to make a tiny kitchen. The shared bathroom was a floor below, and the water was cold.

'It's as bad as The Court,' said Mara, bad-temperedly flinging herself down in the lumpy armchair. 'But with rather less style. Why can't I have plumbing that works, and central heating, and power points?'

'In Kenya we have lizards and snakes,' said Edward. 'You'd hate that.'

'No I shouldn't! At least there'd be someone to get rid of them for me. Oh, Edward, I think I want to be rich. I never minded before, I didn't realise how horrible it is to be poor. Are you going to take me out to dinner or do we have to starve?'

Edward rummaged in his pockets. The deposit on the flat had taken all his month's allowance, he was down to a few notes and small change.

Mara looked at the cash with distaste. 'I suppose we could have fish and chips,' she said distantly. 'We shall have to live on salads. I can't imagine cooking in that grubby little kitchen.'

She rose languidly from the chair, reaching for her jacket. As always, Edward had to watch her. When she moved, every time she moved, he couldn't look away. Her beauty, her grace, enthralled some part of him that wasn't anything to do with sex, or brain, or anything he could define. Like a sunset, like a leopard hunting in the grass, she touched the very essence of him. If we are put here by God, he thought, to love the beauty of the things He made, then I must love Mara.

They sat on the Embankment and she fed him chips out of the paper. Afterwards they walked, and in a dark alley she let him make love to her, while the taxis roared past yards away, taking people home from the theatre. It wasn't what he wanted, all rushed and fumbling, and he couldn't understand why. They had a room now, they could have spent hours giving each other pleasure. He wanted to love her, and all she gave him was a quick fuck.

When it was done she went and stood where she could see the lights, brilliant white and orange and blue, and beneath them women in furs and diamonds. She looked sad.

59

Back in the flat she sat up while he lay down on the bed. He watched her, turned away from him, her chin resting on the palm of her hand. Her hair fell around her like mist.

'I think this is the most wonderful thing that has ever happened to me,' he burst out suddenly.

She didn't turn her head. 'Then you're very easily satisfied.' She got up and came to the bed, stripping off her clothes and leaving them strewn across the floor. He wanted her again, urgently, but she pushed him away. 'I'm tired. Leave me alone, Edward.'

He lay down, feeling again the familiar bewilderment.

Over the next week Mara telephoned everyone she knew. Most were still on holiday, but she left messages and wrote casual little notes. Their money soon ran out and Edward was forced to take an advance on next month's allowance, although what would happen next month he could not think. Mara needed money, she almost absorbed it. Her tights were renewed daily, her clothes, screwed up on the floor each night, had to be cleaned and pressed. They ate out every day, and she bought flowers, bunches and bunches of them.

When he protested, she was amazed. 'You can't expect me to live here and not have flowers, can you? They aren't expensive.'

'Orchids are very expensive.'

'Perhaps that's why I like them. I can't bear to be ordinary and housemaidish.'

She sighed, and stared at the spotted blooms. By their very grandeur they transcended the milk bottle in which they stood. Desperately untidy, Mara nonetheless placed her mark on her surroundings. With her in it, the flat took on an air of almost Parisian glamour.

In no time at all there was no money. Mara couldn't believe that there was nothing, she couldn't understand why he didn't just appeal to his mother. 'You can simply say that London's more expensive than you expected. The visit didn't work out as planned, it wasn't your fault.'

Edward shook his head. 'She gave me what she could afford. We'll have to get jobs, that's all.'

Mara rolled on her stomach on the bed, eating a chocolate. She had gone out and bought a box of chocolates and a magazine when they had no money for the electric meter and nothing to pay the rent. He felt genuine, fierce annoyance.

'You might at least show some concern! You might at least acknowledge that it's your problem as well as mine!'

'You can't complain. I let you sleep with me, don't I?'

60

He was amazed. 'Look — I love you, Mara. I think you love me. I'm not keeping you in return for — for that. Don't I please you? Isn't it what you want?'

She gave him a sideways look. He crowded her so. If she was kind he came on so strong she felt like a dog backed into a corner. He forced her to snarl at him, and then complained when his feelings were hurt. It was time to be honest. 'You assume too much,' she said lightly. 'I like you, Edward, and I like the sex. But I'm not going out to get a job cleaning or something, so we can come back each night to our little lovenest and enthral each other. This is a stop-gap. It doesn't mean a thing.'

'You don't mean that. You think you want other things, but you don't. Why don't we get married and earn some money and go back to Kenya together — '

'Oh my God!' Mara swept her legs off the bed. 'I've had enough of this. I'm getting out.'

'You know you can't. All you want is for me to get a job washing dishes so you can lie in bed all day — and eat chocolates!' A sudden charge of anger, rushing through him like a lit fuse, made him swipe the chocolates in a shower across the floor. He rubbed a hand across his eyes.

Mara saw that he was close to tears. She felt a rising irritation and choked it down. 'I don't want to hurt you, Edward,' she cajoled. 'But I've just got to go. All right?'

'You've got no more sense than a child! Of course you can't go. You'd starve in a gutter.'

She stood, swinging to and fro on her stockinged heel. 'Somehow I doubt that very much. Are you going to help me pack or must I do it myself?'

'I won't lift a finger for you. Ever!' His voice shook with rage.

'And this is the man who told me he loved me. Oh Edward!'

He couldn't bear her laughter, her mockery. She knew what she was doing to him and she didn't care. He stood by the window, arms folded to prevent himself rushing to her, and watched her stuff clothes erratically into a suitcase. Right to the last, when all that was left that belonged to her was the chocolates scattered over the floor, he didn't believe she would go. And then she was ready: tall, golden, unutterably lovely.

'You can't go. You mustn't.'

'I'm sorry, Edward.' For the first time she did seem sorry. He felt a grain of hope, that she might love him after all. But then she said, 'Would you carry my bag down, please?' just as if he was a porter, or one of the footmen at The Court. He shook his head, and stood listening, as she dragged the case down stair by stair. At the next landing someone came out of a room and met her. He heard her laugh, her gracious request. It wasn't Mara who carried the case downstairs. In the world there were butterflies and there were beasts of burden. However the oxen laboured, nobody ever asked the butterflies to help.

That night, hungry, cold, with a grey fog inside him that seemed to wall him off from the life all around, Edward walked to St John's Wood. The porter remembered him.

'Ah yes, sir. To see Miss Venables is it? She came back just this morning. Who shall I say's calling?'

'Edward Demouth.' To his own ears his voice sounded strange, harsh and weary. But the porter telephoned to the flat and after a moment he pressed a security button to permit Edward to use the lift.

'Number six, sir,' he said encouragingly, but waited in vain for a tip.

The door was open when he reached the flat. Diandra stood there, very brown, in a woollen dressing gown. 'Edward? I couldn't believe it was you. Come in, do.'

She looked at him anxiously. He wondered what he must seem like to her. He hadn't shaved, he remembered, and his shirt was dirty.

He went into the flat, a clean, pastel-shaded box with Diandra's cases by the door and her sunhat on the table. 'I thought − is Mara here?'

'No. No, she isn't. I didn't even know she was in London. What's the matter, Edward?'

His throat closed, but he forced out the words. 'She's left me. We were living together, God knows I should have known she didn't love me, but − she spent everything. I've no money and nowhere to stay. I can't ask the Hellyns and I'd die before I called my mother. I've got to get a job and earn the money home.'

Diandra huddled deeper into her dressing gown. 'You must have known Mara wouldn't stay. You did know.'

'Yes, yes!' He walked violently around, so young, so distressed. 'But not like this. I never thought she was cruel.'

Diandra swallowed. For some reason she wanted him to believe the worst of Mara, although for herself she didn't. Mara had paid, in her own way. She hadn't asked for Edward's love, he had given it freely.

'Why don't you stay here?' she said diffidently. 'There's a spare room. You should eat something, bacon and eggs perhaps. Mummy stocked the fridge for me, she thinks I'll starve by myself.'

'Would you do that for me? Honestly?' After Mara, Edward couldn't believe in uncomplicated generosity. He went across to the girl and took her small, brown hand in his. 'I knew you'd help me,' he said softly. 'I don't think you're the sort of person who'd ever let anyone down.'

Chapter Ten

To begin with, Mara was undecided about what she should do. She hadn't planned to leave, not immediately anyway. But people were coming back into town, she knew that somewhere in the ranks of her friends would be sanctuary. That was what Edward didn't understand, that she wasn't alone. Provided you stayed within certain narrow bounds, the members of her class looked after each other.

She thought of Clare Payne, a rather distant cousin of her parents' generation. At The Court, when she hadn't understood about London, she'd decided not to bother with her. But that was before the money ran out, before she discovered how much it cost to maintain clothes and shoes, even to eat. Clare's attraction had increased many times since then.

The taxi drew up outside number 41, Tavistock Square. Mara got out, leaving her bags, and ran lightly up the steps. The bell jangled within, and a minute later the butler answered the door.

'Lady Payne, please, Jennings. And would you see to the taxi for me? I'm completely out of cash. Do bring my bags up.'

'Certainly, Lady Mara.' The butler ushered her through to an exquisite, oval-sitting-room, painted duck egg blue and overlooking a tiny garden.

'Good heavens, Mara!' Lady Payne rose from her desk and came to her. Mara pressed her own fresh cheek to the maquillage.

Once a celebrated beauty herself, at nearly sixty Clare Payne remained worth a second look. Slim to the point of emaciation, her carefully tinted hair and precise dressing were heralded in fashion magazines the world over as the model for the older woman. Little did they know the dedication that Clare expended on herself. Not for nothing had Mara delayed her arrival until the afternoon. In the mornings Clare was dressing.

'Darling Auntie, I'm sorry to descend on you like this! I've been

64

staying with a friend in an absolutely squalid little flat, and I simply can't stand it another moment. I've a forest of invitations and it's just so embarrassing when the person you're sharing with can't come! Can I possible foist myself on you, Aunt Clare?'

The older woman patted her on the shoulder. 'Do sit down, Mara. You know how I hate being rushed. Jennings will bring some tea and we'll have a little chat. How is your poor mother?'

Mara lifted her shoulders in a shrug. 'As well as any of us, I suppose. It was such a shock. Such a cruel shock.' Despite herself, her voice trembled.

'Of course. My dear, you know how sorry I am.'

Mara recalled that Clare, although quite close to the family, had not found it possible to attend the funeral. She lost all compunction in that second. 'I'm really quite a waif at the moment,' she confessed artlessly. 'The estate's in turmoil, of course. I didn't think it fair to take on a decent flat of my own right now, but sharing's just so difficult!'

'Indeed.' Lady Payne took a cigarette from a silver case, and Mara obediently lifted the onyx table lighter to ingnite it. The older woman had caught the flash in Mara's deep blue eyes, not for a moment deceived by her polished charm. Girls were taught it at school, like algebra. She wondered why Mara had come.

Of course everyone knew that the Hellyns were under strain, but until now Clare had not suspected that it might be acute. Were they then financially embarrassed? Very little else would send Mara looking for free lodgings; in the years Clare had watched her turning from spoiled little girl to wilful beauty she had never once thought her eager for guidance. But this association could hold benefits for both of them. She was herself at something of a low ebb, in the social sense that is. She was being herded into old age before she was ready for it, and everything in her rebelled.

'How was your cruise?' asked Mara, opening her eyes wide with feigned interest. The butler was struggling to place the tea tray on the overcrowded coffee table, but neither woman felt disposed to move anything to help him. They barely noticed he was there.

'Wonderful, as always,' lied Clare. She hated the sun, and had suffered the ignominy of seeing her escort courting another, younger, woman. She had only gone to keep an eye on him, and it had come to nothing. She wanted something fresh, something different. Could this girl provide it? Instead of endless tea parties with people she had known forever, she could join Mara's whirl of fun. She need not, after all, learn to knit.

As the butler prepared to leave, she lifted a finger. 'Jennings, have the guest room made up for Lady Mara, please.'

65

'Very good, ma'am.'

When he had gone, Mara said quietly, 'Thank you, Aunt.'

Clare dipped her head in acknowledgement. 'Well, we must see you safely launched. Be good and get married right away, it's so unpleasant to have a girl rattling about for years.' She got up and collected a large, embossed book from a side table. 'We must discuss our diary.'

Shit, thought Mara, sipping a cup of tea and crumbling a piece of madeira cake, I shall be saddled with the old bag night after night!

It would almost have been better to have kept Edward in tow – but that wasn't possible. The evening stretched ahead, endlessly polite, with no Edward to satisfy her every whim. He had looked so stricken, like a shot deer, reproaching her. She almost wished she'd been a little kinder. But he was a boy, and he wasn't enough. Restlessness gnawed at her, a longing for something, anything. She was alive and lovely, and the world should know it. She had stayed with Edward too long.

The very next evening Mara and Lady Payne went to a ball. The invitation had been extended and accepted when she was at The Court. All the time she and Edward had been together she had watched the date approaching, knowing that by then things would have changed. And they had. She bathed in gold-tapped luxury, wrapping herself in towels as soft as thistledown. Warm, sensual pleasure soothed her nerves. Her father's death meant she hadn't been to half the things she had planned, and now she was to make up for them. This was to be a grand ball, a festival, in which Mara could launch herself upon the London scene. It was the day the weather broke.

She stood at the window, looking out on to Tavistock Square. From the main road beyond came the sound of tyres swishing through the wet, and the plane trees planted in the pavements hung down their leaves under the onslaught of water. The trees at The Court never drooped like that, they stood and fought the weather, tirelessly. Suddenly she could almost smell the earth, the very essence of home. Her dress tonight was the one she had worn on the night her father died. Left to herself, with money enough, Mara would never have worn it again. She resolved that when she could, as soon as she could, the dress would be cut to ribbons and burned, because it was beautiful, and must always remind her of that night. A lump of tears burned in her throat.

Lady Payne came in behind her. She was wearing a St Laurent sheath in ruby silk, of stunning elegance. 'You should wear my pearl necklace,' advised Clare. 'The dress needs it.'

The dress needed nothing of the kind, but Clare had never been

66

able to view another pretty woman without a twinge of jealousy. If she could dress Mara up like a Christmas tree, she would be happy.

'You really are so kind,' said Mara, and waited while Clare went off to get the necklace.

'It goes perfectly,' said Clare.

'So it does – but I really think it's going to irritate my neck. Mother has the same problem. But I do appreciate it, Aunt.'

'Call me Clare,' said the other woman thinly. 'You're not a child any more. I do hope you're not going to be one of those debs that almost suck their thumbs at one.'

Mara choked on a giggle. 'I do hope not, Aunt. Clare.'

They took a taxi to the ball, and hurried the few yards to the door canopy under a screen of umbrellas held by staff. Nonetheless both women stopped beneath the lights, tilting their heads and leaning close to one another, to give the cameras a better shot. Lady Payne, seething with precious stones, clips and bracelets, was in startling contrast to Mara's simplicity.

'Mara dear, I'm so glad you could come! And Clare – how kind of you to look after dear Mara.' Their hostess welcomed them, a quivering mound of flesh jammed into a corset. Mara greeted her daughter, a girl she genuinely liked, and then rustled on into the room. Heads turned on all sides.

Muted pops sounded all around as waiters expertly removed champagne corks. A string quartet began to play a waltz, and at a signal from the master of ceremonies the heavy velvet curtains began to be drawn on the wet evening outside. Mara felt a warmth, and a certainty that had been lost recently. She hadn't known where she was going but now she thought, 'It's here that I should be.' Someone offered her a glass of champagne and she accepted almost mechanically, already half drunk on the excitement of the evening to come.

Dancing, drinking, laughing, she was a princess in a brilliant circle of light. The admiration washed over her like warm milk; she fed on it, drinking it in. 'You're the prettiest girl here – you will come with me to the races won't you?

'Do come and stay. My mother would love to meet you, I'm sure.'

Was it towards midnight that it started to pall? The rain didn't help. She remembered The Court the night her father died. The drops, falling heavily against the windows, they had tapped to the rhythm of his breathing. She felt so sad suddenly. Everything seemed banal and childish.

She went into the cloakroom and ran cold water on her wrists. Loneliness lapped at the edges of her mind. No-one would ever love her as her father had done. He had taken with him her one certain source of constant love, and it could never be replaced – not here, not anywhere. Sarah, an older girl, dark, exotically coloured, said: 'Are you coming, Mara? We're going to a club.'

'All right. I'd like that.' She dried her hands and pressed them to her cheeks. Only when she stopped did the thoughts crowd in, so she must not stop until she dropped, exhausted.

Six of them crammed into an expensive hatchback, laughing, and at the club Mara swept to a table. She was learning to hold her drink, not for her the giggling stupidity of other girls. Although alcohol caused barriers to fall, with Mara they were invisible ones.

They danced for hours, moving in a crush of the well-heeled and well-connected. A fat man, very drunk, fell across their table. He fixed Mara with a bleary eye. 'You're the most beautiful girl I've ever seen,' he burbled.

'Fuck off, will you?' said one of the boys. 'She's with us.' He tried to kiss her neck but she put up a hand and pushed him away.

Another man, much older, came across the them. There was a sudden sharpening of interest amongst the group.

'Hello, Dermot,' said one, and Dermot grinned at them.

'Want a good night, boys?' he asked, and at once two of them stood up. They went out towards the cloakroom and Mara said, 'What is it? What's he giving them?'

'Just some coke. Jimmy heard he was here, that's why we came.'

Minutes later the boys came back. One of them slid his hand down the back of Mara's dress, feeling her backbone. 'I feel fantastic,' he purred. 'Come on, girls, have a snort.'

Sarah passed him her bag, he slipped something inside and passed it back. She and Mara got up and went to the powder room.

The room was pink, lushly carpeted with a low, glass-topped table and velour chairs. A couple of other girls were talking quietly, but Sarah took no notice. She went straight to the table and knelt beside it. Carefully, meticulously, she took a packet of white powder from her bag and poured it out in two narrow streams. Then she took out two straws, one made of silver, the other plastic. 'You can have your own made,' she told Mara, handing her the plastic one. 'I'll give you the address if you like.'

'Thanks.'

Mara watched as Sarah bent over the table. The other girls watched also. Brisk, firm sniffs and the powder disappeared up first one nostril, then the other. Sarah sat back on her heels, her mouth wide and grinning. 'It's good stuff. You'll love it.'

Mara knelt beside her, taking up her own straw. The first sniff, she wasn't firm enough, the powder dissipated. 'Don't waste it,' said

Sarah, and again Mara sniffed. A burn in one nostril. She moved the straw to the other and sniffed again.

Her mouth came open. She sat back on her heels and her eyes were wide with shock. A tremendous ebullience bubbled inside her, the pink of the walls seemed superb, an inspiration. She waited for the fuzziness of drink, but there was none. It was pure, undiluted pleasure.

'Let's go back.' Sarah snapped her bag shut and went out. Mara followed, feeling as if her feet were floating across the floor. The boys had ordered champagne. She drank some quickly, to assuage the dryness at the back of her throat. All thought of sleep left her, she wanted to dance and laugh forever.

At four o'clock they left. The boys and Sarah had all snorted again, but Mara refused. It frightened her a little. Such power in so few white grains. She wouldn't use the drug regularly, she decided. Just now and again, to enhance an evening, a mood. Jimmy, crammed next to her in the back of the car, was trying to put his hand up her dress, but she fended him off.

'Why won't you?' he moaned. 'I gave you the coke, didn't I?'

'You don't buy me with one snort,' said Mara, and leaned across to brush his cheek with her lips. Her breasts pressed briefly against him. 'That's to say thank you,' she murmured.

'I think I love you,' said Jimmy, and one of his friends said, 'Shut up, old boy. You'll hate yourself in the morning.'

Mara looked out of the window. Lights gleamed on water, the stars were strung across the sky as if they were Christmas decorations. They passed a brilliant shop window, models in autumn suits striking angular poses.

'Where are we going?'

'There's an all night diner by the river,' said Sarah. 'We'll have some tea and bacon sandwiches.'

Taxi drivers and fruiterers used the place, it was no more than a couple of old caravans parked under the arch. The food was prepared in one and you sat down in the other. Tonight it was full of tired men in donkey jackets, so they stood outside on pavements drying in the morning breeze and laughed and munched their sandwiches. The men stared at the girls, as if watching exotic birds.

Jimmy said drunkenly to Mara, 'We ought to get engaged. My people would like that.'

She offered him a sip of her tea. 'I couldn't, Jim. You're not old enough.'

He hiccupped. 'I'll be twenty next month.'

'Will you?'

The other boys were throwing paper cups full of tea up into the air, like children. Sarah was laughing and calling encouragement, but Mara stood in silence. They seemed so young.

Clare Payne lay in bed and studied Mara. The girl had been out till dawn, last night as every night for the past week, and yet she seemed to thrive on it. The morning light showed clear skin and bright eyes, the glint in them almost feverish.

'Don't you think it's time you stayed in one evening?' asked Clare, without real conviction. It was her habit to come home at one or two in the morning, leaving Mara to find some more than willing escort at five or thereabouts.

'I'm having a wonderful time,' declared Mara, and settled herself on the end of the bed. She was wearing cord jeans and a shirt, unbuttoned just enough to show the cleavage of her magnificent breasts.

'I hope you're not letting those young rams get out of hand,' said Lady Payne, sharply.

Mara laughed. 'Of course not.'

She was undoubtedly a success, uncrowned queen of this season and, it was said, ten previous ones. It was what she had intended — but somehow she wasn't pleased. The money was a problem, of course, a constant irritation. It meant no new clothes, however much she needed them, not even a Snoopy T-shirt for which there was currently a craze. She had to be devious, almost two-faced, persuading others to take her, pay for her, buy her things. Just a little cash would help. A little money and perhaps she wouldn't be quite so tied to the circle in which she found herself.

'Clare — I'm running rather short of cash,' she began.

'My dear, you surprise me.' Clare extended a hand for her cigarettes, deliberately giving herself time. Did she really have to fund the girl as well? She decided not. 'Have you asked at home?'

'Not really, no. It seems rather frivolous when Marcus is up to his neck in demands from the tax people.' Mara took care to keep financial embarrassment within carefully marked bounds. They were in temporary difficulties, which would disappear once the estate was settled. In fact, she almost believed it.

'Are you sure it's wise to leave things in his hands?'

Mara's face flamed. She would say what she liked about Marcus, but to hear Clare talking as if he was an idiot — she clenched her teeth.

'He's perfectly competent,' she said stiffly. 'I can't imagine why you should think he wouldn't be.'

70

'Just so long as he doesn't start seeing things again.'

Holding her temper on a tight rein, Mara said, 'All he sees are bills and more bills. And I don't want to bother him, so I would be grateful if you could let me have a loan. I really do need some more clothes.' She tossed her head, sending her curls swinging across her shoulder.

Clare closed her cigarette case with a snap. 'I really don't think I should take on such a responsibility,' she said sweetly. 'Speak to your mother, darling, I'm sure she'd love to help.'

'Yes. Of course.' Mean old cow, thought Mara waspishly. She could afford dozens of dresses.

Back in her room she felt jumpy and harassed. Inexorably, in a way that puzzled her, she found herself thinking of sex. A seventeenth-century pamphlet the girls had circulated at school came back to her — 'Once a girl has tasted the sugar-stick, she cannot live without suck.' Perhaps it was true. When she danced with a man, even someone she barely liked, and his thigh rubbed hers, or his hands felt hot on her back, images flashed across her brain. She saw herself naked with him, she felt him crushing her with his weight. But if she slept with any of the boys she knew, the Edward problem was inevitable. Young men were too intense, she decided, heirs to every-thing except virility, which they had in full measure. They were too young to be rich enough, or powerful enough, or to possess the allure of sophistication.

Her mood persisted into the evening. She and Clare were dining together at a private house, although the atmosphere between them was almost frosty. As usual the party divided after dinner, the older members playing bridge and the younger going off to a club. Mara felt bored. She sat, leaning her elbows on the little cluttered table while the others danced and shrieked and threw champagne corks. Sarah slid into the seat next to her. 'What's up?'

Mara shrugged. 'Bored. I've heard all the jokes and none of them are funny.'

'I'd watch it if I were you. People are starting to say you're just too damned superior for words. You don't join in, you see.'

Two of the boys were dancing, doing Indian war whoops complete with napkins as tomahawks. Mara watched grimly. 'Why did you do the season if you didn't want to have fun?' demanded Sarah.

Mara sighed. 'I thought it would be fun. But it isn't, somehow.'

'Well, you just watch it.' Sarah put a hand on her shoulder, and prepared to drift away. 'People don't invite you if they think you'll sneer.'

Mara was left alone. She was wearing the grey sheath, and her hair

71

tumbled around her bare shoulders. A man, tall, greying, came up to her table.

'Lady Mara? You won't remember me. David Selmer.'

'Of course I remember you.' In fact her memory for names was poor. A City tycoon, she thought. Married, or divorced or something.

'Do you mind if I join you?'

She didn't care either way, but mindful of Sarah she said, 'Please. I should like that.'

The music was loud and it wasn't easy to talk. He sat and simply watched her, after a while clicking his fingers for the waiter to bring champagne. Mara studied him just as openly. Early forties she guessed. Heavy gold jewellery – a little too much for someone of her class. Definitely nouveau riche, with that slightly aggressive confidence born of social insecurity. She knew she ought to get rid of him, but somehow did not.

The wine came and they sipped in unison. He was watching her breasts. She leaned back and put her arms beneath her hair, sweeping it away from her neck. Selmer grinned. He had a slightly olive skin, as if he had Greek blood in him. What would he be like in bed? she wondered. The drink ran in warm ripples through her veins.

'Why don't we go and eat somewhere.'

'Thank you. I've already eaten.'

'Well then – let's go on where we can talk.'

'It is a little noisy in here.' She got up smoothly, deliberately cool. The man made her nervous, a feeling she found not entirely unpleasant.

His car was waiting, a Rolls, brand new and somewhat too opulent. He made no move at all to touch her, making only light conversation about people he thought she might know. 'I was in Cannes recently, for the film festival. Did you go? No, I can't believe I wouldn't have seen you.'

'My father died. I was tied up for most of the summer.'

'I'm so sorry.' Said with an utter lack of remorse.

She began to wonder where he was taking her. In coming in his car, had she tacitly agreed to something? What was going to happen?

They stopped at a dark house, somewhere in Mayfair. They got out and Selmer had a brief word with the chauffeur before escorting Mara to the door. 'Is this your house?' she asked.

'It is indeed. I'm here alone, except for the servants.'

'I see.'

She didn't know what she should do. She hardly knew the man, he wasn't even of her class. Yet she was filled with a desperate

72

excitement, as if she was driving too fast and might at any moment crash. When he opened the door she paused, pulling back. 'I'm not sure I should come in.'

'What? Not even for a drink?'

She gave him a half smile. 'Well then – but only a drink.'

He led the way through the hall – and up the stairs. 'Where are we going?' she asked nervously, for he had hold of her hand and didn't let go. 'I really don't know you well enough for this.'

He laughed. 'We won't do anything you don't want, Lady Mara. But we should talk about it in comfort, don't you think?'

It was of course possible that the drawing-room could be on the first floor. Yet when he opened the door and she confronted an expanse of deep blue carpeting, in the centre of which was a giant bed, she lost her breath.

She turned, and he was right behind her. 'Don't you think this is going a little too fast?' she said quickly.

He shook his head. 'Not at all. I want you. You're the most sensual woman I think I've ever seen. Why waste hours making small talk when we both know this is what we want.'

'I think you're mistaken. Why should I offer myself to someone I don't know? I thought we would have a quiet drink. Get to know each other.'

'And so we shall.' He slid an arm around her waist and guided her into the room. His thigh met hers. Her body flamed, betraying her, because she wanted a man and he was hard, through and through.

He left her standing in the midst of the carpet and went to a cupboard. 'Gin?' he asked. 'No, let's have wine. Good red wine.' He took out a bottle and uncorked it, then suddenly swung the bottle to his lips and drank. Droplets ran down his chin and stained his shirt ruby red. 'You.' As if mesmerised she took the bottle and drank also. He watched her.

'God. Oh God, but you're wonderful. Let me undress you!' His hands went round to her zip, but she pushed him away, the bottle still in her hand. 'No! I don't want to. Why should I?'

He stared at her for a second. Then he laughed. 'You realise I can make you do what I want? You could scream all you like, no-one would hear.'

She felt the blood draining from her face, she sank her teeth into her lip as if she could halt it. Every instinct told her to keep her nerve. 'This is hardly a seduction,' she said slowly. 'I thought I'd be offered a little more than threats and cheap wine.'

'Oh! So you know what's cheap and what's not? How cheap are you then, darling?' He moved quickly around her, she felt his breath

73

on her neck. Suddenly his fingers jabbed into her. He had her by the waist, his teeth grazed her shoulder. When she tried to move he grunted and drove his knee into her back. There was no trace of gentleness. He had brought her here to humble her.

Out of terror came inspiration. Selmer had the upper hand. Unless she fought back now she was at his mercy. 'Give me three thousand,' she said suddenly.

'What?'

'Three thousand and you can do what you like.'

'God!' She'd managed to take him by surprise. He looked her up and down, revising his assessment. 'A high class whore. I swear I'd never have known. God, you girls get everwhere. I fell nicely into your trap, didn't I?' His voice was softer, less grating. She was no longer the aristocrat, superior, despising him. She was a girl on the make, on his level. Smiling, playing her part, Mara said, 'You did indeed.'

To her amazement he made no quibble about the price. He walked away quickly, pulled his wallet from his jacket and wrote out a cheque. 'Here.' He held it in an outstretched hand and she took it, scanning it briefly before putting it in her bag. She turned her back. The whole scene set her on fire: she felt wild, unreal. 'Unzip me,' she whispered.

He kissed her neck, her shoulders, sinking his teeth into her flesh. 'Don't bite where it shows!' she hissed, writhing out of her dress. He said nothing. His hands were everywhere, his mouth was everywhere. Suddenly he picked her up and flung her down on the bed. He was ripping at his clothes, careless of buttons, zips, anything. God help me when a man takes time to undress, thought Mara. Suddenly he turned and picked up the bottle from where it stood in the middle of the floor. He drank, came to her, and pushed it up between her legs. The cold glass brought a gasp, she could feel the wine rich, warm inside her. The bottle rolled away and a strange man straddled her, naked, grinning down at her need. She closed her eyes.

It was lunchtime the next day before Mara arrived back in Tavistock Square. Clare was pacing the drawing-room, smoking a cigarette with furious puffs. She waylaid Mara in the hall. 'Come in here at once, please. Jennings, you will be good enough to cancel Lady Mara's engagement this evening. She is indisposed.'

Mara said, 'Thank you, Jennings, I should much prefer that you did not do any such thing.'

The butler looked from his immaculate employer to the dishevelled girl, her evening dress crumpled and stained, her hair imperfectly

74

hiding a bite mark on one shoulder. He knew who paid his wage. 'Of course, Lady Payne.'

Mara lifted an eyebrow and followed Clare into the drawing-room. 'Do please spare me a lecture,' she said, sinking into a chair.

'Rather more of an inquisition. You were seen leaving with David Selmer – I have no doubt that some enterprising photographer has snapped you coming in just now. I don't care what little games you got up to last night, my girl, but I will not have your name, and by association mine, plastered all over the Fleet Street gossip columns. You are barely nineteen, and you could be cited in a divorce case! What price a good marriage then may I ask?'

The colour had risen to Mara's hairline. She wasn't used to being taken to task, and in this case, she knew, justifiably. If she'd known what would happen, she would never have gone with the man. She gritted her teeth. 'I'm sorry, Clare. I didn't think.'

'You may be even sorrier! Do you know what sort of creature Selmer is? The man you slept with last night is a regular at Bangkok whorehouses, God knows what filthy disease he could be carrying!'

Mara went as white as before she was red. 'He couldn't! I couldn't –'

'I shall give you the address of my gynaecologist.' Clare scribbled on a sheet of thick notepaper and thrust it at Mara. 'I suggest you make a call at once.'

She sat with her head bowed. 'Yes. I will.' God knows what had possessed her last night! She had wanted a little fun, a little company; this morning she had even felt truimphant. But three thousand pounds was nothing for this. She felt filthy, humiliated and ashamed.

Chapter Eleven

The affair made the papers, but in muted form. There were no pictures of Mara either leaving with Selmer or arriving home, although the gossip columns were determined not to miss the next episode. A cadre of photographers camped desultorily in Tavistock Square and lurked around nightclubs where they thought Mara might go. For a week they were disappointed.

Having been washed out, lectured and dosed Mara went to nothing but the most prim luncheons. In the mornings she shopped, replenishing her wardrobe on the bargain rails at Bruce Oldfield, Jean Muir and Agnes B. She wandered round Harrods, picking up bags and shoes, silk nightdresses and sheer underwear. At Liberty's she had coffee with friends and bought beautiful print dresses and scarves. At night she went to bed and read until she slept, the book still propped before her.

The sounds of London intruded on her dreams. In the country, at The Court, the owls whispered around the chimneys and pheasants called in the woods. What was she doing here, so far from home? Sometimes she woke early and Selmer's face hovered in the dark, but when she struck at it, her fists closed on nothing. Her heart pounded and she lay very still. Such a horrible, vulgar man! She disgusted herself.

She went to talk to Clare, knocking on her bedroom door at ten in the morning. 'May I come in please, Aunt?'

'By all means.' Clare was sitting up in bed, made up, in a frilled bedjacket, with a silver tray of tea and toast on the table beside her. The room was a riot of fabric and lace, an explosion of somewhat excessive femininity. Great swathes of cream muslin fell from a half tester round the head of the bed, the quilt was thick with ribbons. It was impossible to imagine a man there at all.

Mara perched herself on the end of the bed, spreading the skirt of her new floral dress.

'I see your mother did manage to send you something,' said Clare.

Mara grinned. 'Yes, she was wonderful. Clare, about last week – I am sorry, truly.'

'What did the doctor say?'

'I didn't catch anything, the tests came back clear. But I might have. It was stupid of me, I admit it.'

The older woman picked restlessly at the frills on her bedjacket. 'God knows what you wanted with him anyway. In my day girls had no desire until they were at least twenty-five. Then they deceived their husbands.'

'I think I must be rather precocious.' Mara paused, wondering how to go on. 'I don't want to embarrass you again, Clare,' she said at last.

'I should hope not! If you're interested in that sort of thing, there are lots of older men who have the sense to be discreet. Younger men of course can't be trusted. Why don't you get engaged, dear? You could be caught in flagrante delicto in the Royal Enclosure at Ascot, and provided you were engaged no-one would give a toss.'

Mara sighed. 'They're all so young. Young and silly.'

'My dear, if you wait until they're old and sensible they will all be married to someone else.'

'I suppose so.' Mara shelved the question. She had never met anyone to whom she would like to be married for even five minutes. But of course she would marry, and put up with it. It just seemed to her an evil day that was best postponed.

'Clare, if I asked you about someone, would you tell me?' she said frankly. 'A man, I mean. You know everyone, and I wouldn't want to make that silly mistake again.'

'Has he contacted you?'

'What, Selmer? He rings now and then. I don't take the calls.'

'I see.' Clare reached for a cigarette, lit it and studied Mara through the smoke. The girl really was utterly lovely, and it seemed that sensual quality was entirely deserved. 'Do you enjoy having men make love to you?' she asked suddenly. 'One does it, of course, but personally I find it greatly over-rated.'

'I – I enjoy it, yes.' How to explain the ache that arose in her some days? When she was at her most lonely, tense and isolated at even the grandest party, then she wanted it. Afterwards she always felt different. Quite obviously Clare thought her wildly promiscuous; she almost seemed to admire her for it, although one boy and one rake scarcely added up to a wild and careless life. Let Clare imagine what she liked, Mara was not about to confess the prosaic truth.

Clare stubbed out her half-finished cigarette and yawned delicately. 'I think it's time you returned to circulation, Mara. I've accepted tonight's party, and I gather the Shandons have invited you for the weekend.'

Mara knew the Shandon daughter, though they had never been friends. But their fathers had known each other, years ago in the army, and on the strength of that she had been invited for a Friday to Monday visit. There would be spare young men, and Mara's name had been pulled out of the hat.

'I did think I might go. Will you come?'

'I think I'd better, don't you?' They exchanged a smile of grim understanding.

They motored down to Sussex in time for lunch. The weather was fine but blowy, and Mara felt happier than for weeks. She was wearing a new dress and she was making a fresh start. Beside her Clare nagged for the car window to be shut, because the breeze made her hair untidy. She irritated Mara more than a little.

Pre-lunch drinks were in the conservatory. Not everyone was there, quite a few people wouldn't arrive till the evening. But at once Mara felt her spirits fall. There were two distinct groups. One was the parental generation, headed by the tight-permed, well-fleshed Lady Shandon; the other Mara's age. There were two or three callow Guards' officers, one of them still with acne, a plump boy from a stockbroker's office who stammered, and a collection of girls who took against Mara on sight. She felt like a lioness amongst chickens, trying to fit in and deceiving no-one.

Two of the officers detached themselves from the group and set upon her. 'My name's Philip – this is Tony – we've been longing to meet you. I'm really surprised we haven't met before actually. Did you go to the Redford ball, I feel sure I must have noticed you?'

She was cool and discouraging. Yet the more distant she became the more she enthralled them. They were used to girls giggling and gasping and keeping their handkerchiefs screwed up in the palm of their hands, not this ill-concealed boredom. The harder they tried to interest her, the more silly they seemed to become.

At least Clare seemed to be enjoying herself. She was talking to a grand and rather forbidding man who had a vague job in town and also doubled as master of the local hunt. He was paying her extravagant compliments and every few seconds Clare gave a high, tinny laugh. It grated on Mara's nerves, and, it seemed, on those of her hostess. Lady Shandon cast frequent grim glances in her direction.

Mara extracted herself from her corner and abandoned the boys. She drifted across the room, wondering why it was that the best families always had shabby furniture. The Shandons imported their own sherry and owned a yacht, but the carpet was worn down to the canvas and the chintz on the armchairs was faded to a lifeless cream. Mara disapproved slightly. It was ugly and unnecessary, except in so far as everyone did it. She disliked the thought that in certain matters they all conformed.

A tall, burly man came into the room. He had a big, rather genial head, covered in thick greying hair. As so often with men of that age, Mara was at once reminded of her father. Like him, trained in the army, he stood very straight. It was Shandon himself, twenty minutes late and in trouble with his wife. He avoided her eye and saw Mara.

'Good heavens! You must be Henry's girl. My dear, I should have known you anywhere, you have all his good looks.'

He could have said nothing that would more endear him to her. 'Nobody ever said we looked alike — do you think we do?'

'I don't suppose it is likeness really. But I would have known you anywhere. He must have been delighted to have such a beautiful daughter.'

'I do miss him,' said Mara softly. Her eyes filled with tears.

'Now, now, let's not have this.' He took her hand, patting it firmly. 'It's my fault for upsetting you.'

'It isn't you — I like to remember him, but it does make me cry.'

Suddenly she had the urge to confide. 'I don't think I'm nearly over it yet. I go to all the parties, but I don't seem to have fun. It all seems awfully stupid.'

'Well, that isn't any wonder. He was a fine man, the finest. You'll come round.' He looked over her head and saw that his wife was ushering people through for lunch. 'Come and eat something, my dear. At the very least we can make sure you have a good time this weekend, can't we?'

Tears hung on her lashes as she looked up at him. He made her feel like a little girl again, dependent and safe. 'Thank you. You're very sweet.'

All that day Shandon took special care of her. When she went for a walk he sent someone after her with a jacket, when she came back muddy he took her shoes at once to have them cleaned. Jane Shandon glared and his wife looked daggers, but Mara didn't care. She had almost forgotten what it was to be babied.

She went along to Clare's room after changing for dinner. Mara had chosen white that evening, a short strappy dress with a bolero jacket, heavily encrusted with scrunchy beads. Her hair was caught up in a wispy knot on top of her head, courtesy of Lady Shandon's

79

rather solid lady's maid, who had, she said, "Put up hair on the crowned heads of Europe."

'How very difficult,' said Mara ironically, and the maid glowered.

Clare was smoothing cream over her cheekbones, delicately filling in the tiny lines radiating down from her eyes. She painted her face as delicately and carefully as any great artist with a major canvas, and to stunning effect. Half an hour could see her transformed from a pale, too thin older woman to a sophisticated lady with marvellous bones. Mara watched her, fascinated.

'How do you make your eyes stand out? I sometimes think you've put eyeliner on, but I can't quite see it.'

'I put dots around the eye, and blend them together with a brush. Definition without being obvious, you see.' She glanced beyond her mirrored reflection. 'What a delicious dress.'

'Thank you. Are you wearing the grey? It's superb.'

They complimented each other like knights saluting before a joust.

'Those two boys are very sweet don't you think?' said Clare.

'Quite possibly. One was already tight when we arrived and the other kept putting on this fake German accent. "Ve have vays of making you talk!" Once would have been no more than mildly amusing and he did it non-stop.'

'I think you make boys nervous,' said Clare, turning to look at Mara. 'You should give them time to get used to you.'

Mara wandered to the window and gazed down on the circlet of perfect gravel before the front door. 'I hate Guards' officers. So arrogant.' She turned and faced Clare. 'Vivien Shandon's nice, isn't he?'

'Oh, good heavens, you can't be serious! He must be fifty. And look at his wife. She'd carve you up and serve you as a canapé if you so much as breathed on him.'

Mara laughed. 'I thought her the archetypal country lady. Dogs, horses and good works. Sex when she can fit it in between committee meetings. He knew my father. He's quite good-looking really.'

Clare fixed her with a steely glare. 'You'll get yourself into an awful lot of trouble if you keep playing these games! You should join in more. Once you make some real friends you'll meet them again and again, and then you'll have some proper fun.'

Mara swung back and forth on her heel. 'I don't think girls like to be friends with me.'

But Clare had no time for Mara's little difficulties. 'I'm sure you're wrong,' she said decisively, indicating that the subject was closed. 'Let's go down. Samuel will be waiting.'

'The MFH? I think he's smitten, Auntie.'

'Do you?'

Clare allowed herself a satisfied smile. A mild romance was just what she needed to raise her spirits, which Mara seemed determined to depress. How had vague, ineffectual Charlotte produced such a girl? She was Henry's child through and through this one, as attractive and unfathomable as he had been.

At dinner Mara sat between Philip and Tony, leaving Jane, on Philip's other side, very much neglected. Mara was sweet to them, flirting with one and then the other, mocking them both. Even when Philip was talking to Jane he was listening to Mara. But every now and then Mara's gaze would stray to the head of the table and she would see Shandon looking at her, smiling encouragement. It sent shivers up and down her spine. 'Are you cold, Mara? Shall I get you a wrap?'

'No thank you.' Why did boys always give you such doglike, fawning devotion?

She turned her head to look at Shandon's wife, presiding at the far end of the table. She ruled her husband rather too forcefully, decided Mara, although she knew nothing at all about it. The poor man was utterly wasted on her.

At the end of the meal the ladies withdrew, leaving the men to port and cigars. As they settled in the drawing-room, one of the girls said in a low voice, 'I wish my season was over. I've been everywhere and I hate it!'

'So do I,' said another. 'The same stupid boys and Mummy looking anxious when you get home, in case none of them liked you. And if you want them to like you you have to sleep with them, and then they tell all their friends.'

'Why?' asked Mara. The girls looked at her and she went on. 'I mean, isn't it better not to sleep with them? Then they continually want you to.'

'Or they go off and find someone who will,' remarked Jane Shandon. 'It's all very well letting them make the running, but if nobody runs anywhere near you, what can you do?'

'Leave the race,' said Mara simply. The other girls stared at her.

'What it is to be absolutely fascinating,' said one in tones of heavy dislike. They turned away, leaving Mara on her own. She felt miserable suddenly, and lonely. Whatever Clare said, she wasn't wrong. Girls always shut her out.

To her surprise Lady Shandon also seemed determined to ignore her. Mara was hurt, not realising that Jane had sobbed for most of the afternoon. Philip had almost certainly been going to propose that weekend, and now it would come to nothing.

81

'And all because of bloody Mara Hellyn! I don't know why you had to invite her, Mummy!'

'Darling, I know her mother,' pleaded Lady Shandon. She had never expected the girl to be quite so ravishing, or the boys to be quite so entranced. Neither the Shandon mother nor daughter would have regretted seeing Mara fall in the lake.

When at last the men came in, Mara was sitting by herself in the window. 'You two boys, come and play cards with Jane and Louisa,' commanded Lady Shandon. 'And you others, come along.' She made up brisk foursomes. But as Mara rose, expecting to be included, she found herself deliberately left out. Everyone was to play except her.

Her head came up. She looked round the room and caught Shandon's eye. She shrugged, expressively, and he came across.

'Did you want to play? I'm sure my wife didn't intend – '

'It's all right. I don't mind.'

Since clearly she did, Shandon said, 'I do apologise. I imagine the girls do rather feel you're putting them in the shade.'

'Hardly.' Mara never needed to boast about her looks. She couldn't remember a time when she hadn't been lovely; it was impossible to imagine a day when her beauty would be gone.

Shandon smiled down at her. 'Well, we don't have to worry about them. What would you like to do?'

She had a sudden, intense desire to put her arms round him and rest her head on his broad, warm chest.

'Actually I'd like to see the stables,' she said.

'Would you? Good heavens, you're the last girl I'd think was the horsey type.'

'I'm not really. But it's a lovely evening and the bats are out. I like stables at night.'

'So do I. Lovely time of day, everything quiet and sleepy. None of the clatter.'

She smiled up at him. He could see the soft down on her cheek. He felt reckless suddenly, and said, 'Why don't we go out this way?' He leaned across to open the window at which Mara had been sitting. It was not meant to be a door since it was three feet from the floor and led on to a flower bed. He stepped through on long legs, holding out his hand to help her over the low seat. She laughed and followed him, her skirt riding well above her knees, noting with a delicious sense of pleasure Lady Shandon's amazed stare.

The evening air was soft and humid. Mara's heels caught in the gravel and Shandon put out his hand to steady her. 'I'm sorry you're not having a good time,' he said.

She glanced up at him. 'But I am! I don't mind at all not talking to

82

the boys. They really are so impossibly silly.'

'Well. They are at that age.'

'Aunt Clare says I should marry someone even though they are silly because they might turn out all right when they're your age. But suppose they don't? I'd rather marry someone older. Much older. Except of course they're all married to someone else.'

They rounded the corner of the house and before them stretched the formal gardens with the stables beyond. 'How I wish we had a house like this,' she murmured.

'But The Court is in a different league. This can't be a tenth of the size.' Shandon allowed himself a fatherly hand on her shoulder.

'Probably not. Perhaps what I really wish is for The Court to be this manageable. It's a nightmare keeping the place up, you can't know!'

'Poor you.'

She turned to him. 'Not me. My brother. I see those two in there being so stupid and I think how much Marcus has to cope with at home.'

'They'll have responsibilities too, one day. One has to keep a sense of proportion, I always think.'

'I just do so hate talking to people who don't understand. You do. Don't you?'

'Yes. I think I do.'

They walked on to the stables. The gravel was thicker on the garden paths and Mara kept stumbling. He took her hand to help her, and somehow it seemed perfectly natural to keep it once they came to the stable cobbles. There was no-one there, if you excluded the horses, leaning mild-eyed over the doors. Sure enough, the bats were swooping and diving high above the roofs.

Mara turned to Shandon. 'Please kiss me.'

'My dear − I can't!'

'Why not? No one will know and we both want to. I'm lonely tonight. I don't feel I fit in anywhere. I like you so much and I just want to be kissed.'

It wasn't the first time Shandon had been approached. He was a good-looking man. He'd had a fling once with a woman about his own age, but it hadn't been serious. There had never, ever, been anything like this. The girl was young enough to be his daughter. And she was − irresistible. 'I can't,' he said hoarsely. 'One day you'll find someone who's right for you. You don't fit in because you're so lovely. You threaten us all.'

'Not you. Please, not you.'

She lifted up her face and he couldn't help but kiss her. His tongue

83

in her mouth was big and warm, it aroused her. They kissed again, then she pulled away to lay her head against his broad chest. She had such a feeling of warmth and serenity, she would give anything to keep him like this. There was only one thing that would suffice. She whispered, 'I want you to make love to me. It's all right, I'm quite experienced.'

'I can't – I absolutely can't!'

'Please! I won't tell anyone, I won't make any trouble. I just want to be close to you.' She was nearly crying. Her breasts swelled from her dress, he could almost feel them in his hands. She pressed herself against him, breathing kisses against his lips. 'Please! Please!'

'My God. My God.' Shandon was beyond resistance. He looked wildly round the yard, then pulled some keys from his pocket. 'We'll go into the stable office. For God's sake don't let my family find out.'

'I promise. Oh please, please love me.'

In the office there was only the floor or the large, bare desk. Shandon took out a horse blanket and threw it across the desk. Mara drew off her jacket and stood for him to unfasten her dress. It was so strange, because Selmer had done this too and that had been utterly different. Shandon loomed over her, his big hands cradling her breasts.

She stepped out of her panties and lay on the blanket, waiting until he had taken off his trousers. 'Say if I hurt you,' he said, and stood before her, nudging at the entrance to her body. She spread her legs, and put her hands down to open herself. He grunted, pushing in, making slow, shallow thrusts. It was uncomfortable, she had to hold on to the table to prevent herself from falling off.

For some reason she couldn't understand, the excitement was fading. She wished she wasn't doing this, she wanted it to end. Her head struck the table rhythmically. Suddenly he reared up, clutching a breast in each of his massive hands. His mouth was open and his eyes stared into space. Blood flushed his skin a dark red, he grimaced as if in agony and the thing within her began slow, steady pulsing. For five seconds he hung there, his fingers biting into her flesh, and then he came down on her, sagging like a pricked balloon. Slowly, wearily, he got off her. He looked almost ill, quite exhausted.

Still half naked, he slumped into a chair. 'My God. What have I done?' he whispered.

Mara sat up, rubbing her head. 'It's a bit late for regrets,' she said sharply.

'Do you have to be so hard? Imagine if your father had done this to Jane! What would you think of him if he'd done such a thing?'

Mara said, 'That's just ridiculous.'

Shandon looked about him, as if amazed to find himself in this situation. 'Why don't you put some clothes on?' he muttered. 'Are you going to blackmail me? Is that your game?'

'But — there isn't a game. I was lonely. I wanted you to comfort me.'

'No you didn't!' He was vicious. He stared at her almost as if she was loathsome. 'I couldn't believe what I heard about you, but I do now. The way you behaved — you've had some men! I suppose tomorrow there'll be someone else, I wouldn't put it past you to make a play for the vicar!'

Shocked, Mara whispered, 'I only wanted you. I'm not like you think.'

'I know what I think!' Shandon extended a shaking, guilty finger. 'You're just like your father. One after another he had the women, nobody was safe. And you are just the same!'

'Am I?' Mara got up. A flame of anger seemed to scorch her throat, she could almost taste it. The man was a great slimy worm; she had given him all she could and he had turned on her. 'Does your fat wife like you in bed?' she asked coldly. 'I didn't come, you know. But you didn't notice. I suppose it makes you feel better to put the blame on me. That's all right. I'll find a way of getting my own back.'

She began putting her clothes on. Damn, she felt as if she must smell. She didn't care. If Lady Shandon suspected then it was no more than the woman deserved. And she would revenge herself, the best way she knew how. Her throat felt hot with tears.

As she left, Shandon extended a hand to her. 'Mara —' he said huskily. 'I don't want you to make any trouble.'

She stared for a long minute. How could she have thought him attractive? He was a tall, greying, somewhat paunchy man. 'You revolt me,' she whispered, and left him there.

Chapter Twelve

Vivien Shandon was a man of limited imagination. His life was generally a worthy one, not from any positive choice but because he had never felt the need for it to be otherwise. He was kind to his wife and children, civil to his tenants and emotional with his horses. The standards by which he lived had seldom been challenged, he had simply done what he wished. That it was never anything he shouldn't was simply because he never thought he might like such a thing. He was a man who could be relied on to give a fiver to a tramp or write a letter of recommendation for someone's ramshackle son, and he was loved for it, even though the money meant nothing and the letter was written by his staff. An uncomplicated man, who should never have fallen foul of Mara Hellyn.

It wasn't too long before he realised that he was in the wrong. In the drained aftermath of their encounter he had wanted to hit out, rub it away, undo this appalling thing. Men of his standing did not, simply did not, seduce their daughters' friends. He wasn't used to seeing himself as badly behaved and he had no mechanism for dealing with it.

But the damage was done. Mara stormed back to the house, her anger smouldering like a banked fire. Every word he had said came back to her, every moment of ecstasy gained at her expense. Shandon had deceived her; she had wanted love, and kindness, and he treated her like a scheming slut. Her head ached. Her throat felt raw with screams she could not let out. It took every ounce of her strength to contain her rage and pain.

She wondered what she had thought, what she had seen in him. Whatever it was had vanished in a second, and yet before, she had felt − that she had found something. Someone. Was she searching then, was that what it was all about? How stupid to lose your father and think he could be replaced. That love was gone forever.

Reason persuaded to go upstairs and wash before joining the others in the drawing room. She sat and looked at herself in the dressing-table glass, her eyes were like brilliant blue stones. 'They won't forget me,' she whispered to her reflection. 'They'll remember Mara Hellyn for a very long time.' She sprayed perfume in the cleavage of her breasts. A faint blue mark showed above the top of her dress, but she made no attempt to hide it.

They were all still occupied when she went in. At once she went over to Jane's table, and settled herself on the arm of a chair. She started to chatter in a bright, over-heated voice and every now and then she glanced nervously towards the door. Philip, Jane's boyfriend, showed her his cards. They began to play the hand together, and after a while she leaned across to her other neighbour and engaged him in just the same brittle way.

The girls across the table fumed in silence, until Jane said, 'Oh, for God's sake, Mara, why don't you get the hell out of here? You're spoiling the game.'

Mara ducked her head. Philip said, 'Damn it, you're upsetting her. You can be bloody rude, Jane. Rude and unkind.'

'It's all right,' said Mara in a low voice. 'It doesn't seem to be my night tonight. I'm in trouble wherever I go.'

The door opened. She glanced up. Shandon was standing in the doorway, looking desperately embarrassed. Mara almost shuddered. 'I'll go to my room,' she said urgently. 'Is there another way out?'

'What are you implying?' demanded Jane. The colour came and went in her face. She put her cards down face up.

'Nothing – nothing,' hissed Mara. She pressed her hands together and leaned forward, letting her jacket hang open. The bruise was darker now, a clear fingermark across the white of her breast. Mara pulled the jacket closed.

'I'll take you upstairs,' said Philip in a grim voice. 'Can I get you something?'

'No – no. I should have gone straight to bed, but I didn't want – ' she looked down at her hands.

Jane said shrilly, 'You're being ridiculous, Mara! What are you talking about?'

'I'm not talking about anything! Will you please just let me go to bed.'

They all watched as she and Philip left the room, deliberately choosing the doorway furthest from Shandon. His eyes were like those of a dog caught out in crime.

On the stairs Philip said, 'Did he try something? Is that it?'

Mara seemed to shudder. 'He seemed so fatherly. He was the only one who seemed to want me here. I didn't realise why.'

'Did he hurt you?' asked Philip throatily.

'No, no! Not badly. He seemed to think — was it my own fault do you think? But a man that age — '

'I'd never have thought it of him.'

Outside her door she turned to face him. 'I'll be all right now. I'll put a chair under the handle, there isn't a lock you see.'

He ran a hand through his dark hair. 'My room's quite close. I'd hear if you cried out or anything.'

'That's awfully kind of you.' She hesitated. 'I know it's an awful lot to ask but — would you look after me tomorrow? I'd go home but Clare obviously wants to stay. I can't tell her. I don't want to tell anyone, and if I left I might have to.'

Philip swallowed. 'Of course. Anything. I won't let him get near you.'

'Thanks. You're very sweet.'

Alone in her room she subsided on to the bed. She had not one moment's regret. In the space of ten minutes she had broken up Jane's romance and blighted Shandon's reputation, making that cow Lady Shandon look an absolute fool. How dare he say such things about her, about her father? Like Selmer he would pay for what he received, but in coin of her own careful choosing.

A shoot had been organised for the following day. The wet spring had taken its toll of birds, so no-one was expecting a big bag. Somehow breakfast was late, and none of the Shandons appeared before nine, so everything got off to a shambling start. Shandon himself was haggard, and his wife, usually a head-scarved accompaniment, stayed at home. Jane had red-rimmed eyes and a spot forming on her chin.

In contrast Mara looked glorious. She wore brown cord knee breeches with cream socks, and a dark green wax jacket. Her hair was up, a soft knot that seemed in danger of falling down at any moment, and her eyes were the deepest blue. She was wearing make-up but no-one could tell.

'Are you all right?' asked Philip, taking her arm in a proprietorial grasp.

She grimaced bravely. 'Yes, I'm fine. Bit of a head, that's all. I didn't sleep very well.'

'No.' He glanced at Shandon. 'He doesn't seem too bright, either.'

'Huh!' Mara cast him a glance of pure venom. 'Probably terrified. In the bath this morning, I felt — you can't imagine how I felt. I wanted to rub my skin raw.'

Philip glanced at the guns, and then at Mara. He could imagine her capable of murder. 'Do you think you ought to come out?' he asked. 'If you like we could go into town, have lunch perhaps.'

'It's all right.' She smiled, aware that she had let out too much. One didn't, of course. 'I'll feel better once we get going. I love a shoot.'

Henry had taught her to manage a gun when she was eight, and over the years she had become more than competent. But nobody ever noticed women shooting — they ignored it, like some weird abberration. If they hung on then over the years their husbands got used to the idea until it became an eccentricity, like breeding wolfhounds or inviting Russian revolutionaries to stay. Women Mara's age didn't shoot. Nobody ever expected them to.

So to her surprise she and Jane Shandon were left sitting on the Land Rover while the men went away across the fields. It was quiet, almost hushed. A thrush was hammering a snail on the road and the tap, tap, tap might almost have been high heels walking along. A faint smell of cows and silage drifted towards them from the farm.

Jane said, 'Would you like a sandwich?' in a stiff, unnatural voice.

'No thanks.' Mara felt awkward. She hadn't expected to confront her enemy quite in this way.

'Do you — do you really mean to have Philip? Because if you do I'd like to know.' Jane had an abrupt way of speaking, like her mother. She didn't know how to prevaricate.

Mara caught herself in the act of feeling sorry for her. But if she hadn't been such a cow none of this would have happened. Jane didn't deserve sympathy. She said lightly, 'I barely know him. Why? I wasn't aware there was anything special between you.'

'Weren't you?' The girl looked drawn, hopeless.

'No. Actually, I don't think he's my type.'

'And my father is, I suppose?'

'Good God!' Mara leaped off the bonnet of the car and went to the hedge, pulling out a long, thin branch. She stripped the leaves and twigs from it, then brandished it like a whip under Jane's nose. 'I shall hit you with this if you dare say such a thing! The man mauled me. He got me by myself and touched me and tried to make me touch him. I don't care what he says to you, or your mother. Don't you believe me?'

Jane looked into Mara's flushed face. 'Yes,' she whispered.

'Good.' Mara let the stick fall.

'But it's you, you!' burst out Jane. 'You're the cause of it all! You make them all stupid!'

She started to cry, long shuddering sobs. After a moment Mara went into the back of the Land Rover, amidst the boots and coats and

89

gun cases, and got out the sloe gin. She half-filled two plastic tumblers.

'Here. We both need this.'

'Thanks.'

It was sweet, with a harsh and heady back-taste. Mara was tired suddenly, because she had hardly slept and because anger was such a wearing emotion. The booze went straight to her head.

'You ought to marry Philip' she said suddenly. 'He's OK.'

'The choice isn't mine,' said Jane.

'You should stop sniffling and being horrid to people. Anyway, you'll be all right once I've gone.'

Jane sat up drunkenly. 'I think – I think you don't know the damage you cause. After you, everyone seems second-best.'

Mara laughed and went to refill her cup. A man in a shooting jacket was walking up the road towards them, carrying a shotgun, a labrador at his heels.

'Did we leave anyone behind?' she asked Jane.

'What?' She looked and sprang to her feet. 'Oh God! Oh God, he can't see me like this! We thought he wasn't coming.' To Mara's amazement she was off, like a rabbit, over the gate and into the wood.

'Hello,' said the man.

'Hello,' said Mara. She waved a hand towards the wood. 'Jane felt she should make a hasty exit for some reason. I don't think we've met. I'm Mara Hellyn.'

He lifted his shooting hat half an inch and replaced it. He was about thirty, she decided. A thin, lined face, wide at the temples and narrowing to a long chin. 'Jay Denham. Bit dull for you, isn't it, sitting here?'

'Entirely.' Mara didn't care how she disparaged her hosts just then. 'They seem to think women shouldn't shoot. I thought I'd take a gun, but apparently not. So, Jane and I were drinking the sloe gin and having a heart to heart. She thinks I've pinched her boyfriend.'

'And have you?'

'My dear man.' Mara opened her eyes very wide. 'One has only to see him to know the answer to that. He has appalling buck teeth.'

He went at once to the wing mirror and pulled his lips back. 'Worse than mine, you mean?' His were uniform and white, with long eye teeth.

'You look very similar actually,' said Mara. 'Why don't you have some gin to console yourself?'

'Do you think I'd better? I'm supposed to be shooting.'

But Mara was holding out a tumbler. 'You can't leave me here on my own. Up to now this has been the worst weekend of my entire life,

90

I'll have you know. Everybody hates me.'

She was wide-eyed, her lips stained purple from the gin. 'I don't believe that,' he said flatly. 'Unless you've been breaking hearts.'

Mara sighed. 'They think I mean to, even when I don't. It's all very silly, and I'm so damnably tired of it all. I do wish my father was still alive.'

'Do you? I often wish that too.'

She put her face close to his. 'But you didn't know my father.'

Even closer, so close she could smell gin and talcum powder, he said, 'No. I don't suppose I did.' And they began to laugh.

Mara's head was swimming. With an effort she stepped away from him. 'I think we'd both better have something to eat,' she declared.

'Let me get it.' He reached in past her to extract the hamper with its chicken legs and pasties and elegant smoked salmon sandwiches. Mara took out a pasty and began to munch, and Jay chose a chicken leg, perching up on the tailboard beside her. Mara tossed a bit of pastry to the dog. 'I wonder where Jane is. Perhaps she's being sick.'

'Don't get a conscience and go and look, will you? She's the most tedious girl.'

She giggled. 'You don't know how tedious! She always seems to be buttonholing me to tell me how horrible I am.'

'She's a force for moral good,' he declared. 'Just like her mother.'

'Shall I tell them you said that? They'll never invite you again.'

He looked amused, and chuckled. 'They will, you know. It might be your lot to upset everyone, but I can say what I like and no-one ever gets offended. Bloody ridiculous, don't you think?'

She didn't understand him. Nonetheless she leaned back, stretched out her booted legs and said, 'Offend me.'

'Er — I take it you mean verbally?'

Looking at him beneath her lids, she said, 'Yes — for now.'

'And no wonder you get in so much trouble! Mara Hellyn, you're a scheming, immoral — would you mind if I called you a cow?'

'Not at all. And I am scheming, and I am immoral. Try again.'

He sprawled beside her, his hat half over his face, clearly enjoying himself. 'Mara Hellyn — you're a stupid, boring girl who reminds me of many a gatepost.'

'Take that!' She gave him a quick, mild slap on the ear, whipped off his hat and sent it wheeling over the hedge. The dog started barking, he lay back and roared with laughter, and the shooting party arrived.

Everyone else was a great deal more embarrassed than either Mara or Jay. Shandon flushed in red blotches and Samuel said, 'Good heavens! How good of you to come, sir. I see you've met Lady Mara —'

91

'We ate a pasty together,' declared Jay expansively.

'No, no,' contradicted Mara. 'You had the chicken leg. It's swimming around now in half a pint of gin.'

Samuel fixed her with a glare. 'Lady Mara — if I might introduce you to Prince John?'

She put her hand over her mouth and chuckled. 'I see. I'm most sorry I insulted your teeth. Do you think I should go and get the hat?'

'Definitely not.'

She watched the laughter draining out of him. Philip went away behind the hedge to get the hat and as if by common consent, Mara found herself herded to the outside of the group. She petted his dog.

'I'm so glad you managed to get away, sir.' said Samuel.

'I'm sorry I wasn't here earlier. Are you breaking for lunch?'

'No, no,' lied Shandon, 'just moving along a bit. Delighted to have you join us — ' He gesticulated frantically to the keeper. People began to run about aimlessly in all directions; it was farcical and desperately undignified. Mara would not join in.

'Lady Mara's been keeping me amused,' said the prince, and looked around for her. 'She's been telling me all about her weekend.'

She stayed in the distance, merely lifting an eyebrow.

Shandon cast her a look of almost horrified loathing, seen by both the prince and Mara. Their eyes met and they chuckled.

'I don't see your detective,' said Samuel loudly.

The prince said tartly, 'You wouldn't. I left him at home,' and everyone laughed as if at a brilliant joke. The sycophancy took Mara's breath. She walked away, shaking her head, and went back to the house.

Clare was passing the day sitting elegantly in the conservatory, leafing through *Horse and Hound* in lieu of *Vogue* and waiting for Samuel to come back. When she saw Mara pass the door she jumped up and summoned her. 'Mara? Mara, come here at once. I want to talk to you.'

Obediently Mara complied, but before the lecture could begin she said: 'Prince John came on the shoot. I didn't recognise him, but Samuel seems very thick. Does he move in those circles?'

Clare blinked. 'Good heavens! I suppose he might, he talks a lot about Scotland. What's the prince like?'

Mara shrugged. 'Very nice. A bit bored, I think. He told me his name was Jay Denham.'

'Denham's one of his titles. I think his friends call him Jay. He's a cousin of the queen. Whyever didn't he tell you who he was?'

'I imagine he gets very tired of people falling back in a state of shock. Isn't he married to that woman from — where is it? — one of those mid-European places.'

'Havenheim,' supplied Clare. 'They've got two little girls. But, Mara dear, I think it imperative that you apologise to Lady Shandon. I don't know what happened last night and I really don't care, but she's wandering around like something out of a tragedy. Everybody is just dying to get away and tell the tale, and you've only yourself to blame.'

Mara set her jaw. 'Oh no I haven't' she said tightly. 'It isn't my fault that the Shandons don't know how to behave. They're reaping the harvest of their own bad manners. Perhaps next time they won't be so damned arrogant!'

'Coming from you, Mara, that is rather too rich,' commented Clare with acid point.

Quite unexpectedly, instead of simply taking his leave after the shoot, the prince returned to the house. It was as if a bomb had dropped in a fish-pond, with frantic terror and dead fish in all directions. Normally Lady Shandon would have been more than capable of taking it in her stride, but today she rushed about, her hair on end, and confused the cook with ambiguous instructions. They were to have salmon, no trout; they were to rush to the village for broccoli, and to hell with Cook's speciality of marrow in spiced sauce. Since every time Lady Shandon saw her she became more distraught, Mara retired to the library. The only books of any prominence were volumes of Churchill's biography, all apparently unread. She picked up one at random.

After no more than ten minutes the prince came in. Mara glanced up. 'Hello.' She noted his shooting gear. 'What are you going to do when tonight's feast is served up and you haven't got a dinner jacket?'

He sighed and threw himself down a leather sofa. 'Try as I might, they insist on sending a car to collect one. I could have borrowed or done without.'

Mara wagged a finger at him. 'They're busy being honoured. It would have lowered the tone.'

'So it would.'

She went back to her book, acutely conscious that he was watching her. 'What are you reading?' he asked at last.

'Life of Churchill. I'm appalled at the man's confidence. I don't understand it. He had no reason to be that sure of himself.'

'Aren't you?'

She glanced up. 'No. And neither, I suspect, are you.'

93

He was silent for a moment. She watched his face, so strong and angular, with that lean, narrow jaw hung on to it. He said slowly, 'If you asked everyone here who was sure of themselves, they would say me and you. Wouldn't they?'

'Yes. Yes, I imagine they would. But we're not talking about confidence, are we? I mean, Churchill always knew what he wanted, and so he could be sure of himself. If you don't know, then you can't be sure that what you're doing is right.'

'How do you know that fits me?'

She wrinkled her nose. 'I made a guess, I suppose. I thought you seemed very like me.'

Suddenly he got up, walking to the window with angular grace. He had long, long legs, stretching endlessly within his loose moleskin trousers. 'I've been warned about you already,' he remarked.

'Not by Samuel, surely? He doesn't know me.'

'But he knows your aunt. Apparently you leave a trail of broken hearts and empty beds.'

Mara flushed, absolutely scarlet. 'What an absolute − fucking − lie!' She picked up the book and flung it across the room, sending it skidding across the floor and into a huge flower arrangement. 'They have absolutely no taste in this house,' she added inconsequentially. 'Those flowers are just so dull.'

He came across to her and lifted a strand of her hair. 'Don't be cross. I didn't mean to upset you.'

'Yes you did! You wanted to see what I would do. And I've done it. I hate these bloody Shandons, they're middle-class as hell.'

He was so close. She felt her breath catching in her throat, and yet she knew she would do absolutely nothing to encourage him. It must all come from him, he must walk every inch of the way.

'I'm only staying to see you,' he said.

'Yes, I imagined you were. And all the time they tell you I'm a loose woman, you think how admirably that suits your purpose. What a pity for you they got it wrong.'

He stepped away from her, laughing shakily. Mara knew, as if it was written in the sky in letters of fire, that this was a man who had never had to reach out for anything he wanted. He said, 'I don't impress you very much, do I?'

'*You* do. Your being a royal doesn't at all. I'm a Hellyn, we own a house that's bigger than most palaces. Queen Elizabeth was the last monarch that stayed there, because ever after we vowed not to let another in the door. She left with half the furniture, you see. We wouldn't even let the cavaliers stay during the Civil War, and a very good move that turned out to be. Until the Restoration, of course.

94

But you can't win all the time, can you?'

'Will I win now?'

She spun on her heel and turned her back to him, folding her arms across her breasts. Then, slowly, she reached up and unfastened her hair. The golden curls fell like a curtain. She half turned, and saw his face, hot with longing. She chuckled. 'Before you win, you have to fight a battle. I shan't surrender. And I always admire valour.'

She moved slowly towards the door. As her hand touched the handle he said, 'When I saw you today I thought you were the loveliest woman I had ever seen in my life. And now I think you are one of the most exceptional.'

Mara smiled. 'Oh, such flattery! You of all people should know the value of that.'

'I don't think it is flattery. I think it's true.'

'Then it's up to you to see if you are right.'

She went out, leaving the door ajar. She knew, without turning her head, that he stood in the doorway, watching her go.

Chapter Thirteen

It was late when the prince returned home, well after midnight. The wheels of his car scrunched on the long gravel drive, and the watchman switched on the floodlights. There was never any possibility of a discreet arrival at the house; he might as well screech in blowing the horn and singing sea shanties. Jay allowed himself a silent curse and halted on the immaculate and weedless circle before the door.

Although he tolerated this house he wasn't fond of it. Anna's father had made the choice, impressed by the over-sized pillars that ranged along the front. There was an enormous ballroom, too, with six giant chandeliers, but they had never put it to use. All in all the house was too grand and too vulgar for Jay's taste, although he accepted that it was more than suitable for a Crown Princess. When you were heir to somewhere quite as insignificant as Havenheim, modesty was not advisable. Two countries only needed to expand a little, almost take a deep breath, and Havenheim would disappear into the great maw of Europe – another place that once was, and was no more.

He wondered if Anna would be awake. They entertained very little in the country and went to bed early. His wife loved the days there, clumping round the garden in her boots and taking the children for rides in the park. To her, brought up with all the pomp and stiffness of a Germanic court, it was a wonderful liberation. But Jay was often bored. He longed for his London life – opera, ballet, National Gallery committee meetings and Picasso exhibitions. In the country he swam, endlessly, up and down the private pool. Sometimes the girls swam too, splashing about with shrieks and rubber rings, but never Anna. She was much too shy of her body.

The watchman was standing in the doorway, and as Jay passed he dropped his head in a bow. Many of the servants were from Havenheim, and they were incapable of anything except strict formality. It had the advantage though that the girls were fluent in German as well as English, and talked of Havenheim very much as if it were home. Sometimes, in the country, Jay felt the exile.

Thank God his valet was English. He at least understood that it was no service to wait up for someone until the small hours of the morning like an aggrieved mother-in-law, and he obeyed the order not to do it. Anna's maid, Greta, would die rather than go to bed before her mistress, but then she had been with the family for over thirty years, like her mother before her. She slept on the same floor as Jay and Anna, and as Jay crept along the corridor he imagined her lying there listening.

His bedroom was furnished with almost Japanese absence of clutter. The walls and curtains were white, the carpet a dark steel grey against which the black oak of the bed, the table and the chest of drawers stood out like fingermarks. All the paintings were stark and modern, often disturbing, possibly in protest against the extravagant romanticism of the rest of the house. Suddenly he thought of Mara Hellyn there. He almost laughed. She was entirely a creature of curves and softness; she and this room were diametrically opposed.

The connecting door to his wife's room stood slightly ajar. He closed it silently, wondering what on earth he should say to her at breakfast. They had been going to plant up the new rose bed in the afternoon, and he had run off like a wayward schoolboy. But he felt himself grinning. Separated from Mara at dinner by the ever vigilant Samuel, he had watched her playing games with everyone, like a bored goddess. She picked people up, turned them round a few times for her own amusement, and discarded them all dizzy and bewildered. And afterwards he had stopped by her chair. He leaned over her shoulder and whispered, 'Well brought up young ladies don't dine on human flesh, Lady Mara.'

She raised her eyebrows at him. 'Fancy! I must remember to confine such things to the bedroom.'

'Will you be staying in London?'

She leaned her chin on her hand. 'I really couldn't say. Look, you should go away. Your posse of bootlickers is after you.'

He laughed and straightened up. Sure enough, Samuel and Clare were advancing, determined to save him from Mara. She was watching him, her wonderful eyes quite steady. He licked his finger, reached out and ran it across her bare shoulder, walking instantly away.

Now, thinking about it, he was on fire. They had touched and it had been electric, he had heard her sharp intake of breath. Everything about her heightened sexuality; his lower belly ached with unslaked

97

lust. He thought of Shandon, watching her with miserable, hopeless sheep's eyes, the mooning boys, even Samuel who had developed a quite unreasonable dislike of the girl. He had no doubt that Samuel, too, secretly found himself drooling.

He undressed and sat on the edge of his bed, trying to relax and turn his mind to sleep. It would not come. All he saw was Mara Hellyn. He got up and went to the connecting door, opening it silently. He never went to Anna like this. If he wanted her he knocked soon after coming up to bed. Sometimes Greta was still there and she would grin and leer like the madam of a brothel. He imagined her listening to him grunting, for Anna never made a sound.

She was fast asleep. He stood beside the bed looking down at her. The pillows were fringed in rows of cream lace, her diamond stud earrings gleamed in the midst of her hair. All at once he caught himself thinking how ordinary she seemed. He reached out and touched her.

She woke up slowly, and when she saw him, naked, she blushed scarlet.

'Jay – it's so late.'

'I know. I'm sorry. I came home thinking of you. I had to be with you.'

'Yes.' She moved across the big double bed, making room for him to enter. As he lay down at her side the lace of the pillows cut into him, the sheets felt heavy and cold. Anna always wore silk in bed. He ran his hands over her gown, feeling her body stiff and unresponsive beneath it. She was half asleep still, he had taken her by surprise. He pulled one of her long, flat breasts free. The flesh was soft, it resisted him not at all, only half filling the bag of skin. Mara Hellyn had breasts that could smother you. They swelled above her dress as if at any moment they would burst out. And on one was a dark, black bruise.

He got on top of his wife, unable to wait a minute longer. She closed her eyes, he watched little spasms crossing her face. He was coming, he couldn't help it, he had no more control than a boy.

He slid off her and lay for a moment, panting. 'You didn't come,' he said.

Anna gave a short, embarrassed laugh. He had never said that before. Sometimes Jay courted her, spending an hour, two hours in her room, kissing her feet and her neck. Then she might come, biting the backs of her hands to prevent herself crying out. For the rest she didn't mind. It wasn't important to her.

He was reaching between her legs. He was touching her, stroking her.

'No! Stop it, Jay, I don't like it.'

'Yes you do. I want you to come, Anna.'

'Not with – not with you watching.'

'Yes. Me watching.'

He half sat up. He knew the sex had aroused her. He pushed away her protesting hands and began gentle, circular stroking. He wet his fingers in his own discharged semen. It was like bathing her in oil. She put her hands over her face, hiding as the pleasure began. He put two fingers of his other hand into her and he felt her begin to convulse. Her breath was coming in gasps and spasms. She rolled violently aside.

'That was good for you, wasn't it?' he asked. She shook her head, not looking at him. 'I'm sorry,' he said stiffly.

After a moment she turned over. 'What happened tonight, Jay? Where did you go?'

'Didn't you get my message? I had dinner with the Shandons. There was a shoot and it went on rather.'

'But what happened? Who did you see?' The German accent was always thickest when she was upset.

'No-one special. Anna, I simply came home and wanted to make love to you. We don't do it enough.'

'But I am always here, Jay. You don't have to – embarrass me.'

He said harshly, 'I wanted to give you pleasure. Not such a crime, surely!'

'I'm sorry – I was not pleased.'

He felt like hitting her. His hand twitched as if he really might strike a blow. He pulled himself up, taking short, strained breaths. To give her pleasure had been an apology for his thoughts.

What had gone wrong? When he left home this morning he had been calm and happy. Tonight he was wild enough to violate his wife. It was the girl, of course. All his wisdom and sophistication were no protection against the heartbreaker. He knew, with a stab of sharp regret, that he must never see her again.

Days later, in London, Mara waited for him to contact her. She had laid her trail, she had spiced it with promise, and in the fullness of time he would come to her. But as the weeks went by and nothing happened she went on as before, going to parties and dinners, to the opera. Sometimes she saw Jane Shandon, thinner and rather white, occasionally with Philip in tow. They were both wary of her, as if they could blame her for everything. She had little sympathy. The wolf had blown on the little piggy-wigs' straw house, and it had come tumbling down. It was time they learned brick-laying, she decided.

99

But the old feelings were coming back. Why didn't he call? Why, at the opera, was the tenor out of tune, the orchestra out of time and the scenery dull? Why was there never anyone interesting to talk to? Sometimes she drank too much, vomiting discreetly in the toilet. One of her dresses became splashed and the marks refused to clean out; she tore another on the handle of a door.

Once more she needed money. She considered asking Clare again, but since the Shandon weekend Clare had been less than friendly. She was seeing Samuel, and no doubt reported that all was well – the prince was in his marital bed and standards remained pulled up to the chin. So she wrote to Marcus, a brief, friendly letter.

A week later she received a reply, scrawled in his distinctive black ink:

Dear Mara,
I received your letter. We trust you are well and enjoying yourself. You can't have the money because they've taken it. Don't let them know about me. I escaped last night down the ladder, but that won't always work. If you hear that they've got me, don't try to help. They'll come for you as well. You'll be all right as long as they don't find out.
Yours ever, M.

Her hands shook as she folded the paper. Madness came off it like a foul smell. She grabbed the 'phone and dialled home, though usually she asked Clare before she made long distance calls. The expected ringing tone did not come. Instead there was a high-pitch whine. She rang the operator and complained, and they put her through to the engineer, who tried again and still failed to get connected.

'Fault on the line,' he intoned. 'We'll investigate.'

She sat holding the silent 'phone in her lap. She was so broke there wasn't even the money for a ticket home. And really – did she want to go home? What could she do, what could anyone do?'

If only her father was alive. If he hadn't died the world would be fun again, there would be no demons that couldn't be tamed. Without him The Court was a desert, with disappointment round every corner, because you remembered him and he couldn't be there. If he was here Marcus would be well. He was never this bad when Henry was alive!

Gradually she began to rationalise the letter. Marcus had been drinking again, he was always very odd when drunk. He started and finished quite sensibly. And after all, was it so bad? They all knew he hallucinated, they had known for years. He had turns, days when he would be wild and unbalanced, peopling the world with strange things. Afterwards he was different, tired, sleepy. The letter wasn't unusual, merely unexpected. Away from him she had forgotten.

She decided to write to Lisa. Getting out paper and pen, assembling her thoughts, it all began to seem very exaggerated. Marcus had written a letter when drunk, and the 'phone was out of order, that was all. She wrote a light, chatty page, at the end adding, 'PS − how is Marcus? I got a very odd letter from him, do let me know if he's OK.'

That night she went out to a club with Jimmy. Nowadays she knew lots of people, young men dragged her off to their tables and introduced her to actors and film producers. Everyone thought she should be in pictures, it seemed, except those who might put her there. She was the wrong style. They wanted waif-like girls with small, high breasts and she would not, absolutely would not, submit to the indignity of being assessed by people she despised. So she was cold and unimpressed and men used to being courted took against her. It made Jimmy cross. 'You could be famous, Mara. Another Marilyn Monroe.'

'And why should I want to be anything of the sort?' All she wanted was some money.

On the pavement outside she broke the heel of her shoe. Her heart sank, resting in the pit of her stomach in sad, grey dismay. 'Bad luck,' said Jimmy, holding her against him. 'Shall I carry you?'

'No,' snapped Mara. 'Look, Jim − can you lend me a hundred quid? I'm rather short at the moment.'

His mouth fell open. He seemed to be struggling to find words. 'Well − yes,' he said finally. 'But I'd need it back by the end of the week. I spend every penny of my allowance myself.'

Mara sighed. She wouldn't take what she couldn't pay back. 'I'll manage, Jim,' she said dismally, and hobbled along.

The others wanted to go on somewhere, only Mara wanted to go home. Everyone piled into a cab, but she persuaded them to go via Tavistock Square and drop her off. As usual she had to avoid paying and her dependence enraged her. Money was such a stupid, vulgar obsession, she didn't deserve to be obsessed by it.

The square was quiet and the house dark when the cab drove off, Jim's arm waving wildly out of the window. She stood for a moment, feeling the evening wind on her cheek, listening to the night.

'Good evening, Lady Mara.'

She spun round on her broken heel and almost fell. Selmer reached out and caught her arm; she found herself looking up into his face. 'What are you doing here?'

He didn't smile. 'What do you think? A little business, perhaps. A worthwhile transaction. If of course you're at home.'

101

It was a reference to the many wasted 'phone calls. Mara pulled herself upright, standing on tiptoe to compensate for her heel.

'I'm going in,' she said coldly. 'I'm sorry.'

He still held on to her arm. 'I don't want to alarm you, Lady Mara,' he murmured, 'but it would be in your interest to comply.'

'What do you mean?'

'Well — his fingers gripped a little harder — 'London's a rough place, even for the aristocracy. A pretty girl could get hurt. Might be a car, might be a couple of blacks looking for a good time. A knife, anything.' He reached up and touched her cheek.

Mara held herself rigid, refusing to flinch. 'You don't frighten me,' she said sneeringly. 'I'll tell you why I won't do business. I hear you have very bad habits, and I never go anywhere I might catch something.'

A muscle twitched in his cheek. 'OK. I'll take care of that. Three thousand.'

'Four,' she said, yawning with nerves. Oh God, how was she going to get out of this? The man's Rolls, parked in the shadows, suddenly purred into life.

'Get in the car,' said Selmer.

She thought about screaming, but he could kill her before anyone came. They wouldn't miss her in the house, she wasn't expected until at least three o'clock. 'Four thousand' she said desperately, playing for time.

'All right. Four.' He was pushing now with real force and instinctively she knew she must not fight. He wanted to hurt women, he took pleasure from it. She must take the greatest care not to push him over that cliff.

A car was driving into the square. Suppose it was a photographer? Selmer could cook up a brute of a story and Clare would throw her out. The only hiding place was the Rolls, but once inside she put her face against the window to see who it was. The car stopped close by and the driver got out. She found herself looking straight at Samuel. He raised his eyes, touched his hat and went to knock on Clare's door.

Mara turned to Selmer. 'I can't come. My aunt will know, it's no good.'

'And what kind of a fool do you think I am?' He rapped once on the glass. The Rolls pulled away.

In the dark before dawn, Tavistock Square was utterly silent. Not a light showed in any of the houses, the street lamps were no more than small yellow pools in the gloom. Early falling leaves rustled in the gutters as a breeze gusted across the hard London pavements. The dull drone of cars somewhere behind the endless grey roofs seemed to speak of a machine-like, loveless world, as if all was in the grip of a never-sleeping monster.

Mara opened the door as quietly as she could. If she could get to bed Clare might never know where she had been, or who with. Explanations were simply not possible.

Her leg hurt. He had kicked her just once, an experimental jab, and she had come back at him with a bottle. That had stopped him. As for what else he had done, she preferred not to think about it. She had simply survived.

In a sudden flash of realisation she knew that she hated Selmer more than she would have believed possible. Every fibre in her was set in loathing, and in the midst of it she hated herself. Her body had been his to use, he had wiped himself on her as if she was of no more importance than a bath towel. Her hand hurt; an experimental burn from a cigar. Her throat hurt. If only she could run to someone, anyone, and cry and cry and tell them everything – but there was no-one at all. The price of sin is loneliness, she thought to herself. You live with it quite alone.

She lay in bed all morning and dragged herself downstairs for lunch. Clare was already in the drawing-room, her hair in an immaculate French pleat, wearing a neat Chanel suit from the latest collection. Mara glanced down at her own tired afternoon dress.

'You must have been quite late last night,' said Clare nervously.

'Yes.' Mara wondered if she should apologise, or launch into a complex explanation. But she would not justify herself.

'I gather you saw Samuel,' burst out Clare. Her hands came together and she began twisting her rings.

'Yes. Yes, I believe I did.'

'I wouldn't want you to imagine – he came to borrow a book.'

'Oh. I see. An inspiring volume, I trust?' Despite herself Mara's lips twitched. Here was Clare, caught out in a fling.

'Very inspiring,' said Clare in a dead voice.

'One so often finds the urge to read coming upon one at that time of the night.'

Clare flushed a delicate pink. Then she said, 'And where were you going? You didn't come in.'

'Well, indeed no,' agreed Mara. 'I broke my shoe. We were going on, I came home to change, but under the circumstances – please don't apologise Clare, I quite understand.'

Clare got up and walked in agitation round the room. 'I don't think you do at all. I don't personally – It isn't something I myself – but he is so insistent! One cannot – '

103

'Indeed,' agreed Mara with heavy irony. She took a sip of water to ease her aching throat. 'Please, Clare, there's no need to explain.'

'One lives in absolute dread of Jennings finding out,' whispered Clare. 'One would scarcely be able to meet his eye.'

Mara grimaced. If her secrets were only that small! 'If Samuel had any sense he'd invite you to stay with him. Are you sure he's not being an awful nuisance, Clare? There's never any point in inconveniencing yourself for people. For men.'

'I'm very fond of him,' said Clare. 'Very fond indeed.'

Gazing at her across the salmon terrine, Mara wondered what she saw in Samuel. He was abrasive, dictatorial and, to her mind, cold. Perhaps Clare was simply lonely, and put up with things that disagreed with her because they were better than nothing at all.

Loneliness, that was the enemy. Sometimes Mara felt as alone as the last person on earth. And if perfection was not to be achieved, if there was only going to be a scale that ran from misery up to mild content, was it not better to settle for mild content? If she married someone, Jimmy perhaps, everything would be simple. No Clare, no Selmer, and with access to Jimmy's trust fund no more money worries. If Clare could put up with Samuel, why not she with Jimmy, who hadn't the brains to be unpleasant?

Just then, gazing down at air bubbles trapped in the fish glaze, she gave up trying to be happy. She had gone on hoping, even after her father died, and after Edward, and Selmer, and Shandon, even beyond the point when she ceased to believe that the prince would 'phone. It had not survived last night. She felt changed, like metal in a fire, and not for the better. In the centre of her being there rested an impermeable core of pain.

As soon as lunch was over she went to the 'phone and called Jimmy. 'Jim? It's Mara. I wondered − would you take me to dinner tonight? I wanted to talk, just the two of us.'

He agreed with commendable speed, hesitating just long enough for her to guess that he would have to cancel something else. Jim at least was prepared to put her before everything.

When the call was finished she sat for a while, wondering what she should do. All energy was drained out of her, she lacked even the will to cash Selmer's cheque. Tomorrow perhaps. The afternoon sunshine made speckles on the carpet. She watched them change, and flicker, and disappear one by one as evening approached. God forbid that she should dream tonight.

When Jimmy arrived she was dressed in boots, a long blue wool skirt and a white jumper, tucked in at the waist. He went slightly pink, as he often did at the sight of her. 'You look wonderful. But you always do, don't you?'

'I hope so. Are we going somewhere quiet? I'm a bit tired.'

'Didn't sleep too well, I suppose? Neither do I when I have an early night.'

Mara allowed herself a wry smile.

In the restaurant, Jimmy said, 'What have you done to your hand?'

'I burned it. Oh, Jim, you don't know how pleased I am to be with you tonight.'

He covered her injured hand with his own. 'That goes for me too. When I'm with you, I can't believe it's true. Me. And you. I mean, anyone would want to be here.'

She smiled and withdrew her hand. He was coming to the point too quickly, she had no wish to spend the evening pretending to be starry-eyed with happiness. So she emptied her glass and drank half another and asked Jimmy to tell her his newest jokes. And thankfully the food arrived to divert them.

The cuisine was French and involved a great deal of silver serving and flaming puddings and fish slices. Jimmy said, 'Have you noticed that waiter? He keeps looking at you. Do you know him?'

Mara glanced across. Tall, blond with a smooth brown skin: Edward. Their eyes met and she felt her stomach heave on the mussels she had just eaten.

Everything seemed to be conspiring at once to upset her. He looked malevolent, it was the only word for it. But then she would think that – last night had made her know things, believe things that she could never have imagined. She could see evil in anything today.

Jimmy was looking at her. She swallowed. 'I know him well. It's Edward Demouth, he stayed with us for a while. His people have a big farm in Kenya.'

'Has he upset them then? Must be a bit pushed to dress up in a white jacket and grovel round tables scraping egg off the cloth.'

'I imagine he's been living it up, don't you?'

'I'll call him over.'

She put up a hand to stop him, but it was too late. Jimmy had summoned the head waiter. 'Could you let that chap off for a minute? We know him and we'd like a word.'

'Certainly, sir.' French politeness masking French disdain. He sent Edward to them with a grim flick of his head. Grudgingly, he put down the cloth he was holding and came across.

'You know this could lose me my job?'

'You ought to be glad to lose it, old chap.' Jimmy adopted the tone that had seen him through years at Eton, condescending to lesser

105

mortals. 'Friend of Mara's, I gather. What are you doing slumming about down here?'

'Earning money,' said Edward.

In a low, rushed voice, Mara said, 'Is it your fare home? I can lend you some if you like.'

'Lend it? I don't remember ever asking for anything back from you, Mara!'

'Have it then! You can have it. I didn't mean – '

Edward's voice was bitter. 'No. But then you never do, do you? If I wanted to borrow money, I'd get it from Diandra. But I'd rather earn it.'

'Diandra? Are you seeing her then?'

'You could say that. She's coming home to Kenya with me, for a visit. A very long visit.'

'That sounds absolutely splendid,' broke in Jimmy, aware that antagonism was in the air and doing his best to disperse it. 'Hunt lions, do you? Or is it conservation now and all Grandad's trophies stuffed in the attic?'

'Jimmy, do shut up!' snapped Mara.

'You know, Mara,' said Edward thoughtfully. 'I could have understood it if you'd dumped me for someone worthwhile. But for this?' He gave a neat, waiterly bow and walked away.

Mara dropped her forehead into her hands. Jimmy said, 'What did he mean? Did you have a thing going with him?'

'No, of course I didn't. He was in love with me. I didn't let him down very lightly.'

'Oh, if that's all.' Jimmy's false manner fell away and he sipped his wine. 'I don't suppose you'll be kind to me either, will you?'

She glanced at him. This was the moment to say that she never meant to let him down at all, but somehow the words stuck in her throat. Eventually she said, 'Don't be silly, Jim.'

Just the same, he screwed up his napkin and said tightly, 'We ought to get spliced, you know. Everyone would like it. And it's not as if you're doing all right on your own.'

'What?' She didn't understand him. Jim leaned forward, trying to explain. 'You're not like the other girls. You ought to settle down. Everyone has their fun but with you it's different. Sometimes I think you go a bit too far. I can't explain it – '

'Don't try.' She reached out and put her hand over his, then remembered Edward and withdrew it. 'Let's go and see that friend of yours. Dermot, wasn't it? Cheer ourselves up.'

'You're not using the stuff, are you?' Jim looked suddenly anxious. 'You shouldn't Mara.'

106

'You do.'

'Not much any more. Look, are you sure you want to?'

She got up, taking him by surprise. 'Come on, Jim. If you don't take me, I'll go by myself.'

Later, in her room, she lay on her bed and saw a world tinged with pink. It softened everything: Edward's angry face, Jimmy's disapproval, Vivien Shandon, who petted her like a father and then skewered her like a barbecued fish. Selmer lurked in the dark somewhere, but she was safe from him now, for the moment.

She sat up and her hands were shaking again. They hadn't stopped trembling since Selmer pushed her into the car. The night stretched ahead, empty, black.

Kneeling in the bathroom, trying to chase the white line with her little straw, she felt rising hysteria. It was all the fault of the shoe. Without that he would never have caught her, and that was her father's fault, for leaving them poor! And if you looked at the cause of that it was the house, the damnable, beautiful house! Suddenly she wished she was there. The sharp, fierce burn hit her nostrils. Her head hung down, her long hair trailing on the floor. Thank God. For a while at least, she had tranquillity.

In the morning she drank milk at breakfast, to combat the dryness in her throat, and dressed in a red wool suit. Her skin looked like marble against it and slightly swollen eyelids gave her a brooding, heavy look. Clare was bad-tempered because they were to lunch at Samuel's house and she had been forced to get up at eight.

'You look exhausted this morning, Mara! I thought you were going to have an early night.'

'I'll be all right in the fresh air.' Her hands were shaking again. An unreasoning panic seemed to be nibbling at the edges of her vision, although everything was under control now. She was safe, here, today. On her way upstairs the telephone rang. Usually Jennings answered it, but the ringing went on.

'Do answer that damned telephone, Mara!' yelled Clare.

Mara caught it on the 'phone at the top of the stairs, where Clare had put a French antique desk, purely for effect. 'Hello,' she said abruptly.

'Er — is that you, Mara?'

She straightened up. Her fingers twisted in the telephone cord. 'It is indeed,' she said throatily.

'I am glad. It's Jay. If you remember, we met before.'

Chapter Fourteen

There was a smell of burning. Lisa hitched up her too long dressing gown, pushed the dog aside and rushed into the kitchen. She was too late, the toast was flaming, a veritable conflagration. She threw it into the sink, turned the taps on and then fought her way to the back door through the smoke. It billowed across the kitchen garden, like a steam train going up hill. Marcus came in, started and went to the door. He shut it firmly, casting Lisa a look of reproach. 'They'll get in,' he said.

'They can't with the smoke, they don't like it. Let me open the door, Marcus.'

She went to try but he caught her wrist, easily restraining her. Struggling, she tried to get free, but his grip tightened until the bones felt as if they would crack. 'Marcus! Let me go at once!'

'Don't − open − the − door!'

'I won't. I promise I won't.'

He let her go and she retreated across the smoky kitchen. Her heart was beating wildly, and her wrist throbbed in giant pulses in time with it. He began to pace up and down, his head lowered, staring at her out of brilliant eyes.

'Would you like porridge?' she asked jerkily. 'You liked it yesterday.'

He said nothing but she went to the range to begin cooking. It seemed ridiculous to keep it lit with only two of them in the house, but with summer at its end they needed its warmth. When she lifted the iron cover to check on the fire, Marcus raced across the kitchen, yelling, 'No!' His hand slammed the cover down. She could smell burnt skin. 'You want to let them in,' he whispered. 'It's you. I should have known, you let them in behind my back.'

'No, I don't. Marcus, I wouldn't do that.'

Trapped against the range, her brother's face inches from her own,

Lisa was aware of irrelevant thoughts. Who would feed the dog when he had killed her? She hoped very much that he wouldn't kill the dog as well, he was old and used to kindness.

Very gently the back door swung open. Marcus shrieked and fell down, his arms folded over his head. Through the billowing smoke Lisa saw a tall man in brown cord trousers and Arran sweater. He looked vaguely apologetic. 'I'm so sorry,' he said. 'I tried to 'phone but there was no reply. I've come about the grant.'

Lisa put her hands up to her face. She had the urge to fling herself at the stranger and sob. After a second she mastered herself. 'I'm so glad you came,' she whispered.

He was Professor Chandler, of the Historic Buildings Trust. Marcus had written a letter asking for their advice, and he was here to give it. 'I'm afraid you contacted me some weeks ago,' he apologised.

Lisa grimaced. In those weeks her life had spiralled down, down, down. She had prayed for someone to come. But she had expected Angus, not this hawk-faced Professor.

Marcus was moaning, scrabbling around on his knees, his arms over his head. If she wasn't careful Professor Chandler would think they were both mad as hatters. 'He had the 'phone disconnected,' she said hoarsely. 'And he's drained the petrol from the car. I thought my other brother would come back, but he hasn't. I thought someone would realise. If we need something he locks me in and walks to the village; he wears two balaclavas in case the monsters get him. The horses are going mad in the stables. There's no-one to see to them, and it's all I can do to make him let me out to throw them some hay. I thought he was going to kill me.'

'Good heavens.' The Professor was clearly trying to appear matter of fact, but his long hand flexed, thoughtfully. 'How very worrying for you.'

'Yes,' agreed Lisa, feebly.

Marcus was clinging to the table edge, sobbing, 'Don't let them get me!' in the most piteous way.

'I think – a doctor?' suggested the Professor. 'I'll call in at the village.'

Despite herself, Lisa burst out, 'Don't leave me here! Please don't leave me!' Fear, bottled up for weeks, suddenly became all-engulfing. She tried to get between the tall visitor and the door. Marcus turned his head, fixing her with a stare of terrifying intensity. Suddenly he got up and ran out of the room, his footsteps sounding thunderous in the corridors. The performance astonished the Professor, and he turned to Lisa in sudden sympathy.

'My dear girl – what do you want to do?'

'We'll go together.'

They slipped out and locked the door behind them. The Professor's car was parked in the drive, a pre-war Bristol Bentley. Even as Lisa tried to run towards it, stumbling in her slippers, she thought how well it suited The Court. It had the same air of faded magnificence. A rook cawed and instinctively she flinched, she lived in horror that Marcus might get hold of the guns. She had locked the cabinet and hidden the key but he was more than capable of breaking in. She imagined the shot blasting out from one of the windows, and only when she was safely cushioned by the car's deep leather seats did she let out a long sigh. 'Thank God. Thank God.'

The Professor glanced at Lisa's nightclothes. 'Would you like to borrow my jacket – or something?' He looked dubiously at the old tartan dog rug in the back, that currently sheltered a large piece of porcelain.

'No,' said Lisa flatly. But then she glanced across at the man beside her. He was too young and too good-looking for her to feel comfortable beside him in this condition, half-dressed and hysterical with fright. She ran her fingers through her tangle of hair, fighting to appear a little less distraught. Her teeth were chattering, and she too thought about the rug on the back seat. But she didn't want to bother this strange man, unfairly involved in her mess. Try as he would to hide it, his clean profile exuded distaste. He didn't want to get involved.

She knew she ought to be thinking of what she should do, but her brain felt as flabby as wet cottonwool. Telephone Angus, perhaps? Term had barely started, but he had gone back over a month early to try and do some work. Why had he left her? But then, he couldn't have known. She turned to Professor Chandler. 'We must drive straight to the doctor's surgery. I don't want people to realise, you see.'

He hesitated. 'If you'll forgive me – his appearances in the village must have given rise to comment. It's not every day someone shops dressed up as a member of the provisional IRA.'

She was not amused. 'I see no reason to confirm vulgar suspicion,' she said coldly.

The surgery was on the edge of the village, a matter of great inconvenience to pram-pushing mums and the elderly alike. But it suited Lisa's purpose. She hardly knew the doctor, apart from his visits to Henry. She had never bothered to speak to him.

The Professor accompanied her into the waiting-room, and she swept past the curious faces with barely a glance. The receptionist looked dumbfounded. 'Lady – Lady Eloise?'

110

'I must see the doctor urgently, please,' declared Lisa.

'He has someone with him – '

'I did say it was urgent.'

She didn't care what they thought of her, all these staring people. They only wanted to gloat, she thought, to see the Hellyns dragged down. She had waited, thinking Marcus would come round, and now everything was as terrible and embarrassing as it could be. A man cleared his throat. It was the landlord of the pub, he had known them all for years. 'If there's anything we can do, miss,' he said awkwardly. 'Happy to oblige.'

She felt tears pricking her eyelids. She tried to mutter, 'Thank you,' and could not. The publican nodded.

The surgery door opened and the doctor came out, looking distinctly annoyed. 'Well?'

'I did rather expect a private consultation,' said Lisa frostily. She was finding that dudgeon was her best defence against tears.

'I was told it was urgent,' snapped the doctor.

'And so it is.'

Gracelessly he ushered her into the room that housed the afternoon baby clinic. All over the walls were pictures of bouncing babies, and notices saying "Breast is Best". Perhaps that was the root of the problem: bottling by nanny. They started unhinging him at Day One, and had continued right up to date. The job was very nearly done now.

'Well? I do have a surgery to run. People, ordinary people, are waiting.'

She tried to speak. 'It's – It's my brother. I'm sorry, this is very hard for me.'

'Difficult as it may be to believe, whatever problem you have is likely to be twice as bad for anyone else,' snapped the doctor. 'After all, they don't have your advantages.'

'Really?' She glared at him, hating him for the inverted snobbery that despised her without knowing her. 'My brother's gone completely mad. He hasn't let me out for three weeks. I thought – I thought he was going to kill me.'

The doctor's face changed. 'I see. And where is he now?'

'Locked in the house. But there are guns, he could break into the case. I feel I must –' she swallowed, trying to control herself. 'I shouldn't like people to know. It isn't his fault, you see.'

'Indeed.'

The doctor picked up the telephone and began dialling. Lisa sat down on one of the little chairs designed for toddlers. It brought her knees to her chin. She rested her head on them, wondering how she

111

could contract Angus when she couldn't remember his number. She sat, cradling her knees, and after a while she heard police sirens and fire engines in the road outside. Poor Marcus, she thought distantly. He always knew that sooner or later they'd come to get him.

Angus arrived after lunch, his dark hair on end and his face drawn. Lisa was mucking out the horses, making up for the days of neglect. She leaned on a fork and watched her brother striding towards her, wondering again what had gone wrong. Calm, sane Angus, and his twin a lunatic. She said the word in her head, trying to come to terms, to believe it. Such an unkind, unloving label.

'Lisa! Are you all right?'

She shrugged, wearily. 'Just about, I think. I turned the horses out. He wouldn't, you see.'

'Where've they taken him?'

'High Top. It was horrible. Four policemen had to hold him down while they drugged him.'

'God. Oh, bloody God!'

Angus sat down on a straw bale and Lisa put an awkward hand on to his shoulder. They weren't a demonstrative family, on the whole. 'Have you told Mother?' asked Angus.

Lisa shook her head. 'I can't think of any point, can you? He might get better with drugs. We could tell her then.'

'What about Mara?'

'We've had the odd 'phone call and a letter to Marcus asking for money. He sent back one of his essays on paranoia and Mara wrote me a cheerful little missive asking if something might be wrong. The least she could do is come up to see!'

'I was coming at the weekend,' said Angus in justification.

'I thought you had to come eventually.'

They worked together for a while, brushing the cobbled floors and pulling chaff out of the drains. The stables were almost better built than the house, or at least better maintained. The hay racks were made with the Hellyn crest worked in iron, there was even a stone trough let into the floor where horsemen two hundred years ago had bathed their charges' strained tendons and bruised heels. Even the weathervane was lovely, a bow of seven stars pierced by an arrow. It creaked nowadays and was probably soft with rust.

'It was the money that finally upset him,' burst out Lisa suddenly. 'Everyone seemed to be getting at him, the bank, Father's tailor, the caterers for Mara's ball. And the stockmarket's down. Father had loans on everything, you know. God knows what he was hoping, perhaps he meant Mara to marry some horrible millionaire. I think I

112

should tell you — we sold some of the Georgian silver. And it made hardly any difference at all.'

Angus cleared his throat. A sense of doom had grown on him the nearer he came to The Court, a sense of entrapment. 'What was Marcus going to do then? Did he have a plan?'

'Just selling land,' said Lisa. 'The man at Home Farm's giving up and going to live with his daughter. Marcus was going to sell.'

'Good God! That is absolutely out of the question!'

He got up and began to walk furiously, going nowhere. He stopped at one of the neglected flower barrels and kicked it. One of the slats fell out, followed by a little avalanche of worm-infested soil. Everything was falling apart. Angus swung on his heel. 'Look,' he said to Lisa. 'There's only one thing for it. I'll have to leave Oxford and get a job. In the City perhaps. And you'll have to open the place up, like it or not.'

Lisa closed her eyes. She looked pathetic standing there, dirty fists clenched, her hair in unattractive slabs on either side of her thin, white face. A little, stringy girl in faded jeans and an oversized shirt. She opened her eyes, blinking away the tears. 'I think I'd rather sell up,' she said tightly. 'If it's all the same to you.' She was shy and stiff with strangers, she couldn't bear the thought of hordes of them trampling over the house.

Angus said, 'We can't possibly sell. The Hellyns belong at The Court, I won't be the one to finish it. Look, forget about the visitors. We'll think of something. All right?'

She nodded, wearily, and went back to her work.

Lisa went to bed in the afternoon, falling dead asleep in seconds. She needed it. Since Marcus's breakdown she had slept in snatches, locking herself into her room. He had hardly slept at all, sitting up at a lighted window, watching the night, or striding about banging on the glass, yelling at his enemies. She had dreamed, restlessly, of being burned alive, and now she was thankfully dreamless.

Angus decided to exercise his hunter. It irritated him to have to groom and saddle all by himself, and his own irritation annoyed him. He had spent all his life in a feather bed, and now that he was tipped out on to the floor he was damned if he would winge and whine. All the same, it was infuriating to have to work for an hour on a nag before you could ride it.

The horse was full of himself, wild from lack of exercise. Every other stride was a fly-buck, and Angus gritted his teeth and hung on. That was another thing. If you had a groom, he rode exercise. You could live in London and come back for the weekend to find a calm

113

and well-mannered horse. Who in God's name was to see to the hunt? He'd have to go down to the kennels and see old Tom, and talk about things.

Up on the hill the wind was blowing, stripping leaves from the trees. A spiral of smoke was being whipped into rags. The gypsies again. Such was his mood that Angus almost relished the confrontation, he wanted someone to savage. He rode fast down into the valley, the horse taking hold and forcing him to curse and saw at his mouth. A gypsy boy stood by the hedge watching him, and for once, instead of the sullen stare, the boy laughed. It was infuriating. Angus felt mocked.

'Why are you all camping here again?' he demanded loudly. 'How long have you been here?'

The boy said nothing. They never did, just stood and watched you like idiots. You couldn't fight that.

The caravans were further on, the lad was about his own affairs, poaching probably. When Angus rode round the bend he saw the camp – ancient vardos with the paint peeling, a collapsing fibreglass van with a hole hacked through the top for a chimney. The gypsies stared at him, all black and smoke-stained. It was mostly women, he realised. A baby was crawling near the fire.

'Somebody pick up that child,' he ordered. No-one moved. At the last moment the infant put out a hand to the fire, and then turned away. Presumably gypsy children learned early to leave the fire, or else they died horribly. Angus felt a sudden and unusual dislike of them. 'You know damned well there's been trouble in our family,' he snapped. 'Yet here you are again, abusing the kindness we've shown to you in the past. Look at this place – rubbish everywhere, and there's a sapling snapped in two down the lane. Tethering your blasted horses, I suppose. It's got to stop. I want you off, today. For good.'

One of the young girls turned her head and looked at him. She was filthy, her hair a mat, and she wore a man's shirt tied round her waist with a piece of gold plastic chain. Angus felt a stab of unexpected desire. Her nipples were visible through the shirt. He felt himself going hot, though he knew she would stink to high heaven.

'Hitch up your wagons AT ONCE!' he yelled, and his horse cavorted sideways, almost trampling the baby. Angus cursed, but still no-one picked up the child.

One of the women, fat, her head in a scarf, said, 'Tomorrow, sir. Go tomorrow. We've a girl, birthing.'

Angus hesitated. But of course it was a ruse to delay matters. 'I want you out, today,' he snapped.

114

The old woman went to the back of a wagon, dragging the curtain aside with her horny hand. A girl lay within, pregnant belly mountainous. She was biting a cloth to prevent herself crying out, her bare legs were like sticks of white asparagus. Angus swore. He felt conspired against. 'You have until the end of the week,' he rapped, and swung his horse round.

The hunter was keyed up from standing. He skittered across the road, putting a back leg into the ditch. Desperately trying to control it, Angus saw the gypsy boy again. He was grinning to himself. The horse half reared, taking it into his head to refuse to go forward. Angus's cap fell off — he wished to God he had put on a crash hat. Then the boy chirrupped, a small, unimportant sound. The black horse stopped, shuddering. The boy chirrupped again, picking up Angus's hat and holding it out to him.

'Thank you,' said Angus awkwardly. His horse moved calmly and quietly away.

By the time he had unsaddled, mixed a feed and settled everything for the night, it was growing dark. Lisa was in the kitchen, cooking. He smelled garlic and herbs. Three breasts of duck were waiting to be sautéed.

'No need to send you on a cordon bleu course,' remarked Angus, flinging himself into one of the elm chairs that had been there forever. The kitchen was warm and welcoming, they barely went beyond it nowadays. The drawing-room fire took an age to light and an age longer to become hot. Without help The Court was an impossibility, he reflected.

'Professor Chandler's coming to supper,' remarked Lisa. 'I said I'd show him round afterwards.'

'At night? You're becoming very brave.' As children none of them went into the dark parts of the house, because of the ghosts. Lisa's mouth twisted a little. It would take more than a ghost to frighten her nowadays.

She spread a lace cloth on the table, and set wooden circles on it as place mats. They were thin pieces cut from the boles of some of their trees when they were felled earlier in the year. She had saved them and sent them away to be polished. The colour varied according to the type of tree. She wavered momentarily on whether to use the damask napkins. It seemed odd when eating in the kitchen, but scruffy to use anything else. She resigned herself to hours spent soaking them in salt and ironing them wet, and fetched them from the dresser. The table looked charming, she had arranged some late-blooming roses in a water dish and they moved about, like galleons.

There was a knock on the door. Angus got up and went to answer it, but instead of Professor Chandler it was the doctor. He stood in the doorway, clutching his bag, his jaw set aggressively.

'Do come in,' said Angus after a pause. 'I was about to have a whisky. Perhaps you'll join me.'

'I won't, thank you,' said the doctor. 'I'm sorry to intrude. I see you're enjoying yourselves.'

It was an obvious reproof. Lisa remarked, 'Do please accuse us of heartlessness straight out, doctor. Marcus is in a lunatic asylum and we are having a party.'

'I had thought you might wish to visit him today. The charge-nurse intended to call me when you came, I wanted to talk to you.'

'Isn't he still drugged?' asked Angus.

'Yes. Entirely. But it's hardly natural to dump a brother in hospital and think that's the end of it. He can't stay there forever, you know!'

The energy that had built up during her sleep drained out of Lisa. She sat down heavily. 'But he'll never be better, will he?'

'At this point it's extremely difficult to say.'

It seemed he had come there simply to accuse them, and Lisa couldn't bear it. 'Do you think he'd want us staring at him?' Her voice was unnaturally shrill. 'They put him in a straitjacket. He isn't an animal for us to go and peer at, drugged to the eyeballs to keep him from savaging people. I shall visit when he knows me. When he has some dignity.'

'He may be ill, but he still needs to feel loved,' declared the doctor.

Lisa swung round on him. 'You pompous little man! He thinks I'm in league with his enemies, he hates me! And you produce your platitudes and your off-the-shelf solutions. You only came here to make us miserable.'

The doctor had the grace to look discomfited. 'Actually I brought some forms for you to sign.'

Angus sighed. 'I see. Well, for God's sake have a drink while we get on with it. A job like this needs a strong stomach.'

They were committal forms, Marcus was to be incarcerated until the hospital deemed fit.

Professor Chandler arrived as the last form was being signed, giving permission for Electro-Convulsive Therapy if required. He wandered about the kitchen, poking into corners and opening doors in the range, irritating Lisa. At last, with the forms finished, they all had a drink. The doctor was thawing, and Lisa remembered that her mother had never considered it proper to socialise with the medical profession. They had offended him, and were now having to make amends.

'Why don't you pop in and see me on Friday, Lady Eloise?' he

116

advised. 'We can discuss things, see how you're feeling. I can explain a little more about your brother's condition.'

'Yes. Thank you.' She realised that he wanted to be on good terms with her, to be a trusted friend of the family. People at school latched on to her for the same dubious reasons, because she was titled and lived at The Court, because they were descended from one of William the Conqueror's nobles and on her mother's side could go back to Agincourt. The people who liked you for yourself were few and far between.

When he had gone, she made the sauce for the duckling and tossed the salad. The Professor got in her way, discovering ancient fish kettles in cupboards and a cast iron ladle that thrilled him. 'Fantastic. Absolutely wonderful. Ladles seldom last, you know, and this is very old.'

'Actually it has a hole in it,' remarked Lisa.

'So it has! But what an interesting artefact. This kitchen alone is a treasure trove.'

Angus got out the newspaper and started to read it. Lisa was reminded, horribly, of the old man, their grandfather, who considered himself so far above other mortals that manners counted for nothing. He had been known to abandon boring dinner guests and go to his room to listen to his gramophone, at intervals yelling to Curtiss, 'Have those bloody curs gone?' So she demanded that Angus help her place the dishes on the table. He obliged somewhat grimly. They were both having to learn to do things that had previously never been in the least necessary. Like washing clothes, and cleaning silver, and wiping the dog's paw marks off the kitchen floor when before it had all happened, magically. She should have been more grateful, she thought fiercely. They had taken so much for granted.

The food was very good. Lisa had discovered an aptitude for cooking, and kept at the back of her mind a plan to cook dinner parties for people if things really did become desperate. It was what girls of her class did, of course, an amusement before marriage. She would be a backroom girl, doing the work whilst others had the fun. It did not appeal.

Over coffee she said to the Professor, 'I'll show you the house, if you like. We'll have to put our coats on, it's very cold.'

He got up at once, leaving Angus to the paper, and they started along the passages, switching on lights and using a torch where the bulbs had gone. In just a few short months the air had became dank and lifeless. The house might have been empty forever.

'Has much been sold?' asked the Professor, tramping a long, bare corridor.

'Some, yes,' replied Lisa. 'Not by us, yet. We'd have to clear whole rooms to get anything worthwhile. All the good pictures have gone, I'm afraid. And the Hellyns built, they didn't go in for collecting quite as much. They furnished the rooms but they didn't buy the best. So we haven't the best to sell.'

The Professor tweaked a pair of ancient, dusty curtains, faded in streaks by the sun. 'It still has the feel of a home though – don't you think?'

She didn't, actually. Without the family, the servants, the constant bustle of activity, it seemed dead. Her spaniel sighed and flopped down, but almost at once they began walking again. The dog grumbled but got up, following them with a patient pad, pad of his feet.

'Perhaps you might like to see the tapestries?' said Lisa. 'But the rooms are quite shut up.'

'Oh ... well, perhaps we should,' said the Professor, who was inclined to spend the evening peering up at an ornate, if cracking, plaster ceiling. 'We must be thorough, must we not?'

She led the way to the great hall, and they stood with their necks straining, gazing up at the banners that hung from the roof.

'One imagines they would fall apart if one so much as attempted to remove them,' sighed the Professor. 'I know so little about textiles. Of great interest to a medievalist, no doubt,' he added, thinking that he might have appeared unimpressed.

'We do have others,' ventured Lisa. 'Some of them are quite large.'

He followed her along the maze of passages and stairways to the long gallery on the opposite side of the courtyard. The room was in darkness, and when she switched on the light only one staghorn chandelier lit up. So she walked round the walls, shining her torch up and along, explaining: 'They've been here centuries. The rooms were designed with them in mind, they're French mainly. One or two English, I believe. Some of them suffer from moth. And one or two got wet when the roof leaked. We took those down and rolled them up somewhere.'

Professor Chandler stood in silence. He stared up at Lisa's flickering torchbeam, seeing faces, figures, the wild eyes of a running deer, the red of a cloak, a dress. An old woman leered at him with consummate lewdness, a man knelt sobbing at the foot of a cross.

'This is my favourite,' said Lisa, softly. Her torch stopped on the figure of a little girl. She was laughing, her small fat hands over-flowing with flowers. They cascaded down her skirt and on to the grass. 'I wanted to be her once. She looks so happy.'

They stood looking up. The shutters enclosed the room entirely; it

118

was ghostly, a million miles from the world. But the little girl triumphed over the darkness, she lit it up with her flowers and her smile. The Professor said, 'But why are they shut away? You keep them like a secret.'

Lisa nodded. 'Marcus hated them, you see. All his life. He said the people were alive, and evil, he said they would come out in the night and hurt him. It was the first sign. My father thought – well, it's understandable. He thought if he shut them away then Marcus would have nothing to fear. But of course he found other things, everywhere. It isn't what Marcus sees, it's what he is.'

'Do people know they're here? Experts I mean?'

She turned off her torch and made her way to the door by the feeble overhead light. 'I believe they're mentioned in one or two books. No-one ever asks to see them though.'

Walking back through the house, the Professor seemed pre-occupied. 'They're the reason for the courtyard, of course,' he said finally. 'It was built with the hangings in mind. It would be out of the question to move them.'

She agreed. 'You do realise it's the great hall roof that's most important, don't you?' she insisted, because he seemed to be forgetting why he was there. 'Father had it surveyed. Two of the hammer beam supports are completely rotten, and the main roof truss is suspect.'

'Yes.'

He looked at her thin face, which hardly ever seemed to smile. The burdens of care seemed to be falling rather too solidly on her frail shoulders. 'The grant will of course be forthcoming,' he said gently. 'But in return we do expect the house to be open. Not all the time, but perhaps one afternoon a week during the summer. And on request, to academics. When convenient, naturally.'

She took a deep breath. 'And that would be all? We wouldn't have to hire guides and build a coach park and rows and rows of loos?'

He laughed, and pushed his forelock back out of his eyes, taking what seemed to her to be his first real interest in their plight. 'I think you can rest easy on that score. You're quite a long way off the beaten track. You might only get half a dozen people in an afternoon.'

Lisa sank her hands into her coat pockets. She was cold, and the dog was grumbling about this pointless evening jaunt. The house was so quiet when you were alone in it. Pushing aside the kitchen door, she walked into warmth and light. She stood blinking, watching Angus reading his paper, the dirty plates still on the table. 'We're going to open the house,' she said.

Chapter Fifteen

The morning smelled of autumn, with blue skies, fresh winds and the swallows gathering on telephone wires all over London. By midday summer had made one last push to gain ascendance and the owners of cafés were putting tables on the pavements and selling ice cream. Mara wandered about, strolling down Bond Street looking into shop windows. One or two names caught her eye, discreet salons where you had to be known to be admitted. But no-one ever denied her entrance. Gold lettering on white marble plaques. She chose one at random, rang the bell and went in.

She went upstairs to a long, hushed room, littered with spindly sofas and pier-glasses. A girl at a desk rose to meet her, and a middle-aged woman dressed in black lifted her eyebrows almost to her hair.

'Excuse me − ' said the girl, and then looked to her mentor for advice. 'Madam Neal?' she asked hopefully.

'Do you have an appointment?' asked Madam, with ice.

'Lady Mara Hellyn,' replied Mara. 'Perhaps you know my mother? The Countess of Melville.'

Deference was immediate and irritating. 'But of course,' oozed Madam Neal. 'And I do believe we've been fortunate enough to see your photograph in some of our more select magazines? Bettina, we must rearrange our schedule. We shall take tea.'

They drank thin Earl Grey out of thinner porcelain, whilst a mannequin paraded dresses. Designed with English society women in mind, they veered between dullness and elaborate overkill. There were debs' dresses, covered in flounces, and dowager eveningwear that hadn't changed in thirty years. Mara sighed. 'Something less formal,' she said. 'Something more relaxed.'

Madam Neal glanced at her. She had been clothing every shape, size and style of woman for over forty years, for functions as diverse as parties on Italian yachts and Royal balls. 'An intimate occasion?' queried Madam.

'Indeed.'

A pair of double doors were thrown back, and racks of clothes wheeled into the showroom. There were long coatdresses with sparkling buttons, an emerald green cheong sam — 'Quite a few ladies like the Oriental touch,' said Madam Neal — and a host of trousers. Almost everything was silk, cool and shiny. Madam held out a pair of heavy, cream silk pyjamas. 'If you have your pearls in London, nothing could be more exquisite, Lady Mara.'

The girl tapped her long fingers against her lips. She didn't care how much the pyjamas cost, they were entirely what she wanted. When she realised that they were priced at over a thousand pounds she felt a certain thrilled delight, like a gambler putting all on one roll of the dice.

Mara began to get ready at around four o'clock. She lay in the bath and let her mind drift, imagining this or that conversation. Time seemed to drag. At one point she thought her watch had stopped and got out to telephone the speaking clock. But at last it was six and she could dress.

Clare came in as she was fastening long pearl drops into her ears. They were her last birthday present from her father.

'Good heavens, you do look luxurious. Where are you going?'

'Dinner,' said Mara casually. 'Jimmy Carruthers.'

'Again? This is getting interesting.'

Mara half smiled, refusing to be drawn. The buzz in town was that she and Jimmy would tie the knot, but until she had attended the ritual Friday to Tuesday at his home in Norfolk no-one expected to hear anything. Provided Clare did not meet Jimmy tonight, she was perfectly safe. She glanced at her aunt's beaded cocktail dress. 'Where are you going?'

'Actually —' Clare almost blushed ' — I'm dining at home. Samuel's coming.'

'I see. Please don't worry if I'm late in, will you, Clare?'

'No, no. I won't at all.'

When she had gone Mara made a face at herself in the dressing table glass. It made her uncomfortable to have Samuel so close at hand, perhaps taking his leave just as she came in. It brought her to his notice, when she knew that if he could he would stop this thing before it started. She sprayed scent on her wrists and throat, moving from side to side to see if her breasts hung down too far under the camisole without a bra. They did not. As a last act, she powdered the back of her hand, where the burn mark still showed faint pink. It was

121

an automatic gesture, symbolising her mental rejection of that night. She would rub it out, powder it away.

Jennings called her a taxi. Nowadays she never left the house without ensuring that he was at the door. She hated crossing the square. The space from front door to busy street felt like enemy territory. In the butler's hearing she gave the driver the name of a restaurant, and then appeared to change her mind and ask for Chelsea when they reached Hyde Park. Neither did she give the exact address, but made the driver drop her just off King's Road. She walked the rest of the way, hearing her high heels clack on the pavements, attracting stares and wolf whistles. Number ten, he had said. She tried to see some magic in the number, some portent. The whole mews was smart, full of brass and flower tubs, expensive cars parked here and there. Outside Number ten was a large grey Ford. It could have been anyone's. Her heels slipped on the cobbles.

He opened the door before she had time to knock. Taller than she remembered, with that long, lean jaw.

'Lady Mara.'

'Hello.'

She went in and they stood in the tiny hall, embarrassed and unsure of what to say. 'You look absolutely marvellous,' said the prince at last.

'Thank you.'

He rubbed his hands together. 'Why don't you come into this room here? This house is awfully pretty but there isn't the space to swing a cat. It belongs to my — to a friend of mine. He's quite appalled at me, I'm afraid.'

She went before him into a tiny sitting-room, with space enough only for a narrow, chintz-covered sofa and an armchair. Although not particularly cold the fire was lit, and a table-lamp was casting a soft glow. The prince went to draw the curtains but couldn't find the cord. Mara did it for him, and their arms brushed against one another.

'I'm sorry,' he said 'I'm not very good at fending for myself, I'm afraid.'

'Neither am I, actually. Since my father died I'm having to get used to it, though. We're broke you see.'

'What, absolutely? I mean, are you selling up?'

She shrugged and went to sit down on the sofa. 'We couldn't even if we wanted to. And, of course, we don't. Nobody wants The Court, it's too precious to be turned into anything and too big to run. I came away the day after we dismissed everyone — the butler, the chauffeur, the lot.'

An opened bottle of champagne was discreetly positioned in an ice bucket. Mara wondered whether he had opened it himself. He said, 'Is that why you live with that peculiar woman?'

'Clare? Yes. I don't think her particularly odd.'

'Good God, but she is. As carefully presented as any prize Jersey cow, rather bony in parts but with tremendous eyelashes.'

Mara laughed. 'Samuel's very enthralled. They're sleeping together you know.'

'Are they?' He paused in the act of passing her a glass of champagne. 'That is reassuring. One sometimes feels that one is quite alone with the necessity for sin.'

'Do you count it as sin then? This?' She looked straight into his face. Her golden hair tumbled around her shoulders, her eyes were sapphire blue. He turned away suddenly.

'Mara – don't misunderstand me, but I doubt if this is right. Obviously I'm married. My wife's a Roman Catholic, we have two children. And of course she is heir to Havenheim – a very toy soldier place, one must admit, but nonetheless one of the few remaining monarchies. Whilst you are – young, and free and desirable. There must be a dozen men who would marry you tomorrow.'

'Quite a few, yes,' she agreed.

He came and took her hand, looking down into her face. 'Perhaps that's what you should do. I ought not to spoil that for you.'

Mara tried to laugh. 'Don't worry,' she said breathlessly. 'I shan't be difficult, I promise. For both of us this is – a diversion. We shan't allow it to affect our real lives. In a while I shall marry someone, and with a bit of luck he'll let me shoot. I'm quite a good shot, you know.'

'I'm sure you are.' He took a long breath, still looking at her. A pulse in her throat beat rapidly. 'Shall I put on some Mozart?' he asked.

'Yes, please.'

She drank her champagne while he struggled with the unfamiliar machine. The gentle notes of piano concerto number one drifted into the little room. Mara curled herself into the sofa, feeling that they were alone in a little, padded box, with just the fire and the music. He came and sat at her head, and let his fingers rest on her temples. She leaned against him, feeling the warmth of his chest through his shirt, hot on her cheek. His thumb trailed across her lips. Her mouth opened slightly in a long, slow sigh.

'You're not a virgin,' he said softly.

'You wouldn't want that,' she said, and he laughed and agreed. 'No. I wouldn't.'

His hand slid into the camisole of her pyjamas, lifting her breast.

123

He heard the sharp intake of breath as he brushed her nipple, she hung her head down and let her hair cover her face. He caressed her until she began to groan, then he bent his head, pushed her hair aside and pressed his mouth to her neck. Violent, sustained kisses, sucking at her flesh. As he pulled suddenly away, dragging at his clothes, she opened her eyes and stared out through a mist of hair.

He stood in front of her and she looked at him. Then she sat up, reaching for him. She rubbed him against her cheek, as if he was something beautiful, something she almost worshipped. He kissed her head, her hair, he knelt before her on the floor and undressed her like a child. When at last he pushed her back on the sofa and entered her, they looked at each other and smiled.

When it was finished they lay together, their skins sticky and hot, so tangled it was hard to tell that they were two people and not one, wildly endowed with heads and arms and legs. The prince's face was slack with pleasure, his eyes blue slits beneath weary lids. This is love, thought Mara. This is what everything is about. She felt a bursting contentment.

He drove her home around one in the morning, each of them wondering if the other felt as they did. Mara felt drunk, on almost no alcohol, and she unfastened her seatbelt to lean her forehead against his arm.

'This is madness,' said Jay.

'Yes.'

He drew up outside Clare's house, well out of the light.

'I will see you again?' whispered Mara.

'Of course. Soon.'

She turned towards him, reaching out her arms. They began to kiss, wildly passionate, although at any moment the door of one of the houses could open to disgorge guests on to the street, there would be lights and noise, recognition. But the danger excited him, he revelled in a delicious spice made up of risk and wild desire.

Suddenly the door of Clare's house opened. They froze. He hid his face against Mara's shoulder.'

'It's Samuel,' she gasped. 'He might know the car. You've got to go.'

She opened the door and flung herself out, but he caught her hand for a brief second. 'When shall I telephone? Tomorrow?'

'At ten. I'll wait for you.'

She slammed the door and ran the few yards along the pavement. Samuel was on the point of leaving, Jennings was still holding the door. 'Good evening, Samuel,' said Mara wildly. 'One so often sees you going the other way.'

He looked at her oddly. She pushed her hair out of her eyes, wondering if her neck was marked, if in some way he could sense the past hours. Her whole body vibrated with well-being, for a second she didn't care what he thought. But he was looking at the car driving quickly out of the square. 'I've been out with Jimmy,' she said unnecessarily. 'Jimmy Carruthers.'

She pushed past Jennings and ran up the stairs to bed.

Chapter Sixteen

Prince John of Denham, thirty-one years old, father of two, sat at breakfast in his London flat. On his nineteenth birthday he had been voted the world's most eligible man. On that day he had been declared rich, well-bred, intelligent and charming. He liked motor racing and leggy blondes, although thankfully he was just as interested in the art world. There had been talk then that he might drive in Formula 2, but nothing had come of it. The feeling was that it wasn't quite suitable.

What a long way he had come since then. So many unsuitable things had fallen by the wayside, first the cars, then the model girl-friends, then the wild parties mixing dukes and scrapdealers, painters and popstars. He realised now, though he hadn't then, that there had been subtle and relentless pressure. To make him what he was now, the solid, respectable, photogenic husband of Princess Anna of Havenheim.

He looked over his newspaper at her. She smiled anxiously back. 'Is something the matter, Jay? You look rather cross.'

'It's just the news. The bloody Irish, as usual.'

Anna nodded and sighed. She had much sympathy for everyone in the Irish question, and could see all points of view. But then, Havenheim had been rent by all manner of conflicts over the centuries, both their own and other people's. A mixed race country, the people were united only by their loyalty to their crown. To her mind the lack of an Irish link with the British crown was more than half the problem, whereas in Havenheim everyone could claim that she was theirs, as her father was, as her children would be after them. Although of course it would be so much better if she had a son. Havenheim tolerated women on the throne, but no more than that. Anna sighed. She had been pregnant twice since the girls, and each time miscarried. Now she was unable to conceive at all.

'I'm going to see the gynaecologist today,' she remarked.

Jay grunted and did not lower his paper.

'He's going to start me on the pills I told you about.'

Now the paper did come down. 'You do know I'm going to Scotland on Friday? I'm stalking.'

'Are you? I think I'd forgotten. Oh, well, perhaps we can start the pills another day.'

Jay went back behind his newspaper. He felt vicious, and ashamed for feeling that, but he was damned if he would be put off. Clearly she wanted him to postpone. But in September the Scottish heather was a carpet of purple, and the deer were restless, filled with the excitement of the coming rut. He had a lodge up there, tucked under a mountain of rock, with flagged floors and huge fires and peaty whisky. It was accessible only by tractor or Land Rover, and then not in snow or heavy rain when the track was like a river. A woman came in to cook and her husband saw to the house.

They used to go there together. In fact, when they first married Anna had adored the place, or at least said that she did. Nowadays she said she was bored and it always rained, so he went on his own, with just his valet, and even the detective had to stay in the town. And this time he would take Mara.

He tried to avoid thinking of her when he was with his wife. It seemed the ultimate disloyalty. But again and again he found himself storing up interesting stories to tell her, jokes that she might like. If he was involved in an art exhibition he made sure she was invited to the preview, and he gave her a marked catalogue so she should not miss the paintings he considered important. She had a good eye, had Mara, far better than his wife's. She rejected the overblown and the pretentious at a glance. In fact they agreed on many things.

'If I might have the preserve?' asked Anna.

Irritation flashed. After all these years she still had not learned to call it marmalade. He passed it across, surreptitiously watching her neat table manners. Mara ate messily, as if she was bored, and would be still less interested if she had to worry about crumbs or a tidy plate. He had kissed her, last night, as she was eating cream. A delicious cocktail of wine, and cream, and Mara. And she laughed at him and made him wait till she had finished, scraping her bowl absolutely and untypically clean.

'Did you enjoy yourself last night?'

He picked up his coffee, and found it was half cold. 'Not really, no. A very dull meeting.'

'What was it about? I thought the festival had been cancelled.'

His stomach contracted. God, of course it had. Why had he forgotten that? 'Did I say it was about the festival? I must be getting old.

127

It was Glasgow artists or something. I haven't seen any of their work, I can't judge. We're staging a show.'

'When will it be? I must put it in my diary.'

'Er – I'll get my secretary to give you a note.'

He threw his newspaper down and got up. 'I'm sorry darling, but I have to dash. Busy day.'

'Of course. Do go in and see the girls, won't you?'

'Don't worry, I will.' He caught her hand and raised it to his lips. Her eyes watched him, nervously. She suspected of course. But he did what he could to make her happy, trailing back and forth to Havenheim at least four times a year, standing useless for hours while she reviewed the goose-stepping little army. She was always so careful of him, so anxious that he should not be offended. And that in itself offended him.

His daughters were preparing to go out, Marie-Christine to a dancing class and Isobel to school. They jumped on him, squealing, while the Havenheim nanny clucked. 'Princess Isobel! You will crease your skirt. Don't tread on your father's shoes, Marie-Christine.'

'Don't fuss, Nanny,' said Jay. He perched on the edge of the table, his girls against his knees, and he tweaked their hair ribbons and teased them. 'They're not teaching you to read at this school of yours, are they? Don't they know princesses don't read?'

'Yes, they do, Daddy, yes they do!' they shrieked.

'I don't read yet,' said Marie-Christine, very solemn at almost four.

'But I read very well,' said Isobel complacently. 'When I read, everyone notices.'

Jay snorted. At what age was it that you realised you were surrounded by sycophants? As long as they conformed, these children need never strive for perfection, they could muddle along, being applauded for whatever mediocre standard they achieved, in a warm bath of falsehood. If nothing else, he wished he could spare them that.

He got up, pushing them away with the abrupt change of mood that so confused them. 'Goodbye, Daddy,' they quavered, but he was gone without a word.

Mara went up to Scotland by herself on the train. Clare was very anxious that she should be leaving the promising situation with Jimmy Carruthers, apparently in mid-stream, to go jauntering off stalking with some friends of her father's. But they were people Clare knew well, and there was no rushing marriages. Far too many matches, contracted in the excitement of a season, fell apart under dull routine. She confined herself to advice on deer stalking. 'My dear, don't whatever you do cough! No-one will speak to you for days. And be sure to drink lots of whisky, otherwise you catch a raging cold. Take a hot water bottle, they never have enough.'

'I'm looking forward to it,' said Mara ingenuously. 'I do hope someone remembers to meet me off the train, though.'

'Oh, they'll do that. But it could well be in a shooting cart, pulled by some ancient and smelly pony, with an even more ancient and smelly driver. Don't expect to keep your fingernails for a moment.'

Right up to the last minute, Mara was rushing around London shopping. Amidst the nighties and silk underwear were presents: books, a waistcoat and even a miniature teddy bear, long enough and thin enough to be a caricature of Jay. She wanted him to know how special he was. But on the day before she left Jimmy telephoned.

'Mara? I thought I mightn't catch you. Are you going to Scotland?'

'Yes. I'm off tomorrow, Jim, and terribly busy.'

'Who are you staying with? I thought I might try and wangle an invitation.'

'What?' She almost shrieked into the 'phone, then covered it up with a tense laugh. 'What a lovely idea. But I don't think there'll be room.'

'But who are you staying with? Is it the Fergusons?'

It was the name she had given Clare. Everyone knew they had a huge house and never minded people filling up the turrets. The ghillies were always run off their feet looking after broken ankles and heart attacks, they rarely had time for the sport.

'It isn't anybody you know,' said Mara firmly.

There was a silence. Then Jimmy said, 'You shouldn't, Mara. You're getting in too deep.'

'Too deep for what? Into what?' He couldn't know, she told herself. No-one could.

'It's all right if you're not too involved, of course. With him.'

She took a deep breath. 'Jimmy — does everyone know?'

'There are rumours, but not that it's you. I just guessed, that's all.'

'Clever old you,' said Mara thinly. 'But I'm going, Jimmy. Nothing on earth could stop me.'

He gave a heavy sigh. 'Well, if you must I suppose. You can trust me not to spread it about, you know. After all, you'll need someone to take you out afterwards.'

She laughed. 'You are sweet, Jim. But don't hold your breath.'

The train left London at mid-afternoon the next day. A sleeper had been booked and she had never travelled in one before. She opened all the cupboards and played with the taps. It seemed all of a piece, the strangeness, the secrecy, travelling to her lover in brand new clothes.

She was wearing a blue tweed skirt and matching beret, with a long wool coat over her crisp shirt. Jay's first sight of her would be in these clothes and she had longed to look exotic and different. But she dared not stand out and draw attention to herself, so she was simply pretty and stylish. By lunchtime tomorrow she would be with him. The very next day they would wake up in the same bed. Ripples of excitement ran through her belly, she almost felt sick. From now until a distant time, days away, weeks away, she would be happy.

The train rattled through the night. She was hungry, because at dinner she had been too excited to eat. Half-waking dreams beset her, the faces of men – Jimmy, Edward, Selmer – never Jay. Why not Jay? At three she got up and drank some water. It was hot, airless, she was deafened by the endless clacking across the rails. What if he isn't there? she thought. What if he doesn't come? The pain was like a blow, she pressed her fists between her breasts to crush it. Tears of anticipated horror ran down her cheeks. Everything ended, everything turned into dust. The end would come, and she knew it. Please God, not yet, she whispered.

After a while the noise of the train became soothing, soporific. She sank back against the pillow. His face came easily now, with that long, hanging jaw. She loved it more than her own. Only a few more hours, she told herself.

The guard and the porter helped her off with her bags, and she stood on the platform while the train slid away behind her. He wasn't here. He hadn't even sent someone. It was her nightmare so she assumed it must be true. Speaking tightly to control the tears she asked the porter to bring her bags to the gate, she must get a taxi. He chatted as they walked, about the weather, the late sunshine. A Land Rover stood at the kerb, dried mud caking the sides and half the canvas back. A labrador peered out at her. She glanced and then glanced again.

'Er – I'll go in this,' she said jerkily. 'Put the bags in the back, please.'

'In here, Miss?' He looked dubious. There were boots and ropes and the dog.

'Yes.'

She fumbled in her purse to give him money, she hadn't enough change and gave him a note. Then she ran round to the front and scrambled up into the passenger seat. The porter saw the man at the wheel lean across to kiss her, and he wasn't surprised because she was lovely. But then, as they drove away, he thought – but of

130

course, he must be wrong. For a minute there it looked like –
him.

It was cold on the hill, and at this time of year the sun barely rose high
enough to touch every hollow. Patches of ice crackled in the bracken,
and some of the highest tops of all were touched with snow. They
walked half the day and saw nothing. The ghillie was upset, first by
Mara and then by the paucity of deer. He mumbled about a heather
burning, it had stripped an entire hillside. Perhaps they were feeding
on new growth . . . they would see tomorrow.

He was a small man, who walked the steep slopes with a measured
stride, never faster or slower. At lunch he ate apart from them, his
back deliberately turned. Mara made a face. 'He doesn't approve.'

Jay shrugged. He didn't care. He felt the blood of other days in his
veins, other times. When had princes stopped doing what they liked?
Once there had been a balance, duty and pleasure keeping each other
in check, but it had all gone wrong. They gave in too easily, accepted
the strictures of others with barely a fight. Well, he was fighting. But
he wished the ghillie wouldn't look at him like that.

On a steep bank Jay and the ghillie forged ahead, and then waited
for Mara to catch up. She looked lovely, struggling up to them, her
hair blowing like golden threads against her dark green jacket. 'The
deer don't like that head, maybe,' said the ghillie blankly.

Jay glanced at him. 'She's a lady, Andrew,' he said. 'She's used to
our ways.'

'Aye, sir. And so she is. Would the Princess be a mite too foreign
then? You'll be thinking of a change.'

'What the hell do you mean by that?'

The ghillie said nothing, merely turning away to scan the country
with his binoculars. Jay said furiously, 'You know very well I should
never do anything to hurt the Princess Anna. I have the greatest
respect for her. As should you!'

Mara, staggering up to join them, heard what was said but for a
moment barely understood it. Then her face went white. She looked
at the two men, and neither of them met her eye.

'We'll be getting on then,' said the ghillie and began to climb once
more. Jay followed and Mara, still out of breath, scrabbled after.

They got back to the lodge at around four in the afternoon. Mara
went straight to change, and minutes later Jay followed. He burst into
her room, scarcely bothering to knock.

'Mara! Why are you hurt? Andrew was upset, he wanted me to set
his mind at rest.'

'He wanted you to deny me. And you did.'

131

He stared at her. She slipped off her shirt, and the crispness of her movements told him not to touch her. The bra she was wearing had thick elastic straps, to hold her great breasts in check. He was suddenly impressed by the confidence that allowed her to let him see even her most unlovely clothes. Mara knew she was beautiful, and nothing could make her ugly.

He came across and unfastened the hooks, trying to slip his hands around her. She pulled away. 'Stop it. If you have such respect for your Princess Anna, you can have some for me.'

'Mara! This is ridiculous.'

She knew it and she didn't care. He didn't know how she loved him, he didn't care that she wanted to hear lies. Darling, darling, you're so much more to me than her, I'd leave her tomorrow if it wasn't for this or that or the other.

He put his hand on her hair, and she tried to shake him off, but he kept his hand there and turned her round to catch her shoulder.

'Mara, Mara, don't you know how much I love you?'

She ducked her head, trying to hide her tears. 'You don't love me at all. You should have told him you loved me.'

'You know that I couldn't.'

He waited. After long seconds Mara nodded. He kissed her then, letting his tongue tangle in hers, feeling her stretch herself against him. The kiss went on and on, until he picked her up and carried her to the bed.

Downstairs in the kitchen, Mrs Kinnair, the cook, cocked an ear to the rhythmic thumping above. She and her husband exchanged glances, and then, when the moaning started, she went red and clattered saucepans.

'The filthy hussy!' she whispered, and her husband nodded. What had he done with Princess Anna and the wee bairns? To behave like this might be all right in London, but to come here, and expect them to condone it, that was something else again! They would never feel the same about him.

After dinner that night, curled up on a sofa, lulled by the fire and the whisky and love, Mara said, 'Does anyone know about us, do you think?'

Jay let his fingers drift through her hair. 'I don't think so. Why?'

'You know I told you about Jimmy Carruthers? He's sweet actually. I think he knows that there's someone. That it's you.'

He sat up. 'Christ! Have you been talking, Mara?'

'Of course not! But I know he watches what I do. And lots of people must know you're having an affair − the man you borrowed the house from for one.'

132

'They're all my staff. They're totally discreet.'

She laughed at him, still nettled by the afternoon. 'You are naive. They mightn't say in so many words but they're bound to hint. "The old boy's got himself a bit of stuff at last." They've probably been expecting it.'

He turned round to stare full into her face. 'What on earth do you mean?'

'Oh, really, Jay!' Mara knew she should be quiet, but just could not. 'I saw her on television the other day, opening something. She's plain and dull and ordinary.'

He took a shuddering breath. 'In contrast to you, I suppose? I won't have you talk about Anna like that.'

'But you don't mind what your ghillie says about me! Or the looks from Mrs Kinnair, and her husband glowering as if I was committing a crime! They can say what they like to me, but not to your precious wife!'

'No-one's said anything to you.'

'It's in every word. Hatred dressed up. My God, it takes two to tango, I don't exactly tie you to the bed and impale myself!'

He got up to pour himself another whisky. A muscle in his jaw was twitching. 'I made it plain at the start what this would mean, Mara. We can't − it isn't possible. I could never divorce.'

'Yes you could.' She turned her face away as she said it. The unmentionable thing.

'My God. You know I can't,' he said at last.

'Would you? If you could?'

He thought of Mara, ruling his life, his home. Capricious, passionate Mara. She was as instantly noticeable as Anna was insignificant. If he had seen her first − but he had not. And he should test her. See what she wanted from him.

'No. No, I wouldn't.'

She sat stunned, staring at him. 'You said you loved me. You don't mean that.'

'I mean I would never marry you.'

In an instant she was up and at the table, snatching up the fruit knife. Her first slash brought blood welling up out of her wrist, and he was almost too late to prevent a second. He gripped her hand. She fought him with eyes blazing, her teeth clenched on the effort. 'Let go,' he hissed. 'Mara, let it go.' She clung on till she could hold no more. The knife fell.

'Let me see that! You fool, you reckless child! Can't you see how much I love you?'

'You don't, you know you don't. You said you wouldn't marry me!'

He wrapped a napkin tightly round the wound and rang the bell. Mrs Kinnair hurried in.

'There's been an accident,' said the prince tightly. 'Look at this please, Mrs Kinnair.'

The woman looked at Mara, shaking and white as a ghost. When she unfolded the napkin, blood spurted. 'I'll get the doctor,' she said.

'Yes, please. Right away.' said Jay.

'Can't we just bandage it or something?' begged Mara. 'I don't want a fuss.'

In front of the woman, Jay put his arms around her. 'It was my fault. You need stitches, it's very deep. God, but I never thought – '

'I'll go and telephone, sir' said Mrs Kinnair, and hurried out.

Mara said, 'So now you know. I would have done it, Jay, if you hadn't stopped me.'

'But – why? Why, Mara?'

'Because I love you. I don't really care if you stay with her. But you should want to be with me. I want to be loved back.'

Viciously, angrily, he knotted the napkin on her wrist. The blood seeped slowly through, staining it bright, arterial red. 'You don't know what it's like,' said Jay. 'The toadying, the endless praise. In the end you believe nothing about anyone. They all want something from you. I thought you loved me a little. But I still believed you were one of those.'

She laughed, such a soft, indulgent sound. He filled up her whole life, and he didn't know it. 'We ought to make a blood pact,' she said. 'Like the Indians.'

He was caught off guard. He gasped and almost chuckled. 'All right. I'll take my punishment.'

He picked up the fruit knife, opened his shirt and slashed his belly. He let out a grunt. For a second the cut remained bloodless, but then it began to fill. Mara took off her bandage, kneeling at his feet and pressing her wrist against him. He felt her blood, his blood, running into his groin.

'God! You're driving me mad,' he said wildly. 'I don't know myself. Oh, Mara, Mara. Don't ever give up on me.'

She was growing light-headed. She reeled back and he caught her. He bound up her wrist again, and held her close until the doctor came.

134

Chapter Seventeen

It was a wet afternoon. Clare was sitting at her desk in her drawing-room, writing letters to her friends. A small fire burned in the grate, and she knew that in a few minutes Jennings would bring tea. The house was quiet without Mara, but on the whole she thought she preferred it. The girl was very intense, she decided, up one minute and down the next, for no apparent reason. Just like her brother, she thought grimly. It was to be hoped the Carruthers family had no such tendency.

The door bell rang. She ignored it, assuming that it was the Jehovah's Witnesses again, but then Jennings came in and hard on his heels, Samuel.

'Clare! I'm so sorry to intrude, my dear. I've something rather important to discuss.'

She was flustered. It was many years since men rushed in on her unannounced, and she had never liked it. One was given no opportunity to replenish lipstick, or adjust a sweater, and the first moments were taken up with twitching and smoothing. She felt sure her hair was coming down.

'Jennings — tea, I think?' She cast a sideways look into the glass by the door. Yes, her lipstick was gone. Damn. She nibbled a little, to try and make her lips pink.

'I'm afraid this is no time for tea. Thank you, Jennings.' Samuel waited rather pointedly for the door to close, and then for Clare to settle herself prettily on the sofa. 'I won't sit down, if you don't mind. I confess I'm somewhat agitated. Clare, do you know where Mara is?'

Clare lifted her shoulders. 'Scotland. With the Fergusons, I believe. Why?'

'Do you — is it possible do you think — that she's gone somewhere else?'

'Where else? If it's the Carruthers boy I'm delighted, he's quite smitten with her. And she can be rather rackety, I've found. She ought to settle down.'

Samuel sighed heavily. 'Could she be with the prince?'

'Oh my God, Samuel! You don't think − oh my God!'

'He's taken a week to go up to his lodge. Leaving the princess at home, needless to say. Nothing odd in that, of course − but I have a place up there myself, and when I telephoned today I heard the most worrying rumours. A girl picked up at the station apparently, a girl seen out stalking − and an accident. The doctor was called out to the lodge at ten o'clock last night.'

'What makes you think it's Mara?'

'The prince knows her. Obviously he admires her. And I saw his car here one evening. Mara saw me, shot into the house like a rabbit and the car screamed off. I could have sworn it was the Ford he sometimes uses − but she said it was Carruthers. And if he can afford a car like that in London, his father's giving him a damn sight too much money.'

Clare dropped her forehead against her hand. She had almost no feeling of surprise. First the wildness, then the gloom, and these last weeks, the euphoria of love. Yes, the girl was in love.

'Why are you so frantic?' she asked. 'You're not required to guard the prince's morals.'

'Good God, Clare, don't you understand? Suppose this gets out? It's within a whisker now. The princess would be devastated. And you know what these tinpot states are like, they might not stand for it in Havenheim. He might even be assassinated, I'd put it as strongly as that. I hate to be cold-blooded, but that might be the best outcome. There's a strong communist element in Havenheim, but they remain romantically attached to the crown. You can imagine how the Americans would take it if the monarchy was deposed and a communist state set up right next to Germany! Once you take the lid off something like this, it doesn't stop boiling.'

The door opened and Jennings brought in the tea. Samuel, who sometimes forgot he was no longer in the army, opened his mouth to order it away. Then he noticed crumpets, and cucumber sandwiches, and two sorts of cake. Clare's house was always enormously comfortable. He settled down in an armchair and prepared to do the food justice.

He felt better after he had eaten. Clare was silent, she wasn't nearly so fluffy as she liked to pretend. At last she said, 'Do we know what the accident was?'

'A cut, I think.'

'Not an abortion, or anything like that?'

136

'She'd be in a Swiss clinic, not stuck on a Scottish mountain. Look, I want you to telephone and ask to speak to her. Tell her she has to come home.'

'Suppose she won't?'

He spread his hands, helplessly. 'God knows. They take their chances, I imagine. She either obeys or we contact her family. I'll speak to the prince when he comes back to London. A bit on the side is one thing. One doesn't expect a man to lose his head.'

Clare flashed him a dagger look. 'You, of course, would never be in any such danger. I take it I am your bit on the side.'

He was appalled. 'Clare – my dear – you're no such thing. My dear, I do apologise.'

But the damage was done. Clare's sympathies, once wholly with Samuel, took a definite lean towards Mara.

A capercaillie was strutting about outside the window. The lodge had no real garden, just a stream shored up by stone walls, and a pond scooped out so long ago that it seemed entirely natural. For the rest there was grass, bracken and heather, with a hawthorn tree as crabbed and twisted as a witch.

The bird went on its way, pecking like a wound-up toy. Mara stayed by the window, watching, waiting for Jay. Her wrist throbbed and stung. Such a stupid thing to do, in cold blood. In the heat of the moment she knew now she might do anything. She knew how people could murder.

At last she saw him, coming down the hill. They were sending the pony up, so they had killed somewhere. She knew he might go back with them and prayed he would not, he had to come to her. When she saw him start towards the house she let out her breath, and ran down to meet him at the door. He took her by the shoulders and kissed her.

'Jay! There was a telephone call. From Clare.'

'Good God! How did she know you were here?'

'That's just it – Samuel told her. There's the most almighty row brewing. She wants me to come away at once. I said no.'

His face became set. She watched the happiness drain out of it, the lines become a little more pronounced. It was as if every part of him was known to her, she could read each separate thought in the turn of his head, the curve of his shoulder. She put her good hand on his neck. 'I'll go in the morning. I know I must.'

He kissed her fingers, leading her gently into the sitting-room. He poured them each a measure of whisky. 'It was great today,' he said. 'We picked them up about six miles away, trailed them for three. I took an old stag, quite massive. A clean kill.'

137

'That's good.'

They stood very close together. Mara felt warm suddenly, she felt safe. He wouldn't desert her.

'Does your wrist hurt?'

'Yes. It doesn't matter.' She put her hand on his belly, where he had slashed himself. The closer they became the less they needed to make love. The link was there in tenderness, a magic kingdom to which they had found the key.

'Will you go to The Court?'

She nodded. 'Until my wrist heals.'

'I'll come as often as I can. My God, I've danced to their tune for long enough, I don't come to heel as soon as they jerk the leash.'

She turned her head to press feather kisses on his mouth, to brush away the anger. 'I used to despair,' she whispered. 'I don't any more. And neither should you.'

He put her away from him and looked at her. She was pale still, the colour just visible beneath her skin. Her eyelashes were golden, he realised, a dark gold like toffee. The curve of her cheek made him catch his breath.

The next morning he drove her to the station. It was early, few people were about. They sat in the Land Rover, gazing straight ahead. Suddenly Jay said, 'I wish this was over, I wish you were gone. This hurts just so damned much!'

'Yes. Yes, I know.' She was exhausted, they had hardly slept at all. The night had passed in love and exaltation. Everything had been spent.

'I bought you a present,' he said wearily. 'For the end of the week. I meant it to finish then, you see.'

'That was silly,' said Mara. 'I knew that couldn't happen.'

'I see that now. You don't shovel love into a box and close the lid, it isn't possible. I thought it was. I feel rather a beginner at this.'

'Can I see my present?' – asked Mara.

He reached into his pocket and brought out a blue velvet jeweller's box. The hinge was too strong for Mara's weakened fingers, he had to open it for her. Glowing on velvet lay a pair of hoop diamond earrings, set in platinum. Mara grimaced. 'What a very mistressy sort of present.'

'I suppose it is really. Very Mrs Simpson.'

She turned to look at him. 'You know, I'd much rather have the money. We are just so ridiculously poor at the moment, it's the greatest nuisance.'

He laughed at her. 'Isn't that even more mistressy? A kept woman.'

'I thought you wanted to keep me.'

He put his hand up to her face. 'I do. Oh, I do.'

Later, in the train, she felt the warmth start to ebb from her heart. The chill was almost physical. She pulled her coat round her and rang to ask the steward for some tea. It was a terrible thing to depend on someone for all your happiness.

Chapter Eighteen

The Hunt Kennels stood about a mile from The Court, built by the Hellyns a scant hundred years before. But, as with everything they touched, it was extravagant, a crenellated fortress of a place with kitchens and larders and benches for a couple of hundred hounds. The current twenty rattled around noisily, their howls echoing in the empty space.

Angus stood for while, watching. He felt disorientated, because he'd been in London all week job-hunting and only this morning he'd been in Oxford settling the details of his departure. He wasn't adaptable enough, he thought, and grimaced. Oxford had proved all too adaptable, his tutor expressed polite regrets, his friends sending their good wishes, but already he was forgotten. He was no longer one of them.

Tom, the kennelman, was calling up his hounds. 'Here Bell, Bell, and Raider, Raider, get back!'

There had been a Raider in the pack for generations – was this last season's hound or a new entrant? Angus waited until the gate opened, and hounds poured in a flurry into the lane. Tom, seeing him, lifted his cap.

'Well, hello, sir. I heard you was back.'

'Yes. Not for good though, I'm afraid. Hounds look well.'

'So they should, sir, amount they eats. Ware Melody. Ware Bracken!'

He flicked his leather whip at an errant pair trying to sneak off into the fields.

Angus bided his time, thinking how difficult it was to slow to this pace the instant you came home. Ground must be covered, but slowly.

'How's your wife?' he asked. 'And your daughter, is she still at home?'

Tom answered, but Angus barely listened. That had been Marcus's forte. Not only did he listen, he remembered. When he was about ten, and home from school, one of the tenants had complained about slugs on his cabbages. In the next holidays, quite without prompting, Marcus had eyed the vegetable plot, remarking, 'Still got the slug problem, I see, Mr Baines.' It had become a family saying.

Angus realised Tom had fallen silent. 'You'll be starting cubbing,' he said.

'Aye, sir. Like I said, two weeks off.'

Damn! He really must try and pay better attention. 'What will you do without a Master? Would anyone like to take over temporarily, do you think? Until my brother's well again.'

'Bad business, sir. A very bad business.' Tom hawked and spat, a habit that Angus found nauseating. He looked up to the trees, where a pigeon clattered into flight, large and bulbous as a jumbo jet.

'There's a new man from town,' went on Tom at last. 'Dripping wi' brass. Hunted a fair bit. He's rough, like. Rides a bloody great bay, t'old earl knew him. Your father, like. Name's Maythorpe. Reg Maythorpe.'

That evening Angus said to Lisa, 'How do you fancy our new Master? A Mr Reg Maythorpe, of all the Godawful names. What have we come to when we have a Reg Maythorpe leading the field, I ask you!'

His sister observed him from the ironing board. 'You really are an appalling snob, Angus. He's a cracking rider. Impossible to live with.'

'Perhaps he'll break his neck and leave his millions to the hunt. I suppose he'll do now and then. I'll get back when I can, of course. Can't have the man ruling the roost.'

Lisa thumped the iron down on a shirt collar. 'I don't think Mr Maythorpe will appreciate being jocked off whenver you feel like it. Either he's Master for the season, or he isn't.'

'We don't want the bloody man there permanently! He'll never let go.'

Angus got up and went to the cupboard, pulling out a brandy bottle and two glasses. He poured a measure for himself and a smaller one for his sister. Quite suddenly he felt very depressed, as if someone had pulled down a shutter and excluded every glimmer of sunshine. Everything seemed to be piling up at once, in a gathering heap of disorder. He wondered if the job would make any difference. Henry's old stockbroker had offered him a place in the firm, an old boy arrangement, worryingly insubstantial. Angus suspected he was to be paid on commission. He took a large gulp of brandy, letting it burn his gullet.

'Everything's changing, isn't it?' he said tautly. 'You alter this and that and think everything else will stay the same. But it doesn't. The balance has gone. We may never get it back, you know.'

Lisa looked down at her hands, the forefingers stained with vegetable peelings and the nails broken. She nodded. 'Perhaps we never will.'

The next day they were in the orchard picking apples when Mara came. They saw the taxi approach and wondered who it might be. 'Perhaps it's Edward,' said Angus. 'We haven't heard from him in months.' They gathered up their baskets and made their way to the house.

But it was Mara in the kitchen, warming her hands at the range. Lisa at once noticed the bandage. 'What on earth have you done to your wrist?'

'Nothing. Aren't you surprised to see me?'

Lisa sniffed. 'Very. They've sent Marcus to hospital. He's gone bonkers.'

Mara went white. 'For God's sake, Lisa!' said Angus, and pulled up a chair for Mara to sit down. 'It's all right. He's better than he's been in months. Years perhaps. They have new drugs, it'll make all the difference.'

Mara swallowed. 'It's just – I didn't think. I didn't expect it. I cut my wrist, you see, I lost a lot of blood, it makes me dizzy. Does Mother know?'

They shook their heads.

Lisa made some tea. She found herself watching her sister, aware of many subtle changes. Mara was much better dressed, her hair bound up in a chignon encased in a black silk net. She seemed svelte, almost luxurious, as out of place as a Samovar in an English tearoom. And at the same time, she was quintessentially English, so perhaps it was the tea that was wrong. Sitting there, wrapped in a coat of rich red wool, Mara provoked thoughts of pearls and champagne.

'How did you cut your wrist?' Try as she might Lisa could not keep the antagonism from her voice.

'I was in Scotland. A knife slipped. Look, what is wrong with Marcus? He will get better, won't he?'

Angus looked at Lisa. 'You're the one who's so friendly with the doctor.'

'No, I'm not! He's a bit of a social climber, actually. Doesn't care how broke we are, he just loves getting over the threshold. He says it's schizophrenia,' added Lisa, almost as an afterthought.

Mara was silent. 'They can't cure that,' she said finally.

142

'I never expected that they would,' said Lisa. 'Did you?'

'Surely — surely they can do something?'

'They might be able to control it. Apparently sometimes people lead quite a normal life.'

Angus took a long breath through his nose. 'Bloody doctors,' he muttered. 'Put a bloody label on something and they're happy.'

Lisa turned away. She had thoughts sometimes, perhaps they were mad thoughts, she didn't know. When Marcus was at his worst, she believed in demons. She thought of them whispering, conspiring, driving his real self away. But where did he go? Was he somewhere in this room, like a cloud of invisible gas, locked out of the body they had sent away? Or was he inside all the time, hidden in some corner of his mind, looking out at her through terrified eyes, calling uselessly for help? Thank God they had a name for it at last. Even if you could do nothing, a name assuaged some of the terror.

They visited the hospital the following day. Leaves lay in heaps on the drive, because this year there was no-one to clear them. The car skidded harmlessly once or twice, and Mara grabbed for a handle and banged her wrist. 'Damn! That hurt.'

'It almost looks like a suicide attempt,' remarked Lisa.

'Not on one wrist only,' said Mara. 'It needed stitches, though. I thought about Lisa's head.'

The others shuddered. When she was small Lisa had hit her head against a wall and split the skin. The doctor had come to sew it, declaring it quite unnecessary to use an anaesthetic for such a young child. Her screams went unforgotten to that day.

'Marcus brought me an apple,' said Lisa suddenly. She hadn't remembered until then.

They didn't recognise him. In all the shambling, stoop-shouldered figures there was not one that could be Marcus. He was so tall, so broad in the chest, and everyone there seemed thin and slack-skinned. Eventually they found him sitting in the corner, in a cardigan that wasn't his, turning and turning a card in his hands. It was a wheel design, colours merging into one another.

'Hello, old chap,' said Angus. 'How are you?'

He didn't look up. Mara reached out and touched him, and for a second he stopped turning the card. But then he began again, quite absorbed.

Lisa took a deep breath. 'Do they give you enough to eat?' she asked. 'We could always bring things in for you.'

'I'll have it, Missy! I'll have it!' A small and demented old man danced at her elbow. She shrank away and he leered at her, mouthing

143

'I'll have it! Don't feed us enough in here. Not enough jam.'

They left quickly.

'He will come round, you know,' said the charge nurse, a hefty man with a prison warder grip. 'He'll be ready to come home pretty soon. You'll be amazed.'

Outside they said 'Home?' and looked at one another.

'We ought to get Mother back,' said Mara. 'It isn't our responsibility.'

'Don't be ridiculous.' Angus passed a hand over his face. He felt rather sick. When he looked at Marcus it was like seeing himself, old, ill and mad. 'I would stay,' he burst out. 'But I've got this job and God knows, we need the money. He's my twin, I know I'm the one responsible.'

'No more than us,' said Lisa tightly. 'You're not more of a brother just because you're a twin.'

'Aren't you?' Angus looked at her out of bleak, tired eyes.

'I can stay till Christmas,' said Mara. 'I don't really want to go back to London just yet, actually.' They both stared at her and she blushed. 'I'm rather involved. Someone may come and see me from time to time, that's all.'

'Good God,' said Angus. 'Are we going to have to fork out for a wedding then?'

She swallowed. 'I don't know. Something like that, perhaps.'

They got into the car and drove thankfully away. Mara felt tired suddenly, as if her lack of sleep for nights past was at last catching up with her. She dozed in the back, while Lisa and Angus talked.

'What will you do?' asked Angus.

'Stay, of course. I've got to. Professor Chandler wants me to arrange noticeboards and arrows for the visitors. Car parking spaces and so on.'

Angus sighed. He had no wish to do that, or to incarcerate himself in the City, none at all. He wanted to go back to Oxford and finish his degree. The life had suited him down to the ground.

Suddenly he envied his brother. At least Marcus had got himself parcelled off to a place where nothing was demanded except that you ate and slept and didn't break things. Only Angus was looked to for solutions, but then everyone asked too much of him, and they always had. He felt a stab of aggression, and jabbed his foot hard down on the accelerator. The car wasn't up to it and the engine whined. 'If there's one thing I'm going to do before I go it's get rid of those damned gypsies.' snarled Angus.

* * *

144

It wasn't that the gypsies never left, reflected Angus. Each time he ordered them off they went, more or less as requested. But back they came, at shorter and shorter intervals, like car drivers ignoring the notices saying "Return Within One Hour Prohibited" and dashing once round the block. He wondered where they went. Towards Leeds perhaps, or up towards Appleby. They all had their different rat-runs.

He breakfasted early, before the girls came down, noting that since Mara's arrival mess had proliferated. Lisa wouldn't put up with that. At least he was going away, and would not have to stand umpire for his sisters' endless squabbling. Tramping out to the stables he noticed that the weathervane was hanging limp and crooked. If someone didn't mend it before the winds began in earnest, it would be beyond repair.

He stopped in his tracks. With a sense of helplessness he thought – there is only me. No faceless personage was about to appear and mend anything, not the weathervane, nor the fences the gypsies broke, or the loose hayrack or the rocking cobbles. A few builders would fix the roof, but nothing more. Exhaustion came over him before he had begun the day; he was swamped by the hugeness of the task. If he could master just one small area of the situation he would feel more in control. 'The gypsies,' he said again, and forced himself to move. To hell with the weathervane, the cobbles, even the leaves choking the gutters – he would succeed somewhere today.

They were eating when he rode up. He realised that always before he had come in mid-afternoon, when most of the day's tasks were completed. Now there was washing soaking in a tub, a fire burning down scrap, and they stood around eating white bread sandwiches out of dirty hands.

'Good day to you,' said Angus. No-one answered. He got down from his horse and then wished he had not. Two skinny, yellow-eyed lurchers leered at him and bared an exploratory fang.

'Now we really have to talk about your visits here,' said Angus firmly. 'Each time I instruct you to leave I find you back here in less than two weeks. It's got to stop. This isn't a place where you can pitch just as you like. It's private land, Hellyn land.'

One of the men stepped forward. 'Ussen's been here forever. Slates Lane, we allus been here.'

'You're supposed to be travellers, damn it!' snapped Angus, losing his temper. 'If you want to stay somewhere permanently, why don't you bugger off to the council estate? Then at least you could wash those poor brats once in a while.'

The man chewed silently. Angus realised that he had put paid to

145

any talk he might have had with them. But God, they infuriated him so, with their sullenness and their stupidity. They lived like animals, he thought, and that human miracle, the brain, was less use to them than if they were cows.

He turned to get back on his horse but as he put his foot in the iron, the gelding spun round fractiously. The gypsy man took hold of the bridle, none too kindly. The hunter yawed and fought for its head, and as Angus looked down he saw anger pass across the man's face. Impotent, frustrated rage. The man wants to kill me, thought Angus in amazement. He felt no fear, only surprise.

He was trotting away when he heard a horse cantering down the track behind him. At once he thought of the gypsy's face, but he saw immediately it was not a gypsy horse. A bright chestnut gelding, quite fine, careering along half out of control. He halted and the chestnut slithered to a stop too, in a lather of feet and earth. The rider was no-one he knew, a girl, almost smothered by her vast jockey helmet.

'It's you, isn't it?' she said breathlessly. 'You've been at it again!'

'What?' He was bewildered. He felt sure he had never met her before. As far as he could judge she was rather short, with square hands and a round, smooth face. Her round brown eyes were glaring at him in indignation.

'Don't look so bloody innocent.' She gestured back towards the gypsies. '"Get off my land?" Ring a bell, does it? Riding out of your fine big house on your fine big horse to go and persecute a lot of cold, ill, uneducated people. They don't do you any harm. But we all know about breeding, don't we? Do as your ancestors did, get the poor off the aristocratic table, and if they fall on the floor, tread on their fingers.'

So many words battled within Angus that he could utter none of them. In the end he said, 'Would you mind telling me who you are?'

'Jean Maythorpe,' said the girl. 'And you don't know me, though we're all supposed to know you. What a pity we all gave up curtseying, it would suit you down to the ground to watch us all bobbing up and down.'

'Are you Reg Maythorpe's daughter?',

'Oooh, sir, I'm honoured!' She fluttered her eyelashes in wholly mocking dismay.

'You can tell your father that I was going to ask him to take over as Hunt Master this season. The offer is as at this moment withdrawn.'

She laughed in his face. 'He will be cut up! Let me tell you that it would have been only common courtesy to come and ask him before it was all round the neighbourhood. And don't pretend it's some big favour — he's the only man rich enough to keep the pack going, and

146

you know it. If you want him, you ask him, don't involve me.'

Angus, completely bewildered, retreated into cold disdain. He touched his hat. 'You will forgive me, madam. I must take my leave.'

'Oh, no you don't!' She pushed her unmanageable horse alongside him, fighting to hang on as it tried to run away with her. Angus's hunter favoured a superior, aristocratic trot. 'You're to go back now and tell those poor people they can stay.'

'Don't be ridiculous. They're filthy, lazy, they steal, they poach, they break fences, pollute the water, leave scrap and litter everywhere, they break trees, let their horses on to crops – and a dozen things I probably don't know about.'

'Yes,' said the girl. 'Yes, they do.'

He stared at her. 'Then what possible grounds do you have for telling me to let them stay?'

Her brown eyes met his. 'Humanity. Christian charity. That rare impulse to help someone less fortunate than ourselves.'

Angus drew rein. 'Look,' he said, 'Miss Maythorpe. You obviously have no understanding of the situation. I'm perfectly within my rights and I've shown more tolerance than either my father or my grandfather would have done. Now, I don't intend to discuss estate business with you any longer. As I'm sure you're aware, this is a bridlepath, but as I now intend to leave it I should be grateful if you would observe the rules and confine your ride to the prescribed route. And,' he added nastily, 'get yourself something more suitable to ride. That nag's far too strong for you.'

'Get stuffed,' said Jean Maythorpe. And as he rode away towards The Court, she yelled, 'I hope your patrician vowels choke you.'

Cantering back across the park, Angus boiled with rage. God damn the woman! God rot her! What on earth did she think she was doing, charging up and demanding – yes, demanding – that he do as she said? The words he might have spoken formed in his mind, in clear and decisive paragraphs. But she had left him dumbfounded.

His horse was dealt with in record time, every forkful of straw, every sweep of the brush, punctuating some telling phrase in Angus's mental discussion. When the horse was fed, groomed and rugged up, the stable set for the day, he looked up at the weathervane. He'd do that. It would be such a tragedy if it was ruined.

He went to the coach-house and found a ladder, setting it firmly against the wall. Climbing up to the gutter was quite simple, but once there he found the gutter itself was loose, hanging on by a few rusted brackets. It was clogged, too, with leaves, and Angus spent a few minutes scooping them out with his hands. Then he began the long, precarious scramble up to the ridge and the weathervane.

His first slip had him clinging on, with flat hands and crooked fingers, even his face pressed against the greasy slates. He fell back about three feet, his toe wedged in a broken slate. The thought of the drop turned him cold. He'd break a leg, possibly his back. But he went up again, and slid again, less drastically. Climbing a roof was a knack, like rock climbing presumably. He reached the ridge and tentatively straddled it, humping himself along to the weathervane. Now what was he to do? The support was broken but the screws that held it to the roof were rusted solid. Without tools he could do nothing.

'Can't you get it off?'

He looked down. A short girl with shiny brown hair, wearing jeans and a bright red jumper. It was the voice he recognised. Jean Maythorpe.

'What on earth are you doing here?'

She shaded her eyes to look up at him. 'I thought I'd better apologise. I lost my temper. And if you're not careful you'll lose your grip.'

'I already have,' confessed Angus. 'Gave myself one hell of a fright. Look, I'll have to come down, I need hammers and things.'

Going down was harder than going up. His feet had to search for a ladder he couldn't see. The girl guided him, shouting, 'Put your left foot down – not so far – you're there now, within an inch – don't worry, I'll hold the ladder.'

'Is that supposed to fill me with confidence?' He tried to look at her and slipped.

'Will you concentrate?' she said in an agonised voice. He did.

Once on the ground they were both embarrassed. Angus was covered in moss and leaves, his jodphurs streaked with rust.

'Why didn't you change?' asked Jean. 'You'll never get those clean.'

'Won't I?' He never thought about things like that. Someone, people, would deal with his washing. He went to plunge his hands in the horse trough. 'Have you come to berate me again?'

'Not unless you're difficult. I don't think I explained very well.'

'Only that I'd go to hell if I didn't do as you said.'

She went red. 'I didn't say that!'

'That's what it sounded like to me. Look, why don't you come in for a drink?'

She looked at him. 'All right. My father says you can always tell a nob, they booze from morning till night.'

'Then I don't imagine he knows many nobs. I was thinking of sherry before lunch.'

148

'Ooh! Aren't we twee!'

She was deliberately teasing him and it flicked him on the raw. He always became very public school when on edge, and she set him on edge. He stumped to the house, holding the kitchen door to allow her to enter.

His sisters were having a row. Mara stood with a vase of flowers in her hands, her cheeks brilliant with colour, while Lisa sat at the table slicing beans, as white as her sister was red.

'How dare you say this is Father's fault?' thundered Mara. 'You'll be blaming him for dying next! You always hated him, just because I was his favourite!'

'What absolute rubbish,' said Lisa coldly. 'If you could ever – '

'Excuse me,' said Jean, timidly.

Mara looked at her, snorted, and handed her the vase. Then she stalked out of the kitchen.

'That was my sister, Mara,' said Angus. 'Lisa, this is Jean Maythorpe. My younger sister, Lady Eloise.'

The girl looked at him. 'Now that does put me in a difficult position.'

'Whatever do you mean?' Angus was genuinely puzzled.

'You haven't given me any name that I can use. Do I say Lisa, and be too chummy, or Lady Eloise, and sound like a creep, or tug my forelock and say ma'am?'

Feeling awkward, Lisa said, 'Just Lisa, please. I heard your car, but by the time I'd got out you'd wandered off somewhere. And then of course Mara wanted to express an opinion or two.'

'While you remained resolutely silent,' remarked Angus. 'Do I have to go and dig in the cellar for the sherry?'

Lisa directed him to a cupboard.

'What a wonderful kitchen,' said Jean, gazing up at the high, arched ceiling studded with meathooks, the range with the old smoke oven in the chimney. 'You could feed an army in here.' She put the flowers on the table.

'Are you staying for lunch?' asked Lisa. 'I'll do some more beans.'

As always she was blunt, almost abrupt. It was shyness but it made her quite forbidding. Angus said, 'Yes, why don't you stay. We can take a vote on the gypsies.'

'I don't know why you bother chasing them away,' said Lisa. 'They're so pathetic, and they don't really bother us.'

'On second thoughts, we won't take a vote,' said Angus, and poured the sherry.

The sherry glasses were eighteenth-century and exquisite. When Jean commented on them, both Angus and Lisa looked surprised.

149

The only people they ever expected to remark on their home were valuers and art historians. For the first time Jean began to feel rather intimidated. She pushed her hair behind her ears and said, 'I've got to tell you about the gypsies! I mean I must, before you make me feel it would be shocking manners, when I've drunk your sherry and everything. They've got to stay you see – there's a boy in prison for theft, on remand, they're waiting for the trial. And one of the women gave birth in one of the wagons, in the most filthy conditions, and it was underweight of course because they never eat properly. It's in hospital with pneumonia. And at least while they're in Slates Lane we can given them some proper health care, and try and do something about the children. They've got worms, and permanent colds, and none of them ever goes to school. When they were travelling all the time, of course, there wasn't anything you could do, but now they've begun to stay longer and longer here we can try and bring them up a bit, you see. The headmistress at the village school has promised to take the younger ones, provided they come the day before for a bath. Otherwise it's impossible, the parents all complain.'

'I wouldn't like to sit next to one,' said Lisa distastefully. 'It's like a lesson in social history, the poor in days gone by.'

'Exactly,' declared Jean. 'They've been left behind. Well, if they'd had anything about them they'd have been into chrome caravans and lorries, not struggling along in vardos with the odd chicken in a cage.' She laughed. 'You know what they say?'

'What?' asked Angus.

'That they belong here. They're Hellyn people. That they and the Hellyns prosper or fail together.'

Angus put down his glass rather too hard for such a fragile vessel.

Lisa cleared her throat. 'What a neat bit of superstitious blackmail,' she remarked. 'We can buy our good luck back by helping the gypsies.'

'And how do you know so much, Jean?' asked Angus belligerently. 'I've never been able to get two words out of them.'

'Well. You wouldn't.'

To Lisa's surprise Jean began to clear the table, ready for lunch. She held up a silk and lace bra. 'What do I do with this?'

Lisa took it and tossed it into a corner. 'It's Mara's. She's never got used to living without help. None of us has actually.'

'Yes,' said Jean, as if it was all too apparent.

As always, Lisa's food was surprisingly good. Mousseline of chicken done with herbs and a wine sauce. Mara had cooled down and was sweet and amusing. 'But what do you do, Jean?' she asked. 'What's your job?'

'I don't get paid for anything.'

150

Angus said, 'But all this gypsy stuff. Are you in social work?'

'Only in a voluntary capacity.' But they were determined to get to the bottom of her, so she said, 'I don't need to work, you see. My father's very well off. And it wouldn't be fair to take training and a job that someone could have who needed it more. So I sort of clean up round the edges where the Welfare State falls down. The gypsies, alcoholics, that sort of thing. And I do political work, of course. I want to stand for Parliament.'

Mara put her hand up to her face to hide a smile.

'I don't exactly see you as our local Member somehow,' said Angus.

'Oh, not here! Liverpool perhaps. I'm in the Labour Party.'

Lisa began to chuckle. 'Angus, you've invited the devil to sup. Someone go and see if Grandfather's revolving in the tomb.'

Ignoring her, Angus burst out, 'You don't really support those clowns, do you? They couldn't possibly run the country!'

'And I suppose you're quite happy to have gypsies shunted from place to place, off the edge of the earth if possible, and the homeless left to die in the streets in winter, and old ladies perish in their homes for lack of money, and – '

'I do always feel,' broke in Mara, loudly, 'that it is so wise never to talk about politics. Don't you, Jean?'

The girl's cheeks flamed. Angus said stiffly, 'I'm afaid that was my fault.'

'Don't be so pompous,' snapped Jean.

'Oh, for God's sake!' Angus flung his napkin down and stood up. 'Is your father as bad as this? We'll be the only hunt in England demanding a union show of hands before we draw a covert!'

'Actually, he's a Conservative,' said Jean. 'Does it count as talking politics if you've stood up and I haven't?'

'God knows,' snarled Angus. 'And I'm going to get that weather-vane off.'

He stomped out, slamming the kitchen door. Mara and Lisa exchanged glances. 'You have put our Angus in a tizzy,' said Mara, mimicking their old nanny. 'He's normally the most placid of us all.'

'I think one of you ought to go and help him with the weathervane,' said Jean. 'If I went, he'd throw it at me. He ought to have a crawling ladder on the roof really, he doesn't seem to have the faintest idea how to go on.'

'I'm sure we shall learn,' said Lisa, her voice tinged with acid.

'By the look of this place you're going to have to,' said Jean. They had ruffled her and her manners had gone completely. She pulled herself together. 'Thanks for lunch, it was delicious. Can you tell him

151

if he wants my father to be MFH he'll have to ask him himself? Dad won't lift a finger otherwise.'

'I'll tell him,' said Mara.

When Jean had gone, the sisters started to laugh. 'Well!' said Lisa. 'Where did he find her?'

'Down a very left-wing mineshaft, I should imagine. Flung there by one of her victims. It must be a great problem for her that she was born rich.'

Lisa sighed. 'I wish she'd offload some of her cash in our direction. Just a little more money, and one or two people to help, and we could start living in the house again. The only difference between this and a bed-sitting room in London is that we have to run down miles of freezing corridors to bed.'

'There are a few more difficulties,' said Mara, remembering. 'Actually I meant to talk about money today. I'm not too badly off just at present. Why don't we try and find someone to help outside, and someone to char? You can't slave away doing everything and I don't mind paying. We can run the inside fires on wood, surely, there's masses on the estate.'

Lisa blinked. 'How much have you got? And where from? Have you sold something out of the house?'

'No, of course I haven't! I was given it. It's this friend of mine, we're rather serious about each other, and he knew how hard up we were —'

'Who on earth is it?' demanded Lisa. 'It isn't someone horribly vulgar is it? Some Greek shipping magnate that we'll hate?'

Mara turned away. 'No, of course it isn't. And it's quite all right. You never know, he might sort everything out once we're-settled.'

She was softer, Lisa realised, more vulnerable. Were the holes in her confidence new, or was she simply prepared to let them be seen nowadays? 'Is he nice?' she asked.

'Yes. Oh, yes. He's very witty, you know, and very sweet. The first time we met I was quite squiffy. He did make me laugh.'

'You said he might visit us. Do give me some notice, I'll make an effort.'

Mara linked her fingers together. 'I'm sure he'll come. If he can get away.' She had a momentary picture of his face, as vivid as if he were there, in the room with her. He had neither written nor telephoned since she arrived, but she knew it was difficult, she understood. Sometimes she felt as if he was very close, and again that he was far away, and had forgotten her. If that were so, if she was to go from day to day and never see him, she thought she would rather be dead.

Chapter Nineteen

In November the weather was bright, cold and dry. Most mornings Mara could look out across the park and see pheasants pecking at the iron earth, and sometimes geese flew on to the lake, fifty at a time. The ice was thin still, glittering on the surface like an oily sheen until the birds smashed it.

Angus was in London, working. He'd come back once or twice at weekends, but it cost money to travel and besides, he found it irritating to see the Maythorpes taking such a hold on the hunt. They had taken over with reforming zeal, sending a wave of repairs and new leather coursing through the kennels. Even the whipper-in had a new horse, and his old stager was at last retired. To the Hellyns, everything they did seemed like a criticism.

Mara flexed her wrist, testing it for strength. It still hurt, but she didn't care for that. Maythorpes or no Maythorpes, she would hunt today, and rid herself of this terrible, dragging lethargy. The days passed, on leaden feet, and now and then Jay either wrote or telephoned. When he did it was wonderful, but afterwards, surprisingly soon, she was down again. There was so long to wait between calls, and he never wrote more than once a week. She didn't care how much her wrist hurt, she would hunt and be happy.

Reg Maythorpe had decided to hold the opening meet at The Court as before, but on a Saturday. It was a departure from tradition, because Saturdays brought out big fields, all teenagers and businessmen. But as Reg said, 'You want to make some money, don't you?'

'It goes to the hunt, Reg, not us,' said Mara. Reg liked to talk to her. With Angus he bristled; with Lisa, although he wouldn't admit it, he was intimidated. Only Mara made him feel right. A man of standing, worthy of respect, as he respected her. She wasn't afraid to tell him what she thought, nor was she so blunt she set his back up. Her sister did that.

153

He sent his gardeners over the day before, to smarten things up. He didn't like the mess the builders left, mending the roof, and he even considered asking to have the scaffolding taken down, because it spoiled the look of the place. Maythorpe lived in a big, modern house on the far side of the village. He had stables and a few acres, two gardeners, a groom, and since his wife died, a housekeeper. He did not know that Angus thought the place loathsome, too new, too neat, too flashy, but then even without the scaffolding Maythorpe eyed The Court with distaste. 'Nothing but a bloody barrack,' he told anyone who would listen. It gave him the chance to let them know he was a frequent visitor.

Mara stood at her bedroom window, watching him ride up the drive. His daughter was with him, still on that hot Anglo-Arab, but Maythorpe himself looked every inch the country Master, big, solid, and his horse up to weight. Although she should go down and welcome him, she did not. She stayed at her window, watching, braving the cold. Downstairs Lisa would be laying out trays of drink and plates of food; they had been bothering about it for days. Last year of course Curtiss had seen to it, there had been no necessity for anyone to do more than socialise. How odd that she hadn't known she sat on a mountain of other people's effort.

Hounds arrived on foot, noisy and full of themselves. Lisa's spaniel blundered out, barking crossly, and old Tom whipped hounds off. 'Get you this cur dog, Miss Lisa!' he yelled, and she ran out, all wet hands, to catch the thing. Mara shivered and rubbed her arms. She supposed she should go down.

The whole house smelled of woodsmoke. Jay's money paid for a lad from the village to come in part time to help with the horses and cut wood with a chain-saw, and they built roaring fires downstairs that spat out shards of flaming bark and filled the chimneys with soot. She wondered if she ought to ask Jay for more, so they could run the central heating. It had been installed fifty years before just in this end of the house, but it had pipes the size of drains and was hopelessly inefficient. Even at full blast the upstairs radiators gave off the merest breath of warmth.

And everywhere, endlessly, she was reminded of her father. Every time she came down to breakfast she felt a new surprise that he wasn't there. She wouldn't stay after Christmas, she decided, she'd go back to London and get a flat. Jay would visit her then.

In the passages, far from the fires, her breath formed clouds. Immaculate in her black coat, golden hair wound up into a heavy bun, she hurried into the kitchen.

'Twenty minutes too late, as usual,' snapped Lisa. 'Everything's done.'

154

'So it is. Aren't you clever?' said Mara. Then, as Lisa glowered, she said, 'Look, I'll do my bit clearing up afterwards. Why don't you go and get tidy?'

'I suppose I should.' Normally Lisa liked herself dressed for hunting. But who could compete with Mara, who put curves into clothes that had never before seemed to need them? She went and got changed, feeling tired.

The morning dissolved into a mêlée of drinks and food and conversation. So many people came that Lisa dragooned foot followers into passing round trays, and stood in the kitchen frantically slicing fruit cake and putting cheese on biscuits. Mr Maythorpe beamed and Mara circulated while Lisa ran in and out like a billiard ball potted out of sequence.

'Pity Angus couldn't be here to see this,' said Maythorpe to Jean. 'He'd feel better about things. Everything going on just as before.'

'Oh, I hope not!' said Jean. 'This is the new age, Dad. We want everything to be different.'

'Like hell we do! I didn't get here to have this and then find they're giving slices away free to everyone. I don't mind a bit of privilege as long as some of it's mine, and that's the truth.'

She snorted and left him. 'And take it steady,' he roared after her. 'You know that damned horse of yours is a fool!'

He glanced at his watch, a Hunter on a fob he had bought when he became Master. No point in being someone if you didn't look the part, after all. Time to go. He signalled to his huntsman, and Tom began gathering up hounds. Honest chap, Tom, and worth his good new horse. Maythorpe knew horses and for once Tom had something decent, something that wouldn't stop at the first ditch.

He noticed that Lady Mara was on her brother's nag, and he waved jovially. The right sort of nob, she was, pretty as a picture and a do-as-she-liked air that had the boys mad for her. And him, Reg Maythorpe, on familiar terms!

'Right, ladies and gentlemen,' he called, and took out his horn. He could hardly prevent himself grinning with pleasure, and to control it he clenched his lips tight in a scowl.

In the kitchen with the washing up, Lisa felt her head spin. Drinking on an empty stomach, she'd downed a fortifying whisky the moment everyone rode away. Damn Mara, damn her to hell. If they were dying of thirst in the desert you could be sure Mara would have the last swig at the water bottle.

The dirty glasses and plates piled up in daunting mountains. There was no way this could be left until they came back, wet, cold, and wanting supper. If Mara had a shred of decency she'd have stayed

155

behind and let her sister go off with the hunt.

Lisa stood for a moment, thinking. Who was this nameless man who telephoned, wrote letters and sent Mara money? Every time she asked questions Mara lowered the shutters, as if Lisa was a little girl, prying into adult concerns. It was infuriating.

She began spreading the final drying cloths out on the range. The house was quiet and she felt rather forlorn. They had all gone off without one thought for her. But her horse was ready to go, full of oats and eager, so there was nothing for it but to put on her hat and follow them.

Of the four children, Marcus was the best horseman, followed by Angus, then Mara, and Lisa was bottom of the class. She inherited their ponies, always too big, and she was carted over hill and dale with no hope of stopping. The end result was a less than enthusiastic horsewoman. Today the mare was keen, and chased after the field with worrying enthusiasm. At the first gate the horse wanted to jump while Lisa was determined they should go through. When she got off the mare danced and stood on her foot. Tears filled her eyes. Damn it, this was the last straw!

She got back on, turned the mare and bullied her back to the stables. No-one helped, no-one could be bothered to wait, and no-one cared if the beastly animal killed her. Lisa was fed up, sick to death of work and ordinariness. There was nothing to look forward to except a long, cold, builder-filled winter, followed by a visitor-threatened spring. Nothing exciting ever happened, nothing different. The chances were no-one would even notice that she failed to appear today.

Trotting briskly up the drive, she saw someone wandering along the front of the house. 'If you're looking for the hunt, they've gone,' she shouted. Damned townee, she thought, wearing smart clothes in the country.

The man walked towards her. 'I was looking for Lady Mara, actually. Has she gone out?'

Lisa pulled off her hat. 'I'm her sister. She'll be out for hours, I should think. You should have told her you were coming.'

'Would you mind awfully if I waited?'

'Oh. All right.'

She put the horse away, hurriedly throwing it some hay. Was this the one? Whose contributions were paying for Peggy from the village and a boy to help outside? Whose letters sent Mara up to her room for an entire morning? Who 'phoned, but never came, and whose name she did not know?

He was waiting in the kitchen. She switched on the light, trying not to stare at him. 'Would you like a drink perhaps? We've some rather good dry sherry – ' She stopped and looked at him properly. 'Do I know you?'

'Er – I'm not sure that we have met actually. My friends call me Jay.'

'And you're a friend of Mara's?'

'Yes. I'm extremely fond of her. Sherry would be delightful, thank you.'

As she poured her mind ran through a filing cabinet of faces. His, quite good-looking, very long in the jaw, was familiar. Had she seen him on television? she thought. He turned his head as he reached to take the glass. Lisa said, 'Good God. You're the prince.'

He nodded. 'I'm afraid so. I have rather stolen a day off to come here. There's no way I could contact Mara, is there?'

'They could be anywhere,' lied Lisa, who knew pretty well where they must be. She felt sudden, hot antagonism. 'What do you want to see her about?' she asked.

His mouth twisted in a cold smile. 'It is personal.'

'Is it?' Lisa surveyed him thoughtfully. He had an odd jaw, long and narrow, but he really wasn't bad looking. He was annoyed, she realised, because she was here and Mara wasn't. 'I wish you'd go,' she said.

'I'm sorry. I have to see Mara.'

The words would not stay unsaid. 'But don't you think you ought to go? I'm not surprised you've fallen for Mara, lots of men do. But you're married. It isn't fair.'

He sighed irritably. 'My dear child, this isn't something I want to discuss with you. Mara and I have talked. She's an exceptional woman.'

'She can be very silly too. If you loved her you wouldn't spoil her life.'

Jay lost his temper. 'Look, little girl, this has nothing at all to do with you. I want to see Mara, and I suggest you take me to her at once. Immediately!'

'I'm nearly nineteen years old,' said Lisa thickly.

'I'm sorry. You look much younger.' He stood glaring at her, a man used to having his lightest wish obeyed. 'I warn you, I intend to see her,' he said tightly.

Lisa took a scornful breath through her nose. She glared back at him. 'Very well. Far be it from me to stand between my sister and ruin. We'd better go in your car.'

The first covert was hanging wood, at the edge of the moor. The nearby lane was crammed with cars and bicylces, so they might not yet have found. If that was the case, Maythorpe would be restless by now. They'd be moving soon, to somewhere more productive.

'Do you hunt?' asked Lisa briskly, as he drove the car slowly up between parked cars.

157

'Not often, no. The security people get nervous. Look, I'd like you to go across to her if you would.'

'Of course. I'm sorry, I'm not used to clandestine meetings, you'll have to explain things. You're very lucky my brother isn't home.'

'I thought he was coming home soon. Mara told me.'

'That is my lunatic brother,' said Lisa kindly. 'We have one of everything in our family.'

'Including a viper,' said the prince with a grim smile. He stopped the car. Lisa got out to run across the field.

She spotted Mara at once, talking to Jean Maythorpe and ignoring several hopeful men. When she saw her sister, Mara said, 'Good heavens, have you fallen off already?'

'Not exactly,' said Lisa. 'Look, I'll take the horse. There's someone come to see you.'

'Who?' All the tension, all the hope, showed in her face.

Lisa turned away. 'He's in the car.'

So she joined the hunt after all. Jean Maythorpe's wild chestnut took off on the first run, and Lisa was swept along too. She jumped and she galloped until she was exhausted, and still it was too early to go home. The horse was in his element, following hounds, listening for the horn, even Lisa could barely damp his enthusiasm. At four o'clock, in the twilight, they ran a fox to ground at Hell Rocks.

'I'm going home,' said Jean. 'If they dig it out, I shall hate it.'

'Yes.' The horses turned together, weary now and cold as their sweat dried. Lisa was shaking with weariness, and at home she would have to face Mara. If only he was gone.

Jean took the bridlepath off to the village, leaving Lisa to ride to The Court alone. The building was almost completely dark. On winter's evenings the lack of light repelled. It was a gloomy, dying monster. How wonderful it would be to switch on every light in the place, every bulb in every table lamp, and sit up here to watch. It would look like a ship, sailing in the night. In all her life Lisa had never seen that.

The boy they hired on hunting days with Mara's money was waiting to take the horse. As Lisa slid to the ground, her knees buckled and he had to catch her arm to steady her. 'Have a good day, ma'am?' he asked.

'The horse ignored me. He should go out on his own, he'd enjoy it more.' She shouldn't say things like that, it led people to think that madness ran in the family. Which perhaps it did. In trepidation, she went into the house.

The sisters sat either side of the drawing-room fire. The only light came from the table lamp, and the fireglow. Mara's hair, loose about

158

her shoulders, was a thin net of red, like threads of steel in the furnace. She wasn't lovely tonight. Her face, blotched with crying, was drawn into long, miserable lines.

'We can't use the money any more then,' said Lisa, sighing.

'Why not? Nothing's changed.'

'But before I thought − well, it would have been family money in the end. We've been living off immoral earnings.'

Mara pushed back her hair, blowing her nose hard on a handkerchief. Jay's handkerchief. 'You can damn well go on living off it! It's only instead of diamonds and things, the usual mistress stuff.' She was crying again, slow tears that oozed out of her eyes without so much as a sob.

'I mean, it's just so stupid!' burst out Lisa suddenly. 'It isn't as if he's ever going to leave his wife. He's treating you like − like some little slut! Hiding you away, locked up in the country, in case there's a scandal. What he's really worried about is that in town you might find someone you like better.'

Suddenly Mara smiled. She leaned across and rested a hand on her sister's knee. 'You don't understand at all, poppet. It's as bad for him as it is for me. Everybody watching, waiting for him to take a false step, nudging him back on course the moment he does something *he* wants which isn't what *they* want. I think −' she took a deep breath ' − I think he's going to change, you know. He's not going to put up with it. Sooner or later he's going to break out. And then − we can be together.'

Lisa found herself wondering if she had ever really known Mara. How was it possible to live with someone for so long and find that they have hidden themselves from you almost completely? Mara controlled people, yet here she was quite dominated by this man. Mara never allowed herself to be inconvenienced, and here she was, sobbing and alone.

'Suppose Angus finds out?' she said. 'And Mother? What are they going to say?'

'I don't care. Lisa, I absolutely don't. People can say what they like and it won't stop me. I love him, you see, and even if he was cruel to me, if he only came to see me once in a blue moon, I'd still wait. I can't be happy without him.'

Lisa was aware, suddenly, that she loathed the man who could do this to her sister, who let her destroy herself in this way. All her life Mara had seemed strong, so much stronger than everyone else. She had never seen that Mara's great need, her life force, was in loving and being loved. She didn't see it now.

159

Chapter Twenty

At the beginning of December, Marcus came home. They brought him in an ambulance, and when they opened the back dors he sat and looked out at his home with an expression of blank incomprehension.

'Now you will make sure he has his pills?' said the doctor, rubbing his hands at the prospect of regular visits. Lisa found that, as usual, he was standing too close to her, but whenever she took a step back he took one forward. He was becoming very keen on chummy little chats in the kitchen over coffee. She had the feeling that he wanted her to confide in him. He was cultivating his position as the trusted family practitioner.

Alone with Marcus, the sisters felt uncomfortable. He didn't seem to know what to do with himself. For the rest of the morning he sat in the kitchen, watching Lisa cook or wash, and Mara peel carrots until she got bored and spent half an hour arranging a posy of flowers. Marcus kept looking around, as if he couldn't believe that he was home. He sat, twisting and untwisting his fingers. The girls talked in bright, unnatural voices.

'I think we're in for a hard winter.'

'Yes, a very hard winter. It's cold now, actually.'

'Yes, isn't it.'

'At the hospital,' said Marcus slowly, 'they don't like winter. All the tramps get sent in. Patients, you see, often turn into tramps.'

'Well, you won't' said Lisa. 'There'll always be someone to take care of you.'

He grinned then. 'Not a bloody baby, for God's sake!'

They celebrated. Mara went down to the cellar and found a bottle of vintage champage. 'We're down to the last three,' she declared as she came out. 'And the sherry's almost gone. I think we're going to have to start visiting the off-licence.'

'The whole village will say we've taken to drink,' said Lisa. 'They won't know we've been guzzling our secret supplies all along. You are allowed champagne, aren't you, Marcus? Do have some.'

Officially it wasn't allowed, but he had a glass and got squiffy. He told tales of the hospital, of the doctors going madder than the patients so that visitors ran away from them and begged the lunatics for help.

Halfway through the evening they rang Angus in London, to tell him the news. When Mara came off the 'phone, she shrugged. 'Sounded a bit strained. I think he had someone with him.'

'I do hope he isn't drinking,' said Lisa owlishly. 'He's got to save his money. The bank statement looks absolutely disgusting.'

'Again? It would help if they'd stop putting the bloody interest rates up. Perhaps they'll let us buy on tick at the off-licence, I do hope so.'

'We could go and barter,' said Marcus. 'How many bottles for a silver fork? At least that way we'd enjoy selling up.'

'Until eventually we'd be sitting on bare boards, singing sea shanties,' said Lisa, waving her glass. 'There must be worse ways to go.'

Angus put down the telephone rather slowly. He had no wish to hurry back to his visitor. It was Stanley Westerley, the head of the firm, whose friendship with Henry had got him the job. He had also found Angus this flat, which took rather more of his salary than he would have liked. Living in London was proving inordinately expensive.

'That was my sister,' said Angus in explanation. He sat down again in the grim, grey functional armchair. The furniture came with the place, a rather passé blend of Danish light wood and tubular steel functionalism. Never in his life had Angus lived in such universally ugly surroundings.

'No bad news I hope?' A thin, spare man, Westerley had a falsely genial manner. He had the instincts of a shark.

'On the contrary. My brother's come out of hospital. He's very well, much recovered.'

'Yes.' The tone let Angus know that however recovered Marcus might appear he would do well to keep him right away from the firm. They had more than enough home-grown oddballs.

'As I was saying, Angus,' went on Westerley, 'I do rather wonder if you have entirely found your feet.'

'I'm sure I've still got an awful lot to learn, Stanley. But I've grasped the systems pretty well I think.'

'Do you?'

Angus flailed around, trying to think of an error he might have

161

made that could have caused this visitation. As far as he could recall he had been running a relatively tight ship. As yet he dealt only with smaller clients, overseeing their portfolios, advising them on trends and specific purchases. The firm produced its own company reports and Angus translated the general recommendations into something suitable for his clients. Actually he thought he was doing rather well.

'Have any of my clients complained?' he asked.

'Good God, no. We'd chase them off pretty quickly if they did. Angus, dear boy – forgive me, but how are you managing? Financially, I mean.'

Angus considered telling him to mind his own bloody business. But, he needed the job. 'Well – obviously I'd appreciate a little more,' he said stiffly. 'I can't expect to start on a huge salary.'

'How very pessimistic of you,' said Stanley, and put his fingers together in an arch. Then he laughed. 'Don't look so appalled, Angus. I'm not expecting you to rob a bank. But you are such a boy scout, dear boy. For instance, why have only five of your clients taken up our company recommendation? It was marked as a definite buy.'

Angus clear his throat. The frog persisted. 'I studied it, naturally,' he said huskily. 'It seemed rather risky. Most of my clients are on small incomes. I don't like advising them to take up positions which – obviously my attitude would be different if the client was happy to speculate. Most old ladies and retired schoolmasters aren't.'

'I see. Angus, did you ever wonder why we made the recommendation?'

'Yes. Yes, I did.'

'And what conclusion did you come to?'

'I thought perhaps you were being rather optimistic.'

Westerley began to laugh. 'Henry's lack of acumen is a very potent gene, I see! Please don't be insulted, dear boy. Your innocence does you a great deal of credit. We had very good reason to recommend as we did. To those who work for us it wasn't just a recommendation – we expected you to buy that stock for every single one of your clients, even to override their personal opposition to it. The market's very slack at the moment. Those deals, small in themselves, coming within the space of a week, would stand out on the screens at once. The price would rise. We might even be able to encourage some rumours about a takeover. And then, unaccountably, some large-scale selling would take place and our little boom would be over.'

'Leaving my clients with a loss.'

Stanley shrugged. 'Not a huge loss, in most cases. But a killing for us. We'd been setting it up for months, buying a little here, a little there, building up enough to make it worth our while. And your efforts, Angus my boy, turned our firework into a damp squib.'

Angus hardly knew what to say. The firm was trading on its own account, and that was obviously illegal. It was deceiving its clients, rigging the market . . .

'We always cut our boys in whenever something like this pays off,' said Stanley gently. 'It's only fair. All those little old ladies telephoning and complaining – you deserve some recompense. And, of course, if you wanted to take up a position yourself, have a discreet word with the office manager. He'll rig up an account for you.'

'I take it you get inside information,' said Angus.

'Of course. In the course of time, if your brother maintains his recovery, he may well be asked to sit on a number of boards. Amazing how many firms love a title. Anything of interest to us would be most gratefully received, you'd be fascinated to know how much we learn that way. And how many declining families get back on top,' he added happily.

He got up, and Angus automatically rose with him. 'Now,' said Stanley, tapping Angus's arm, 'You have a little think. You couldn't keep a dog alive in London on your salary. A bit less work and a bit more fun, that's what you need. A chap like you could be drowning in parties if he had a mind. We'll be complaining next that you can't keep awake at your desk! Let's keep this between ourselves. I've marked your card, and we'll look forward to some improvement.'

Tapping Angus again, he put on his hat, picked up his umbrella and left.

Looking round his gloomy little flat, Angus thought how neatly he had been set up. Even the flat was designed to make him both miserable and poor. He had no doubt that if he resigned now then Westerley would spread the odd rumour – "Too like his brother for comfort, if you take my meaning. Thank God we got rid of him in time" – and if he informed, then he could look forward to life as a social pariah. The firm might get a roasting, but Angus would never get a job.

On only one thing did he agree with Stanley Westerley: he wanted some fun, some good, honest, get drunk and get happy fun. From the moment he arrived in London he had been swamped with invitations. There was no more sought after creature in town than an unattached man under forty. His address had been passed round like a secret code.

He picked up four cards for tonight. One was thicker than the others, and properly engraved. A large, society ball. Black tie. Well, they were celebrating back at The Court and he would join them – in spirit.

* * *

163

Usually when he stood tying his bow tie he felt pleasurable thrills of anticipation. Tonight he felt shivers of anxiety. If only Mara would hurry up and name the day. If she could land a millionaire their troubles could be over. Perhaps he ought to sniff around some rich girl, he thought dismally. He had a mental picture of a nightmare woman, short, dumpy, and determined. Damn it, tonight he was out to enjoy himself, not court the girl with the biggest diamonds.

He walked into town, to save money, and the commissionaire looked dubious until Angus showed him his invitation. As he took off his coat and silk scarf, a voice at his elbow said, 'Good evening, Mr Angus.'

It was his old butler. Angus took his hand, shaking it vigorously. 'How very good to see you, Curtiss! How marvellous. Are you working for Lady — whoever's party I'm at.' He fumbled for the invitation.

'Netherington, sir. As it happens I'm doing agency work now. Lot of Americans, very exciting. How is everyone at The Court, sir?'

'Pretty well, I think. Good Lord, Curtiss, what a surprise. And you look remarkably fit.'

'Good of you to say so, sir. Rather hard on the feet, these evening parties. One often finds things amiss, and too late to change. One adjusts, sir, one has to.'

'Yes. We've all had to make one or two adjustments.'

'What a pity Lady Mara's become ill, sir. She was such a hit, spoken about everywhere.'

'What makes you think she's ill?'

'Is she not, sir? Lady Payne's been putting it about.'

Angus blinked. 'I see. Would you know why that might be by any chance?'

Curtiss lifted his chin, stretching his neck like a chicken. 'Only gossip, sir. Prince John much admired her, I do believe.'

'Good God.' Angus reached into his pocket and brought out his note case. He tried to slip Curtiss a fiver, but the old man said, 'I'd rather not, sir, if you don't mind. Do very well out of the embassies, I do. I often think of the old days at The Court.'

'So do I,' Angus withdrew the money. 'If ever we get back on our feet again, I'll get in touch right away. And you will let me know if you have any problems, won't you?'

'That's very kind sir. Do give my special regards to Lady Eloise.'

Curtiss went on his stately way, rebuking waiters, uncorking champagne, sending a girl at the buffet to change her grubby apron. Angus felt better suddenly. The world was a jungle, but in unexpected corners you might come across a friend. As if to emphasise the point, he saw a man he had been at school with, and across the room his second cousin who was waving and yelling: 'For God's sake, Angus! Thought you were still nose down at Oxford. Come and have a drink.'

He drank and he danced, and the mothers of two of his partners invited him to dine. In the interval a girl dropped ice cream down his jacket, went beetroot red and scrabbled at it with her handkerchief, so to cheer her up he had to dance and chat. Her mother promptly invited him to dine as well. And he'd had a hard day, and what's more Westerley's words kept sounding in his head. Would it matter if he did as he suggested? Weren't all the people that mattered people like this, here tonight, that Westerley would never dare to try and exploit?

He went to get his coat. It was blessedly quiet in the cloakroom. He realised that he had been nursing a headache for most of the evening. What wouldn't he give to be back at Oxford now, in his study, chatting about some abstruse moral point that was light years away from whether you should or should not defraud old ladies. And when he looked at it like that, the answer was clear. But he couldn't see any way out.

In the street the wind was gusting noisily, funnelled between the buildings. He began to fasten his coat − but it wasn't his coat. It was a great deal too big and the buttons were completely different. He turned to go back, and met someone coming out. He held Angus's coat.

'Here, mate,' said the stranger. 'You've got my coat.'

'Yes, so I realise. I was about to come and change it.'

'Bloody well hope so! Mine's a sight more expensive than yours.'

'Is it?' Now that he observed the coat properly he saw that it had satin lapels, very large buttons and a contrast lining. His own was some years old, but made to measure, and utterly discreet. The man was obviously Australian, and that explained it.

Having exchanged coats, they walked along together. 'Name's Toby Ledbetter,' said the Australian.

'Angus Hellyn.'

'Guess like me you've had enough of that charade. Fancy a drink? Don't look so bloody anxious, I'm not a shirt lifter.'

Angus grinned. It was exactly what had crossed his mind. But he wouldn't mind a drink.

They went to a drinking club in a tasteful, velvet-padded basement. A few hostesses were desultorily working the tables, but the Australian waved a girl away and they weren't pestered. He ordered a bottle of scotch and a jug of water, poured them both a good measure and sat back. He was really huge, thought Angus, with a barrel chest and

165

thighs like trees. His head was big too, with a shock of dark brown hair.

'I'm sick of bloody London,' said Ledbetter. 'Poncy people and no bloody honesty.'

'You're bloody right,' said Angus, and picked up his drink. 'The place is full of crooks. And women.'

'I thought the women were one of the better bits. Some real lookers at that bash tonight.'

Angus nodded. 'Couldn't agree more. But every time I danced with someone her mother invited me to dine. I couldn't say no. And I'll feel a bastard if I go and then never see the girl again, so I'll have to take her to the theatre or somewhere. And that means another dinner invitation and round we go again. I don't want to and I can't bloody well afford it.'

'Down on your upper class uppers, are we?'

'To the eyeholes of the leather. What did you say your name was?'

'Toby Ledbetter. And I'm very well wadded, as it happens.'

'Couldn't lend me a few quid, could you?'asked Angus ironically. 'Sure.'

Instantly Toby was feeling in his pocket. Angus stuttered, 'I didn't mean that you should – you don't know me!'

'Well, no, and if it was my last quid you wouldn't get it. What do you need?'

'Far more than you could possibly lend! Please, I was only joking. Honestly.'

The other man shrugged and put his money away. 'Bet all those ladies don't know you're strapped.'

'I'm sure they do,' said Angus. 'But I'm good family, you see, and there's a long shot on a title, so obviously they're keen.'

'Well, if the broad's well-heeled, I don't suppose it matters,' said Toby. 'Not that I'd like to be kept, but there you are.'

He leaned forward and topped up their glasses. Angus knew he should go home to bed, he had to face work in the morning. But he didn't much care if he went or not. He took up his glass and sat back.

'Only tonight,' he said, 'I found out that I'm working for a crook, that my elder sister's having an affair with a married offshoot of the royal family, and our butler's in love with Lisa. That's my younger sister. Fortunately I don't have to worry about the butler, he's nearly seventy.'

'You must have very nice sisters,' remarked Toby.

'Nice.' Angus considered the word. 'Mara is beautiful.Charming, too, but not nice. Lisa's quite nice though.'

'But not pretty.'

166

'No, not at all. Perhaps it's a pity the butler's so old.' He dropped his head back on his shoulders. 'God, but I'm pissed.'

'You sure are.'

Toby put the top back on the bottle and slipped it into his pocket. Then he hitched an arm under Angus's and hauled him to his feet. 'What a good thing you met me, Angus,' he declared. 'You certainly need taking care of.'

They met about once a week after that, for lunch or dinner. As far as Angus could find out Toby had some sort of holiday complex in Australia and was in England to try and finalise the finance for another. He suspected the man was being deliberately evasive, but it didn't bother him particularly. After that first night, when he had the feeling that Toby must have engineered the meeting, he too was cautious. But Toby was useful to him. Angus included him in quite a few of his invitations, and mothers were torn between trapping Angus for his name and Toby for his money. 'But what does he do, Angus dear?' they would purr to him and he would say, 'Property. Deals in property.'

As Christmas approached Angus became aware of a subtle pressure. Toby wanted to come home with him. He resisted, turning aside each broad hint with a joke or a change of subject. At last, Toby sat back at the lunchtable, puffed on his cigar and said, 'OK. We're mates and we've stood by each other. Why the hell won't you ask me back?'

'Why the hell do you want me to?'

'Because otherwise I've got a sodding awful time on my own in London. And I want to see this gorgeous sister, and your nutty brother, and the sweet little one that the butler loves, and this bloody big mansion you keep talking about. I'll bring a crate of champagne and two turkeys, all right?'

Angus sighed. 'You don't know what's involved. First, the house will be freezing – half the roof's off. Second, my brother's not in the least amusing when he has one of his attacks, he's terrifying. Third, my mother's coming back from her sister's, for the first time since my father died. Fourth, Lisa is anything but sweet. She's very shy, she wouldn't know what to say to you.'

'Brother, do you need me!' said Toby. 'Without something to lighten the atmosphere, you'll have stabbed each other by Boxing Day.'

Laughing, Angus gave in. 'All right, you bastard. Champagne, two turkeys and a present for everyone. And don't say I didn't warn you.'

Toby reached acros and gripped his shoulder. 'Thanks, mate,' he said.

167

Chapter Twenty-One

Christmas at The Court had been the same for as long as anyone could remember. A twelve foot tree was cut in the park and brought into the Great Hall, to be decorated with candles. Specially seasoned logs were put on the fires, Cook laboured for days over the food and on Christmas Eve the family drove to the village for the midnight service. They walked back across the frosty ground, each child joining in as soon as they were old enough, and when they arrived home they drank mulled wine, ate mince pies and stood around the tree to sing 'O Come, O Come, Emanuel' in parts.

On Christmas morning the farmers came and were given a drink, with gifts for their wives and children, so the family's presents waited until lunchtime. Christmas Dinner came in the evening, at five o'clock, so that the children could go to bed afterwards while everyone else had a party. But this year, the first since Henry died, there was no money and no excitement. It was as if they had all suddenly grown up, and found there was no Father Christmas.

The girls were determined that this year should be something like the ones that had gone before. The Great Hall was swathed in polythene and unusable, so they persuaded Marcus to dig up a six foot tree in the park and they all dragged it into the drawing-room through the French doors. For convenience they invested in a string of fairy lights, because candles had always been a worry. Everyone lay in bed at night and worried about the tree catching fire.

'Angus says he's bringing two turkeys,' said Lisa. 'With this friend of his. I do wish he wouldn't bring someone strange, we'll hate it.'

'We always used to have lots of people,' said Mara. She sat back and looked at the tree. It seemed rather bare, but people always had presents to put round it, and some to hang up.

She wrapped her arms around herself and went to the window. Some mornings the frost was so heavy it looked like snow, but they never had snow before January. She felt rather desperate. Jay had gone to Havenheim for Christmas, but soon, soon, she could go back to London and they would be together again! She turned to her sister.

'Where's Marcus? I haven't seen him for hours.'

'I thought he went out for a walk.'

They exchanged glances. He'd been unsettled that day, unusually restless. Mara said, 'I've got to meet Mother off the train.'

Without a word, Lisa went to put on her coat and boots, and tramped across the park. Faithful as ever, her spaniel waddled behind, grumbling about his arthritis.

She went to the folly first, because that was often Marcus's haunt. Today there was nothing, just the low, eerie crackle of frost in the trees. Fog had hung over the earth since early morning, barely lifting all day, and now at evening it sank down again, a cold, ghostly blanket. She began to call and the sound bounced back off the trees and the mist. 'Marcus! Marcus!' Nothing.

She began walking again, past the folly and up towards Slates Lane. The gypsies were still there, although the baby was long since out of hospital and the boy presumably sent to gaol. As she walked she called, until out of the mist a voice said, 'Aye.'

Her heart stopped. 'Who is it? Who's there?'

A man stepped forward. Just one of the gypsies, and she'd known they were there, she was looking for them.

'Have you seen my brother?' she asked. 'He's gone wandering.'

'We got him safe,' said the man.

He turned down the lane and she followed, stumbling on the ice in the ruts. She wondered how they lived in these short winter days, without warmth, without light. But when she came to the camp they seemed comfortable. The wagons were drawn close together, and between them they had made sack and polythene huts. In the centre was a fire, blazing up, driving away the fog. All around sat children, slatternly women, dogs, men – and Marcus. He was hunched by the fire, a sack over his shoulders, mumbling, shivering.

'He ain't well, missy,' said a girl.

'No. He's ill in his head,' said Lisa. Her spaniel, eyeing the dogs, sat on her boot.

'We found un wandering,' said the man. 'Wandering un crying – we don't know what to do with 'un.'

'It was very kind of you to take him in.'

She went to Marcus and tried to persuade him to get up. He shook his head, eyes tight closed, making a high, crushed, stammering noise. Why couldn't he be well for Christmas? she caught herself thinking. Just for Christmas! The gypsies stood around and watched

169

interestedly until at last she said, 'Could one of you help, please? To get him up?' And one of the women came to life and hauled Marcus to his feet. He calmed then, and seemed prepared to walk.

A thought struck Lisa. 'You people have been here an awful long time. Aren't you ever going to move?'

The man sunk his head between his shoulders, looking up at her under his hair. 'The gal — she say we to stay.'

'Jean Maythorpe, you mean? Good heavens! She is getting above herself. If she invited you on to *her* land I'd be more impressed.'

She realised how ungrateful she must sound when they had been so kind to Marcus. 'Don't move yet, of course,' she said hurriedly. 'But in the New Year you must. I'll have a word with Miss Maythorpe and find somewhere for you. Thank you again for your help.'

Walking back in the gloom, with Marcus stumbling and shivering at her side, she saw the shadow of a fox slipping quietly down the hedge. A pheasant clattered his way to his roost, making her start. It was such a little step from reality to imagination, before the shadows of the night became shadows in your head. She turned to her brother. 'Why aren't you cured, Marcus?' she asked dismally. 'We gave you the pills.' But he moaned and gibbered, and even the spaniel drew away.

Christmas in Havenheim was utterly extravagant. They were famous for their Christmas Fair, held in the castle grounds. There were stalls for wood crafts, wine, Christmas biscuits, toys, and every evening there was a procession in which a statue of the Christ child was carried aloft.

'There's nothing like Christmas in Havenheim,' said Anna happily. She was wrapped in fur, a short and rather dumpy figure. Her cheeks glowed like apples.

'The children love it, anyway,' said Jay.

'So do you! You used to say it was perfect,' accused his wife. 'You know you did.'

And he had. But he had seen too many Christmas Fairs, each one exactly like the last and followed by an identical Christmas. Anna's Father, Crown Prince Ferdinand, was host, Anna was hostess, and Jay was a bit part player. God, what he wouldn't give to have his own Christmas in his own house with his own family.

They went back into the castle, and all the guards saluted like toy soldiers. It was childish he knew to object to the fact that they never saluted when he was alone. So childish that he couldn't mention it, although he knew the remedy would be instant. He shouldn't need to mention it.

Anna said, 'Sometimes I wish we lived in Havenheim all the time. Don't you?'

'Not while your father's alive, dear,' he replied, with deliberate mildness. Over his dead body.

Ferdinand was waiting for them, warming his legs in front of the fire. He was tall, bearded, and insisted that a footman should always be on duty both outside and inside the door. He ignored them totally and expected that everyone else should. The door was opened, closed behind them, a chair was drawn up for Princess Anna, a drink procured for Prince John, and the footman returned to his place by the door.

'Now,' said Ferdinand, 'are you trying, Jay, to give Anna a son?'

Jay blinked. 'Is this entirely a subject for public discussion, sir?'

'Oh, the fool probably doesn't speak English. Anna tells me you're not trying. She takes her pills and you don't come to her.'

He ought to have known she'd go to her father. Anna was bred in her father's shadow, and in all her life he had never failed to give her what she wanted. Jay shot her a glance and saw that she was looking at him with an expression of deadly sincerity.

'I really cannot discuss my marital relations with you, sir,' said Jay.

'What about your extramarital ones then?' Before Jay could say a word, he went on, 'We know all about your little frolic in Scotland. A pretty girl, I believe. Perhaps even a great beauty. Next time I come to London, I shall make sure I am introduced.' He laughed to himself, a throaty chuckle.

Jay found he was trembling. It was all he could do not to leap up and strangle the man as he stood, choke the life out of him!

Ferdinand stopped laughing. 'I am well aware that this is over. You had yourself the good sense to finish it. But I will not − *will* not! − have my daughter neglected. She needs a son. Havenheim needs a son. If Anna has a son soon she need not ever rule. Her son can rule in her stead, for I shall live to be a very old man. She would like that. She would prefer it. And for Havenheim it would be best.'

Jay thought, The old fart's right. To give him his due, he was right. The admired woman in Havenheim was a wife and mother. Even the school hours were so constructed that it was well nigh impossible for a woman to have children and a job. The royal family would retain far more respect if Anna was seen to be tending to her home, if her son could rule in her stead.

'I am not a stud bull,' said Jay thinly. 'I will not perform on command. Even royal command.'

'You managed twice before. A third time should not inconvenience you,' said Ferdinand.

That Anna should be sitting listening to this was amazing. If he told

171

this story in England no-one would believe him, and if that did not emphasise the bloody foreignness of these people then nothing did. Why in God's name had Havenheim seemed so damned attractive six years ago? He'd married to be its prince, and they wanted no more of him than his cock.

He got up. To hell with restraint, to hell with good manners, to hell with the bloody footman with his ears wide open by the door! At the last moment he hung on to the coat-tails of his temper. 'In my marriage,' he said slowly, tightly, 'I will not be told what to do. If I wish to have an affair, it is my wife's concern and not yours. If I wish to father a child on her, that too is my concern, whether it's heir to this tinpot kingdom or not. And if I find that she has spoken to you about these matters again, or if you speak to me on your own behalf, then it is over. I shall not live with her. I shall not father a child. And I will shake the dust of this place off my feet forever.'

Anna began to sob, but he deliberately looked away. She deserved this, God but she deserved it! He'd believe anything of her now. Her father probably hid under the bed while they were making love.

As he made for the door, the footman opened it for him. Jay stopped.

'Do you speak English?' he said.

'Yes, sir,' said the footman.

Jay laughed.

Later he went to Anna's room. Her maid, Greta, was brushing her hair and in the glass he saw that Anna's face was blotched with tears.

'Leave us,' he told the woman. She took her time, insolently. He roared: 'Get out of here, damn you!' and she went.

'There is no need to take it out on Greta,' said Anna. 'None of this is her fault.'

'I think some of it might well be,' retorted Jay. 'She invades our privacy, she creeps around your bed like a voyeur. The madam of a goddammed brothel!'

'You would know more about that than me, of course,' said Anna.

He paused. 'How long have you known? About the girl?'

She turned her face away. 'Just yesterday. My father told me. Until tonight I didn't believe him.'

'What a pity you didn't see fit to ask me about her yourself.'

Spinning round she said, 'Why? What would you have said? That it was just sex, is that it?'

'No. No, I wouldn't have said that.'

He walked towards the window, opened the curtain and looked out. The fair was closing, but strings of lights still gleamed prettily in

172

the dark. Was he angry enough, stupid enough, to destroy her world, and possibly his? They were trapped in this marriage. 'She's very beautiful,' he said quietly. 'You can't imagine — I was never affected by looks in that way before. When the light falls on her face — she's like a painting, she could bring you to tears.'

'But you didn't love her. You didn't, Jay, you didn't love her?'

He spun round. 'You don't know how angry you've made me today. I would like to say yes, I loved her very much. But that would hurt you. And though you deserve to be hurt, you deserve to be deeply hurt, I will not do it. Those words are therefore unsaid.'

Anna's face relaxed into a look of joyous, blissful relief. 'I knew you could not! Oh, Jay, I am so sorry. My father asked me about these things, I did not want to tell him! I wanted to speak to you, but you have been cold to me, and cross, even with the children. I knew something was wrong.'

He sighed. 'I find playing second fiddle very wearing, my dear.'

'If there's something that upsets you, you must tell me! I will have it put right at once.'

'And why can't I put it right myself?'

She went rather pink. Her fingers began playing with the brush on her dressing table. 'Because I am a princess of Havenhein — and you are not its prince. If my father were dead it might be different, but he does not want it to be different. But if you tell me, the things will be put right.'

'They will do what you say, even what my three-year-old daughter says, but they will not do what I say.'

'Jay, that is so silly! What do you want that they will not do? There can be nothing.'

In the material sense there *was* nothing. But the people of Havenheim disliked him, and he would always be excluded from their life. Oh God, he thought, if it wasn't for Mara I'd go mad! He felt a wave of desire, hot and insistent, and he would not spend it on his wife. She would think she had won. And since they knew, the need for discretion was gone ...

He went to his room, and placed a call through the castle switchboard. It took minutes, the onyx of the telephone grew warm in his hand. But at last someone answered. Thank God, it was Mara.

'Hello?'

'Darling! Oh, darling, I have never wanted you so much.'

'Oh, Jay, where are you? Are you in Havenheim?'

'Yes, and going mad missing you. Look, after Christmas we'll go away, just the two of us. Abroad somewhere, Italy perhaps. Would you like that?'

173

'More than anything in the world. Are you sending me a present?'
He leaned back, grinning. 'I thought presents were too mistressy.'
'Not Christmas presents! Did you get mine? I sent it with the letter.'
'Yes, and I unwrapped it early.'
'That is terribly unlucky! You shouldn't!'
'Oh yes I should. It might have been something I didn't like.'
'And was it?'
'No. You never do anything I don't like.'

When he rang off he went to his bedside drawer and got out Mara's present. It was a book of love poems and in the front she had written: 'J. To you, for you, with you. Only ever you. M.'

He was terribly lonely suddenly. Sleeping alone, living alone, even when surrounded by people. They weren't his people, they never could be. Their jokes seemed foolish and obvious, they thought his corrupt and snide. Their generosity overwhelmed, they thought him cold, and yet he would never attack his worst enemy as he had seen them do. At the beginning he and Anna had been very close. There had been affection, on both sides. They had not known each other, they had not understood that they were essentially foreign, and different, that when they said this or that it meant neither that nor this to the other. They missed each other constantly, like bad tennis players.

He flung himself down on the bed. There had to be some way out.

Despite Marcus, despite everything, The Court began to take on a life of its own that Christmas. It was as if a great dog shook itself and determined to play, lumbering around surprising everyone. The beginning was the arrival of Charlotte, much greyer, rather more wispy and every bit as vague. The girls were on edge, feeling a threat to their independence, but it was very soon clear that Charlotte did not mean to take over. She was a dispassionate observer.

'I'd forgotten how large this house is,' she complained, returning from a sortie to her bedroom. 'All my married life it took me twenty minutes to fetch a handkerchief.'

'We should have organised the servants into relay teams, like African messengers,' said Mara wryly. 'The doctor's here about Marcus. Did you want to talk to him?'

Her mother looked anxious. The problem of Marcus was one which she had shelved again and again, and if the girls appeared to have it in hand then she was not about to interfere. 'He won't want to speak to me, will he, darling?' she asked hopefully. 'He always seemed to be the most pushy little man.'

'Lisa knows what it's all about,' said Mara. She sat gazing at the fire, her long arms spread wide along the sofa. The happiness inside

174

her seemed to bubble up as if from an inexhaustible spring. She felt as close to Jay now as if he were there in the room, and she needed not a particle more.

In the kitchen with the doctor, Lisa said, 'You can stabilise him, can't you? At least for Christmas?'

'Well. Nothing's ever certain, is it?' The doctor leaned across and squeezed her small hand comfortingly. Lisa's spaniel growled. 'What a jealous old thing he is,' laughed the doctor and Lisa managed a sick smile. 'Yes.'

This was all getting out of hand. She fixed the doctor with a piercing gaze and said, 'This stuff you've given him? He won't wake up in the night and start yelling about Them again, will he? We've people coming.'

'The knock-out pills work a treat. You won't hear a peep till morning. Possibly even lunch-time. Lisa, I've been meaning to say – '

'Why don't we have a drink? A Christmas drink? Come along, doctor, it is the festive season.' She ran to the cupboard and got out the brandy, sloshing two large measures into tumblers.

'Do call me Stephen,' said the doctor.

'Righto.'

But the drink was a mistake. It extended the visit and gave a sensation of intimacy that Lisa had not anticipated. An odd dance began. The doctor stood too close and Lisa moved to perch on the edge of the table. The doctor perched too, so she leaned on the range, and he leaned with her. Round and round they went, getting faster and faster until at last he pinned her by the door. 'Lisa! Don't keep running away from me!'

'Do let me go. This is against the Hippocratic oath, isn't it?'

'No. But you know how I feel about you, you must know!'

'You've been very kind about Marcus,' she quavered.

He looked down at her indulgently. 'And to think I once thought you such a cold-hearted little person!'

She pushed him then, hard. 'I am not a little person! You make me sound like an idiot child. Now, go and stand over there and finish your drink.'

To her surprise, he went, saying, 'What a pity there isn't some mistletoe.' He had the grace to be embarrassed, she noticed.

She said, 'I hope you're not offended, Stephen.'

'Me! Good heavens, no. A woman of your position – I should know better than to imagine you'd tolerate this sort of thing.'

'We do still function in the normal way,' remarked Lisa. What did he think she was? Perhaps he thought that blue blood was frozen to ice.

To her relief, she heard a car driving fast up to the house. 'Visitors,'

175

she declared, and pointedly put down her tumbler.

'Well. I must be off. Can't have the local quack cluttering up the place, can we?'

With that honesty that often led her astray, Lisa said, 'I'm always very glad to have you to clutter us up, actually. You're so good with Marcus.'

'You don't know how glad I am to hear you say that.' She opened the door wide, but he stood planted before her.

Angus, coming through the herb garden, called out: 'Hello, Lisa! Not having a heart attack, are you?'

Rescued, she beamed at him in relief, and Toby, bringing up the rear, saw her at her best. A small, thin, almost waiflike girl, clearly in need of help. Something in him responded.

He pushed past Angus and unceremoniously elbowed the doctor aside, dumping bags and cases on the floor at Lisa's feet. He seemed to loom over her, huge, smelling of the cold night and petrol. 'How d'you do?' said Toby. He stuck out his vast hand and Lisa tried to shake it. Her fingers disappeared completely, leaving just one small stained thumb wiggling in view. She felt helpless. 'I didn't expect – well, you're so big!'

'I'm not much bigger than Angus.'

He was perhaps only a couple of inches taller, but Toby was built like a tank while Angus had all the length and leanness of his forbears for generations past. Next to Lisa, Toby suddenly felt clumsy.

The doctor, at under six foot quite eclipsed, said petulantly, 'I was just leaving. If you'd excuse me.'

'Did you want to kiss her goodbye?' asked Toby, and Lisa's face flamed.

'No of course he doesn't! He's the doctor!'

'But you might know him very well.'

'Not that well,' said Lisa hurriedly. 'Goodbye, doctor. Stephen. I'll telephone at once if there's any change.'

'Call on me at any time, my dear. Any time at all.'

At last, he was gone. Lisa fell into the kitchen and sank into a chair.

'Bloody cheek!' said Angus. 'You've been encouraging him, Lisa.'

'I can't be beastly to him, I need him for Marcus. Anyway, he wants to marry a title. He'd make up to a horse if it had one.' She ran a hand through her hair. It needed washing and hung in limp hanks round her face. She was acutely conscious that peeling chestnuts had stained her fingers and that her jeans were covered in woodash. 'Mother's home,' she said, justifying herself. 'It's been a busy day.'

She got up to brew tea and Angus said, 'We had a fantastic drive up. Toby's got a Porsche. We hardly touched the brakes right up to Leeds.'

176

'Really?' Cars did not impress Lisa. She had no mechanical bent whatsoever, taking an age to learn to drive, though like all the children she had learned at fourteen on the estate.

'Marvellous car,' said Angus

'I do hope you're not going to be tedious and spend all your new lolly on a bright red boy racer.'

She could feel Toby watching her, following her about with his eyes. Angus shouldn't have brought someone they didn't know, already it had made things awkward. She set down two of her wood slice table mats and topped them with mugs of tea. Then, because the table looked rather bare, she took an arrangement of dried grasses from the window and added that, and as an afterthought a deep blue bowl filled with home-made biscuits.

'You have made that pretty,' said Toby.

Lisa flushed and Angus said, 'She's always fussing. How is everyone?'

He meant Marcus. Lisa said, 'Not too good. Had an attack last night.'

'Bad?

She shook her head. He had been controllable, which was the main thing.

Toby was watching them both, his big head moving from side to side, following the conversation. 'Don't you want to say hello to your mother, Angus? Or your sister?'

Angus grinned. 'You want to get a look at Mara. I'll go and hunt them out.' He went off, leaving Lisa and Toby alone.

For almost the first time in his life, Toby was lost for words. This little, plain, somehow refined girl intimidated him. She fought her shyness with such brittle courage. 'I've got the feeling I'm making a lot of work, descending on you like this,' he blurted.

'Not at all. I like cooking. Did you remember the turkeys, by the way?'

'Yes, I did. They're free-range, probably tough as hide.'

'Probably.'

He laughed and she felt stupid. He was making her stupid, far more than usual. She ought to meet more people, she wasn't used to it. Taking the initiative she asked, 'What is it that you do exactly?'

Smoothly, as if reciting, he said, 'I've a holiday complex. Hoping to start another, I'm here to raise finance.'

'But you've been here months, Angus says. You must be doing something else.'

He was completely surprised. There was silence where his reply should be. But to his relief, Angus opened the door and called, 'Come on through, old chap. I'll introduce you to everyone.'

Toby went out quickly, almost galloping. Lisa followed more slowly, wiping her hands down her jeans. Like everyone else, he was sure to be bowled over by Mara. She felt tired suddenly, and dispirited by the amount there was to do. Toby would need sacksful of food to maintain that massive frame. She wondered what she had said to upset him.

In the drawing-room, Toby perched on the spindly-legged sofa, a fragile piece that felt as if it might break under his weight. Charlotte engaged him in polite conversation. 'Australia is such a fascinating country. I went there on my honeymoon, you know. The High Commissioner was charming, I remember. I do believe he took us to the Melbourne Cup.'

'Really?' Toby looked as if he thought she might be making it up.

'Mara, dear, do you know anything about Australia?' asked Charlotte, wrinkling her brow.'

'He may be a colonial but I don't imagine he only wants to talk about the place.' Mara smiled at him, and Toby grinned briefly.

'You know us colonials,' he said. 'In all that space we don't get together often enough to have much conversation.'

'So I imagined,' said Charlotte.

The fire was dying down. Lisa went across and began to sort out a fresh log. 'Here! Let me do that.' Toby put his hands lightly on her waist and moved her aside.

'I can manage, honestly,' she said stiffly.

'Of course you can't. We colonials are brilliant hewers of wood. Why don't I see to the fires while I'm here?'

'How very practical of you,' said Mara with a yawn.

That night they ate supper in the kitchen. Marcus stayed in his room and Angus and Mara took turns taking trays up to him. Lisa served green pea soup with home made bread, beef in red wine with shallots and deep fried garlic mushrooms. The pudding was jam roly poly, served on to plates so that each swirl of pudding nestled in its own clear circle of jam.

'You make everything look so nice,' said Toby. 'I can't believe it.'

'Thank you.' Lisa tucked her hair behind her ears, and then wished that she hadn't. It was so schoolgirlish.

'That's why everything takes so long to arrive,' grumbled Angus.

'Was Mrs. Matthews the cook who always served cold food?' enquired Charlotte. 'Or that other one?'

'It certainly wasn't Mrs. Matthews,' said Lisa. 'She was brilliant. It's only now I realise it.'

They finished with cheese, and went into the drawing-room for

178

coffee. Lisa wandered back to the kitchen and began clearing up. It was quiet and warm, with soft hushing noises coming from the range as logs disintegrated into ash. She picked up the rake and flicked open the firedoor.

'I said I'd see to the fires.' Toby was standing in the doorway.

'I didn't think you'd remember this one.'

'First one I thought of.' He came across and commandeeered the poker, raking the fire through with decisive strokes. He left a bed of glowing wood, then tossed logs on to it in a tight stack. 'That should keep till morning.'

'Yes. Thanks.'

How she hated being alone with people she didn't know. Even the doctor wasn't as bad as this. 'What did you think of Mara?' she asked suddenly.

'What am I supposed to think?'

Lisa shrugged. 'That she's lovely. Irresistible.'

'I must be made of the wrong stuff. Don't get me wrong, she's a lovely girl. Very pretty. Not very soft, though.'

'What do you mean? Soft?'

He picked up a pile of plates and dumped them in the sink. 'Sort of − vulnerable. There's a girl that doesn't need anyone to stand between her and the world. She's got it sized up, and she can do what she likes with it. Not a weak spot anywhere.'

'Oh, she has,' said Lisa. 'I mean − you wouldn't know, but − well, she's terribly in love. It makes her quite miserable.'

'And I bet she enjoys every minute.' He turned on the taps and started to fill the sink. 'And how come her fingernails are perfectly varnished? Yours are like a navvy's.'

'I suppose she hasn't got used to not having help.'

'Well, it's about time she bloody well did get used to it! Get in there and sit down and have some coffee. You can talk to your mother, the rest of us will do the washing up.'

'You needn't look at us as if we chain Lisa in the cellar to work,' complained Mara, as she and Angus were herded out to the kitchen. 'She just never waits for anyone else to get round to things. Do it at once, that's her motto, and it gives her appalling indigestion.'

'You shouldn't let her do it at once,' said Toby.

'I can see you won't!' Sighing, Mara reached into a drawer and delicately pulled on a pair of rubber gloves. 'She likes being competent. It makes her happy.'

He gave her a rather jaundiced look.

179

Chapter Twenty-Two

Christmas Eve brought a flurry of preparation. Angus and Toby cut armfuls of holly and the girls made red ribbon bows so that sheaves of the stuff could be stacked on the kitchen dresser and stood in wicker log baskets with the bows arranged like flowers. Out in the woods, loading their haul on to an old forester's sledge, Toby stopped to look down on The Court. It was framed for him like a Christmas card itself, turrets and battlements, arrow slits and gargoyles. Even the polythene flapping above the Great Hall could not spoil it for him.

Toby turned. 'Thanks, Angus,' he said abruptly. 'I shouldn't have made you bring me but I'm damned glad I did. If I'd known it was like this, I wouldn't have dared ask.'

'Glad you came actually,' said Angus. 'You do indeed lighten the atmosphere. Though I think we'll all be driven insane if Mother insists on talking to you about kangaroos. She only knows two types of Australian: one dines with the High Commissioner, the other with Crocodile Dundee.'

'I struck out with the High Commissioner,' admitted Toby.

The sledge was full and he wrapped the rope around himself, hauling at the front while Angus pushed from behind. They proceeded steadily across the frosty ground. In the house, watching, Charlotte said: 'What a splendid type of man! So willing.'

'Like a horse' murmured Mara. 'I wonder what he talks to Angus about.'

'Very little,' said Lisa, adding a bow to a growing pile. 'I imagine that Angus talks to him. And he listens to everything.'

Even Marcus attended midnight Mass. He insisted, fretfully, and Charlotte gave in. Lisa knew that it wasn't sensible, but with Toby there she wouldn't argue. He made her uncomfortable, she had the feeling that he was watching them all, making his own private notes.

180

'Put on your coat, Marcus,' said Charlotte, and when he didn't obey her immediately, she cried shrilly, 'Will someone make him put on his coat!'

'I'm not an idiot,' said Marcus sullenly. Lisa went to get his coat, sensing Toby's criticism. He thought Charlotte ridiculous, with no strength or consistency. He thought they all pandered to her. His thoughts were infectious: once or twice Lisa found she was thinking them herself.

They drove down to the church, Lisa and Mara crammed in Toby's Porsche, the rest driven by Angus in the old car. The night was cloudy, with few stars, and a breeze stirred up fallen leaves like living creatures in their path. Lisa wanted to go to bed. She blinked and widened her eyes, trying to keep awake and revive her Christmas spirit. Mara was humming, a low, contented sound. That afternoon a messenger had roared up on a motorbike, to deliver a small, weighty package wrapped in gold. It lay now beneath the Christmas tree, waiting.

They parked and got out. The cold began to wake Lisa up a little. She yawned and stamped her feet. Toby said, 'Have my gloves.'

'No thank you. I'm not cold.' She went ahead into the church.

The light of candles, the hush of many people knelt in prayer. The organ playing softly, without any real tune, like Mara's humming. Holly and Christmas roses, and lilies at the font. Charlotte thought of Henry's funeral. All the things that had gone wrong since he died. She couldn't understand it. Before, everything had been perfect. And now nothing was.

The Hellyn pew was at the front, and lined with cushions. Angus held his mother's arm, guiding her, and Lisa took Marcus's hand. Toby was left with Mara, and people nudged each other and nodded, thinking that he was her young man. It irritated them both. They knelt briefly to pray. As soon as they sat up, the organ lifted its voice. The service began only when the Hellyns had arrived.

Ancient carols, ancient prayers. So many years in which Henry had sat with them, warming Mara's hand in his pocket, giving everyone sweets. On this first bereaved Christmas they all thought of him. And they prayed, every one, for Marcus, and themselves.

They sang, finally, 'O Come All Ye Faithful', a crashing bellow that rolled around the stone walls like a wave. The vicar roared the verses, beating the organist by a short head on every line. The congregation split, those who disliked the vicar keeping with the organ, the vicar's contingent bellowing with him. In the end the organist defeated everyone, playing bass notes loud enough to drown the devil himself. When at last it stopped, the air trembled.

181

Everyone gathered in the churchyard to wish each other Merry Christmas. Last to leave, the Hellyns made the rounds, shaking hands and acknowledging good wishes. Toby tagged along, bobbing in the wake of Hellyn prestige. Lisa felt him watching them, forming a judgment. She wished very much that Angus had never invited him.

Suddenly she spotted Jean Maythorpe. She went across. 'Jean? I thought it was you. Merry Christmas.'

'And to you.'

'About the gypsies. They seem to think you've given them permission to stay.'

Jean crammed her red wool beret firmly on to her head. 'Angus said they could. We discussed it.'

'I think he meant that they needn't move at once. Obviously they can't stay forever, it's unhygienic for one thing. There's only so long all those people can keep popping behind the nearest hedge. They'll probably get typhoid.'

It was an argument that took the wind from Jean's sails somewhat. Nonetheless she said, 'Trust the Hellyns to find some very good reason for evicting them! You don't give a damn about their welfare really, you just want them to be someone else's problem.'

'I wouldn't mind at all if they were yours, actually. I said you'd find them somewhere else. They can stay till then.'

Taken aback, Jean flared at her, 'And this is a fine way to start Christmas. Evicting those poor people without a second thought! It's damned disgusting.'

'Have you tried to find anywhere else for them?' Toby's voice cut across both girls. Jean said stiffly, 'Not as yet, no.'

'Been taking advantage of the Hellyns then, haven't you?'

'They've got more than anyone else,' retorted Jean. She turned on her heel and stalked off, the red beret defiant.

Lisa laughed ruefully. 'And they've got millions! However little money we have, everyone still thinks we're rich.'

Looking down at her, Toby said, 'But you are! With the house, and the land.'

'And the loans and the mortgages. We can't make nearly enough to pay off the debts. We don't pretend to be hard up, we damned well are! And if you're going to tell us about our treasures, we've got nothing of any value except the tapestries, and they are so incredibly valuable that they can't be sold. Belong with the house, you see.'

'Show me. In the morning, show me.'

He really was the most presumptuous man. 'I'm far too busy. You'd better ask Mara.' She turned away, and went to exchange the obligatory few words with the vicar.

Walking back across the park, saying little, Lisa let her mind wander. Perhaps they were rich, not in money but in power. However long the Maythorpes lived here, however much they contributed, they could never match the Hellyns. They carried the weight of centuries. Take tonight; in the beginning some tough Hellyn lord had threatened mayhem if the service began without him. Today, it was a treasured tradition, and the Hellyns were obliged to turn up to allow it to continue. Their existence gave the village, and its people, an identity, a sense of times past and times to come. No-one else could give it that. And if the Hellyns themselves could no longer sustain that existence, if they needed or wanted to change, then the chain would be broken. Something complex and irreplaceable would be gone.

Marcus stopped in front of her. He put his head in his hands and began to wail, softly keening. Charlotte said, 'Oh no. Not tonight, surely. Lisa, can't you do something?'

Lisa went to her brother. 'Have you got a pain? You'll be better at home, love.' She reached up to pull his hands away, but he shrieked and cowered. Angus put an arm round him. 'Come on old chap. Come on home.'

'I can't, I can't,' wailed Marcus.

Charlotte said petulantly, 'I thought the pills were supposed to stop all this. Why on earth can't you be sensible, Marcus? When you promised your father you'd behave.'

'I don't think he's doing it deliberately,' snapped Toby. 'The poor guy's frantic.'

'Do try to mind your own business,' said Mara thinly. 'Come along Mother. We'll go home. The others will see to him.'

Toby couldn't believe the desertion. He waited until Charlotte had disappeared into the gloom, then he said, 'That's his own mother! He's like this, and she leaves him!'

'She isn't very capable, I'm afraid,' said Lisa. 'Look, why don't you both go on. He's better just with me.'

It wasn't true. At moments such as this Marcus barely noticed other people. Angus said, 'You should never have brought him, Lisa. You could have guessed this would happen.'

'You heard Mother. She agreed.'

'I hardly see that as of the greatest importance. My God, you'd think we could get Christmas over without something like this! You go back Toby. We could be hours.'

'No, I'll hang around,' he said. He took a deep breath, puffing out clouds of steam. He seemed to be savouring the night, the cold, the rising mist, as much as any hot summer's day.

Angus let his impatience rip. 'I don't think we need to hold a party.

If you're not back in half an hour I'll have to 'phone for someone to bring the car up from the village. So for God's sake try to get him home!'

He walked away, swallowed up almost at once by the night and the mist. Marcus began whimpering to himself, but when Lisa tugged at his arm he went rigid. She sighed. Sometimes this could take hours. She settled herself down on the ground, huddling her knees to her chin, to wait till the spasm passed.

Toby said, 'You shouldn't let them do this to you. They dump on you like a load of babies.'

She let out her breath. 'Mother can't cope, she never has. Probably because she never had to. We had nannies, and then we went away to school, all of us. And Father liked her to ignore Marcus's little problem. He thought it was some adolescent phase.'

Toby laughed. 'Like masturbation.'

She said nothing. He realised that he had embarrassed her very much. He stood over her, gazing down at her narrow head. 'You know, you're far too young to be left out here in the dark, on your own with a lunatic. And you do it. I can't believe it.'

'Which one's the lunatic?' retorted Lisa in a clipped voice. She got up. 'Come on, Marcus. We must hurry, or the dog will be worried. If they let him out he might come looking for me and get lost. Come on, old chap.'

To her relief he began to walk, stumbling a little. Toby took hold of one arm and Lisa the other. They were all frozen, and Lisa's teeth were chattering. 'Have my gloves,' said Toby.

'No thanks.'

'Damn you, girl! Have the bloody things.'

She struggled to put them on as they walked. Then she said, 'You shouldn't shout. It doesn't help Marcus.'

'And you shouldn't bloody well annoy me. Will you put on a dress tomorrow? I'm sick of seeing dirty jeans and a wool skirt that doesn't fit.'

'You've only been here two days. I've been busy.'

'Nobody's *that* busy. You trail around like a poor relation.'

'We're all poor relations, we just don't have any richer ones to sponge off.'

She felt ruffled. He was bullying her for some odd reason of his own, and she wasn't used to it. She said, 'It isn't my fault if Mara doesn't like you.'

'Why the hell should I care if she does or not? She's a bit of a cow, if you ask me.'

'You don't mean that.'

184

'Bloody hell, Lisa, of course I do! And I don't fancy her either – she's all tits and arse.'

There was a faint glimmer of moonlight, lighting the grass to a pale silver grey. 'Don't you like girls?' asked Lisa, thinking perhaps he was homosexual. Perhaps that was why he was so odd.

She heard him chuckle. 'Of course I do. You know I do.'

'What sort of girls do you like then?'

She saw the flash of his teeth. 'Just at the moment it's thin, little delicate ones. With long, superior, aristocratic noses that make them look like very well-bred fawns.'

Her breath caught in her throat. 'I think you're being quite dreadful,' she said stiffly, and clung tight to Marcus's arm.

At last they reached the house. Marcus tried not to go in, and Toby manhandled him through the door. 'Don't be so bloody rough!' snapped Lisa.

Mara, who had made cocoa and was waiting for them, said, 'Please don't pick up his habits, Lisa, darling.'

'I didn't think Australians had a monopoly on swearing,' retorted her sister, and went to warm her hands at the range.

Toby said, 'I'll put him to bed if you like.'

'Would you?' Lisa was suddenly dropping with weariness. It was so late, she was so tired and so confused. Her last act must be to slide the giant ham into the range, to leave it simmering overnight. Then, regardless of anything, she would fall into bed.

When she woke she lay cocooned in warmth. She turned her head against the pillow, blissfully, and reached down to snuggle the covers more closely about her ears. Her hand touched the silky edge of an unfamiliar bedspread. She stared at it, her eyes too close to focus properly. It was one of the spares that they kept in the blanket chest in Toby's room.

Lisa flung out of bed, shuddering in the cold. She would have to lock her door. What had he been doing, sneaking around her while she slept? What did Angus know about him? He might be a murderer – anything.

It was early but she couldn't sleep any more. She ran a shallow bath, because the water was always tepid nowadays. A wood fire lacked the power to heat vast quantities. She sat splashing herself, feeling goosepimples like a rash on her arms and legs. Cold as she was, she stared down at her own body. Thin, yes. But delicate? Narrow wrists and ankles, blue veins just under the skin. And breasts that were no more than goosepimples themselves.

Lisa got out quickly. She was shy of her body. At school she always put on her clothes in the shelter of her dressing gown. Her face in the

185

glass over the basin caught her attention. A fawn, had he said? She had large, heavy-lidded grey eyes, but who would notice them beside that nose? He must be the only man in the world who could admire it, but then his was crooked, as if it had been broken at some time. All in all, he had a rough, cheerful sort of face, he looked like a man with no time for indecision or cowardice. And she was always undecided. And quite often afraid.

She dressed defiantly in jeans and a sweater. But as the most subtle concession, she caught her hair up in a ponytail and tied it with bright red ribbon. And she put the merest touch of mascara on her lashes, so little that she was almost sure no-one would notice it. And then, when she went down, he was in the kitchen before her. They were alone.

'Good morning, Lisa. I've done the fire. Did you sleep well?'

She glared at him. 'Did you come into my room?'

'Sure. Your door was open. You looked cold, I fetched another cover.'

'You had no reason to come near my room! What did you want?'

His face was ingenuous. 'To say goodnight to you. You were knackered, I thought you might have gone to sleep in a chair or something. If you did that in this house you'd wake up dead.'

'I'm sure Angus must have told you it isn't the most comfortable home.'

'He said it was cold, but he had two lovely sisters, one of them nice. You were the nice one.'

She blushed then, and banged the kettle on to the range. Toby said, 'I've made a pot of tea.'

'I prefer Earl Grey,' she snapped.

'That's what I've made.'

She poured herself a cup and stood sipping it. If she held it near her face and closed her eyes, the steam played pleasantly on her eyelids. The smell of the ham filled the kitchen, making her hungry, though she never ate breakfast.

Her dog, let out by Toby, was scratching to come in. She went to open the door but he stopped her.

'Just a minute.'

'What?' He was standing in front of her, very big and male. He wore a dark green hairy sweater.

'I want a Christmas kiss.'

Her cheeks began to colour again. 'I know perfectly well why you're here — to size up the place. Are you an antique dealer? I don't think you have to make up to the family to quite this extent.'

'I'm not out to rook you. And you know what I think about you. It shows in every supercilious flick of your head.'

186

She was blushing furiously now, and the dog was whining and scratching at the door. 'Let me get to that door, please.'

'Just as soon as you kiss me.'

He took hold of her shoulders and she ducked her head into her chest. His face came down to hers and she turned her cheek this way and that, until her head fell back. His lips fastened to her throat, she felt his tongue, licking her. She cried out. His mouth came down on hers.

It was an invasion, vile sensation forced into her mouth. His tongue was huge, like a giant piece of muscle. The kiss went on and on, his breathing quickening, the hands on her shoulders moving rhythmically. She tried to pull her head away, but his mouth pressed down, trapping her. She closed her teeth on him.

He pulled back, instantly. After a second blood began to run over his lip. He closed his eyes for a moment, and when he opened them he laughed. 'My God! You might be small but you've a helluva bite.'

'What on earth are you doing this for? Why don't you leave me alone?'

She flung herself at the door and let in the dog. He bounded up to her and she bent down to hug him. Toby said, 'Show me round, will you?'

'No. You're a bloody vulture. You want to pick pieces off the carcase, whether it's quite dead or not. Holiday complex indeed!'

'I have got a holiday complex. It's worth about three million dollars. And I've got a yacht, five cars, four houses and a small chain of restaurants.'

'I don't believe you.'

He shrugged.

Lisa began furiously to assemble breakfast, spreading a cloth, putting out bread and cereals, orange juice and yoghurt. 'Did you want porridge? I'll make you some.'

'OK. Can I ask you something?'

'What?'

'I bought you a scarf for Christmas. Can I change it and buy you some clothes?'

She turned with the pan in her hand. 'But − of course you can't! I don't need any. And you can't look smart at The Court, it's too cold.'

'It doesn't have to be like this. You don't have to shuffle around like a Russian countess after the Revolution. You choose to.'

To her horror, her eyes filled with tears. 'Why don't you shut up? There's no use pretending. You're making up to me to get your hands on the silver, or the chairs or something.'

187

'Oh, for Christ's sake! It's not the furniture I'm interested in. It's the house.'

Angus came in, muffled up in an Aran sweater. 'Good God, Lisa, what's the matter? Are you peeling onions this early?'

'Yes. Yes, I am,' she said and turned back to make the porridge. Toby stood three feet away, watching her, and that was annoying. It advertised that something had happened. But at last the porridge was made and she could serve it, and Toby moved away. Angus looked from one to the other, wondering if he should say something. But then Mara came in, and Charlotte, and the moment was lost.

Marcus got up in time for the dinner. He had slept for most of the day, and when he woke, with one of those changes that so disconcerted, he was diffident, humorous. Everyone got dressed up, Mara in a luxurious white cashmere sweater with a glittering, beaded neck, Charlotte in a warm red tartan dress. Lisa wore neat navy blue, and navy blue stockings with flat shoes. She looked like a child.

Angus opened champagne and poured glasses for everyone. 'Some for me, old chap?' queried Marcus. His smile slid off the end of his mouth. Angus poured him a glass, quickly, although he was up to the ears with pills. He didn't want a scene, not now.

'Let's open the presents after dinner,' he said suddenly.

'But we never do that.' Mara could barely wait to see what Jay had sent her.

'Let's do it tonight.'

They agreed, doubtfully, wondering why. Lisa went to put on her apron.

She excelled herself that night. The turkeys were succulent with crisp brown skin, the stuffings piquant and interesting. A gusty wind rattled rain on to the windows, and they piled logs on the fire and opened another bottle. Angus set the pudding alight, and carried it round the room in a blaze of blue flame. No-one could look at the Stilton.

Afterwards they sank into lethargy in front of the fire. The champagne, mixed with Marcus's pills, made him drunk and sleepy. Angus put him to bed. There was nothing now to stop them opening the presents.

'Open your surprise, Mara,' advised Charlotte. 'Who is it from?'

'A very good friend of mine.' She took up the parcel, balancing it on the palm of her hand. The gold paper was smooth and even, and it was tied with a complicated bow of gold string. She tugged the end of the string. As it fell off the paper began to unfold. Inside was a jewelbox, dark blue embossed leather.

'Go on, then,' said Angus.

188

The catch was delicate, a small gold lever set into the leather. Mara struggled, found it, and flicked it with her fingernail. Inside, on a bed of velvet, was a ring.

'Oh my God!' said Lisa.

'Is that real?' asked Toby.

'Darling, you can't accept it. Who is this man? You'll have to send it back.' If Charlotte was firm about anything it was the impropriety of such gifts: one huge solitaire diamond, that fractured the light into greens and blues and silver. The setting was elaborate, a web of plaited gold on a thick gold band.

Angus took a deep breath. 'Mother's right. That's not something you can keep.'

'I don't think it's up to any of you to decide,' flared Mara. 'It's mine.' Quickly she slipped it on to her left hand. 'That's where I shall keep it.'

'No,' said Lisa. 'People will talk.'

'You are not to keep it,' said Angus. 'Mara, take it off at once.'

'But who sent it? Who is this man?' Charlotte was utterly bewildered.

Mara got up. She wouldn't sit and be questioned. Angus caught her arm. 'I didn't mean to talk about this now, but if I must then so be it. Send it back, Mara. Send it back and have done with him.'

She glared at him. 'I'll to what I damn well like, thank you, brother mine. You're only my brother, not my keeper.'

'Can't you have a little thought for someone other than yourself for once? You're dragging our name into the muck, behaving like a common prostitute!'

'Angus!' Charlotte was outraged. 'Don't you dare say such things to your sister. Mara would never do anything dreadful.'

Mara cupped her hands over the ring. 'It isn't dreadful to love someone,' she said shakily. 'It isn't dreadful to want to be with them. All he wants is to give me something special, because he loves me and we can't be together. I might as well tell you, Mother. He's married. But he's going to get a divorce. It's difficult because of who he is, and that's why he's sent me this ring. It's a promise.'

'Or a payment for services rendered,' said Angus.

Mara drew back her arm and hit him across the cheek, her fingers clenched into a fist. Charlotte screamed and Lisa got up and ran between her brother and sister. 'Stop it, stop it both of you! We can talk about it tomorrow.'

'There's nothing to talk about,' said Mara shrilly. 'It isn't anything to do with anyone but me. I love Jay and he loves me, and we'll go on doing that whatever anyone says or does. If I was married and had an affair with him you wouldn't turn a hair, so you're nothing but a lot of damned hypocrites!'

She turned on her heel and ran out of the room. Angus dabbed painfully at his swelling cheek. 'She'd make a wonderful boxer,' he said, trying to laugh it off.

'Angus, you must stop her,' said Charlotte urgently. 'Your father would never have stood for this. He used to say she'd make a brilliant marriage.'

'Well, he would,' said Lisa. She surveyed the remaining presents. 'Are we going to bother to open these or not?'

Dutifully they exchanged gifts. Toby gave Lisa the silk scarf. 'I'll buy you something else as well,' he offered. 'Something you'll really like.'

Charlotte said, 'Mr. Ledbetter, this evening may have misled you. We don't expect vulgar extravagance at Christmas.'

'What about tasteful extravagance? I think Lisa could do with some.'

It was as much as Charlotte could stand. Squabbling, violence, with no-one to make the beds or tidy the rooms, Mara disgracing herself and Angus bringing this terrible man to witness it – she gathered her shawl around her and went off to bed.

'I'm sorry, Toby,' said Angus.

He leaned luxuriously back in his chair. 'No worries, mate. Happens in the best of families.'

'We are the best of families,' said Lisa. 'Though if Mara goes on like this, we won't be for long.'

'Who's the bloke? Do you know him?'

'Yes.' Lisa tried to avoid her brother's eye. 'Oh, there wasn't any point in telling you, Angus. He came here once. We can't do anything, no-one can. Mara does what she wants. And he'll leave his wife and there'll be a terrible scandal and in the end it won't matter a damn.'

'If he does leave his wife,' said Angus. 'But knowing Mara, he will.'

He felt depressed suddenly. Problems and difficulties seemed to crowd in on him. Marcus, his job, and now Mara, hellbent on trouble. He drank a whisky and wished that Marcus was still up. When they were boys they had talked about everything, their lives had been lived in tandem. It was lonely like this. He got up wearily. 'Put the guard on the fire, won't you? No point in burning the place down just yet.' He went off to bed.

Lisa and Toby were quite alone. She sat silent, watching the logs fall into caverns of red fire. The wind roared in the chimney, like a

190

thousand ghosts. Toby said, 'Lisa, I want to see the tapestries. You promised.'

'Not in the dark. And not with the wind blowing, the polythene rattles.'

'You're not scared, are you? I'll hold your hand.'

She looked at him then. There was something about him that made her relish his company, and something too that made her afraid. But she couldn't now go off to bed and leave it at that. 'All right,' she said.

They walked in silence down the corridors, up the passages, in and out of doorways. Their feet clattered in the empty spaces, through huge rooms, galleries, solars. Toby stopped now and then, opening doors at random, to find perhaps a bathroom, or a panelled study, or a bedroom with Chinese wallpaper peeling off in the damp.

'It's horrible, left like this,' he said suddenly.

'We're supposed to have dozens of ghosts.'

'Not surprised. Does it affect your brother, do you think?'

Lisa shrugged. Toby was coming to recognise the gesture, there was something very Gallic about that shrug.

She turned a corner, and marched down a long hall. At the end were the doors to the Great Hall, and she tugged on the huge handle without waiting for Toby. He put his big hand over hers. 'Let me do things like that for you. I don't like to see you struggle.' His palm burned against her cold hand. They turned the handle together.

In the Hall she flashed a torch up to the roof. Rain was beating on the polythene, and the wind tore at it, sounding like a hurricane. She showed the beams, new wood spliced into the old. All the banners stood drooping against the wall, tattered and filthy. She touched one and fragments fell away into dust. 'One day we'll get them restored,' she said.

'If you wait much longer, they'll have fallen apart.'

They went on into the galleries. Of all the people she had brought here over the years, friends of the family, relatives, Professor Chandler, not one had made the entire inspection without comment. Toby did. They went from hanging to hanging and he said nothing. All the glory of past lives, that seemed to her pictured for them, as if by some wonderful magic, moved him not at all.

At the end she said, 'Well. That certainly inspired you.'

'You don't need me to tell you they're fantastic.'

'Are you going to offer us money? We won't sell, of course.'

In the dim light his face was no more than a blur. She began to feel nervous, in the dark, surrounded by noises, and this big man looking at her. 'I keep wondering if the Hellyns were always this stupid,' he

191

said suddenly. 'They can't have been. There must have been someone with some sense to build this, keep it. And here you all sit, like dogs with the guts bred out of you. Waiting for it to rot.'

She was taken aback. 'We do what we can. It's too big, you don't understand.'

He said, 'All it takes is some courage. You've got that, more than the rest put together. Can't you see what a priceless, precious thing you have here? People should see it, they *need* to see it. And you're going to open the door on Wednesdays, let a few old ladies trail around in the filth and the cold?'

'We'll close in the winter' said Lisa, shrilly.

'So in winter it's back to this, is it? Dying by inches. Letting the house die. Watching the loans eat up everything, hoping for the best. Selling a bit here and a bit there. How long before the tapestries have to go? Five years, ten? If you don't do something Lisa, soon there'll be nothing left.'

She wrapped her arms around herself. 'I wish you wouldn't say things like that,' she whispered. 'Of course we'll have to go in the end. It isn't a real tragedy, but to us it seems like one. We've been here so long, you see. I hate to be the generation that lets everyone down.'

'I knew you'd understand. I knew you were the one.' He ran his hands through his hair and went on excitedly, 'I've thought of something. I admit, when I first came I was going to buy the place. When I saw it I knew it wouldn't work. The world doesn't need a hotel this big, or a conference centre or anything I could make it. But it's special, these hangings are special.' He let out a breath, and it formed clouds. 'I want a partnership. You put up the house, I put up the money. We'll do up some of the house, do it up fabulously. And we'll take guests.'

'You said you didn't want a hotel.' Lisa was bewildered.

'Not a proper hotel, no. More a sort of house party. You'd entertain them, just like friends. People staying, who happen to pay. You wouldn't have to bother about them all that much. You'd have staff again, of course. And the way you do things, Lisa, you make everything look like class.'

'Do I?'

'Yes. Oh, Lisa, Lisa, I never met anyone in the world like you before – ' He caught hold of her and dragged her towards him. She dropped the torch and heard it break, and he put his hands in her hair and pulled her head back to kiss her. She closed her eyes and let her head fall back, wondering how she could let this happen when she knew it was all for money. He was so big. She had an almost claustrophobic feeling of helplessness.

192

'Stop it. Stop it!' She tried to push him away, but he was ten, twenty times stronger than she. Unless he wanted to let go there was nothing she could do to make him. Suddenly his big hand closed on her breast. Her nipple went rigid with shock, and he rolled it against his palm, murmuring, 'Lisa, Lisa! Oh, my darling girl.'

'No!' She struck out at him, pathetic little attempts at freedom. For long seconds he held on, refusing to believe she didn't want it. Then he let go.

'Bastard! Creep!' She was shaking with heat and emotion. She turned and ran for the door, and began to run back through the house. After a moment she heard him running after her.

She knew her way and he didn't; he saw her disappear out of each gallery the moment he arrived in it. When he called her, his voice echoed in the empty spaces, sounding alien, frightening. She fell into the drawing-room. It was warm, quiet. No-one was there.

Lisa crouched by the fire, spreading her hands to the logs. The man was a fool, a rogue, he wanted to fill the house with strangers who would look at them all and laugh. When he came in her head jerked up, as if she expected him to hit her. He closed the door, quietly, and came to the fire.

'I'm sorry,' he murmured. 'I wouldn't ever hurt you.'

She shook her head. 'It's my fault. I never could bear to be cuddled. When they gave us a lecture about sex at school, I was sick.'

He sat on the floor in front of her.

'You don't have to make up to me you know,' she said. 'If I like your scheme, I'll like it whatever you do.'

'Will you? Why don't you like me and the scheme together?'

She shrugged. 'I might. Have you really got the money, Toby? It would cost a fortune. And we'd have people here all the time.'

'If I don't have to buy the place, I can afford it,' he said. 'I thought we'd do up the medieval rooms and this just for now. You'd have a separate sitting-room and so on.'

She looked earnestly up at him. 'I'd hate people all the time. Forever.'

'Honey, it needn't be forever. Just for now, we'll make some money. We'll draw up an agreement. When you're rich you can buy me out and go back to rattling around like peas in a drum.'

She kept thinking of the problems. 'But we'd have to entertain them as if they were house guests. I'd be far too shy.'

'Of course you wouldn't! And your mother would be marvellous. A real Countess to impress the visitors.'

'It would work if Mara was here,' agreed Lisa.

'For Christ's sake!' His face was an inch from hers, dark red, with

193

spittle at the corners of his mouth. 'Why are you so timid? She's one sort of glamour, you're another. I wish — I just wish you could see yourself! OK, she's beautiful. Like a big, golden dog. And you're a little, thin Italian greyhound, all nerves and big eyes. Some people don't like big dogs! They like fragile ones. That need cossetting, and cuddling, and keeping warm — '

She turned her face away. After a moment he said, 'Well. You certainly know how to give a bloke the cold shoulder.'

'I didn't mean to! Really I didn't. Actually I like you an awful lot.'

'But you don't like me kissing you.'

She swallowed. 'I might,' she said slowly. 'When I know you a little better.'

His face split in a relieved smile. 'Is that all? I'm a bull at a gate, I should be ashamed of myself. You — you make me lose my head.'

She laughed because it was ridiculous. How pleasant she found it, sitting there by the fire, when she knew he wasn't going to touch her. Firelight played upon his face, like warpaint.

'Why are you two sitting here in the dark?'

Lisa turned and saw Mara. She had been crying. The ring still sat defiantly on her finger.

'We've been talking,' said Lisa. 'Toby's got the most brilliant idea. He's going to invest some money in the house so we can take guests, a sort of paying house party. I'm going to run it.'

'You? My God, Lisa, what are you talking about?' Mara put her hand to her mouth, and caught her lip on the ring. She breathed on it, taking in some sense of security, some sense of Jay. Since Henry's death everything was changing, even Lisa. She said, 'He isn't at all the sort of person we want here, Lisa. I couldn't understand why Angus brought him. He's got no conception of the way we live. Do you want to live in a house with jacuzzis and fitted carpets?'

'My God!' Toby flung a hand up to his head. 'A fate worse than death!'

'We've got to do something,' cozened Lisa. 'We can't go on chopping up trees for the fires.'

'We are doing something, we're taking visitors! We're going to have notices everywhere saying "This way to the Great Hall", and we'll serve tea at fifty pence a cup.'

'It won't make anything,' said Lisa. 'It's a sop to persuade the Historic Buildings people to stop the place falling down. This way we're doing something. Oh, Mara, you must help persuade Mother. It's the best idea anyone's ever had.'

Mara snorted. 'Are you sure it's the idea and not his Australian playboy charm?'

194

When she had gone Lisa got up to follow her. It was very late, almost two. From the trees across the park came the hoot of a tawny owl, and then the harsh cry of his mate.

Toby said, 'This place is another world. You ought to share it.'

She swallowed. 'I'm sure they'll come round. I'll do my best, I promise.'

He had a sudden sense that he must stake his claim. 'But you will try to like me? There's a chance that you will? I don't want to do it otherwise.'

Her heavy-lidded eyes stared at him. 'That's blackmail.'

'Is it? I know what I want, Lisa. I might not be the cleverest bloke in the world, but I know what I want and I never change my mind.'

She drew away from him. 'I don't like to rush into things,' she said.

'You're rushing into this hotel thing.'

'Isn't that different? That's just business, it isn't the same.'

He looked down into her clear face, so white, so pale. He thought that he was probably making the biggest mistake of his life.

Chapter Twenty-Three

The Boxing Day meet was to be held at the Maythorpes'. Only Angus and Mara rode, since none of the horses was up to Toby's weight. But he followed on foot, taking the short cut across the fields, crashing through ditches and streams with hearty abandon and causing Mara to curl her lip whenever he chanced in view.

'I think this is a lesson, Angus.' She offered Toby a chill shoulder and turned into the Maythorpe drive. 'Don't ever bring a creature like that home again. Not only does he try and price the furniture, he's tiresome and embarrassing.'

'Don't you think it's a good idea then? About the house?'

She grimaced. 'No, I do not. He's doing it to flatter Lisa. She seems to have an amazing ability to impress the lower orders with her aristocratic disdain. And, of course, she's only shy.'

'He does seem rather smitten. But I can't banish the thought that he's had something like this in his mind from the moment he met me. He could be any sort of a profiteer. We ought to get the money from someone we know.'

'The whole idea is stupid. We shouldn't give it a moment's thought,' snapped Mara. She couldn't understand why they didn't see how dreadful it would be. It was bad enough having to open the house at all, but she knew Toby wouldn't rest until everything was spoiled. He was that sort. To him The Court was just a problem, an investment opportunity, he saw nothing special in the dust, the ancient pall of neglect. He thought it would all be fine brightly polished and good as new. His ruthless scrubbing brush would decimate the place. Besides, what would Jay think if they were running some kind of a guest-house? He would never be able to come near her.

Angus sat his horse on the periphery of the crowd, and drank two stirrup-cups in quick succession. How could he put his mind to schemes for The Court when he had to go back to work and face

196

Stanley Westerley? Nothing much had happened in the pre-Christmas lull, but he had been left in no doubt of what was to come. A test was coming up, and he was like a man in the condemned cell, waking every night from dreams of escape. The first false move was the one you shouldn't make, if he did as they asked he would be forever in thrall. The market was well down, there was no money to be made by honesty. The whole business sickened him.

Slumped in gloom, he became aware that Jean Maythorpe was approaching. As usual her horse's mood bordered on the manic, it skittered and fussed constantly.

'Angus! I wanted to talk to you.' The horse swung round and tried to rear, but as usual she hung on. Although barely in control she never seemed to be aware of it. Her nerve disturbed Angus, he doubted very much that he could do as well.

'If it's about the gypsies, I don't want to know,' he said coldly.

'Of course it's about the gypsies! Your sister says they've got to go. And the only place I can find for them is an absolutely grotty site halfway to Hull which the council's trying to close. So I think we'd better put in some sort of chemical lavatory, don't you?'

'What? In Slates Lane?'

She nodded, bright-eyed with defiance.

'You can put your chemical loo where the monkey put his nuts.'

He swung his horse round and into the throng, determined to get rid of her. She followed, bashing into people and lurching against a pony. Its child rider started to cry. 'Will you stop, Angus! Look how you're upsetting people.'

He pulled up. In a low, vicious voice, he said, 'I'm not in the mood, Jean. I warn you, I am just about at the end of my tether, and if you dare say one more word about gypsies I shall strangle you with my bare hands!'

She looked taken aback. He wondered how it was that she could force him to lose his temper so easily, and then was so hurt. 'I'm sorry,' he said stiffly.

'Did you have a bad Christmas, is that it? We had a terrible time after my mother died, we didn't know what to do with ourselves. I expect it's like that, isn't it?'

Angus looked at the opulent Maythorpe house, every inch of its double-glazed rooms cluttered with furniture. Everything they owned was new. Even the antiques had been restored to sparkling freshness, as if they were made last week. Perhaps death mattered to them more, he thought. The Hellyns were balanced on a pyramid of death. They sat on its top, the few survivors, and beneath them lay centuries of Hellyn bodies. In contrast the Maythorpes were new-minted. The past was lost to them, except in the odd family story and memory of a grandparent. When a death came they adjusted to it as if it was the first, they had no tried and tested formula. But the Hellyns knew what to do. They went on, as they had always done, and didn't care.

Jean was watching him, her round face puzzled and rather anxious. 'Is it your brother?' she asked suddenly. 'Is he bad again?'

He shook his head and then thought, Yes, let her believe that. He said, 'I suppose it must be that. Hardly ever seems to be his old self. One notices it more, at Christmas.'

'Yes. You must.'

They trotted together to the first covert, letting out a reef across the first field. Jean's horse corkscrewed and her hat fell over her eyes. 'Stop it, you bugger!' she cursed.

Angus grinned. She had almost no imagination. It cheered him up. She was her father's daughter, as ebullient and opinionated as Reg himself.

Mara went home after an hour or so, and Angus assumed that Toby had gone as well. When he saw him on the moor, mud-splattered and panting, he rode across.

'Didn't think you'd keep up. We've come some distance.'

'Don't I know it! First thing, I'll buy a horse and ride out.'

Angus slid down to the ground, leaning on the hot neck of his horse. Hounds had lost the scent, they were covering the heather like hoovers. 'Are you serious about The Court? Exactly what do you want to do?'

Toby grinned, showing flat, square teeth. 'We can't go on meeting like this!' he declared, and Angus had a strong urge to hit him.

'Will you stop playing the fool!' he snapped.

Toby eyed him. 'I play anything I damn well like, Angus. I think you should remember that.'

Suddenly it seemed as if they hardly knew each other. Angus said, 'I'm not asking you to become involved at The Court. It's our home, we have a right to take it seriously.'

'It's my money, and I can be as stupid as I like with it. I made every penny myself, which is more than can be said for you. But like I told Lisa, I'll put forward enough to do up some of the house. I'll advertise for guests. We'll employ staff, but the family will do most of the entertaining.'

'Who gets the profit?' asked Angus.

'I do. It's my investment. The family gets to live in their home for free. And you'll have to keep the Wednesday visitors − that way we still get the grant for the roof. My guests won't mind. They'll see it as really living like a lord, open house and all.'

198

'I want a share of the profits after three years,' demanded Angus. Toby scratched himself, clawing at the thick mat of hair inside his shirt. 'Make it five and you're on. It'll take that long to recoup the investment.'

'Very well. Five.'

Toby withdrew his hand from his shirt and held it out. Angus had no wish to take it. He felt deceived, tricked by a pretence of friendship. But good manners prevailed. He shook hands.

'There you go then,' said Toby. 'Nothing like a fucking colonial to liven things up. Be more grateful, Angus. It ain't every day you get dragged out of a hole.'

'You think I'm a bloody fool, don't you?'

Toby considered. 'Yeah, you're not sharp. But why should you be? No-one ever started out that way. If you'd been where I've been, you might have learned the same lessons.'

Somehow Angus doubted it. Hellyns had made money and Hellyns had lost it, essentially from doing the same things. They seemed incapable of adapting to changing times; they stayed in the same place, in the same tired soil, generation after generation. And he wasn't the man to break the mould.

Hounds found and took off towards Hell Rocks. Angus swung up into the saddle again, and Toby swore and spat. Angus looked back at him from time to time, and saw him labouring doggedly in their wake. Jean, whose horse was tired at last, said, 'You've got to hand it to him. He keeps on trying.'

'He thinks I've had a cushy life,' remarked Angus.

'So you have.'

Rage took him by surprise. As hounds swept on past the rocks he leaned down, grabbed Jean's bridle and hauled her out of the field.

'What are you doing? Let go! Angus, let go!'

He kicked on, dragging her weary horse on outstretched neck. It was dark in the lee of the rocks. The sound of the hunt faded across the moor. 'You think you're so bloody clever! You and your fat father, what do you know about hardship? When do you have to do things you hate, live a life you despise, just to keep things going? And you can do as you like. Be what you like. Today's hobby is good works, tomorrow it's bloody flower-arranging! Don't you think that I might like to be that free?'

She put her head on one side. 'You don't like your job.'

That was, after all, the bottom line. 'Yes. I don't like my job.'

'Dad always says you shouldn't put up with anything you don't like. You should get out, whatever the consequences, it always works out best in the end. And it must be foul being a stockbroker, just

199

pushing money around. You ought to be doing something that does someone good.'

The headache that had been nagging at him all day suddenly seemed to clear. 'You must think me very muddle-headed,' he said.

'I don't know about that. It's difficult to think straight when you're in the middle of something.'

He saw his opening and went on the attack. 'Glad you realise it. It's time you understood that the gypsies have to go. They're travellers, and if that's what they choose you haven't the right to stop them.'

'They can't stop travelling if someone doesn't help. They can't even read. Now, if the Hellyns had got to grips with this in the past there wouldn't be any need for all this today. It's your fault entirely.'

'You cannot dump all their problems on me! I've done more than my fair share, it's time everyone helped.'

Jean tossed her head. 'You haven't done anything. A bit of tolerance, that's all you've contributed.'

He was looking at her, smiling, as if somehow she delighted him. She felt uncomfortable suddenly. He said, 'Come out with me tonight. We can have a drink somewhere.'

'You'll not soften me up,' she said breathlessly.

'I won't try. Pick you up about eight?'

She nodded.

The hunt was long gone, and it was getting very dark. They both turned their horses for home. Jean glanced at him once or twice, letting her eyes linger on his long, slim thigh. Oh God, she thought, Oh God. In the dark, in the car, would he kiss her? She wanted it more than anything in the world, more than anything ever. And all he would do was walk beside her into the pub and sit and talk about the bloody gypsies in that way he had, hardly opening his mouth, flattening every word. He didn't see her as a woman at all.

Angus picked her up sharp at eight. There had been a scene at The Court, and he hadn't wanted to delay. Charlotte had taken against the country house scheme, and she and Mara threw their combined weight into its opposition. Angus argued, Lisa argued, and Toby, slumped in a kitchen chair, went to sleep holding a glass of whisky.

'That vulgar man!' declared Charlotte.

'He was a fine figure of a man two days ago,' remarked Lisa, and Mara snarled, 'Trust you to take his part. You don't have to believe every word of flattery, he's got more than a little to gain you know!'

So he'd been glad to get out. He put on his battered sports jacket with the leather patches on the sleeves, and his cord shooting trousers.

To his amazement, Jean appeared in the Maythorpe sitting-room wearing a dress of tight black lace.

'Where the devil are you going?' demanded Maythorpe, looking from one to the other.

'Nowhere special,' said Jean, making pointedly for the door.

'Then get back and put on something warm,' declared her father. 'Weather's bitter. Enjoy your run, did you, lad? Fair nithered I was when I got back in.'

'It was a good day, Mr. Maythorpe,' said Angus stiffly. The hunt was running on oiled wheels since Maythorpe took over, but it irked him to admit it. Nowadays all you needeed was money, it seemed.

Jean was waiting to go. Angus gave her father a polite nod and withdrew, but on the way to the car Jean said, 'You don't have to behave as if you're dismissing the waiter. He's my father. You should be polite.'

'How dare you correct my manners!'

She sniffed. 'I don't like you giving him the brush-off. He notices and it hurts him. I know he's an old fool but I love him, and I won't have it.'

Absolutely punctilious, Angus held open the car door for her.

'Madam.' She didn't smile. As he got in, Angus said, 'Your father's right, you know. You look quite lovely but you'll freeze.'

'I've got my wrap,' said Jean, pulling a shawl around her shoulders.

'Did you want to go somewhere special? I thought perhaps the Carpenters' Arms.'

She nodded. 'Fine.'

Everyone stared when they went in, but Jean marched defiantly to a corner table, daring Angus to be embarrassed. But of course he wasn't. The Hellyns did as they liked, and expected others to accept it. Jean could have worn a bunny suit and Angus would merely think it odd. They'd have come to the Carpenters' Arms just the same.

She wished that she'd worn something more sensible. The dress had been tight when she bought it, but then she'd meant to lose weight. Sitting down was very uncomfortable. And she was wearing her father's Christmas present to her, a pair of large diamond earrings. It occurred to her that Angus might think them in extremely bad taste.

'What would you like to drink?'

'Sherry, please. Dry.' She preferred it sweet, but dry was more sophisticated. Angus had a scotch, and they sat sipping their drinks in silence. Jean crossed her legs invitingly, and was amazed at herself. What was she doing here trying to impress this man? If he said he only liked blondes she'd be out of there and into the bathroom with the bleach before you could say peroxide.

'Have you been to Slates Lane lately?' she demanded. 'They really are getting themselves organised. They're running a television off a car battery.'

Angus sipped his scotch. 'Any lingering charm they may have possessed for me has now been destroyed. The last thing they need is a television. They're lazy enough as it is.'

'At least the children can hear people talking,' defended Jean. 'They have this terrible thick accent, no-one understands a word the little ones say. And they'll see the way other people live.'

'Shooting each other and drug peddling!' Angus laughed. 'You really are incorrigibly optimistic. Tell me – ' he leaned his elbows on the table ' – how's the politics? Have you been taken up as a candidate yet?'

Her face became wary. He said, 'Go on, you can tell me.'

'I suppose I'll have to. I was rejected. They've taken on a woman from a factory, the union convener there. Thick as a brick but with the right socialist credentials.'

'Poor Jean! Tarred with the brush of affluence.'

She glared at him. 'I knew you'd make fun. Dad did too. But I want to help, I want to do things! They said I should get a job doing something worthwhile, otherwise the voters wouldn't stand it.'

'And will you? Get a job I mean.'

She shook her head. 'I can't you see. I can't leave Dad on his own. If I was a candidate I'd have to, but it seems to me there's no point in trying to do good to people you don't know if you do bad to people you do. There isn't any useful, politically conscious work round here.'

'Except bothering me about the gypsies.'

She grinned. 'Well. You deserve to be bothered. It makes you think.'

She was right. Jean made him look at himself, at his life. He said, 'Next Monday I'm going to hand in my notice.'

'Are you? I knew you should. They're all sharks in those places, I'd hate to see you turn into one as well. What are you going to do instead?'

'Actually – I thought I might stand for Parliament.'

Her eyes widened. He saw her fingers gripping the stem of the sherry glass until he thought it would snap. Then she stood up, picked up her shawl and stormed to the door. Angus followed, completely disconcerted. 'Jean! What on earth is the matter?'

Outside in the car park, with drizzle blowing in the yellow glow of

202

the arc lights, she turned on him. 'You bastard! You smug, privileged bastard! What will you campaign for then? State maintenance of the aristocracy, complete with Rembrandts and butlers? How about a levy on taxes, so that women who work in canning factories can know they're supporting people like the Hellyns on their country estates? Of course you're bound to get the seat. Who wouldn't want this aristocratic sprig to grace their constituency? It'll be all your bloody friends on the selection committee for one thing!'

'That isn't what I want at all.'

She was rigid with scorn. 'It wouldn't sound like that, isn't that what you mean? Wrap it up in soft language. Campaign for the government to help with cleaning paintings, and it will just so happen that all those paintings will be in the hands of people like you, for the pleasure of people like you. Just like the opera, and the ballet. Why don't you hold string quartet concerts at The Court, then you can get the Arts Council to shore up the walls!'

He was appalled. 'I don't know why you hate me so much.'

'I don't hate you. If you must know, I adore you! But I just wish you would think.'

They stood, looking at each other. Jean put her hand to her face, horrified by what she had said. She tried to laugh. 'Oh God, just look at me. All dolled up in lace and diamonds, making a complete fool of myself.'

'Would you like to go on somewhere? We could find something to eat, I imagine.'

'Thanks. I'm not hungry.'

She went to the car and Angus rushed to open the door for her. He hadn't locked it, and that in itself typified the gulf that lay between them. If the car was stolen he couldn't afford another, yet Jean, who could afford a dozen, would never leave a door unlocked. Tears were clogging her throat, she knew that if she said one more word she would sob. Angus still held the door, looking down at her.

'Did you mean that? About − what you felt?'

She nodded. Everything was ruined, what was one more brick on the pile?

He got in the car and drove off in silence. Jean realised they weren't going back, he was going up on to the moors. He pulled off the road, heather scrunching beneath the wheels. She wondered if they would be stuck there.

As the engine died he said, 'I ought to explain − this job in the City, I got it a damn sight too easily. The senior partner knew my father. He was his broker, actually. They're a very flash firm, most people seem to have fast cars and boats. I never thought to ask why.

I assumed either they'd been there much longer and earned a great deal more than me, or it was family money. Of course it's nothing of the sort. They're crooked, through and through. Stanley Westerley — that's the senior partner — he's suggested that it's time I joined in. They set up little coups now and then, and one's coming up after Christmas. If I stay I have to do as I'm told. If I leave no doubt there'll be a few words in certain quarters, letting people know I'm as dotty as my brother. And if I turn them in there's no certainty that anything can be proved. But I'd be certain never to see another job.'

'Bloody hell!' said Jean, with feeling.

'I'm going to leave,' said Angus. 'I decided this afternoon, talking to you. It's the lesser of all evils. And I always meant to go into politics. I took it at college, you know. I mean, obviously I'll have to start at the bottom, but at least I'd be working at the right thing. I was a lousy stockbroker.'

Jean turned in her seat to look at him. 'You need the money though.'

He grinned. 'You'd be amazed at what turns up. I think I've been let off the hook. Toby's got a scheme under way to turn The Court into an upmarket hotel, complete with resident earl. The family can live almost free and the farm rents should just about service the loans. If it takes off we might eventually make something. So I've decided to try and find someone to take me on in London while I sniff about trying to find a decent seat.'

'It could take years,' said Jean. 'You're far too young.'

'So are you. Didn't they tell you that?'

She nodded. 'That's why I'm telling you. Oh, Angus, forget what I said. I'm proud of you, even if you are going to be a Tory with a paunch!'

'You'll have to keep a close eye on me and stop me running to seed!'

He put his arm awkwardly along the back of her seat. His other hand landed like a squid on her knee. 'Are you going to try and seduce me?' asked Jean in a high, breathless voice.

'Yes. Yes, I was actually.'

'Oh. Well, go on then.'

His hand slid up the inside of her thigh and he turned to kiss her. She tasted of sherry and bread, her mouth gaped wide under his. He touched her crotch and she moaned gently. 'You've done it before, haven't you?' he asked.

She nodded. 'Only twice, though. He was married and I didn't know. I didn't love him or anything, I just wanted to do it.'

They kissed again, but this time she pulled free. 'What about you?

There must have been lots of girls at Oxford.'

'Not many,' he said quickly. 'Well, quite a few. I'd go to parties and get pissed and jump into bed with anyone who'd have me. Damn stupid. Comes from being locked up at boarding school for years. The first time a woman lifts her skirt, you go crazy. By the way, are you on the pill?'

'I'll go on it tomorrow if you like. Let's take a chance.'

'God! Are you sure?'

She nodded. At that moment pregnancy attracted her like a loaded gun. If the bullet struck home everything would change. The shot would blast across the chessboard, scattering the pieces into new and different patterns. There was the spice of danger.

They began to struggle out of their clothes. Angus dragged Jean's dress down to her waist, hauling on the zipper. She had neat, pert breasts, round and firm, like the rest of her. He unfastened her bra and began caressing her, rather inexpertly. At college he'd always been too drunk to care what he was doing. 'Will you please get on with it?' groaned Jean suddenly.

'I thought women liked to wait.'

'I don't care what you thought, I want it now!' She wriggled out of her tights and pants. Angus tried to pull her across the front seats, and then found the gear lever in his way. They began to laugh, hectically trying to manoeuvre arms and legs into matching positions. Her head was down against the toor. As he lay across her he saw that her face was turned away, eyes shut.

She came within seconds, convulsing rhythmically. Angus felt a great sense of power. She could have done nothing that pleased him more. He was miraculously free from constraint, free to wallow in pleasure, with no lingering doubts about what he should or shouldn't have done. It felt absolutely right.

Afterwards, everything seemed different. She lay across his lap, naked, legs apart, utterly relaxed. Her pubic hair was darker than that on her head. He teased it into spirals and curls.

'I'll come round in the Land Rover tomorrow afternoon,' he said. 'You won't be in danger from the gear lever, we can do it in the back.'

She yawned. 'I'll go to the doctor in the morning. You can pick me up after lunch. We can go and see the gypsies, fight, and then make it up like this.'

'Let's make it up again.' His fingers strayed down between her legs. She writhed. It was too direct, she didn't like it. Much better for her the slow grinding of two bodies one against the other. She wondered if she should tell him that she'd never come before tonight. He wasn't so brilliant a lover either. It was just that ever since she first saw him she'd longed for this, she'd lain in bed and sweated thinking of it. He could touch her anywhere, even on her elbow, and at once it became an erogenous zone. It made her rather ashamed.

A car went past on the road while they were locked together. It lit them brilliantly but neither of them so much as blinked. There was a cocoon around them, a brief shell of fascination.

London was at its worst in January, a maze of grey streets, funnelling a vicious wind. The taxi drivers drove bad-temperedly, wipers constantly fighting a sleety rain. The shops looked sad, their Christmas decorations suddenly tawdry.

Angus arrived late on the Monday. He had given notice at his flat and registered with a couple of agencies, hoping to find somewhere cheaper. When he arrived at the office, he was chilled through. He stood in the sumptuous foyer, his wet shoes soaking the thick blue carpet, enveloped in expensive warmth, and almost gave in. He thought, The broad road to hell is not paved at all, and certainly not with good intentions. It has deep and luscious carpeting, and on either side stretch acres of polished desks, with friendly faces and solid brass table lamps. If he went to his desk now there would be no acid comments about lateness, and at lunchtime everyone would gather for a pleasant meal, cooked by the daughter of one of Stanley's many friends, and they would crack a bottle of decent claret.

It would be so easy to give in. 'Resign tomorrow,' whispered a voice, 'It doesn't have to be today.' But if he didn't do it now he never would. He turned and strode up the stairs to the executive suite.

Stanley's secretary was leaning languidly and glamorously across her desk. She wore Hermès scarves and Gucci shoes, but her manners had the slightly rough edge that meant she had learned them rather late. Her father was a pork butcher in Morden, and he had spawned a daughter employed by Stanley because she was not only bright but also unscrupulous. She beamed at Angus. 'Hello, Angus. Have a good Christmas?'

'Yes, thank you. May I see Mr. Westerley, do you think? It is rather important.'

She grimaced, pressed the intercom button and carolled, 'Angus Hellyn to see you, Mr. Westerley. A matter of some importance.'

Nonetheless he kept Angus waiting ten minutes or so. The secretary said, 'How is your poor brother?'

'Quite well, thank you.' He picked up a copy of *Horse and Hound* and pretended to read it.

'You must be so anxious, having mental instability in the family. And especially in a twin!' She laughed merrily.

206

'I'll let you know if I intend to start climbing the walls.' Angus was icy cold.

She put her hand up to her mouth. 'Oh dear, have I blundered? Perhaps it's something you don't like to talk about. I mean, when you get people like the Yorkshire Ripper wandering about mad, it must turn an awful lot of heads your way, don't you think? He looked so normal. It could have been anyone. Even you, Angus.'

Angus thought how much he would love to wring her neck. She had a smile like a piranha fish. Stanley buzzed for him and he got up and went in. The office was a symphony in pink carpet and dark wood, with small original oils grouped in clusters on the walls. Stanley reclined at a vast desk, repellently new and shiny. Angus thought how intensely Lisa would dislike the place. What on earth had possessed him to work for someone who had such grandiose ideas in decoration?

'Angus! How was the country?'

He had the wild notion of replying, 'Well sir! I have put down the revolt! The Marches are quiet once more.' But his only revolting peasants were the gypsies, and they were contemplating a move to an inner city rubbish dump. Under the influence of Jean, he had relented and said they could stay.

'Very well, sir,' he replied and then wished he'd omitted the 'sir'. It was the public school training. Put him the wrong side of a desk and subservience throttled him.

'What can I do for you? Important, was it? Do you need a loan?'

Angus cleared his throat. 'Not exactly, Stanley, no. I'm afraid I've come to hand in my notice. Over Christmas I've thought about it and decided stockbroking isn't quite what I'm looking for. I'm finding I have rather a lot of family commitments just now.' He wondered if he was being cowardly. He ought simply to say he didn't fancy being a crook.

Stanley leaned forward helpfully. 'Good Lord, Angus, surely you know how flexible we can be? We're not one of your nine to five sweatshops and if you need a freer schedule I'm sure we can come to an agreement! We don't find people of your calibre on every tree, now do we?'

'I'm sorry, Stanley. I've quite made up my mind. I'm thinking of going into politics.'

There was a pause. Then Stanley put back his head and roared with laughter. 'Politics! You? It would be like throwing a baby among lions. You'll never get a seat and you'll starve even if you do. Have some sense, boy. Make your fortune first and then play your games. In your position, you can't afford this sort of thing.'

207

'It's up to me to decide what I can and cannot afford. I'm sorry, Stanley. I'd like you to accept a month's notice from today.'

The older man leaned back, looking at him. All the false bonhomie was draining away. 'I see,' he said at last. 'Obviously this is unexpected. And, if I'm honest, as I feel I must be now, Angus, you haven't done so well in your time with us. A very erratic performance, erratic in the extreme. But, we were prepared to give you time, for your father's sake. He was a client of mine all his life.'

Grimly, Angus said, 'So I understand. What a pity his investments did so uniformly badly.'

'You can't put the blame for falling markets on my shoulders.'

'Not for the markets, no.'

Stanley got up, indicating that the interview was at an end. 'One month it is, then. Let us know if you want any references. We'll say what we can, of course. I'll put the word round that you're looking out for something rather less taxing.'

'Is there any point in asking you not to?'

He smiled. 'None at all, dear boy. None at *all*.'

The cold wind in the street felt clean and fresh. Angus drew in great gulps of it, trying to counteract the slime that seemed to cling to him. Westerley wallowed in it, and Angus despised his own gullibility. He should have seen it from the first. But he was furious with himself for antagonising the man, it had been an unnecessary self-indulgence. He wouldn't work today, he decided. The notice could start tomorrow. Today he would get round and try and find a job. If he could put his side of the tale before Stanley's rumours began, he might be in with a chance.

But he felt sadly in need of comfort. He went to his club, finding instant solace in the somewhat shabby warmth. When he had come here as a child with his father he'd hated the place, he couldn't think why anyone would want to spend time where you couldn't shout or run or play games. Now it closed about him like a warm and familiar cocoon, sheltering him from the world and its unpleasantness.

He took coffee in one of the rooms, warming his hands in front of the fire. The brass fender gleamed with polish, though the leather on its top was cracked with age. A sudden gust of wind slashed sleet against the windows and Angus grinned to himself. He felt better already.

'You're looking cheerful, Angus.'

He looked round. It was Nicholas Branbury, a man of about fifty, and Lisa's godfather. Angus was delighted. 'Hello, Nicholas! How are you?'

208

'Better out of this godawful weather. My arthritis is playing up.'

Angus glanced at his hands, gnarled and swollen-jointed. 'You ought to go to the sun,' he advised.

'Can't afford it, old thing. Four girls still at school and so pretty I'll have their weddings to pay for in no time. You still working for Westerley's mob?'

'No. I handed in my notice this morning. Not well received, I'm afraid. I'd like to get out of stockbroking altogether and get into politics, but it's not going to be easy. Stanley's keen to be as difficult as he knows how.'

'Always thought the man was a shit. Used to tell your father the same, but he wouldn't listen. Thinks he's God, does Westerley. Look, Angus, I'm lunching here today. There might be one or two people that could help you. Will you leave it with me? I can't promise anything very grand.'

'Just at the moment I'd be grateful for anything. He rather gave the impression that I might never work again.'

Branbury snorted. 'Bloody conceit of the man! Don't you worry, Angus, he's done more than enough damage for one lifetime. About time he came a cropper.'

Angus's relief spread and grew until he was wrapped in a glow of well-being. He had felt so alone, and he was nothing of the sort. Those of his class protected each other, they stood together and defied outsiders. Westerley, for all his flash bravado, could never wheedle his way into this charmed circle. He glanced quickly at Branbury's mild, plump face. Perhaps the tide had turned for him. Perhaps at last he was starting on the right track.

Chapter Twenty-Four

The interior of a Rolls-Royce always smelled special, thought Mara. She snuggled down into the fur to which she had treated herself. Leather, fur, silk ... she thought of the creatures who had died to cosset her so, and felt rueful. What a pity that pleasure had to be gained so bloodily, in everything.

There had been a terrible scene at home. For once no-one believed the easy lie, they all suspected the truth. In the end she screamed, 'All right! I am going to him, and I don't care who knows it. And you haven't the right to stop me. It's his money we've been living on for the last three months!'

'Mara! Is that true?' Charlotte had gone white.

'Yes,' she said defiantly.

'Angus was right. That is prostitution. You cannot possibly take money from someone like that, it's utterly, utterly wrong!'

'We had to have money from somewhere. For God's sake, Mother, we had to live!'

'There isn't any point in rowing,' said Lisa. 'Why don't you just go? Nothing we say is going to make you change your mind.'

So she went, Charlotte refusing to speak to her.

She was going to spend the night with Clare Payne. The thought soothed her, more than she understood. They had an odd, shifting relationship – rivals, friends, enemies – with none of that inbuilt antagonism that scarred her dealings with her mother. With Charlotte, the bridges of understanding that should have been built over the years simply weren't there. In a perverse way Mara was glad that her mother knew, that she was angry. It was a small revenge for years when she looked the other way.

Her father would be ashamed of her. A fierce blush started in her belly and worked upwards. She put up her hands to cover her burning face. But it wasn't her fault! She loved Jay, and he loved her, and

210

besides, weren't the family ruining everything, letting strangers trample about The Court, wrecking it? Since Henry died home had become a place of turmoil, with no rest or peace anywhere. No wonder she was running to Jay. The hot blood in her face began to recede. She dropped her hands and tried to compose herself. Of all people, her father would have understood.

They were coming into London. The sky was dark, lowering, full of snow, but the shops were bright and cheerful, all with 'Sale' signs in the windows. God forbid that she should ever become one of those women who haunted sales, rummaging desperately through rail after rail of tired pre-Christmas stock, trying to save money. As far as Mara was concerned there was never anything worth buying until at least March.

The front door of Tavistock Square opened with a flourish. Mara ran up the steps, thanking Jennings with a smile. Clare, coming out of the sitting room, almost blinked. The girl was radiant, the gold of her fur reflected in her eyes. Her excitement was almost tangible.

'Mara, dear — I didn't expect you to arrive in quite such style.'

'Didn't you? Jay sent a car for me, he hates me to rattle about on trains.'

'Yes.' Clare led the way into the sitting-room and closed the door firmly. 'Samuel has asked me to speak to you.'

'So I imagine.' Mara smiled at her. 'Please don't mind, Clare. Obviously everyone has to try very hard to get us to be sensible and stay in our proper little boxes. And we won't, of course.'

'You — you've seen him since September.'

'Yes. And we've written and telephoned.' Instinctively her right hand went to the ring on her left. She fingered it.

Clare's eyes followed the gesture. She swallowed. 'My dear — I'm not at all sure that the prince is within his rights in giving you that ring. Samuel mentioned to me — it has become known — it's one of the royal jewels of Havenheim.'

'Is it?' Mara looked at it in surprise. 'I imagine Jay feels he has a right. After all, that silly little kingdom has done its best to beat him down. They don't consider him at all. So they do owe him something, Clare.'

The older woman walked to the window, jerking the curtains shut, although normally she left that sort of thing to Jennings. She felt the need to exclude the world, to ensure that no-one heard what she was about to ask.

'Is he going to leave her, Mara? I have to know. Samuel says — he believes — that it would unsettle the Havenheim throne. There isn't a son yet, and of course she couldn't divorce. The monarchy would

211

lose face. Mara, it could be that Havenheim would become a communist enclave on the German border, and God knows, there's been more than one war started by something far less trivial!'

The girl snorted. 'What absolute rubbish! She'd be a fat little queen, and she's got two fat little princesses to follow after her. They'd be glad to be rid of Jay actually, he has no real role there. They bring him out on ceremonial occasions, like some embarrassing spare part. He's hilarious about it.'

'But is he going to leave her?'

Mara fingered her ring. 'I don't think I want to discuss that. It isn't something Jay and I have discussed. I shall fly to Italy tomorrow and he will be there. We'll have a holiday. After that we might have some idea of what we want to do.'

When Mara had gone to her room Clare sat, her fist pressed to her mouth. The affair bubbled at the edges of public consciousness, and every day more and more people knew. That no-one had spoken out was due solely to the closed nature of their world, which instinctively turned its back on journalists. It was said that even the princess knew, and this trip to Italy might have been calculated to flaunt it in front of her.

Samuel was waiting for her to telephone. He snatched up the receiver almost as soon as it began to ring. 'Clare? What did she say?'

'Very little, I'm afraid. But I can't imagine that he'll spend two weeks in Italy with Mara and come back determined to go back to his wife. She really is so – so happy!'

Samuel's voice cut in sardonically. 'My dear, we can do without sentiment, don't you think?'

Clare snapped, 'No, we can't. The princess has clearly made him absolutely miserable. She has no-one to blame but herself.'

'For God's sake, Clare! I am relying on you to talk some sense into the girl! This romantic twaddle helps no-one.'

'How fortunate that *you* are so sensible, Samuel,' she purred nastily. 'You never have to consider people's feelings. Goodbye.'

She slammed down the receiver. If Samuel wanted her to attempt to influence Mara he would have to ask her nicely. He seemed to think he could come to Tavistock Square as and when he chose, satisfy himself in bed and the very next day yell at her down the telephone. He kept her isolated from his particular circle of friends, brought her dull presents and nagged about Mara. But, in one of those stupid twists of circumstance, if he asked her to marry him she would accept at once and forgive him. If he wanted to behave like a husband he should become one, but if he wished to remain a lover he ought to learn the rules. One did not take one's mistress for granted.

212

Mara left for the airport early in the morning. Clare saw her off, and suddenly Mara thought how like mother and daughter they must appear. Clare's elegance, that in Mara became glamour; the barbed conversation. 'Please don't do anything you're likely to regret,' hissed Clare.

'I can't tell what I'll regret. I have to do what I feel like, and so does he. Be pleased for me, Clare! I'm so excited.'

'How I wish you were marrying Jimmy Carruthers.'

'But you know we'd be miserable!'

Clare smiled ruefully. 'Not at once, perhaps. And you wouldn't be so very miserable. Whereas this — ' She tailed off, helplessly.

Afterwards, when Mara had gone, Clare went back to bed and tried to sleep. A sense of doom hung over her. Suddenly she wished very much that she had tried harder to persuade the girl not to go. She would have failed, of course, but it would have been better to try.

She was still dozing when Samuel arrived. He stormed up to her bedroom, barging in without knocking. 'My God, you can't have let her go!'

Clare gathered up her dressing gown and began to put it on. 'I wasn't aware I was supposed to chain her to the bed. How dare you come in like this, Samuel!'

'You knew I wanted to talk to her. It was vital.'

'What ever makes you think she would have paid you the slightest attention?'

Clare slipped off the bed and rang the bell for her breakfast. While she waited she did her hair with the silver brushes on her dressing table. Outwardly calm, inwardly she seethed with rage. Samuel was utterly perplexed. 'What is the matter with you Clare? Don't you see how important this is?'

She cast him a cool glance. 'Everything appears to be more important than good manners, it appears. Since when have you had permission to invade my bedroom as and when you please?'

'I'm sorry, my dear. I must apologise. Why on earth didn't you say she was leaving?'

'Because you didn't ask me! And I will not stand by and see you hounding Mara in this way. What about your precious prince? He's old enough and experienced enough to know what he's doing. If he wants to leave his wife, that's entirely his affair. Have you promised to scotch it by any chance? Perhaps it's your reputation that's on the line.'

'Well, of course it is!'

Breakfast arrived, and in the lull Samuel seemed to pull himself together a little. When they were alone again, he said, 'I'm sorry to be

213

so stupid about this. I have to tell you — Ferdinand's been on to me. Princess Anna's father. He wants it stopped and he's going to be damned unpleasant if it isn't. He's threatening to encourage the communists, which will give the Americans a heart attack, and they'll take a very dim view of a situation resulting entirely from Lady Mara's escapades. It's all going to get very unpleasant, I'm afraid.'

'You shouldn't promise what you can't deliver,' said Clare.

He grinned ruefully. 'How right you are, my dear.'

She gave him toast and coffee. All in all, as rows went, it had been quite civilised. 'Do you think we might — take a nap?' murmured Samuel. His moustache twitched.

'I don't know if I want to. You're being so horrid to me. And to Mara.'

'Clare! I wouldn't want to hurt you for the world.' He coaxed her gently to the bed. As she lay beneath him, her legs spread wide, she caught herself thinking how pleasant this was. He expected nothing of her, just her compliance. Knowing that, it was far from unenjoyable. And she was making things too easy for him, providing too much. When he subsided, with an old man's sudden flaccidity, she put her fingers on his cheek.

'Samuel dear,' she said. 'If you want to continue this, we really must get married.'

His face fell. His neat, compartmentalised existence was about to collapse. 'But you'd hate to live in the country, Clare!'

'Not nearly so much as I dislike being the subject of gossipping servants.'

She had chosen her moment well. He was so comfortable beside her. She was attractive, intelligent and she satisfied him. On the debit side, she wasn't nearly so biddable as he had once supposed but then, he thought, he had no wish to lose her. And when she discovered just what he intended to do to Mara Hellyn, if there was no public commitment, he would. 'My dear Clare,' he said. 'If I'd know you would accept, I'd have asked you long ago. You've made me very happy.'

Jay was waiting in a chauffeur-driven limousine with tinted windows. She recognised his shape, the triangular head narrowing down to his long thin chin. An Italian in a plain suit opened the door for her and passed a signal to an outrider, who raced away in front. The door closed with a heavy, decisive clunk and she sat, not daring to look at him.

'You're wearing the ring.'

She nodded, and the car began to move. Even the panel that

separated them from the chauffeur was coloured. They were enclosed in a dark box. Mara's heart thundered sickeningly. She put out her hand and found his. The fingers were cold, the palm hot and anxious.

'Oh Jay, Jay!' She turned and flung herself at him, clinging like a child. She was crying, he was crying, they tangled tearfully in a net of her hair.

'I thought they wouldn't let you come!' She pulled back to look at him, wiping her face with her long fingers.

'They couldn't stop me. Mara, I've given up pretending, I don't care who knows we're together.'

'Where's – her?' She hated asking about his wife, she hated the woman herself.

'In Havenheim, with her father. He knows we're here but fortunately he doesn't seem to have enlightened Anna.'

'Why didn't you?'

He looked into her eyes. 'There's no point in upsetting her unnecessarily. Of course, in the end, she must know.'

They kissed. Mara's desire flamed, as hot and vivid as a fire receiving oxygen. She felt desperate suddenly, to love him and be loved, to know that she was still precious to him, would always be so. He began to touch her everywhere. She hung on to his kisses. They sprawled across the seat as if they were wrestling. Then the car stopped. Slowly they disentangled, trying to pretend normality. A pulse beat steadily in Mara's belly, a deep, throbbing urge. The door opened and she stepped out of the car.

They were in the courtyard of a house. On three sides were windows, the fourth, through which they had driven, was simply a wall with high wrought iron gates. All the buildings were pale, sun-bleached pink, the shutters darker and slightly sagging. Water ran through stone gulleys, cascading out of the mouths of lions and dolphins into a dark pond. Huge carp swam lazily around, bumping the lilies. At its edge there stood a sundial, made of crumbling stone, and so tall that Mara could not see the top. The edge of the pool was worn from centuries of feet that had climbed there to look, at the moon and the stars casting their shadows on to a green copper plate. Someone, a maid perhaps, was singing in a rich Italian voice, quavering the top notes and lingering long and sentimentally on others. Mara felt strange, lost; she burned to make love and be transported to paradise.

She followed Jay into the house. She gained an impression of much dark wood, of a room with an enormous fireplace flanked by jars large enough to conceal Ali Baba and many of his forty thieves. Everything smelled heavily of flowers, hyacinths perhaps. As she

215

looked about her, Jay took her hand and made for the stairs.

'Everyone will know,' she whispered guiltily.

'I don't give a damn.'

A maid was coming down. She stopped and curtseyed, making a face to herself once they had passed. Well, she could understand his haste. The girl was beautiful — so beautiful.

Jay opened a door and pushed Mara through. Never in his life had he felt so wild, so utterly determined to do something. The bed was high, curtained in white muslin and heavy white linen. The floor was highly polished wood, with only one or two small rugs here and there. Mara went to the window and watched leaves blowing around the courtyard in the thin winter sunshine; the room was slightly cold, and rather strange.

'Mara — Mara, please.'

She turned and smiled at him. Her heart was in her eyes, he knew then that she gave him everything, her love, her trust, her happiness. As he went to her, claiming her, he had not a moment's doubt.

Theirs was an idyll played out in the winter of the year. Some days it rained, and they sat by a fire watching the lions and the dolphins in the courtyard spew water frantically. On fine, cold afternoons they walked — in the gardens, round the town — a detective pacing a scant three paces behind. Mara bought sweets and bangles, hair clips and shoes. She bought a pair of tan and green boots, trimmed with gold, and she adored them and him and everything.

In the evenings they ate *fritto misto* and pasta. Sometimes they went out and bought pizza and ate it like children, sitting on a wall. Jay watched her laugh as she spilled wine on her fur; she was so young, and so happy.

He kept thinking of Anna. Such a stolid, worthy woman, who never saw how she oppressed him. Mara sparkled like diamonds set in gold; she was a filigree of nerves and emotions, dark and light. He had felt so old for so long, as if life had nothing new or exciting to offer him. And here was Mara, who made him young again, who made every day taste like new wine, sharp on his tongue.

After a week he had to say something. She lay against him in bed, naked, sticky with love. Her hair was in a thick plait on the pillow because last night he had tangled it into a nest and she didn't want that again. He chuckled. In a moment he would unfasten that plait and spread her hair out like a golden curtain and she wouldn't dream of stopping him.

She gave him a new opinion of himself, as someone highly sexual. He was surprised because he had never imagined himself quite this virile. But the act itself was only a vehicle, a means of expressing what

216

they meant to one another. Was that a feminine view of sex? He wondered. Or was it what every man came to, once he loved, completely?

'Mara. Are you asleep?'

She stirred against him, warm and smooth. 'No. I'm too happy. I don't need sleep, I just need happiness.'

'I've decided what I'm going to do.'

She rolled over, putting her arms around his neck and her face against his chest. Her breasts, soft and mobile, rested against his belly.

'Don't spoil this,' she whispered. 'We don't have to think about it yet.'

'I'm afraid I must. Look, it isn't going to be easy. I shall leave Anna at once, I shan't go back. I've no wish to turn everything into a wrangle. We'll have a legal separation and eventually I'll get a divorce. After that, you and I can be married.'

She was wide awake now, her pupils large and black. 'What about the children?'

'I'll try and insist on an English education. I can't visit if they're in Havenheim, I'd be asking for trouble.'

'And the house? That's hers isn't it?'

'It is indeed. But I'm moderately wealthy in my own right. We won't starve.'

She lay on him and kissed him, teasing his tongue with her teeth. He felt light-headed, liberated, as if he had been let out of prison. No more toadying, no more Havenheim with its indifference and veiled insults. Everything seemed simple suddenly, as if with one effort of will he had cast aside all the chains that others had shackled to him. It was in everyone's interest for him to do as he was told, everyone's but his. Why had he endured it so long?

The newspaper article appeared the very next day. The timing was no coincidence. Samuel's spies kept him well posted on how things were progressing. He hadn't gone so far as to bug the bedroom, but then it was hardly necessary. The most perfunctory observation could detect the way of the wind. A little digging, some discreet pressure, and he conjured up an absolutely vicious storm.

EARL'S DAUGHTER SELLS HERSELF TO MAKE ENDS MEET!
Mr. David Selmer, a respected financier with a taste for the girls, has revealed to us the true nature of his relationship with top deb Lady Mara Hellyn — daughter of the late Earl of Melville. The Earl's tragic death from cancer left his family destitute — and lovely Lady Mara did not intend to starve!

217

'She picked me up in a very high-class nightclub,' says Selmer. 'I couldn't believe my luck − and when she asked for money I couldn't believe that either.'

Selmer paid several thousand pounds for his night of love.

'Worth every penny,' he told us, grinning. 'She's an amazing girl, highly experienced. I learned more in one night than in the rest of my life.'

Such is Lady Mara's fun-loving schedule that Selmer only managed to book her once more −

'She'd run out of cash and needed to work. She spends a fortune on clothes and cocaine.' But David Selmer admits he's been passed up for someone else. 'He must be paying one hell of a lot. She likes it in hard cash, she won't take gifts of any kind.'

Our sources tell us that Lady Mara is at present in Italy with the British husband of one of Europe's richest women.

'She's very discriminating,' says Selmer. 'I'm really quite flattered that she added me to her list of clients.'

There was an enormous picture of Mara, wearing a flowing silk dress. She looked magnificent, tall, icily smiling, entirely proper except that her nipples showed like buttons through the silk.

On the same day the quality papers carried small articles on their front pages, briefly stating that the Director of Public Prosecutions was considering papers relating to a vice and drugs ring operating in London society. On the following day there were inside features hinting at the pressures affecting today's debs, and the crippling cost of the London season. Pictures of Mara began to proliferate. The ball began to roll.

A packet of cuttings arrived with breakfast three days after the tabloids first broke the story. Neither Jay nor Mara had been reading the papers, and they were happily unaware of anything. At first Jay thought it must be some horrible sort of joke. Pictures of Mara, everywhere. The story − he couldn't believe the story.

'My God. This is just − my God!'

'Jay? What is it?' She leaned across to see what it was. She went white.

'Don't look,' he said quickly. 'It's some ghastly smear campaign, you don't want to know.'

But she was reading the tabloid article. As she scanned each line her colour ebbed still further until her face was almost yellow, stained purple beneath the eyes.

'We'll sue,' said Jay. 'Obviously they want to discredit you. Look,

218

they're just hinting at me. They're hoping I'll cry off and behave myself. Don't worry, darling, we'll crucify them in the courts.'

'But — we can't.' He was looking through the rest of the papers, cursing at every one. 'Jay — we can't even deny it. It's true.'

He didn't understand her at first. He looked up in puzzlement, but what he saw in her face arrested him. 'Mara? What do you mean?'

'Come up to our room. I'll tell you everything.'

She sat on the bed while he stood at the window, looking out into the courtyard. Birds were pecking around on the stones; when they flew across the pool their wings were reflected up to him. Mara said, 'I didn't sell myself. It was before I met you. I went to his house, I was drunk and miserable. I didn't care. I realised he wanted to humiliate me. Because of who I was, what he thought I was. So — I pretended I was a prostitute. I said he had to pay me. He thought it was funny. He paid, and we spent the night together — if I hadn't said that he'd have hurt me, he might even have killed me. And of course I spent the money. I needed it.'

She ran her hand through her hair, and still he didn't turn round. In tones of rising hysteria she went on, 'The next time he just grabbed me. Pushed me in the car. He threatened me if I didn't go with him. He did — horrible things. He abused every part of me, every inch of skin — I wanted to die. I thought he was going to kill me and I didn't care if he did.'

'But he gave you money.'

'Yes! Four thousand pounds. And I needed it, desperately.'

'For cocaine.'

'Sometimes. Only sometimes, when I was down and unhappy, and after that night I needed it, God how I needed it! He raped me, Jay!'

'He gave you a good price. You can't complain.'

She was struck dumb. He swung round on her, his face black against the light from the window. He said, 'I pay you! Is this what you give to the best customers, your command performance? She won't take jewels, he says, she only likes cash.'

'I took your ring,' she said shrilly.

'Are you still up to it then? How many while you were at The Court? Country prices there, I suppose. A tenner for a quick screw at the back of the tennis court.'

'Jay! How dare you? How can you dare?' She came off the bed towards him, alight with rage. As she raised her fist to hit, he caught it. She struck out with her other hand and he caught that too. They wrestled wildly, until Mara was forced to her knees.

'Who else has there been?' His voice grated in his throat.

'No-one! There was a boy, Edward, he was the first. Two virgins

219

together in the stables at a party. I couldn't find love so I had sex instead. It took a while to realise how many men will screw you and not care. Vivien Shandon did it to me. That's what all the fuss was about the day we met – he did what he wanted and then called me names. But then, that's what you're doing. Isn't it?'

His thumb ran across the scar on her wrist. How beautiful she was, how lovely. She had that rare combination, a beauty that was sexually enticing. With her lack of caution, too, inevitably she would get into trouble, starting things she couldn't finish, making enemies. Some very powerful men had turned against her.

'Mara –' he tried to explain what was in his head. 'It can't be as we hoped. Not now.'

She seemed to crumple. He let go her wrists and she folded in on herself, crouched on the ground with her head covered by her arms.

'Mara, don't, please listen! I mean to leave my wife. It's something I must do. If this hadn't blown up we could have lived together quite openly. My family wouldn't have liked it but not a lot would be said. But with this – there'll be a great deal of disapproval. I dare not suggest that we get married.'

Mara uncurled a little. 'But we can live together discreetly. We could marry later, when it's all blown over.'

Jay laughed. 'And all the headlines would read "Royal prince weds call girl". They're worried enough about the royal image in Havenheim, God knows what would happen here! I have a duty to my family not to inflict this sort of thing on them.'

She scrabbled to her feet then, and ran like a hare into the bathroom. The door slammed shut. There was the sound of sobs and running water.

Jay was terrified. She might kill herself, she was more than capable of it. His razor was in that bathroom, with a new set of blades. He began to hammer on the door. 'Mara! Mara, open this door!' The water kept on running, all the taps, full on. In a panic Jay picked up the bedroom chair and struck it against the door. The chair broke but the door, solid mahogany, only scarred a little. He ran out of the room and bellowed for help. The detective came. 'Quick, help me break open the door,' ordered Jay. 'She could kill herself.'

They threw themselves against the wood, their combined weight thudding against the lock. On the third attempt the wood shattered and the lock burst. They saw Mara, in a cloud of steam, sitting on the floor by the bath. The razor blades were arranged on the floor around her.

'I couldn't,' she said softly. 'I kept thinking that you might not leave me alone.'

'My God, of course I won't!' Jay knelt down and held her, rocking her backwards and forwards against him. 'How can you think we'd be parted? I never meant you to think that.'

'But we can't live together. You said that.'

'Not officially perhaps. But we will. Of course we will.'

She looked up at him through her hair. Everything had gone wrong, from perfection to disaster in less than an hour. They were the same people as an hour ago, they had done nothing, and yet everything was changed. Instead of marriage and children they faced a life full of sleazy meetings, dogged by journalists with nothing better to do than destroy them. She got up wearily. It was difficult to think. 'What's going to happen?'

'I don't know. Darling, I honestly don't. I'll fly home tomorrow and talk to a few people, try and put the lid on this thing. Will you stay here?'

She shook her head. 'I'll come with you. I can't stay on my own.'

Mara let the maid pack. A strange numbness made everything seem remote and unreal. She re-read the newspaper cuttings again and again and couldn't believe they concerned her. Selmer's face eluded her, although there was a small inset picture in one or two of the papers. She remembered him only at some moments, when something Jay did triggered the memory of that night. Life scarred you, leaving marks that nothing could eradicate, and she had known then that he would haunt her. The man was utterly foul.

But she had survived and been happier than she had ever thought possible. This was a test perhaps, arranged by fate, to see if they had the strength to hold on. But what else could she do? All she had was Jay, he was all she ever wanted. And in her heart of hearts, she doubted him. He had a wife, children, a position in society. He was the one with everything to lose.

Chapter Twenty-Five

Clare's sitting-room was warm, an oasis of comfort far from the biting wind and sleet of an English winter. A large arrangement of hothouse flowers stood on the table, matched by another in the hall, and there was a little pile of letters by her side, in muted cream and ivory, a small avalanche wishing her well on her engagement.

Clare herself sat turning Samuel's diamond on her finger. She was upset, and confused. All her life had been spent avoiding serious thought, dealing in the trivia of clothes and make-up, houses and staff. After her husband's death even her lovers had been no more than amusements. Strong emotion was quite alien to her. And yet here she was feeling deceived, stupid, and above all angry. Only days ago Mara had been euphoric, and from that to the crushed and crumpled girl she saw now seemed obscene. Samuel had manipulated everyone, even her, but the engagement had to stand, unless she wanted the entire world to know what went on in her home. Clare watched the pale blue of her Chanel wool dress reflect in her diamond and it gave her no pleasure.

'Darling, I'm so sorry,' she said heavily. 'If I'd known what Samuel was going to do, I promise I'd have tried to stop it. But I can't understand David Selmer. It's not as if any amount of money would make much difference to him. He's easily a multi-millionaire.'

Mara sighed. 'Jay thinks he threatened him. Selmer's got something to do with pirating spare parts for planes. That's why he goes to the Far East so often. And he hates me. He hates all women.'

'You should sue. Deny everything in court.'

Mara shook her head. There was no point. Samuel had achieved a scandal, he had blackened her irrevocably. There could not now be a discreet reshuffling of bedmates, it was out of the question for Jay to marry a public slut. She put her fist to her teeth and bit it. It was all very well not caring what people thought, provided you never had to

222

live with that opinion. People watched, and they were unforgiving.

Clare said, 'Why don't you change, Mara? Have a bath before dinner.'

Mara looked down at herself. This morning she had dressed to impress Jay, determined that his last sight of her should be memorable. Such silly clothes: a cream silk top, stained now with coffee, showing three inches of cleavage; a short black skirt, like a tart's, and huge high heels. Only desperation could have driven her to such vulgarity, in broad daylight and before chauffeurs, stewards, maids. The photographers had caught her at the airport, because Jay had abandoned her, whisked away in haste in case anyone saw them together. Reporters thrust microphones under her nose, the flash bulbs popped, and thank God Clare had come.

'I don't care how angry Samuel is,' she said curtly. 'I will not leave you to these vultures. You can come and stay with me for a few days.' Mara was hustled to the Rolls and away.

Upstairs in her room, Mara could not settle. She wandered about in her dressing gown, arms wrapped tight about herself. If only Jay would telephone. She felt abandoned, lost. If only he would let her know that he loved her. Yet however often he said the words it wasn't often enough; he said them because he was kind and nothing more. How could he love her now?

Hysteria was rising in her throat. She went to her address book and leafed through the pages with shaking fingers. When she picked up the telephone her knuckles were white. 'Jimmy Carruthers please – it's – a personal call.' How odd to know that your name would open no doors, only close them. After a long pause, Jimmy came to the 'phone.

'Jim? It's Mara.'

'My God! I thought it could be you. Darling, are you all right? You've no idea of the flak. Reporters round here night and day trying to get the inside story. Except I've only ever been on your outside, haven't I? Oh God, Mara, I'm sorry. I'm a bit pissed.'

'That's all right, Jim. You didn't believe it all, did you?'

There was a pause. Then, loyally, he said, 'No, of course not. Look, I'd invite you out but I absolutely daren't. The family would kick up one hell of a fuss. But it's bound to blow over, old girl.'

'Is it?' She took a deep breath. 'I wondered – that friend of yours. Dermot. I'm in a bit of a state at the moment and I really would like something. Do you have his number?'

In a low voice he said, 'No, I haven't. And you know what I think about you taking the stuff. If you ask me it's what got you into this mess in the first place. You didn't know what you were doing.'

'You're the one who started me off,' she said tearfully. 'I'm going mad, Jim, I can't stand it! Jimmy, please!'

223

Agonised, he said, 'It's for your own good, Mara. If you keep on with the stuff you'll end up really mad, just like your brother. Look, I can't talk any more. I'm sorry.'

He put the 'phone down and Mara was left stranded. He wouldn't help. Perhaps no-one would. She had stepped outside the limits of her small, aristocratic village and become a pariah. Folding her arms around herself she went to bed, curling up on it like a snail, crying into the covers. If only Jay loved her she wouldn't care about the rest. If only Jay cared.

The telephone rang. She fell off the bed and grabbed it.

'Mara. It's me.'

Her world, spinning wildly like a planet out of orbit, began to steady. 'Are you all right? I thought − I didn't know what to think. At the airport −'

'I know. Darling, I'm sorry. Look, there's a terrible row going on here, everyone keeps trying to persuade me we're on the verge of an international incident. Even the American Ambassador wants to talk to me. I've told them you're going to The Court.'

'I can't bear to! I can't bear to go and not see you, I've waited months and months there for you already. Don't send me away.'

His voice dropped almost to a whisper. 'I'm not going to. One of my aides has found a flat in St. John's Wood. I want you to stay there. I'll come as often as I can, but no-one must know. Absolutely no-one. Do you understand?'

She managed a tearful giggle. 'Only too well. You darling, darling man.'

'I'll send the keys in the post. Don't let anyone know. Promise?'

'Brownie's honour.'

The relief was exquisite. Like a drowning swimmer, she'd been hauled back on the boat. She looked down and saw that her hands had stopped shaking. How stupid to be so dependent, she thought. But she was, and there was nothing she could do about it.

Jay sat in the study of his London house, long legs crossed on the desk. Samuel stood uncomfortably opposite him, but he would not be asked to sit down. The room was rather cold. Jay never kept his own apartments warm, although Anna liked her house stifling.

'Would you like to explain why you felt you should act as you did?' asked Jay distantly.

Samuel cleared his throat. 'I can't lay claim to any specific actions, sir −'

'Oh, stuff it, man! We both know what you did. Spies dredging the dirt, a little discreet blackmail, a word in the ear of one or two

224

newspaper proprietors. It wasn't even difficult. But why?'

'I think, sir, with due respect – it has been felt that you were unaware of the implications of the break-up of your marriage.'

'Not at all,' purred Jay. 'The implicatiions escaped me when I got married, not now that I contemplate divorce. Oh yes, Samuel. I do still contemplate it. And if Havenheim goes communist, which I consider unlikely, I have no doubt that you will enjoy yourself hugely trying to restore that which you laughingly call democracy. You know what I mean – the system that tries to deny its citizens freedom of speech, freedom of action, even freedom of thought. My freedom, in fact.'

'With respect, that freedom was sacrificed when you married Princess Anna. You have an obligation to maintain the monarchy there.'

'Balls! As far as you're concerned, all I have to do is act as a stud bull for the Princess. My own thoughts, feelings and personality are simply an inconvenience. Good God, man, I'm an insignificant sprig on a very large tree. Why can't you bugger off and worry about something important instead of my love-life!'

Samuel shifted from one foot to the other. He would have liked to pick up his walking stick and thrash the randy young fool! Coldly he said 'The Americans, sir, have made it clear that they do not want a country so close to the Eastern bloc de-stabilised by something so trivial as your desire to have sexual intercourse with Lady Mara Hellyn. A senior American has said, sir, and I quote, "Why can't he fuck them both?" And I confess I am of much the same mind.'

Jay's feet came off the desk with a thump. He stood up. 'Get out, damn you! Get out of my house. You've got a cold heart and a filthy mind. You understand nothing of what's been going on. I don't believe you even know what you've done. You could have destroyed that girl and you never gave it a thought! She's passionate and lovely and young, but all you can think to do is take all that and throw it in the muck. You don't see the beauty and the innocence.'

'Not a word I would apply to Lady Mara, sir,' retorted Samuel.

Rage suffused Jay's face. He came round the desk with murder in his eyes, and Samuel backed towards the door. He wasn't quick enough. As he turned the handle Jay's fist caught him on the cheek, as he fell into the hall he got a boot in the gut. He lay groaning and gasping, an aide hovering uncertainly.

'Get him out of here,' said Jay thickly. 'If he stays here a minute longer I'm likely to kill him.'

As they helped the old man away he knew he should experience remorse. But Jay felt cold, relentless. In some small way Samuel should be made to suffer, he should know what he had done to others.

225

He had smashed something quite beautiful, something quite perfect: Jay's innocent trust.

The days dragged until the weekend. He was supposed to be going shooting, and indeed would depart as if he was. Instead he would shed his detective and drive to St. John's Wood, and Mara. The week was turning into an extended round of recriminations and ghastly warnings, it was as if no-one would be happy until he could be witnessed performing his marital task in Anna's bed. And in fact he felt desperately randy. He woke in the night dreaming of Mara, of making love to her, and in the day he could barely read a line without her face swimming before him. He missed her warmth, the way she smelled in the morning before her bath, of love and sweat and happiness.

And he imagined, sometimes, other men. The thought excited him, though he despised himself for it. Was she the same with them? Mara was profligate, she gave and took pleasure all the time. He imagined her lying beneath his detective, or his aide, even the chauffeur. Had she really been faithful to him at The Court?

The thoughts kept him in a state of preoccupied tension. And to his surprise, on Friday, Anna arrived.

At first he thought she didn't know. She bustled in, her shortness surprising him after Mara, and she threw off her fur hat and coat.

'Darling Jay!' She put up her cheek to be kissed. 'The children are coming on later, they are skiing. It was snowing so much I feared soon the airport would be closed, and I do not want to stay in Havenheim for weeks.'

Jay snorted. She wanted the next baby, it was obvious. And to his horror he felt himself respond. 'You're going to be very bored this weekend,' he said quickly. 'I'm going shooting.'

'Oh.' She looked a little upset. 'I thought perhaps – wouldn't you rather come to the country? With me?'

The coquetry was obvious and rather pathetic. He turned away. 'I'm sorry, Anna. I can't. Another time perhaps.'

There was so much between them that was known and so little that they could discuss. 'My father sends his good wishes,' quavered Anna, and Jay turned on her. 'I bet he damn well does! Will you never learn that I will not have him meddling in my affairs?'

Anna ducked her head and turned away. 'How was Italy?' she asked stiffly.

'Pleasant, thank you.' He was enmeshed in a web of pretence, he felt strangled. He had to cut himself free. 'You know I wasn't alone, I suppose.'

'I – I did hear something.' Her hands were tangling themselves

226

together. She had put on weight over Christmas, he thought. Anna always ate when she was unhappy.

'Don't upset yourself,' he said gruffly.

She gave a short laugh. 'My husband is in love with another woman and he tells me not to be upset! Why did you pretend not to care? I asked you and you lied.'

'That isn't true.'

'But it is! Oh, you played with the words, but you meant me to believe that you didn't love her. I never thought that you would lie to me. And she's a slut, a prostitute! If you leave me for her − I should be so ashamed.'

Jay turned away. 'She isn't that,' he said tightly. 'You don't know her and she isn't that.'

Suddenly Anna lost her temper. Not once in all their married life had she done so, but now she did. Her arm struck the table lamp, sending it crashing to the floor. She kicked out at a footstool and it careered across the carpet. 'Oh, and she is a nun I suppose! It's the convent where she learned all her little tricks, the ones to please a man. What a pity I did not go to the same convent, I could have learned how to suck and lick and wriggle, and it would not matter that I am not beautiful or clever, that I do things I don't want because of who I am, that I can't do as you and take this man, that man, any man! Here I come, running back to see you and all you can do is pretend to go shooting when I know you are going to HER!'

She hit out at an ornament and Jay crossed the room. 'Stop it, Anna! Have some dignity, can't you?'

She was crying, harshly. 'I don't want dignity. I want not to be alone. I want not to be left with nothing while you have all you want. I want not to be a woman left alone, Jay, left alone!'

'God Almighty!'

At that moment he would willingly have left her forever. The marriage had been arranged for her convenience: he had danced to her tune for years. And now that he wanted to change things, she had the temerity to make him feel guilty. All these screaming, crying women . . . he wanted none of it! For a desperate second he wished he really was going shooting.

He left the room. All the staff were wearing the masks they reserved for family upsets, when they heard everything, were aware of every-thing, and pretended blocklike ignorance. Anna's maid, Greta, was standing in the hall. 'Go to my wife,' snapped Jay, and watched her lugubrious face take itself off. That was one perfect instance in which Anna should have given way, and had not. He hated the woman and she hated him, yet Anna refused to part with her. She would not therefore be left alone at all, she could have bloody Greta and like it.

He drove the car out of the gates with a savagery that scattered tourists like pigeons. Defiantly alone, he hardly cared who knew his destination. But sense prevailed, and he took care to set off towards the M1 before doubling back in the Edgware Road. He hardly wanted to go to Mara now, his thoughts tumbled in space.

But he was calm by the time he reached St. John's Wood. The luxury block had its own car park and he sat for a few minutes, thinking, before going in. He was exhausted. His neck ached and his eyes blinked as if full of ground glass. When he got out of the car he thought the thick, fume-laden air would choke him.

There was a porter to be negotiated, and he put on his reading glasses and pulled his hat well down over his head. 'Miss Denham,' he told the man. 'I'm her brother.'

Without waiting for a reply he went straight up in the lift.

Mara was waiting for him at the door. She was wearing jeans and a loose blouse, only half-buttoned. Jay had thought himself exhausted, but when he touched her he flamed. She was warm and firm and luscious. When she kissed him he tasted oranges and wine. 'You've been drinking,' he accused.

'Just a glass or two with lunch. I daren't go out, people stare. I'm in purdah. For you.' She dropped to her knees in front of him, rubbing her breasts against him. The remaining buttons fell open and she reached up to touch him. Laughing, he joined her on the floor, wrenching at the zip of her jeans. But Anna's words whispered to him; Where had she learned these tricks? Who had taught her? The thought excited him. He was rough, rougher than he intended. He dragged at her jeans and had her.

She tousled his hair. 'Why are you so angry?'

He closed his eyes. 'I'm not.'

'Yes you are. Everyone's getting at you. But I won't. If we have so little time then I won't waste it howling.'

'Promise?'

She nodded. He felt a wave of love for her, because she was beautiful and understood.

He rolled on his back and told her about Anna. It was a ridiculous situation, both of them half-naked on the hall floor of a rented flat, surrounded by the muddle that was Mara's constant accompaniment. A handbag nudged against his elbow, a shoe rested between his feet.

'I'm going to leave her,' said Jay, harshly. 'I'm sure of that. But if I got her pregnant again there wouldn't be nearly the fuss.'

Mara rolled away from him. She got up, dressed only in the shirt, and fetched a bottle of wine. She poured herself a glass, giving him nothing.

228

'It would make things easier,' said Jay. He was almost enjoying this, he realised, he felt well again. He wanted to discuss everything, without secrecy. Amazing how sex changed his perspective.

'It would take years,' snapped Mara. 'And I won't have you going back there and doing it.'

'If she had a girl everyone would accept we'd tried. And if it was a boy they'd let me go instantly, no-one would even notice.'

She dug her bare heel into his side. 'You'd better not.' He laughed.

Later, over dinner delivered from some local restaurant, Mara said, 'The porter knows who I am, by the way.'

'I thought he looked a bit odd. Didn't you wear a hat or anything?'

She nodded. 'But I was here once before, looking for a flat. When I first came to London. He knew my name the moment I came in.'

He breathed out through his nose. 'If the newspapers get hold of it, we're in trouble.'

She leaned her head on her hand, looking at him. She didn't care who found out. It seemed then that great forces were ranging themselves against her, and she could defend herself with nothing more than Jay's affection. If the world knew that he loved her, at least then there might be others who thought she should win. Her position was being constantly eroded. In Italy he had been going to tell his wife and leave. A week ago they had planned to live together in secret. Now she was hidden in a flat, with nothing to do but wait for him, and he even talked about making his wife pregnant!

'I'll make sure the porter doesn't say anything,' she murmured.

'What on earth do you mean?'

She shrugged. 'I'll be sweet to him, that's all. Flatter him and so on.'

Jay swallowed. For a moment he thought she meant to sleep with the man. God, but it was strange after the tensions of the last week to feel sexually satisfied. He wondered what else they could do. There was the whole weekend ahead and they were confined to this one small flat. 'I wish we could go to the theatre,' he said.

'Yes. We'll just have to watch television. There's a video, we could get a film.'

She leaned her elbows on the table, looking at him. Suddenly he thought, there was nothing in the world that would make him happier than an evening alone with Mara, with or without the television. He smiled to himself. In a life of shifting sand, for once he seemed to stand on solid ground.

Chapter Twenty-Six

Lisa hooked her thumbs into the waistband of her jeans and stared about her. She seemed slightly disdainful, looking down her long nose as if what she saw was not entirely wholesome. The room gleamed with newness, from its tasteful wallpaper, a copy of the original Chinese, to its restored and lacquered cabinets, to the four poster bed covered with an embroidered linen quilt.

'What's the matter with it?'

Toby was in the doorway behind her. He looked resigned, as if he had been through all this before.

'It's all so disgustingly shiny.' She ran a hand through her hair and went to inspect the books placed invitingly on the table. New, all of them. 'We've got a perfectly good library, why are these here?'

'Aren't they Shakespeare or something? Give the place tone.'

Lisa withered him with a glance. 'We have reams of Shakespeare. If we have to have new books they should be newly published, not tarted up editions with illuminated capital letters, like some fake medieval manuscript. They're out. And the paintings . . . no-one ever needed ancestors in a bedroom. They go back to the gallery where they belong.'

'But there won't be anything on the walls!'

She shrugged. 'Buy some good modern stuff. We used to have impressionists, of course, and they would have been lovely. But the Hellyns always sell at the wrong time. We could have lived forever on the sale of one Monet today.'

'I don't suppose − prints? Copies?' He saw her face and sighed. 'This is costing one hell of a lot, Lisa.'

'I told you that from the start.'

She stomped out, and he followed her. The hallway was warm, sunny with yellow paint. It had seemed to him too modern a choice but Lisa was adamant. They were offering a home, not a museum piece. The Court was a mishmash of styles, medieval chests sitting cheek by jowl with eighteenth-century elegance. Lisa chose and rejected with what seemed to him arbitrary firmness, but the result, he had to admit, was stunning. She had created a guest wing of enormous charm, full of idiosyncratic touches; there was a doll's cradle in one room, complete with battered china doll, and in another a vast wooden jigsaw puzzle set out on a table.

'It took us two years to finish it,' she remarked.

Looking at the thousands of pieces Toby said, 'Won't it attract dust?'

Lisa replied, 'Of course. And someone will dust it.'

Following her downstairs, he wondered what exactly it was that he had taken on. The girl was an autocrat, insisting on things with a certain stilted determination. Her shyness helped, it made her seem stiff and unbending. Toby wished that he knew her better.

The doctor had been to see Marcus and was waiting in the kitchen.

'Hello, Stephen,' said Lisa, and went to put the kettle on.

'Everything looks very grand.' The doctor picked up a cloth and began drying cups, and for some reason it annoyed Toby intensely. It was a definite statement of feet-under-the-table intimacy. He picked up another cloth and dried a cup, then they both wrestled over the remaining one. Toby won.

'We're getting a dishwasher,' he said grimly.

'I can't think why' said Lisa. 'The porcelain's far too good to go in. And the silver and the glass.'

The doctor smirked. 'When are you opening, Lisa dear?'

'Next week. The staff's coming on Wednesday. And, do you know, our old butler's coming back – Curtiss? Angus met him in London and enticed him.'

'I had to offer him a decent screw, of course,' said Toby.

Lisa winced and the doctor said, 'Really.'

Between them they made him feel vulgar.

Charlotte came in, wearing a skirt and cardigan in drooping lavender crochet. 'Have you asked the doctor, Lisa,' she said.

'No, not yet.' The girl made coffee, assembling some home-made shortbread and fruitcake as if from nowhere.

'Asked me what, Lady Melville?'

Lisa said jerkily, 'She wants Marcus to go back to the hospital. She thinks the visitors might upset him.'

'Don't you mean he'll upset the visitors?' interrupted Toby. 'Let's be honest, shall we?'

Charlotte coloured. 'I don't mean that at all. But any disturbance seems to make him worse. And it's all bound to be very disturbing –'

231

The doctor said, 'I'm sure we could arrange for a temporary admission. If that was requested.'

It seemed that they all waited to hear what Lisa had to say. She looked tired, thought Toby, and rather strained. But, if the furore over Mara had done little for their nerves, it had done wonders for the bookings. They had a full house from day one.

'I'd rather he stayed,' said Lisa at last. 'They drug him more at the hospital.'

'It doesn't harm him,' said the doctor. 'You do understand that?'

Lisa avoided his eye. The twitching, drug-induced lethargy into which Marcus sank seemed to her just as harmful as his mental torment. It was like a ham-fisted giant trying to mend a watch, and all her instincts urged her to let the watch run, keeping the wrong time, ringing alarms at strange intervals, but nonetheless still a watch, still going. They couldn't cure him, and in trying they seemed each time to break him a little more, kill him just a little.

The telephone rang and Toby went to answer it. He came back in a second.

'Reporters?' asked Lisa. He nodded. It was almost the end of March and they were down to several calls a day now, when at the start they had been unable to think for the telephone. In the end they had taken it off the hook.

Charlotte said, 'I can't understand why these people keep bothering us. One would have thought that tabloid scandal-mongering could only go so far.'

'It's bound to die down, Mother,' said Lisa. But week after week the story hung on, refusing to go away.

She turned her back on them and went to the sink, starting to wash a pan with unnecessary force. Charlotte never doubted for one moment that the articles were lies, but Lisa suspected otherwise. Mara took money from men without conscience, and whether she did or did not take money for favours was hardly the question. To give the one and take the other was entirely in character, and there need not have been any question of a straight exchange. The events would have happened, separately, and it was only in linking them that Mara looked so bad. It was the explanation that Lisa preferred and she clung to it.

When the doctor left she took the dog for a walk. Toby came with her, though she would have preferred to go alone. The day was cold and grey, with a frost that would not lift from morning till night. The newly installed central heating battled with the temperature, the Historic Buildings people still hadn't finished the roof and money was draining away as if through a sicve. At that moment Lisa saw Toby

232

not as a saviour, but as a fellow casualty of the shipwreck, unaccountably choosing to join them in their leaky boat.

'Hellish cold,' he remarked.

She grunted and trudged on. They rounded a lake, frozen now except for a small centre hole where dozens of ducks squatted miserably. Tiny flakes of snow blew on the wind.

'Lisa —' He caught her arm.

'Please don't. We can be seen from the house.'

'All right. Let's go in the trees. I want to talk.'

He was not about to be put off. They climbed the slope, the dog puffing grumpily in their wake. A few snowdrops nestled in the shelter of the first bare oaks.

'That's a sign of spring,' said Toby.

'Not really. They're a winter flower, people never realise that.'

'Trust you to look on the black side. Right bloody pessimist, that's you.'

She put her hands in her pockets and faced him. 'I feel pessimistic. And so should you. You're going to go bankrupt.'

He scratched his ear. 'I don't really think so. I admit, it's costing more that it should, but it's my problem, not yours.'

'Don't be ridiculous! I told you it would cost a fortune to do the place up, and it has. We can't possibly get it all back from guests.'

He grinned. 'If I believed that we'd have given up long ago. The sums still add up, even if it is only just. We're going to be full for at least six months. We'll get out alive.'

'You forget, I'm not intending to get out.'

She watched him, her eyes so clear and grey. He said, 'OK. I am thinking of something else, but I'm not abandoning The Court. The two can work together. I want to start a club somewhere incredibly flash and exotic, a real jet-set watering hole. People can be discreetly fed down the line to The Court, the right sort of people.'

'A club in London, do you mean? They've got loads already.'

'That's why I'm thinking of somewhere else. Rio perhaps.'

'Good God!'

She turned away, hunching her thin shoulders. 'Are you leaving then?' she said stiffly. 'You can't set up that from here.'

'I'll have to go soon, yes. Will you mind?'

'Of course not! We couldn't expect you to stay forever.'

'I only want you to say that you'll miss me.'

She glanced at him. 'Of course I will.'

He came close to her and put his hands on her shoulders. She ducked her head, as she always did, rejecting his kisses every time. 'Lisa.' He nagged at her. 'Lisa!'

233

'I don't want to be mauled.'

'I just want to kiss you. Come on. Please.'

She put back her head and he kissed her, slowly, expertly. She began to respond, uncurling like a flower in the sun. Each time he went a little further, forcing himself to gentleness. He touched her breast and she tried to pull away. He held her close, his hand under her coat, his palm huge and hot. Her head fell back from him, she was breathing in short, harsh pants. He crushed his groin into her, letting her feel his erection. In an instant she had broken free.

'Why do you always start?' She turned away, pulling her coat together. 'All you want is to get me into bed.'

He caught his breath. 'You've got to grow up some time, love. Do you think I'm just too bloody vulgar, is that it? I'm not the right sort?'

'It's not you! It's anyone. I don't like to be touched.'

'But you can't stay like that. You can't go through life never letting anyone touch you. It isn't being good, it's being dead.'

She turned her back and began walking up through the trees. He and the dog followed, unwilling both of them. He felt a rising desperation, because she was so stiff and strained, and nothing he did seemed to get to her. If he went away forever she might not care, and if she did he would never know. 'You do understand,' he said urgently. 'I'm not just trying to get laid. I care about you. I want to make you happy.'

She spun round, looking down from six feet further up the slope. 'There's no need to lie. I don't believe the things you say to me. I know I'm dowdy and plain, with a big nose and no proper bust. You say you like those things but that's only to be kind. I think you're too kind to be honest.'

His mouth fell open. For a moment she almost laughed, because he was so big and baffled. He didn't realise that people saw through his little, kindly strategems. She saw him swallow. He said, 'Kind! I can think of a hundred men who'd think you were talking about somebody else. "Tough shit Ledbetter" is what they call me.'

She blinked. 'Whatever for?'

'Because — because I walk in, cut the feet from under them, and say, "Tough shit".'

'I suppose people are different in business.'

He didn't know what to say. She had him caught between two stools. If he was to be believed then he had to admit himself a brute, and if he let her think him lovable she credited him with lying. A little desperately he said, 'I really do mean what I say. I think you're beautiful. And everyone else would think so too if you didn't hide

234

yourself in oversized clothes and shooting jackets. You've got more taste than anyone I've ever known, and the one thing you don't apply it to is you. I'll tell you the truth — if the guests see you the way you are today they'll think you're the governess, not what you are.'

'And what am I?' Her voice croaked.

'The beautiful daughter of the house.'

She put her hands up to her mouth, but the words came just the same. 'That isn't me. That's Mara.'

She had the power to make him absolutely furious. He reached up and grabbed her by the shoulders, shaking her like a doll. 'Like fuck it is! Your father was a stupid and ignorant man. He had a love affair with his favourite daughter and left everyone else out in the cold. Even you mother's scared of Mara, because Mara was queen. But your father's dead! Mara's fallen off her pedestal. She's shacking up with some guy for cash and she doen't matter any more! Grow up, little girl.' He spun round, pointing at The Court through the veil of leafless trees. 'Look at that house. You've done what she never could. You'll be what she can never become. And if you don't you'll be here forever, getting stiffer by the year, looking after your mother and your loony brother until you die.'

Lisa shivered. Sometimes that seemed her inevitable fate. Everyone else seemed to find opportunities, so why not her? Perhaps it was simply that she didn't recognise them. 'I'll go shopping,' she said jerkily. 'Isn't that what you want?'

Toby laughed. 'Yes. I suppose that is what I want. And I don't care if it does take every penny I've got.'

Walking back to the house he wondered if he was entirely stupid. The more he gave Lisa the less seemed his chances of getting her into bed. He could persuade her to anything, he thought, but not that. Looking down at her narrow head he wondered what sort of man her father could possibly have been. There was something daunting in the power of a man to reach out from the grave, filling one daughter with a sense of her own loveliness, another with her own lack of worth. He felt suddenly that it wasn't Lisa he was fighting, but Henry, whose dead hands gripped more strongly than any that lived. It was up to Toby to hack Lisa free.

If anything was to emphasise Lisa's smallness, it was shopping. Everything swamped her, from sleeves that fell past her knuckles to hems that caught in her shoes. Her clothes seldom fitted because she was impossible to fit. Lisa trailed from shop to shop, visiting each and every exclusive bolthole within reach of The Court. The necks of silk blouses gaped, the seams fell off her shoulders, the waists of dresses

235

were bunched around her hips. All that she bought were two skirts from the children's department of Marks and Spencer.

Toby took her to lunch. The restaurant had spindly chairs, and he overflowed on all sides, while Lisa perched on hers like a bird. She had left home this morning all pink and bright with excitement, and now she drooped. He could see that she was very disappointed.

'Why don't we get you something made?' he said.

She stretched her lips in an attempt at a smile. 'Perhaps we'd better. There's a woman in the village makes dresses, I think.'

'I was thinking more of couture. Look, Lisa, you never settle for second-best in the house, so why for yourself? It's an investment. Vital for the hotel. If you don't look good the whole picture's going to be spoiled.'

'You're being silly. Nobody's going to notice me, and that's that.'

Toby set his jaw and signalled for the bill. He would not be put off by that distant air she knew destroyed him. He was determined to buy her some clothes. He had to prove that she was beautiful. 'We'll go to Paris,' he said. 'This afternoon.'

She didn't believe him, not even when he marched in on Charlotte's afternoon nap. Her mother had taken to stretching out on the chaise longue in the drawing-room after lunch, and snoozing until four. When Toby crashed through the door, she was jerked rudely awake.

'Charlotte!' he declared. 'Something's come up.'

She struggled to lever herself upright. Lisa said 'It isn't important – Toby, Mother's resting.'

'Of course, it's important. Good God, if we don't take in the exhibition now we'll miss it. Vital stuff. So we're taking the Paris plane this afternoon.'

'What exhibition?' Charlotte looked in bewilderment from one to the other.

'Interior design,' decided Toby. 'Lisa's longing to go. Thought it was too expensive, but now she's so short of ideas it's essential. Closes on Saturday.'

'But where did you say? Paris?' Charlotte patted at her sleep-tousled hair. 'Lisa can't possibly go to Paris.'

'Of course I can't,' added Lisa.

Toby, stopped in his tracks, stared at them both. 'But it's in the contract. The family has to pull its weight. I'm sorry, Lisa, but there's simply no alternative.'

He saw the ghost of a smile twitching her mouth. He turned to Charlotte. 'I'll take the greatest care of her,' he promised. 'We'll be back on Saturday.'

But even when Lisa sat in the plane, with her suitcase packed and

236

a washbag borrowed from Marcus, she thought it was impossible. It was unreal. People didn't take her to Paris. As the plane careered down the runway, she began to panic. 'I can't go! Mother won't know where I am.'

'We told her we were going to Paris.'

'Yes, but I didn't mean it! Who's going to see to Marcus?'

Toby sighed. 'Your mother. Look, it'll do her the world of good. Her whole life's been spent finding someone else to do her dirty work, it's about time she faced up to something serious.'

The plane bounced in the air. It was a small provincial shuttle flight, with none of the armchair security of a large jet.

'I don't want to go to Paris with you.' Lisa stared at him in alarm. 'I don't want you coming into my room in the middle of the night.'

'We're going to buy clothes, not fuck each other stupid!'

The stewardess, leaning over them with coffee, jerked and almost spilled it. Toby glared morosely. He didn't know the first thing about couture, except that it happened in Paris. He eyed the stewardess's varnished glamour, and mentally superimposed it on Lisa's shapeless, colourless form. He couldn't imagine anything less lovely. Suppose he turned Lisa into a creature of blonde streaks and sticky lipstick, and still didn't make her happy? However hard he tried he never seemed to succeed.

Over the years Toby had acquired the habit of luxury. When he made his first million he resolved never to stay in anything other than the very best hotels, no matter how much they irritated him. He would have preferred a family run pension with good food, but like most self-made men he wanted the world to see how far he had come. So he stayed amidst flunkeys and gold leaf, with sauces that gave him indigestion and room service that cost more than the room. Arriving in Paris, with Lisa, he took a suite of three rooms in the Hotel George V.

Lisa wasn't impressed. 'Rather too much, don't you think?' She wrinkled her nose in that way she had. 'Why on earth should we wish to eat smoked salmon sandwiches an hour before dinner?"

'I thought you might like them.'

'No, thank you.'

She turned her back on the gold filigree plate of assorted delicacies and went off to bathe. Toby munched smoked salmon morosely. Champagne was cooling too, but she'd ignored it. He got up and hammered on the bathroom door. 'Lisa!'

She opened the door a crack. 'What?'

'I just want to tell you that you're being a bloody wet blanket.

237

You're just about the most boring girl I ever met, you've got no idea how to have fun!'

She blushed. 'Just because I won't sleep with you!'

'To hell with that! Just because you won't eat a sandwich or play with the taps or drink a glass of bubbly or do anything that might be construed as having a good time! You hate the plane, you hate the hotel, you hate the food. And you hate me, I suppose.'

She scooped her hair back behind her ears. 'No, I don't.'

'Then you surprise me.'

He turned back to the sandwiches, but she opened the door again and came out, wrapped in a huge bathtowel. 'I'm sorry, Toby. I don't hate it, really. I mean – I'm sorry. I will have a good time, I promise.' She sat down in the chair opposite him, her shoulders like fine marble above the towel, her little feet protruding at the other end. She took a glass of champagne and nibbled at a sandwich.

She smiled at him. 'Why are you looking at me like that?'

'Because you're lovely. Even serious about enjoying yourself. I never knew any girl as hard to know as you, Lisa.'

'I'm perfectly simple. What you see is what you get.'

'And if only I was getting it.'

She tossed her head and stuck out her tongue. When she relaxed she was young and adorably innocent. For one thing she was completely unaware of her own sex appeal. Seeing her sitting there in that towel tormented him. He drank another glass of champagne in one gulp. She leaned her head on her hand and said, 'This room doesn't suit you. It's all far too flimsy.'

'Suits you a treat.'

'Does it?' Reaching out for her glass of champagne, her little breast rose to the edge of the towel.

Toby got to his feet. If he stayed a minute longer he wouldn't be able to control himself, and then she'd never speak to him again. Tonight was the time, when she was tired and drunk and happy.

'I'm going to get some air,' he said loudly. 'I'll be back in time for dinner.'

'Oh. Now? But I thought –' she tailed off in bewilderment.

'There's business to attend to. Can't stay here all day, wasting time!' He made for the door, wondering if this was the most idiotic thing he'd ever done, or simply the most hopeless. When he looked back she was sitting disconsolately in the chair. Why couldn't she see what she was doing to him?

Out in the street he thought of looking around for a whore, an eager tourist, anything. But he couldn't face it somehow, not in place of Lisa. What a fool she was making of him. He walked the streets,

238

freezing without his coat, trying to cool his blood.

They dined early, because he intended to take her out on the tourist trail, to the Folies Bergère and the Left Bank cafés. But by eight o'clock he was sneezing.

'I knew you shouldn't have gone out without your coat,' remarked Lisa.

'I'm perfectly all right.' He sneezed again, and his eyes began to water. My God, he'd planned a night of charm and amusement, only to be struck down by the common cold. He took a gulp of wine and found he could hardly taste it.

'I wouldn't if I were you,' advised Lisa. 'You'll get a headache and feel much worse. I'll get you some aspirin.'

So the evening was spent in the suite, watching an old film on television, dubbed into French. Expecting lechery, Lisa was delighted. The night held nothing more daunting than a mug of cocoa and a packet of Kleenex. She stood behind his chair and stroked his head. 'I think you might go bald one day. Hair this thick never lasts.'

'You'd better make the most of it then.' He leaned back and closed his eyes. His head was throbbing, his eyes felt like red-hot coals.

'I really do like you,' murmured Lisa.

'Do you?' Her hands were delicious, soft and cool.

'Of course I do. And it's very kind of you to bring me to Paris.'

'Would you have said all this if I hadn't caught a cold?'

'Certainly not. You were going to make love to me, weren't you?'

'Course I was. Were you going to let me?'

She considered. 'I don't know. But I'm awfully glad we can't.'

The film ended. Toby coughed miserably into his handkerchief and Lisa helped him off to bed.

In the morning he was too ill to go shopping. He lay in bed and let himself be babied, finding it surprisingly pleasant. She fed him croissants and raspberry jam, and sent out for papers that he might like. She had only to enter a room, he thought, to make it smell fresh and good. When she came in everything settled itself down in its rightful place and looked attractive.

'What are you going to do?' He gazed at her blearily.

'Well – I'm going to Chanel. Clare Payne wears a lot of Chanel and she always looks right.'

'Will you manage on your own?'

'Oh, yes. Mother used to come here when we were very small. They might remember her name. It is OK, isn't it, Toby? I thought we could take some of it out of the business perhaps.'

If there had been anything in the business he might have agreed with her. His coffers were funding this spree. But she was doing what

239

he had suggested and he couldn't complain. 'Get what you need,' he told her. 'Anything.'

Outside, in the bright, fresh Parisian day, Lisa felt light-headed. It was so long since she had spent any amount of time away from The Court, and she was in Paris, and all around were people who looked as she wished to look and didn't. She needed neat, tailored clothes, with set-in sleeves and tight waists, clothes without frills or bows, merely perfectly cut. Strong colour diminished her too. She was best in peaches and greys, and gentle blue. Suddenly she despised herself for her weak-mindedness. Why, if she knew how she should dress, did she not follow her instincts? As Toby said, there was no Mara to overshadow her, making her efforts seem futile, no Henry to notice some little alteration and make some trivialising remark. How often had he done that. 'Good Lord, Mara, your little sister's trying to be grown-up. She'll be challenging you next!' And everyone laughed, because it was so obviously ridiculous.

For a moment she stopped, frozen into immobility by the memory. Toby said she was stiff, and she was. She had learned to protect herself. Being with him, laughing with him, she sometimes felt that for the first time in her life she could lower her guard.

She arrived back at the hotel in the afternoon, laden with packages. Toby was in a miserable mess of used handkerchiefs, but to his delight Lisa dropped everything and tidied him up. 'Poor old you, your nose is all red. Here, let me do your pillows.' She turned them on to the cool side.

'What's all the shopping? I thought you were buying made to measure.'

'One suit. All this is the prêt à porter. I seem better suited to French sizes.'

'Going to put it on then?'

She hesitated. Then she picked up her packages and went into her bedroom to change.

She had bought three silk shirts in different colours. She put on the peach one, with a tight, short grey skirt in grey wool. She wore peach tights and grey shoes, and the sides of her hair were swept up and caught in combs high on her head. Her ear-rings were large paste clips, like lumps of coral.

Standing shyly by the bed, she said, 'What do you think?'

'Er – is that the dressiest thing you got?'

'Just about, yes. Don't you like it?'

He considered. She was neat, elegant – and somehow expensive. Every line and bone seemed to be hinted at: the perfect fall of silk across her breasts was interrupted only by the briefest, most tantalising amount. It wasn't at all what he had expected. It was better than he had expected. She had an air of well-bred fragility. He struggled for words. 'You look French.'

Lisa's face split into a beam. 'That's the nicest thing anyone ever said to me in my whole life.'

They flew back to England next day. Lisa fussed over him and Toby began to wonder if he liked it as much as he had thought. At a stroke his cold had turned him into an object, like her dog, or Marcus, or even her mother. He felt very close to her, and knew that if he hinted at desire, that closeness would go. She liked him like this. She liked him emasculated.

He let out a long sigh, coughing as the air irritated his sore throat. His manhood was an embarrassment to her, making him demand what she could not give, making her turn away from him. Her little hand rested on his huge knee as she leaned across to reach a magazine. Soft, shiny hair brushed his lips. Suddenly she turned her head and touched his cheek in a kiss. 'You're so kind to me,' she said. 'I think you're the kindest man I've ever known.'

Kind! When he was nineteen he had pulverised a guy in a fight, he'd had to leave town before the police got hold of him. Kind! He'd lived with a girl for six months once, and when she got pregnant he got her an abortion and dropped her with never a backward glance. If he'd had any true kindness in him, he wouldn't have a cent. He tried not to think of the things he'd done to get this rich. He'd started out intending to bully her family into selling up. Couldn't she see that? Didn't she know that?

He sank back in his seat. Of course she didn't. She thought he was kind.

Chapter Twenty-Seven

Charlotte was quite bewildered by Lisa's sudden departure. She and Toby flitted off together at all hours of the day to see about this or that, but Paris? She vaguely assumed it was something to do with curtains or furniture perhaps. As the day wore on and darkness began to fall she began to feel somewhat aggrieved. No fires had been lit, no food cooked. Marcus came in. He had been painting, but as always tore up anything he created. It was never good enough, never right.

'Marcus, do you know why Lisa has gone to Paris? She just swept in and swept out, without so much as a by your leave.'

'I was painting. I didn't know.' He walked towards the dead fire-place, rubbing his hands together. 'We'd better light a fire, hadn't we? It's dreadfully cold and dark tonight.'

He began to struggle with sticks and paper. The drugs sapped his co-ordination and he was hopelessly inept. Charlotte got up and went to the window. The gardener was gone, the decorators had finished, the builders had abandoned the roof while they waited for further supplies of some special sort of tile. They were alone, she and Marcus. And where had Lisa gone? Paris? It was ridiculous.

'Would you like to watch television?' Her voice sounded jerky and strained. How foolish to be afraid of your own son.

'No – no thank you.'

The fire was starting to blaze. He began to walk around the room, touching things, picking them up and putting them down too clumsily. He was clumsy about everything now; he even walked as if the floor wasn't where he expected it.

Charlotte snapped at him, 'Why don't you leave things alone, Marcus?'

He put down a vase and it slipped and fell against the hearth. It shattered. Marcus put his hands up to his face and shook with sound-less sobs.

She didn't know what to do. Lisa would be firm, matter-of-fact. She would say it didn't matter, that he was to stop at once. And by pats and little strokes she would comfort him. But Charlotte couldn't bear to touch him, she hadn't in years.

Sitting there, watching her son, she felt unbearably lonely. Henry had been the centre of her life, she hadn't needed more. All that she wanted she found in him, and strange though it was, the children had spoiled things. Marcus, with his problems, Mara, from her earliest days squeezing between them to make her way to her father's knee. And the four of them squabbling amongst themselves, making alliances and treaties, a tangle of connected emotion.

Marcus was crying harder now, working himself up. Dispassionately Charlotte said, 'To think I was so pleased when you were born.'

Harshly, through the sobs, he said, 'Do you want me dead, Mother? Is that what you mean?'

She was taken aback. How dare he feel and understand, and yet be so out of control? She said briskly, 'Of course I don't want you dead. I want you to stop being so silly, that's all.'

He reached in a pocket for a handkerchief and mopped his face. 'Would you like me better if I was crippled perhaps? You don't know what it's like, you don't know any of us. You never wanted to. You always sent us away.'

'Why don't you go and lie down?'

'I know you wish I wasn't here. You can't bear to be with me, with any of us. And now Father's gone you've no-one else.'

Charlotte angrily began putting her writing things together. 'You do talk such nonsense! It was difficult when you were small. Your grandfather was alive, and your father always liked a great deal of attention. And of course Mara was such a nuisance. Always – always getting in the way. Taking up your father's time.' Suddenly, unexpectedly, she was crying. 'What did you think I should do? Whenever you children were home it was always the same! Henry was angry because you were so odd, and Mara was so absolutely ingratiating – and I never meant to have Lisa at all. We didn't want any more children. We particularly didn't want another girl, not like Mara! She was the only daughter Henry ever wanted.'

'Didn't you think how it was for us? For me?'

Charlotte got to her feet and faced him. 'You had Nanny. You didn't need me.'

'But I did. Honestly, I did.'

His mother's voice became shrill. 'What did you expect? Your father couldn't bear you, he only wanted Mara! You were perfectly

243

well looked after. I came and saw you often.'

In the centre of the floor, Marcus seemed to crumple. His knees buckled down to the carpet. 'I wasn't loved,' he whispered.

His mother stood looking down at his distress. She put a tentative hand on his hair. 'I tried, Marcus,' she said. 'There wasn't room for you all, somehow. But I'll try and love you now.'

They both knew that it was far, far too late.

In the evening Marcus had one of his fits. He ran through the corridors, screaming and crying. Charlotte stood in the kitchen, her hands clenched in her hair, hating him. Where on earth was Lisa? How dare she go off and leave her mother alone with a lunatic? She picked up the telephone and dialled the doctor.

'This is Lady Melville. You must come at once. My − my son is beside himself. I want him committed. At once.'

The doctor mumbled, he was halfway through his meal. He talked about pills and calming influences.

'I tell you, I want him committed!' shrieked Charlotte.

She put the 'phone down. Her heart was pounding against her breast, an erratic thumping. She wondered if it was a heart attack, and hardly cared if it was. Life had been fraught since Henry died, he had caused everything and left her to face the consequences. Marcus was screaming now, 'No, No, No!' his voice echoing in the upstairs rooms. Against her will the image came again, of him new-born, pink and wailing. Yet when she reached out her arms they put him away, because there was another child coming, and besides, she must rest. She hadn't nursed him, she hadn't loved him. He was supposed to grow up tough and strong, a credit to them. Poor little pink and screaming baby.

She went out of the kitchen, called, 'Marcus! Marcus where are you?' He came to the top of the stairs, gaunt and wild-eyed. She swallowed and put out her arms. 'Don't worry, darling, Mother's here.'

He fell on her, clinging like an enormous octopus. Together, they reeled against the wall and for all his size he was a child to her again, the baby she hadn't nursed. What had she done to him? What had she missed?

Ten minutes later the ambulance came to take him away.

The house was eerily quiet when Lisa and Toby returned. The kitchen bore the marks of Charlotte's efforts at cooking, and a bottle of Marcus's pills was spilled on the table.

'They'll be here somewhere,' said Toby.

They walked through the rooms together, and found nothing.

Although she said not a word, Toby could sense Lisa's rising hysteria. When they opened Charlotte's door, expecting nothing, they saw her lying on the bed. Her face was bloated with weeping.

'Mother! Thank God!' Lisa ran forward, putting out her hand to touch and then withdrawing.

'They took him away,' sobbed Charlotte.

'To the hospital?' Lisa let out her breath. 'That was what you wanted, wasn't it?'

Toby said, 'I'll get her a sedative. And I'll make a cup of tea.'

Charlotte struggled to sit up. 'Why is he here? How dare he take you off like that? You're needed here, you have to stay here! He isn't at all the sort of person I want you to know.'

Lisa said, 'That's silly. Toby's here to help, he's been so kind – '

'But I don't want him here! This isn't his house. Your father wouldn't have let a man like him over the threshold. Vulgar, jumped-up sort who thinks he can take you away – '

'I'll get the pills' said Toby, and Charlotte flared, 'You'll do nothing of the sort! I won't have you staying here. The least I can do is ensure that one of my children is properly protected.'

'But, Mother, he's got to stay here! He's paying for everything.'

'Then he can pay for a room in the village. I won't have him under my roof.'

Toby went out and Lisa followed him. They stood whispering in the passage. 'She's really got a bee in her bonnet. Will it do if I keep out of sight until tomorrow?'

'I don't know.' Lisa was at a loss to understand what had happened. 'Perhaps you'd better go to the village for now. She'll calm down.'

He ran a hand through his hair, and then smothered a sneeze. 'I wouldn't mind if I was doing what she thinks I am,' he muttered. 'I didn't actually think she'd noticed.'

'She's upset because of Marcus, that's all. I knew I shouldn't have left her.'

'Don't give me that! It's blackmail to keep you running around doing as you're told.'

'All the same, you can't stay now. Please, Toby. It's only for a few days.'

He blew his nose violently. 'This is farcical. I don't care what she wants to think of me, but I'm damned if I'll be turned out. I'll stay as long as I damn well like.'

Lisa hung on to his arm. 'Toby. Please.' Her eyes were misty with tears.

He went to his room to pick up a few things and then went out to the car. It seemed he was always doing what Lisa suggested. He felt

245

he was wriggling under the pressure of her small but muscular thumb. And he hadn't done as he was told in years, perhaps ever. If only, if only he could get her away from here, out of this strange climate of duty and heritage. It was as if Lisa shouldered obligations for Mara, Marcus, perhaps even Angus, as if she was the scapegoat, the sacrificial lamb. And here he was, turned out of his comfortable bed to rack up in the village, nursing his cold in a pub. God knows why he put up with it.

Lisa stood dismally at the window and watched him go. All the fun and friendship of Paris was gone. A thousand and one tasks lay before her, all to be done before the staff arrived and the hotel opened. Her mother was calling. 'Lisa? Lisa, where are you?'

She rubbed her arms. If there was one thing she really liked about Toby it was his optimism. He never believed the world would turn against him, and it never did. Her mother was right, of course. He was vulgar and opinionated and exactly the sort of man her father disliked. But he had been lovely in Paris.

Toby took a room at the village pub. It was a jolly sort of place, low-ceilinged and cramped. The Hellyns had owned it a century ago, when there was barely a cottage that did not come under their hand, but all that had long since gone. Nonetheless the village still bore the marks of ownership, in its uniform style and extravagant walls and railings. Hellyn patronage had produced it, but planning laws preserved it, forcing people like Reg Maythorpe to build further out than they would have wished. No collection of new modern boxes had been put up within ten miles, and because of it the pub wasn't prosperous enough to redecorate. The brewery kept it on as an example of how things used to be, with sloping floors in the upstairs rooms. Toby's wardrobe wouldn't stay shut.

His cold was still just as bad. He felt resentful that Lisa should so easily have despatched him here. Why hadn't she stood up to her mother, told her that he was ill? He would have liked another evening being pampered. Instead he went down and sat in the bar, drinking whisky and feeling morose.

Every now and then the outside door opened, bringing in the cold night and freezing him in its icy blast. Would spring never come, he wondered? Tomorrow he must get on to his office in Sydney, check on the publicity for The Court. They were just about ready for photographs and he wanted Sunday colour supplement coverage to really gee things up. Did any of those damned Hellyns appreciate what he was putting into their house? Did Lisa?

The door opened again and he shuddered. What a benighted

country. But it was a girl this time, Jean Maythorpe, and she was alone. Toby was still enough of a chauvinist to be surprised.

'Hello, Jean. Get you a drink?'

She looked pleased. 'Thanks. Gin and orange.'

She hitched herself on to a neighbouring bar stool and slipped off her coat. She was a trim little thing, he noticed, with a nice pair on her and an open, friendly face.

'Often come in here on your own do you?'

She nodded. 'I have to get away from Dad. He gets going on marriage and settling down.'

'Thought he seemed fairly settled as he is.'

She grinned. 'For me, silly! He wants me to have children.'

'Marrying first, I presume. Unless he's very liberal.'

She ignored that and sipped her drink. 'He says I'm wasting my life.'

'And are you?'

She nodded. 'I might be. You see — well, I've fallen for someone. And he's working away and doesn't think about me at all I don't think. And my career's going nowhere. Nothing I do seems to work out just now.'

Toby sighed. 'I know the feeling. Bloody frustrating, this country. Everything takes so long, the weather's lousy and the women won't let you screw them.'

Jean laughed. 'You've been asking the wrong one. She's much too snobby.'

He grunted. That thought had occurred to him more than once.

He lifted his finger for the barman to refill their glasses. 'Have you heard the latest on Mara?'

'Only that she's with some Arab. The paper said he pays her in rubies, weighing them by — well, it was quite disgusting.'

'We can discount that one. Not the sort of girl to have rubies stuffed up her, I would have said. Though you never can tell.'

Jean took a gulp of her drink. Toby was ordering doubles and she felt rather light-headed. 'Angus knows where she is, actually. He's got a new job, working for Conservative Central Office, and he sees her now and then. But he doesn't tell me anything.'

'She certainly isn't sending rubies home, I know that much.'

He watched Jean surreptitiously. Her cheeks were flushed and she was drinking hard. Was she in love with Angus Hellyn? He could imagine Angus having a stab at her, she was so sane and wholesome. If there was one thing he knew about Angus it was that he could not bear any hint of emotional disturbance. Like a dog who had lived through snakebite, he was terrified of snakes.

247

He drained his glass. 'I'm going to London in the next few days. I'll give him your best wishes if you like.'

'No − no, don't do that. Could you say − well, yes, give him my best wishes. Don't tell him I was here on my own, will you? Say I was with someone.'

'Male of female?'

'Oh, male definitely. Someone tall and very good-looking.'

Toby laughed. She was so utterly straightforward. 'Look,' he said, 'I've been so damn busy lately I never got round to buying a horse. Could you help, do you think?'

She finished her drink. 'I can do better than that. Dad's thinking of selling one of his hunters, he's well up to weight. But he's a bit long in the tooth now, the horse that is, and Dad thinks he needs something younger now that he's Master and goes out every time. Come out tomorrow and try him.'

'I've got a bloody awful cold, I'd better not.'

'Best thing for a cold, some fresh air. Come on. Half-past ten at our house, I'll even take you to the meet.'

The whisky was lighting a small fire inside him. What the hell? One wasted day wouldn't kill him. What was life for if not enjoyment? He was sick of The Court and the Hellyns, he would spend a great day with someone who simply didn't notice life's complications. 'Sure thing' he said.

The morning air was cold and crisp, but for once the sun shone, gleaming on puddles and spiders' webs. Toby felt better, his head less thick and some of the weight of depression lifting from his soul. The Maythorpe hunter chewed his bit like an old gentleman mouthing dentures, and he skipped a little with pleasure at being out. Toby patted his neck. He wasn't much of a horseman actually, though he saw no reason why that should stop him hunting.

Jean turned and said, 'Are you OK? He's quite fresh.'

'Oh, I'm fine. How come you haven't got a headache this morning?'

'I never get headaches. I didn't have that much, did I?'

'Quite a bit, yes.'

At the meet Jean talked to everyone. Toby was happy just to sit and relax, marvelling at being there at all. There was more than half a world between this and the beach kid he'd once been, missing school to go surfing. He'd wanted to be the best, and for some reason had fixed his sights on tubing it in Hawaii. One broken nose and two cracked ribs did nothing to deter him; he watched the surfing movies and yearned to do it like that. But you didn't get to Hawaii on beans, so he started to trade in this and that, fruit at first, and then domestic

248

appliances when he discovered the meaning of the word perishable. There was quite a bit to be made in buying up old washing machines and fridges, fixing them and selling them on. And you didn't have to be too scrupulous. When he had enough he bought a bit of land on the beach, put up a few shacks for a surf shop, and somehow he got more land and the shacks turned into chalets and he found himself a millionaire. He never had been to Hawaii.

He flexed his huge feet in their expensive boots. He was too big for this game really. The surf suited him better, and so did the climate. What was he doing in this old, dead world, pouring money into a house he couldn't buy just because of some runty offshot of an old and worn-out tree? She didn't deserve him.

He gathered up the reins and pushed his horse on. He was obliged to find the brakes rather sooner than he had expected, but then he never could abide slugs. 'Hey, Jean!' His roar summoned her from her group of friends.

'Yes?'

'Stick close to me, will you? I feel in need of some intelligent company today.'

She laughed. 'Once we start going, you'll just have to try and keep up. I don't hang about for anyone.'

'You try and lose me, sweetheart.'

They rode off together just behind Jean's father. Hounds found almost at once, and took off at a cracking pace. The field hung back endlessly, Toby almost rammed the bit through his horse's back teeth to keep him still. As soon as Reg gave the signal Jean's firebrand took off, and Toby was after her, three parts out of control. Earth came up and hit him in the face, he saw the first hedge and knew he had to leave it to the horse. He took it like a trooper, Toby thumping down on his neck, and they thundered away again. This was something, thought Toby, this was living. As he crashed on in Jean's erratic wake he looked at her tight, neat bottom bobbing ahead of him and felt a great affection.

Angus surveyed his table. The flat was so small that with the table extended it was impossible to sit anywhere except at it, so they would be forced to eat almost straight away. But despite the lack of space he was quite pleased. He had remembered to buy candles, one of the girls at the office had been only too pleased to cook the food, and all that was required of him was some elementary re-heating and re-membering to take the cheese out of the fridge. The entire office thought he was entertaining some lady love, whereas the reality was much more delicate. Mara was coming.

249

He recognised her step in the passage and opened the door before she could knock. Not having seen her in weeks, he felt a slight shock of surprise. She seemed taller, thinner, with an air of dramatic tension, possibly caused by her trench coat and dark felt hat. But even when she came in and threw her coat and hat aside, he was aware of something. He had grown up with her, but for the moment she was unfamiliar. Suddenly he realised that this must be how she seemed to others, and he was briefly allowed to experience it. She really was incredible.

'Sorry to be so furtive,' she apologised. 'People point at me in the street and ask for my autograph, it's quite dreadful.'

'My heart bleeds for you.' Angus handed her a glass of dry white wine. 'The family's having a hell of a time. And so am I. You can imagine how difficult it is to get taken seriously politically when your sister's starring in the tabloids.'

She slid neatly behind the table, rested her elbows and looked up at him. 'Am I here to be given a lecture? I wouldn't have come if I'd known.'

Angus sighed. He would much rather not stir the water, but something had to be said. 'Look, there isn't any future in this, Mara. Not only does it harm me, all of us in fact, it harms you. In the end you're going to be left high and dry.'

Coolly, she said, 'All you're really bothered about is your career. A batty brother and a scandalous sister don't look good on the election leaflets.'

'Oh, for God's sake! If you must know I left my job under a cloud. Stanley Westerley's been doing his damnedest to shoot me down, but I was lucky. He's got more than a few enemies himself. But this on top of everything is pushing it a bit too far, and I'm not in the least sure that you're not going to make things worse.'

Mara sipped her drink. She was very pale, with pink blusher painted a little too fiercely on her skin. 'Perhaps I will. I didn't plan this, Angus, but Jay and I can't stop being us just because you want to be you. In the end it doesn't matter what other people think. You've got to do what's best.'

'And I will not get selected as a prospective candidate if you make any more scandal.'

'Yes you will! Honestly, Angus, they'll be mad to turn you down. You must be the nicest, cleverest potential candidate they've ever had. Anyway, you aren't old enough yet. By the time you get selected, no-one will remember the slightest thing about me.'

Angus struggled with himself. Somehow he didn't want Mara to be the first to know. 'Look,' he said finally, 'I've got the chance of something. I mean, the seat's totally unwinnable, it's a total Labour stronghold, but there's a by-election coming up and the candidate's bound to get lots of media coverage. I'm in with a chance, Mara. I can get known. Can't you at least make sure nothing dreadful turns up in the papers until after the tenth of June?'

'Good Lord, this is exciting! We'll see you bravely smiling after your defeat, claiming the moral if not the actual victory. Don't you dare wear an outsize rosette, they look so terribly vulgar.'

'I'm not even the candidate yet,' murmured Angus.

He went into the tiny kitchen to bring out the first course, rubbery prawns set in some kind of white sauce. Mara picked out the prawns and left the rest.

'How I do miss Lisa's cooking,' she said wistfully. 'I'm having to learn, you know? Jay and I can't go out very often, only if some of his friends invite us both, and then they turn down the lights and we aren't allowed to sit together.'

Angus grunted. He disliked the way Mara seemed to think the situation a perfectly appropriate subject for discussion. His predicament had of course been endured by many another relative of a royal mistress down the ages. Some made the best of it and demanded money, others took umbrage, while the majority pinned sickly smiles to their faces and tried not to mind. The last alternative seemed the only one to survive healthily into modern times, and he had best adopt it.

'So you're not going on holiday together again?'

She glanced at him, and quickly dropped his eyes. 'I don't know what we might do. I'm sorry, Angus, I know I'm being an awful bore. I promise we'll try and steer clear of June, anyway.'

They fell to talking of other things. Angus overheated the casserole and it was dry and tough, but the pudding was nice enough. He said, 'The Court's going to start taking people next week.'

Mara sighed. 'You do realise I can't even go home? I might not be thinking of anyone else, but nobody's given a thought to me. You've tarted the place up and filled it full of strangers and I can't show my face. I'd have to wear a label, like an exhibit. "Lady Mara Hellyn, well known adventuress".'

'Well, you can't hide forever.'

She dropped her eyes. Forever was a word she was coming to hate. There was no forever in her life, only tomorrow. She lived from day to day, staring at the walls of her flat, waiting.

She went back quite early. There was someone talking to the porter, a man with the slightly seedy air of a reporter. Mara ducked her head and hurried to the lift, while the porter said loudly to the stranger,

251

'Now see here, I won't have you disturbing my residents. Be off with you, at once!'

Perhaps she hadn't been seen. Mara leaned back in the lift, closing her eyes briefly. If someone offered the porter more money than he could decently refuse then no amount of graciousness would protect her. Jay had to do something. He must act, and soon.

She was lonely in her flat. She threw herself face down on the bed, still in her clothes, giving herself up to wanting him. The 'phone sat silent on the table. He hadn't rung her today. It was all she could do to make herself go out and not sit there, waiting. Usually she had no choice but to stay home, because no-one invited her anywhere. Society was locking her out, walling her up in this place. Jay must do something, he couldn't let her go on like this!

It was late, he wouldn't telephone now. At the start he had called at two or three in the morning, just to tell her how much he cared. Now, he visited on the days he had no engagements, or he came to stay at weekends, and he had no reason to talk to her. Besides, what could she say? Her life was empty, there was nothing in it of interest. Occasionally she suffered the dread thought that she might be boring him.

She picked up the 'phone herself and rang down to the porter.

'Trevor? It's me. I know it's asking an awful lot, but could you get me something? I don't need very much. That really is most terribly sweet of you, I can't imagine how I'd manage if you weren't here. Pop it in the box in the lift, I'll pick it up. Thank you so much, Trevor. Love and kisses.'

After a few minutes the lift began to whine. She went out into the deserted hallway, and when the lift arrived she stepped in and clicked open the control panel. Slipped behind the electronic circuitry was a neat packet of white powder. Mara took it, slammed the panel shut and went back into her room. Already she felt relief.

Chapter Twenty-Eight

Left alone, Angus began the slightly obsessive clearing up that sometimes typifies men living by themselves. He liked things just so, and was coming to feel that entertaining sometimes came a bad second to tidiness. His life was neat, orderly, and he could do without Mara's profligate habits, leaving chairs covered in crumbs and lipstick on every glass.

When everything was shipshape he sat down and finished a letter to Jean. He wrote once a week, setting down all that had happened to him and making polite enquiries about her father. It was nice to think of her at home, keeping an eye on things. He felt that he had a champion in the field.

There was a knock on the door. It occurred to him that it was probably Mara, collecting something she had forgotten, and he glanced round the room wondering if he could have overlooked an earring or a bracelet. When he opened the door he was taken by surprise. Toby stood there.

'Hi there, Angus, my old mate. Got a scotch anywhere?' Toby leaned hugely against the doorpost. He was wearing evening clothes and looked already the worse for wear.

'It's damn nigh midnight.' Angus moved aside to let him in and Toby reeled across to a chair. He blinked up at his host. 'You ought to be pleased to see me. Done you a bit of good tonight, my son. Been talking to a few editors, setting them straight on a few things. You are cast as the reliable member of the family, steady as a rock.'

'Is this publicity for The Court?' Angus went into the kitchen and poured them both drinks.

The flat was so small that conversations from one end to the other rarely needed raised voices.

Toby yawned. 'We're going to have pages and pages of colour photographs. Your mother can look aristocratic, Lisa Parisian, and

Marcus can occupy a sort of Byronic role, moody and mean.'

For a moment Angus was silent. Then he said, 'I don't want my family exploited for your profit. Confine your photographs to the house, please.'

Toby gave a crack of laughter. 'Too late, sunbeam. You should have had your scruples at the start. Lisa's got to be in it, I've been bullshitting all night about her. She looks fantastic, an absolute cracker. And she should, I spent thousands on her clothes.'

'What on earth − ?' Angus stared at him in angry bewilderment. 'Who gave you permission to buy my sister clothes?'

Toby gave a lazy, sharklike smile. 'I don't think I need permission. For anything I do.'

'Well, that's where you're wrong! We didn't give you rights over the family, for God's sake. The Court's our home. We won't be dressed up and paraded like a cartload of monkeys!'

For a moment Toby watched him, his face thoughtful. He had the disconcerting ability to sober up almost at will, it seemed. He said, 'If you read the contract, as you should have done, or at least as your solicitor should, you'll find out that what I want I get. If it's for the good of the hotel, you do it. All of you.'

'We never agreed to anything of the sort.' But even as he said it, Angus felt his confidence waver. He hadn't read the small print and neither, he would bet, had the family solicitor. An old and doddering firm, they had served his father and grandfather with pedestrian incompetence, and now saw fit to pass on the curse even to the third generation. 'Shit!' he burst out. 'Shit, shit, shit!'

Toby laughed, got up and rested a heavy hand on Angus's shoulder.

'Don't fret, old son. I'm not going to have naked fan dancing on the lawns. The old place is looking wonderful, you'll be delighted. By the way, Jean sends her best wishes.'

'Oh.' Angus wondered how much he knew. 'Have you seen much of her?'

'She takes me hunting. Lovely girl, straight as a die.'

'Yes.'

Angus felt rattled. Toby gave and withdrew friendship in accordance with some obscure code of his own. An occasional glimpse of the iron hand and it was back in the velvet glove. Next to Toby he felt helpless and inexperienced. He took refuge in stiff formality.

'Well, if there's nothing further you want to discuss − I do want to get to bed.'

'Your narrow, lonely couch. Ought to find yourself a human hot water bottle, the big city's teeming with 'em. Look, Angus, I don't want to beat about the bush. Your brother's a nice guy, I really like him. When he's not climbing the walls. Even then, you can't take against the bloke. Your mother's shoved him back off to hospital, and it's probably best, he can be bloody impossible sometimes. But with all this publicity I would like the earl to be around. Just shaking the odd hand, posing in the Great Hall, if we can get rid of the fucking scaffolding by next week. Why don't you come? And be the earl?'

'You mean — impersonate my brother.'

Toby shrugged. 'Why not? You look the same, give or take a twitch or two. And believe me, at the prices we're charging, we need all the glitz we can get.'

Angus put down his glass and got up. He would have liked to stride about, but in the flat it wasn't possible. He felt trapped in an airless room. 'You don't understand a bloody thing about us,' he said angrily. 'We're not acting, damn it! My brother *is* the earl, it's what he *is*, not some damned silly part in the school play. We agreed to have a few guests, as a house party. And now you think we should all star in your pantomime, complete no doubt with a pantomime horse. We are not an all-singing all-dancing group of players, and the minute we start acting like one we are dead!'

'You're dead anyway. If this doesn't come off then you will be back where you started, Angus, my son. You may be too posh for this money-grubbing stuff but if you don't start doing it you will end up in the gutter.'

'If that's so then it's no concern of yours.'

'For Christ's sake, Angus, all I'm asking is that you get off your backside and help!'

After a moment, Angus said, 'Very well. Obviously you can insist I come and I will. But as myself. Anything else would be an insult to my brother.'

'Just don't go around telling everyone who you are, OK? I'll do all the misleading that has to be done.'

'I'm warning you, Toby —'

'What?' The big man looked down at him mildly. Angus felt a tide of impotent rage. 'I'm sick to bloody death of you pushing me around!' he burst out.

Toby said, 'If you joined with me in this, I wouldn't have to push. Come on, Angus. We used to be friends. I've got another day in town, why don't we have dinner together tomorrow night? We could take in a show.'

It was an olive branch, and at any other time Angus would have accepted it. But he said, 'Sorry. Previous engagement.'

'You don't say. Some other time, perhaps.'

Angus listened as Toby ran heavily down the stairs. He shouldn't have been so abrupt. He really did have a previous engagement, the selection committee, and Toby was the last person he wanted to tell. When he was with Toby he felt slow and dull-witted, like a beginner at chess playing the grand master. But the difference between them wasn't great. It was only confidence. Unlike Angus, Toby had no conception of what it was to fail.

But, nonetheless, Toby was offended. Hide it as he might, he felt vengeful, as if the Hellyns were taking all that he had and giving nothing in return. Months ago he had stood amidst bare trees and marvelled that anyone could have built so preposterous a house as The Court. He had been charmed then, and now knew the place well enough for the charm to have lost some of its power. It was as if he had been in love and was waking up, embarrassed about all that had gone before. Toby didn't think he had been rude enough for Angus to be really upset. The least he could have done was to offer another drink, or even a bed on the floor. He wouldn't have accepted, but the offer should have been made. Instead Toby trudged morosely back to his impersonal and grandiose hotel.

That same night, Jay and Anna attended an official dinner. There were signs of strain, however bright the masks they tried to wear. They avoided speaking to one another, and conversed too intently with their neighbours. The food was over-elaborate and very rich. Anna ate too much, while Jay left his and drank the wine.

To his surprise, as they prepared to leave a swarm of policemen seemed to descend on the hall. They stood at every exit, and plain clothes men with suspiciously blank faces were out in the street, watching the roofs.

Anna touched Jay's arm. 'Is something happening? There is a policeman over there with a rifle.'

'So there is.'

Jay walked across to his detective and raised an eyebrow. 'Well?'

The man looked unhappy. 'I think − not wishing to alarm the princess, sir − we've received an IRA threat. We're taking all precautions.'

'So I should hope.'

A policeman in peaked cap and braid strode in from the street. He bustled across to them. 'If I could ask you both to wait for a few moments, sir − we're bringing the dogs in. Some sort of explosive device appears to have been planted.'

'Where? Do let me see.' Anna tried to push her way to the door but Jay restrained her.

'Darling, the police want us out of sight. There could be a gunman out there.'

256

'I can't be bothered to worry about gunmen.' She shook off his hand and walked to the door, looking this way and that with interest. One of the plainclothes men grabbed her and hustled her back. She was distinctly ruffled.

'Come into a private room, Anna,' said Jay grittily.

This time she did as she was told. Coffee was brought on a tray, and a further supply of the little marzipan sweets Anna had gorged on earlier. But she didn't look at them.

'How dare that man push me so?' she declared furiously. 'You must have him reprimanded.'

'I think he's in the SAS,' remarked Jay.

'I don't care if he's in the boy scouts. If I wish to risk my life then it is mine to risk. All my life people have threatened me. I am not now going to be timid.'

Jay chuckled. It wasn't a sound she had heard recently. Her face lightened. 'Am I being very silly?'

'Yes, quite. But brave too. Someone could be about to blow us up.'

She threw up her hands. 'Let them! I don't mind dying. I think I should be happier dead.'

He let out his breath. 'Have I made you so unhappy?'

'Yes. And you know it. And the pity is that first I made you unhappy, and I do not know how or why. Or at least I did not know. Perhaps now a little better. But it's too late, isn't it, Jay?'

She picked up the coffee pot and poured them each a cup. As she handed his across her hand shook. Brown drops fell in a line across the encrusted seed pearls on her long white dress.

'I hate that dress,' said Jay, suddenly vicious. 'It makes you look a hundred.'

She seemed to shudder. 'It is not my fault I am not a great beauty. I don't have style, I know that. And I have no friends here to advise me. This girl of yours, she was born beautiful and she has all her circle around her. Nobody who is English and well-born is ever alone.'

'Mara isn't what you think her,' said Jay heavily.

'You always say that!'

She tried to drink her coffee, but spilled it again. The dress was quite ruined, a spreading stain marked the front. 'I wish I was dead, I wish I was dead!' she whispered suddenly.

He couldn't bear it. 'Oh, Anna, don't!' He put his arm around her and she clung to him, shaking. 'It isn't so bad, you know,' he said gently. 'We've got the children.'

'I want another. I want a boy, for Havenheim and for me. Your boy.'

He could feel her soft breasts against him, but within all was fierce

257

determination. The way she hung on, holding him as he twisted and turned to be free. This side of Anna was quite new to him.

'To hell with the bomb, or the gunman or whatever,' he said suddenly. 'Let's go home.'

She put back her head. 'Yes. Let fate decide what happens to us.' They laughed, and opened the door.

The hall was full of policemen and soldiers, and one or two alsatians sniffing about enthusiastically. 'Is there a car to take us home?' enquired Jay. 'We're sick of sitting around waiting, I'm afraid.'

A storm of protest arose, muted out of politeness. Jay longed for someone to tell him not to be so bloody silly, but of course no-one did. So out they went into the street, walking past two amazed snipers lying down in the ambush position. He tapped on the window of one of the police cars, and Anna stood in the light, looking around.

'This is so exciting,' she said happily. 'It is like being in a film.'

'Bloody horror movie if you get yourself shot, missus,' said one of the snipers lugubriously.

The policeman who had spoken to them before came rushing up. 'Get 'em in the car, get 'em in the car,' he yelled, and they were hustled into the back of the police car. The doors had no handles.

'It's like being arrested,' remarked Jay. 'Do you know where to go, officer, or are we on our way to the Scrubs?'

'Er — we'll try and see you right, sir,' said the driver. He sped off, the radio crackled with panicky messages, and a couple of motorcycle outriders swung in from somewhere to escort them. As they drove away, a mighty explosion sounded. Looking back, they saw the street covered in a pall of dust.

'Good God,' said Jay. 'There was a bomb.'

Anna said, 'People will be hurt. We must go back.'

But of course the policeman drove on. They listened to the radio all the way home, and afterwards, in their apartments, they telephoned to discover what had happened. Jay stood at his desk, a glass of brandy in his hand, and Anna sat in the chair next to him, her balloon glass cradled like an infant. They felt a guilty elation.

Jay was saying, 'I see — and ten people injured — we'll visit tomorrow if we may. Convey our deepest sympathies. Thank you.'

Anna looked up at him out of huge eyes. 'Well?'

'Four people dead. Two of them clearing up in the room where we took coffee. If we'd stayed we'd have certainly been killed. The bomb was in a cloakroom just behind.'

She put her hand to her mouth. 'We were spared. I can't understand.'

'Yes. We were spared.'

Suddenly he felt desperately aroused. Anna seemed like a stranger, a wide-eyed stranger. All he knew was that he wanted sex with her then, at that moment, to dissipate some of his excitement. She saw what he wanted. He realised she wanted it too. They put down their drinks and began tearing at each other's clothes. He ripped off her ghastly dress sending seed pearls like rice scattering across the carpet. He pushed her down on top of them, aware of a deep, shameful urge to hurt. She clung to him, gasping against his shoulder. In a moment it was done.

'You see,' said Anna triumphantly. 'It need not be finished.'

He pulled away. 'I wish you wouldn't think — I shan't stop seeing her. If you want, we can live like this. We'll try for a son. But you have to understand — you can't expect me to be faithful.'

He saw her face stiffen. Words burned within her, but she said nothing. In silence she began to gather her clothes, bundling the dress into a heap in a corner. She left the room, she went upstairs. He heard her maid, Greta, start babbling at her. In English Anna yelled, 'Will you leave me alone, you stupid cow? Why can't you ever leave me alone!'

He almost felt shocked.

Chapter Twenty-Nine

Once the publicity photographs were taken and as winter moved into spring, Toby stayed away from The Court. He went abroad for a few weeks, and when he returned he stayed in London. Lisa was bewildered. She hadn't realised how much a part of her life he had become, and now he was gone she almost felt abandoned. But when he was there, she often wished he wasn't. She didn't understand herself.

Spring came with a rush. One day the wind had teeth, freezing the hedgerows and keeping snow under the rocks on the moor, but almost the very next day there were primroses, a blue sky dotted with scudding clouds, and the dog fox barking at night in answer to his vixen. Marcus, whenever they visited him, said, 'I must come home soon. For the swallows. I shall come home before then, shan't I?'

They were getting ready for the opening. Ten people were coming to stay, and Curtiss had arrived from London to supervise the servants and the cleaning of the silver. To Lisa's surprise, because she had imagined everyone eager to return, only a few of the old staff had come back, and they treated the newcomers like troglodytes. It seemed they were in danger of faction-fighting in the kitchen even before any of the guests arrived.

They were all terribly nervous. 'I shan't eat with people who don't dress for dinner,' declared Charlotte.

'Of course they'll dress,' said Lisa. 'It's just like having people to stay. We can do as we like. If we want them to dress, we say so.'

'And suppose they call us names? They could be awful people. What sort of people pay to stay in other people's homes?'

Lisa went to the conservatory and paced the flags, turning each time she encountered a bank of the new, wicker furniture. She was sick with fright. Where was Toby? Why had he worked so hard only to leave just when everything was coming together? Someone had arranged huge pot plants between the chairs, great ferny things from some hothouse, that would surely wither and die in The Court's ancient draughts. What were they doing here?

Lisa went in search of Curtiss, locating him in the wine cellar. He was happily racking up dozens of bottles of Château Margaux.

'Curtiss, the plants in the conservatory. Did someone order them?'

'Mr. Ledbetter had them sent up from the village, my lady.'

'Mr. Ledbetter? Is he in the village? Now?'

'I do believe he's at the pub.' Curtiss placed the last of the bottles lovingly in its hole, and stood back to admire the ranks and ranks of good wines. 'Hard to remember when we last saw the cellar as well stocked,' he mused. 'Not even in your grandfather's day, my lady. We've even got pink champagne.'

'Pink champagne is vulgar,' said Lisa, a great deal less sweet than the champagne. She turned and went back up the cellar steps.

So, at least he was back in the village. Why had he bothered to come, if he was simply going to inflict things upon her, with no thought for her wishes? She had always thought that he at least took notice of what she said, that he considered her opinion. But he was dumping on her just like the rest.

The whole point of everything seemed to have been lost. She thought suddenly that Marcus should be here. They were saving his heritage and sending him away to do it, and just at that moment she couldn't remember why. Her head ached. Soon there would be hordes of visitors, and people wanting things, needing things, and she was too tired and too worried to cope. How dare Toby leave her like this? How dare he go hunting with Jean Maythorpe and then leave her for weeks, and come back only to put his feet up in the village? He should know that she needed him.

Her spaniel, very bored, sat down wearily on the hard wood floor and sighed. He could do with a walk, and on impulse she fetched her coat and started off. She would go towards the village and see what Toby had to say.

She felt better out walking. The algae on the statues was brilliant green today, like verdigris on copper, putting the dull, winter-beaten grass in the shade. How she wished she had the money to re-design the gardens; they had never been great and neglect only made them incoherent. Lisa liked order, structure, she wasn't happy with decay.

As she neared the village she took off her headscarf and dragged a comb through her hair. A local woman had cut it for her, neatening its customary ragged edges into a sleek bob. In the evening she wore it with slides, but by day she brushed it straight back, a severe, chic fall. Some things Toby said made sense. There was no point in aping

261

Mara, or even despairing because she couldn't. Just as well compare poodles and labradors, who might both be dogs but were otherwise totally dissimilar. She knew he would hate her coat, a Burberry found in the dog room. She had turned the sleeves back into huge cuffs, but the hem almost trailed on the floor.

She found him almost at once. He was sitting in the bar, having a lunchtime drink. He looked very brown. When he saw her, he was taken by surprise. A flush rose up under his tan, and he stumbled to his feet, knocking over a stool.

'Lisa! What are you doing here?'

She swept the skirt of her coat in an arc and perched on one of the remaining stools. 'Hello, Toby.'

He swallowed. Why was it that Lisa could rattle him more effectively than anyone he had ever met? Two minutes ago he had felt calm and in control, yet she managed to make him feel a clumsy oaf.

'You look — you look fantastic. I like the hair.'

'Thank you.' It was her turn to go pink. She said, 'The plants look good. But I think they'll die, the conservatory's not at all warm.'

'Yes. I'd have got plastic but I didn't think you'd like that.'

'No.' She fiddled with a beer mat. He offered her a drink, but she refused. At last she said, 'We haven't seen you for ages. Everything's chaotic at home.'

'Is it?'

She caught the edge to his voice. But what had she done, why was he angry with her? 'Are you sorry I spent so much money on clothes?' she asked bluntly.

'Good God, no. I'm not the sort of bloke who gives with one hand and takes it back with the other.'

'Oh. I see.'

The conversation faltered and died. Toby sipped his beer, watching Lisa over the rim of the glass. He was struck again by her slightness, and that gloss in her hair, he hadn't noticed that. Like dull gold.

'How's your mother?' he asked jerkily.

Lisa made a visible effort. 'Rather nervous, I think. So am I. Suppose we don't like these people? Or they don't like us? All those photographs in magazines ... we might get hundreds of people wanting to come, and we won't want them.'

'You'll want them,' said Toby harshly. 'After what I've spent, you'll want them if I have to disembowel every one of you.'

'I don't think that would make us very much keener,' she commented wryly.

He laughed. When he was away from her he forgot how much he enjoyed Lisa's dry humour. He forgot her air of highbred tension,

262

making the air around her hum and crackle.

'I'm sure Mother wouldn't mind if you wanted to come back,' she murmured.

He couldn't think what to say, and it was not often he was lost for words. 'So you do know what I'm upset about?' he said at last.

She flushed and said quickly, 'I thought it might be that. But you're not the sort of person to be bothered by someone like Mother. You're much too tough.'

He gaped. 'Not so tough you can't hurt my feelings! I do have feelings, you know. I'm not some rough-hewn lump of timber!'

To his amazement, her eyes filled with tears. 'And neither am I! You didn't have to go like that. But I suppose you're happy now, swilling beer and going hunting with Jean Maythorpe. I suppose that's what you want.' She got off the bar stool and started to put on her scarf.

'I took her out to dinner once as well,' retorted Toby. 'I am allowed to do that. After all, *you* don't want me.'

'I suppose she's only too willing to take up with you. I suppose she's that sort of girl.' Lisa swung on her heel and marched to the door. Toby abandoned his beer and followed her.

'Why are you being so bitchy? You didn't want to know me and Jean did.'

'I didn't tell you to go! My mother did.'

'You didn't try to stop her, as I remember it.'

'I said to go for a day or two, not weeks and bloody weeks!' She sank her hands deep into her pockets and began stumping down the road, the skirt of her coat catching her heels. Toby kept up with her easily, walking backwards to see her face. He trod on the dog.

'Now look what you've done! You could have broken his foot.' She bent down to cradle the shaking dog.

'You think more of that damned animal than you do me. You've broken my heart!'

'You haven't a heart to break. You can't have or you wouldn't be so mean.'

Neither of them spoke. The dog whimpered pathetically, he was a tremendous actor. Toby said, 'I feel like going away and never coming back.'

'Just because you can't get your own way.'

'No! Just because I give you everything and it isn't enough! What more do you want? What I've done to that house, it's for you, all of it's for you! You could have had anything you wanted, it would have been yours.'

'That isn't true! You do it to make money, you can't pretend not.'

263

'I can make money a hundred better ways, I don't have to flog myself to death here. And once, only once, I ask something of you and I don't get it.'

'But you didn't ask! How do you think I should know if you don't ask?'

'And you think I'm the one without the heart?'

Lisa pushed her hair back from her face. 'I'm sorry. I've been unkind and I didn't mean it, I promise. Come back now and I'll tell Mother she's not to be rude to you. I've kept your room just as it was, with flowers and everything. I'm sorry I don't seem − that I seem rather cold. I don't mean to be.'

He put his arms out and she went into them, even though they were in the village street and people could see. She put her arms round his neck and he hugged her. 'I have missed you,' she whispered into his chest.

'And I've missed you, honey.'

He drove her back in his Porsche, the dog crammed in the tiny rear seats. Halfway up the drive he stopped and turned off the engine. They sat and stared at The Court, today sprawling benignly in the sunshine.

'Magnificent. Not beautiful,' said Toby.

'There isn't anything else like it,' said Lisa.

'Unique. Like you.' He reached across and took her hand. 'The world's full of blokes like me but I never saw anyone like you anywhere.'

'I think you're quite different, actually.'

His hand felt very hot and big. 'Me? Blokes like me are ten a penny.'

They sat, quite silent, as if they were waiting for something to happen. A small bird landed on the bonnet of the car.

'I've bought a place in Rio,' he said suddenly. 'I didn't think I'd get it but I did. The pictures look ghastly, a rundown club on the side of a hill.'

'So why did you buy it?'

He shrugged. 'I needed a club. I think I can make it into something. Lisa − when The Court's up and running, come out with me. You can help put it together.'

'Me? You mean you want me to come to Rio? To Brazil?'

'Yes.' He tried to twist to face her, and the steering wheel got in his way. 'We could get to know each other properly, without your bloody mother or Angus or anything.'

'You mean we could sleep together.'

Toby let out a long sigh. 'There isn't anything wrong in wanting to

264

do that. It seems to me you Hellyns have no bloody idea of how much you take and how little you give. And I'm not buying you, God knows I'm not, but everything in this world is something for something. I want to get close to you. I think I've bloody well earned it!'

The colour in her face was gathered in two bright spots on her cheeks. A strand of hair fell forward and she scooped it back behind her ear with a gesture so feminine that he almost felt stabbed. She was so delicate, so far from prettiness and yet so much something he desired. Never in his life had he waited so long for a woman. Silently, not meeting his eyes, she nodded.

Angus arrived that evening, the first time since the photographs. He didn't see Toby until they were drinking sherry before dinner, and the two men stiffened, like challenging dogs.

'Glad to see you could make it,' said Toby crisply.

'It is my house,' retorted Angus.

'You surprise me. I always thought it belonged to Marcus.'

Charlotte let out her breath in annoyance. The man always said something unpleasant, and yet she had to tolerate him, him and his appalling schemes. She ignored him and turned to her son. 'Have you seen Mara? We haven't heard in weeks, she could have disappeared off the face of the earth.'

Angus took a sip of his drink. 'I see her quite often. She's well.'

'She always is. Whatever she does, she never falls ill. Quite the most dauntingly healthy girl.'

'She'll have babies like shelling peas,' remarked Toby.

Charlotte visibly shuddered. 'What a fascinating expression,' she murmured. Her eyes were a clear, cold grey. She rang the bell.

After only a few minutes Lisa began to wonder why she had dreamt of including Toby. Angus took sly swipes at him and Charlotte treated him with all the courtesy she would afford a bad smell. Lisa subsided into unhappy silence.

'Nervous about tomorrow?' asked Angus.

She gave a brief smile. 'Of course she is,' said Toby. 'She's no need to be, of course. Everyone will think she's wonderful.'

'I do think Lisa can speak for herself,' said Angus.

Her head came up. 'Don't be rude to Toby. It seems to me that everyone's favourite pastime is bashing Toby! He didn't have to get involved here. He's doing us a favour, if only someone could appreciate it.'

'I'm sure that we all appreciate Toby,' said Charlotte with heavy irony.

Angus cleared his throat. 'I've got some news,' he began. 'It's not something to shout about. At least, it's very good news from my point of view, but in the long term.'

265

'You're a candidate in a Labour stronghold?' said Lisa.

'How the devil did you know that?'

She shrugged. 'We all know already. You wrote to Jean when you heard from the committee. Jean told Toby and Toby told me.'

'Oh. Oh, I see.'

'We're all very pleased for you,' said Charlotte, as if a little surprised that she should be expected to be pleased at something so doomed to failure.

'I don't know why Jean had to tell anyone,' said Angus. 'And why you Toby?'

'She likes talking about you,' he said smoothly. 'Reads your letters into rags.'

'Why on earth do you write to Jean Maythorpe, darling?' demanded Charlotte. 'You'll be giving the girl silly ideas.'

Curtiss served coffee in the family drawing-room, and as always once they left the table whatever net of common interest they had woven seemed to break. They were restless, and could think of little to discuss. Angus said, 'If you don't mind, Mother, I'll go down and see old Reg. Talk about the hunt. He'll want to go over his first season.'

'Oh. If you must, darling.' Charlotte looked dubiously at Lisa and Toby. There were few things she disliked more than the prospect of an evening spent with That Man.

Angus went out quickly. He felt restless, and cross with Jean. She had no right to tattle their private correspondence. He wouldn't write to her if nothing he said was safe.

At the Maythorpes', all the outside lights were blazing. Angus allowed himself to be mollified. She was hoping, if not expecting, that he would come. The front door opened as his car drew up and Jean was there, in a dress of silk jersey that could have done a turn at a cocktail party. Angus like the way she dressed, the rather brash overstatement, the diamonds. When he went up to her, he bent and kissed her cheek. She went pink with delight.

'Oh, Angus! I thought you might come. Dad said you'd be too busy sorting things out at The Court, but I bet Lisa's done everything. How does it look?'

'Like an oasis in the desert,' he remarked crisply. 'A few respectable rooms in the midst of a crumbling pile. If someone strays from the beaten track they could be lost forever.'

'We'd find their skeleton, years later,' said Jean in a thrilling voice. 'Fingers clawed against the door – gone mad with hunger! Oh, sorry.' It always seemed tactless to talk about insanity with the

266

Hellyns and yet the subject always cropped up. It was very odd.

They went through to Reg, who was waiting in lordly style before the copper canopy of his gas fire. He had placed two brandy glasses and a decanter on the table, and next to them was a pile of photographs. The record of his hunting year, in pictures.

'Sit down, Angus, lad,' he said cheerfully. 'You'll take a glass? Right good season we've had, though Mrs. Stacey's mare had to be shot last week. Broke a leg in a ditch. She says she's giving up, but I'll lay money we'll see her out next winter.'

'Oh. Yes.' Angus shot a pleading glance at Jean but she merely grimaced and sat down. The hunting saga was obligatory, it seemed.

It took forever. Photograph after photograph had to be explained, the story recounted and the right comments made. Jean watched indulgently, and at last Angus could bear no more. He stood up.

'Would you mind awfully, Reg, if Jean and I went out for a while? I know she wants to talk over one or two matters. I'm a candidate, you know.'

'Aye, and for a decent party too.' Reg reluctantly closed his albums. 'Get her round to your way of thinking lad, I'm sick to bloody death of socialist twaddle. "Let's all lie in the gutter and starve together" – that's their motto.'

'And yours is, "You can stay in the gutter, I don't give a damn",' retorted Jean. 'My only hope is that Angus will have some compassion. He's not quite beyond prayers.'

She picked up a fur jacket and Angus helped her to put it on. It made her look older, perhaps a little hard. In the car he said, 'I don't like you in fur.'

'Dad bought it for me. He said I needed keeping warm. And actually I don't approve of fur all that much, but I can't hunt and disapprove, it doesn't match.'

Angus laughed. He liked Jean's honesty so much, the direct pithy way she got to the heart of things. 'Look,' he said, 'I'm full of brandy. I probably shouldn't even drive.'

'Well, then. What do you suggest?'

Angus raised his eyebrows. They drove slowly out into the road, turning right away from the village. The mouth of a track opened up beside them, and twenty yards down it curved to hide them from the road. Angus turned off the engine. In the dark the whites of their eyes gleamed. 'You shouldn't have told everyone my news,' he whispered.

He heard her swallow. 'I know. But I wanted everyone to know you wrote to me.'

'Why?'

'I don't know. Oh, yes I do. Because I don't want to be your low-

267

class bit of stuff. Something you keep secret because your family wouldn't approve. The girl you dump when you marry Clarissa Pethick-Smythe.'

'Who the hell's she?'

'I don't know. But I bet there is one.'

He moved across and slid an arm around her shoulders. 'There's only you. I'm working too damned hard for anything else, and besides, with Mara's antics it pays to keep my head down. I'm not much of a catch. Scandal, poverty and insanity all in the same family do tend to put people off.'

'They don't put me off.'

He put his lips against her neck, feeling her hand reaching to cradle him. 'How fortunate.'

At The Court, Lisa was yawning ostentatiously. 'I think I'll go to bed, Mother. Did I tell you Toby's staying the night? He's got to be on hand first thing in the morning.'

'Yes, I thought it best,' he agreed, stretching his long legs and grinning, in that way he had, as if he was totally guileless.

'I don't think the pub is unacceptably distant,' said Charlotte. 'I'm sure Mr. Ledbetter would prefer the surroundings.'

'He's staying here,' said Lisa through gritted teeth.

Charlotte shot her a look of fulminating rage. Then she put away her emboidery and prepared to go to bed. 'Then I think we shall all retire,' she said tightly.

When they reached the landing, Toby bent and kissed Lisa's cheek. 'Night, sweetheart,' he said.

As he went off to his own room, Charlotte said, 'Lisa. I think we should talk.'

She followed Charlotte to the grand bedroom that for so long had belonged to both her parents. Nothing had changed since Henry died. His tall ship's table still stood at the bedside and on it rested copies of *The Field* and *Shooting Times*. Even the pillows on the bed were the same, as if Charlotte had not moved to take up Henry's space but still confined herself to half the available width.

Charlotte seated herself at the dressing table, while Lisa stood in the centre of the worn rug, like a child being told off at school.

'Lisa, dear,' her mother began. 'I know you feel very grateful to Mr. Ledbetter. I'm sure we all feel grateful. But he is not the sort of man I like to have in the house. Altogether too brash.'

'I can't exactly throw him out,' said Lisa.

'I think at least you can stop encouraging him to make up to you!' flared Charlotte. 'Trips to Paris, kisses, cosy little tête à têtes — I

268

think this has gone quite far enough. I want you to tell him his advances are not welcome.'

Lisa swallowed. 'He's just friendly,' she murmured. 'He doesn't mean anything.'

'Indeed.' Charlotte began to take combs from her hair. 'I imagine he's got his eye on the tapestries. No doubt in his ignorance he thinks marriage to you would give him a foothold in the family and a say in what happens to our treasures. Set him right on that score and I'm sure you'll see the last of him.'

Lisa giggled. 'I don't think he wants to marry me,' she murmured.

'Then what on earth do you think he does want?' Charlotte pressed her fingers to the bridge of her nose. 'My dear, it's often the lot of plain women to be flattered by men who want something. Think! You're not a beauty. A man like that must have dozens of glamorous girls fawning on him. You're young, you're innocent, it's easy to be deceived.'

'He — he likes the way I do things. The house — '

Charlotte took off her rings, shaking them into a cut glass tray. 'I imagine you saved him the cost of a decorating firm. Don't be so gullible, Lisa. The man's a common rogue.'

She began to cream her face, as she had every night since she was a girl. The cream itself had never changed, it was pale pink and gave her skin a high, greasy sheen.

'Why did Father marry you?' asked Lisa suddenly.

Her mother shot her a surprised glance. 'We were in love. He was so wonderfully good-looking, he could have married anyone, but he fell in love with me. I was very pretty in those days.'

'But you had money, didn't you?' snapped Lisa. 'He wouldn't have married you if you didn't. And for a while you lived high on the hog, until it was all gone and you were back where you started.'

Charlotte's reflection stared at her. 'You're becoming very bitter,' she said. 'All I want is for you not to make a terrible mistake. That man doesn't care for anything except himself, and here you are deceiving yourself into thinking he loves you. Not everyone can have love. Not everyone's suited to it. And those that aren't should learn to be happy as they are, without twisting themselves inside out with envy.'

Lisa turned and ran. She felt ill, almost sick. Her parents had indeed loved each other, but Charlotte had given ten times more devotion than Henry in return. What did her mother know about love and need, the bargains struck by people other than herself? All the same, Lisa felt sick. Perhaps it was true; she was plain, unlovable, doomed to spend her life alone. Toby was only out for what he could get.

She put on a nightdress of the thinnest silk. Her body showed through it only as a darker stain, so thin and sticklike. She saw nothing that Toby could desire. What was she to do then, turn her back on this one chance? Perhaps she was only fit for the crumbs that others left. Other people. People like Mara who gorged on all that life had to offer. But even the crumbs were sugar on the tongue.

She made up her mind entirely. She would go to Rio with Toby, she'd do everything that he asked. It wasn't real, and she knew that. But if she wasn't to have love, then a pretend emotion was better than nothing. If this was all she was offered, then so be it.

Breakfast was taken as it used to be, from silver dishes set out in the dining-room. No more burnt toast, no porridge hot from the pan. Everything was kept warm, and tasted quite different.

Charlotte was first down, followed by Angus, full of beans on a fine spring morning. As Curtiss brought coffee, Angus said, 'You don't know how glad I am to see you, Curtiss. Breakfast hasn't been the same since the day you left.'

'We've all been adventuring,' the butler agreed cheerily. 'But it's certainly pleasant to come back safe to harbour, sir.'

'If it *is* safe harbour,' said Charlotte. 'I hate to think what your father would think of this scheme, Angus. And the old earl would never have imagined we could do such a thing.'

'We all have to move with the times,' remarked the butler.

When he had gone, Charlotte made a face. 'He certainly hasn't improved! Are we to find him serving at table and joining in the conversation, do you think?'

Angus swallowed a mouthful of bacon. 'He's just feeling cheerful. And so am I. Where are Toby and Lisa, for goodness sake? They can't lie in today.'

They came down as Angus was finishing his coffee. Lisa looked white and tired, in contrast to Toby's infectious enthusiasm.

'Ready for the big day, are we? Beautiful morning, I think I'll go for a ride later. Do you fancy coming Angus?'

'All right, if there's time. We could go out with Jean. Whatever's the matter, Lisa? You look exhausted.'

She poured herself coffee and sat down. 'I didn't sleep very well. I was worried about everything.'

Toby rubbed his hands together. 'No need for that, Lisa. Look at your mother. Cool as a cucumber, aren't you Charlotte?'

'I hope I am neither so green nor so indigestible,' she said.

Toby grimaced. 'Glad to see we're all in such spirits,' he said thinly. 'Are you sure you're OK, Lisa?'

'I'm fine.' She sipped her coffee. Without asking, Toby went and fetched her a plate of bacon and egg. She didn't eat it. He watched her anxiously, his pleasure in the day visibly dimmed.

Lisa went to her room straight after breakfast. Her head ached and she felt almost tearful. Her spaniel scratched at the door and she let him in, and then sat on the bed cuddling him, hating herself for being so easily depressed. Her mother had said nothing she didn't already know. But somehow she hadn't expected it. Some part of her still hoped that her mother at least saw her as intrinsically lovable.

After a while she got up to go downstairs and check with the cook about dinner. There was to be salmon, an enormous beast poached in one of The Court's giant fishkettles. Timing was certain to be a problem, because the kettle was so heavy and they hadn't wanted to indulge in an extravagant trial run. Also the fish was wild, and slightly marked, so presentation would be important. She fixed her mind on the day.

As she opened the kitchen door, she jumped. Toby was there, giant fist raised to knock. He was carrying an orchid. 'Er − I was keeping it for later. But I wanted to give it to you now.'

'Mara likes orchids.'

'Oh! I didn't realise. I'll get you something else.'

She grabbed his arm as he turned to go. 'It's all right! I didn't mean I don't like it. I was just saying.'

'Good. Good.'

They stood uncomfortably together. Toby couldn't understand why yesterday everything had been so good between them when now it had turned so sour. 'It's too late to change your mind about Brazil,' he said truculently.

'I don't want to! But if you −'

'I've booked the tickets. Six weeks from today.'

'I don't know what we'll say to Mother.'

Toby grunted. 'If that's all you're worried about! It's another conference. A hotelier's conference. Or a health trip, or a shopping spree, or even a goddammed orgy. We don't have to report to her on everything we do.'

'No.'

She smiled at him, for the first time that day. 'Don't be nervous,' he said. 'It doesn't matter that much.'

'It matters a hell of a lot and you know it!' she retorted. 'I'll be all right. In fact, everything will be fine.'

'Good girl.'

She moved to go past him and he caught her hand, lifting it to brush his lips lightly across her fingers. Then he let her go.

*   *   *

271

The first guests arrived in a Rolls. The family, and Toby, were assembled to greet them, Charlotte in drifting blue silk, Lisa an elegant doll in tailored gray. As for Angus, he wore a suit, blue shirt and red polka-dot bow tie.

'What the independent aristocrat is wearing nowadays, I take it,' said Toby nastily. He himself was in white shirt and Savile Row pinstripe. Were it not for his pugnacious face anyone could have been excused for confusing them.

Angus said, 'I'll wear what I like. As I told you before, this isn't fancy dress.'

'Actually it feels like a play,' said Charlotte nervously. 'Are these the Americans? The Batchelders? At least they look presentable.'

The man was tall, greying, with a pearl-handled walking stick, while his wife exuded quiet style. But at the moment when Charlotte should have stepped forward with a welcoming hand she stood frozen in panic-stricken immobility.

'How do you do?' said Lisa, stepping desperately into the breach. 'How kind of you to come.'

'Delighted.' The Americans shook the hands before them.

'Good journey?' asked Angus in the manner of someone who would have preferred them to suffer a fatal accident rather than arrive.

'Wonderful. Quite wonderful.' Mrs. Batchelder smiled hopefully at everyone.

Lisa gathered her wits and moved aside to let them into the house. This was becoming quite ridiculous. These people were here to stay, they were guests. Friends almost. 'Come into the drawing-room. Curtiss, is it too early for tea, do you think?'

The butler inclined magnificently. 'I shall bring some at once, Lady Eloise.'

En route to the drawing-room, Toby and Angus deserted. Lisa battled on, she and Mrs. Batchelder sustaining a desperate conversation.

'Eloise. What a charming name.'

'Do please call me Lisa.'

'And we are Phyllis and Steve.'

Lisa shot a horrified glance at her mother. God defend anyone who called her Charlotte on first acquaintance. 'My mother, Lady Melville,' she murmured apologetically.

Mr. Batchelder wandered over to the window and gazed out across the lake. 'Get much fishing around here?' he enquired.

'Not a lot, no' said Lisa. 'Do you fish?'

'Er – no. No I don't.'

'We have horses,' broke in Phyllis. 'You have horses, don't you?'

272

'We breed,' added her husband. 'We're from Kentucky.'

At last Charlotte seemed to come to life. 'Do you mean race-horses?' she enquired. 'My husband used to own one or two. We weren't very successful, I'm afraid. Do you have any success?'

Steve looked thoughtful. 'Some. Some.'

'We – er – we won the Triple Crown last year,' murmured Phyllis apologetically.

'We rub along,' said Steve. 'We're just folks.'

Relief was spreading visibly across Charlotte's face. These were the right sort of people, her sort of people, with the added attraction of foreign glamour. She could almost forgive them for coming here. 'I wonder if you'd like to see the gardens later?' she murmured. 'Or the park? What a shame it's still so dark after dinner. By the way, we do dress.'

'Dress?' Steve looked disconcerted.

'Evening dress.'

Curtiss came into the room, wheeling a tea trolley groaning with porcelain and silver. Lisa got up. 'If you'll excuse me – let me know when you've finished, Mother, and I'll show Mr. and Mrs. Batchelder their room.'

'Lisa –' her mother wailed in faint alarm. But even as the door closed behind her, Lisa could hear Charlotte saying, 'You have English relatives? How interesting. How did your family come to be in America exactly?'

It was a preliminary to Charlotte's favourite genealogical conversation. After hours and possibly days of interrogation she would find some remote connection with somebody she knew.

More people were arriving, this time an elderly Dutch couple, tired and rather anxious. Lisa cossetted them, taking them at once to their room and ordering tea. 'We must find some Dutch newspapers,' she told Curtiss. 'Get someone to telephone the station, or the airport or something. Warm scones I think, please, Curtiss.'

She bustled downstairs again, to meet and greet the next arrivals. It was all a great deal easier than she had anticipated. But then, as Toby had said at the start, it was only a house party. When she was small, before the decline really began to bite, every weekend had meant strangers wandering in the passages and a dull supper in the nursery while a feast took place downstairs. The house absorbed people, it took them in without any fuss at all.

Late in the afternoon, when everyone had arrived, Toby came looking for her. 'Sorry I sloped off. Felt a bit of a spare part.'

Lisa grimaced. 'It was all right. Angus should have stayed though. He's being very unco-operative.'

'Isn't he just? He's so damned half-hearted about things. Never takes control, never grabs life by the throat.'

'I don't think you can expect Angus to be like you,' retorted Lisa. 'He isn't any sort of a sharp go-getter. But he's good and kind and he does his very best.'

'He'll get eaten alive in politics.' Toby reached out and tucked an errant strand of Lisa's hair behind her ear.

She sighed. 'That had occurred to me. Poor old Angus. I can't see him making any impression on thousands of Labour voters, or at least not a favourable one. Unless they want someone nice. Someone who means well.'

She thought about it as she changed for dinner. Angus always shied away from difficulties, almost from habit. He was a natural peace-maker, the rock upon which the rest of the family leaned when their mercurial natures got the better of them. Lisa could just about see him as a steady backbench MP, but as an innovator, a man of decision, that was something else again. And yet he seemed absolutely set on it. The best she could hope for was a gentle disappointment.

She put on a dress of lilac silk, severely cut except for flowing panels in the skirt. There was no time to admire herself, not if everything was to be perfect. She ran downstairs and caught Curtiss putting an unpleasantly tall flower arrangement on the dinner table, when she had made one specially and put it in the dog room. Tonight had to be perfect: for Charlotte, for Toby, for the staff who had worked so hard. But most of all for the house. Somehow, she thought, the house deserved a celebration. It had suffered so much.

The dinner was magnificent. Angus sat at the head of the table, Charlotte at its foot, and everyone drank champagne. Above them the chandelier tinkled in the rising warmth.

'How much is that worth?' someone asked.

Charlotte fixed him with a dreamy stare. 'I really have no idea. No doubt the eighth earl would have told you. He was always obsessed with money. Such an unfortunate trait, I always feel.'

There was a brief silence before Phyllis Batchelder launched bravely into an anecdote about the President. Charlotte understood none of the politics and knew no names, but took the absorbed interest of someone hearing about life on Mars. Lisa almost snorted down her highbred nose. Could she really go to Rio and leave her mother here, leave people like this exposed to her? She had changed since Henry died, become set in a curious enclosed world. Yet she appeared to be enjoying herself, and as for the guests — they were enthralled. They were like visitors to a zoo, and Charlotte was a pet anachronism wheeled out for their amusement.

When the meal was at last over Lisa slid away into the garden. So early in the year it was still cold and she shivered. The moon was shining on the lake and one of the barn owls from Home Farm swooped across the park on silent wings. She heard someone coming. It was Angus.

'My God! It's a bit exhausting.' He leaned against a tree.

Lisa said, 'Mother's doing well. I haven't seen her so happy in months.'

He nodded. 'It's what she was brought up to do, I suppose. I can see her swinging smoothly into summer, and the shooting season, and hunting weekends, just as it was when we were small.'

They stood listening to the night. Tiny creatures rustled across the lawns, there was the plop of a rising fish. 'They could always fish the lake,' said Lisa. 'We could stock it with something.'

'And have anglers standing up to their waists at all seasons of the year? God, I'm glad I'm in London. This is all so bloody social.'

She put her hand on his arm. 'Thanks for coming. I wanted to ask you but it seemed a bit unfair.'

'Toby insisted, actually. Says it's written in the contract.'

'Oh. I didn't know.'

Her hand dropped and she turned away from him. They had never been close. As children there had been the triumvirate, Mara, Marcus and Angus, with Lisa as the outsider, too young to join in. He found it hard to assess what she had become. She was trim, with an almost delicate elegance that sat oddly with her bony face. Her manner too, verged on self-possession, mixed with a touching reserve. She was an interesting girl, and he wouldn't have noticed if it wasn't for Toby. He treated her as purest glass, and when he managed to make her laugh he was happy all day, which was odd when the man was such a bull about everything else.

'Do you ever wonder what would have happened if Father had lived?' asked Angus

She nodded. 'Yes. Yes, I do. It wouldn't have been good. He died just before it all began to go wrong. And dying made it worse.'

'I don't think he did it on purpose!'

She sighed. 'If he'd lived another year, he would have. What is it with the Hellyns? They don't know how to adapt.'

It seemed very true. A cloud covered the moon, and took the light from the lake. A soft wind shook the tops of the trees and a dog fox barked again, up on the moor. They turned and went into the house.

Chapter Thirty

Daffodils were thick against the walls. Anna looked down from her bedroom, thinking that all in all, she was lucky. It was spring and they were still together, still breakfasting in uneasy politeness, and even occasionally dining. Sometimes he came to her room, always angry, always abrupt. He blamed her now for many things, and one of them was being shy about sex. So she tried, as best she could, and despised herself.

She couldn't go on like this. She was short-tempered with the children when they nagged and pestered to go to the country. If they went they went alone, because she must stay here with Jay, clinging on to him. If her father ever found out that she knew, and condoned, the situation, he would act at once. He would bring hell crashing about them before he permitted his daughter to be so insulted. And she worried about him; sitting in Havenheim he thought of himself as so much more powerful than he was. If he invoked the wrath of the truly great, he would be no more than a nut between the crackers.

Suddenly weary, she sat at her desk, pulling out one of the many tiny drawers. Folded inside, small as a postage stamp, was a piece of paper. On it was the address of Mara's flat. If had been gained so easily, through a simple question to the detective, and yet she had agonised about asking him. Jay thought he was being so discreet, quite unaware that a radio detection device was fitted automatically to his car, and to hers, in case of kidnap. That it also served as a neat method of surveillance was conveniently overlooked, except in this case, when clearly surveillance was called for. How she hated the thought of faceless men knowing that her husband kept a mistress.

Sighing, she dragged herself to her feet. There was no use planning if you did not act, however weary and dispirited you felt. She would borrow Greta's small car and launch herself off into the London traffic, praying that some of her driving skills would return. It was time to see the girl for herself.

Mara was weary. Jay had stayed until almost dawn, seemingly tireless. He left her sticky and sated in bed, and when at last she woke, around eleven, she simply bathed and pulled on a silk robe. When the porter buzzed she was drinking coffee and nibbling toast, the newspaper propped up messily before her.

'A visitor, ma'am. Come to collect something your friend left last evening.'

Mara looked round the usual clutter of the flat. Jay left many things, she couldn't imagine what he would want urgently. Perhaps it was one of the gold and pearl cufflinks his wife had given him, and his valet was in a panic. She yawned. 'Send them up, please. Thanks.'

The lift whined and a soft knock came on the door. Mara pulled her dressing gown roughly closed and went to open it. She was surprised to see a woman. 'Oh. Was there something you had to collect? I'm sorry, I don't know what it is.'

'If I might come in.'

A pronounced foreign accent. The woman was short, unremarkable in a dull green suit and her hair showed signs of grey. But she walked calmly past Mara into the flat, her head held oddly high. As Mara closed the door, the woman said, 'I am Princess Anna. I believe you made love with my husband last night.'

Mara almost shuddered. She felt the blood draining away from her skin. With a huge effort of will, she controlled herself. 'Perhaps you'd like some coffee?'

'Thank you.'

The princess sat rigidly in an upright chair while Mara found a cup. She poured from the pot with a hand that barely shook. The princess declined milk and sugar, sipping as if the brew contained hemlock. Mara felt wildly defiant. She threw herself back on the sofa, extending her legs to show off endless tanned skin. The woman was a frump, stiff as wood. No wonder Jay couldn't stand her.

'You realise how bad this is for Jay,' said the princess.

Mara laughed. 'He's happier than he's been in years! I'm sorry if that upsets you but it's true. We satisfy each other in every way. Sexually, emotionally, everything.'

'Even intellectually? You appear to have led a life of endless whoring, I cannot imagine you have much other conversation.'

'You shouldn't believe everything you read in the newspapers. I know that is hard for you to understand, but a great many men want to sleep with me. Some like to pretend they have done so.'

277

Anna set down her cup. 'Come, come, Lady Mara. Your exploits with Mr. Selmer were well documented. My father has many accounts from his staff, even one from a man who entered the room while you and Mr. Selmer were – engaged.'

To her horror, Mara's cheeks began to burn. What else did the old witch know? 'What an amazing command of English you have,' she snapped.

'And also German, French, Italian and Spanish. The day will come, Lady Mara, when there are no men that will sleep with you. I am not surprised that my husband became entrapped, you are very beautiful. But it is time for you to realise that this can go no further. My husband remains my husband, come what may. He still sleeps with me, you know.'

Mara's eyes narrowed. She would have liked to claw the woman's eyes. 'Jay's a virile man,' she murmured. 'I've no doubt that he manages to do his duty.'

The princess gave a grim smile. 'Perhaps I should tell you that I am pregnant. I have told my husband that I have no objection to him using you for relief until the child is born, but after that I want him to desist. He has promised that it shall be so. I feel you should be told. You are young, you might not like being employed for such a purpose.'

'He would never agree to such a thing!'

Anna rose to her feet. 'I know him so very much better than you, my dear. He is a charming man who finds it difficult to be as strong as he might wish. Perhaps he will not give you up. Perhaps he will visit you, once, twice, in a week. But it will become less and less, and you will grow older and older. If he left me, which he will not, he would be an outcast. He has made *you* one already, I think.'

Mara dragged herself to her feet. She almost tripped over the trailing edge of her dressing gown. 'I shall tell him you were here. I shall tell him everything you said.'

Anna smiled. 'I very much hope that you will do so, my dear. Naturally he will deny many things and you will wish to believe him. Please think about whether you should believe me instead.'

The dignity remained up to the moment Anna sat again in Greta's little car. She put her hands on the steering wheel and found that they were violently shaking. She could barely close her fingers. Oh, by the Blessed Virgin, what had she done? She wasn't even sure she was pregnant, she was only two days overdue, and three previous babies had been lost a week after a missed second period. And Jay would deny that they had ever talked; he would come to her and rage that she should have upset his darling so. No wonder he loved her! She was

278

breathtakingly lovely, so tall and golden, all rounded flesh and soft, sweet face.

Anna hated her, hated so violently that she pressed her fists into her body. She tried to calm herself. If she was growing a baby let it not be filled with hate, with loathing of that woman for being what Anna could never be – beautiful, sexual, adored. Tears began to seep beneath her closed eyelids. How hard it was not to be loved. All her life love had surrounded her and now, in this strange place, that was not hers and never could be, she felt abandoned.

Suddenly the door to the flats opened and Mara came out. She was wearing trainers and a battered raincoat, her hair like a cloud of gold. Anna shrank down, but the girl looked neither to right nor left, simply running out to flag down a taxi. Anna's heart thundered in her throat. Was she going, even now, to Jay?

Gradually she began to calm. She tried to remember the controls on the car, what Greta had said about the choke. At last she drove hesitantly out into the traffic.

Mara headed straight for Tavistock Square. She dared not ring Jay, and she wasn't even sure that she wanted to. As the woman said, he would deny everything. But suppose he truly meant to leave? Ever since Italy she had felt herself pushed further and further away.

To her relief, Clare was at home. She stood up as Mara came rushing into the room. 'My dear girl! Has something terrible happened?'

'It was his wife – she came to see me – oh, Clare, if he leaves me I'll die!' She fell sobbing on to the sofa. Clare fished for tissues in her handbag, and rang for some brandy.

The whole story poured out. Mara offered it up like a sacrifice, begging Clare to put some favourable slant on the facts. At last the older woman sighed. 'If he really meant to leave you as she says, she wouldn't have come. But not meaning to go doesn't mean he won't.'

'He promises that we'll be together. I'm sure he doesn't lie.'

'Well, he certainly doesn't seem to want to divorce his wife,' remarked Clare. 'Samuel's delighted, I have to tell you. They appear to be living together in some harmony. What's more, you have gone into purdah, and even more fortunately the newspapers seem to have lost interest.'

Mara leaned her aching head on her hand. 'You all think it's just going to fizzle out, don't you?'

'Don't you? Mara, my dear, you must be sensible. He should never think of asking you to sacrifice you life in this way. At the moment everything's perfect for him. His wife is desperate, you are desperate,

279

and he can flit from one to the other feeling wonderful. You are both flattering his very considerable ego.'

'He hasn't got an ego. And even if he has, it wouldn't help if I didn't flatter it. What should I do, Clare? I must fight her, I must win.'

The girl was unbelievable, utterly single-minded. Clare sighed. 'You should leave him at once. Get a job abroad, perhaps. If he means to leave his wife then he must, otherwise you refuse to see him again.

'Mara, dear, she has everything on her side and you have so little! Men get over these sexual things, they come to their senses. And she has two children and expects another. In the end it's the children that count.' Clare spoke with all the sadness of a barren woman. She felt as if she had only lived half a life, on one side of a great divide. If she had borne children her life would be so different now. But then, if she had children, she would value Mara less. With Mara, she reached out a tentative hand towards motherhood.

'I never wanted to be anyone else in all my life until now,' said Mara miserably. 'And I'd give anything to be her.'

She went back to the flat quite early, because Samuel was coming and Clare did not want him to know about Mara's visit. A lonely evening stretched ahead, without Jay, who was going to the opera with his wife. How wonderful it would be to dress up tonight, and go out into the world. She remembered standing with Edward, watching the lights, and she had felt then that the world was waiting for her. Now, in her opulent flat, she was shut out.

Without knowing it, her thoughts followed Clare's. It was the children, of course. If he had no children, he wouldn't stay with his wife a minute. Was it totally loathsome to wish the creatures dead? Of course it was. She didn't wish that, though by all accounts they were being brought up to be prim and silly and staid. What did she wish? That they were hers perhaps. That she was the one with the unbreakable hold over Jay's heart.

She went into the bedroom and stood, looking down at the packet of pills. They looked so insignificant in their pretty pink wrapper, a girly foible, like vitamins. She picked them up, took them into the bathroom and flushed them away.

Anna waited and waited for him to lose his temper. But the days clicked past, one after the other, and things were as before. Why had the girl not told him? She didn't care, that was all, she knew the wife could not defeat her. As if a mere wife could ever hope to eclipse something so lovely! Mara's image seemed burned on her brain, she saw her constantly. Why did she live in such mess, and more to the point, why did Jay not mind? At home he was utterly meticulous.

One morning, over breakfast, she said, 'Jay, I have some news.'

'Mmmm?' He continued to read the paper.

'I'm pregnant.'

The paper came down. He looked quite amazed. 'Good Lord! Well, that's wonderful. I'm so pleased for you, Anna.'

'You should be pleased for us. It isn't only mine.'

'No, indeed. Well, you're going to have to take things fairly easily, I imagine. Why don't you go down to the country? You know how much you love it.'

'But I should much rather stay here with you.'

Silence grew, like a wall. Eventually Jay said, 'Don't you think it would be better not to torment yourself?'

Anna tried to sound calm. 'But I prefer to know what you do. My child must have a father in more than name.'

'That wasn't what we agreed.'

Her voice almost rose to a shout. 'I agreed nothing! My only agreement was in marriage, before God! It is you who have changed things, not me! You leave me clinging to hay!'

'You mean straw.'

She was in danger of tears. 'Hay, straw ... I don't know. Oh, if only you would give her up. We could be as we were, and happy.'

'Haven't you learned anything? The happiness was yours, not mine.'

She found herself staring at him, willing him to believe her. In a low, anguished voice, she said, 'I would do anything. I know how much I ask. If it is in my power, I will give anything to you.'

He got up and went out. Her pain tore at him, he couldn't bear to see it. The child had been a hostage, instead of himself, but she was greedy. She wanted more, she would always want more. He whipped up his anger, but no amount of heat could quite extinguish his thoughts. My God, but she was brave! Six months ago, if asked, he would have said his wife was ordinary in the extreme. But even in her greatest pain she had dignity. He couldn't help but offer her respect.

He went to Mara often that week, tormented by his wife's white face. But even there she intruded. Mara had the habit of questioning him when he was at his most eager, leaning her head back to look into his eyes. 'You do this with your wife, don't you? You can tell me, I won't mind.'

'It's never like this! Don't talk about her.'

'Does she talk about me? I bet she does.'

'No! Be quiet and let me love you, darling. Darling –'

281

'Please leave her, Jay. Please come and live with me.'

'Be quiet!' He took hold of her shoulders and slammed her down on to the pillow. His lovemaking was violent, almost cruel. It made him think of Anna. He thought, Why can't she leave me alone?

Afterwards Mara watched him, almost wary. In Italy she had been a cat with the cream, entirely satisfied. She was a cat still, but full of watchfulness. What did he think, what did he want? Once they had seen clearly into each other's minds, and now, even in passion, she felt shut out.

The weeks passed. Anna was given a hormone implant and instructed to spend half the day in bed. Her specialist wanted to draw some fluid from the womb, to establish the baby's sex and the likelihood of abnormality, but Anna refused. She so wanted it to be a boy. If it was a girl she didn't think she could endure the days. An announcement was made in Havenheim, and the apartments were deluged in flowers and tiny model cradles, a traditional Havenheim symbol of good luck.

Jay took the girls for a drive, to cheer them up. They were quite left out of all the excitement; even Ferdinand was sending presents for the new baby and not for them.

'If it's a boy, we won't matter any more,' said Isobel.

'That's ridiculous! You're very important little girls. You're my little girls, and Mummy's.'

'Boys are more important.'

'Everyone in Havenheim thinks we should be boys,' added Marie-Christine.

'Who tells you these things? Who is it?'

Marie-Christine put her thumb in her mouth, but Isobel swung her legs and said, 'Nanny.'

He went back and demanded that Nanny should be sacked. Anna was resting, lying down on her bed under a quilt. 'She's feeding those girls with idiotic sexist nonsense!' he told her. 'Do you think that only boys count? Does anyone today?'

'In China they do,' remarked Anna. 'And in Havenheim. It is very English of you to mind.'

'Since Havenheim considers me of rather less importance than a good horse, I find it difficult to believe in their principles,' snapped Jay.

He started to leave, because of course Anna wouldn't dismiss her Havenheim nanny. But she hitched herself up in bed and said, 'She could leave by the end of the week. Do you have anyone else in mind, Jay? I think you should find someone you like.'

282

Quite taken aback, he said, 'At the very least we should have someone who's prepared to let the girls get dirty. The woman's quite neurotic.'

Anna swallowed. 'How you've changed. You always used to be so precise.'

'Was I? Anyway, it isn't good for children.'

The search for the nanny took a lot of time; he found he could only visit Mara one evening that week. She made a special effort, which was a pity because he could only stay till about ten. The table was laid for dinner, with candles and tall thin glasses. She had cooked, and made serious attempts to tidy the place up. She was wearing a new kimono, the neckline plunging almost to the waist. Her breasts ballooned out, beyond the point of indecency, and all he wanted was to get her into bed. But she wanted to eat first, which annoyed him. Why was she dressed like that if it wasn't on offer?

'I want us to talk,' she said, sipping at a glass of mineral water.

'What about? You know I can't do anything yet. Anna has to keep calm, she has terrible pregnancies. Every complication in the book.'

'Poor Anna,' said Mara thinly. 'Actually, I wanted to talk about a holiday. I thought we might go to Italy again. Very discreetly, of course.'

Jay sighed. 'You know we can't. If people begin to think we're still absolutely serious about each other, then someone will blow the whistle. We'll be all over the papers.'

'So what? I'm sick of pretending, Jay. I'm sick of being on the sidelines. You don't seem to care how long we go on like this.'

'Only until the baby's born. If it's a boy, Anna and I will quietly separate.'

Mara looked at him oddly. Her eyes seems very blue, he noticed, like medieval stained glass. 'And if it isn't?'

He sighed again, irritably. 'If I could arrange life to suit us I'm sure I would, darling. Anna is pregnant. I don't know what the sex is, I'm not sure I want to know. All I can say is that I will do nothing to upset her until the baby is born. I have a duty to a woman who is carrying my child, and I won't shirk it, darling. You wouldn't want me to.'

Those eyes, blue pools into which all light seemed to fall and die. 'You've got a duty to me, Jay,' she said softly. 'I'm pregnant too.'

Time seemed to freeze for him. He thought, I should have known she would do this. Like a goddess she entrapped men, enchanting, deceiving, robbing them. She had stolen this child, taken it without his knowledge. He was unutterably furious.

'You − bitch!'

He was on his feet, coming at her. She scrambled up, hampered by

283

the kimono, and ran headlong into the bathroom. He was at the door before she could slam it. They fought and he won. She retreated against the bath, one breast and shoulder quite bare, her skin white against the dark red fabric of her dress., 'Don't touch me,' she said softly. 'I deserve your child, I'm owed it.'

'You'll get an abortion, damn you!'

She took a long, dragging breath. 'You don't mean that! You're angry, you're not thinking. Jay, you want our child, you must want it! No-one will try and stop us being together now.'

'But why now? My wife is pregnant, why now?'

'Because now you owe me as much as her.'

He went out into the sitting-room. How could she do this to him, force him into this situation? This was no act of love, it was blackmail, and his worst enemy could do no more. Did she not see the world of difference between a baby planned, with consent, and this – this trick? All his trust in her seemed to shiver, as if it rested on lies. He wondered what else she might do. Whatever else it was, it could never be as bad as this.

He picked up his coat, and cast a grim look back at Mara. She had never looked more luscious, half-naked, brilliant with colour. 'I don't think you have any idea of your own selfishness,' he said. 'And you don't begin to understand what you've done.'

Jay stayed away for a week. He took Anna and the children down to the country, and the girls and he played cricket in the garden with a tennis racquet. His wife sat at the window and watched, cheering and clapping at every shot. It seemed peaceful there, and undemanding. He felt like a man on leave from battle.

During that week he took journeys, but only in his imagination. He found a house, and put himself and Mara in it, with the child. He couldn't put a face to the child, or even a name, though the baby in Anna's belly seemed quite real to him. If it was a boy it would be John, and if a girl Anna Frances, though Anna wouldn't think of a girl. He remembered those other times, the births, the miscarriages, the times of joy and grief; Anna's face lit up from within, and again the days when the light seemed almost put out.

He tried to visualise Mara's tall body swollen with pregnancy. He couldn't see it, any more than he could see years at her side, in this house that he imagined, somewhere, anywhere. Mara was heat, passion, life lived to the full, with nothing held back. There was no pleasure for her in quiet days; she would not lie as Anna did, sewing as her children played.

He stood on a seesaw, caught between two betrayals. Sometimes he woke in the night and couldn't believe his situation. How had it happened? At the start every minute without Mara was a little death within his life. He had loved her, oh, how he had loved her. He put his fingers on the scar on his belly. Had he really done that? He had been mad, and the memory of it appalled him.

Yet he missed her. Sex with Anna was forbidden, and in that week he was quite without release. It wasn't only the act, it was the closeness afterwards, the sleepy, murmured intimacies. He needed that. He found himself sitting at Anna's side in the evenings, longing to say what he was thinking, to let loose the thoughts bottled up in his head.

On the third night, they sat by the window after dinner, watching darkness fall. Jay was silent. In the background some Verdi was playing. Anna said, 'Are you thinking of her?'

'I don't know. Perhaps in an indirect way I am. We always talked at this time of night.'

'What about?'

He sighed. 'Love, sex, that sort of thing. Silly things, lovers' things. We missed all that you know, you and I. We were always far too sensible.'

'I think I was too shy. I am shy still. I can't − I can't look at your body and feel comfortable within myself. I was brought up too strictly, I think, with too many warnings.'

He got up and walked a few paces away, as if going to change the record. But he stopped. 'I wish I knew what I felt,' he said desperately. 'I wanted to live all my life with her, we were like two halves of the same thing. I wasn't happy unless I was with her, I couldn't live without seeing her, touching her, loving her. I still feel a great deal of that. But I'm so happy here with you.'

Anna took a deep breath. She gathered all her courage, all her strength. 'Go and see her then,' she said. 'I won't hold you here against your will, I won't threaten this or that if you don't stay with me. We've lived together so long and we haven't known each other. It's different now.

'Next time I go to Havenheim I shall ask Greta to remain there when I leave. This is your house, you are master here, if you do not like my maid then she must go. And when the baby comes, perhaps he might be in your room. And you could be in mine. We should be closer, we should understand each other more.'

Jay said, 'It isn't so easy! If only you knew how difficult it is.'

She turned to look at him. 'There is nothing hard. We love each other, I know that is true for me and I believe it is true for you. And this girl, you have loved her too. I don't ask you to put her aside now, this minute, but in the end, yes, I want you to finish. If you feel it is wrong, then how much more wrong is it to leave me, and the girls, and the son growing here within me?'

He thought of Mara, perhaps growing another son. He and Anna had agreed to have a child; it was Mara who had deceived him. He felt a thud in his gut, of rage and pain and desire.

At the end of the week he left Anna and the children and drove back to London. He went straight to Mara's flat, passing the porter with his usual cursory grunt and rather less cursory ten pound note. The man put out a hand as if to stop him, but then shrugged and buzzed up to the flat.

As he stepped out of the lift, Mara stood at the door, waiting for him. Although it was mid-afternoon she was wearing a dressing gown, and her hair was tangled about her shoulders. She grabbed his hand and kissed it, falling on her knees to kiss, to put her arms around his waist and bury her face against him.

'Oh, darling, darling! I've waiting so long. Love me, please love me.'

He couldn't prise her away. She seemed wildly drunk. He said, 'For God's sake, pull yourself together. What's the matter with you?'

'Nothing. Oh God, I'm so glad to see you! Do it to me. Now. Now.'

She dragged off her dressing gown and started to wrench at his fly buttons.

'I think I would rather you shut the door,' he said coldly.

She fell back, away from him, and lay on the floor, laughing. 'You prude! Don't you want little Mara? Why don't you take that stupid look off your face and shut the door? Come and lie down here, I can tell you want to. I can tell you can't wait.' She put her arms above her head and stretched her legs out across the carpet. Her eyes glittered feverishly, as if she was ill. She was stretching, writhing, like someone possessed.

Jay was sickened. He went to the door and slammed it, standing with his hands to the wood, trying to control his own disgusting lust. She was naked, lying spreadeagled on the floor like a madwoman.

He reached down and grabbed her wrist, and she laughed hysterically. 'What are you on?' he demanded. 'Have you taken something?'

She wagged a finger. 'Nothing that you need worry about, you're such a good boy!'

He dragged her up and she hung by her wrist, her eyes suddenly bleary and unfocussed. After a moment he let her go. She sagged to the floor; he had to force himself not to kick her. Her breathing seemed to steady. She put her hands over her face and whispered, 'Oh God.' Jay went to make her some coffee. The flat was a tip, complete

286

and utter chaos. Even the dishes left from last week still sat in the sink, growing mould. Mara crawled, shivering, to her dressing gown and pulled it on.

'Are you really pregnant?' he asked.

'Yes. I think so.' She closed her eyes suddenly as tears began to run. They glistened on her long lashes, like dew.

'You know you could be harming the child?'

'It's only cocaine. And why should you care? I bet you want me to get rid of it.'

He sighed. 'I don't know. Honestly, I don't know. You should see a doctor, you might have done terrible damage. Mara, didn't you think?'

She pushed back her hair with a shaking hand. 'Why didn't you? Leaving me here all week, just going, not a word, no kindness, nothing. You didn't care how it would seem to me. You'd have been happy if I died.'

'That's stupid and melodramatic and you know it.'

Suddenly, everything about the place revolted him: Mara, the mess, everything. If he stayed, he knew, he'd get over that. She would cry, they'd talk, he could come back to the intimacy they had made their own. There was only a little distance between them.

But he didn't want that. He wanted to go on, not back, to widen the space until neither of them could ever reach across. Now one embrace would bridge the gap, but if he went now in no time the gap would be a chasm and there would be no crossing it. He could go home, to Anna and her world.

'You can do what you like about the child,' he said. 'If you have it, I'll give you money of course.'

'What? What do you mean?' She was still fighting wooziness.

'I'm not coming back, Mara. I've had enough. You can keep the flat, of course, and I'll settle any hospital bills. If you have the baby I'll support it, but I strongly recommend you to take some advice. There aren't many women who'd so lightly play with the health of an unborn child.'

'I was miserable. I was beside myself! Jay, don't go, I want to talk. You'll come on Wednesday, won't you? Please?'

She followed him to the door. He didn't know if she truly did not understand. He put his hands on her shoulders, so straight and strong. Who would have thought that Anna's would be stronger?

'It's over, my love,' he said. 'I'm sorry.'

He took the stairs down, and she stood at the top, quite bewildered. Perhaps she had dreamed it, perhaps he hadn't come at all. Back in the flat she went to the window, putting her hands against the glass.

She saw his car, saw him get in and begin to drive away.

She ran to the bathroom but all the cocaine was gone. She put her hands over her belly. God, what had she done? Left alone, quite alone, the baby hadn't seemed real, she had forgotten it. Just a counter, just a ploy in the game, she had picked it up and mentally put it down. Had she killed it? How could you tell?

She spread her dressing gown and stood sideways to her reflection. Her belly was no more than the slightest curve. Was it all right? She ran to the telephone book and scrabbled about for a number, the gynaecologist, Clare's man. She would make an appointment for tomorrow morning, first thing. Jay had been right to be angry. He'd stay away until he realised that his baby was loved and cared for, that she'd been silly and mad. He would never stay away for good.

Later she went and lay down on her bed. All of a sudden she felt terrible, dragging weariness. The past week had been all frenetic tension, waiting, worrying, and he had come and he had gone, leaving her drained. A fog seemed to cloud her mind. She closed her eyes, putting a hand on her belly, thinking how strange it was that she was no longer alone. Someone lay with her, closer even than Jay.

She knew she mustn't think about anything. Her only safety was in lying here, quietly, letting sleep lap at her, letting peace enfold her, quite still. He was gone. She must lie there, with this quiet other life, until at last she could bear it.

Chapter Thirty-One

Lisa said nothing about Rio until the week before her departure. By then her mother was enmeshed in guests and arrangements. She had forgotten, or chose not to remember, that this wasn't a genuine house party, and just as Toby had planned, she ran it as one. There was the formal greeting, the ritual appearances at meals, and between times a vague assumption that someone would look after these people. That someone was Lisa, and latterly Curtiss, arranging shoots and rides, cocktail parties and nature walks. By the time she came to leave Lisa was almost sure that everything would be all right. Except, of course, Charlotte.

She went to her room early one morning. 'Mother,' she began hopefully, 'you are enjoying all this, aren't you?'

Charlotte, still in bed with the newspaper and a breakfast tray, glanced up over her half-moon spectacles. 'I hardly know what you mean, Lisa. I'm doing my best, at all events.'

'Yes, of course you are. But it is better than before, isn't it? So much more comfortable.'

'I don't know what you want me to say. The house is permanently full of strangers. One does one's best not to complain.'

'Really, Mother! You might at least give Toby some credit. It was a brilliant idea and it isn't nearly as dreadful as you thought. Is it?'

Charlotte took off her spectacles and said irritably, 'I'm sorry, but I will not hold any kind of brief for that man. He's quite rapacious, and whatever spurious charm he possesses never succeeds in concealing it. Your father knew the type, and avoided them. Businessmen with bites like sharks. They think of nothing but money.'

'It wouldn't have hurt Father to think of it occasionally.' Lisa sat on the bed with her chin in her hands.

'That's a stupid and unkind remark.'

Charlotte shook out her paper, replaced her spectacles and made it

289

clear she expected Lisa to go away. For a minute the girl's courage almost failed her. Then she braced herself. 'I'm going to a conference,' she said shrilly.

'Are you, dear?' Studied disinterest.

'Yes. On Thursday. I've given Curtiss a list of all the arrangements.'

'I should hope so. Please don't come the martyr. After all, you were the one who wanted to open the house. Nobody else was in the least keen.'

'Absolutely. That's why I'm going to this conference. I need to learn about all those organisational things, like portion control and visitor numbers.'

Her mother shuddered. 'How appallingly commercial.'

Lisa left. If Charlotte didn't want to know where, when, or for how long, then she wasn't going to tell her. She would go to Rio for three weeks and to hell with everything. She felt a brief and delicious rebellion.

On the day of the departure she said to Curtiss, 'I'll be three weeks, I think. If Mother notices I've gone you can tell her I'm having a few days' holiday as well.'

Curtiss cast a grim eye at Toby. Lady Melville might not have much idea of what was going on, but he certainly did. And how much he wanted Lady Eloise to marry brilliantly and do down her glamorous sister. Curtiss had established his favourite on his very first day at The Court, when Mara was out riding with her father and Lisa played tea parties all alone in the house. He gave her cake for her dolls and she had hugged him. Now here she was, getting mixed up with someone who would use her and hurt her, a man too hard and clever for anyone's good, and her as innocent as a newborn babe.

'Just get in touch if there's a problem, my lady,' he said meaningfully. 'Things don't always work out as we expect.'

Lisa went pink. 'I don't suppose they do,' she muttered. 'Goodbye, Curtiss. Thank you so much.'

In the car, Toby said, 'What the hell was he on about?'

'No idea,' she replied. 'Or at least − he thinks you've got designs on me. He doesn't approve.'

Toby snorted. 'The day one of that lot approves of me is the day I lie down and die.'

She wasn't listening. As The Court receded she felt her tensions dropping away. Freedom beckoned, with all its promise and terror.

When she came out of the airport building Lisa almost cringed. Light assaulted her, harsh and brilliant, hotter than Hades. She put up her hand to shield her eyes, feeling the world spinning sickeningly. The flight had lasted forever, and here they were, like flies pinned out under an enormous light bulb, squirming.

'My God! Smells incredible, doesn't it?' Toby drew in great gulps of air, full of petrol and heat, flowers and earth, and underneath the taint of something rotten and foetid.

'It's so bright.' Lisa fished for her sunglasses and Toby chuckled, put an arm round her and hugged her.

'Didn't I tell you it would be exciting?'

A porter was loading their bags into a taxi. Toby thrust money at him, without looking at it. He seemed so experienced, thought Lisa, in everything. Perhaps it was just confidence, in his wealth, in his ability. Nothing seemed to worry him.

On the drive to the hotel she hung out of the window. They passed a market, reeking of overripe fruit, and tall busty women slunk past on stiletto heels, overtaking short fat housewives in sweaty black dresses. The place gleamed and glittered, with too much concrete and too many cars.

'You OK?' asked Toby, glancing down at her.

'I've got culture shock,' she said wryly. 'It's so foreign.'

'Not nearly as foreign as Blighty. I was bewildered when I first arrived, couldn't work out why no-one wanted to know me. But then, I was a wildboy from the outback and shouldn't have expected anything else.'

'How fortunate that now you're so cultured,' teased Lisa.

The driver leaned back to talk, driving with one hand and half an eye. 'Tour of city?' he asked gutturally. 'Copacabana?'

'Why not?' said Toby. 'We can have a bath any day, let's see Rio!'

Lisa, who wasn't at all sure that she wanted to get to the hotel, said 'Yes, let's!' enthusiastically.

The city came almost to the edges of the sea. The beach people were beautiful, with skins like tanned silk, the girls tall and lovely in highcut swimsuits. Young men did flamboyant exercises, and then strode along the sand with macho exhibitionism. Their swim trunks were tighter than skin and bulged obscenely.

Toby said, 'This is all very liberated. Let's have a swim later on.'

For a second she closed her eyes. The place was strange, sexual, lustful almost. Everywhere she saw tight clothes and brown, moist skin.

He gripped her hand tightly and waved the driver on, on. They passed shanty towns perched on gravelly hillsides, with women queuing at a standpipe for water. A couple of boys were wrestling with a giant lizard, hanging on to its tail as it tried to run away. Lisa was haunted by its pale, blinking eye. What did it think, dragged cruelly from its quiet home?

'I hate that sort of thing.'

'No point in being provincial,' said Toby. 'Don't look.'

They went on again, into the baking city streets, where the lizard's eye seemed to blink in a thousand luxurious shop windows. Over it all, like a watchman, loomed the mountains. The place was unreal, yet more vivid that anything Lisa had ever known.

The dust was caking their skins, drying their throats. Lisa's clothes felt glued to her with sweat. The hotel began to seem a haven, whatever else she might have thought.

'Where now?' said Toby.

She tried to swallow. 'Don't you think we could go to the hotel?'

'What? It won't be very special, you know. One hotel's the same as another the world over. Bed, bathroom, expensive restaurant and lousy room service.'

'I just want to get washed and have a drink.'

'Are you tired? For God's sake, why didn't you say?'

He leaned forward to give the driver the name of their hotel. Lisa marvelled at him. He never seemed to tire, and his enthusiasm bubbled to the end. Suddenly he yelled to the driver to stop, sprang out and bought some slices of fresh pineapple. It was like cool, sweet water, and the juice made sticky rivers in the dust on Lisa's hands. She caught his eye and smiled.

'I'm sure that's the sort of thing you're not supposed to eat.'

'Is it? Christ! I'll give you some whisky as soon as we get to the hotel, pickle the bugs.'

The hotel was very smart, the lobby lined with mirrors and perspex, reflecting its rioting green plants again and again until it felt like a chrome and glass jungle. Toby had booked luxury, a vast suite with a wide view of the city. In the centre of the bedroom stood a huge four poster bed.

Toby tipped the porter. When he had gone, and they were alone, Lisa said, 'I'll have a bath if I may.'

Toby said, 'It's your room as much as mine. Here, have that whisky.'

'Are you sure it doesn't just make the bugs drunk?'

'Buggered if I know. Perhaps if they're drunk they forget to make you sick.'

She took a glass in her sticky hand. It didn't taste like real whisky, but then she rarely drank it. Toby knocked back his in a second. It occurred to her that he might be nervous, which was ridiculous. Nothing frightened Toby.

'I'll have a bath' she said again.

'OK. I'll follow you.'

He sat drinking whisky, looking out over the city and listening to her movements as she washed. Long trickling sounds as she lifted an arm or leg from the water, soft swooshing noises as she soaped herself; little sighs of pleasure, that turned him on more thoroughly than any blue movie he'd ever seen – the things that girl did to him without even trying!

Toby looked down at himself. God, what was he thinking of? She was so little, so delicate, and he was such a great brawny brute – he hated to think of what he must do to her. Must do, because he couldn't bear to hold back. She seemed to imagine that desire was something that came upon him from time to time, that intruded into their otherwise calm relationship. Yet the desire was constant, kept under exhausting control. He couldn't live like that. She made him live like a monk, made him feel that he should try and live like a monk, made him feel guilty about something that had never given him a moment's pause before. He almost felt that he was corrupting her. And perhaps he was. There has to be corruption in growing up.

She came out of the bathroom wrapped in one of the hotel's bathrobes, her arms lost in the sleeves, tripping over the hem. Her hair clung damply to her forehead and beneath it was her beaky nose. She looked at him defiantly, as if daring him to think she looked pretty. He thought, She's like a small, fierce hawk.

'I'll – I'll wash,' he said jerkily. 'Have a lie down. Have a sleep.'

'All right.'

She lay on the bed, and her heart bumped against her ribs. Was it to be now? Jetlag disorientated her, she felt exhausted and yet could not sleep. Would she ever be able to sleep with him beside her? A giant body, hot and close; she would wake whenever he stirred. Slowly she drifted into a doze, not quite awake, but not even half asleep.

Air conditioning made the room cool. When he climbed on to the bed beside her she felt the warmth radiate from his skin. She turned her head, looking through half-closed eyes, and saw that he was naked.

'Toby – ?'

'It's all right. Honey, it's fine, it's going to be wonderful.'

His body loomed above here, his head blotted out the light. When he kissed her, his tongue roaming her mouth, she heard him moan.

He pulled open the bathrobe and touched her breasts. Lisa closed her eyes, pressing her hands against his shoulders, trying to push him away. But he was touching her, stroking her, whispering words of

293

love. 'You're so thin — there's nothing of you — darling, do you like that, do you like me to touch you?'

For a big man he was wonderfully gentle. But she hated herself, hated her breasts, that were no more than slight humps against her chest, the nipples swollen as raspberries under his hand. She closed her eyes, shutting him out, trying to shut off her own sickening responses. He was asking her to give up, let go, let him take control, and she couldn't.

When he rolled on top of her, she fought. 'No. No! I can't breathe!' He lifted himself up on his elbows and she put her hands against his shoulder and looked at him wildly. 'You're smothering me. I can't bear it.'

He was breathing hard. 'Do you want to be on top? I never heard of anyone losing their virginity that way, but you could be the first.' An obscene picture of what he meant formed in her brain. She, on top of him, balanced like a little monkey on his great body. 'No. No, it's all right,' she murmured.

His hand went between her legs. She forced herself to part them, and then lie still, waiting. Something hard touched her thigh, and his fingers groped blindly. He touched a raw nerve and she squealed. He touched again and she began to fight him, trying to get him off. Feeling lay between her legs, skinless and exposed, as near to pleasure as it was to pain. She writhed, twisted, but he was holding her down, pushing hard and harder still between her legs.

Her mouth gaping, she saw his face above her, slicked with sweat.

'Stop — stop — you're killing me!'

Something in her gave. She was hurting, badly, she could feel hot blood, and still he pushed into her, creating space where none had been before, huge in her small frame. Toby grunted, looking down at her with eyes that didn't see, and she lay helpless with pain and shock. God, would he ever stop! Would he ever get it out of her?

He gave a mighty shout, rearing up with his eyes wide open and his mouth stretched. She felt shudders racking his whole body, felt the thing inside her twitching with a life of its own. Toby fell to the side, gasping, helpless, still joined to her at the crotch. Gingerly, she wriggled herself free. Every part of her was shaking, even her teeth chattered. But he put out an arm and gathered her back to him, holding her in a circle of muscle and sweat.

After a while they got up. They were hungry and went down for dinner. Lisa found herself watching him, watching everyone. How could the world be based on something so animal? How could it go on, how could people be civilised, knowing that this was at the heart of everything? She felt that everyone had known except her, that she was the last to be admitted to the secret. She felt changed, as if someone had torn down a gauze between her and the rest of humanity. She saw clearly, and wasn't sure she liked it.

'All right?' Toby kept saying. 'You don't hurt, do you?'

She was stiff, that was all. The bruising was in her mind. She watched as Toby leaned back in his chair, letting out a huge, contented sigh. He looked calm, and rich. Waiters scuttled here and there at his bidding, though he was never other than polite. He was watching her with an expression of great satisfaction.

'You're wonderful,' he said. 'Just wonderful.'

She couldn't meet his eye. For minutes at a time she would forget, and then a vision of what they had done flashed into her mind and her whole being cringed in embarrassment.

She forced herself to look at him. 'Shall we go out? We could see the club.'

'Not unless you feel up to it. I thought you'd want to rest.'

'Toby, I'm not made of glass!'

'You're not made of the same stuff as I am, that's for sure.' He grinned, rather sheepishly, and threw down his napkin. 'Rio at night. That's something special.'

Was it the city, was it the day or was it him? Lisa took deep breaths, tasting the warm night air, tasting excitement. They couldn't get a taxi and the commissionaire wanted them to wait, but Toby set off along the street, regardless of muggers. But then, he was like a rock, thought Lisa, huge and solid. It would be so easy to cling to him and yet so wrong, because when he went away she would have nothing. He held tight to her hand, she felt like a child in his care. Everything was different here, new and exciting. She looked up at him and smiled. Perhaps after all it was going to be all right.

They found a cab rank some streets away, with one small, brown driver looking through a film magazine and smoking. His cab smelled of garlic and the seats were ripped. Toby gave the name of the club and the driver nodded, starting the engine in a belching cloud of smoke.

At the beginning they drove through drab suburbs, but soon they gave way to squalor. When they passed a bar wild music blared out at them, and prostitutes sprawled on the steps, their skirts well up over their knees. Street vendors cooked fish and snacks, and there was the smell of overflowing drains. The cab began to climb, travelling up into the hills.

'By Christ' said Toby. 'I've bought a bloody climbing hut.'

'We don't seem to be too close to the beautiful people,' murmured

Lisa. 'The report said it was in a fashionable district, didn't it?'

She saw his teeth flash in the dark cab. He chuckled. 'Too true. I'll console myself with tearing the agent limb from limb.' They both laughed.

The slums fell away but the cab still climbed. From what they could see they were in wasteland, ground despoiled by the city and left to rot. The driver swung the wheel and stopped. They got out. Before them slumped a shabby, dirty-white building, lit by a single light bulb outside the door. Huge moths fluttered in the dim glow and mosquitoes whined like enemy divebombers.

'What a stinking hole,' said Toby. 'I don't believe it.'

Lisa stood in the hot wind, letting her hair blow. 'But, Toby — look.' He turned to follow her eyes. There, stretching for miles below them, were the lights of Rio. Like a great jewelled carpet, there the city lay, and beyond was the sea, the surf gleaming silver in the moonlight.

'A slum with a view,' said Toby.

'But what a view!' Lisa looked out into the gloom, trying to focus. 'Do you own all this? There's masses of space, it's huge.'

Toby sniffed. 'I wonder if I own all the clapped out cars and oil drums. I never saw such a mess. The agent said it was lawned.'

'Perhaps it is. Underneath everything.'

The taxi driver was babbling, he didn't want to wait. Toby loomed over him and glared and the man subsided. They went cautiously forward into the light, and Toby rapped on the peeling paint of the door. When there was no reply, he turned the handle and they went in.

It was a bar, with shutters at the windows and a floor of bare boards. Four men sat slumped at a table, playing cards and drinking. A thin, gingery dog curled its lip and Lisa bent down to talk to it.

'Watch it!' snapped Toby, but the animal was already wagging its tail. Lisa always got on with dogs. One of the men put down his cards and got up, ready to pour them a drink.

'My name's Ledbetter,' said Toby. 'I own this place.'

The man stopped in mid-stride. Then he turned and rattled out a fusillade of Spanish to his companions. In a second they began to fold up the cards and leave. The dog scratched at the door and Lisa went to let it out. The mosquitoes buzzed in a cloud around the light bulb, and the men talked in a quickfire exchange of Spanish. Toby waited in silence until they left, slinking out guiltily. The barman stood in front of his dusty row of bottles, his sweat-stained shirt hanging outside his trousers.

'Senor,' he said. 'Welcome.'

'Thanks.' Toby scanned the room. One corner of the ceiling was

296

stained brown with damp and the far end of the room was cluttered with tables and iron chairs piled high. He said coldly, 'Let's have a drink, shall we? Let's celebrate.'

Lisa drew in her breath and he reached out and put a proprietorial arm round her. 'You'd better have two,' he commented. 'The dog probably had rabies.'

'I think you're a hypochondriac,' she remarked.

'Yeah. I probably am.'

The barman looked hopeful. 'Good, strong place,' he said. 'Wunnerful views.'

Lisa sipped the drink he offered. Raw spirit scorched its way down her gullet, the fumes filled her head and made it spin. What a strange, disorientating day. Tonight, suddenly, Toby frightened her. But then he looked across and smiled and she felt safe again.

Back at the hotel they lay on the bed and laughed. 'What a night. What a hole,' said Toby. 'Am I totally off my head or did that place have potential?'

Lisa was drunk. 'Potential,' she said blearily. 'Defnite potential.'

'Glad you agree.'

They had taken off their shoes but nothing else. He swung on top of her, nuzzling and murmuring. When she closed her eyes there was no light at all, she was walled in by black. Not again, she thought, please not again. She was sore and torn, he couldn't! But there was an urgency about him, a blind determination. Whatever he pretended, he wasn't pleased with that club. And he was territorial, making sure of establishing his rights to her.

In his eagerness he tore her skirt. She lay underneath him, her teeth clenched against pain. But she could envisage the day when it didn't hurt, when there would be no need for endurance. It wasn't the pain that frightened her. It was the loneliness, lying close, heart to heart, and sharing nothing.

The club looked terrible in daylight. It stood amidst sour wasteland, on which weeds could barely summon the energy to grow. A few scrubby trees did their best to shade it, but everything else was stark and ugly.

'It's big enough,' said Lisa. 'Though you'd have to build a kitchen on the back.'

'Needs a glamorous front,' added Tony. 'And the roof's gone.'

'And you'd have to make gardens. You could have a pool with exotic fish, and a terrace for people to dance outside. With a giant mosquito fizzer,' she added, looking ruefully at the bites on her arm.

'Why don't I just pull the whole lot down and rebuild it?'

He squatted down on his haunches, picking up pebbles and tossing them from hand to hand. Lisa said, 'But will people come? It's completely out of it.'

Toby shrugged. 'Only takes twenty minutes. With the right publicity we could get all those gorgeous girls off the beaches. And that should bring the fat cats. Cabaret, good food, your style and your name — we can do it, sweetheart.'

'Yes.' She suppressed a sigh. As her mother said, she was useful to him. Toby liked to work efficiently and with her he had workmate and bedmate wrapped up in one tidy, if unattractive, parcel.

Toby went to see the agent, Senor Artimez. He worked from a building downtown, a man on the fringes of prosperity. He was small, brown, rather slimy Lisa thought, when he came into the foyer to greet them.

He took Toby off at once to his office, leaving Lisa behind. She was offended. It was as if Toby was keeping secrets from her, and she had none from him. Or at least — she had many secrets, she realised.

When Senor Artimez came back, he seemed changed. All the ebullience was gone, and his colour had turned from brown to greenish grey. On the other hand Toby was absolutely calm, frighteningly so. Senor Artimez put out his hand for Toby to shake and it was ignored. 'I hope we understand each other,' said Toby gently. 'Now that we know each other better.'

'Yes. Yes. Absolutely.' The man stood, trembling, as they went out into the street.

'What on earth did you say to him?' demanded Lisa. 'He was terrified.'

'Then he scares damned easily.' Toby took her arm and led her across the road, dodging hooting cars. 'He thought I was far enough away for him to be able to do as he liked. And he thought he could pull the wool over my eyes if ever I got here. He's stupid, made no attempt to find out who I was, the way I do business. Now he knows.'

'How do you do business?'

He glanced down at her. 'I don't get taken for a fool.'

Lisa said, 'Are you getting some money back? Is that it?'

'He's standing a percentage of the improvements, yes.'

'Suppose he can't afford it?'

'Then he goes bankrupt.' On the far pavement he stopped and grinned down at her. 'Don't get nervous, sweetheart. I know what I'm doing, I promise.'

'But it's not that much money. It doesn't matter all that much.'

'It isn't the money. It's — oh God, we don't have to talk about this. Let's go swimming, let's go to bed.'

298

She hung on to his arm. 'I wish you wouldn't be so hard on people, Toby.'

For a second he looked bewildered. 'I'm not hard on you. Ever.'

'It's just − the poor man looked so frightened, Toby.' She held on to his arm, tightly. It took both her hands to encircle it.

'Let's go back to the hotel,' he said throatily. 'Please.'

So they went. A maid was cleaning and Toby gave her a handful of money to go away and come back later. Lisa wondered how he could be so generous, and at the same time so unforgiving. When he was making love to her he held her head between his big hands and whispered, 'I love you. Lisa, I love you, I want you to know that I love you.'

She murmured back, unintelligibly, not believing him.

On the surface, things went well. They looked at the sights, they swam, they ate strange food and went to clubs, to dance and size up the opposition. When he entered a room with Lisa on his arm, so small, so erect, Toby felt choked with pride. Who would ever have thought that he could have a girl like this, delicate, the perfect lady?

He was filled with new and buoyant energy. At night he made love, in the day problems dissolved before him, there was nothing that could stand in his way. The club was to be gutted, stripped out, the roof replaced and extensions built front and back. Day by day, the junk was hauled away to be replaced by bricks and piles of sand.

One morning they got up early to talk to a landscape gardener. He was a tall, brown man with a skin like creased leather. All three of them stood on the hillside looking down at the city, watching the sunshine on the sea, catching the gleam of perspex and metal in the buildings below.

The gardener blew his nose noisily on a bright red handkerchief. He was the younger son of a rich family, and had disgraced himself by refusing to enter the family firm. He gardened for amusement, taking only those projects that amused him. He spoke English with a heavy South American accent.

'I'm sorry,' he said. 'I think you've been deceived, Mr. Ledbetter. I'm surprised your agent hasn't advised you. There's no water. Jose gets a trickle from a pipe, enough to wash a few glasses, but no more. Someone should have told you, saved you from so much expense.'

They both stared at him. 'No,' said Toby. 'No, I wasn't told.'

Lisa had a sudden vision of the agent's grey face. No wonder he was scared. He hadn't dared tell Toby the full scale of his crime. She swallowed, and looked resolutely ahead,. 'How do you get water here then?' she asked.

The man shrugged. 'Pipe it. But there's nowhere it can come from.

299

Dig for it. But here that won't do any good. In ten, twenty years, if the government pipes some in, then you could do something. Now it's a waste of time. You can't run a club, you can't grow a lemon tree. All because of water.'

Toby said, 'We'll sort out something. If necessary I'll bring it in by tanker.'

The man laughed. 'You could never bring enough! I'm sorry, Mr. Ledbetter. If there was water this would be the most magnificent place. I could plant a garden here that would astonish you.'

When he had gone, they looked at each other. Lisa said, 'Oh dear.'

Toby sniffed. 'It's a problem, that's all. Perhaps we can build a water tower, collect rain or something.'

Lisa drove her heel into the dust. 'It looks terribly dry. But there are springs further down the mountain, why don't we try digging?'

'Doesn't look too promising, does it? Wonder if they have diviners out here.'

'I'm not sure I believe in them.'

He glanced at her. 'Oh, I do. Seen it work, in Oz. Little Abo, got a twig bending itself in two right over a spring.'

She watched his face, stiff, unsmiling, avoiding her eye. 'What are you going to do?' she murmured.

'Find water, of course. Nothing else *to* do.'

'But about the agent. Leave him alone, Toby, please.'

'He doesn't deserve to get away with this.'

'You could take him to court! You could, Toby. Wouldn't that be best?'

He turned and looked down into her anxious face. 'You shouldn't worry so about people. But all right. If you want, I'll leave it to the lawyers.'

She put her arms up round his neck and hugged him.

Toby sent her out to look for a water diviner. A lot of people said, yes, they'd known of one once, but somehow no-one could give her a name or an address. She trailed about the city, from air conditioned office to boiling street, from shanty town to the newsdesk at the local paper. No-one could help.

Toby had hired a car. She began to think he had sent her on a wildgoose chase while he got up to something behind her back. Perhaps it was many things. Suddenly he seemed to be busy, taking 'phone calls, making deals, talking to people. The work at the club came to a complete standstill, for there was no point in pouring more money into it until the water problem was resolved.

On the afternoon she gave up her quest for a diviner, she demanded that Toby take her out to the club. He glanced up from his papers. 'What for? There's no point in staring at it.'

She sighed. 'Toby, I wish you wouldn't take this so personally. What are you doing here? You're rushing around everywhere proving what a bigshot you are. You don't talk to me. We don't seem close.'

'If you want more sex, you've only got to say so.'

'More! You never stop!'

A silence developed. Lisa said desperately, 'It's not as if the club matters. It doesn't. It's only your pride that's hurt.'

'That happens to be a pretty important part of me.' He went to the fridge to get a beer, and came back with it unopened in his hand. 'You know how stupid I've been. Buying something I knew nothing about, trusting someone I'd never met, going through third parties. I'm ashamed of myself. Bloody ashamed. I can't even put it all on the agent, I left myself wide open to be swindled.'

'I don't think any less of you,' said Lisa.

He put the beer down. 'I wish I knew what you did think.'

'At the moment I just want to go and have another look at the club.'

She knew what he wanted her to say. She knew he had wanted to make love. They went out to the car in silence, and if it had been hot in the morning, now it was a furnace. Lisa wandered about, kicking up dust and stones, while Toby sat on a rock and watched her. If only there could be water here, it would be a lush, green paradise.

She began to look for a twig. She knew it should be forked, but of course there was nothing like that up here. All she could find was a whippy branch off one of the spiny bushes, its leaves dried into dust. One spur could vaguely be described as one of the prongs of a fork, albeit eight inches shorter than the other. Defying herself to feel silly she began walking up and down, pointing the stick at the ground. Of course there was nothing. Her footsteps making patterns in the dust, she walked up and down, up and down, taking care to make each line exactly parallel with the last.

'You're wasting your time.' Toby stood watching her, his face grim. 'If you want separate beds then say so, don't stay out here playing games.'

'I wish you'd be quiet. I'm concentrating.' Her hands tingled from holding the stick. She flexed her fingers and went on, and they tingled again, they felt hot. 'Toby,' she called out cautiously. 'Toby!'

'What is it?' He was back at the car, ignoring her.

'I think I'm doing it.'

'Doing what?'

'Water divining.'

He came across and watched her. She took slow, small steps across the patch of ground. 'My hands tingle,' she explained. 'They feel hot, hot on the inside. But only here.'

'The time I saw it before, the stick bent.'

'I know, but I can feel something. Honestly, Toby, I can. There's water here.'

'Go and try somewhere else and see what happens.'

So she went on, round and round, up and down. But the tingling only came in that one place. Finally she flung the stick down. 'I won't do any more! I'm so tired I could drop. It's there, it's absolutely there, and you won't believe me!'

Toby sighed. 'Oh, for God's sake! What's a drilling rig on top of everything else? What's a few more thousands down the drain?'

She watched while he marked the spot with a small cairn of stones. The car was like an oven, and he opened all the windows to cool it. As they drove down the hillside the noises and smells drifted in to them. Lisa closed her eyes. He realised suddenly that she looked grey and ill.

'Lisa? Are you all right?'

She opened her eyes and nodded. 'It's just the heat. It was so hot.' He looked as if he thought she might be pretending. At the hotel, she trailed up to the suite, and gulped down orange juice from the fridge. It made her head swim. She went and sat in the shower, letting water rain down on her head.

Toby said, 'I'll call the doctor. You shouldn't have insisted we go.'

She sat on the edge of the bed, swathed in a towel. 'I'm all right.'

After a moment he sat beside here. 'I didn't know you didn't like the sex. I thought you were getting used to it.'

'I am. Honestly.' The lie hung between them.

'I always get it wrong with you,' he said.

Her head came up. 'It isn't you, it's me. I'm no good at touching, I always want it to stop.'

He said, 'I do what you want, I'm as sensitive as I know god-dammed how! Just for you I let Artimez go, and he's the nastiest little crook in town. I love you and I want a little love back, what's wrong with that?'

Exhausted, she leaned back on the pillow, her hair in wet strands about her face. He put out his hand and reached under the towel to put his palm hard against her belly. Instinctively she flinched.

Angrily Toby said, 'If you'd just try! You lie there as if I'm trying to punish you!'

She opened her eyes and stared up at him. He was such a hard man. How could she believe in his softness? It seemed to her that he was a lion and that when they lay together he asked her to believe he was a

302

lamb. And he was a man of the world, big, attractive, rich, he'd had dozens of women. All her caution, all her sense of her own survival, told her to hold something back.

The next day a drilling rig began work at the club, and at the same time they received an invitation. It was to a dinner party, held at one of the luscious, expensive houses that overlooked the bay.

'Why have they invited us?' asked Lisa. 'Do we know these people?'

'I spoke to the husband last week,' said Toby. 'Put some money into a venture of his. They like new people, gives them something to gossip about.'

'I don't know if I want to go.'

'Hard luck. We're going.'

Lisa watched him with apprehension. When they were alone he was angry, abrupt, and then suddenly he would be sweet to her. She knew with certainty that she didn't understand him.

The drilling rig worked on and on. She went to watch it most mornings, standing in the dust as the screw bit further and further into the earth. No-one had any hope of finding water, not even Lisa herself any more. But one Friday morning, when she went up the mountain and got out into the hot morning sunshine, there was a pool of sloppy mud spreading around the drill.

'Senora, we found him!'

'Are you sure?' She stood doubtfully to the side. But the mud was certainly wet. An hour went by, and the drill boss made her wear a hat against the sun. A foot further down, and mud was spouting out of the borehole. Just before noon they hit water.

She filled a bottle with it, and once captured it was a murky liquid full of sand and floaters. At once she went back to the hotel, still wearing the battered hat the drill boss had given her. She stood in the lift, itching with excitement, and when at last it arrived at their floor she raced down the passage and burst into the room. 'Look! Toby, look!'

Too late she realised they had a visitor, a man in a cream suit, his panama set carefully on the chair beside him. But Toby leaped up, crossed the room with huge strides and swept her round so hard that her feet took the panama and sent it flying. 'You clever girl! You clever, clever girl!'

'Wasn't I? I was right, wasn't I?'

'Of course you were. You're the cleverest girl in the world.' It was such sweet praise.

They picked up the panama and Toby made introductions. The

303

visitor was a lawyer, overseeing the negotiations with the agent. Lisa shook his hand politely and made conversation, though she wanted to go out and dance, frolic away the rest of the day and the whole of the night. She went into the bedroom while Toby and the lawyer concluded their business. When at last he was gone she rushed out and hugged Toby's neck. 'I can start designing now. I know just what I want to do, it's going to be wonderful.'

'And so are you.'

He took her by the hand and led her back into the bedroom. Today, she thought, today it will be good. Nonetheless anxiety tightened her muscles, she felt on trial, her pleasure demanded on pain of rejection. The days when women weren't supposed to enjoy it beckoned insidiously. He was so gentle he made her skin twitch, he waited so long that she almost screamed for him to get on and get it over. All the time it went on he was watching her, monitoring her responses. And, of course, she failed him.

The day was spoiled for them. Try as they might they couldn't revive their spirits. Toby wandered back into the sitting-room and picked up the bottle of water, trying with false enthusiasm to recapture the joy. 'Doesn't that look good? What we can't do now! Well, Lisa, you've excelled yourself this time.'

'Toby – don't.'

He caught her eye and subsided. The mood was broken and there was no way to mend it. He felt a certain dull resignation.

They both went to work, Toby telephoning contacts and Lisa finalising her design. The theme was to be strongly Brazilian, with a blend of greenery and glass, marble and Indian art that was wholly her own. She went out to buy pictures from galleries: the occasional piece of sculpture, two dozen sets of tables and chairs. Every bill was given to Toby, and he never told her to stop. In a way he was buying her, and if she could have given him what he wanted she would. She was beginning to think she hadn't got it to give. Instead she worked on the design, worked non-stop, late into the night. She was trying to make amends, and Toby of course thought she was avoiding him.

By the evening of the dinner party they were reduced to treating each other with careful politeness. Lisa dressed in a white sheath, her tiny waist belted with a red peasant scarf, gold earrings hanging like miniature chandeliers. Toby was in a cream tropical suit, and somehow it made him seem almost gangsterish. Lisa had a drink before she left, a gin for Dutch courage.

'You want to be careful,' said Toby. 'That's a very bad habit.'

Lisa shrugged. 'It's either that or I don't go. I don't know anyone.'

Their hosts lived in a wide house commanding views out across the bay. Huge windows were draped in sheer curtains, powered by small electric motors, so that at the touch of a button they could be swept aside. They were last to arrive, and some ten faces turned as they entered. Lisa's step faltered and Toby caught her elbow and propelled her into the room.

'Lady Eloise! I am Maria Rontuffi, I'm so glad you could come.' A tall spare woman leaped up and engulfed her. She was wearing black, the neckline dipped almost to her waist and a gold pendant swinging in the cleavage of her breasts. 'My husband, Miguel.' Lisa was passed down the line. The husband was much older, his skin dead-white against his wife's mahogany. He patted Lisa's hand, smiling without animation, watching Maria flatten herself against Toby to reach up and kiss his cheek. As she moved her dress shifted on her narrow body, at intervals showing a nipple. Lisa accepted a drink, finding herself placed far away from Toby. Maria sat on the arm of his chair, throwing her head back and laughing.

'You've been very lucky finding water,' someone said to her. 'The price of land on that ridge is going to double.'

Toby glanced up. 'I've taken options out on a few properties,' he remarked. 'Just as well, really.'

'I didn't know that,' said Lisa in amazement.

'Didn't you honey?'

She felt ruffled. That woman was pawing him and she didn't know half his thoughts. It was time to go through to dinner, to a white marble table on a white marble floor. Lisa was placed at her host's right hand, and he talked to her now and then, watching his wife and Toby. Every now and then her hand disappeared below the table. Toby's face was utterly inscrutable.

Lisa found it hard to eat the food. These people all knew each other, they shared jokes and acquaintances. She was almost sure that one couple, married to others, were having an affair; there was an electric buzz when they talked to each other. People touched, a man got up and kissed a woman's shoulder. And Maria kept on reaching below the table.

When the cheese arrived, Maria got to her feet. 'We will swim,' she said. 'We shall all swim naked in our pool.'

Lisa glanced in horror at Toby. 'No thank you,' she declared. 'I'd rather not.'

'But others will.' Maria grinned round at them all, a lascivious smirk. 'Come along everyone. We will swim.'

To Lisa's horror everyone got up, including Miguel. He said, 'You can sit and watch if you like. Or you can stay here. I shall stay here and read. My wife enjoys these things best by herself.'

'Does she?' Lisa looked at him in horror. 'I think I'll go and watch.'

The pool was in the garden, a huge baroque affair of fish-head fountains and blue glass chairs. The lighting was subdued, with black shadows everywhere. Changing rooms stood to one side, but Maria, leading her guests, threw off her clothes at the poolside. She stood on the edge, wearing nothing but twin diamond bracelets. Her body was brown and firm, and the men whistled and called out. Toby stood and watched.

'Come on, Toby,' called Maria. 'Come swimming.' She lifted her arms and executed a passable swallow dive.

Lisa stood quite still. The others began taking off their clothes, all except she and Toby. He turned and looked at her. 'Come on,' he said, and soundlessly she shook her head. He came close and whispered, 'I'd like to swim with you. I want to make love.'

Loud samba music began to play over the speakers, and people began to jump into the silvery water. Maria swam up and down, lying on her back. 'Toby,' she called again. 'Why don't you come swimming?'

'You know what she wants?' murmured Toby.

Lisa nodded. 'You couldn't.'

'I bloody well could! Lisa, come in the pool. Wear your bra and pants if you must, but loosen up and come in.'

'I didn't know I was coming to an orgy,' she said shrilly.

'Neither did I. And if you ask me you need one, you need something to turn you into a woman!'

He turned, dragging off his jacket and throwing its Savile Row tailoring in a crumpled heap on the ground. His trousers followed, shirt, tie, underpants, and lastly his socks. 'Toby! Toby!' called Maria. He walked unconcernedly to the end of the pool, stood back from a little springboard, took a run, bounced, and jack-knifed into the water. He made barely a splash. When he surfaced, half the pool away, he flicked the water from his eyes and swam with powerful strokes to Maria. She turned to him, laughing, her arms outstretched. As he kissed her the water cleared, and Lisa could see the woman's legs, twining around his hips.

Lisa fled. She ran through the house, past the room where Miguel sat reading, out into the road. The car was there, and she fumbled in her bag for her set of keys. As she drove off she scraped the bumper on the gate, but she didn't care, she didn't stop. Her heart was pounding against her ribs, and her stomach churned as if she might be sick. That was it, then. The end. It was over.

In the hotel she sat for a while, trying to control her shaking. When

306

she realised it wasn't going to stop she got up and tried to pack despite it, dropping bottles and packets in the bathroom, forgetting her birth control pills and having to unzip her suitcase to hide them discreetly in the bottom. But of course she couldn't leave at night. Still in her clothes she lay down on the bed. At four o'clock he came in.

He leaned on the doorpost, looking at her. 'I'm bushed,' he said. 'Do you mind if I come there and lie down?'

'All right.'

She moved across and he took off his shoes and jacket to get on to the bed. He wore no socks or shirt, and he smelled of the pool. After a while he said, 'Why don't you get angry?'

'There isn't any point. I can't love you properly.'

Toby let out a long, painful sigh. 'On the way home tonight I stopped off and knocked up Senor Artimez. Then I knocked his teeth out. He was almost relieved, he's been expecting me to kill him.'

'Why are you telling me this?'

'I don't know. So you don't feel too bad, perhaps. So you can leave in the morning with the whole thing closed, finished, done with.'

After a moment, Lisa said, 'Did she — did she like it?'

'Oh, Christ, yes. That sort always does, they've got a permanent itch.' He lay very still, and she began to wonder if he was asleep. Gingerly she lifted herself up on her elbow to look at him, and found he was looking right back. 'I couldn't give any more' he said.

Suddenly her eyes flooded with tears, and she put her hand over his face so he wouldn't see. 'Go to sleep,' she said thickly.

In the morning, while he still slept, she picked up her cases and left for home.

Chapter Thirty-Two

Angus stopped his car at the top of one of the endless streets of terraced houses. A couple of children were kicking a ball in the ten-foot, the bleak and unimaginative name for the gap between two sets of stone backyards. They eyed him warily, in case he was the school attendance officer.

There was a smell of stale fish. This was a fishing port, once great, but the fish stocks had dwindled and the trawlers grown, so that men who had once owned seine net boats had to sell up and go on the dole. There was money still to be made in fish, but in freezer ships bristling with radar and sonar. Men were out on them for weeks, and for every dutiful woman left sitting by her fire there was another out dancing while her teenage sons were up in court for theft.

The place was cosmopolitan too, with a thriving Polish club and many Dutch, typified by their excessively clean houses. This terrace looked weary and down-trodden. Dull grey washing flapped against walls, and a woman walked by pushing a child in a buggy, tossing it an occasional chip.

Angus drove on. The place intimidated him utterly. What was the point of preaching self-reliance and individual struggle to people here, who knew that promises were hollow, life was hard, and prospects bleak? They hadn't the money, they hadn't the strength, and most of all, they hadn't the hope.

He arrived at the station early and hung around, too restless to read or drink coffee. Jean's train was five minutes late and at first he couldn't see her. When at last he spotted her brown, curly head bobbing jauntily through the crowd, he felt a surge of delight.

'Jean! I'm so glad to see you. Here, let me take your bags.'

'Aren't you going to give me a kiss?'

'Not here, no. I'm the candidate, I'm being exemplary.'

Once in the car he took her in his arms and kissed her properly.

Jean gave a happy sigh. 'You're not going to play this as a stuffed shirt, I hope. It's quite the wrong image.'

'Not if I want to impress the powers that be.'

'Votes impress them, nothing else. Don't be all stiff and starchy.'

She was at him already, barely five minutes off the train. He rammed the car into gear and said briskly, 'My darling girl, they wouldn't vote for me if I was the most popular stand-up comic in the country. The place is a nightmare. The only new business that's started up here in the last ten years is a chemical works that belches out fumes that might or might not cause cancer.'

'Well then,' said Jean.

'Well then, what?'

'That's your campaign platform. A proper study to find out what's in the emissions, and a clean-up programme. Or closure. And a business initiative. It's no use saying telling them the rest of the country's having a ball, so hard luck Heslington. You've got to say, ''Look where voting Labour's got you. Put me in and see some real improvement. We don't promise, we perform!'' '

'You've got it all worked out, haven't you?'

She nodded. 'We can give them a run for their money.'

'God help me if they find out you're a member of the Labour Party.'

Jean laughed and settled in her seat. She didn't mind helping Angus avoid complete humiliation. He couldn't possibly win, this was the Labour heartland and always would be. It was a bright, sunny day and in the High Street a group of street artists in T-shirts were performing a mime. The shoppers stared at them in horror, many still muffled up as if they hadn't yet noticed the sun was shining. Further on came the drab terraces that Angus had seen earlier, and the docks, quiet now after the early morning fish landings. Last of all was the chemical works, huge, already rusty, covering the streets in a thin, sulphurous pall.

'It's a bloody disgrace,' snapped Jean.

'Employs over a thousand people though.'

'Then they can employ a few more to stop all this gunge. What are people thinking of? What's the M.P. been doing? It shouldn't be allowed.'

She was still fulminating when they reached the pub. Angus had reserved two rooms for them, bare, functional, slightly beery cubicles usually occupied by commercial travellers. Last night had been his first, and he had lain in bed turning things over and over in his mind. He had a month before the Heslington by-election, and in that time he had to learn about the place, organise his workers and make himself heard in a fundamentally hostile arena. It had seemed impossible. But now, suddenly, Jean brought it all into focus. In the end what mattered in Heslington was what needed to be done.

They had sandwiches and beer in the bar, then retired upstairs to write reams and reams of notes. At eleven, Angus leaned back and ran his hands through his hair. 'I just wish I could promise them investment. But I've scrabbled around and the most the poor devils can hope for is a grant for insulating a few lofts, and that's limited.'

Jean tapped her pencil against her teeth. 'You could tell them that. Say you couldn't believe what you discovered. And if they do the decent thing and elect you, then you'll campaign night and day for some proper development.'

Angus grunted. 'It's a bit woolly. I wonder if they'd like a fish packing station or something? Or better motorway links.'

'Don't you dare suggest a museum,' said Jean. 'That's what always happens. Bit of inner city deprivation — forget the jobs and give them art classes and museums instead. It's a cop-out.'

Angus got up and stretched. He went to the window and looked down on the pub car park. It was starting to rain, but he felt suddenly as if he had never been quite so happy. At The Court he felt helpless, surrounded by need and yet unable to begin to fulfil it. In the City, all that grubbing and dealing and back-scratching left him cold. But here, in Heslington, he felt a fire in his blood, he wasn't daunted, he was challenged.

He turned. 'For the first time in my life, I feel as if I'm doing something worthwhile,' he burst out.

Jean pulled a face. 'Don't fool yourself. You won't get in. But it's groundwork for when you do, and you'll remember Heslington, and how it was. Then you can do something worth crowing about.'

He nodded. 'I'm really glad you're doing this, Jean. I don't know how I'd have managed on my own. Look, we'd better get some sleep. I don't know if you want to — I mean, they're only single beds.'

Jean went pink. 'Do you want to? It'll be awfully cramped.'

'I don't mind if you don't. The landlady doesn't bring us tea or anything.'

'I bet she will while I'm here. I'll scuttle back to my own room early on, just in case.'

Sure enough, next morning the landlady knocked enthusiastically on their doors, and was disappointed to find both Jean and Angus just where they should be, in separate beds. Angus was incredulous. How on earth could Jean have known? For a moment he saw her almost as a creature from another planet, with powers of communication lightyears beyond him.

310

'They call it the common touch,' said Jean, munching bacon and egg. 'And you haven't got it. Don't worry, I've enough for us both.'

At ten they met the party workers. Middle-aged, dispirited, they viewed Angus with something less than enthusiasm. Angus felt memory stir, of the cadet corps at school when he had been put in charge of a weary, miserable and unathletic group of depressed new boys and was told to build a bridge to cross a deep and fast-flowing stream. He hadn't bothered with the bridge, he'd taken them to the tuckshop and cheered them up. They responded, every one, by dragging their parents over to meet him the moment they were allowed a visit. He wondered if Mars bars would do as much for this lot.

He stood up to speak. 'First of all, thank you very much for welcoming me as you have.' There had been no welcome, merely a letter giving him the address of the pub. 'Obviously we have a hard task ahead of us. We don't expect to win. But we shall give them a damned good run for their money!'

A sigh went up from Mrs. Wentworth, a rotund lady who chaired the local Townswomen's Guild. She had heard it all before and was beyond patience. The last idiot who had fought this seat, on being grilled about unemployment had declared that people could get work if they only tried, and they were probably lazy. He had almost been buried under the loads of rejected job applications sent from the farthest flung corners of the constituency and very nearly lost his deposit.

'It seems to me,' went on Angus desperately, 'that there's no use telling people here that the government's doing a wonderful job. Clearly it isn't. There's no investment, no work, declining industries and terrible waiting lists at the hospital. And the last Labour member did nothing about it! Now, he was ill, and as we all know he died, but even when he was well he didn't achieve much. Heslington needs someone in government to represent them, someone with the ear of ministers.'

'And you think you've got that?' murmured a retired colonel.

'I've certainly got a darned sight better chance than this bloke they've got now. He's more interested in sanctions against South Africa than getting the chemical works cleaned up. He'll promise to change the world, but he can't change Heslington.'

'Well said.' Mrs. Wentworth nodded vigorously.

The colonel leaned back in his plastic chair. He stared at Angus, his eyes as hard as flint. 'If you'll forgive me, am I right in thinking that your sister has featured rather heavily in the newspapers over the past few months?'

311

Angus had been dreading this question. His answer was ready. 'I hold no brief for my sister, sir,' he said. 'And I must point out that almost nothing in those articles has any basis in truth. Added to which – ' his voice dried to a croak and he had to pause to cough. He took a long breath. 'Added to which I think I should tell you that my brother – my twin brother – is confined to a mental hospital with a serious mental illness. I felt that you should know at the start, in case it emerges later on.'

There was a stunned silence. 'They certainly found us someone colourful, at least,' said Mrs. Wentworth, snapping her handbag shut. 'It is a National Health hospital, I hope?' The colonel almost cringed waiting for the reply.

'It's National Health,' agreed Angus. A collective sigh of relief went round the room.

Mrs. Wentworth got up. 'This has all been very constructive. We'll be knocking on doors and licking envelopes with a will. By the way, I do the press releases, and I'll be sending them out sometime tomorrow. Get your hair cut for the television, won't you? Over the collar looks really Sloane Square wine bar, I always think.'

Angus and Jean slipped out for another pub meal. Over the next few weeks they were to live on pub food, an endless diet of chips and suspicious beefburgers. They stared gloomily at a picture in the local paper, of the Labour candidate. He wore baggy denim trousers with braces and turnups, a collarless shirt and hair shaved down to the skin. 'I think he's a member of Militant,' said Jean.

'Looks more like an off-duty storm trooper to me. I can't turn up next to that in a waistcoat, he'll crucify me.'

Jean considered. 'How about sort of country gear? Cord trousers and a chunky sweater.'

'Suppose it keeps hot?'

'A shooting jacket then. You're a solid, aristocratic countryman with old-fashioned values of care and responsibility. Keep on telling everyone you have to take paying guests at home. They won't know it's a luxury hotel.'

'It isn't.'

'Of course it is! About as luxurious as you can get, complete with resident dowager.'

They spent the afternoon wandering around the park and then the library, looking up local history. It seemed that little of note had happened in Heslington since the lifeboat sank, and that was blamed on the Tory government's lack of spending on lighthouses. When they got back to the pub an envelope was waiting for them. 'Thought it best to gct moving,' said a note. 'Sent this out to television, radio

312

and all papers. Regards, T.E. Wentworth (Mrs.)' It was the press release.

It read:

Angus Hellyn is a remarkable young man. His strong character has been forged in many fires. Raised in penury at his ancestral home, the strain proved too much for his brother, who is now confined to a mental hospital. His sister, Lady Mara Hellyn, has been involved in scandal at the highest level. It is this that sent Angus into politics. 'I feel I must do good,' he says.

He has firm views on development in Heslington. Closely related to many members of government, he is sure that he can persuade the powers that be to provide cash for our suffering community. He is particularly interested in facilities for the mentally ill and enforcing the regulations against under-sixteens in the red light area of the town.

Angus and Jean looked at each other. They began to shake with silent laughter. Set against the Labour man's promises of social security reform, it read like a thriller. 'She means to get you noticed,' said Jean, wiping her eyes.

'I shall be infamous! I wondered at the time if I was supposed to vet press releases but I didn't want to upset her.'

'That's what you're here for, I suppose. To learn.'

The telephone began ringing halfway through dinner. The radio stations wanted him the very next day, the newspapers were requesting interviews and the local television news wanted to film him door-stepping. He put them off until Friday; he didn't want to learn how to do it with the cameras breathing down his neck.

As he put the 'phone down yet again he saw Jean's face. She looked glum, and for a second he couldn't think why. When she saw him staring she put on a brave smile, but it wavered at the edges.

He said, 'I'm sorry, Jean. I know you could do this miles better than me.'

She swallowed and tried to fasten the smile a little more firmly. 'And I could. And better than the twit they've got on the other side. But if I'd really wanted it, I'd have tried harder, wouldn't I?'

'I didn't try all that hard. I got this through a family friend, Lisa's godfather, as a matter of fact. I didn't want to tell you, it sounds so bloody spineless.'

'No, it doesn't.' She sighed, and for a second her face was bleak. 'The world isn't fair. The people in Heslington know it isn't fair. You're prepared to live with it, but I'm just stupid enough to think I can try and change things.'

313

'But so do I! I'm just as keen to improve the place as you, surely you can see that?'

Jean finished her drink and got up. 'I'd be a pretty mean person if I begrudged you a break, wouldn't I? I'd better ring Dad. He'll be wondering what's happened to me.'

He watched her as she talked, making the effort to tell Reg what was going on, listening with interest to what he had to say. She was like a tea-cosy, he though, wrapping herself around people she wanted to keep warm. He knew that she thought him rather helpless, the child of endless privilege. It pleased her to mother him, and some part of him was soothed by that, but it wasn't something he needed. You didn't survive prep school at eight without developing some sort of strength. You didn't watch your own twin's suffering without forming a steel hard carapace. Suddenly, sadly, he felt that she didn't know him.

Chapter Thirty-Three

Lisa had been away for more than a month, and when she returned home her mother wouldn't speak to her. For three days they communicated through the butler, until finally, passing on the stairs, Charlotte said, 'What's happened to the Ledbetter creature? I thought he'd be hanging around again, out for what he can get.'

Lisa said, 'I think he's got better things to do, Mother. He's – he's very busy. I don't know what he's up to.'

Charlotte snorted. 'At least some good's come of this stupidity then.' And that was all that was said.

Rolls-Royces were once again a familiar part of the scene at The Court. When Lisa, hands full of fruit, glanced out of the window and saw the Silver Shadow she ignored it and went on her way, setting down bowls in the drawing-room, morning room, and the hall. No-one ever ate any, they behaved as if it were made of wax, but they always provided fruit for guests, and she would continue. The kitchen was kept well supplied with browning bananas and shrivelling apples.

Home soothed her, the routine took her mind off things. She stopped to admire the morning room, newly decorated in pale yellow and white, with a painted French chest in the corner from one of the upstairs rooms. Professor Chandler had found it, buried under a pile of sheeting, and it gave just the right air of muted grandeur. Part of the moulding needed replacing on one side, but Lisa didn't mind. When it was new it must have shouted with self-importance, now it merely muttered, and let the room speak for itself.

As she set her bowl down and adjusted some flowers to balance it, Curtiss came in. 'Lady Eloise – would you come please? Lady Payne's arrived, with your sister.'

'Mara? Here? Good God.' Lisa hurried out, her grey silk skirt rustling about her. The day was warm, summery, and most of the guests were out enjoying the weather. It was all so English, and so very far from Rio.

At her insistence they had wrenched some of the downstairs windows open, even in the disused rooms, and there was the scent of lavender from the bushes just outside. It pleased her, and the pleasure remained, out of place, when she looked at Mara.

'I had to bring her home,' said Clare Payne.

'Yes. Yes, I can see. Mara, whatever's the matter?'

'Please — just leave me alone.'

Her face was puffy, blotched. She had put on weight and her hair needed washing, and her clothes were a mess, as if she had thrown on anything, clean or dirty. Above all there was an air of utter misery.

'I knew it,' said Lisa. 'I did warn you.'

'Well, it's happened and you can be glad! I don't know why I'm here, I wanted to stay in London. Clare wouldn't let me.'

Lisa turned to Curtiss, her face a mute plea. 'Why don't you go up to your room, Lady Mara?' he murmured. 'I could bring you some tea.'

'Yes, darling, do,' said Clare. 'You must be so tired.'

Mara spread her hands hopelessly. 'So you can talk about me, I suppose. I am tired. So terribly tired.' She wandered away, her step heavy, like an old, old woman.

Lisa and Clare went into the morning room. The sun had left it, but it was still bright. Lisa sighed. 'She looks terrible. Half dead. I knew that man would do this.'

Clare sat down, crossing her elegant legs with a swish of nylon. 'It's rather worse than you think, my dear. Is your mother here?'

'I'd much rather you told me, Clare. Please.'

'You girls grow up far too quickly.' Clare leaned forward and whispered, 'He's made her pregnant.'

Lisa's face felt rigid with shock. 'That is terrible. Why hasn't she — I mean, it's obvious —'

'My dear, she won't. He's offered to pay for Switzerland, anything, but she won't listen. And she took some drugs, cocaine I think, so there's a perfectly good medical reason for getting rid of it. She refuses to listen, and she cries and lies in bed and does nothing at all. I'm at my wits' end! Samuel wants us to marry at the end of the month, and here is Mara, quite desperate. I couldn't possibly leave her.'

Lisa put her hands together. 'It's very kind of you. We never hear from her. She's seen Angus once or twice, that's all. Aunt Clare — it's not like Marcus, is it?'

Clare rapped Lisa's wrist with an admonitory finger. 'Absolutely

316

not! It's simply love, and there's nothing so destructive. People get beyond themselves. I blame this man entirely, he took her up and then abandoned her. Samuel, of course, believes he was entrapped, but that's men for you. They think women can help being desirable.'

'Can't they?'

'Not in the least.' Clare leaned back and looked at her. 'Lisa dear, I have to congratulate you. You've acquired a certain elegance. And the house – I've never seen The Court so prosperous, not a single mouse trap anywhere. Where is your Australian millionaire? I must meet him.'

'Mr. Ledbetter's away,' said Lisa stiffly. 'Once he starts a project he doesn't often linger. We've been left very much to our own devices.'

'What a very odd way to do business.'

'Yes.'

Clare was to stay the night, and there was no room that was not occupied by guests, or servants, or the mice that still prospered in the unrestored parts. So Lisa gave up her own suite to Clare and arranged for a bed in Mara's room.

She packed up her night things and went in to her sister. Mara was lying on the bed, tear-stained, silent.

'You look terrible.'

Mara wiped her eyes with a ragged tissue. 'I don't care.'

'How long have you been crying?'

'I don't know. Since he went. It feels like forever.'

'Look – ' Lisa sat on the edge of the bed ' – why don't you come down to dinner? We're crawling with people at the moment. You just have to sit there and listen while they tell you how wonderful the place is. They've all heard about you.'

Mara sat up suddenly. 'I bet they have! They think I'm some sort of prostitute. Even *he* thought I was! He did, you know. In the end he despised me. How dare he! Going back to that prissy wife of his. She's a good woman, a woman fit to bear his child, while I'm just a good lay, to be used infrequently, to cleanse the pores. Lisa – I don't know how he could!'

She put out her arms and Lisa held her. She patted, she soothed, she searched her mind for something to say. 'Has he contacted you?' she said at last. 'He must be worried about the baby.'

'He doesn't give a damn!' Mara pushed her hand through her hair. 'He only cares about her. He thinks I'll toddle off to Switzerland and get a quick vacuum job, and save him so much trouble and embarrassment. And why the hell should I?'

'Is the baby all right? Do you know?'

317

Mara flushed and ducked her head. The bloom had quite gone from her, she looked tired and ill. 'Did Clare tell you what I did?'

'Yes. It wasn't much, was it?'

'As much as I could get my hands on. I was going mad. And every time I think about it, I feel so ashamed. You shouldn't speak to me, Lisa. I've been horrible, mean and selfish and cruel. But I didn't think! I just wanted to stop being miserable. It − it hurt so much, you see.' She looked desperately up at her sister.

'Drug addicts have babies all the time. It could be perfectly all right.'

'That's what the doctor says. He says it's OK. Oh, Lisa, I'm so sorry. I never meant to be mean. When it was all settled, when we were together, I was going to come back and stop all this silly guest business and put the house right again. I was, I promise. And you could have fun. And we'd be happy. All of us.' Her voice trailed away dispiritedly.

Lisa said, 'It wasn't your fault. And it's bound to come right in the end.'

They sat together in silence. Sunlight spattered the carpet with jewels of colour, and the curtains swayed back and forth in the lazy afternoon breeze. 'I've been in a tunnel,' said Mara at last. 'A long, dark tunnel.'

'And now you're home,' said Lisa. She put out her small hand and held her sister's larger one. Mara said, 'You look fine. Is it Toby? Is he being good to you?'

'He's not here.' Lisa felt her throat tighten. 'He's got other things to see to. He's starting a nightclub in Rio, he hasn't got time for anything as mundane as this.'

'So we're both abandoned.' The thought seemed to cheer Mara up immensely.

'Yes,' said Lisa. 'So we are.'

Mara bathed, washed her hair and came down to dinner. Her new shape was almost Rubenesque; she was forced to borrow one of her mother's wrapover dresses. Make-up hid the shadows under her eyes and if she was less lovely than before, she was still lovely enough to astonish. The guests stared at her in awe, and she stared back, gloomily. Clare fussed over her, making sure she sat out of a draught and had a cushion for her back. In contrast Charlotte took no notice of her daughter whatsoever.

The storm broke after dinner, in the family sitting-room. Charlotte came in last, and shut the door. It had been Clare's unenviable task to give her the reason for her daughter's return. 'Well,' she said thinly. 'Would you like to explain yourself, Mara?'

318

The girl leaned back in her chair. 'I'm pregnant. I don't think that needs a great deal of explanation.'

'I'm so glad your father's not here.' As Charlotte's pale eyes fixed on her, Mara flushed. Her mother went on, 'And what do you imagine you're going to do? The Court's full of people, you can't stay here.'

'How very kind of you, Mother,' said Mara thinly.

Clare stepped in. 'Perhaps you ought to go away, darling. You don't want to be on the front pages of the tabloids all over again. Couldn't you go abroad, just until the birth?'

'And then what?' wailed Charlotte. 'What are we going to do with it? A nameless illegitimate brat ... no-one's going to marry her with that in tow.'

'I'm sure I'll find someone desperate enough to take us both,' remarked Mara. Her eyes glittered, defiant to the last.

Her mother looked at her consideringly. 'You might be right. I suggest you start looking. If you can marry before the birth you might manage to give this byblow a cloak of respectability.'

'You really are appallingly bourgeois,' snapped her daughter.

Charlotte clenched her fists. 'Don't you dare call me names! How could you do this, when I can't cope, when your father's dead, when there isn't anything we can hide behind? It didn't matter once, when we could do what we liked and no-one knew. But, my God, to do it now! As if you haven't harmed us enough.'

'And what about me?' screamed Mara, her throat tight with un-shed tears. 'Don't you care about me at all?'

There was a crashing silence. Lisa said, 'Don't you think we should discuss where Mara could go? Obviously she can't stay here.'

'Perhaps France?' interposed Clare. 'Or is that too near?'

'Far too near,' said Charlotte, tensely. 'She can go to Kenya. Genevieve can look after here. We had her tedious son for months and months. He's married that girl Diandra, and a very good catch for him – he's got absolutely no money.'

Mara's face was schooled to blankness. Edward. If only she had thought more of him, been less young, less silly. But she had, and that was that. So she couldn't go to Kenya.

The telephone rang. Charlotte picked it up, wrinkling her brow as if expecting further bad news. She listened, sighed, and said, 'How tedious for you, dear. No doubt you'll do better next time. Goodbye.'

Lisa grimaced. 'The by-election. I forgot.'

'I don't think it deserved our full attention,' said Charlotte heavily. 'He lost of course. He seems delighted.'

'He must have done much better than expected,' said Clare. 'Shall

319

I turn on the television, Charlotte? We might see him on the late news.'

Sure enough, there was a report of the by-election, and Angus was filmed thanking his party workers.

'He's done brilliantly,' cheered Lisa. 'He's halved the chap's majority! Well done, Angus.'

'What on earth is Jean Maythorpe doing there?' demanded Charlotte. 'That girl is so vulgar. Look, she's wearing diamonds.'

No-one took any notice. Even Mara sat forward to watch Angus shaking hands and waving, and to hear the commentator declaring him an exceptional candidate. Charlotte had a headache. Noise stabbed at her, relentlessly. She didn't understand anything. Mara was pregnant, Angus was on television and the house was full of people she didn't know. They came and went, week by week, wearing her down. She had exhausted her capacity for friendship, and even politeness. Suddenly she felt angry, at Henry, at the world, most of all at her ungrateful children. 'Why doesn't anyone listen to me any more?' she burst out.

They turned surprised eyes on her. Clare said, 'Shall I take you up to bed, Charlotte? You seem very tired.'

The two women went up the stairs together. Charlotte stumbled once or twice, she had to rest on the landing. When she reached her room she sat on the bed. 'When I was first married I had a maid all to myself,' she told Clare. 'I wouldn't dream of trying to undress. The men got rid of the maids, they didn't ask us.'

'I don't suppose they wanted it to happen.'

'But it wasn't important to them. They kept their things on much longer. I've wondered lately − I shouldn't have let Henry had all his own way. I don't think Marcus should ever have gone away to school.'

'Marcus?' Clare was taken aback. 'Whyever do you say that now, Charlotte?'

'I don't know.' She sighed heavily. 'He needed me. Perhaps they all did. And I let Henry push them out, I let him tell me to send them to Nanny, or to school, just anywhere! He wanted me for himself, you see.' Suddenly she fixed Clare with an unblinking stare. 'Did he sleep with you? I always wondered. There wasn't a pretty woman for miles who was safe. That's where Mara gets it from − one here, one there, he would go from one to the other like a prize stud. I had to be as he wanted. Otherwise I knew he'd go.'

Clare took a deep breath. 'They never meant anything to him, you know. They were just flings.'

'It was that time in Monaco, wasn't it? I always knew. Your

husband safely in business meetings on a yacht, and Henry pretending to be talking business too. He was with you, of course.'

'It didn't last beyond that week,' said Clare urgently. 'I want you to believe that. He loved you, Charlotte.'

'Yes. Yes, I always believed he did.'

She began to take off her rings, the small, insignificant diamonds that were all the Hellyns had left. Clare helped her with her dress, and then with her underclothes. It was strangely intimate, and yet Clare felt detached, as if she was a maid. Charlotte sat like a child while Clare fastened her nightdress ribbons. 'I should never have sent Marcus to school,' she said again. 'But it wouldn't have made any difference. The damage was done by then.'

Clare helped her into bed and left her. Why now, after all these years, had she remembered that week in Monaco? Perhaps it had been Mara's pregnancy, Charlotte had been carrying Mara then. Oddly, she couldn't remember much about Henry, or his lovemaking. She'd wanted a child. Her husband couldn't give her one and she'd have taken Henry's if she could. Her husband might have known, she wasn't sure. They'd both so wanted a baby. Unexpected tears pricked her eyes and she blinked very quickly to stop them falling. Life had been relatively kind, all in all.

Someone had turned the light out on the stairs and she couldn't find the switch, so she clung to the banister and descended carefully in the dark. The Court was the darkest house she had ever known, night filled the place as if it was coming home. A small shiver ran up and down her spine, when she reached the hall, and the lightswitch, she stood in the glow and felt panic recede. It had been such a terribly strange evening.

Angus would not have believed it was possible to feel victory in defeat, yet he felt it, fiercely. In a few short weeks he had made his mark on Heslington. The local television channels had begun it, filling in dull bulletins with pictures of Angus knocking on doors and kissing babies, looking handsome wearing his tattered old shooting jacket. His opponent, bristling with street credibility as offputting as the stubble on the top of his head, wasn't in the same race. When interviewed he produced worthy and irrefutable statistics about housing benefit, while Angus brushed back his long dark hair and yelled, 'To hell with benefits! People need jobs, not handouts!'

In the background he always saw Jean, and knew she was longing to yell, 'I don't think jobs are going to do our pensioners any good!' but thankfully she kept silent. Her principles were a torture to her, like a close-fitting hair shirt. He watched the women on the Labour side and saw why Jean couldn't fit in. They were strident, often unattractive and badly dressed. Jean's tendency to flashiness infuriated them, added to which she was too down to earth, too practical. Not for her any socialist rhetoric, and under her guidance he gave up Tory platitudes himself. 'If you don't know, admit it,' she counselled. 'You don't want them to drag it out of you.'

The worst, the absolute worst moment of the campaign, came in a debate between the two main candidates in the Town Hall. To the outsider it must have seemed amusing, a tin-pot version of the American presidential election, with drains and shopping precincts in place of Star Wars and global domination. The Labour man knew Heslington inside out, he even knew half the questioners. 'Well, Frank,' he'd begin, 'as you know, I've been trying to get something done about your council flat for months. But under this blinkered Tory government — ' and so on and so on.

Prepared for this sort of emergency, Jean handed Angus notes about council house spending. At one point, pinned against the ropes, he saw her mouthing the words, 'ADMIT! ADMIT!'

He took a deep breath. 'Of course we need more spending,' he said forcefully. 'If elected I guarantee Mr. — Thornton, is it? — to look closely into your case. And even if I don't become your Member of Parliament, you can rest assured that if you write to me I'll do my best to get something done. I don't pretend concern, Mr. Thornton. I mean to achieve something in Heslington.'

Back came the Labour man, like a bull terrier scenting victory over some effete pedigree showdog. 'How in God's name can you be concerned about us in Heslington, Mr. Hellyn, when there are gypsies on your own land in need and squalor? I don't suppose you notice on your thousands of acres, but there are women giving birth in wagons, on filthy rags. Children with pneumonia. Last winter six of those gypsies were taken into hospital. In this country! On your land! Children who can't read, children who don't get enough to eat. Don't talk to me about concern, Mr. Hellyn.'

Angus was dumbfounded. Out of the corner of his eye he saw one of the Labour workers smirking; they had worked night and day to find something discreditable that he hadn't already admitted. He said weakly, 'Obviously we'd prefer those gypsies to be properly housed. They choose to live in the way they do — ' and the Labour man interrupted, 'Oh yes! If they chose they could live in your bloody great luxury mansion, I suppose!'

It lost him the seat. Without that he might just have scraped home. Heslington had been Labour for years and nothing had changed, the people fancied something new. And it was a by-election, so it wasn't as if they were voting for a government. They wouldn't have minded giving Angus a try, but not after that.

Back at the pub, Jean did her best to console him. But in the end she said, 'He was right, you know.'

Angus sighed. 'Yes. I do know. We have got to do something about those damned gypsies! They certainly don't travel any more, they just stay there. Unless one of them's wanted by the police. The odd one skips off now and then.'

Jean lay back on the bed. 'Nag the council to build them houses. They'll be difficult tenants, of course, but you've got to expect that.'

'We don't have council houses in the village.'

She turned over and glared at him. 'You should have.'

He reached out and tweaked her nose. The more they were together the more he liked her. There was nothing hidden, everything she was lay clear for all to see. Did she think that she saw all of him? Just then he didn't care. They were very close, he'd never been so close to anyone in all his life except Marcus. And that was like the clinging of a drowning man.

After the vote Mrs. Wentworth came up to him and gave him a resounding kiss. 'Well done, young man!' she declared. 'You won't have any trouble getting a seat. Wonderful performance.'

'He could have won,' complained the colonel, thwacking his walking stick on the ground. He contemplated Angus out of a wild blue eye. Then, taking him by the arm, he drew him to one side. 'A word in your ear, my boy. That girl of yours. Not quite the right sort. Ideal for Heslington, man of the people and all that, but not if you get in. Biggest mistake a man can make, marrying beneath him. Saw a lot of it in the army, nice girls most of 'em. Made them damned miserable. Doesn't do to swim against the tide. Let her down gently and find someone of your own sort.'

Angus felt as if someone had thrown a bucket of water over his head. He glanced across at Jean, in her diamonds, wearing a blouse trimmed with Brussels lace. She was talking to someone, laughing, and when she felt his eyes on her she turned and smiled. He smiled back, but with the colonel still at his side he felt total betrayal.

'Nice girl,' said the colonel dispassionately.

That night Angus got drunk. He sat in the bar of the pub long after closing time, downing whisky chasers and trying to sing. Jean sat with him, her head propped wearily on her hand. At half-past one, she yawned. 'Let's go to bed.'

'No! The night is young. Besides the landlady doesn't like us sleeping together.'

'I'm not sleeping with you tonight. I'll put a bowl by your bed and leave you to it.'

'Sweet Jean! Sweet practical Jean. A girl that likes beer and ham sandwiches.'

'When I can't get champagne and quails' eggs, yes.'

She eyed him unhappily. The antagonism of the party workers had been all too apparent to her, if not to him. They wanted an aristocrat, someone they could boast about. No-one was ever thrilled when she came to tea. She imagined what they would think of Mara, arriving like an exotic animal from some South American fastness, or even Lisa, with her highbred, spare good taste. Girls like Jean were ten a penny, but the Mrs Wentworths of this world would walk a thousand miles to talk to people like that. Snobs abounded it seemed, even the most charming individual might despise you underneath. But never Angus. Surely never Angus?

He tried to get up, and almost fell. She hung on to his arm, supporting him. 'The colonel says you're a nice girl' he said blearily.

'He hates my guts,' retorted Jean. 'Don't make so much noise, you'll wake everyone.'

Suddenly he stopped. 'You'd think the family might have been interested. Your father was.'

'I don't think your mother understands, do you?'

'Sure she doesn't. Never understood any of us, if you ask me. Times like this she makes me bloody angry! You'd think she'd have been pleased. A little bit pleased. I know I didn't win.'

He looked so young and bewildered. She reached up and put her arms around him. 'I'm pleased,' she whispered. 'Pleased and proud as Punch!'

He had the devil of a hangover in the morning. His head pounded, his mouth felt dry as dust. When he looked in the cracked bathroom mirror he saw the face of a man twenty years older, a debauched and repentant roue. Jean did the packing, throwing the detritus of weeks into bags and boxes. She put all the press cuttings, the rosettes, the handouts, into a large pile. 'I'll get a plastic sack and sling those out,' said Angus blearily.

'No, you won't! They're souvenirs. You'll be glad of those when you're a minister.' He felt too ill even to laugh.

By the time they neared home the hangover was giving way to weariness and mild depression. It was only to be expected, he supposed. The last weeks had been fuller and more exciting than any he had ever known, and now it was over. Next week he'd return to his mundane job and his little achievement would be forgotten, mouldering like his press cuttings in the bottom of a box.

He dropped Jean off at her bungalow and drove off quickly. He couldn't face Reg today; in fact he wondered how Jean could bear to face him every day. Not a failure would go unavenged nor a success untrumpeted, however embarrassingly. Angus felt sudden affection for his own undemonstrative family.

The bustle in the drive surprised him. There were cars everywhere, and at the side gate, an ambulance. Angus parked quickly and got out. To his surprise he saw Mara, wearing an old black dress. Her face was chalk white.

'Mara! What a surprise! Why the ambulance? Has one of the old duffers had a stroke in the night?'

She didn't smile. Her eyes, he noticed, were ringed with black. 'It was a heart attack,' she said softly. 'We just found her this morning. Angus, Mother's dead.'

He thought about laughing. But it wasn't like Mara to joke in such terrible taste. And then again, he wanted to laugh until his sides split, because it was such a ghastly irony, for his mother to die just when he was deciding to appreciate her. He put his hand out and caught Mara's fingers. Her face crumpled. 'Oh, Angus,' she wailed. 'I'm so terribly afraid it's my fault!'

Chapter Thirty-Four

Charlotte's funeral brought Hellyn family connections flocking to
The Court. Dowager aunts, uncles stricken with gout, even some
strange people from a Scottish fastness that no-one had ever heard of.
It was odd because they hadn't come when Henry died. Perhaps they
had thought about coming, decided not to and then regretted the
decision. Charlotte's death gave them a second chance.

They buried her in the family plot, with all four children at the
graveside. Angus and Marcus stood side by side. They didn't look like
twins any more, reflected Lisa. Marcus looked old, thin, his suit
hanging limply from his shoulders. Halfway through the service he
began to cry.

Lisa felt cold, and rather detached. Next to her Mara looked
deathly, the shadows under her eyes thrown into relief by her black
dress. The colour suited Lisa rather better. An old aunt, wearing one
of those fur stoles that still possess head and claws, tapped her on the
arm and said, 'My dear, you remind me so much of Coco Chanel!'

Henry's headstone still looked fresh and new. Mara said, 'We
ought to have brought Daddy some flowers. He oughtn't to be left
out.'

'He always did hog the limelight,' remarked Lisa.

'Don't be so catty!'

Angus hissed at them, 'Not now, girls!' and they fell silent. They
would rather squabble than stand there, thinking, listening to the
dreadful rattle of earth on the coffin. They each took a handful and
cast it in, and Marcus stood for long seconds on the very edge,
looking down. 'Come away, old chap,' said Angus and drew him
aside.

Back at The Court there was an odd mingling of funeral guests and
others. Bewildered family members found themselves talking to
South American industrialists, amazed that Charlotte had apparently

326

possessed such a cosmopolitan acquaintance. Lisa kept wondering where her mother was. Everything seemed to lack cohesion without Charlotte at its head, however nominally. For the first time she thought about the future. What was to happen now? Who was to look after the guests? Suddenly everything seemed dreadful. She went out into the garden, sat down under a juniper bush and wept.

After a while, when she was tired of crying, she reached into her pocket and pulled out Toby's letter. He had written first, a brief note, and she had replied. It was the start of an occasional correspondence, each putting up a fa`ade of happy and fulfilled days. Lisa told him a great deal about the running of The Court, because of course it was her duty to keep him informed. And in return he told her about the club.

It had opened barely a month after she left. Today Toby wrote, 'You ask about the club. Looks fantastic, crammed every night. The folk of Rio consider it the height of glamour, even if the food is less than great. We could do with some help from you on that score. The waiters are sloppy and every band I hire plays La Bamba. Every bloody night. And the people yell 'Ah! La Bamba!' as if they'd never heard anything so wonderful. It makes me want to kill someone.'

Lisa chuckled to herself. She could just imagine his big head slumping between his shoulders, the picture of disgruntlement. Toby liked his own way, he had no instinct about letting others have their heads. But if the crowd wanted La Bamba, then they should have it. He would be driven comprehensively nuts.

A shadow fell across the grass. 'Glad to see you're amusing yourself,' said Mara thinly.

Lisa put the letter back in her pocket. 'It was just a letter. It's so hot in there.'

Mara sat on the grass next to her. 'I thought you were making quite a hit with the relatives. I'm the black sheep, of course. Lips curl every time anyone looks at me.'

'So difficult to get used to, after all that adoration,' retorted Lisa.

Mara dropped her chin on to her knees. 'Don't be so catty.'

Bees hummed in the grass, feeding on clover. Sunlight casting through the leaves laid a tracery of lace across their faces. Mara said, 'I can't get used to it. I'm not even used to Father being gone. Lisa, do you think it was my fault? Truly? I never meant to upset her so much.'

'If you ask me it's a family tendency,' said Lisa matter-of-factly. 'Her own mother died of a heart attack. Any of us might. You can't expect the world to walk on tiptoe in case you pop off, now can you?'

Mara grimaced. 'I just wish — we could have been closer. All of us.

327

Now they're both gone it's all settled and done with. I hate feeling that we can't change anything, that there's never going to be a day when it all goes right.' She looked anxiously at her sister, as if seeking approval.

Lisa said, 'You are silly. You can't always have a happy ending.'

Gradually the house emptied of everyone except immediate family and the guests. Clare was staying on, she couldn't bring herself to leave until something was settled about Mara. And then the ambulance came to take Marcus back to hospital and he refused to go.

He stood on the step, calm and very white. 'I'm well at the moment,' he pleaded. 'I don't need to go back. I want to stay at home and do what I can.'

The two male nurses glanced at each other. 'Come along, sir,' coaxed one, without conviction. They had a lot of symnpathy with the patient. It wasn't as if he was going to be sharing a bedroom in a council flat, now was it?

'Marcus, old chap, there's no-one to look after you,' said Angus. 'I've got to go to London and Mara's going away. Lisa's got the house to run, you know that.'

'She's going to need help,' insisted Marcus. 'Please, Angus. It was Mother who didn't want me here. I made her uncomfortable.'

Lisa's eyes became very large. 'I don't mind,' she said tensely. 'If everyone thinks that's best.'

She waited for someone to say no, it was too much of an imposition. But no-one did. She felt a rising tide of anger. No-one questioned her role as the one to stay at home, no-one considered her feelings at all. And of course, she didn't mind having Marcus, not when he was like this. But which of them would be there to help when he was pacing a room, up and down, up and down, endlessly muttering, fidgeting, unable to rest or sleep?

Lisa opened her mouth to say that on second thoughts she couldn't cope. That they must think of something else, someone else, perhaps find the money for a nurse. But Marcus looked so happy. He was like a balloon, moments before flat and shrivelled, inflated now with the wonderful gas of hope. So she said nothing.

Clare, Lisa and Mara sat in the garden. Curtiss had served them tea, and none of them had eaten very much. They were sleepy in the afternoon warmth, drugged with the scent of the old-fashioned roses. The bees were out again. They came from the village, and when you passed the hives in this rare, good summer the smell of honey hung in the lane, like a rich, golden haze.

Clare yawned delicately. 'Your mother said Kenya, Mara. It's ideal, nobody who's anybody lives there. And I don't want to be melodramatic, but it was almost the last thing she said to you.'

'So it was. But I never did what I was told before and I can't see why I should start now.' Mara twirled a teaspoon in her empty teacup.

'It is rather your last opportunity. And, Mara dear, you have to go somewhere. You're too visible here, you can't possibly give birth at The Court.'

Lisa said, 'It might be difficult staying here on my own.'

'With Marcus, you mean?' Clare grimaced. 'There's always the doctor. And Curtiss can help, it's not as if you're quite alone.'

'I meant without Mother. I'll have to be here all the time, welcoming people and so on. Jean Maythorpe thinks Angus should stay.'

'She would,' said Mara. 'That girl is getting ideas. But she of all people should understand about Angus's career.'

'He isn't working very hard at the moment,' murmured Lisa.

Her sister rounded on her. 'You know perfectly well he's got to stay in London, or they'll forget him! You can't expect him to hang around here greeting rich Arabs and dusting the silver, can you?'

'Well, since I have to, I don't see why the hell he shouldn't!'

'Lisa dear, I seem to remember it was your idea.'

Clare intervened. 'Girls, we haven't decided anything. Is it to be Kenya, Mara? Do make up your mind about something. Don't you like the Demouths? I know Diandra quite well, a very sweet girl.'

'Absolutely charming.' Mara threw herself sulkily back in her chair. 'I take it I do have to go?'

'Of course you do. You've waited a month and he still hasn't made any attempt to contact you. You're starting to show, it's absolutely vital that you take yourself off until the birth.'

'And then what?'

Clare paused. 'I think you should decide about that when the child's born. We can't make any assumptions, can we?'

'No. No, I suppose we can't.'

Mara's face became set against pain. Suddenly she got up. 'I'm hot,' she declared. 'I'm going to swim in the lake. Coming anyone?'

Lisa said, 'No, it's full of weed. Do be careful.'

But Mara was off, leaving her long dark skirt and white blouse strewn across the lawn. She ran to the lakeside, dipping her toes in and shaking them with cold. 'She shouldn't,' said Clare. 'She'll lose the baby.'

'Perhaps she ought,' murmured Lisa.

She watched her long-legged, beautiful sister, her hair falling from a knot, underwear doing nothing to hide her. When she turned sideways her stomach was clearly distended, but she looked like a goddess, fertile and blessed. She threw herself in and began splashing wildly about, this way and that. 'Mara,' called Clare. 'Do come out. Don't be silly.'

Mara began to swim further and further out. Then she lay on her back, her hair floating like weed itself. She lay quite still.

Lisa ran to the edge. 'Come out, Mara! If you don't come out I'll get someone to fetch you!'

But Mara lay in the water, letting the cold seep into her, letting the weed wrap around her legs. Lisa pulled off her shoes, threw off her skirt, but before she could plunge into the water Mara seemed to wake. She sighed, turned, and began swimming back to the bank.

When she came out, she saw her sister standing there half-dressed. 'I thought you were going to drown yourself,' said Lisa.

'For a minute I thought so too.' Mara swallowed and tried to smile. Her face was dead-white with cold, blotched here and there with purple. 'The lake's a horrible place to swim. It's full of weed.'

Clare ran up, and bundled her into a blanket. 'I've had just about enough,' she said hysterically. 'I shall telephone this evening and arrange your flight. We'll send you out to Kenya and see how they cope with you!'

They went into the house, leaving Lisa to pull on her shoes and skirt. There were faces watching at the windows; the guests had witnessed another real-life Hellyn drama. Soon they would leave, and so would Clare and the family. Everyone came, everyone went, only Lisa seemed doomed to stay forever.

Chapter Thirty-Five

The Demouths stood together at the airport, a sun-bleached, weather-worn group, seemingly without colour. Europeans lacked colour in Africa, they took on the look of desert earth, pale and dry. In contrast the Africans were a riot of primary shades, the rich reds and blues and yellows of shirts and dresses and headscarves, the deep black of their skins. Even in her short time there Diandra had taken on the look of hot country whites, and on her occasional visits home her mother shrieked at her burnt skin and dry, splitting hair. But she had been happy, blissfully, unbelievably happy. Until she heard that Mara Hellyn was coming.

Genevieve was delighted. It was an opportunity to do something for Henry, and indeed for Charlotte. Her friends were dead, but their child needed help. 'It's good to be able to repay a kindness,' she told the family, folding the letter decisively back into the envelope. 'The girl's got herself in trouble and doesn't know where to turn. She can stay as long as she needs to.'

Edward sat, cold with shock. He could feel Diandra's eyes on him, watching for some telltale sign. He cleared his throat. 'I'd rather she didn't come, Ma,' he said stiffly. 'She's a difficult sort of girl. Causes a lot of trouble.'

Genevieve laughed. 'She's got herself pregnant, she can't cause much more trouble than that!'

'I do agree with Edward though,' broke in Diandra, breathlessly. 'I mean, we're miles away from a doctor here. It wouldn't be safe.'

'I had all my boys here, and it didn't kill me,' said Genevieve. 'We'll take her into town now and then for a check-up, she can always go into hospital if there's a problem.'

Richard and Tim, her younger boys, were goggling. Genevieve snapped, 'And you two can make sure you're civil to her! Get off and

331

do some work, you can't spend the whole day stuffing yourselves with food.'

When they had gone, Edward said, 'Ma, I don't think you quite understand. The boys are bound to fall in love with her. She's stunning to look at. I've never seen anyone like her.'

'Really, Edward! What a thing to say in front of your pretty wife.'

'It's true,' said Diandra. 'When she walks into a room, men's mouths fall open. She'll be the most terrible nuisance. All the women hate her and all the men fall in love.'

'But not you, Edward?' Genevieve cast an alarmed glance at her son.

'No. Not me' he said shortly. 'I knew her at home. She was spoiled rotten, an absolute cow. Most people only see her party manners.'

'I liked her at school,' said Diandra. 'She'd lie like a trooper to keep you out of a scrape.'

'There then,' declared Genevieve. 'You can have a friend to keep you company. A bit of a crush won't do the boys any harm. I admit I'm longing to see this gorgeous creature, I can hardly wait.'

But, whatever she was expecting, it was less than Mara herself. She was wearing trousers and top in a vivid print, the top shaped like a ragged edged poncho, loosely hiding her stomach. She wore a wide hat on her head and high-heeled sandals on her feet, and tendrils of hair fell down from the hat like strands of pure gold. Her expression was sad, heartbreakingly so, but when she saw them she smiled. It was like sunshine after rain.

'Dear God,' said Genevieve and stepped forward to meet her. 'My dear, I'm Genevieve Demouth.'

Mara shook hands. 'It's terribly kind of you to let me visit you. Mother and Father spoke about you so affectionately.'

'Yes. Well.' Genevieve blinked rapidly. 'It only seems five minutes since they were staying with us. We must get your bags, where is everyone?'

Edward was standing in stony silence. Diandra stepped away from his side. 'Hello, Mara.'

'Diandra! Darling, it's lovely to see you. And Edward. It's really kind of you to let me come. I was so horrible and bratty when you stayed with us, Edward, I didn't think you'd put up with me for a minute.'

'I'm sure you knew Mother would let you come,' remarked Edward.

She gave a brief half-smile and went on to Richard and Tim. 'You boys are enormous!' She rested a hand on a bicep of each. 'I hope you won't get too bored with me.'

'No! No, we won't' stammered Tim, going bright red.

'Let's go and get the bags.' Edwards shepherded his brothers off in the direction of the baggage carousel.

The boys and Genevieve chattered to Mara on the drive back, while Edward and Diandra sat silent. Mara was to have the guest bungalow for the duration of her stay, and Diandra took it upon herself to show it to her. They said nothing until they stood in the large, airy sitting-room, with zebra skins on the sofa and the floor. The head of a wildebeeste hung on the wall, glassy-eyed. There was a stone fire-place, for the evenings were often cold. Mara stood in front of the empty grate and sighed.

'Don't you like it?' asked Diandra. 'The trophies are old, nobody hunts any more.'

'Yes. Yes, it's fine.' Mara went to the sofa and flung herself down. 'I'm sorry, Diandra. I didn't mean to inflict myself on you. There aren't many people willing to house unwanted pregnancies, I had to come.'

'Who's the father?'

'Someone. Someone I love very much.'

'You can't still love him if he's done this to you!'

Mara closed her eyes. 'You won't stop when you can, and by the time you know you should it's too late. I'm glad about the baby. It's something to hang on for.'

Diandra giggled. 'I'm sorry, Mara. I just find it very strange that you of all people should lose someone. I've never known a man yet that didn't want you forever.'

'Neither had I until now.' Mara opened her eyes. 'Don't worry. I'm a pregnant cast-off, Edward won't take a blind bit of notice of me. I won't be horrid, I promise.'

Diandra pushed back her soft brown hair. 'Well. That's a relief. I'd hate to have to claw your eyes out.'

'Would you? For Edward?'

'I think I would.' Her eyes were wide and anxious. 'If you lay one finger on him, I will.'

To begin with Mara and Edward saw little of each other. She stayed in bed late in the mornings, while he breakfasted early and went off to the farm. He made excuses to be absent for lunch, and in the evenings everyone was there. For over two weeks there was no opportunity for a private conversation.

For Mara the days passed in heat and tedium. She slept, she read, she walked around the gardens until the sun became oppressive. Gradually, with nothing to do, she became more and more bored. All those months in the flat in London, what had she done then? Waited,

333

that was all, Waited for Jay, made herself ready for him, and that was not boring at all. Once, twice she wrote to him. Desperate letters, that she didn't care who might read. There was never any reply. Money was put into her bank account, but apart from that he might have been dead.

She lay in the hot afternoons, watching her belly swell, feeling the flutterings of the child within. Had she damaged it? In her memory that one short week expanded to a lifetime, every minute lasting an hour. Perhaps the baby was maimed, horribly maimed. The nightmare haunted her.

Genevieve was always busy, going here and there, supervising the kitchen or the grain store or the village vaccination programme. Genevieve did it all and didn't look for help, not even from Diandra. But of course, Diandra had Edward. In the evenings Mara would see them looking at each other, see the signals that she knew so well. That which she and Edward had learned together he was now teaching his wife. They went early to their room, shut the solid wood door and made no effort to get any sleep.

All the same, Edward got up early, though Diandra always slept late. Mara was sick of sleeping. She began to rise just after dawn, when it was cool, when what energy you possessed seemed concentrated and strong. Edward and the boys wore bush trousers and shirts, and Mara did likewise, letting the shirt hang outside her trousers. They sat together in the house, drinking orange juice and eating toast, watching the sun burn the shadows from the earth.

The farm worked on around her, the cattle driven from field to field down the dusty road, hens scratching in the yard. Somebody was always watering the garden it seemed, creating a shell of greenery. It was an escape, a place for Genevieve to wander and remember the land of her birth. However many years she lived in Kenya, however much she loved its brilliance, there would always be a longing for England. And if she returned, thought Mara ruefully, she would be so disappointed. Out here they romanticised all that, and saw nothing at all romantic in their own wide skies.

'There's been talk of some rhino poaching,' said Edward one morning. 'I'm going to ride out and see what's what.'

The others grunted, but Mara said, 'What will you see?'

'Couple of dead rhino perhaps,' said Edward. 'But I hope not. Our rhino have been poached for years, they're pretty difficult to get close to. If we see any tracks we'll get on to the wardens and get them out with guns.'

'Why don't the wardens come out now?'

Edward withered her with a look. 'This isn't England. We don't

334

have policemen on every street. Preserving rhino is everyone's business, yours as much as mine.'

'Can I come then?'

Genevieve sat up. 'Don't be silly, Mara. You're pregnant.'

'You rode when you were pregnant, Ma,' said Tim.

'You've got a quiet horse, haven't you?' said Mara. 'I only want to jog along and watch.'

'No,' said Edward, and got up from the table.

He was almost ready to go when Mara came out to the stables. She leaned against the wall and watched him. 'I wish you'd let me come. I'm going crazy here.'

'You should have thought of that before you came. Learn to play patience or something.'

'What are you frightened of? Do you think I'm going to make a pass at you? In this condition?'

He tied a water bottle to his saddle. 'Don't be ridiculous.'

'You're a married man, you're obviously happy. You should be grateful to me. If I hadn't educated you, there's no telling what might have happened. You might never have realised what a smasher Diandra is.'

Edward sniffed. Then he said, 'She is, isn't she? I mean, you don't expect to find a girl like her. Loyal and good and sweet.'

'And pretty,' added Mara. 'Not in an obvious way though. I hope you tell her you think she's pretty.'

'Not often enough, I suppose. You don't when you're with some- one all the time.'

'No.' She stood looking at him for a moment. Then she said, 'I'm sorry, Edward. I made you very miserable and I'm sorry.'

'Don't be. I was a bit of a baby about things.'

'Yes, you were a bit. Friends? I don't want you to have to avoid me all the time.'

'OK. Friends.'

She waited a scant second, then said, 'Does that mean I can come?'

'For God's sake, Mara! Do you never give up?'

'Not when I want something. I want to ride, I want to do some- thing! Edward, I'm going mad.'

He leaned against his horse, his eyes creased from the sun, as if she amused him. As if he took pleasure in looking at her. He really had turned into a terribly attractive man, she thought. 'All right,' he said. 'I'll get the boy to saddle the mare.'

They rode out across the veldt, into the empty space that seemed to stretch forever. The horses trotted, a swinging stride that covered miles almost effortlessly. The dust began to burn in Mara's nose, and

335

her thighs hurt, from months of idleness.

'I'm so damned unfit,' she panted. 'I should be ashamed of myself.'

'Should you?'

She glanced at him. 'All right. I've done a lot of things I shouldn't. But I've decided having this baby isn't one of them. I want it. It's something very special to me.'

'It's not that twit I saw you with at the restaurant, is it?'

'Who, Jimmy? No. His family's notoriously infertile actually, always on the verge of dying out. If he'd made me pregnant married or not they'd have hung out the flags. It wasn't him. It was someone – someone I miss every day.'

'Did you ever miss me?'

She laughed. 'Oh, Edward! Of course I did. But it wasn't right and we both knew it.'

He thought how he'd wanted to die. But that had been a childish thing, an urge to show her, make her sorry. Mara was such a contradiction. When she was good she was very, very good, and when she was bad she was – exciting, infuriating, unbelievably entrancing. He was suddenly glad she was with him, glad that she was riding at his side, her hat falling off the back of her head and sweat running down into the dark cavern between her breasts. He found his eyes straying to her pregnant belly; he thought how it would be to run his hands over that hard, swelling mound.

The sun rose higher. They stopped in the shade to drink, sharing the same bottle. It tasted of her lips. He knew, without a doubt, that he should hever have let her come.

He stopped speaking to her. They rode in silence, towards the far, curved horizon, seemingly aimless. But soon they came to some scrub, bushes set here and there, and as they went on the scrub thickened into tangled thornbushes. They came across rhino spoor, distinctive piles of droppings, and the tracks of a mother and her calf. Edward signalled to Mara for quiet. If the rhino were here they could charge at any moment.

They pulled the horses to a walk, hooves making almost no sound in the dust. Suddenly Edward stopped. Slowly lifting his hand, he pointed, and there, like grey smudges against the thicket, stood the mother and her baby. They were close, so close Mara could see ears twitching, wrinkled faces and little, piggy, short-sighted eyes. Edward turned his horse and led her away.

'Why didn't they see us?' she asked when they were clear.

'Poor eyesight. We were quiet and we were upwind. One windshift and she'd have been on us like a tank.'

'Do we go back now?'

'Not yet. We look for signs of poachers. She had a lovely horn, they'll be after it.'

'I find it hard to imagine Chinese men swallowing down powdered rhino horn and trying to get it up,' remarked Mara. 'There must be a million things more useful. Naked dancing girls, dirty magazines, early nights.'

'They ought to put you on prescription,' said Edward. 'You'd cure anyone.'

The words hung in the air between them. Mara felt a familiar heat. She put back her head and stretched. Her breasts, heavy with pregnancy, lay like ripe melons ready for plucking. Edward said, 'Mara, – '

She turned and stared at him. 'Would you really? You've got Diandra, you love her. You make each other happy. Would you really put all that at risk for one tumble on the ground with me?'

'She wouldn't know. I'd never do anything to hurt her, surely you can see that?'

Mara pulled her horse over to the shade of a tree. She slipped out of the saddle and looped the reins loosely over a branch. Edward followed, and they stood, an inch away from one another. He put his hand under her shirt.

'Don't.' Mara pulled violently away. 'I don't understand you!' she said hysterically. 'I don't understand men at all. How can you want me when you've got someone you love? Or do you think because you want this that you love me too? I've got a man's child growing inside me, because he said he loved me! Do any of you love?'

'Don't pretend you don't like it,' said Edward thickly. 'I remember how it was.'

She turned on him. 'Oh, I enjoy it all right. I can't help wanting a man. But what do you want? a body, that's all. You don't even like me, and the first chance you see you're trying to get into my pants.'

'For God's sake, Mara! You can't play the innocent, you came out today to make me screw you!'

She snatched at her hat. 'I might have done. I don't know. I don't want you now. I've had enough of married men, using me, lying to me, lying to their wives. Would you give up Diandra for me? Would you leave all this and live with me alone?'

He grinned suddenly, a wide, hard smile. 'You must be joking.'

'There you are, you see. I've been a whore, first for money and then for love. I won't say I'm giving it up, because we're all whores one way and another. But my price has gone up.'

Edward's face became stiff. 'I'd have given you anything once,' he

337

said harshly. 'It wasn't the sex I was buying, it was you!'

Briefly she put her fingers against his cheek. 'Believe me, you're so much better off with Diandra.'

Riding home, neither of them speaking, she wondered if that was her biggest mistake. Edward had grown up. Whatever he said, he still loved her a little, and lusted rather a lot. A big, attractive, risk-taking man, someone she could have lived with, someone whose children she could have borne. But she'd wanted more. And all she had was a fatherless child and a great well of loneliness.

In the long, dark evenings mosquitoes buzzed against the screens of the porch. Mara played board games with Tim and Richard. She let them show off, practising their charm. They adored her, and so did Genevieve, because Mara was a free spirit, she never cared what people thought. It reminded Genevieve of Henry.

Unknowingly, without intention, Mara eclipsed Diandra. The girl simply wasn't a match. She didn't have that way with her, of easy intimacy, she didn't have that calm confidence that let Mara announce to a cocktail party at a neighbouring farm, 'I'm an unmarried mother. I think I'm abandoned, but I'm not sure in which sense.' Everyone laughed of course, everyone admired her. Except Diandra.

Sometimes in the afternoons Diandra would drive into town. She bought fruit, and vegetables that they didn't grow on the farm, and sometimes a special beer that Edward liked. And she went to the market where they sold native jewellery to the tourists and she'd find a bracelet to send to her mother, or something for herself.

One day Mara asked if she could come, she had an appointment at the hospital. Since there was no good reason for refusing, Diandra agreed. The car was hot, airless. Diandra wound down the windows and let her hair blow in the dust. Mara took out a scarf and wound it turban fashion around her head. She looked exotic.

'I wish you wouldn't preen so much,' snapped Diandra.

'What? Do you mean putting on a scarf? I don't like dust in my hair.'

'Last night, you leaned across the card table and gave both boys a wonderful view of your cleavage. And you let down your hair, and loosened your belt and really made yourself at home.'

'You were taking notes, weren't you? I'm pregnant, I get very hot and uncomfortable.'

'Those boys were writhing, and you know it. I don't know what gets into you with men around, you're ridiculous.'

'It isn't the boys you're worried about. It's Edward.'

Diandra changed gear unnecessarily. Her face was set in angry lines. 'I knew I'd hate it if you came,' she said jerkily. 'You've spoiled everything.'

'Diandra, I didn't want to come, there just wasn't anywhere else I could go. I'm not here to cause trouble. I haven't slept with him. And I won't, I promise you.'

'What good's that? He wants to. He can't take his eyes off you, he watches you all the time. And at night – he's different. We can't talk the way we did. He holds things back, as if he's got something to hide.'

'He has,' remarked Mara. 'But it isn't so terrible. A bit of lust for another woman. He'll never do anything about it.'

The first traffic lights at the edge of town showed red in front of them. Diandra jerked the car to a stop. 'I wish you'd go away,' she said fiercely. 'I wish you'd go and never come back.'

Mara went wearily to her hospital appointment. Diandra had depressed her, she reminded her of Jay's wife. Women never liked her, whatever she said, whatever she did or didn't do. And Jay hadn't stayed. What was he doing now? Surely he must feel some of this terrible, dragging loneliness.

The hospital was light and airy. They settled her to wait in a cool, white-painted room. She leafed through a magazine, glancing at the photographs. And there he was. Tall, thin, with that curiously wide forehead and narrow chin. He was coming out of an art exhibition and he looked bright and interested. A wave of rage washed over her. How could he look so happy? She was exiled, alone, bearing his child and he – he didn't care. She took hold of the page and quietly crushed it in her palm, ripping it silently into shreds. When she was called to see the doctor she stood up and let it fall like used confetti on to the floor.

Her blood pressure was way up. She was at once admitted into the hospital and put to bed. They telephoned Genevieve but of course couldn't reach Diandra, who eventually arrived at the hospital when Mara failed to turn up at their rendezvous. She came up to visit.

'Are you ill, Mara? How long are you going to have to stay?'

She shrugged. 'They don't know. Till the blood presure goes down. I could almost believe you willed this on me, Diandra.'

'I'm sorry. I didn't mean to.'

Mara leaned back against the pillows, putting her long hand over her eyes. 'It's probably for the best. You and Edward can get back to talking to each other.'

'It isn't that I don't like you Mara,' wailed Diandra. 'If it was just you and me we'd be friends. When men are there you're different. You can't let them ignore you.'

339

'What do you want me to say? I've told you I don't want Edward. If you go on at me like this, I might as well have him. You hate us just as much as if we were really sleeping together.'

'Bitch!'

Diandra turned on her heel and went out. When the nurse came to read Mara's blood pressure it had gone up again. They kept her in for a month.

She went back to the farm shortly before Christmas. The boys had made a 'Welcome Home' banner for her, and she was unaccountably touched. Her belly seemed vast, growing with no reference to her at all, an attachment. She found it hard to remember the love-making that had caused this, just as she could hardly remember that last day. If only she hadn't been stoned, he would never have gone. If it was a boy, if only it could be a boy, he would come back.

The family included her in their round of Christmas parties, but as they extended on into January, a feverish round of celebration at which you met the same people time after time, she preferred to stay at home rather than trek off across miles of dusty roads only to drink orange juice. It was peaceful, she could wander about as she pleased, eat what she liked, with no Edward or Diandra to make her the object of their own personal war. The family became used to leaving her behind.

Towards the end of the month they took off on a seventy mile drive to a neighbour, leaving Mara on her own. The baby wasn't due for at least four weeks, but she tired easily, and didn't want to go. The farm was quiet, almost all the servants were off about their own affairs. In the barns she could hear the horses stamping, and a cow in the pasture started to moo. Suddenly she heard an engine, revving hard, approaching at speed. She got up from her chair on the verandah and stood looking towards the road. A cloud of dust hung in the air, like a rolling, extending balloon. Her hand went to her throat. Were the Demouths back early? Or was it something else?

Edward had a gun but she didn't know where it was. She thought about hiding but then imagined how ridiculous she would seem if it was nothing at all. It might be the game warden, and at first, as the jeep roared into view, she thought that was so. Five, six men with guns. Too late she realised that game wardens they were not. They were poachers.

Courage that she hadn't known she possessed stiffened her backbone. She stood behind the verandah screen as the men got out of the jeep, walking carefully, as if they expected no-one but might still be ambushed. They must have watched and waited until the family left. All at once a man noticed her. He let out a yell and fell

340

backwards in a heap. They all stood, staring up at her.

'What do you want?' asked Mara shrilly. 'I'm not alone. The family won't be long.'

'What your name?' A man wearing a battered bush hat stepped forward. His rifle was held across his body, and his finger caressed the trigger.

'I am Lady Mara Hellyn.' Try as she would she couldn't keep her voice steady. 'I'm staying here. If you hurt me there'll be a lot of trouble, I'm very important.'

'We don't hurt you. My brother, he hurt.'

She looked towards the jeep. On the back seat lay another man, unconscious, perhaps dead. Blood, turned almost black, soaked his side. Flies buzzed over the wound.

'Do you want water?' asked Mara. 'I can give you water and bandages.'

'You got medicine? Pills?'

She nodded. Genevieve kept penicillin as a basic stand-by, both for the stock and the people. She was prepared for anything from snake-bite to septicaemia.

Mara went into the house, fetching the first aid box from Genevieve's bedroom. The man followed with his gun. He stood very close to her, smelling of sweat and blood. She felt her own sweat break out cold all over her. Never in her life had she been so afraid.

They carried the man on to the verandah. When they peeled away his clothes Mara's stomach heaved; his side was a mass of chopped flesh, as if something, presumably a bullet, had raked across him. His brother washed it, trickling water from a bowl, letting it drain away almost to Mara's shoes. The patient never moved, the only sign of life was an occasional flicker of an eyelid. They dusted the wound with antiseptic powder, bandaged it roughly and carried him back to the jeep. Finally they took all Genevieve's penicillin.

Even as the jeep roared away down the track, she couldn't believe they had gone. She had seen their faces, she could identify them. Why on earth hadn't they shot her? It seemed imperative suddenly to get rid of the blood. She carried bucket after bucket of water to the verandah and swabbed it clean. The day faded, she wondered when someone would come. Her back hurt. She went into her sitting-room and lay on the sofa, but her back still hurt and she lay on the floor. The wildebeeste head stared down at her from the wall. She felt a wild sense of unreality, as if she was dreaming and wasn't here at all.

Hours passed, and she lay there. Pains began, and at first she ignored them, but as they increased she felt a rising sense of panic. It was the baby and she was alone. If it came now, far from the hospital, both she and it would die.

She pushed herself up to the sofa, half-sitting against it. The wildebeeste looked quizzical now, as she puffed and panted and strained. Every now and then a pain came that was diabolical, cutting through her control. It wasn't supposed to be like this. Nowadays childbirth wasn't supposed to hurt!

At last, at long last, she heard them come home. She tried to call, but a pain came and silenced her. She lay with her teeth clenched, fighting it, and when at last it subsided she called, 'Genevieve! Genevieve!' pathetically. It wasn't Genevieve that came. When she looked up she saw Edward. 'Mara. Oh, my poor darling love,' he said. And behind him, white-faced, stood Diandra.

At last they called Genevieve. 'Diandra, get some sheets,' she commanded. 'And, Edward, call the doctor. He's got to come out, we're going to have a premature baby on our hands. Did you fall, dear? Has it been going long?'

'Some poachers came,' gasped Mara. 'And when they went I started. Hours ago.'

'Oh, yes. I heard the wardens had shot up a gang,' remarked Genevieve.

'Poachers? You were here, alone, with poachers?' demanded Edward.

His mother fixed him with a steely glare. 'Get out, Edward. You can't be the slightest use and you've got to call the doctor.'

The pain came in waves, great surges that crashed over her and then trickled away into nothing. In between she could hear Edward and Diandra rowing. 'Why did you marry me if you still want her? Don't deny it, I heard you.'

'Can't I be civil to someone under this roof?'

'Civil? Is that what you call it? When you can't talk to me for mooning about over her. I hate you, Edward. I absolutely hate you.'

Genevieve got up and went to the door. She said something in a low voice. There was the sound of Diandra sobbing wildly.

'I don't know what's got into that girl,' said Genevieve, coming back. 'I've never seen such jealousy. If she's not careful she'll drive Edward away.'

'I hope not,' gasped Mara.

'Did the two of you never think of making a match of it?' enquired Genevieve. 'You wouldn't have got yourself in this scrape.'

'No.'

Mara closed her fists until her nails dug into her hands. Her head spun with a riot of confused thoughts. Jay, and then Edward, and then Jay again, grinning at her with the face of a poacher, a wild nightmare of images, coming at her from all sides. 'Genevieve! Genevieve!' she yelled, and the woman held her hands.

'It's all right. Push, dear, push it out. Come on. Push.'

She put her chin on her chest, trying to focus on this one thing. But she was tired, so tired, she couldn't bring herself to struggle. The nightmare sucked at her, how easy to slide back into that. Like death. Like entry into hell. She jerked herself away, and the breath caught in her head, swelling it like a football as she pushed. Every part of her strained, ached, struggled.

'Dear God,' said Genevieve. 'Don't stop, girl, not now.'

She pushed again, and now it hurt to go on and hurt to go back, there was no end and no escape. If she'd known it would be like this she'd never have let it happen. It was the single most terrible thing she had ever endured in all her life!

And it was over. A gasp and a slither and there on the sheet lay a wailing, pink little boy. 'There! There! There!' crowed Genevieve in delight. 'He's beautiful. So beautiful.'

Mara gathered him up. The cord snaked away from him, joining them still. Outside Edward was shouting and Diandra was crying again, but she heard nothing. Every fibre of her being was lost in love.

Although premature, the baby weighed a respectable six pounds. 'Count yourself lucky you didn't go full-term,' commented the doctor. 'You'd need the calving ropes.'

'He is all right, isn't he?' asked Mara anxiously.

'Doesn't he look all right?'

'Oh yes.' she smoothed the tiny, downy skull. 'Just like his father, actually. His head's the same shape.'

Since the entire community was speculating on who the father might be, the doctor took a good look at the child. But he saw no resemblance to anyone, least of all Edward Demouth, who was popularly supposed to be the guilty man. Why otherwise would he give the girl a home, when he knew it was driving his wife to despair?

Mara stayed in bed for a week. On the fifth day Edward came to visit her. He sat on the bed looking sombrely down into the cradle.

'Diandra's going home,' he said suddenly.

Mara looked blank. 'For a visit you mean?'

'No. She's going home to her mother. She's leaving me.'

The words took a moment to sink in. At last Mara said, 'Do you mind?'

'I don't know.' He put his hands together, as if trying to force himself to think. 'She says I took her as second best. Perhaps I did,

343

I don't know any more. I thought we were happy. But you remember that day? When we went riding. You wanted me to give up everything for you. Do you want that now?'

'Do you mean − do you want to change Diandra for me? Is that it?'

He stared at her miserably. 'I don't bloody know. I'm not rational with you around. When you were having the baby − I wanted to be with you. I wanted it to be ours! I'd make it ours, Mara. I'd treat it as my own.'

She looked from Edward's fair head to the baby's darker one. 'He has a father, thank you,' she said softly. 'I don't want you and I don't need you either. That day in the bush, I never meant anything to happen. I just wanted to see what you'd do. If you'd do it.'

'You can always make me do anything. You know that.'

'We wouldn't last a week. It was only a bit longer last time, then you started yelling at me. You've conveniently forgotten.'

'Have I? I don't know anything any more.'

He looked crushed and dispirited. Mara felt tender towards him, as if the love she had for her baby had overflowed to lap around the room and all that was in it. 'Look,' she said softly, 'you can have your own family, you and Diandra. I want − I want something different. We wouldn't be happy, you know. And Diandra loves you, she really does.'

'But what about me? I loved you from the start, from the very first day. I can't love Diandra like that. I thought I could. But then you came along and I saw it for what it was. Nothing.

Mara set her jaw. She would not let Edward do this, and his persistence was annoying her. 'I should have let you screw me that day,' said Mara casually. 'That would have cured you. I thought I was being moral for once and not breaking up your marriage, but the trouble with you, Edward, is that you are a very randy man.'

He flushed a dark red. 'You don't have to say things like that.'

'Don't I? Here you are telling me all about your heart-searchings and you can't take your eyes off my breasts. If I was in bed for any other reason than this, I'd get you in here with me and cure you in five minutes flat. Just think what would happen if I took you up on your kind offer! I wouldn't be faithful. A few kids and a lot of affairs later you'd be wishing with all your heart you'd never lost Diandra. And she'll be married to someone else, making them a good and loving wife.'

'She say's she won't divorce me.'

'I don't suppose she will till she finds someone she likes better. Someone who doesn't dump her when he feels like a change.' Mara leaned back in bed, her hands behind her head. Her breasts, swollen with milk, bulged over her nightdress. Go away, Edward,' she murmured. 'I don't like you enough to put up with you.'

Blindly, he got up and stumbled out.

Mara tried to laugh and could not. Instead she fought tears. She could have had Edward, could have put the clock back and begun again. Why then hadn't she? Of course she didn't love him, not as she loved Jay, but he need never have known. In time she might herself have forgotten that this wasn't love. She'd sleep discreetly with this or that neighbour, if she got bored. But the children would be Edward's, one after another, to thank him for taking both her and her child. So why hadn't she?

It was Diandra of course. She might hate Jay's wife, see her as an enemy, but how could you hate someone who all through school brought you Mars bars from home, and let you copy their prep? You couldn't. And if you injured them you wouldn't be happy. Mara put her hand down to the cradle, inserting her finger into the baby's tiny fist. You couldn't teach someone to be kind and loving if you yourself were otherwise.

She asked Genevieve to send Diandra to her. 'The girl's packing,' declared Genevieve. 'Good thing too, if you ask me. I'm sick of her mooning about the place.'

But Mara insisted, and at last Diandra came. She was white-faced and weary.

'You look ghastly,' said Mara. 'Haven't you made it up yet?'

Diandra shook her head. 'We won't. It's gone too far. He never really wanted to marry me, you see.'

'Why do you say that?'

'For God's sake, Mara, don't play the innocent! It's your fault and you know it. He was all right till he saw you again.'

'And he'll be all right when I'm gone. Is the end of next week OK?'

Diandra sighed. 'It wouldn't make a blind bit of difference. We're finished whatever happens with you. I thought his mother liked me, but it seems she doesn't. Everything's spoiled.'

Mara snuggled down beneath her covers. 'The old cat's jealous. She had him to herself for years and then she lost him – no wonder she'd like to give you the boot. She doesn't like me any better, or at least she wouldn't if I was in your shoes. Why don't you get Edward to build a separate house? At least you could fight in peace.'

'It's too late,' sobbed Diandra. 'It's all far too late.'

'I'll go tomorrow,' said Mara wildly. 'Don't give in so easily, Diandra! You never did know how to hang on and win.'

345

'I'm so miserable I can't try.'

There was a knock on the door. It was Edward, come to fetch Diandra for supper. 'I don't want any,' she sniffed.

'Of course you don't,' agreed Mara. 'Why don't you take her into town, Edward? Why don't you talk? I can't understand why you're letting go so easily, either of you. When I first came I was jealous because you were so happy!'

'You're the one that spoiled it' hissed Diandra.

'She didn't mean to,' defended Edward. 'It wasn't her fault.'

'When does she ever mean anything? It just happens and she blames everyone else. Oh, how my head does ache.'

'You ought to go and lie down.'

'How can I with your mother glaring and thinking things? She doesn't want me here, Edward. Tell me what I ought to do.'

She looked up at him like a sad, weary fawn. She seemed helpless and young, her soft brown hair straggling around her face. Suddenly Edward thought of the day he'd come to her, penniless, distraught, and she'd comforted him. How could he have forgotten that? How could he now not comfort her? Everything had been so simple and clear to him, and somehow it had all got confused. Mara watched him from the bed, golden and lovely, and she had always confused him. There was no right or wrong any more, no up or down, no clear broad path to happiness. You did what you could and what seemed best at the time. You didn't afterwards think it should have been different and go back on it, because all you did was make worse and muddier messes. Look what a mess he had made of this. He put out his arms and drew Diandra's head on to his shoulder.

Chapter Thirty-Six

In England, Christmas had been mild. January brought the first sharp frosts, and in the mornings snow dusted the fields. Farmers complained that the land was sodden, drowning the winter crops, but as February came into sight the weather changed. Overnight the temperature plummetted. Rivers congealed into ice, and at The Court they opened the door one morning to find a dozen small birds frozen to death against it. Then came the snow, two sustained heavy falls. The earth became quite still. It seemed as if nothing at all could move, that the world was held in a cold, white circle of light.

Marcus sat in his room. He was motionless except for his fingers, which twisted and turned against each other, a constant machine, making nothing, running on nerves. His thoughts were as tumbled as the fingers, twisting, tangling, a maze that turned in on itself and never ended. At least this time he knew he was sick, knew that the misery was in his head. If there was a God, if there was anything good in the world, why in God's name wouldn't it stop?

There was a knock on the door. Lisa, come to see what had happened to him. He thought about getting up, but at once he knew, absolutely knew, that if he moved he would be in danger. All that kept him safe was immobility. At last, after long minutes, she came in.

'Don't you want to come down? We'll be serving dinner.'

Of course he couldn't reply. If his voice left the confines of his body he would be in deadly peril.

'Marcus? Marcus, please?'

He sat, not even his eyes moving. It was one of the things she found most frustrating, this withdrawal from the world. He could never explain, so no-one ever understood. Even though she said nothing he saw the thinning of the skin on the bridge of her nose, the telltale loss of blood. He could feel the force of her anger.

Lisa went out, closing the door hard. He couldn't help it, and yet if he couldn't no-one could. And downstairs she had to face the guests' curiosity, putting their large faces down at her and pretending compassion.

Curtiss met her at the foot of the stairs. 'My lady — one of the guests has spoken to me. She asked if Lord Melville was entirely safe.'

Lisa bridled. 'Well, of course he is! Of all the cheek.' She wrapped her arms around herself and said in a hard, brittle voice, 'I thought these people wanted to see how we live. This is it. Freezing weather, a foot of snow and the earl cracking up. Has anybody managed to thaw the drains yet?'

'Not as yet, ma'am.'

'Shit!'

Tonight was a night for foul language. The weight of snow had cracked a beam over a gallery in the old, unrestored part of the house. A three foot hole had appeared in the roof, and no-one could do so much as stretch a tarpaulin over it. Snow and wind blew around the deserted gallery and all day Lisa had struggled to remove chairs and chests, and Curtiss had tried vainly to block up the doors to prevent wind and weather gusting into the rest of the house. Added to which half the drains in the guest rooms were frozen and no-one could empty their bath. And of course, Marcus was beside himself.

She took a long breath through her nose. It was time to go and join the guests for drinks, and to hope that good manners would prevent them from berating her. The cold was making her shiver uncontrollably, no amount of fuel or expense seemed to warm the house. She was wearing a thermal vest under her evening dress, and was considering adding a cardigan over the top. But the hostess at least must pretend that all was well. She would have to sit and freeze.

As soon as she entered the room she knew the Gibsons would be trouble. He had taken well-paid early retirement from some manu-facturing firm and she was a clothes horse with four suitcases and at least two fur coats. As they said themselves they knew how to appreciate the finer things in life, and clogged up drains in a cold stately home did not deserve their appreciation.

'You seem to be having one or two problems, my dear,' began Mr Gibson.

Lisa smiled a wintry smile. 'Another whisky, Mr Gibson? Curtiss?' The butler bore down on them, but to no avail.

Gibson went on, 'It isn't good enough you know. The bath's stinking. Absolutely stinking. It's not something we're used to, I can tell you straight. And you know what my wife saw? With her very own eyes?'

'Not the ghost?' said Lisa hopefully. You could market spooks, she'd been told.

'A mouse! Running along the corridor, bold as you like. What have you to say about that, may I ask?'

'Good heavens,' said Lisa weakly. 'I'm sure Curtiss can find you a trap. If you like.'

'Trap? Did you say trap?'

'We used to use a shotgun but it made a terrible mess of the skirtings.'

He eyed her with fulminating disbelief. Then he went back to his pin-thin wife, shivering in Dior silk. Oh God, thought Lisa, that was a refund if ever there was one. But she was damned if she would fawn on these people. They would have to love her or hate her, she couldn't mould herself in some false and ingratiating image.

The meal passed in chilly politeness. Although piping hot when it left the kitchen, by the time the food reached the plates the sauces were congealing. Scallops sat on clammy china as if washed up on some isolated beach, and every time Lisa lifted her wine she felt a small shock as her lips met icy glass.

'There's a bone in my fish,' complained Mrs Gibson. Let it be a magic icicle, thought Lisa, let it pierce you in the heart and finish you off. But she dragged her good manners back into play.

'What a dreadful day you're having with us, Mrs Gibson,' she murmured. 'It is so good of you to be so tolerant. Curtiss, shall we have mulled wine? We'll have it in the drawing-room.'

'At once, my lady.'

He raised a quizzical eyebrow and she replied with an imperceptible shrug. Anything to restore good humour and some vestige of warmth. Cold as it was now, it was nothing to the thought of sliding between icy sheets. Hot water bottles and electric blankets were powerless to ward off the chill. As a child Lisa could remember putting a blanket inside the sheets, and sleeping in that.

Half the guests clearly thought that bed was still the warmest place, and withdrew after only a glass of hot wine. But the Gibsons sat on, huddled over the fire. Mrs Gibson shuddered audibly in an almost constant quiver. Her husband stood directly in front of the fire, obstructing the heat from everyone else. Lisa allowed herself to hate them, knowing full well that they were justified. In the soft days of summer she had chosen to forget what a hard winter was like. They shouldn't be open at this time of year, it was foolhardy.

Far away, down long corridors, the front doorbell jangled. Lisa ignored it, although she had no idea who it could be. No-one called at this time of night, no-one at all. Perhaps it was the police, she thought idly. Come to arrest her for running a disorderly house. Could clogged up baths and freezing rooms be considered disorderly? They certainly weren't good order, that was undeniable.

Minutes later, when she had forgotten all about the visitor, the door opened. Cold air erupted into the room, bearing with it a tide of people and noise. Curtiss, a taxi driver, and in the midst of them, golden and tanned and healthy, Mara. She cradled a screaming infant.

'What on earth — ?' Mr Gibson leaped protectively towards his wife, who uttered little, terrified cries.

'Hello, everyone,' declared Mara, smiling her glorious wide grin. 'Why are you all sitting around in evening dress? You must be frozen stiff.'

'I see you managed to run over a rabbit or two,' remarked Lisa, looking pointedly at her sister's mink jacket.

'My darling, what is the point of immorality if it doesn't pay well?' carolled Mara, and held out her wailing child. 'Do have him, Lisa, my arms are cracking. He's been bawling ever since we left Nairobi. Oh, and could you pay the taxi driver? I've no English money at all.'

Lisa stood with her arms full of baby. Dreadful, unrepentant Mara. She felt a bubble of happiness that she was there, and that alone should prove how desperate things had become. 'Could you pay the driver please, Curtiss?' she said feebly. The child in her arms screwed up his face for yet another harrowing shriek.

'Shit,' declared Mara. 'He must be hungry. Give him here, do.' She scooped him up, swept to the sofa and sat down. Without a shadow of embarrassment she unbuttoned her shirt and began to breastfeed.

The room emptied miraculously. Even Curtiss, who felt himself very much one of the family, felt it incumbent on him to leave. When the door closed behind them all, Mara chuckled. 'My God, what a bunch. Do they always look so frozen-faced, or is it just the temperature?'

'The drains are clogged up,' said Lisa. 'And part of the roof's collapsed. It's in the old bit, but we still get snow on the landings in the mornings. And birds come in. And the windows freeze on the inside.'

'Just like it used to be,' said Mara contentedly. 'A bit of paint and a few radiators don't begin to tame February at The Court. It is so lovely to be home. Ouch! Don't chew.'

She carefully detached the baby from her nipple, and plugged him in on the other side. He guzzled greedily. Lisa averted her eyes from her sister's naked breast, distended, brown, with a large wet nipple. She ought to have known Mara would be like this. There was never anyone more sensual than she.

'What do you call it?' asked Lisa stiffly.

'It's a boy. He's called Drew. Short for Andrew Henry Denham Hellyn. And he's absolutely beautiful. Don't you think so?'

350

Lisa stared at the pink, absorbed face, sucking with an almost incandescent joy. Not beautiful, no. But quite wonderful, she couldn't deny that. She sat beside her sister and trailed a finger across the baby's hair. 'You oughtn't to have Denham, you know. Not wise.'

'It's his father's name,' said Mara sharply. 'He has a right to it. And I shall write and tell Jay, and I'll send pictures.'

Suddenly Mara's eyes flickered to her sister's. For an instant her confident front wavered. 'Have you heard?' she asked stiffly. 'About – her?'

'Don't you know?'

Mara shook her head. 'I could have found out, I suppose. But the antics of minor royalty don't rivet the entire Kenyan nation, I can assure you. I didn't see anything in the papers.'

'There wasn't much here.' Lisa pleated the lilac silk of her skirt. It was a dress she wore too often, because its wadded and sequinned shoulders gave her a feeling of some importance. 'It was another girl.'

Mara said nothing. But her face, pale as marble beneath the tan, spoke for her. Triumph, despair, rage and hope, fighting for ascendancy. Her grip tightened on the baby. 'I gave him a son,' she whispered. 'She couldn't and I did. A beautiful, perfect son.'

'I don't think you ought to contact him' said Lisa quickly. 'Just a note to tell him of the birth, that's all.'

'Rubbish! You can't shrug off responsibility with a cheque, you know. And he won't want to. I know Jay. He'll be longing to see his child, and for that matter, me. We finished on a silly row, with everything changing and difficult. And – and I do so want to see him.'

'Have you written to him?' asked Lisa quietly.

Mara flushed. 'The letters were returned. But they were opened! You see, he had to know what I said, he had to read them.'

'It might not even have been him. Suppose it was his secretary, or some aide?'

'He couldn't. Not my private letters.'

Her face shadowed. She shouldn't have come back, she knew that with hard certainty. In Kenya she could have been someone else, living a new and hopeful life. Here, she was taking up everything again, the old passions and miseries. All she had was her baby, but it wasn't all she wanted. Still, like an addict with a drug, she needed Jay.

The baby had finished. He was lying in a milky doze, so full that droplets oozed from the corners of his mouth. Even his eyes rolled, as if bobbing on a sea of milk. 'You're drunk,' said Mara softly. 'And I've got to change you. Where do I sleep, Lisa? You can't be full at this time of year.'

351

'We are,' snapped her sister. 'We're full right through to the summer. But there's a maid's room you can have. They leave because they can't get to the shops.'

'I'm not at all surprised.' Mara stood up, balancing the baby across her shoulder. 'By the way, how is everything? Marcus? Everything?'

Lisa bridled. Resentments surfaced, like rotten wood. 'Are you putting him in the same category as frozen drains? As it happens he's in just as bad a state. The technical term is catatonic, I believe. But why concern yourself now? If you'd been really interested you might have written from Kenya, or telephoned, or even sent the odd post-card. Instead of which you bide your time until you can come back and disrupt everything, upsetting the guests, putting the servants out of their rooms, patronising everyone. I know it's a shock to stop sunbathing and come back to real life, but let's get one thing straight: I do the work round here and I take the responsibility. So don't you dare think you can do as you like.'

Mara laughed in her face. 'So, you're in charge. But, little sister, what about dear Toby? You might have crawled your way over the bodies of your family, but he after all is the wallet around here. What does he say about your drains and draughts and disgruntled guests? You're going to be knee deep in letters of complaint. The atmosphere was thick enough to cut with a knife.'

'As far as I know, Toby's still in Rio' retorted Lisa.

'Surely he keeps in touch?' Mara teased. 'Toby wouldn't forget you. Not Toby.'

Lisa shot her a look of loathing. 'We correspond. Infrequently.'

'No wonder you look so mopy.' Mara strode to the door, saying over her shoulder, 'If I were you, I'd be worried. If this goes on The Court is going to earn itself the most abysmal reputation. But of course you've thought of that. You're in charge.' She smiled sweetly. As the door closed behind her, Lisa stuck out her tongue.

The next morning the Gibsons left, and two other couples, and as if that wasn't enough, Curtiss came down with 'flu. The place was in turmoil. Guests took to wandering along the corridors in their dressing gowns, looking for functioning baths, although the thermo-stat on the boiler was having a fit and the water was never more than lukewarm. Lisa had a nightmare vision of the fault being in some frozen pipe, and the boiler eventually exploding, taking half the house with it. Without Curtiss everything seemed to go wrong. Fires were left unlit, dirty coffee cups sat on tables for hours, and over it all, like some ghastly form of muzak, was laid the wailing of Mara's baby.

Eventually Lisa stormed up to her sister's room. 'Can't you shut the bloody thing up?' she raged. 'It never stops! It's driving everyone crazy!'

Mara, still in bed but wearing her mink jacket, cradled the baby protectively. 'He's got a cold. It isn't his fault. We're staying up here out of your way so you can't complain. No-one could possibly hear him.'

'Well, they can. You're over the drawing-room, the noise filters down a pipe or something.'

'I bet you're the only one making a fuss. Jealous cat.'

The baby snuffled and wailed again. 'He's in such a state,' agonised Mara. 'Poor Drew. Poor little man. Dragging you from nice hot Kenya to this.'

'I'll take him, if you like.' Lisa reached out for the grizzling bundle. He lay in her arms, chewing his fingers, his little nose red and snuffling.

'How's Marcus?' asked Mara, stretching her long arms above her head.

'Dreadful. The hospital's coming for him later today.'

'Why couldn't they come before?'

'I think they're busy. In the winter they get inundated with tramps and drop-outs, hundreds of them. And Marcus isn't that urgent.'

'No.'

Mara stared at her sister. Was she imagining it, or had Lisa grown prettier? Perhaps it was simply maturity. Lisa was all bone and fine skin, and even now, bundled in thick woollens and holding the baby, she stood as if she had an iron rod for a backbone. That was her Napoleon complex of course, she had always hated being small.

'Would you like children?' asked Mara.

Lisa glanced up. 'No, of course not. People take enough looking after when they're house-trained. Look at him, dribbling out of both ends at once.'

'Oh, give him back,' said Mara. 'He can dribble on my mink.'

Lisa went downstairs. The sky was so dark that she could barely see the stairs, and she fumbled desperately for the lightswitch. Already the paper round it was worn and ragged, it was amazing how quickly pristine cleanliness degenerated. Soon she would have to ask Toby if they could spend money on redecoration. And God knows, she really didn't want to ask him anything. He hadn't written in weeks.

Once in the hall, she found two more guests checking out. They were arguing the bill with one of the young footmen, and Lisa sent him on his way with a brief nod. She was quite prepared to give a third reduction, but half was too much. Out of a three-week stay, only the last few days had been impossible. They wouldn't have dared try it on with Curtiss, she thought bitterly, and held her ground. The discussion grew more and more acrimonious, and through it all came the high threnody of Drew's wailing.

Finally, just as she felt she was beginning to make headway, insofar as they agreed that champagne drunk last week was consumed in perfect warmth and friendliness, and had not been downed in a desperate attempt to sustain life, there came a clatter on the dark stairs. Lisa looked up in alarm, peering into the gloom. Someone was running, falling, their feet hammering in unstable frenzy against the ancient wood. It had all the horror of a ghost, something heard but not seen, something about to happen. She felt her heart stutter.

Suddenly Marcus appeared. He looked like a gargoyle, his eyes mad and staring. He hadn't washed, he hadn't shaved in days. He crouched on the half-landing, like a wild man, choking on moans and cries. 'Oh my God!' said the guests in unison. The hairs on Lisa's neck prickled. She could no more step forward than fly. All at once Marcus seemed to notice them. He let out a piercing shriek and raced back up the stairs.

The guests paid at once, the full amount. For her part Lisa was prepared to let them off everything, just to have them out. She wanted everyone out, with Marcus like this. Upstairs the baby cried, Marcus howled, and to cap it all, at the very moment the guests stood at the door, their luggage around their feet, Lisa's old spaniel sauntered casually out from his appointed place in front of the drawing room fire, and lifted his leg on one of the suitcases.

Lisa started to laugh. It was either that or burst into floods of useless and undignified tears. These people were so outraged! Perhaps they thought she did it on purpose, that the whole family was bonkers and got their kicks out of tormenting the innocent. 'I'm sorry,' she gasped, 'I'm sorry. I'm just so sorry.' And away she went again, in gales of laughter.

Silent, they struggled out into the snow. Lisa sank into one of the uncomfortable chairs with which the hall was littered, upright dining chairs with lumps of marble set into the backs. Still she couldn't stop laughing. Gradually it subsided. She sat, shaken by the occasional chuckle, wondering what she ought to do. Only six people remained, it hardly seemed worth laying the huge dining table for so few. Perhaps they should go all egalitarian and invite the staff to fill up the places. She put her hand over her mouth. She was in danger of starting off again.

The front door opened. Lisa cringed down, sure it was the guests, back again to demand blood. She folded her arms over her head, they wouldn't dare speak to her, they'd think she was batty too.

'What in God's name are you doing, Lisa?'

Her head jerked up. Gradually she unfolded her arms, smoothing her hair with what she hoped was insouciance. 'Hello, Toby. What on earth are you doing here? I didn't expect you.'

He loomed over her, vast in an astrakhan coat. 'Obviously not. The bloke out there just told me not to go in. He said the family's mad, the house is freezing, and if I saw the dog I was to kick it. From him.'

'These people never do seem to have any sense of humour.'

She got up, putting distance between them. He was very brown, far browner than Mara. She hardly dared tell him her sister was here. 'How was Rio?' she asked, with pretended interest.

'Hot. The Club's making money hand over fist.'

'That's more than we are.'

He let out his breath in a long, exasperated sigh. My God, but he was huge, thought Lisa. How had she ever had the courage to get close to him?

'Are you going to tell me what's been going on?'

She shook her head. Then, as he took one swift and determined step, she burst out, 'It isn't anything! Just the winter. The drains are frozen, Curtiss has 'flu, Mara's here with her baby and Marcus is demented. And the dog — the dog lifted his leg on that man's suitcase.' Giggles threatened to swamp her again. She put her hand to her mouth and they burst through, like high-pitched silver bells.

Toby crossed the floor and caught her wrist. His fingers felt hot, and they held her too tightly, bending her wristbones with the force of his grip. She stopped laughing, and tried instead to pull her arm free, but he held on. Such a strong man she thought, with violence only just beneath the skin.

'Kiss me hello,' he said softly.

It was all part and parcel of that strange, hysterical day. She tilted back her head, letting her hair hang in a vertical fall. Her mouth came open. For a second he did nothing, but she could hear him breathing, like a pair of cracked bellows. When, at last, his lips touched hers she opened her mouth wide, letting his big tongue tangle with hers, breathing the same air. He let out a moan and tried to gather her close, but at once she pulled free.

'I've missed you,' he said hoarsely. 'I came back to see you.'

'Don't be silly. You came back to check on your investment, and I'm sorry I've made such a mess of it. I don't think we should open in the winter. It doesn't work. There's a bloody great hole in the roof and all the snow comes in.'

'Don't talk about that now.'

355

She twisted her hands together. 'No. I can't really. I've got to see to Marcus.'

She turned on her heel and went quickly up the stairs. Toby hunched his shoulders down into his coat. If he lived to be a hundred, he'd never understand her. And if he lived for eternity he would never fail to be moved by that thin, beaky, highbred face. Damn the bitch! he told himself. Damn her for not wanting him yet still pulling strings and striking chords that he didn't want to hear, didn't want to know. The least she could do was to make him hate her.

In the late afternoon, when a cold hard fog covered the ground and the snow crackled with night-time frost, the ambulance came for Marcus. He was cowering in his room, crouched behind a screen, and the ambulance men were firm and matter of fact. 'Having a nasty turn, sir? Best if you come with us then, isn't it? Can't have you sitting here and frightening everyone, can we? No! No, you don't sonny. Watch him Fred, he might bite.'

Lisa stood watching with her arms wrapped around herself. They might as well get lion-tamers, she thought stupidly.

All at once Marcus made a run for it. He was out of the door and away down the corridor before anyone could do more than yell. The ambulance men raced after him, and Lisa ran too, calling, 'Marcus! Marcus!' in a high-pitched, reedy voice. Marcus began to scream and she put her hands over her ears, because it was a terrible, terrifying sound. God knew what the guests would think.

When the screaming stopped, as if a switch had been thrown, she ran faster. It was Toby. He had Marcus on the floor, flat on his face with the breath knocked out of him. 'You didn't have to,' said Lisa wildly.

'Of course he did.' Mara stood in the doorway, the baby in her arms. Her face was cold and set. 'He could have hurt someone.'

'You mean the baby. All you think about is the bloody baby.'

As they hauled Marcus off to the ambulance, Lisa went and poured herself a large gin.

'Make mine a scotch,' said Toby, and Mara added, 'I think I'll have a scotch as well.'

There was no ice in the bucket, but no-one complained. Lisa crouched on a low stool, turning her glass in her hand, watching the firelight splinter against it into miniature rainbows.

Toby said, 'You really have got this place into one hell of a mess.' Lisa sighed. There seemed nothing to add. The logs in the fire cracked and split, sending sparks racing up the chimney. All the flues in the house were too big, fires burned to nothing in an instant.

'It all went very well at the beginning,' said Mara.

Lisa nodded. 'Right up until Mother died, actually. She was what they expected, not quite with it and a bit intimidating. I'm not old enough.'

'Stay in this place and you soon will be,' remarked her sister. 'You're starting to look absolutely hagged.'

'Why don't you fucking shut up?' said Toby.

Mara raised her eyebrows. 'Oh my God, I was mean to his precious Lisa! How do you inspire this devotion, darling? You should train him to the gun.'

Toby said, 'Look, you shouldn't even be here. You give the place a bad name.'

'Are you entirely serious?' Mara let out a yelp of laughter. 'I think the drains and the vermin do quite enough actually. But, of course, if you'd feel better blaming me, then go right ahead. Feel free.'

Lisa looked up. 'Do shut up, both of you,' she said. 'It's the house that's the trouble. It isn't suited to this sort of thing and it never has been. And we're not suited to it. Marcus gets worse and nobody feels they can come home here any more. We haven't seen Angus in ages. The whole idea was a ghastly mistake.'

'Mother and I did say as much from the beginning,' murmured Mara.

Toby looked from one to the other. 'So you want me to pack up and leave. Isn't that it? Roll up my investment, take the losses on the chin and get out.'

'I'm glad you understand it so well.' Mara smiled at him, swinging her baby up over her shoulder. Drew grizzled and kicked.

'Lisa? Is that what you want?'

The skin of her cheek was almost translucent in the firelight. She put her hand up to the bridge of her nose, pressing her fingers hard against the bone. 'Perhaps we should close in the winter. Just for a couple of months, it's impossible with everything like this.'

Toby finished his drink and rose to pour himself another. 'If we shut the place up there'd be mould in every room. Pipes would freeze. Rot in the beams, mice in the wiring. So that's a bloody stupid idea. If you ask me this is just typical of you people. A few problems and you fold up, you can't fight, you can't even hang on. If it doesn't come on a plate, you don't want to know.'

'If you want to get out, you can,' muttered Lisa.

'You say that so easily when you know damn well if I quit now I'd make a loss. All I'd be left with is a hole in my bank balance, whereas you've got the house done up and some nice new frocks, not to mention our little jaunt to Rio.'

Lisa's head came up. 'Where you got your club designed on the

357

cheap. Funny how the favours you do me always seem to benefit you as well.'

Toby's face flushed a dark, angry red. 'But then, I'm only a rough colonial. I don't understand that with the Hellyns there's no give and take, only take and take again.'

Mara laughed. 'What did you expect, Toby? To be gathered into the bosom of the family? Is that it?'

She was so sure of herself, thought Toby. She had all the confidence, style and downright contempt that being born at the top of the heap could give. He felt a sudden surge of hatred. Mara dropped her eyes, for once having the grace to look uncomfortable. Toby made for the door, not trusting himself even to speak. Lisa said, 'Toby? What's going to happen?' But he kept on as if he hadn't heard.

It was early, before moonrise. The night was black as pitch, Toby's headlights reflected nothing but twin circles of white snow. The drive was like an ice rink, but he drove fast down it, hardly caring if he crashed. He kept up the speed all the way to Jean Maythorpe's door.

In such weather, the bungalow was a testament to twentieth-century living. Light spilled out on to a clear circle of gravel, defrosted by means of underground wires. When Jean let Toby into the bright, brass-encrusted sitting-room, insulated from the weather by double glazing and super-efficient central heating, he felt a rising gratitude. Here, people behaved as you expected that they should; they put comfort before style, honesty before manners, and money well in front of heritage.

Jean said, 'I thought you were still away. But I haven't seen Lisa much.'

'Silly girl never goes out,' mumbled Reg, stretching his legs towards the gas fire. 'Locked away all the time in that damned big house, you'd think *she* was the lunatic. Sit yourself down, lad. Have a drink.'

'Thanks.'

Toby had a scotch. He watched Jean slosh it from the bottle to the glass and wondered how much she'd had already. She looked flushed, a little fatter than last time he saw her. Her woollen skirt, old and shapeless, strained round her hips.

'Seen much of Angus?' he asked.

Jean grimaced. Reg said proudly, 'Saw him at Christmas, didn't you, love? And he writes. Not often, he's a busy man, but he writes.'

'So he does,' said Jean and took a gulp of her drink.

'What's he doing?' Toby couldn't resist the probe, but to his surprise Jean coloured to the roots of her hair.

'I can't help wondering myself,' she said tightly. 'I imagine he's got himself some very tall, very thin daughter of a cabinet minister. He's getting well known in the right places, is Angus. In the right company. I imagine his tongue has grown to giant proportions, actually. So he can reach all the arses he has to lick.'

Reg stared at his daughter. 'Bloody hell!' he said.

Jean blinked very hard, as if to suppress tears. 'So now you know,' she said sulkily. 'I hate to tell you, Dad, but the great romance is off. Not that Angus would realise that. He seems to think he can leave me here forever and I'll still be waiting when he comes back.'

'If you ask me you're getting silly,' said Reg. 'Imagining things. Angus is a nice lad. He wouldn't write and that if he weren't serious. You girls don't understand, a man's got to make his way in the world. Can't be all the time billing and cooing.'

Jean swung away from him. 'Can't they? I'm sure you're right.'

Toby said, 'Look, Jean, I wonder if we could go out and talk? To a pub or something?'

'You can talk here, can't you?' said Reg. 'On a night like this you don't want to be driving about.'

'We'll go to the local,' said Toby. He stood up, waiting for Jean to get her coat.

In the car, she said, 'Dad doesn't trust you. But he thinks Angus is marvellous, which just shows you what his judgement's like.'

Toby changed gear, letting the car run a little on the frosty road. 'Have you and Angus had a row then?'

'We stopped having rows when things started going wrong. Now he's terribly polite. Screws me just the same though.'

Toby laughed. Jean was always so refreshingly honest. 'Typical bloody Hellyn, that is. Think the world owes them whatever they want to have. So, how are you passing the time?'

She almost smiled. 'When I'm not moping around here drinking myself to death, you mean? I don't do much, as it happens. You see, the Labour Party didn't like it when I helped Angus with his election campaign. And Dad didn't like it when I got a job with a charity in town. Made such a fuss that if I hadn't left they'd have kicked me out.'

'What did he do?'

'Oh, telephoned ten times a day. Wasting time promising vast donations, ringing up with suggestions, getting some terminal illness he'd read about that had to have me back home by three in the afternoon. He thought Angus wouldn't like a wife who did a job like that, you see. Poor Dad doesn't realise that we're just too nouveau everything for someone like Angus.'

359

Toby said, 'Lot of people make that mistake.'

'Do they?' Jean was too self-absorbed to be perceptive. She went on, 'So I fill the time in as best I can. I do a bit here and a bit there. Go hunting. And I see to the gypsies, of course.' At the mention of the gypsies she brightened. 'I'm getting to be considered quite an expert. Councils ring me up for my advice on gypsies in their areas.'

'Oh. I see.'

Suddenly Toby pulled the car into a lay-by. He turned to Jean. 'Look, do you really want to go to a pub?'

'No. But I thought you did. Why, what do you want to do?'

There was an odd light in his eyes. His big hands rubbed themselves against the leather steering wheel. 'Right now I want to fuck. And you don't owe Angus anything, and I don't owe anyone in the world more than the time of day. Let's give each other a thrill.'

Jean laughed, shrilly. 'You're not serious.'

'Course I bloody am. Here, I'll put the seat back.' He reached across to wind her seat down, putting his free hand on her breast.

Jean laughed again. 'You don't mess about, do you?'

'It doesn't look as if you mind.'

He unfastened his trousers and dragged them down to his knees. Jean said, 'Oh my God! You didn't threaten Lisa Hellyn with that, did you? It's much too big and vulgar.'

'There are no bloody Hellyns here now,' said Toby thickly. 'We can be as vulgar as we damn well like.'

Jean giggled, and it jarred on him. Still, if she wanted to laugh she could, he supposed. She pulled off her tights and he helped her, rubbing his hands on the insides of her thighs. They had the hard resilience of muscle and flesh, horseman's thighs. She giggled again. 'Shut up,' said Toby, and swung on top of her.

There was no mistaking her enjoyment. Jean, uncomplicated Jean. Mouth wide open, eyes opening and closing in time with his thrusts, she let out wail after wail of pleasure. This was the way it ought to be, he told himself. This was what cured you. Bodies. Just bodies, grinding against one another in a mindless sexual thrill. The girl beneath him came to a shuddering climax, only a second before he too was finished. He'd always known they were compatible. He rolled back into his seat.

'Well,' he said at last.

'Well,' said Jean. 'It certainly beats taking things seriously.'

Chapter Thirty-Seven

If Ghenghis Khan had swept down out of the woods next morning, complete with murdering hordes, he could not have achieved much more than Toby. He found Lisa presiding over the remnants of breakfast, with Mara still in bed, and the few guests wandered about looking cold, a little bewildered, asking questions about hunting or walks on the estate.

'Can't hunt, the ground's frozen,' said Toby. 'But you can take the horses out. Borrow the cars, anything. We'll be unblocking the drains today, you don't want to be involved in all that.'

Lisa gave him a sardonic look. 'Don't imagine we haven't tried everything,' she said pityingly. 'We can't unblock the drains.'

'If you'd tried everything it would have worked. A drain company's coming this morning. If they can't unfreeze them they're to put in a temporary bypass. Rubber piping. And a builder's going to put some sheeting over the roof. Get on to the Historic Buildings people. We can't prat about just because the weather's a little on the chilly side.'

'The Lone Ranger rides again.'

They glared at each other. Toby realised it was the first time she had really met his eye. 'Are the tapestries OK?' he asked.

'They aren't yours. They're nothing to do with you.'

'I wasn't going to make you an offer for them.'

'Weren't you?' She swallowed. He saw the fine bones in her throat rise and fall. 'I'm sorry,' she said suddenly. 'I was horrid yesterday. It was Marcus and everything. I know we seem to be in turmoil but really everything was fine until the hunting stopped and the pipes froze. Where did you sleep last night? I thought you'd come back here.'

Toby cleared his throat. 'Er — I was at the Maythorpes'. I called in and Reg offered me the spare room.'

'You'll be staying here tonight though, won't you?'

361

'No. No, actually I won't.'

Lisa said nothing. The air between them was thick with unspoken thoughts. She might forgive him Rio, when they were in such a mess, but at home, here, with Jean Maythorpe? Her own fury amazed her. Suddenly she clicked her fingers for her dog and went briskly out into the hall, summoning maids, footmen, imbued with crisp energy. She knows, thought Toby. If she was a closed book to him he was an open one to her. He felt as if everything he had thought or done last night lay clear for her inspection. He was damned if he would feel guilty about it. It was Lisa's fault. He wouldn't let himself feel guilt.

He followed her out into the conservatory. All his plants were brown and dying, like some primitive tribe catching measles. She was hacking at the foliage, digging up the casualties with a trowel. 'I hope you're not going to follow me about all day,' she said over her shoulder. 'There's a lot to do. A lot of mistakes to be put right. For instance, I would never have put these plants in here, but someone did. And I did hear tell of someone who bought a whole nightclub without any water supply.'

'I didn't say this mess was all your fault.'

She shot him a searing glance. 'Of course you did. I've pandered to Marcus, I've let Mara walk all over me, I've upset the guests and I've let the pipes freeze. All right, I admit it.' She heaved on a fern and brought it lurching out of the soil. 'I wonder what you should admit, Toby?'

Toby said, 'You could have saved that. It had a spark of life in it.'

'So now you're the expert gardener. I'm sorry. I think things that are as good as dead should be killed off without more ado.'

He had a desperate urge to apologise, which was ridiculous. 'Do you want to be left to ruin this by yourself?' he asked suddenly. 'I mean, is that it? OK, we got in a mess but that's done with. We're still business partners. We could be friends. But if you want me out, say so.'

Lisa drew herself up, although with a dying fern in her hand she looked like an extra in a low-budget pantomime. 'I don't think you've been particularly friendly,' she declared. 'But I'm sure if you feel in need of a friend then Jean Maythorpe will make you very welcome!' She thrust the fern at him. He didn't take it so she threw it in a heap, showering him with compost and nitrogen pellets. Then she hit him on the head with her trowel.

The cut bled. One of the guests had to drive him off to the doctor to be stitched. Lisa, white and shaken, went to see Mara. She was sitting in bed, the radio playing, a plate of toast at her elbow, reading a magazine. The baby lay asleep beside her.

'I see you're really helping out,' snapped Lisa.

Mara sighed. 'I was up all night. What's the matter now? Have the public health people come or something?'

Lisa sat on the bed. 'No. It's nothing like that. It's just — oh, Mara, he's — he — he stayed the night with Jean Maythorpe.'

'What?' Mara almost upset her cup of coffee. 'You mean he slept with her?'

'Yes. I'm absolutely sure he did. He didn't say as much but he looks — '

'Guilty,' supplied Mara. 'Well, there you are. It's probably a very good thing, she was getting far too hung up on Angus. And you don't mind really, do you?'

'No,' said Lisa. 'I don't mind at all.'

Mara reached out a hand to touch her. 'And so you shouldn't.'

They fell silent. Lisa's hands twisted in her lap. 'He said he loved me,' she whispered.

Mara sighed and smoothed her sister's hair. 'Then I imagine he did. I mean he's not stupid. I know Mother thought he was out for what he could get, but he must have realised you didn't have some vast dowry hidden away. And he's not like the doctor, with one eye on the title.'

'I thought you didn't like him.'

'I don't. He's one of those men who are always on the make, they don't look at anything unless they get money out of it. But he did have one redeeming feature.'

Lisa lifted her head. 'What?'

'He did seem very fond of you.'

Lisa put her hands over her eyes, but nothing would stop the tears falling. How terrible everything seemed. Toby was a man of the world and whatever he had felt before, he had passed on and forgotten it. She thought she would give anything to have him love her again. But what was the point? He wanted passion and sexuality, that he could never find in her. It was the sort of thing he would discover in abundance in Jean Maythorpe.

Mara abstractedly patted her sister's shoulder. 'At least he's got Angus out of a mess,' she consoled. 'Angus had got himself very involved and it wasn't going to be easy to get out. It's much better if those two make a go of it, don't you think? They're very much the same type.'

Lisa sniffed and pushed her hair out of her eyes. 'Who's going to write and tell Angus?'

'I will.'

The baby began to stir and Mara reached out a lazy hand to soothe

363

him. 'I think I could stay in bed like this forever,' she said sleepily. 'But you needn't look daggers. I don't suppose I will.'

When Lisa had gone she settled down to write her letters. Angus's was quite brief and to the point.

You'll be glad to hear that I'm home again, complete with Andrew Henry Denham Hellyn, known as Drew. I'm thinking of having him christened in the village church in spring, so do try and come. Marcus is unwell again, and back in hospital. Oh, and another interesting thing. Toby is sleeping with Jean Maythorpe. He blew in from Rio and didn't stop until he got between the Maythorpe sheets, which is probably quite a good thing. At least now you won't have to bother about letting her down lightly, will you?

When the letter was finished she sat twirling the pen in idle fingers. The thought of Toby and Jean Maythorpe excited her; she could picture each of them quite clearly. A dull ache of longing began. Was it really Jay she wanted, or simply a man? Suppose she had taken up with Edward? If anything he was the more virile, a night and morning man if ever there was one. If she had him now, would she want Jay? All she knew was that she did want Jay, wanted him with silent desperation. She began a new letter.

Dearest Jay,
I am writing to you now to give you some news. Your son, Andrew Henry Denham Hellyn, was born in Kenya, on 23rd January last. He's a big, strapping healthy baby, quite beautiful, and I think he's going to look very like you. He has the same shaped head.

I hardly need to tell you how sorry I am that we parted as we did. Now that I have Drew I realise more than ever how wrong and foolish I was to jeopardise his future in any way. At that tine I think I was more concerned with our future, because we had so much and yet let it slip through our fingers.

I don't want to ask you to do anything you don't feel is right. But surely it would be wrong, very wrong, for you to let your son grow up not knowing his father, and perhaps feeling that his father felt no bond or commitment to him at all. I know that you will always provide for us both, but my son needs more than money. He is to be christened at the church here in the spring, a small private ceremony. If you came and stood beside us this once it would mean a great deal to me now, and far more to Drew in the future.

I truly hope that you have found some measure of happiness.

Yours ever

Mara

She read it through several times. It was the first letter to him that neither begged, nor reproached, nor promised undying love. It was calm, adult and reasoned. Surely he would reply, even if only to say no?

Mara got up to post her letters, and stayed up to watch the fun. Floorboards were lifted, blow torches used, and one after another the frozen pipes defrosted, only to prove that they had burst. As the short day ended the house rang to the sound of plumbers struggling to get the water turned back on. Over it all Toby presided, with three stitches in his hair. He looked so grim that none of the workmen dared ask for so much as a teabreak.

Lisa's antics did nothing for his temper. For some reason he did not begin to understand, she was organising an extravagant and memorable meal. They were to have caviare, champagne, roast goose stuffed with duck and an ice sculpture made out of a block from the lake. One of the men had spent hours sawing a piecc out while moorhens and guinea fowl pecked delicately and tremulously in the snow nearby. A maid was sent to town to buy hothouse flowers, armfuls of them, enough for a funeral.

The house took on a surreal appearance; in every corner lurked a workman, ripping up floorboards and soldering joints; meanwhile Lisa conducted a banquet, drifting through the rooms in a floor-length dress of fine blue wool. As the guests came back to the house one by one they were met by Lisa with her champagne bottle. By early evening, with dinner still hours away, everyone was squiffy.

Toby cornered her in the front hall. She was wandering through, bottle at the ready, and when she saw him she hiccupped. 'Good heavens. The spectre at the feast. What can I do for you? Champagne?'

He sighed. 'Look. What do you think you're doing?'

She opened her eyes wide. 'Why, I'm holding the fort! Fiddling while Rome burns. Except that it's a little too cold for that, don't you think? Or should we burn it? Somebody tried it once you know, a couple of centuries past.'

'Don't you think you ought to apologise?'

'For your head, you mean?'

365

'Yes. My head.'

She seemed to sober quite rapidly. 'I would if I was sorry. But I wanted to hurt you and I did. I don't think you care any more for Jean Maythorpe than you did for me, but you're using her just the same. What business opportunity does she represent?'

'For God's sake! The girl's lonely, I'm lonely for that matter. We don't need your permission to screw each other.'

Lisa drew herself up. 'Oh. So you admit it then?'

'I don't see any point in denying it. Lisa, I'm sorry about what happened between us. But this is just stupid, isn't it? Getting yourself so bitter.'

'I am not bitter!'

He grinned. 'Looks like it to me. The spinster who won't take what she can but doesn't want anyone else to have it either.'

For a long second she was speechless. When she turned away it was as if all the strength had drained out of her. She looked little, and thin, and sad. Toby took a long, dragging breath. 'I didn't mean to hurt you,' he said.

'Yes you did. And you're quite right, it isn't anything to do with me.' She bent to put her champagne bottle on the ground, as if it was too heavy to be carried a minute longer. From the drawing-room came a buzz of voices, getting louder and more raucous all the time. She really ought to go and see to things. But she had to stay a moment longer. 'I am sorry about your head,' she said quickly. 'And I'm sorry about Rio. I couldn't do what you wanted and I didn't tell you how I felt.'

Toby sighed. 'I made you unhappy. I wish it hadn't been like that.'

'It wasn't your fault. I know you didn't realise it, but the whole thing meant quite a lot to me. I wouldn't have gone if I hadn't − and you were sweet to me, you really were. I'm sorry I made such a mess of it.'

He said, 'I wish you'd said all this then.'

'It wouldn't have made any difference.' Suddenly her eyes were bright with tears. 'And it doesn't really matter now, does it? You'll be much better off with Jean.'

She turned and went quickly away. Toby felt a sudden rising panic. The girl tied him in knots − this one day, that the next − giving him what he wanted only when he couldn't take it. He ran his hand through his hair, wincing as his fingers met the stitches. What a hell of a day! He was expected to dine at the Maythorpes' and he ought to go. The plumbers were finishing for the night and would be back in the morning to lag pipes and put back floorboards.

Footsteps sounded on the stairs, and the swish of silk. He stood and

366

watched as Mara descended elegantly into the hall. She was wearing one of Charlotte's evening robes, an elaborate silk dressing gown that swathed her still ample curves. It had never looked so good on Charlotte. Her daughter had fastened it to show three inches of cleavage, and tied it high under her breasts. It gave the illusion of endlessly long legs. When she was older she would be heavy, thought Toby, and realised that on Mara it would matter not at all.

'You look great,' he commented.

She raised her eyebrows. 'An unexpected compliment. What do you want?'

If only she knew, he thought. He said, 'Not much. Look, I was talking to Lisa. You're her sister. Can you tell me, honestly, what she thinks of me?'

Mara rested her elbow on the gargoyle at the end of the staircase. There was no way she wanted to encourage Toby. He was the wrong class, he was on the make, and without him The Court would be theirs again. How she hated this invasion, this sweeping away of the old, dark mystery that had enshrouded the place forever. What's more, he made Lisa miserable, and that in itself confirmed him as the enemy. He wasn't good for her.

'I think she was fond of you,' said Mara thoughtfully. 'Perhaps even in love. But then, she hasn't had a lot of experience. I think now she knows it wouldn't work. And you do too, don't you?'

Last night he would have said yes, absolutely yes. Now he didn't know what to think. He turned on his heel and went to the door, letting in a draught of ice cold air. Mara drew in her breath and stood on the last stair, looking after him.

At the Maythorpes' Jean cooked shepherds' pie. Reg talked about horses and money, trying to probe Toby's background and financial worth. He talked about Angus a lot, until Jean flared, 'Oh, do shut up, Dad!' when he subsided in a bad-tempered huff. He kept watching them both, trying to detect what might or might not be their relationship.

At eleven Toby yawned, and took himself along the hall to bed. The carpet was brightly patterend, a mixture of reds and yellows that wouldn't fade in a thousand years. The guest room itself was overtly feminine, full of covered lampshades and dainty dressing tables. Toby went and took a shower, wondering what he ought to do that night. Presumably he was duty bound to knock discreetly on Jean's bedroom door.

But, as he came out of the shower, he heard a knock. He threw down the towel and went to open the door, and when Jean saw him naked she blushed to her hair. 'Good heavens! I didn't expect you to be quite so prepared.'

367

Toby shrugged. 'Do you mind? If we're going to do what I think we are we can forget embarrassment, can't we?'

She giggled rather uncertainly. 'I suppose so. It's no holds barred, isn't it? I hope Dad can't hear us.'

Reg slept at the far end of the house, an arrangement established years ago when Jean was small and Reg in the habit of inviting ladies home for the evening. Now the tables seemed to have turned.

Toby felt reckless suddenly. If they were going to do this they might as well enjoy it to the hilt. He went across and began to unfasten Jean's blouse, getting impatient halfway down and popping three of the buttons. Her bra was very expensive lace, but Toby put his big hand over it and broke the straps. 'Bastard,' said Jean, and giggled again as he rubbed his palms against her nipples. She pulled off her skirt and tights, kicking them aside. She looked up at him. 'I've never done oral sex.'

Toby grinned. 'Always knew Angus was a prat. Want to do it?'

'Yes.'

He lay on the bed, pulling Jean face down on top of him. Her knees came either side of his chest, and as he lifted his head and licked her she squeaked and wriggled. He wrapped his arms round her thighs to hold her still. For her part, Jean stared in amazement at the genitals before her face. She would never have believed she could have behaved like this. A tongue was exploring up inside her, like a big, muscular worm. Excitement surged, she was riding a wave and couldn't fall off. Toby's erection touched her face, he was bucking gently, looking for its satisfaction. Could she? Would she? He held her thighs in a tighter grip, pulling her down on to him, nibbling at the edges of her clitoris. With a cry of muffled anguish she bent her head.

When he came she almost choked. She rolled away from him, spitting and dribbling. She wiped her face on the sheet, then ran into the bathroom to wash out her mouth. 'God,' she said when she came back. 'That was disgusting.'

'Come off it.' He lay back wearily and stared at her. 'You loved it.'

She watched him under her lashes. It shocked her to realise that he was virtually a stranger, a big, brown man that she knew no better than a thousand others. 'Are we doing this just to spite them?' she asked, and sat on the edge of the bed.

Toby considered. 'I suppose we are. They've fucked us up so we're going to fuck bigger and better than ever. You have to admit, it's bloody good sex.'

'The best ever.' Jean put her head to one side. 'But all day today I kept thinking what Dad would say.'

He grunted. At least her Dad didn't know what had happened. He

368

leaned up on an elbow. 'I see you found time to think about oral sex. God! I'd never have dared suggest that to Lisa, she'd turn so cold I'd freeze to death. But Angus is into that sort of thing, isn't he?'

'No!' Jean laughed affectionately. 'He hasn't got over doing the basic stuff yet. And he probably never will. I like it. I like the way he finishes, looks down at me and says, "Darling Jean! That was tre-men-dous!"' Her chuckle died away. She looked sad.

Toby felt the cold breath of heartbeat on his cheek. He said loudly, 'Do it again, shall we? Straight in and out, OK?'

Jean shook her head. 'I won't if you don't mind. I'll go to bed. I've got to go and see the gypsies first thing and see how they're managing.'

When she had gone Toby lay in the dark and felt hopelessly wretched. What were he and this girl doing? Would they go on, getting wilder and more desperate, until they were tying each other to the bedpost and drawing blood? He could visualise it. The experience had to be new, more exciting and thrilling than ever before, so they could prove to themselves that it was better, far better than anything they had known in the past. If only it could be, thought Toby. If only it was.

Chapter Thirty-Eight

The thaw came one afternoon, with a rise in temperature so sudden that snow cascaded down from the trees on to the unwary. The deer had come out of the forests during the cold spell, and the new batch of guests at The Court amused themselves laying trails of apples to entice them into the garden.

'And in the summer they'll eat all the rosebuds,' said Mara disinterestedly. 'These people have no idea how to behave in the country.'

'Snob,' remarked Lisa, sorting through the post. Curtiss was up and about again, thanks to Toby the pipes were all lagged and Professor Chandler was sending a surveyor on an urgent visit to discuss the hole in the roof. Everything was in order once again. Everything was very boring. She tossed the bills on to the table and handed a letter to Mara. 'Yours,' she commented. 'And a dozen circulars. Everything's come together. The post office just sits on our letters until they can roller skate up the drive. They are cowardly.'

'Are they?' Mara got up. 'Look after Drew for a moment, Lisa.'

She went out into the garden, although it was still bitterly cold. She hardly cared. In her hand was crushed a thick white envelope, the writing on it black and spiky. She would have known that hand anywhere, known it if she lived to be a thousand. Suppose he said he never wanted to hear from her again? She started to run through the garden, past the silly trails of apples, into the wood. She ran to the folly.

They had come here as children, she, Angus and Marcus. They had played hide and seek around the pillars and in the bare, marble room that had no windows and no purpose. In the summer they sat on the steps and talked, and told Lisa to go away and stop bothering them, she was too little to play. Now, the snow lay in melting heaps everywhere, and water ran from broken gutters, leaving brown stains on the walls. There was nowhere at all to sit.

Mara leaned against a pillar. The cold bit through into her skin. She wrenched at the envelope, suddenly unable to wait a second longer.

My dear Mara,
As you can imagine, I received your news with mixed feelings. Thank God you and the child are well. I want you to understand, absolutely, that there can be no question of the relationship between us resuming. It is over and done. We must lead our lives separately, seeking to find happiness down different paths.

But, I must of course accept responsibility for Andrew. I am very sad indeed that my son must grow up without the support of a loving marriage, the stable home that should be every child's birthright. Under the circumstances I have decided that I shall attend his christening, as a godparent. I expect an entirely private occasion, and if this isn't the case, there will be no further contact between us. I trust that in this one instance you can respect my wishes.

Yours,
J.

She sat down then, regardless of the snow. Her legs were too weak to hold her. Such a formal, angry letter, after all this time. She pressed her palms to her eyes to force back the tears, but in part she was crying with relief. He would come. It was a beginning.

Her skirt was soaked through, icy water was running in streams down her legs. She got up and began to walk back through the wood. Her ankles were deep in mud, water rained down on her from the branches above her head. Now that she was aware of it, she was icy cold, and shivering uncontrollably.

Running back to the house, she saw Lisa at the window, looking for her. 'Are you going mad?' she demanded as Mara staggered in. 'You could catch pneumonia. And then who'd look after Drew?'

'I'm sure you'd manage,' said Mara shakily. 'I'll go and have a bath.'

There was something different about her. It was as if someone had set a match to a candle, she shone from within. Mara had looked like that before. Her sister felt a deep foreboding.

Jean abandoned all thought of driving to Slates Lane. She saddled her chestnut, draped an oilskin over herself and started off through the mud. The horse, stabled for weeks, was manic. He flung himself up the road, bucking and kicking, and finally managed to divest himself

371

of Jean on the main road. She landed with a thud on the tarmac, and a car screeched to a halt inches from her.

'Jean? Jean, are you all right?' It was Lisa Hellyn, bending anxiously down.

'I'm OK,' she said. 'I was keeping my eyes shut in case you were going to run over me.'

'The horse didn't stop. He's heading for home.'

'Bloody animal! He hasn't been out in two weeks. I should have lunged him first, I suppose.'

'Why not sell him and be done with it?' Lisa picked up Jean's whip. 'He's a horrible horse, he'll kill you one day. Look, you've torn your oilskin.'

'Have I? Damn.'

They stood uncertainly together. Lisa was in the Land Rover and obviously it was incumbent on her to offer Jean a lift home. But she said nothing, wondering why she hadn't kept on going and finished Jean off altogether.

'I was going to see the gypsies,' said Jean.

'Oh yes?' Lisa's face became taut and wary. She pulled her headscarf tighter under her chin. 'I imagine they'll be claiming security of tenure shortly. We'll have to build an entire council estate in Slates Lane.'

'That's just stupid! At least now the children go to school and the doctor visits. Actually, if we could only get a few council houses I'm sure they'd get out of the vans. But there's a waiting list a mile long even for flats, and they don't come under anyone's jurisdiction, you see –'

'So we end up with them,' said Lisa thinly. 'We can do nothing for them, and they certainly don't do anything for us. Except, of course, queer Angus's pitch in by-elections.'

Jean's leg was hurting. She had twisted it when she fell, and possibly the horse had clouted her in fond farewell. She wanted to sit down, and she felt also a foolish desire to be friends with Lisa. In fact, she almost wanted more to be friends with Lisa than with Toby. 'Why don't we go and visit them now?' she suggested. 'I was riding there, it's too sticky for my car.'

'If you will buy a Japanese hotrod.' Lisa turned back towards the Land Rover. 'All right, I'll take you. They've probably frozen to death, sparing their last breath to scrawl "Hellyn" on a tattered scrap of paper.'

'Most of them can't write,' said Jean matter-of-factly.

The car journey was circuitous and took far longer than a ride. Lisa was too small to drive a Land Rover well; she peered anxiously over the wheel, perching on the front of the seat to reach the pedals. Jean watched her surreptitiously. What did Toby see in her? That nose, and her thin, wiry fingers. She was Toby's exact opposite. Where he was big she was small; where he was direct she was secretive and devious. Angus wasn't like that. His stratagems were more obvious than sky-writing, and he had the naive belief that she couldn't see through them. Jean shifted in her seat. How many working weekends had he thought she would swallow?

They turned down the cart-track that eventually led to Slates Lane. It was deeply rutted and the Land Rover lurched horribly. The engine roared and Lisa had to use the wipers to keep the screen clear of mud. In the midst of it she said, 'I gather you're sleeping with Toby.' Were it not for the seat belt Jean would have slipped on to the floor. Had she considered Lisa devious? This had all the subtlety of an atom bomb. My God, she thought, if Lisa knew then somebody would tell Angus.

'It isn't true,' she said jerkily.

'Oh, come on, Jean.' Lisa shot her a look full of cynicism. 'You can't imagine you can keep something like that a secret, can you? Toby isn't actually the soul of discretion.'

'Did he tell you? He wouldn't! I don't believe it!'

'There's no need to get upset.' Lisa negotiated a water-filled pothole. 'After all, your father's bound to find out sooner or later. I wonder what he'll think.'

Jean put her thumb in her mouth and chewed on the nail. In many ways her father still thought of her as a little girl. If he found out about her and Angus it wouldn't have mattered quite so much somehow, because that was real. It wasn't like this thing with Toby. Cheap. Revengeful, almost.

'Are you going to marry him?' asked Lisa brightly.

'If I did – would you mind?'

'Me? Mind? Of course not. We had a fling a while ago, but it wasn't anything. One of those things.'

Jean stared at her pale profile. That was exactly the sort of thing Mara would say. So what did Lisa really think? She couldn't tell. They had never been friends, in fact she wondered if Lisa had many friends. She was always on the outside, intent, serious, doing what she did with absolute concentration.

'Does Angus know?' asked Jean weakly.

'Angus? Oh, I should think so. Mara told him.'

She parked briskly against the hedge. The gypsy encampment was a hundred yards further on, but the ground was a bog, chewed up by ponies and vehicles. Empty crisp packets and pieces of paper were

373

blown into hawthorn bushes and at the edge of the sea of mud sat a set of rusting pram wheels. For once Jean was all out of tolerance.

'Why in God's name can't they ever clean up?' she wailed. 'I do everything for them, and still they leave the place a tip.'

'They keep the wagons beautifully sometimes,' remarked Lisa.

Jean glared at her. 'But they never do the same for the kids.'

It was an odd reversal of roles. In fact, everything seemed to be turning upside down. When they trudged through the mud to the vans a couple of men looked up from sorting scrap and touched their forelocks to Lisa, and she nodded and smiled and said hello. Jean felt mounting rage. She it was who visited them all the time, got them doctors and social workers, and still a Hellyn had only to appear and they started curtseying.

A strange van had arrived. It was far from the latest design, but compared with the broken down vans and collapsiong vardos, it was revolutionary. The plump sides were heavy with chrome. Inside Jean glimpsed lace cushions, and a coke stove glowing red. One of the children stood looking up at her, a scrawny kid in a long overcoat.

'Hello, Kev,' said Jean. 'Got a new family come, have you?'

He shook his head. 'That's ourn. Me Da got it. Says we're on the make now, miss. Got a bit of flash.'

'Looks very flash,' remarked Lisa. 'Go to school do you? Can you read?'

'I goes,' said the boy sulkily.

'He's a permanent truant,' said Jean. 'Isn't that right, Kev? You skive off school most days? Go out totting with your dad?'

Kevin grinned, like an also-ran in Fagin's gang. Suddenly one of the women poked a cautious head out of the new van. 'Kev,' she screeched. 'Ask en if they wants to tek tea.'

Kevin looked at them. Jean could think of nothing but the possibility of catching something. She saw Lisa swallow. Still, there was nothing for it. 'How very kind,' she said weakly.

They left their boots at the door and sidled carefully into the spotless van. It had none of the opulence of rich gypsy families, none of the glass and silver, the collections of garish dolls in national costume. Nonetheless for these people it was a giant step upward, a front parlour of a caravan, into which children, food or living of any sort, were never allowed to intrude. However filthy, hungry or miserable they might be, this van would remain a pristine capsule, enshrining their self-respect.

The tea was served in silence, out of plastic picnic cups. The two girls made conversation, admiring the van and the cushions, sipping the murderously strong brew. Outside it began to rain, and two boys, one of them Kev, wandered past with a dog on a piece of string. Lisa felt as if she was in a dream, and it was a shock to see Jean getting up to go. She had begun to feel that in a minute or so she would wake and it would all be forgotten.

They slopped through the mud back to the Land Rover. The men had lit a fire to burn the scrap, but in the wet it was smoking and feeble. 'They would never have invited me in for a cup of tea if you hadn't been there,' said Jean. 'However badly the Hellyns treated them in the past, they still bow the knee.'

Lisa climbed stickily up into the car. 'You have to remember there's a lot of fear involved. In the old days we could have a gypsy hanged. And we could still get rid of them, if we wanted. They don't forget.'

'Will you get rid of them?'

Lisa shook her head. 'I don't know what to do with them. And if they did go, what would you do to pass the time? You can't spend all of it on your back.'

Jean blinked at her. 'You bitch!' she said. 'I think, underneath everything, you hate my guts.'

Lisa said nothing. She struggled with the low ratio gears, grinding slowly out of the mire.

Hunting was resumed at the end of the week. Toby went out, because he hadn't much to do and Reg would like it. He was well aware that Reg would like nothing better than to see him out of the house and out of Jean's life, but then Reg wanted Angus for a son-in-law. He didn't want some rich colonial muscling in.

Jean went out as well, lunging her horse for an hour beforehand. Not that it made much difference. At the meet the animal plunged and reared, and Toby got tired of being thumped. He left Jean to it and took his horse to the far side of the road.

The meet was at a pub, and he knocked back a couple of whiskies before the off. He felt in need of some stimulation. His body felt jaded, his mind stale. Why was he even staying here? Lisa had regained control at The Court, and apart from some serious talking about theme weeks and Mara's role around the place, there was nothing left to do. The Maythorpe bungalow was full of Maythorpes, and every day that passed seemed to drag him further in. If he had any sense he'd leave now, and by the time he came back people would have forgotten that he and Jean had a thing going.

At the off, Jean's chestnut raced ahead. Toby cantered and jumped in her wake, watching the bobbing figure bob with less and less energy until at last he found her standing by a ditch, holding her horse's reins. The animal hung his head in exhaustion.

'He's cooked himself,' she said ruefully. 'I did warn him but he didn't listen.'

'Stupid bloody animal. I'll walk back with you if you like. This is a filthy day anyway, mud in your face and no scent.'

'Ooh, aren't you the expert.'

They walked side by side, in silence. It was in no sense companionable, because they would rather have talked, and could think of nothing to say. Basically they had little in common, Toby supposed, although outwardly they had a lot. Perhaps they were just too similar. They lacked interest for one another.

Jean's boots began to rub. It was a Maythorpe principle to replace anything that looked remotely worn, even leather boots, which meant that they were discarded almost as soon as they became comfortable. These were so new that after ten minutes she was hobbling. 'Ride my nag,' said Toby. He gave her a leg-up, not bothering to shorten the stirrups. They went on, glumly, Toby leading the chestnut, Jean with her feet dangling.

The field gate led them out on to a twisting lane, that eventually led to the village. A car was coming towards them, going quite fast. Toby reached up and caught the reins of his own horse, holding it and the chestnut steady. 'I am capable of controlling this old thing,' snapped Jean, but Angus, in the car, picked up none of the atmosphere. All he saw was Jean, on Toby's horse, being taken care of.

He screeched to a halt and got out. Jean coloured to the roots of her hair, and sat there, in total silence.

'Thought it might be you,' said Toby.

'I imagine you were expecting me.'

Toby grinned. 'No, not exactly. You've been so busy in London, with your parties and your connections, I didn't think you'd find a moment to come and talk to the country bumpkins.'

Angus ignored him. 'Jean, I want to talk to you.'

'Talk away.' She gazed over his head with what she hoped was disinterest. Her cheeks still burned.

'Not here. Look, he can take the nags home. Come in the car with me.'

She was sorely tempted. She shot Toby a look of wild entreaty, but he looked back, expressionless. 'She might be in later this evening,' he said casually. 'Call round then.'

'Jean?' Angus held the car door, sure that she wouldn't say no.

She swallowed. 'I'm busy now. Come round tonight.'

When he had gone, roaring down the road in a pall of smoke, Jean put her hands to her cheeks and wailed. 'You should have let me go! Oh, I wish we hadn't done anything, I wish I could take it all back!

Did you see how angry he is?'

'Not half angry enough, if you ask me. He ought to have tried to knock my teeth out, surely.'

Jean pulled the horse's reins out of his grip. 'Give it here! You can walk the horse home. I don't know why everyone has to know. This is all your fault, he probably was just busy in London. I wish I'd never let you touch me.'

She kicked the horse into a trot. Toby was left in the lane, holding the reins of the weary chestnut. It occurred to him that if you weren't involved, this whole thing would be vastly amusing.

Angus roared up to The Court, storming into the house past a posse of departing guests. 'It's the earl,' they murmured to each other, and stood deferentially to one side. Angus grunted and strode past. He was looking for Mara.

He found her in the small sitting-room, reading a magazine and eating chocolates. She had her feet up, a tray of tea at her side, and the fire crackled merrily. She was the picture of winter contentment.

'You're certainly pulling your weight around here,' said Angus.

'Angus! Dear Angus, I'm not at all surprised to see you. Have you come to tell me to take myself off to a nunnery? I'm not being any sort of scandal, I promise you.'

'You're never anything else.' He leaned down and pecked her cheek. 'Guess who I just saw?'

'No idea. Not Jean already, surely?'

'Yes, Jean.' Angus squatted down and poked the fire vigorously. 'She and Toby, close as anything. I didn't believe it till then. I thought you were making it up.'

'So now you know.' Mara shifted a little in her chair. 'Makes things easier, doesn't it?'

'What things?'

She looked at him meaningfully. 'Be honest, old boy. It wouldn't have done.'

Mara told them about the christening after dinner. They had dined with the guests, on the usual formal and stultifying fare. It was hard to take night after night, and often Lisa ate no more than a spoonful of anything. She was becoming painfully thin. Afterwards the family retreated to their own rooms, and left the guests to talk about them.

'I've got some news,' began Mara. The others looked wary. 'It's rather wonderful actually,' she went on quickly. 'Drew's father's coming to his christening. He wants to be a godparent.'

The others looked stunned. At last Lisa said, 'If Mother had been alive you wouldn't have dared.'

377

'Yes I would! It's only right. He should be there.'

'He should never have got you pregnant in the first place,' snapped Angus. 'Good God, does the bloody man really think he can turn up here and be charming? I won't have him in the house.'

'Suppose the papers find out?' said Lisa. 'Drew's life would be a misery. Our lives would be a misery. Mara, you can't.'

She ducked her head. 'The papers won't find out. I can and I will. I won't let anyone stop me.'

Angus lost his temper. 'Mara, this is just the end! Why don't you think about someone else for a change? I've got a career to worry about, one that depends on some small measure of respectability! If all this comes out, it won't do you much harm, it might not even do your child a great deal, but you'll ruin a marriage, break up a home, and quite possible finish me in politics.'

'And we all know which is the most important, don't we, Angus?' Mara was contemptuous.

Her brother looked at her coldly. He had never been so near to hating Mara in his life, it almost frightened him. 'You play games with other people's lives,' he said. 'You're just like Father. He never thought anyone else mattered a damn.'

Henry's chair still stood in the room. They didn't often use it. For a second they felt as if he might still be there, sitting, watching them. The curtains moved in an unseen draught. They remembered how autocratic he had been, the way he would demand and it had to be done, instantly. But, oh, he had been the sun for them. His warmth gave them life, beyond it was nothing but cold and barren space.

Angus went out. He drove fast to the Maythorpes', but when he got there he sat in the car, thinking. How he wished Toby need not be there. Why in God's name did Mara always have to meddle? It would suit her to have Jean out of the way, and she thought no further than that. As for himself, he didn't know. There was a girl in London, of course. Lucinda. A nice girl, well-connected. Marriage to her would mean entrée into a great political family. Dammit, he liked her! But in the evening when he came home did he want to find her standing in her elegant drawing-room? Did he want to lead that smooth and varnished life? He couldn't see it, somehow. And to know about Jean, now, was cruel.

The front door opened and Jean came out. She was wearing a scarlet dress, with heavy bands of sequins around the neck and waist. Trust Jean to overdo things, he thought.

'Aren't you coming in?' she called.

Angus grunted and got out of the car.

Reg was overjoyed to see him. 'Toby's out,' he explained. 'Don't

378

know quite how we came to have him staying, but there you are. Jean always does like to look after the lame ducks.'

'Is Toby a lame duck?'

'Dunno. Bit of an odd type, if you ask me. Doesn't talk much, to me, at any rate. Dare say he chats a bit to Jean. Gets on a darn sight too well with Jean. If you take my meaning.'

Angus was being tipped the wink, with Reg's usual heavy-handedness. Was there anyone who didn't know that Jean and Toby were sleeping together? He didn't want to think about it, especially when they were all three together, just like old times. Jean fetched whisky and glasses, and the three of them settled round the gas fire. Suddenly Angus wondered what Lucinda would say if she could see them, and knew she would find it tremendously amusing. What would she call it? Suburban. Everything new, everything clean, everything bright.

Jean said, 'People are talking about Mara. You've no idea.'

'He doesn't want to hear that sort of gossip,' said Reg firmly.

'Perhaps I ought,' said Angus. 'I might get the chance of another seat soon. I should know what people are saying.'

'Which constituency?' Jean's face became sharp.

'Home Counties.'

'Oh. I see.'

That was it, then. If she didn't fit in Heslington, she would stand out like a sore thumb in the south. Angus knew that. She supposed, in his way, he'd been trying to ease the blow. 'Any big issues?' she asked feebly. 'Anything you can get your teeth into?'

He shook his head. 'Not really, no. It's a prosperous place, that's all. Lot of sunrise industries.'

'I see.'

'Jean'll have to mug up on technology then, won't she?' declared Reg, determined to breathe life into the situation. 'She was a help before, she'll be invaluable now.'

Jean took a good deep breath. 'Dad, there's something I think you should know. Angus and I have finished. I won't be helping him any more. That's why Toby's staying. We're – well, we're in love.'

Reg looked sharp-eyed from one to the other. 'What about you, Angus? What have you to say to this?'

'He's got someone else,' said Jean shrilly. 'Clarissa Pethick-Smyth. Or something like that.'

'Her name's Lucinda,' said Angus. 'But there's nothing serious.'

Jean grimaced. 'All these weekends, I think it ought to be by now! You don't want to string someone along now do you?'

Toby came in after Angus had left. He'd been to the pub to see if

379

they had a room, but for once they were full. But really, why was he staying on? He might just as well head for London, Sydney, or even Rio again.

Jean was very bright-eyed, and unnaturally cheerful. She got up at once and went to hold on to his arm. 'Toby, I was just telling Dad all about us.'

'What?'

'About how serious we are about one another.'

Toby glanced down at her. She was staring up at him with a look of steely intent. Who was this in aid of? he wondered. Surely not just to spite Angus? No, it was because of Reg. If they ditched the affair now, as they both wanted to, Reg would think she was a slut. He couldn't bear to think that his daughter was the sort of girl who hopped into bed for a cheap thrill. A romance must be created, simply so that they could knock it on the head. What a stupid situation. Still, he supposed he could endure it for a week or two, and then get the hell out.

He patted Jean's hand. 'We're really very lucky,' he murmured.

Chapter Thirty-Nine

Toby wasn't used to being the victim of circumstance. If he fell in a hole it was one he had dug himself, and he climbed out by himself, using his fingernails if necessary. But somehow he felt inveigled into a situation in which he was powerless. And he didn't want to be stuck with Jean, he didn't want to stay in her house, talk to her father or, if the truth were told, sleep in her bed.

And yet, the very morning after their extremely vague announcement, Reg asked Jean if they would like him to move out. 'Don't want to get under your feet, lass,' he said dolefully. 'I mean, now you're getting wed you'll need somewhere this size. I could have a little place somewhere, manageable like. Now I'm getting on.'

Jean said sharply, 'You're Master of the Hunt, Dad, not a bloody cripple! And we're not getting married. Yet.'

'I've got a couple of houses in Australia, as it happens,' commented Toby.

'Australia!' Reg looked outraged. 'You'll not be taking our Jean to Australia!'

God forbid, thought Toby.

He went to The Court that afternoon, in a mood of fulminating discontent, prepared to find fault in everything. Yet when Curtiss opened the door to him he was, despite himself, impressed. The air smelled of beeswax. Someone was playing a piano, Chopin or something, he never did know anything about classical music. A couple of the guests were in the hall, dressed for walking, a maid passed through with a decanter and glasses on a silver tray. The place had an air of relaxed yet purposeful activity. With a shock he realised this was exactly what he had intended, all that time ago: the perfect house party.

He went in search of Lisa. He found her on one of the upstairs landings, arranging flowers in a window embrasure. She was wearing

381

bluc pleated trousers, belted round her tiny waist, and a full blue silk blouse. Like the house, she too was in perfect order.

'See you got everything back on an even keel.'

She spun round. 'Toby! You made me jump.'

'What the hell are you doing putting flowers here?'

She shrugged. 'They look nice. I like them here.'

'Can't you get a florist to do them?'

'If I admired stultified arrangements of rigid predictability, I dare say I could,' she said thinly.

He had to admit that no-one arranged flowers like Lisa. They almost looked grateful for her attention, draping themselves in falls and curves and misty colours. He struggled to regain the initiative. 'We have to talk. A business discussion.'

To his surprise, she nodded. 'I know. I should have spoken to you days ago, but what with one thing and another — is your head all right?'

'Hurts like hell when I comb my hair.'

She eyed his mat of tangled brown. 'Do you comb it? I thought you wet it, shook it, and forgot it. Like a water spaniel or something.'

'Thanks very much!'

They laughed. Too late they remembered that they were on exceptionally bad terms. Toby said, 'Look, why don't we go to your office?'

She went a little pink. 'I've moved it. I work in my bedroom — have a bath and do some paperwork, that sort of thing —'

'As long as we keep our clothes on I don't think it matters, do you?'

She gave him a fierce look. 'I'm not in the habit of taking mine off quite as frequently as you.'

She led the way upstairs, walking with that brisk, upright posture that he always found slightly amusing. It was as if she was playing at soldiers. She marched into her room, flinging the door wide. Her desk, fine French walnut borrowed from the library, stood in the centre, with a thin gilt chair before it. Lisa sat down, leaving Toby the bedroom armchair. He ignored it and lounged on the bed.

'This is supposed to be a business meeting,' she said testily.

'And so it is. I can talk business lying down.'

'This isn't Rome, you know.'

'And you're not the bloody Queen of Sheba.'

Lisa said nothing. She got out a sheet of paper and a pen, and started making headings. Then she stopped. 'We've got a problem,' she said cautiously.

'You've got several. Redecoration, bookings, the cost of running this show, and Mara. Particularly Mara.'

382

'Bigger than that.' She took a deep breath. 'Professor Chandler's been. To look at the roof. In fact we've had dozens of people to look at the roof. Toby, it's going to cost hundreds of thousands of pounds! They say they're not doing patch-up jobs any more. It has to be done properly. There's going to be an annual budget set aside for restoration, they're talking about launching an appeal for the tapestries alone. And − and −'

'They don't see why they should fund the restoration of somewhere that is running a very nice profit-making scheme.'

'They want us to open properly,' said Lisa glumly. 'All the house. All the summer.'

'That's ridiculous! You're miles away from anywhere. You wouldn't get nearly enough visitors.'

'They don't care about numbers. They just want public access, that's all.'

Toby got up. He walked slowly round the room, a man too big for such a delicate and feminine environment. One of Lisa's scarves lay on the dressing table. He picked it up and ran the silk through his fingers. It was like touching water.

'There's a clause in our contract covers this,' he remarked. 'If the house can no longer be used, and I haven't recouped the investment, you pay me out.'

'Good God! We can't afford it.'

He watched her inscrutably. 'Look, how long can we keep on running?'

She wrinkled her nose doubtfully. 'They won't start this summer. We could probably keep on right through to next spring. But I don't think we should. Not after the drain fiasco.'

'Yes. Not exactly cosy when the winds begin to blow ... OK then. We'll finish after next Christmas.'

'Just like that? And you won't want to be paid back?'

'Oh. I didn't say that.'

There was a silence. Two spots of colour stained Lisa's cheeks, she looked like a thin doll. 'You're going to get your revenge, aren't you?' she said softly. 'You're going to make us pay!'

She sat very still. There was a pulse beating in his forehead, and all at once she remembered how it had been, in Rio, in bed together. She winced.

'Let me explain a few things,' said Toby. 'I've been looking through my accounts. The holiday complex, the restaurants, the club in Rio and this place. You are bottom of the league. I can see why. I told you to run the place like a stately home, and you do. Don't think twice about champagne, caviare, flowers in the bedrooms ... for all

I know you're feeding the damned dog on pheasant.'

'He has to have steak,' said Lisa fearfully. 'It's his age, he's really ancient.'

'Oh, I'm not complaining. If the restoration wasn't necessary I'd give it a good five years, bring all my contacts here, use the place for conferences, get one hell of a lot of mileage out of it. And I wouldn't have Mara about the place.'

'It's her home!'

'Every parasite needs one, I suppose. I won't have her sucking my blood, I tell you straight.'

Lisa's chin came up. 'I'm quite sure the contract provides for the family,' she said crisply.

'I didn't think you'd like me to stick too closely to the contract. Actually the family's been a blasted nuisance. Marcus, for instance. Lisa, he isn't to come back while the hotel's open. And I mean that.' He put out a hand and touched her cheek, quite firmly. She knew he was right. You could not inflict Marcus upon people who didn't understand. It was unnecessary and cruel. She nodded.

'Good girl. Now, how am I going to get my money back?'

'You don't need it. You know you don't.'

'My pride needs it. My businesses need it. And I'll be damned if you Hellyns get away with it. But, let's be practical. At the top of my league of earners we have a surprise entrant. Lady Lisa's.'

'What?'

'The club in Rio. That's what I called it. Smash hit. I get two requests a week asking who the designer was. You see, while they're boogeying in a haze of cocaine they stare up at the walls and see all your beautiful rugs. And the tiles, and the mirrors, and the paintings, not to mention the bleeding plates! Everyone tries to steal the plates.'

'Well, that's why you took me there. I did what you asked,' said Lisa frostily.

'And it was hugely successful. I'm going to concentrate on clubs now. And to show my gratitude, I'll do you a favour. The greatest favour.'

She looked at him fearfully. 'What?'

'I'll take The Court off your hands. In lieu of the cash. And you can't tell me it's worth twenty times that, because it's damn nigh unsaleable and you know it.'

'You wouldn't! You can't!'

'Yes I can. Discounting what's been earned, you owe me at least five hundred thousand and you can't pay. Look, I'll be generous and let you stay until I decide what I want to do with the place. Could be years, you never know.'

She was completely lost for words. How like Toby to win every way. He never took a loss in anything. 'Get out,' she said hoarsely. 'You won't get The Court. We'll pay you out somehow. I'll get a loan or something.'

'You couldn't before,' he said mildly. 'And I'm not keen on instalment plans.'

'We'll get a loan. And you needn't go bothering Angus about it either, taking it out on him. You can — you can go and boil your head!'

He laughed at her. 'You'll have to come round in the end.'

'What? And have bloody Jean Maythorpe as the landlady? Toby, get out! Out!' She came at him like a furious gnat, arms flailing. He rolled off the bed, fending off her blows and backing out of the door.

She slammed it in his face.

'Let me know if you change your mind,' he called.

'Go to hell!' yelled Lisa. There was the sound of a key turning in the lock.

Sometimes it seemed as if The Court was the focus of the winds of the world. They howled around the chimneys, chasing each other in a fierce battle for ascendancy, they raced through the park, up into the woods, and screamed away across the moor. Crows were whipped from the treetops and sent whirling in a bundle of feathers into the tumbled air. They almost looked as if they enjoyed it, thought Angus.

He was out with his gun. He thought he might get the odd rabbit, though he didn't expect much in this weather. But, it was good to trudge across wet headlands and around ponds, his cheeks turning to cold slabs of leather. Half the pleasure was in thawing out afterwards.

He wondered if Lucinda shot. He rather hoped not. She was aggressively companionable, believed in doing a great many things together, most of which he would happily have done on his own. She liked to be there, with him. A couple.

A rabbit skittered away across the field, he brought his gun up and fired. The animal fell like a pricked balloon, and when he got to it he saw that it was quite dead. Blood soaked the grass and its eyes were glazed and blank. He left it where it was.

When he looked up he saw a horseman coming towards him across the grass. It was Toby.

'You ought to take that back for Lisa's dog,' he remarked. 'She's feeding it steak.'

'He's on his last legs, poor old thing. One of these days someone's going to have to shoot him too.'

'Just so long as you don't leave it to Lisa. She does everything else.'

385

Angus's head came up. 'I'll thank you to keep your nose out. I've had enough of your damned interference. For some reason I don't begin to understand, anything Hellyn fascinates you. First it was the house, then it was Lisa, and if you ask me the only thing you want Jean for is to spite me.'

Toby laughed. 'Christ, but you are a bloody fool!'

He swung his horse as if to ride off. But he seemed to think better of it. 'I wanted to say something to you. About Mara. I won't have her living at The Court and doing nothing. It isn't a bloody rest home.'

'It is our home. You are overstepping the mark.'

'Am I? You know damned well that if she stays we'll have the papers here. It's a matter of luck that they haven't yet found out that she's had a baby. We'll lose bookings hand over fist. And it's only a matter of time before she starts seducing the guests.'

'How dare you!'

Angus swung the gun up. Toby sat, staring down the twin barrels. He wondered which one was empty. 'Didn't Daddy ever tell you not to point it at people?' he said mildly.

'He'd have shot you himself if you'd said such a thing about Mara.'

'Well, that's something you Hellyns are very good at. Making a bad situation one hell of a lot worse. I'd have thought better of you if you'd been this angry over Jean.'

'Keep your filthy mouth shut!'

'But, my dear chap, she comes out of the wrong drawer! What more can be said, the girl just won't do!' The mocking words echoed Charlotte's. His finger itched, Angus would have given anything to shoot. But reason prevailed. He lowered the barrel.

'So you'll move Mara out,' said Toby calmly.

She ought to go. Angus knew that Toby was right. But for once, just for once, he wasn't going to do as he was told. 'No,' he croaked, his voice sounding harsh in his ears. 'She stays. You can do what you like but she stays. She's my sister, it's her home, and she belongs in it.'

Toby chuckled. 'What do you know? A bit of determination at last. Keep this up and you actually might get into Parliament.'

He clicked to the horse and began to trot away. After twenty yards he pushed it into a canter, forcing himself not to launch into a headlong gallop. Sweat soaked his shirt, it gathered in a pool in the small of his back. For a minute there he thought he was dead.

That night he took Jean out for a drive. She sat silent beside him, gazing out at the headlights coming up and over the hills. Toby hunted for a station on the radio, and could get nothing but Frenchmen and Radio Three. He pulled the car over to the side.

'Look,' he began.

'Oh-oh.' said Jean.

'What?'

'You always say "Look" when it's serious. Don't worry, I'm not intending to drag you to the altar.'

'I could think of worse fates,' said Toby chivalrously.

'Could you?' Jean eyed him with scepticism. He decided he liked her more then than for a while.

'Do you mind if I go away for a bit? I'll send you three letters a day and a dozen red roses if that makes it any better, but this is all getting a bit heavy. Angus tried to shoot me today.'

'My God, why? Was it about me?'

'Sort of.'

Toby rubbed his nose. He had never wanted out of anything as much as this situation. 'I've got some travelling to do,' he said vaguely. 'I'll come back in a week or so, we can play the big romance for a while and then close it down. I won't come to stay again. Your father treats me like Bluebeard.'

Jean said nothing. In a way, she thought, Reg was right. Toby wasn't good for women, certainly not for her. He was thoughtful, he cared about giving her pleasure, but these were superficial responses. She inspired in him no deeper emotion than irritation. She moved restlessly in her seat. That was the danger of uncommitted sex, certainly for women. After a while you began to look for commitment, in the most unlikely places.

The christening was arranged for a Wednesday in March, at the church in the village. Mara went to see the vicar personally, and asked that no announcement should be made, because it was just a small ceremony, for the family only, and she didn't want everyone to know. Anyone in fact. Under the circumstances.

The vicar seized the opportunity to talk to Mara, seriously, about her life. She came back to The Court in tears.

'What on earth's the matter?' Lisa, who had been struggling with a wingeing baby all afternoon, felt that she was the one who deserved sympathy.

'That bloody man. The vicar! He said he wanted me to know that he admired my courage and knew that underneath all my flighty ways I was good and honest and loyal. Bloody man!'

'Made you feel guilty did he? So you ought.'

Mara flounced to the sofa. 'I'm being quite good, really. Jay's coming for Drew. Nothing more than that. Here, hand him over, he must need feeding.'

387

She unbuttoned her shirt and put the baby to her breast. He gave her a baleful stare, because he'd wanted her and she'd gone. 'I don't have to be at your beck and call,' said Mara defiantly, stroking his cheek. 'Some babies have to make do with a horrible rubber bottle.'

'I'm sure we did,' said Lisa. 'Bottle, Nanny, and the door shut, that's what we got.'

'That's what Jay's girls get, I'll swear it,' said Mara. 'But Drew has a proper mummy. A mummy who loves him.'

'I don't imagine his wife actually tortures the brats!'

Lisa stood and watched her sister for a moment. That man ought not to come to the christening. If he saw Mara like this, bent in love over her baby, he would never resist her. Breast feeding had slimmed her down, she was every bit as gorgeous as before. In fact, there was a ripeness about her, and a new, frank softness. Perhaps she had learned about gentleness.

'I got out the christening robe,' said Lisa.

Mara's head came up. 'Did you find it? Do let me see!'

But as Lisa unwrapped the paper she sighed with disappointment. 'It's so yellow! Yellow as anything.'

'We can try and wash it.' Lisa spread the lacy folds out on the carpet. Yards and yards of lace, French she remembered her mother saying. The bodice and the hem were interwoven with satin ribbon, and that would need replacing. Little puff sleeves lined with white silk, and to fasten it twenty-five tiny pearl buttons.

'I'll soak it tonight,' said Lisa.

'Suppose you ruin it? I hate to think what it's worth.'

Her sister shrugged. 'He's got to have it. He's a royal baby. And, rather more to the point, he's a Hellyn!'

Mara rose early on the day of Drew's christening. A fine drizzle was falling, but the sky was becoming brighter. She went and lay in the bath, thinking of the many, many times she had made herself ready for him. What had he told his wife? Surely never the truth.

They had booked the church for eleven o'clock. It was to be an extremely small affair, just the three godparents, Angus, Lisa and Jay, and Mara herself. She couldn't eat breakfast and the baby sensed her unease and wouldn't feed. Suppose he cried in church, she thought miserably, and Jay thought he was just an ugly, screaming brat?

She dressed, hours too early, in a suit. It was blue wool, the same colour as her eyes, with a slight sheen on it. The jacket was fitted and she wore it without a blouse, showing just the tops of her breasts. It was almost decent enough to satisfy the vicar, she thought. She wore a hat too, of the same blue, a flirty fan of lace arranged on a small

388

triangle of velvet. As she made herself up she thought about Clare. If only she could have been there today — but no-one must know Jay was coming.

They dressed Drew in his robe, turned a soft cream in the wash. He was sleepy, quiescent. A rounded child, with the pink bloom of a renaissance painting. Then, at half-past ten, a car drove up.

'Is it a guest?' asked Mara nervously. 'Don't get bogged down with anyone, Lisa, we mustn't be late.'

Lisa glanced out of the side window. 'It's him,' she said.

Mara went white. She had to cling to a side table for support.

'Sit down,' ordered Lisa. 'I must get him through the front hall! Someone might see him.' She rushed out to get to the door before Curtiss. But the butler was prompt. After one startled glance he dropped his head in the required bow.

'Do stop that, Curtiss,' ordered Lisa crisply. 'This visitor doesn't deserve such things. Perhaps you'd come this way.'

'Thank you so much,' said the prince ironically.

Lisa led the way into the sitting-room. Mara was still on her feet, clinging to the table. 'Jay,' she whispered. Her eyes were wide with fright.

'Hello, Mara.' He cleared his throat and stood awkwardly.

'I hope you don't expect me to withdraw,' remarked Lisa.

'Yes, please,' said Mara in a small, strained voice. 'We won't be long. We've got to go in fifteen minutes.'

Lisa shut the door with an outraged click. Jay said, 'Your sister never could stand the sight of me.'

'She thought you'd get me into trouble. And how right she was.'

They stood looking at each other. His hair was a little thinner, Mara thought, and the lines from nose to mouth seemed more pronounced.

'How was it?' he asked. 'You look wonderful.'

She shrugged. 'It was all right. Frightening. Lonely. I would have given anything to have you there.'

It was the wrong thing to say. His mouth tightened, she knew he wanted to heap recriminations on her head. It was all her fault, she had caused the baby to exist, he had had nothing to do with it.

'Wouldn't you like to see him?' she said breathlessly.

'That's why I'm here.'

'Well, he's only behind the sofa. I keep the cradle in here during the day, otherwise I can't hear him. Why don't you look?'

He crossed the room and stood, looking down at the child. Mara knelt on the sofa, trailing one finger in the baby's downy hair. 'Doesn't he look like you?'

'Yes — he does rather. Your hair though.'

389

'Do you think so? Your eyes. You can't see unless he wakes up.'

'Is he − is he good?'

'Very good. The best baby in the world.'

He put his finger against the sleeping child's fist. He gripped, fiercely. 'What a boy!' said Jay incredulously. 'He'll be a sportsman. A rowing blue.'

'I shouldn't be surprised. I haven't put him down for any schools yet. I thought you might like to do it.'

'Not in my name, of course.'

'No. As a godparent.' She grinned up at him, conspiratorially. His heart shifted within him.

They were five minutes late leaving for the church. Angus was to meet them there, and when they arrived he was walking up and down with the vicar, looking strained. When he set eyes on Jay he became positively stiff.

'Sir. We were expecting you direct to the church.'

'Were you? I wanted a few words alone with Mara.'

No hint of embarrassment. Angus choked down his anger. The vicar hadn't recognised him, and was making faces at the baby. Lisa said, 'Shall we go inside?' in tones of rigid propriety.

They gathered round the ancient font. 'I thought we might sing a hymn,' said the vicar happily. 'Our numbers bear no reflection on the importance of the occasion. Shall I start?' He launched reedily into the strains of 'Almighty, Invisible,' and the others joined in, with varying degrees of enthusiasm. Jay proved to be quite a good singer, and Mara had been the mainstay of the contraltos in the school choir. Lisa found the whole thing almost too absurd. Giggles prevented her from giving her all.

But when it came to the christening, she was choked with tears. Such a little child, born in trouble, held safe only by feeble words. To be Mara's child could be the greatest blessing and the greatest curse. They would stand in the shadows, those that loved him, and watch him toddle off into a world that would not be kind. If only they could keep him from harm, keep him as safe as he was today.

When the water touched him, Drew began screaming. Mara folded her hands into her heart, showing in her face how it hurt her. Yes, thought Lisa, Mara was going to suffer for what she had done. Every blow that fell on Drew would fall twice as heavily on her.

Afterwards Mara said to Jay, 'You will come back?'

He said, 'For a few moments only. I haven't given Drew my present.'

Mara brightened. 'Oh, yes, of course. Christening presents!'

Lisa had bought a silver cup, engraved with Drew's name. Angus had asked Lucinda to get something and presented the baby with an entire set of Peter Rabbit plates. Mara could tell that Jay thought them totally inappropriate. Because he gave his son a silver sword.

The scabbard was chased silver gilt, and from the hilt swung a ceremonial tassel. 'It was my grandfather's,' said Jay. 'I thought Drew should have it. He's my only son.'

'The child is a Hellyn. If I might remind you, sir,' said Angus crisply.

'I think we all regret the accident of his birth.' Jay put the sword across the cradle, and the baby reached up to hit at it with his hands. Mara put her hands up to her face and sobbed.

Angus and Lisa left them alone. Jay gave her his handkerchief. 'I'm sorry, I'm sorry,' wept Mara. 'I didn't mean to make a scene. And I'm not. But christenings are rather emotional, don't you think?'

'Yes. Very.'

'I do so want you to see him. To know him as he grows up.'

Jay reached out and took her hand. 'Mara, you know I want that too. More than anything.'

'But how can we? If I don't see you?'

He felt as if a small window was being opened in his soul, a window he had closed and sealed and thought could never open again. There wasn't a woman in the world more beautiful than this, not one as warm, as soft, as vulnerable. People who resist temptation, he thought, have never been tempted enough.

'I've got to go,' he said hoarsely.

'Yes. Yes, you go.' She wiped her eyes and gave him back the handkerchief. He held her hand in his, palm to palm. He let her go, and left.

391

Chapter Forty

The train was late. Stuffed to the doors with passengers from some other train that had broken down somewhere south of Glasgow, it lurched and groaned its way into Kings' Cross. Angus was standing by the door, because he had vacated his seat in favour of an old lady who had got off at Doncaster, only to see the seat seized by a young and very fit man wearing a walkman. So Angus stood.

He dreamed of being a minister and travelling first class. He didn't dare dream about being an MP, because that was possible and might bring bad luck. No, dreams were for the unattainable, life's Holy Grail, visible through the mists of years.

Lucinda met him off the train, though he wasn't expecting her. She was tall and thin, and she wore a narrow black coat buttoned to the chin. An attractive girl generally, though her mouth was too big and her hair very pale and straight. She wore it swept back in an Alice band.

'Darling!' Angus kissed her cheek. 'What a surprise.'

'Was it a horrible journey? They're mending the line or something, everything's delayed. Darling, I had to come, Mummy wants you to come to dinner tonight. An ambassador and a cabinet minister, just the sort of people you should meet.'

'That's really sweet of her. And you, darling.'

The queue for a taxi was endless, so they took the tube to Angus's flat. Lucinda had taken the place in hand, buying posters for the loo and sets of prints from a market stall which she had asked a friend to frame. Angus had black candles on his table now, because they were chic.

'Darling.' Once inside the door Lucinda turned and kissed him. The passion was simulated, she wasn't in the least desperate for sex. But she liked him to think she was. All good relationships were passionate, she knew that, and couples about to get engaged had to

392

sleep together. Her mother had actually asked her about it.

'Darling, are you sleeping together?'

Lucinda blushed and smiled. 'Yes, actually. Angus insists. But, Mummy, it's marvellous, really. Don't worry.'

That milestone passed, the family expected nothing less than the ring.

Angus stripped off his clothes eagerly enough. He liked doing it with Lucinda, she kept up a constant chorus of 'Darling – that's wonderful – oh!' It never occurred to either of them that she was sexually unawakened. She would only consider real enjoyment when she was safely married.

Afterwards, Angus felt sleepy. Lucinda played with his chest hair, calling him Piggy-Poo, her pet name for him. She wanted him to give her a name too, but so far he hadn't obliged. That was the trouble with Angus. It was like dancing with someone whose mind is on something else. They know the moves but have to be reminded all the time.

'Didn't you have a nice time at home, Piggy?' she asked solicitously.

'It was OK. My sisters were both there.' He had told Lucinda about Marcus, but Mara's baby was not something he was going to confide. As far as she was concerned he had travelled home to see to the estate.

'Was that man there? The one you don't like?'

'Toby? Yes, he was there.' Suddenly he said, 'He's getting engaged to a girl I used to go out with.'

'Oh.' Lucinda eyed him warily. She sat up a little and rubbed her small breasts against his arm. 'You don't mind, do you?'

Angus grinned. 'No. Of course not.'

No sooner had he said it than he realised how much he did mind. It was a flame of anger – anger and hurt and disappointment. Not that he could have made it with Jean, but the possibility was there, it was one which they toyed with when they were together. It had added spice to his life, adventure and unpredictability in what was coming to seem a very predictable existence. Safe seat, good marriage, slow progress up the ranks proving that he was a solid party man. Light years from the rough and tumble of Heslington, where the stock answers didn't work and the people didn't believe them. No, he wouldn't spend his time with Jean, nor yet in Heslington. His would be the safe, sure company of people like Lucinda.

'Penny for your thoughts?' She tickled his ear. God, but she never let up. Not that she wanted to know what he thought, merely to think that she did.

'Let's get ready for dinner,' he said. 'If we don't hurry, your

393

mother may suspect what's been going on.'

'Lucinda giggled. 'So she might! If she only knew what fun we're having. Darling Angus.'

'Darling.'

But the dinner dragged. It was all very polished and easy, with everyone making political jokes and intelligent conversation. They took the name of a union leader in vain, and used it for everything from a visit to the lavatory to sneezing. 'Todding again, old chap?' Lucinda's mother was doing her best to be grand, with silver candelabra and fingerbowls. To Angus it seemed pretentious and strained. One of his earliest memories was of dining with his grandfather, on venison, which he disliked. The silver tureen, long since sold, dominated the table like an overweight dog, while the real dogs grumbled and snored round his grandfather's chair. He had been given port to drink, a teaspoonful in a tiny Elizabethan glass. His mother wore her diamonds, he remembered. And at the end the butler had opened the window and his grandfather got up and threw silver coins out on to the grass. People ran about and caught them, he had no idea who or why.

'Bloody vultures,' his grandfather had said. 'Got more than us under their stinking beds at home.'

The cabinet minister turned to Angus. 'Now, I hear you're going to try for Frensham, isn't that right?'

'I was hoping to get selected, yes, sir.'

'Got a good chance, I should imagine. Safe as houses, Frensham.'

'So I understand.' Angus swallowed down a lump of rather soft bread, Lucinda's mother always seemed to assume half the guests were toothless. 'Acutally, sir, I've been thinking. My home's in the north. And if you remember I fought Heslington not so long ago. I've been wondering if I wouldn't prefer a northern seat. Something I can get my teeth into.'

The minister laughed. 'A good bit of northern deprivation you mean. Restoring shipbuilding by the might of your arm.'

'Not exactly. Just a bigger job, really. If I stood in Frensham, they'd elect me if I was half-dead.'

'But you want to get elected, don't you, Angus?' Lucinda looked appalled.

'Naturally. But on my merits. I think I'm going to let Frensham go.'

The minister chuckled. 'Oh God! We'll probably get a woman in. May the saints defend us.'

Angus left rather early. Lucinda stood in the hall with him, furious and trying not to show it. 'Don't you think you might have talked to me first?' she asked in falsely dulcet tones.

'I hadn't made up my mind until just then. But I don't want Frensham. I'd have it for life, and it isn't my sort of place.'

'It might have been mine.' Lucinda's chin came up. It was her first positive demand.

'I think the decision had to be mine, darling. I'm sorry if you're upset.'

'Well, of course I'm upset! You could have been elected in six months! Now what's going to happen?'

'I really don't know. I'll start looking for somewhere northern, I suppose. And I've got the estate to see to. My brother's very ill at the moment, he can't take care of things.'

Lucinda's mouth set in a narrow line. 'If you ask me he's not the only one that's bonkers! I don't think you want to get elected at all. You're playing at it. You've got some big, idealistic vision that can't possibly work out. And you don't give a damn what I might think.'

Angus said, 'Don't you think that was awfully rude? About my brother?'

'I don't know your brother. You haven't let me see him, or any of your family. Are you ashamed of me or them, Angus?'

'Neither. I just don't think you'd get on.'

There was a silence. 'That wasn't just rude, it was unkind,' said Lucinda.

'Was it? I'm sorry.'

'I'm sorry too.' It was an opening for reconciliation, but he did nothing. Tears welled up, she opened her eyes wide to stop them falling. She reached past him to open the door, and turned her cheek away when he bent to kiss her.

'We're not being sensible,' he said heavily. 'I'll ring tomorrow. Goodnight, Lucinda.' She closed the door behind him even before he descended the steps.

When she still did not return to the party, her mother came in search of her. Lucinda was in her room, sobbing.

'Oh darling,' said her mother. 'I knew you were going to have a row.'

'He didn't even think about me, Mummy. I don't think he cares at all.'

Her mother sat beside her. 'I'm sure that's silly. I'm sure he cares a great deal. But darling — one or two people have been talking to me. You know his brother — his twin brother — is schizophrenic?'

'But Angus isn't ill! You don't think he's ill, do you?'

'No, of course not. But, darling — it might be inherited. Now I wasn't going to say anything, but it has been preying on my mind. I went to the library and read about it and really it is the most terrible disease. Unless you're quite sure about Angus — well, I'd much rather you let him go.'

Lucinda blew her nose furiously. 'That wouldn't happen to us! You're just being silly. You think he doesn't love me and you're finding an excuse.'

Her mother looked at her thoughtfully. 'I don't know. It's your decision, darling. If you feel that you care enough, and Angus cares enough, then that's fine. Otherwise — well, there are an awful lot of nice young men with prospects.'

Her daughter took a long, shuddering breath. Why wasn't he outside now, calling back to apologise and make up? He wouldn't. He was at home, going to bed, putting her on his list of tasks to tackle tomorrow. Whatever romance lay at the core of Angus's soul, she hadn't touched it.

The next day, when Angus telephoned, Lucinda was not at home.

Jay loved the spring, especially in London. It seemed to come earlier there, with potted daffodils sprouting outside every Knightsbridge shop and the close city air popping the buds on the trees in Hyde Park. There were spring exhibitions to look forward to as well, and this year's seemed particularly good.

It was a special year. He had gained a daughter and a son. What's more he felt master in his own home, especially since they had not spent Christmas in Havenheim. Anna's pregnancy had made it difficult to travel, she had stayed at home, enjoying the only family Christmas of their married life.

The birth had pulled her down somewhat. She never shrugged these things off easily, and the arrival of another daughter had been a blow. She had set her heart on a son, she was determined on it! Now that it was a girl everything was turned upside down. They both knew they ought not to try again.

She came down for breakfast one morning, the first time since the birth. Usually she had breakfast in bed, dressed and went to see the children. Although clearly she loved the baby, she wasn't enthralled by it. Jay couldn't help noticing how easily she handed her back to the nurse. It made him think about Mara.

This morning though, Anna sat opposite him across the coffee pot, her hair smoothed into a chignon, pretty and neat.

'Coffee, Jay? Don't read the paper, you've got into bad habits! Talk to me.'

'Sorry.' He put down *The Times* and smiled across at his wife.

'What are you going to do today?'

'I thought I might come with you. Aren't you going to a gallery?'

'Yes – but, darling, are you sure you'll be all right?'

'I shall be fine. And if not, I'll come home.'

So they went to the gallery together. It was strange but not unpleasant to take his wife round. She knew very little, but her comments were intelligent and perceptive. On the way home in the car, Anna said suddenly, 'Did you take her to exhibitions?'

He started. 'Why on earth do you ask that now?'

'I thought you had. The way you looked at me in there. You were thinking of her.'

'Anna, that's absolutely ridiculous. I never took her to an exhibition.'

But he had sent Mara catalogues, and she went alone. They talked afterwards, it was one of the things he most enjoyed. 'There isn't any point in talking about her now, after all this time,' he said irritably.

'I don't know.' Anna pleated her skirt uncertainly. 'I have to go to Havenheim, Jay. My father's upset about another daughter. Everyone's upset. I think I should go to the spring festivals.'

Jay let out his breath in a far from patient sigh. 'I suppose I can just about get away. Shall we take the children or not?'

'I thought I would go by myself. For the first two weeks at least.'

'So I don't clutter up the photographs,' remarked Jay sourly. 'But you'd like to make sure I'm not taking Mara to galleries, I take it.'

'You won't see her, will you? Jay?'

He knew he couldn't lie to her direct. Not any more. They had been through so much, they had come to a new and better understanding. But Mara's baby existed, his son existed. That could never be forgotten. 'I wish you wouldn't doubt me, Anna,' he said softly. 'Not after all this time.'

The lake, and the statues, were assuming the bilious green hue that meant an explosion of algae. This year they would have to pond once again, Henry's expression for an orgy of wallowing in which they cleared the banks of the lake of weed. On a hot day in summer everyone who could move donned a bathing costume, took up one of the bamboo booms and waded about in the water dragging curtains of weed to the shore. Perhaps the guests could do it, thought Lisa. They seemed to like anything that smacked of ancestral rites.

She wandered back through the hall, stopping to see what the post had brought. Bills for her, a few uninteresting letters, yet another turndown for a loan. Nothing from Toby. Even when he did communicate, nowadays he commanded some scribe to do it: 'Mr

Ledbetter has asked me to inform you – has requested that you undertake – would like it to be understood – '. And that suited her fine.

There was one letter for Mara, obviously an invitation. Without the slightest hesitation Lisa ripped open the envelope and took it out. Heavy, gold engraved card. 'Lady Birkett requests the pleasure of the company of Lady Mara Hellyn at a Charity Spring Ball, on Saturday, 25th April. RSVP.'

Lisa tossed the card down. It was from Clare Payne, in her new married name, and surely, if she could invite Mara, she could invite the younger sister as well? What had happened to her girlhood? What had happened to being young? Some days Lisa felt old as the hills, bowed down with the weight of need and responsibility. But on a day like today, when the sun shone and the crocuses stood like little spears on every lawn, she would give anything to go to a party.

She took the invitation up to Mara. 'Look, Clare's invited you to a ball.'

'Has she? Oh, dear Clare! She obviously thinks I've been in purdah long enough. I wonder if Samuel knows she's asked me? I'll have to ring her.'

'I wondered – Mara, do you think she'd invite me too?'

Mara glanced up at her. 'I'll ask her if you like. Are you sure you want to go? You always hate big parties.'

'I haven't been to one. Not since I properly grew up, anyway.'

'And when was that?' Mara lay back on the bed, grinning, but Lisa only made a face. 'I think it was Rio, actually. Toby was a very grown-up experience.'

'At least you didn't end up pregnant or broken-hearted. I got both.'

'No. Of course I didn't. Go on, Mara, please ask if I can go.'

Mara thought about it. If Lisa went, could she still manage to see Jay? It might in fact be easier, because Clare would watch her like a hawk and Lisa might prove a distraction. Since the christening he had written twice, short notes about prospective schools. He wanted Eton, but she was stalling. Let him come and talk to her, and then she would agree. She would tell him she was in London, no more than that. She might stay on an extra day or two and do some shopping.

Clare sent Lisa an invitation at once, together with a short note of apology. 'I hadn't thought you'd be able to get away, my dear. We shall love to see you and make it a happy time. Do let me know if you'd like anything made, it is going to be rather grand I fear. Samuel insists!'

398

Lisa wrinkled up her nose. Clare was casting her as a country cousin. But what was she going to wear?

She went up to her room and stood gazing at the row of clothes she wore for dinner with the guests. Familiar. Uninteresting. Not at all the sort of thing to make her feel good. Pride forbade that she appeal to Clare for help. She would not be treated like a deprived relative who had missed her season, was too old for frivolity but must be allowed to watch the beautiful people from time to time. What would they say if they knew she was a famous designer? she thought. She was one, in Rio.

It occurred to her that she might find something in her mother's wardrobe. Charlotte had worn many beautiful dresses over the years and they all still hung there, reminders of her youth. Lisa flung open the heavy oak doors and surveyed the clothes. In the last years her mother had worn limp silks and sensible wool, there was nothing there that would do. Lisa went back in time, sorting through suits and forgotten blouses, tea-dresses and afternoon skirts until she came to the very oldest things of all. They were small, smaller than anything else in the cupboard. Surely her mother had never been so thin? There was one long dress, made up entirely of sequinned beads. When Lisa held it the material swung, heavy in her hands. There was a sequinned cap to match, with beads hanging in clusters all around. Purple and silver and dark, shot green. The dress was quite beautiful.

It was too long of course, and a little too wide, but the dressmaker in the village could see to it. In this dress, thought Lisa, she would be stunning.

The ball filled her thoughts. In the long, busy days, crammed with a hundred different decisions, she kept it as a backdrop in her head. Doing flowers, counting spoons, in the endless marches down corridors from one area of activity to the next, she took up the ball and wove a story around it. 'Who is that elegant creature?' people would say. 'Just as striking as her sister, in her own way.'

Sometimes she wondered why she was going. She felt guilty, too, because none of the family would be at The Court to entertain the guests. It was only for one night, she told herself. Curtiss could manage. Besides, Toby hadn't the right to expect constant, unremitting devotion to duty. It was what they all expected, Mara, Angus, everyone.

Chapter Forty-One

One morning Mara came rushing into Lisa's room. 'Lisa! I've thought of something dreadful.'

Her sister struggled up in bed. The sun was pouring in through the curtains, so she must have overslept. 'What? What's the matter? I'll get up at once.'

Mara flopped down on to the bed. 'No, you don't have to. Place is quiet as anything, one or two people have gone out for walks, that's all. Curtiss has breakfast in hand and the kitchen is full of eager girls peeling things. But I've thought of something!'

Lisa lay back and closed her eyes. 'Is this thought going to change the world, I ask? Are we going to have peace and plenty throughout the land?'

'I very much doubt it. Lisa, if you come to the party there isn't going to be anyone to look after Drew!'

Lisa's eyes flew open. 'I thought you'd take him with you.'

'And then who'll take care of him? Clare doesn't have endless maids, and Samuel's bound to hate having him in the house. Are you sure you want to go? Why not ask Clare to invite you to something else? We can take it in turns.'

'But I want to go! I'm looking forward to it! No, damn it, you'd better find someone to take care of him or stay at home. He isn't my baby.'

Mara glared at her, put her elbows on her knees and rested her chin on her fists. She was wearing a cream linen shirt and tight jeans, and as always managed to seem as if her clothes had been flung on casually and just happened to look magnificent. 'Can you get nurses for just a few days?' she asked.

'I thought you were only going for one night.'

'I thought I might stay. Do some shopping, and so on.'

'Oh yes?' Lisa gave her sister a very old-fashioned look. 'Well, I suggest you find someone who's prepared to come and be a proper nanny. Because it isn't fair to dump him on just anyone and you shouldn't do it.'

'Dump him! I wouldn't. I won't. He'll be fine for a couple of days. You're just trying to make me feel guilty, Lisa, and I won't have it.'

She got up and went downstairs. Drew was in the kitchen, sitting in the sunshine in his chair, being petted by the staff. 'Who's a lovely baby, then,' cooed Mrs Rogers, the cook. 'Who's the cleverest little boy that ever was?'

'Goo,' said Drew, and everyone gasped. 'Knows his own name,' declared Mrs Rogers. 'A kiddie that age, knowing his own name.'

'He's a genius,' said Mara, sweeping through the door. 'Listen, everyone – I've got to go to London for two or three nights. I need someone to look after Drew, do you know anyone? Some young girl perhaps? Someone who could come and stay?'

'You mean a nanny.' Mrs Rogers' brows began to beetle. You couldn't approve of treating a little kiddie like that, it wasn't right.

'Not a nanny. Of course not a nanny. Just someone for a couple of nights.'

The two kitchen girls gathered round. Somebody's niece perhaps, somebody's sister – except she was away and wouldn't be back until June, and she hated kids anyway. 'Just someone who can see to him,' wheedled Mara. 'After all, you'll all be here. He knows you. I wouldn't leave him just with a stranger.'

Mrs Rogers said, 'Yes, we'll take care of him. Little love that he is. A nice girl to wheel him about and that, that's all he needs. Little love.' She put her face down to the child and beamed at him. Drew clapped his hands.

But the nice girl was hard to find. Mara knew she should have thought earlier. She could have advertised, anything. She went into the village to put a card in the Post Office window. Jean Maythorpe was buying some stamps.

'Hello,' said Mara cheerily. 'Got the ring yet?'

'What ring?' Jean was cold as ice.

'Oh dear, he can't have asked you! But Toby's the sort that you can never pin down, I'm afraid. Don't worry, I'm sure he'll come up to scratch.'

If there was any scratching to be done, Jean wouldn't have minded having a go at Mara. But the Post Office was no place for a row, nor even a disagreement. Two old age pensioners were avidly studying birthday cards so that they could stay and listen, and even the post mistress had lifted up her anti-bandit screen. Gossip was worth getting assaulted for, especially when it involved the Hellyns.

'I hear the hotel's going to close,' said Jean.

'Now, how did you hear that? Oh, of course, pillow talk. I quite forget you're in Toby's confidence.'

'As a matter of fact, I heard it out hunting. Is it true? What's going to happen to the place?'

Mara shrugged. 'Some scheme to open it to the public. We'll have to see how it goes. If it's too awful, we'll all move out. Angus thinks it might be less intrusive than the hotel actually. At least we can have the place to ourselves in the evenings.'

'You'll be able to freeze to death again. Just like before,' said Jean with satisfaction. 'But I must be off. You've got your social security to pick up, haven't you?'

The door closed behind her. Mara looked round at her audience. 'I think something I said must have upset her. Can I put this postcard in the window, please, Mrs Higgins? I've got to go to London overnight and I need a nice kind girl to look after Drew.'

The postmistress bustled round to take the card, while the pensioners shuffled to the door. Who would have thought it? Lady Mara on social security!

The encounter put Mara in a thoroughly bad temper. Nothing short of publishing her bank statement would convince anyone that she wasn't being supported by the state. In fact, Jay was remarkably generous. Since the christening he was actually giving her more. She had telephoned Clare and asked her to buy her a new dress for the party, something rich and glamorous. She felt her mood soften. All the knots and tangles in her life were gradually working loose. Soon, soon she would be happy.

The doctor's car was at the door when she arrived back at The Court. She felt a stab of fear and rushed into the house. 'Curtiss! Why's the doctor here? Is it Drew?'

'I understand he came to see your sister, my lady.'

'Oh. Oh, I see.' That man never stopped mooning after Lisa, and she was never firm enough to get rid of him. Mara debated whether she ought to interrupt. Probably so, if not he would stay so long they would have to offer him a drink.

Lisa was standing by the window, her back to the room. The doctor was before the fire, his hands clasped behind his back. 'Goodness me. You look very serious,' said Mara. 'Have I interrupted an intimate moment?'

Her sister turned, almost blindly. 'Mara — something's happened. I don't know what we're going to do.'

'What do you mean? Is it — Lisa, who is it? Tell me!'

The doctor said, 'There's no emergency, Lady Mara. It's the hospital. It's being closed.'

Mara let out a crack of laughter. 'Is that all? Good Lord, I thought someone was dying. I know they're closing the hospital, it's been on the cards for at least twenty years. No-one's ever going to do anything.'

'Well, they are now,' muttered Lisa. 'The buzz word is care in the community. And in Marcus's case, that means us.'

The sisters looked at one another. Irrationally, Mara thought she should have stayed bad-tempered, there was no point in recovering if a day was determined to turn out like this. 'We'll have to write to them,' she snapped. 'They can't discharge someone in Marcus's condition, he needs hospital care. He isn't acute all the time, but we never know when he will be.'

'They're setting up teams of mental health professionals,' said the doctor. 'You won't be unsupported.'

Mara shot him a glance of undisguised contempt. 'Don't mouth platitudes,' she said. 'It isn't support we need, it's somewhere safe to send him. We can't look after him here.'

'I can't look after him here,' said Lisa flatly.

Into the silence the doctor said, 'They'll be sending him at the end of the week. It's a phased closure.'

'Then we'll come at the end of the phase, please,' said Mara. 'We've got to have time to find somewhere else for him. He can't come here.'

'I promised Toby he wouldn't come while the guests were here.' Lisa went across to the doctor, taking his hand in both her own. 'We can't. You do see that, don't you? Stephen, you must.'

She was upsetting him. He would have given a lot to be able to make it right. 'My dear Lisa — if there was anything I could do I would. But you have to consider priorities. You'll find it difficult, no more than that. But there are many people far worse off, without the space or the facilities or the money. Now, if you want to provide for your brother in an institution, I suggest you look for somewhere private.'

When he had gone, the two girls sat and stared hopelessly at the walls. 'Not again,' said Lisa. 'Every time he comes home he's worse. It's the house, he doesn't do well here. The ghosts get at him.'

'Don't you start!' Mara got up and folded her arms around herself, rubbing as if she was cold. 'I wonder if Jay would pay for him. These places cost a fortune, an absolute mint.'

'You couldn't ask him. It wouldn't be right.'

'And he wouldn't pay. Well, who else then? Toby?'

Lisa avoided her eye. 'I don't think he'd pay a single penny piece.'

Mara watched her for a second. Then she said, 'I think you read

Toby wrong, you know. He'd give you anything you asked for. It wouldn't take so much, if you were nice to him — '

'What do you mean?'

'Don't be naive, Lisa! You went with him to Rio. You had a marvellous time.'

Lisa's face flamed. She stared at Mara as if she were a snake, beautiful, glossy, but a snake nonetheless. 'You want me to prostitute myself,' she said softly. 'Give him a good time and then get paid. He's not our sort of person, he's not our class, but he's rich enough for us to ignore all that. Until he's paid up, of course.'

'I didn't mean anything so vulgar,' said Mara patiently. 'You know I didn't. Lisa, the man loves you, he'd give you the money if you just asked. He can afford it. Tell him it's for the good of the hotel.'

Lisa shook her head, hard. 'If he ever did love me he's got over it. He's with Jean. They're very well suited.'

Mara flung herself back on the sofa. 'I wonder if they think so. Lisa, surely you could ask him. It wouldn't matter.'

'For the last time — no!'

It was always the same, thought Lisa. Marcus came home well, buoyed up by his escape from hospital. As a mark of freedom they took away his shapeless, much-washed cardigan and gave him a jacket, but after the first few hours he looked much the same. He stooped and shuffled, he looked at you sideways out of lowered eyes. Even the most unobservant of guests must realise there was something very wrong with him.

She abandoned all attempts at including him in the life of the house. Perhaps the hospital routine suited him, she decided. So she copied it. She locked his bedroom door at night, feeling like a gaoler, and unlocked it again in the morning when she took him his breakfast. All other meals were to be taken in the kitchen, and on Tuesdays and Thursdays a mental health worker came to take him to an afternoon club.

It really wasn't so difficult, she decided, rolling her head around to relieve her tension headache. Somehow she couldn't think without her headache banging away like a man with a hammer inside her skull. How was she to balance everything? The guests were never quiet. If someone hadn't broken their dentures they were allergic to fish, or wanted her to arrange an archaeological excursion to the earthworks high on the moors. A tribe of ancient Britons had lived in splendid isolation up there, far above the damp and wooded valleys, and people still seemed attracted to the site, however cold or windy it might be. If only they would let her alone for a moment she felt sure she would be able to work things out; the new role for the house; Marcus; Toby's money.

But she was determined to go to Clare's ball. Pangs of guilt kept stabbing her, because she was leaving everything in the lurch to go on a jaunt, but if anyone should stay it should be Mara! Although she was certain to go. Even if it did mean leaving Drew in the care of the cook and a gormless sixteen-year-old from the village, a girl too shy to speak. But she had looked after youngsters, her mother assured Mara, giving the girl a dig in the ribs to make her stand up straight; she was honest as the day is long, was their Tracey.

'At least you know she won't steal him,' said Lisa ironically.

'She'll be wonderful,' retorted Mara. 'Drew took to her at once. She's a find.'

'No-one else thought so,' said Lisa. 'I bet she couldn't even get a job on the supermarket checkout.'

'You couldn't either. They only take people with A level maths nowadays.'

A levels. What a long time ago that seemed. When she was going to pass for Oxford and get a brilliant degree, and her father would say, 'Good heavens, Lisa! I never imagined I'd have such a clever daughter. Well done, darling.'

A stupid reason for ambition, and she had had no other. So, at long last, and with adult reason, she knew it didn't matter. She grinned at her sister with real affection. 'Come on. If we're going at all we'd better pack.'

At the last moment, leaving Drew, Mara was tearful. Mrs Rogers was holding him, making his pudgy arm wave goodbye. 'You will look after him, won't you?' sniffed Mara. 'You'll 'phone at once if he's ill?'

'He won't be ill, Lady Mara,' said the cook determinedly. 'The girl's all right. Bit shy, that's all. We'll look after him.'

'Yes. Yes, I know you will.' Mara put her face against her baby's hair, breathing in his warmth. But it was for him she was going, really. Or at least for both of them. They needed Jay.

'Come on, Mara, do!' Lisa was waiting. Without a word Mara turned and ran to the car.

'Oh, Clare! I should have known you'd excel yourself!' Mara spread the mounds of tissue, and took out her dress. 'Oh, Clare!' she said again. It was pale, palest blue taffeta, like clear water, in the style that Mara suited so well; nipped at the waist, wide at the hem, and an off the shoulder bodice that displayed her magnificent bosom.

405

'I used your old measurements,' said Clare. 'I hope you're still the same.'

'A bit more in the bust, if anything,' said Mara. 'I'll have to be careful I don't fall out. What are you going to wear, Lisa? She's been horribly secretive.'

'I'll show you.' She opened her case and took out the beaded gown, holding the head-dress over one hand. Against Mara's taffeta it looked dark and sombre. The sequins glittered like scales on the skin of a fish.

'Good Lord!' said Mara. 'How incredibly sophisticated.'

'Yes.' Clare looked a little odd, thought Lisa, and spun the cap round on her hand so that the beads flew out. She hardly cared what the others thought. She loved the dress, she loved its dark and dangerous appeal.

'It was your mother's, wasn't it, dear?' said Clare tightly. 'I remember her wearing it. The night she met your father. She never wore anything like it again.'

Except in Monte Carlo, she thought. That terrible time when she and Henry had − well, they'd slept together. Charlotte dressed up her pregnant self in the most ridiculous things, trying to get back to that night. This dress. It made her uncomfortable.

Samuel appeared halfway through the afternoon. He glowered at Mara. Lisa had never met him, but to her own amazement she charmed him. She talked about farming and the hunt, neither subjects of particular interest to her. It was the guests, she realised. Exposed every day to people she didn't know and things she didn't understand, she had developed an automatic facility in conversation. Who would have thought it?

'What a lovely little girl,' said Samuel to Clare, later. 'A pity her sister can't be as sweet.'

'Hmm.' Clare had her favourite and wouldn't give her up. 'She's grown up very well, I must admit. And she's not all that young. Her size makes her seem about sixteen.'

'She'll be a hit,' said Samuel. 'Mark my words, she may not be pretty but she's got something the boys'll like.'

'And you would know, wouldn't you, darling?' Clare, seated at the dressing table, glanced at him in the mirror. He was unfastening his tie, with a certain distinctive briskness. She untied her silk robe and dropped it to her waist.

'Clare! Well, well, well! Clare!'

It was for this she dieted and creamed; so that an old man could put his moustached face against her skin and groan with pleasure. How odd to get to this age and only now discover she enjoyed it.

* * *

406

Clare was one of a committee of ladies organising the ball, each calling on their own circle of acquaintance for guests. There was to be a charity auction during the evening, not to mention a collection that bordered on mugging. To compensate, the ballroom was decked out in flowers and greenery, candles stood in iron sconces eight feet high and beyond the French doors were gardens soft with spring scents and summer promise.

Sartorially it was the event of the season. An actress who feared she was falling out of favour appeared with her breasts bare except for a veil of light gauze, her hair streaked black and silver and a smug escort in a dinner jacket who was the much-married chairman of a huge company group. The debs managed their usual mishmash of styles; they went over the top as punks, retreated into Norman Hartnell dresses that aged them twenty years or crammed their school suet pudding frames into tight skirts and tighter tops. Only occasionally did anyone achieve elegance. A society magazine burbled:

Lady Birkett's entrance, accompanied by Lady Mara Hellyn and her younger sister Lady Eloise (know to her friends as Lisa) proved the high point of the evening. Lady Birkett has long been known for her adherence to Chanel, and never has she looked better, in black silk adorned with jet. Lady Mara, whose lifestyle has shocked even the jaded sensibilities of English society, was radiant in powder blue taffeta. As one of the great beauties of our age, her style is entirely her own, and her reappearance on the London scene is welcomed by all those who enjoy colour, charm and grace. Lady Lisa, younger by some two years, could not have provided more contrast. Delicate as a bird, in an antique dress adapted for her elfin figure, she is at once a delightful original.

The photograph showed all three, Clare and Mara smiling, Lisa gazing about in wide-eyed wonder, the beads of her head-dress making her look almost Egyptian. It was the single moment of unity in the entire evening.

'Oh, look!' said Mara. 'There's Jimmy Carruthers. Come along, Lisa, I'll introduce you to him.'

'Mara dear – ' Clare caught her elbow. 'Samuel's coming a little later. Do please remember – ' she tailed off, hopefully.

'I do promise to behave.'

Mara was gone with a flashing smile and a swish of taffeta, Lisa trotting in her wake. The older woman watched them go. Surely Mara was sensible nowadays? No more drugs, no more casual sex? And please God no more internationally embarrassing affairs. The best that could be hoped for now was a suitable romance, into which Drew could be introduced at the latest possible stage. With any luck history would blur the facts until it was assumed that Drew was the product of an early failed marriage, before Mara made her dynastic alliance. A girl with her looks and breeding should make a brilliant match. But Clare would settle for a minor European count or even a rich businessman. Anything to establish her in life.

She watched her talking to Jimmy Carruthers. The boy was dazzled, of course. But his family wouldn't stand for Mara, and no amount of persuasion would change that. Still, for the moment Mara was safe. Clare turned away, looking for Samuel.

'Thing's haven't been the same since you dropped out,' Jimmy was saying.

'You are sweet, Jimmy! Lisa, Jimmy's been my greatest friend for ever so long. Kind as anything.'

'But she never would marry me,' said Jimmy with mock dismay. 'Look, why don't we dance? There's a friend of mine wandering about, absolutely lost, I'll get him to dance with you Lisa.'

'No, you two go ahead.' Mara was already drifting away. 'I've got so many people to see.'

She was lost to them in the crowd, an occasional glimpse of pale blue taffeta. Jimmy stood watching her go. 'I never knew anyone like Mara,' he said wistfully.

'No. It must be very odd having everyone fall in love with you.'

He laughed and looked down at her. 'I don't think anyone ever fell in love with me. What about you?'

It was a strange question and Lisa considered. 'I don't know. Yes, I think so. For a little time.'

'It's you Hellyn girls, all so fascinating. Come on, shall we dance?'

Lisa was an excellent dancer. With her, men who had never felt that they could do more than stagger round the floor suddenly discovered that they could fly. All she did was follow, like a feather on the wind, and at the end of a waltz and a quickstep Jimmy was getting ambitious. 'Shall we try a foxtrot? I could dance with you forever!'

'I think you must be very good,' said Lisa tactfully.

They were almost the youngest couple to attempt the dance. Whirling and twirling between grim colonels advancing steadfastly to their objectives, Lisa's little feet barely brushed the floor, her dress marking the line of thigh and heel in a beautiful swept arc.

'What a charming little girl,' said the matrons, watching her.

'If only she wasn't a Hellyn,' said Jimmy's mother. 'They are the most unstable family.'

'But fertile,' said her husband. 'Isn't she one of four?'

'One of them's mad and another's that terrible creature Mara. Why can't he get interested in the Bellbrooke girl?'

Mara herself was having trouble getting away. At a gathering like this, a sort of junction where the lines of social congress crossed and intertwined, she was a celebrity. Actors, television moguls, businessmen and rock stars all wanted to know her. If a man has arrived, reached the top in whatever field he chooses, he needs a woman to match him, an escort of class. Mara was everyone's ideal, beautiful, notorious, her sex appeal hanging round her like concentrated scent. She found herself pushed into corners by men drunk enough to try and touch her breasts, and a rock musician, wrecked by heroin and prosperity, lifted her hair and kissed the back of her neck.

She pushed her way out into the corridor. She almost felt frightened. It was as if she was suddenly public property, as if she had no defence against men. Why wasn't she protected? she thought wildly. Jay should protect her. He was all she wanted, not people she didn't know, pawing her, whispering obscenities. She had forgotten about parties like this. In the safety of The Court she felt calm and in control, it was a haven on the edge of a stormy sea. Her thoughts turned to Drew, as she had seen him that morning, happy and loved. She wished, suddenly, that she was with him, that she was home, safe and secure.

She glanced at the clock and saw that it was time to go. Her only hope was that no-one saw her, or at least no-one who mattered. A minicab stood at the side entrance, right on time. She went down the steps in a rustle of taffeta. 'Chelsea, please. Quickly.'

'Do you like this stuff?' asked Jimmy, spooning up sorbet disdainfully.

'Yes, I do rather.'

'Makes my teeth ache. I say, how do you manage at home? Mara told me that you were running the old place as an hotel. Bit bloody bloody, isn't it? You should have elephants or something.'

Lisa licked her spoon. 'Most of the estate's been sold. But we are going to open properly next year. We have to, for the repair grants. And I'm going away. Or at least I might be. I thought I'd try and find work as a designer.'

Jimmy sank his teeth into a chicken leg. 'You're just the sort of girl who'd be good at things like that. Doing out people's homes and things.'

'Actually, I've only done a night club. But it's my brother. They've closed his mental hospital and he's had to come home. Someone's got to look after him.'

409

'Can't Angus, or Mara, or someone? If you've got this job.'

'Angus is busy. And you can't rely on Mara, you know.'

'No. I don't suppose you can.' He looked down at Lisa with an almost fierce intensity. She gave him a cautious smile. For some reason she did not understand he appeared to have taken her under his wing, and it looked as if she would be stuck with him for the entire party. He was nice enough of course. But in her dreams, in her imaginings, she had forseen conquest, not one nice young man all night. Good manners prevailed. When he asked her to dance once again she accepted with all the appearance of delight.

Mara stood in the sitting-room of the mews cottage, her dress spreading across the carpet. Nothing had changed. Perhaps the chairs were a little worn, and the ornaments on the window sill needed dusting. But then, in the old days Jay's visits had been expected. Tonight's was very much last minute.

Suppose he didn't come? Her heart beat against the boned bodice of her dress in quixotic rhythm. Her armpits felt clammy, if he didn't come soon she would have to go and wash. But just then a car turned into the mews, driving slowly over the cobbles. She stood at the window, watching, and then as the driver got out, she drew the curtains.

The little room seemed very crowded. 'The house seems to have shrunk,' commented Mara. 'We didn't seem to fill it up quite as much before.'

'Perhaps it's your dress.' He stood apart from her. They hadn't touched at all.

'Yes. Perhaps it is.'

She sank into an armchair, the taffeta overflowing on all sides.

'Drew's very well,' she said.

'I'm so glad.'

'And I've thought about schools. I don't want him embarrassed. I want you to make up something. Or you could be discreet, couldn't you, about his illegitimacy? Let them know he's yours? That would help.'

'Don't deceive yourself, Mara. That's never going to happen.'

She watched him watching her. He had come here to make love to her, even if he didn't admit it to himself. She was willing, more than willing, but if she made the approach would she disgust him? His hands were so long and slender. She reached out and took one, holding it against her cheek. He didn't draw away. She turned her head, took his middle finger into her mouth and sucked it.

Suddenly she closed her teeth. He let out a strangled cry and pulled

410

away. 'That's revenge' whispered Mara. 'For what you did to me.'

'You were the one that ruined it.'

'And I'm the one left alone. I haven't had a man since you. I need someone, I can't live my life alone. I know it's over, I don't want anything more. Just some love.'

'You really are the most incredible woman.'

He took off his jacket and tie, kicked off his shoes and pulled off his trousers.

'Unzip me,' said Mara, turning her back. He did it, matter of fact, as if she was a servant, unloved. She held her breasts up, holding them in her hands; she went up close to him and let them fall against his shirt. His hands closed on her and she cried out, the marks of his fingers would be there for days. A few drops of milk dribbled from her nipples, Drew's night feed, that he still liked to enjoy. Quite suddenly her mind constructed a fantasy, of Drew upstairs asleep, and she and Jay, the parents, together in wedded bliss. It was so clear, so enticing, that she gasped, hanging against him with parted lips and half-closed eyes. If only, if only it could be true! If only Jay would see how right it was. She hung against him, quite still. Abruptly he let her go. She stood in amazement, watching him take out a condom.

'I've taken care of that,' she said, although it wasn't true. She was taking no precautions at all. 'I won't get pregnant.'

'If you do, it won't be mine,' he retorted. 'You needn't look so indignant. I don't blame you for trying again, but you won't catch me twice.'

'I don't want to. I just want to make you happy.'

She half sat in the chair, spreading her legs. God, it felt odd, this smooth plastic thing going into her. And a man, this man, the only man in the world for her, coming down on her naked flesh. Abandon came on her suddenly. She writhed underneath him, clawing at his back under the shirt, bracing her feet against the floor to push herself up, demanding satisfaction. He gave it to her. He was grinning, knowning she would do anything for this, that she loved and would always love, and he could take her when he wanted.

Her orgasm was fierce, followed almost immediately by another, and still one last, throbbing convulsion. Finally he allowed himself to come. He was calm, a little breathless. Mara was almost destroyed.

'Why don't we sit this one out?' said Jimmy.

'Acutally I think I should find Clare.' Lisa stretched her neck to look round plants and pillars.

'You'll never find her in this crush. Not bored with me, are you?'

'No. No, not at all.' She placated him with a smile. It wasn't that

411

she was bored, simply frustrated. In the distance now and then she saw girls she had been at school with, and interesting people looking at her. She had so few chances to go out, and with Jimmy at her side she was chaperoned and helpless.

He found her a glass of champagne and led her away from the noise and bustle. A wide flight of stairs led upwards, and Jimmy said, 'If we go up here we can sit on one of the balconies. Cool off a bit.'

Lisa wondered if he thought her an innocent. What was he going to do, try and seduce her on a balcony?

But as he said, it was pleasant and cool. Down below in the gardens people talked and laughed, fairy lights casting an eerie glow on their faces. For the first time that evening Jimmy was silent. They sat together, sipping champagne, a little tired and sleepy. Once the excitement faded the body cried out for rest, thought Lisa. She turned her head away from an errant moth, and the beads on her head-dress rattled against her cheek.

'You're beautiful,' he said.

She smiled at him. 'No I'm not. But thank you anyway.'

'I meant it. I know this sounds a bit silly, but it seems to me Mara's all earth and you're all spirit. She's like a really good harvest, everything in abundance − and you're like air.'

'Why are you saying this to me?'

He tried to laugh. 'I'm a bit of a plonker, you know. Knocked around a bit, had some laughs. Took drugs for a while, nothing serious but it worried my people a lot. At one time I thought Mara and I − but she doesn't want me. And I could never handle her, never in a million years. I've got to settle down sooner or later. I know this is an odd thing to do when we've only just met, but really I do mean it. Will you marry me, Lisa?'

The realisation of what he was going to say had hit her a scant second before. If she could have stopped him she would have done, and now that it was said she would have given anything to be able to say yes. He was kind and rather desperate, a man longing to be married, adult and a father. He was not longing for her.

'I wish I could,' she said at last.

'Then why not? We'd be very happy, you know. I'd find somewhere for your brother and you could have a little shop in town where you could do your design thing. We'd have people to stay at weekends, and we could ski − really it would be most awfully good.'

'That isn't what I want. Oh, Jimmy, I am so sorry but it's all a bit too neat somehow. I think I'll muddle along on my own for a little longer.'

Jimmy rubbed his nose. 'Oh dear. Don't mind if I ask you again, do you? Because I do think we'd suit each other.'

They went down again to the ballroom, Jimmy holding her hand on the stairs. Suddenly Clare appeared out of the throng and swept her away.

'Lisa dear, where have you been? Has that Carruthers creature been making a nuisance of himself?'

'Not really. He proposed.'

Clare stared at her for a moment. 'Good heavens. Well, Samuel did say you'd be a hit. My dear, have you seen Mara?'

'I think I saw her in the garden,' lied Lisa.

'Thank goodness! Now, let me introduce you to someone — oh dear, here he is again. You're not engaged are you, dear? You didn't say yes?'

Lisa shook her head.

'I needed you so much,' she said weakly, watching him get dressed.

He glanced at her. 'I know you did. It's all right, my wife's away at the moment. Can you be here tomorrow afternoon?'

She nodded. 'Anything. Please love me a little, Jay. Don't be cruel and cold.'

'I can't be anything other than what I am.' He turned away, and then turned back, fiercely. 'It's your own fault, Mara. How can I love you when I can't trust you? Trying this way, that way, anyway you can to get into my life.'

'You wanted me there once. It was what you wanted more than anything.'

He stood looking at her, his face quite pale, the expression almost sorrowful. 'I wish you'd grow up' he said quietly. 'We can't always have what we want. We shouldn't have it, quite often. None of us has a right to ride roughshod over others, and sometimes, just sometimes we have to put up with second-best.'

'Not you.' She was starting to cry. 'Everything works out for you. But it's at my expense!'

'Don't you think I want if differently? What wouldn't I give for it to be the way we planned?'

'Not a lot,' whispered Mara. She put her hands to her eyes, willing the tears to stop. Not looking at him, she got up and pulled on her clothes. 'You can drop me at Clare's party.'

'I couldn't. I might be seen.'

'I don't give a damn who sees you! For once you can do something for me and me alone!'

In the car, anger lay between them like an imprisoned cat. He drove to a dark sidestreet, leaving Mara fifty yards to walk. She accepted it. There was no other way.

413

'What time tomorrow?' she asked.

'Not before three. I'm lunching.'

She got out and walked quickly up the street. He sat watching her, the car in gear, but somehow he couldn't drive away and leave her. All at once he let in the clutch and drove fast up beside her and she turned, alarmed, thinking he was about to run her over.

'Mara –'

'What is it? What is it now?'

'Tomorrow. Come at twelve, I'll bring sandwiches and champagne. We'll lunch together.'

She stood away from the car, the blue dress like a cloud around her. There was some quality in her he realised, something that tempted humiliation. It was as if her beauty gave her power, and in the end, eventually, men wanted her humbled. He was fighting against that urge. 'I might not come,' she said.

But he laughed in her face. 'You will.' He let in the clutch and drove away.

In the ballroom she saw Lisa almost at once, dancing with Jimmy Carruthers. The disco was in full swing, and Jimmy's wild moves contrasted oddly with Lisa's restraint. As soon as she saw her sister, Lisa broke away and came over, leaving Jimmy carrying on alone for a few ridiculous seconds.

'Are you all right?'

'Of course. Yes. Never better.' Mara pushed her hair back from her head, feigning good humour. What was happening to her? She felt shaky, as if at any moment she might faint.

Lisa saw a pulse beating in her forehead. 'Let's go home,' she said.

'It's only just gone one. You're having fun, you should stay.'

Jimmy said, 'I'll take you if you want. Unless you want to go on to a club or something.'

Mara shook her head. Suddenly she looked tired and very sad. 'No. No, I've had enough of that.'

Chapter Forty-Two

The night was thick and black, an enveloping blackness in which the woods and the sky became one. It was like being in a shell, but a shell as thick as concrete. The lights in the house went out one by one, the noises were lost in the night. Every now and then came the thin, anxious wail of a baby.

Tracey couldn't settle him. Mrs Rogers could do it, but after tea Curtiss had come with a message and she'd gone off to her brother's for the night. His wife had had a fall and everything was upside down.

'He just needs a feed and a change, you can do that, can't you?' demanded Mrs Rogers. 'Your mother told you all about that, I'm sure.'

'Yes, Mrs Rogers,' said Tracey, timidly.

'I'll be back by ten, at the latest,' said the cook. 'And I don't want young Master Drew still in his night things. A feed and a change tonight, and a feed and a change in the morning. There's a good girl.'

Tracey hadn't been worried. People made a lot of fuss about babies, and there wasn't anything to it, not really. But now, with the house so big and empty, she wasn't so sure. He kept on crying. Her mother had said there were two things a baby needed, one was food and the other a dry nappy, but she'd poured two bottles down him and changed him every five minutes and still he bleated on. She wasn't even sorry for him any more. He was a stupid kid anyway, not to do like he was supposed to. And she was sick of him. She was going to bed, and he could scream as much as he liked.

The baby, bloated with milk and helplessly miserable, drew his knees up to his stomach and howled. Small gobbets of sick lay on the mattress at his head. He rolled his hot cheek in them, crying for his mother. In all his short life he had never cried and not been comforted. He was in pain, frightened and bewildered.

Gradually the impatient howl began to abate. He cried wearily, a

415

hopeless, desolate wail. Tracey turned over and settled herself down. You just had to leave them long enough and they shut up. There was no point in bringing him up spoiled, he'd go to sleep in the end.

The crying went on and on. Marcus listened to it, assessing the rhythm; three, perhaps four seconds between bouts, and then a fresh start, loud at first, tailing away to nothing. Again, the pause, and once more the staccato wails. He began to croon in time to it, a half-forgotten lullaby.

Waaah. Waaah. Waaah. He stopped singing, he couldn't think. On and on it went, like a drill in his brain, like drops of molten iron on his sore, beleaguered head. Waaah. Waaah. Waaah. Why wouldn't it stop? Why – wouldn't – it – stop!'

Marcus got up and went to his bedroom door, expecting to find it locked. At first it resisted, but when he exerted force the handle turned. He grimaced to himself. That was The Court for you, no-one but the family understood the place. Not even Curtiss knew that the locks had to be turned one and a half times round, or you could force them. All the children knew, of course. When she locked him in Lisa automatically gave the key that extra click. Everything was slack without Lisa, he thought irritably. He'd mentioned himself that there was mud on the stairs, but of course no-one did anything.

No-one ever took any notice of him any more. He might as well not be there for all the power he possessed. Why, he couldn't even ask to have his lightbulb changed because they thought it was part of some wild, mad plan. The place was full of fools and idiots, who thought that what they didn't see didn't exist.

That baby – that noise! Waaah. Waaah. Waaah. The corridor was in complete darkness, the windows black holes in black walls. The baby was quite alone, a microbe, flailing about in dark space. Quite dark. So dark that nothing in it could be seen or known about, nothing that was done would ever be understood. He went down the stairs carefully, feeling the banister rail at each step. White marble treads gleamed in the blackness like bones, stinging his feet with cold. Waaah. Waaah. Waaah. There was no-one in the world but him and the baby. They were alone together.

He had to lean far over the cot even to see the child. The wailing was loud in his ears, and there was the sour smell of curdled milk. He put down his hand to touch and the baby screamed in panic, because this was not his mother with her voice and her love, it was a stranger, in the night, come to hurt him! Marcus put his hands around the hot, writhing body, squeezing. It was an odd sensation. He so rarely touched another human being, and they almost never touched him. He repelled them, with his odd, mad stare. But this baby, this small,

416

wriggling thing, couldn't get free of him. Now he could do as he liked.

He picked Drew up and held him inches from his face. The child wriggled, squirmed and belched. A long string of goo trickled down on to Marcus's hand. 'Waaah,' said the baby, as his stomach relaxed. He put out a pudgy hand and gripped the flesh of Marcus's cheek.

What was he to do? The child couldn't be left here, in the dark. It was one thing for him to be left, he understood the dangers, knew when to sit quite, quite still. This baby couldn't know that. He was here, in the dark, at risk. Marcus held him close, put his cheek against the child's hot head, and Drew snuffled thoughtfully. In a harsh world it was as well to take pleasure where it could be found, and if he couldn't have his mother he'd make do with this.

Marcus went to the window, looking out across the park. In the distance the lake reflected the weak glow of a star. He had a sudden longing for air, for freedom, for the sound of the wind, and if he felt like that, who could walk and run and speak, how must this child feel? He held him roughly around the middle. And went out.

Tracey woke up about an hour later, she couldn't settle in an unfamiliar bed. It was very quiet. Thank God the kid had nodded off. But as she lay there she thought about all the things that could happen to kids that age, and what they would do to her if she had let them. Had he died in his cot? They'd say she'd hit him or something. Grimly she got out of bed, reflecting that nobody would believe how hard it was looking after babies, constant activity, hour after hour.

She switched on the light in the next room and plodded over to the cot. For a minute she couldn't believe he wasn't there. She lifted the covers, the mattress, she got down on all fours and looked up at the springs. No baby. Quite definitely no baby. Tracey opened her mouth and screamed.

Curtiss called the police. There seemed to be no alternative, with an infant missing and no-one with any idea of what might have happened. Thoughts of the Lindbergh baby kept intruding. It was quite possible that someone unaware of the family's financial position might think they could extract a ransom. And when they discovered that Lord Melville was missing as well — Curtiss had to have a brandy. He sat in the dining room, his dressing gown pulled close around him, trying to control his shudders.

The policeman said, 'You've no reason to think Lord Melville is violent, I believe?'

'God knows.' Curtiss took another sip, letting the spirit burn his throat. 'He was a lovely child. Clever and kind, the nicest little boy.'

'Is that Lord Melville or the infant?'

'Er — Mr Marcus. That's what we still call him, you see. Don't know what the baby's like. I mean, you don't when they're that age. Lady Mara dotes on him, of course.'

'And he is Lady Mara's son? Her illegitimate son?'

The old man closed his eyes for a brief second. 'Don't really live by the same rules as us, do they?' he said vaguely. 'Don't have to. She could have a dozen and it wouldn't really matter. Upset her mother, of course. Killed her if you ask me.'

'Who killed her?' the policeman was beginning to get confused.

'No-one did, damn it! She had a heart attack. And I really must telephone Lady Eloise, she's bound to sort something out.'

The policeman wandered about in bewilderment. It looked like a snatch, but in such an odd household someone could have left the kid under a table and forgotten it. The butler kept telephoning London, but they were all out partying somewhere. He looked out across the parkland. He was damned if he was wandering about there tonight, with a lunatic on the loose and probably man-traps hidden in the trees. He went out to his car and radioed in. They needed more men, a great many more, to search the house if nothing else. The whole giant operation began to move.

'Would you ring home, please, Lady Eloise? I gather it's urgent.' The front door was still open, Mara still on the step talking to Jimmy.

'What's happened? It's not a fire is it?' Lisa went to the 'phone, her stomach churning with nameless foreboding.

'Not a fire, miss, no.'

She stood in silence, waiting for the machinery to connect. Mara was trying to get rid of Jimmy, who was hoping for a nightcap, and when she succeeded she came in and shut the door. 'Thank God! All I want now is my bed.' She began to walk upstairs, stopping when she realised that Lisa was not with her. 'Lisa? Who are you telephoning at this time of night?'

Lisa said nothing. She was listening with white-faced concentration. At last she said, 'Yes. Yes, I see. Of course. At once.'

'What is it?' Mara's voice held nothing but dread.

Lisa looked up at her as she leaned across the banister, her hair like a golden curtain. Such an amazingly beautiful woman. 'Drew's gone,' said Lisa flatly. 'He's disappeared.'

Mara hung in the air for a long second. Then she crumpled, falling into her dress like a broken clockwork doll.

They called Angus, waking him at his flat. He sounded bewildered and only half aware. 'I'm sure he'll turn up,' he said at one point, and Lisa raged: 'For God's sake Angus! For all we know Marcus could have drowned him in the lake!'

418

Mara heard and went to the bathroom to be sick. She had changed into trousers and sweater and sat, shaking, waiting for Lisa to be ready to go home. She didn't want to go home. If she got there and Drew was still gone – they almost never found them alive!

There was no train until the morning, so Clare's chauffeur drove them in the Rolls, stopping to pick up Angus at his flat. He was unshaven and bad-tempered. 'What in God's name were you doing leaving him in the first place?' he demanded, as almost his first words. 'Who was looking after him? I bet you couldn't even be bothered to get a decent nanny.'

'It was a girl from the village,' muttered Mara. 'She was useless. I didn't admit it, but I knew she was.'

'It was only for one night,' defended Lisa. 'And Mrs Rogers was keeping an eye on things. Besides, I'd have taken over in the morning. There's no point in blaming yourself. These things happen.'

'Not to people with any sense of responsibility,' snapped Angus.

They reached home just after seven, when it was still not quite light. To their amazement in addition to the police cars and dog vans clustered on the gravel by the front door, there was a posse of pressmen. As soon as the Rolls stopped they crowded forward. 'Is it true the child's yours, Lady Mara? Tell us about the father. Can we have his full name – it's bound to help us find him.'

'Don't listen,' muttered Lisa, and Angus put a hand under the elbow of each of his sisters, propelling them into the house.

Nothing had been found. They didn't need to be told, it was written clear on the faces around them. 'Any news of Marcus?' asked Lisa thickly. Nobody said a word.

The police searched the house, squads of them, crawling in the attics and burrowing beneath piles of ancient chairs left abandoned in unused rooms. 'Could hide a dozen kids in here,' said one man, covered in dust and exasperated by the futility of it. 'If you ask me the nutter's taken him in the park.'

Angus thought that too. But he had already been to the folly, and all their childhood dens; the ivy-grown hut, the stable room, the oak tree struck by lightning years ago and still dying by inches. Nothing.

Mara sat in the dining-room, facing another policeman, holding on to her sanity by the merest thread.

'Is there anyone might want to steal the child? His father perhaps? Who is his father, Lady Mara?'

'It's nothing to do with him. I saw him in London, he wasn't anywhere near here.'

'All the same I think we should speak to him, don't you? He's

419

entitled to know his son's gone missing. Might have got someone else to take him, after all.'

She looked at him then, her eyes brimming with unshed tears. Jay cared about Drew, she knew that with certainty. She wouldn't put it past him to steal Drew away, but he would never forgive her if she told this man his name.

Lisa, standing in the doorway said, 'I'll give you his name.'

'Lisa! It isn't any of your business.'

'I don't care. If he has any feeling for you at all he'll come and stand by you. He has to know.'

'You never did like him,' flared Mara. 'You always did think he was a shit.'

'Well, now we'll find out if I'm right.'

Five minutes later the policeman reeled out of the room. He didn't use his radio, it wasn't secure enough. He telephoned, locking himself away in the library. Afterwards he made neat, careful notes, because he was going off duty soon and had to hand over to the big boys. And when he went home, and his wife was clearing up the kitchen after the kids' breakfast, he said, 'Here, you'll never guess what!'

The lunchtime headlines simply read, 'Baby Snatch' and gave the briefest outline of the case. Even that was too much for Angus. He insisted that the police move the newsmen to the end of the drive.

'Everyone automatically thinks it's Marcus,' he muttered. 'They're just jumping to conclusions.'

'Who do you think it is?' asked Lisa wearily.

'I'm saying we don't know! We can't know.'

As the hours ticked by the tension mounted. Mrs Rogers appeared, hysterical with remorse. 'I had to go! I did!' she wailed, wringing her hands.

Mara looked at her wearily. 'I know,' she whispered. 'It isn't your fault. It's mine.' She turned back to the window, and tears began to roll soundlessly down her face. 'How will he be fed?' she kept saying. 'He'll be so hungry.'

Police teams were beating the undergrowth at the outskirts of the wood. She watched them, terrified that someone would find something, find − him. If he was close by he would be dead.

'Does Jay know?' she asked Lisa suddenly.

Her sister nodded. 'The police in London are interviewing him.'

'Is he coming? Did they say that?'

'They haven't told me anything at all.'

Angus was coming across the park, walking quickly but with none of the urgency that would mean he had found something. Mara turned away from the window. If night fell, the cold spring night, and

420

still he was missing, she would know he was dead.

The sound of hooves made Angus turn. A bright chestnut was galloping across the park, the rider flat on its neck, face in a wild mane.

'Jean!' he shouted. 'Jean! Have you found something?'

The horse, hysterical with excitement, fought against the bit. Jean dragged him to a standstill, and Angus saw that her face was scratched, as if she had ridden through thorns. 'The gypsies,' she gasped. 'I've been to see the gypsies.'

'My God! Did they take him?'

She shook her head violently. 'Of course not! Last night — they were out poaching, it was so dark, you see. They saw Marcus, in the dark, and he was carrying something.'

'Where was he going?' Angus could manage no more than a croak.

'To the moor! He was going up to the moor gate, so he could be at the rocks.'

'Or anywhere. He could be anywhere. Quick, I'll get my horse.'

His hunter had gone, replaced by a cob that suited the hotel guests. Almost before the lad had finished tacking him up Angus was in the saddle, urging the startled animal into a canter. Jean's chestnut, his few brains shot to pieces, bucked and corkscrewed before settling to a gallop that left Angus standing. A policeman, standing in the drive, saw them flying across the grass. 'Where the hell do they think they're going?' he said vehemently. 'Sergeant! Find out what's over there!'

The chestnut tired long before they reached the gate to the moor. Angus's cob was bottomless and could go forever at his own slow speed. He bowled along over the rough moorland track, picking up his feet in a heavy trot. Angus didn't know whether to call or keep silent. He couldn't believe — he wouldn't believe that Marcus was capable of killing. There wasn't a violent bone in all his body. But in his mind — who could say what was in his mind? Demons and dragons, certainly. Who was to say there was not also a murderer?

He reined in to wait for Jean but she shouted, 'Go on, do. I'll catch up.' Her horse was plodding along with its head down, like a child that has played itself out. Odd how he hadn't realised he cared at all about Drew until now. But he cared more about Marcus. 'Let him not have done it,' he whispered to himself. 'Anything but that.'

Hell Rocks loomed up ahead, dark and menacing. They looked like that even on the brightest summer day, when fox cubs played in their shelter. If Marcus had left the baby there — didn't he realise there were foxes? But anyone capable of taking a baby, a little baby, and bringing him here was not in the business of rational thought. The cob slowed to pick his way over the rocks. He was a good horse, sane and sensible. Sometimes you bred well and produced this, sometimes the plan went wrong and you ended up with Jean's hot chestnut. Or Marcus. It was all in the genes. And all his life Angus had known this hung over him, the genetic instability, lurking inside. The bad fairy had waved her wand and missed him by a hairsbreadth. And perhaps she hadn't missed him at all.

'Marcus! Marcus!' He had to yell. His voice echoed back and forth amidst the stones. He could hear nothing, nothing but the wind moaning and whispering in the rocky cliffs above his head. 'Marcus! Marcus!' Again the silence. But this time punctuated by the rattle of falling shale, as if a rabbit had run up a slope. He pushed the horse on, over the broken ground, letting him pop a runnel of a stream. The noise of the water filled his head, he rode further on and listened. And heard it. The hopeless, hungry wail of a baby.

He was lying at the bottom of the shale, on his face, as if he had rolled from somewhere higher up. His head was scratched and bleeding, but none of the injuries looked serious. His eyes, blue as cornflowers, gazed miserably at his rescuer. When Angus passed his hand in front of the child's face Drew seized on it and sucked violently.

'You've got him! Oh, thank God.' Jean was on foot, her horse left on the grass of the track.

'I can't see Marcus,' said Angus. 'Look, take my horse and the baby. Get him back home. I'll try and find Marcus.'

'Why don't we both go back? Leave someone else to do it?'

He shook his head. This was his own task, his own duty. He helped Jean on to the cob, and watched her settle the baby in the crook of her arm. She was one hell of a horsewoman, he thought, watching her cope with horse and baby as if she did it every day. But he turned back to the rocks before she had gone out of sight. He began to climb the shale.

The pebbles cut his hands and he clung to roots and the odd whippy branch. Twenty feet up there was a ledge and he stopped there, panting and looking about him. Nothing. Above him the shale bank grew steeper. He didn't think that Marcus could possibly have climbed it. But even as the thought formed a little shower of pebbles clattered their way down and past. He began to climb again.

Marcus was at the very top. Angus only became aware of him in the agonising second in which he hung at the rim, desperate for a helping hand. It almost made him fall. 'Help me,' he gasped, scrabbling for a hold in the thin grass. 'Marcus, help!'

But his brother sat and stared into space.

Angus made it by himself, as Marcus must have done. At what point had he let go of the baby, he wondered? Had he even noticed? He sat down to recover his breath, stretching his bruised and bleeding fingers. The blood on Marcus's hands had dried. He had been here for hours, perhaps since the night. He put his hand on his brother's shoulder.

'Don't you think you should come down, old chap? Come on, time to go.'

To his surprise Marcus turned his head and looked at him. 'The baby,' he said. 'We mustn't forget the baby.'

The police met them even before they reached the moor gate. Six of them, in uniform, burly and determined. 'I think we'd better take over now, sir,' said one.

'Thank you, officer, that isn't necessary. My brother's mentally ill, it's not a police case.'

'I'm sorry, sir. This isn't the sort of incident we can sweep under the carpet. We'll be taking Lord Melville into custody.'

Angus felt his scalp prickle. 'I rather think you won't. He'll come back for a bath and some food and we'll discuss things. He doesn't need to be frogmarched to some police cell!'

'I'm sorry, sir. We really must insist.'

There was an undisguised air of menace. Angus had a sudden wild longing to be back in the days when no man would dare lay hands on a Hellyn, not if he murdered a dozen babies. And surely still they need not suffer the utmost rigour of the law?

'I think there's been a misunderstanding,' he said carefully. 'The baby wasn't missing at all. His uncle took him for a walk and became ill, that's all. You were called in quite unnecessarily.'

The policeman looked at him with sympathy. 'I know it's hard for you, sir. It isn't his fault. But he must come with us.'

Angus went back to fetch Jean's horse, and walked it slowly down off the moor. The tears ran down his face, endless rivers of tears. Sometimes he could barely see the path.

'Angus! Angus, what happened?' It was Jean, on foot, coming through the moor gate. He turned his face away. He couldn't bear her to see him like this, his defences gone, his weaknesses laid bare. She stopped some feet away.

'They took him,' he said. 'The police. He'll end up in Broadmoor, when it only happened because they closed the bloody hospital!'

'How did he − how did he look?'

Angus lifted up his face, his mouth set in a line of harsh anguish. 'How do you think he looked? Like he always does, blank, helpless. But his eyes − my God, he knows I did it to him, he knows they came for him and I didn't lift a finger to help.'

Jean passed a hand over her eyes. 'He oughtn't to be in prison. That isn't the place for him.'

'Do you think I don't know that? Do you really have to make such a bloody stupid remark?'

'Well, why are you standing here crying and not doing something?'

He began to hunt in his pockets for a handkerchief. Jean held out a neat lace square, monogrammed he noticed. He wiped his eyes, covering the fabric with mud. 'I'm sorry,' he said gruffly. 'You're right, I should do something. The first thing is to contact a solicitor.'

'Ours is red hot,' said Jean.

'I suppose you got him from Toby.'

'Toby? No, of course not. Dad's known him for years. As a matter of fact — as a matter of fact, Toby and I have finished. Well, almost. We've kept it going for Dad's sake. Next time he comes back we'll have a public row and be done with it.'

'Not good enough in bed, is that it?' said Angus viciously. 'Got tired of having him stuff you?'

Jean turned away, going a dark red. 'You've forgotten your horse,' he yelled as she went, but she didn't turn round. He stood and watched her, making no move to follow, until she disappeared out of sight, through the gate and into the trees.

Mara sat holding her baby, shaking and sweating. Now that he was safe her mind enacted every possible horror, from slow starvation to sudden, violent death.

'He really must go to hospital,' the doctor was saying. 'You can go with him. He needs a thorough check-up.'

She nodded, putting her hand on the baby's battered head, closing her eyes to shut it out. 'I feel so guilty,' she whispered. 'It was my fault.'

'I don't think any permanent damage has been done.'

She opened her eyes and looked at him scornfully. 'Except they've got Marcus in a police cell. I dread to think what's going to happen.'

She held the baby close. God help him, born to her, when she knew just how stupid and selfish and unreliable she could be! There was no use thinking she would never do this again. If anyone knew her own weaknesses it was she and if the moment was right, if the temptation presented itself, she would forget all this, abandon Drew just as lightly. She began to cry, choking on hopeless self-loathing.

Lisa came in, carrying a suitcase filled with the things Mara and the baby would need in hospital. She put a hand on her sister's golden hair. 'It's all right. Truly it is. They might find somewhere sensible for Marcus now.'

'It isn't that! It's me. Poor darling Drew, I shouldn't have left him, why did I leave him? When I love him so much. I wanted to go to

London and I went, I didn't let anything stop me. Oh, Lisa, why do I do these things? Jay said I was selfish and I am, I am. I couldn't even put Drew first.'

Lisa snorted. 'If you ask me, your precious Jay needs shooting. Selfish, indeed! He's the one that always comes up smiling.'

'You know he's right. It was selfish to have Drew, and selfish to keep him, and an absolute bloody shame to go off and leave him like that! I hate myself. I do, I do, no wonder Jay can't love me, no wonder nobody loves me at all!' She paced up and down the room, clutching the baby tight, almost beside herself. It was as if the tensions of the past hours were exploding out of her in an orgy of recrimination.

'Mara, stop it.' Lisa blocked her path and Mara halted, panting on sobs, the tears running endlessly down her cheeks. 'You're being silly,' said Lisa, deliberately matter of fact.

'Am I? Why don't you hate me too? I wish you would, I deserve it. I deserve to have Drew taken away, I'm not fit to have him. My beautiful, perfect baby and I let this happen. Oh God, Drew, I'm sorry!' She bent her head to his and pressed kisses on to his bruised face.

Lisa's mouth twisted wryly. Even Mara's remorse was exaggerated. 'It isn't that bad. He's escaped disaster so far, perhaps he's got a charmed life. He's certainly got more than his share of luck.'

'With me for a mother? Not to mention a father that won't acknowledge him.' Mara took a deep, shuddering breath. 'I wish Jay was here. Will they let him come?'

Lisa glanced up into her face. It seemed to her that if Jay wanted to do something no power on earth could stop him. But his inclinations were quixotic in the extreme, certainly as far as Mara was concerned. He might come. And he might not.

'It's all a bit public, don't you think?' she said cautiously.

'I don't care how public it is! In the end he's going to have to stand up and admit that Drew's his, so why not now?'

An ambulance came to take mother and child to hospital. Lisa stood at the door, watching pressmen skulking in the undergrowth at the edge of the wood. Pressmen to the front of her, guests to the rear and policemen prowling about suspiciously, as if there were a dozen lunatics hiding in the cupboards. Suddenly she couldn't bear it. She had to be alone, somewhere quiet where nobody could get at her. When her dog was younger she had taken him for walks at times like this, but these days he wasn't fit for much more than a bronchial stroll twenty yards from the garden door. So she put on her mac and went alone.

She began a circuit of the lake. Waterfowl were nesting in the reeds, and a swan had taken up residence on a tiny islet at the far end. The male rose up hissing as she approached, almost as tall as she from the top of his orange feet to his gaping beak. His wings beat the air with a noise of rushing wind and suddenly Lisa felt tears welling up. Always sensible, that was her, always the one to be relied on to cope. Even Jimmy Carruthers had seen that in her. In an instant he had her categorised as a good type for a wife, well-balanced, competent and boring. Nobody really knew what she was like. The dreams she had, of wild irresponsibility, dancing naked in abandonment. And if that wasn't possible, and she had to live with mundane reality, then she at least wanted parties where someone else worried about the food. She was never herself, she thought dismally. It suited everyone to have her docile and competent, and if that was one side of her, it wasn't the whole.

She went without thinking to the front door. And suddenly she was surrounded. Photographers, and men with notebooks, even a video camera goggling at her while the soundman waved a long black microphone under her nose.

'Lady Eloise, can you confirm that Prince John is the father of your sister's baby?'

'Does he support the child?'

'Are they still friends?'

For vital seconds she was rooted to the spot. 'I – er – I – I don't want to say anything,' she managed, and a reporter loomed down at her.

'So you confirm it then? I gather he attended the boy's christening, so he does still see your sister?'

'You can't know that.' Lisa looked about in dazed bewilderment. It was hours since she had slept, her thoughts moved with painful slowness. 'Why don't you go away?' she said shakily. 'You should go away and leave us alone!' She pushed through the crowd and fell into the house. Even then they barged open the door and would have flooded into the hall had Curtiss not rushed forward and beaten them back. He slammed home the great iron bolts.

'Vultures,' he declared. 'Nothing but common vultures.'

'How do they know?' wailed Lisa. 'Did the police let it out?'

Curtiss sniffed. 'Could've been anyone, my lady. There was a lot of talk downstairs, and there isn't the loyalty we used to have. The papers pay money these days.'

Lisa put her hands to her forehead, trying to fight her way through the fog that clogged her brain. Did it matter that people knew? Whatever harm came to Jay or Mara must be offset by the good done to Drew. If he had to be a bastard, he might as well be a royal one, bearing if not a seal of approval at least an acknowledgement. If it brought down

426

Jay's marriage then so be it. The world ought to know that in this instance Prince John had acted like an absolute shit.

But the scandal had to be lived through. From time to time they appealed to the police and the cameras were driven back down the drive, only for random snappers to appear at every window. The guests began to leave, the first being a German businessman who was enjoying some illicit luxury with the wife of a close friend. Even those who were prepared to appear on every front page and many a news bulletin grew tired of the household chaos. Delivery boys were waylaid on their way up the drive, the telephone interrupted Curtiss in the midst of decanting the wine and one sudden booking turned out to be a reporter, summarily thrown out halfway through dinner. At the end of the second day Lisa asked everyone to leave. As far as she was concerned The Court was closed.

That night the atmosphere calmed. The great house seemed almost to sigh, relaxing back into itself, into its age-old torpor. Dress it up as they might, change it as they would, The Court won in the end. Their schemes and projects rose and died, only the house went on.

Lisa sat in the quiet drawing-room, her head thrown back, a glass of port on the table at her side. The silence washed over her, like the softest water, filling her up until even her fingertips tingled. When the telephone jangled into life she winced, it was as if someone had embedded an axe in her brain.

'Yes?' She was cautious. Newsmen used any lie to penetrate The Court's unsophisticated switchboard.

'It's me.' Angus, sounding curt and dictatorial.

'Have you seen Marcus? Any news?'

'I've seen him. He's going to be charged, they seem to think there's some measure of criminal responsibility.'

'But that's stupid! Surely they can see he's ill?'

She heard her brother sigh. 'I wish they could. All I can say is, he may be ill but he doesn't look any iller than the rest of the blokes in there. In the end they'll get psychiatric reports and so on, he won't come to court. But for the moment he stays in prison.'

'Oh.' She took a long, deep breath. 'Does he mind?'

'Yes. Keeps asking after the baby, and that convinces everyone he knew what he was doing. And he's sharing a cell with a violent half-wit. Lisa we've got to get him out.'

'Can you do it? Honestly?'

She heard him catch his breath. 'I don't know. Perhaps I can get him a room to himself. We'll just have to see.'

427

Chapter Forty-Three

Jean stayed well away from The Court. With her horse still stabled there she went out walking, trudging along roads in an effort to dispel some of her white-hot rage. Angus hadn't even so much as telephoned. What did you have to do to impress these Hellyns? What did you have to do to earn a word of thanks? But of course, they didn't thank people, not really, they applied gratitude like a benediction to the heads of the little people in their lives, forgetting entirely that it was more than manners, more than form. The best of Angus was seen by the people that served him, she decided. The rest was irretrievably corrupted, by school, parents, the very culture in which he lived. Whatever real feelings Angus had had were buried so deep she couldn't find them.

Her father was standing in the stable yard when she got back.

'Where've you been, lass?' he asked. 'I've sent t'horsebox to get chestnut back. That damned butler issuing orders over the 'phone.'

'I was only walking.'

'And you wouldn't have to walk if they had the decency to send the horse back.'

'Well. You don't expect decency there, do you?' She dashed away an angry tear. That was Dad for you, always there when you least wanted him. Sometimes his concern was a crushing weight.

'Why don't you come along in and have a cup of tea?'

She nodded, unable to speak. Only when Reg was chomping his way through a custard cream did she feel she could say anything at all.

'I've got in an awful mess, Dad.'

'Aye. Don't need telling that, do I?'

'I don't know what to do.'

The kettle boiled and Reg threw his usual handful of teabags into the pot. His tea was always strong enough to embalm the dead. When

428

the cosy was safely on the pot, he said slowly, 'I haven't done right by you, Jean. Kept you too close at home, when a girl as clever as you shoulda been out, making her way in the world. A girl your age shouldn't think she has to keep her old dad company. Shouldn't have to worry in case he's getting lonely. And now the damage is done.'

'What damage?'

'You. Pinning all your hopes on someone as doesn't deserve them. Getting in a tangle with men you don't like.'

'If you mean Toby, I do like him.'

Reg eyed her thoughtfully. 'Then you don't like him enough. And I don't. He's too tough for you, a bloody sight too tough. I've met his sort in business. They've come up hard, and they live hard, and that isn't your way. Here and there, wheeling and dealing, open this, close that. Look what he's done to the Hellyns. Lambs to the slaughter! If anyone loses on that place, he'll make sure it won't be him.'

'Perhaps I find that sort of person exciting.'

Reg snorted. 'And perhaps you don't! He's a gambler and you're a home body. You always have been. A big house and a dozen kids, that's what you ought to have.'

The idea, so unfashionable, was deliciously seductive. Jean could see it all, the Aga in the kitchen, ponies in the stables, a baby in her arms and a toddler at her knee. And Angus. Definitely Angus. She put her arms round her father and cried.

He patted her shoulder with determination. 'So you'll get rid of Toby then. Write him a good strong letter, tonight.'

'He doesn't need getting rid of,' wept Jean. 'It never was meant to be anything much, but it all got out of hand. He doesn't want me and I don't want him.'

Reg asked plaintively, 'What do you want, lass?'

But it was something Jean knew she couldn't have.

After only two days the hospital sent Mara and Drew home. Hordes of pressmen clogged the corridors and entrances, repelled by police who couldn't possibly muster in sufficient numbers to stem the tide. 'Even the nurses kept popping in to have a look,' said Mara glumly. She had been brought back in a police car, and the photographers had risked life and limb to get shots of her.

Angus said angrily, 'I suppose you realise this is the end of my political chances? There are only so many scandals I can weather, and this is one too many.'

'I'm sorry,' said Mara grimly. 'I can assure you it wasn't intentional. I've hurt you all – and I'm sorry.'

'My God! An apology. It certainly is a red letter day.'

Lisa got up and went to the window. The sun glinted on a dozen cameras, inadequately hidden in the bushes. 'We're surrounded,' she said. 'When do you think they'll storm the house?'

Shuddering, Mara said, 'Don't! It's like one of Marcus's nightmares, suddenly come true. Perhaps he isn't bonkers at all, he's a prophet. Has anyone been to see him?'

Angus nodded, but said nothing. Thanks to his insistence his brother was alone in a locked room, with bars on the windows, no belt, no shoelaces, and the sheet on the bed made from an unyielding fabric that could not be torn into strips to hang himself. It was a temporary stop, he would soon be sent to 'a secure mental unit' as the authorities euphemistically put it. The community felt he was a danger, and as such he was to be locked up. Quite possibly forever.

'I must go and see Jean and thank her,' said Mara.

'Don't you dare leave this house!' Angus turned on her violently. 'You'll be splattered over every tabloid journal in the country. And you don't give a damn.'

Mara said, 'Actually, I think it should all come out. I shouldn't have to lie about Drew. I'm not ashamed of having him, I'm not ashamed of loving Jay. I know it's causing trouble but in the end it's bound to be for the best.

But the trouble was considerable. To the papers it was scandal, no more and no less, an interesting sidelight on a dynastic marriage. To Ferdinand of Havenheim it was a calculated slap in the face, not only by Jay but the whole British establishment. That such a thing should happen was one thing. That it should be allowed to become public, with so little regard for the dignity of the Havenheim throne, was something his pride could not swallow. And to Anna it was deep, desperate tragedy.

She flew back to England at night, unable to face the cameras in daylight. They snapped her just the same, upright, thick in the waist, her face drawn into a mask of dignified control. Within seconds she was in a car and away.

As they drove into London she sat rigid with tension. Should she have come? Her father wanted her to stay in Havenheim, never setting foot again in this benighted country. But she had to come. She had to see him, if only to give vent to some of her burning anger. It was eating away inside her, feeding on all her courage, all her self-control.

It was late, there were few people in the streets. But she wasn't tired. Neither was Jay it seemed, for he was in the library, waiting up for her. Long seconds passed and she couldn't bring herself to open the door. If only he had had the decency to keep it secret, to keep her from knowing! If he had to do it at least he could have spared her the knowledge.

He was working at his desk and looked up as the door opened. 'Anna! At last.'

'Hello, Jay.'

'You must be very tired. Would you like a brandy perhaps?' He got up and went to the drinks tray, but Anna waved the glass away. 'I don't want anything. Except an explanation, of course. Perhaps even an apology. It was very cruel of you to make me believe in a marriage that was over.'

'But it isn't. Not as far as I'm concerned.'

They watched each other, faces set. In an attempt to soften her Jay smiled and suddenly she went for him. 'How dare you! How dare you!' She struck wild, flailing blows at his head, but he fended them off easily. And in the midst of it she stopped and turned away. 'I think I want to kill you,' she quavered, as if surprised to find herself so murderous.

'If you'd listen to me, Anna! I think you should at least allow me to explain.'

'Will that make it right then? You father a bastard on this woman, you nurture it, care for it, even turn up at its goddammed — stupid — christening — and you want to explain? I am your wife! I don't ask for love, I don't even ask for you to be faithful, but I will not be treated with so little respect as a piece of mud, a rag, a cloth on which you wipe your feet!' Her lips were wet with spittle, her skin blotched. And he couldn't bear to see her pain.

'Oh, Anna. Anna, I'm sorry.' He went and took her in his arms and she stood, rigid against him, until all at once she dissolved into shuddering tears.

They talked through the night. Anna said, 'Money I don't mind. If the infant was there, then you were committed. But to go and see it, to stand by it at the font! That is so terrible.'

'It's the child I went to see, not the mother. I do owe him something, Anna! I care nothing at all about her, she had the baby absolutely against my wishes. I went — because he's my son.'

She gave a low moan. 'Life is so cruel to me,' she whispered. 'I want a boy for you, I want a boy for Havenheim. And because I do not have one I shall lose you and I may lose Havenheim.'

'I don't see why you should lose either.'

'What? You think my people will respect a woman who cannot bear a son and cannot keep her husband in her bed? Anyway, they think I'm too English. I've got to go home, Jay, and take the girls. I know

431

you won't want to come. And you can go and live with that woman.'

Once he had wanted nothing more. Mara made him drunk, she was so exciting, so vibrant with life. But if he went he would have her and nothing else. His family would exclude him, the establishment would lock him out. He had spent years becoming a force in the art world, the person automatically asked to give an opinion on this or that painting, this or that acquisition. If he went to Mara now the publicity, none of it good, would be shattering. All the committees, the judging panels on which he now sat would suddenly feel much happier without him. Overnight he would be an outcast, lost to his friends, his family, even to his daughters. And in their place would be Mara and her – his – son. Not enough any more.

'I couldn't live in Havenheim,' he said. 'Not unless we had a separate house, away from your father.'

'I'm not asking you to come,' said Anna coldly. 'I do not think I want you to come.'

'Look, Anna – I tried to finish the thing before. She was pregnant and it wasn't possible, but the intention was there. There is nothing more between us, nothing except the boy. And I can't turn my back on him!'

'Although you willingly turn it on me and your daughters. How little you think of women, Jay. We are all such a disappointment to you, even her.'

He wasn't a man who made friends of women particularly. The first had been Mara, and because of that he had begun to know his wife. For years they had lived in polite and sterile companionship, and if that should have been enough for them, time had proved that it wasn't. Anna's pride was terribly hurt, but she had slammed no door on him. He had the sense that this was his very last chance.

'I'm giving a statement,' he said slowly. 'Shall I show it to you?'

'Yes.' She held out her hand. He passed her a sheet of typed paper and she scanned it quickly. Then she brought it closer and read it again.

Prince John of Denham wishes it to be known that Andrew Henry Denham Hellyn, born to Lady Mara Hellyn in January of this year, is acknowledged as his son. The liaison between the prince and Lady Mara, which resulted in the birth, is one which the prince has ended and now bitterly regrets. The prince is aware of his duty towards the child, and will undertake generous financial support. He wishes to express his sincere regret for the distress and embarrassment caused, particularly to his wife, whose duties often require her to be away from home. Prince

John has expressed the hope that press harassment of Lady
Mara and the infant will cease, and that they will be permitted to
continue their lives in peace.

'So. It is my fault,' said Anna, and threw the paper down.

'We just hint that we were apart too much,' said Jay. 'It was a
mishap caused by absence, no more than that.'

She looked at him miserably. How many times could she swallow
her pride and let him back into her life, into her bed? This was the
very last time. 'We could live apart from my father,' she said
tentatively. 'But you must never see either of them again. Not ever.'

'I'll be in England a lot, you realise that? You must come too.'

She grimaced. 'Goodness me, now you need a chaperone.'

'No. But you need to believe in me.'

She nodded, wordless, her mouth closed tight on tears. At last,
curbing them, she burst out, 'We have no laughter in our lives! We
must find some for ourselves, I am so sick of tears and squabbles.'

'So am I. My God, so am I. Anna, if you knew what a relief it is to
have you know about this! And if you knew how sorry I am — so
very, very sorry.' He knelt at her feet, put his arms around her waist
and buried his face against her.

That night, out of courtesy, he slept in his dressing room. In the
morning, very early, the telephone rang. It was his private line, used
only by family and close friends. Still clogged with sleep, he picked up
the receiver.

'Yes?'

'Jay? Jay, it's me.'

His stomach contracted. For a moment he thought he might be
sick. 'What are you doing telephoning? You know it's foolish.'

'Darling, I have to know what's going to happen. It all had to come
out in the end, you do see that? It is better, really.'

'Not for me, I'm afraid.' He dropped his voice to a harsh whisper.
'It's the end, Mara. Absolutely the end. I don't want to see you, I
don't want to hear from you. Perhaps now you'll stop using the child
to hold me to ransom!'

'What on earth do you mean?'

'It's your timing that betrays you,' he snapped. 'I don't think
there's anything you wouldn't do to me, my family, anyone, to get
what you want. You are the most completely selfish woman it has ever
been my misfortune to meet.'

He heard her take in her breath. Suddenly it was as if he could see
her, soft, blurred by sleep, her hair tangled and cloudy. 'Do you mean
that?' she asked slowly. 'I don't understand you any more. I know

433

I've been stupid and I'm sorry, there's nothing you can say to me that I haven't said to myself. It isn't all my fault, some of it's yours as well. But you're so cruel to me – '

She made him cruel. If he remembered, if he allowed himself to remember, all that they had been to each other, then they would never part. They would go on, meeting here and there, risking everything. He didn't want that any more, he didn't want the danger and he could live without the excitement. If he looked at it only in cold calculation he could see that Mara had served her purpose in his life. A man bound by convention, prevented ever from doing anything to excess, he had been desperate for adventure. She had provided it. She had even unwittingly given him power, because never again would the people of Havenheim think that they could take him for granted. The converse of Anna's humiliation would be a grudging respect, because he was a man, he had proved himself a man, and their princess should count herself lucky to hold on to him. Look at the girl he'd had! What a ram! The men would nudge each other in bars and chuckle.

'Jay? Jay, talk to me! You are coming to see me, aren't you?'

'No. Don't telephone again, I shall have the number changed. If you write, the letters will be given to my secretary. I am interested only in Drew, and I want you to understand that.'

'Don't be so bloody pompous! It isn't three days since you were screwing me as hard as you could!'

'You always were an easy lay, my dear.'

She almost choked. 'You – bastard!'

'And I wouldn't use that word too liberally. I should warn you, I'm issuing a statement to the press today. No doubt they'll try and get your side of the story but if you've got any sense you'll shut up. For Drew's sake, if no-one else's.'

'Jay – Jay, you can't do this. Darling Jay, please!'

'I'm sorry. Goodbye Mara.'

He found he was bathed in sweat. Suddenly, feeling that he was being watched, he looked up. Anna was standing in the doorway.

'You were brutal,' she said.

'Was I? Somehow she brings out the worst in me, all the stark, uncivilised emotions.'

But he had loved her. Oh, how he had loved her. And even to talk to her made him hate himself, hate the world, because that love should never have fallen apart. He felt old suddenly, old and disillusioned. Whatever strength he showed he knew how weak he was, whatever kindness he displayed hid a deep, inner cruelty. Stitch

434

as he might a cloak to show the world, he despised himself. When he looked at his wife he felt a great and tragic despair.

Mara put down the telephone and went and washed her hands. She washed them again and again, trying to rid herself of a taint. After a while, when the skin was red and sore, she thought that if someone saw her they would think she was mad. Perhaps she was. What other word could sufficiently describe such desolation?

Someone was calling her. Angus. 'Mara? Mara, this baby's screaming the place down. What in God's name are you doing?'

She turned quickly, putting her hands behind her back. But she couldn't hide her face. 'Oh God!' said Angus. If there was one thing he hated it was uncontrolled emotion. His first instinct in a row was to walk out. 'Look,' he began angrily, 'you must have expected it. Everything's against you and has been from the beginning. You never had a chance!'

'He loved me. He told me he loved me.'

'And that's just sentimental claptrap. Grow up, Mara! Happy ever after doesn't exist.'

When she looked at him he seemed to be far away. 'If only Father was here,' she said suddenly. 'Everything was always wonderful then.' Angus gave a brief and mirthless laugh. 'I think you're forgetting a few things. The way he ignored Marcus, and trampled over Mother, and lost interest halfway through Lisa's school reports. I don't blame him entirely. He was the product of the old man, who lived too long and stopped his son growing up. But as far as you were concerned, Father had all the judgment of a besotted adolescent.'

'You make it sound filthy! We only loved each other.'

'Mutual uncritical adoration. You'll never find it again. And you'll cripple yourself looking for it.'

She wandered sightless past him. Drew was bawling healthily in his cradle and she picked him up. How long had he been crying? When only yesterday she'd promised never to let him cry for longer than the time it took for her to reach out her arms. Failure. Always failure. She put her mouth against the soft down of Drew's head and breathed tear soaked kisses.

Angus ran downstairs. Mara enraged him, because she did what she wanted, brought the world on her head and left others to pick up the pieces. Finally, this time, she had lost him his job. They were solicitous, he wasn't exactly out on the street, but it was clear that if he went back there would be no more selection boards, no matter how many strings he pulled. The government was in the business of soothing Havenheim, and Angus was an embarrassment. In the scheme of things, he didn't count.

He felt uniquely thankful that he wasn't still entangled with Lucinda. He couldn't have borne her concern, prattling about his plight to this and that influential personage, desperately trying to get her father to pull the irons out of the fire. She wouldn't have deserted him. But how much she would have wished to.

He decided to go for a ride. It was probably a bad idea, since the photographers might still be in the woods, perched like rare birds in thickets. But since no-one was prepared to be kind to him, he had to be kind to himself. So he took the cob and went up towards Slates Lane.

The sun was coming up over the hill, spreading liquid gold across the fields and the tops of the moors. Blackbirds squabbled in the trees, arguing over nesting territory. Magpies croaked in the hedges. They preyed on the smaller birds, rearing their young on the young of others. Like Toby, thought Angus. The man was a natural predator.

When Angus came out on to the green road the sun was dappling the grass with the patterns of leaves. Angus cantered along, wondering how it was that he felt so numb. His life was in ruins, brought down in Mara's earthquake, and as yet he couldn't despair. Perhaps that would come later. Sparrows fluttered in the hedgerow, and he passed two gypsy horses, tethered on the wrong side of a fence. They whinnied after him, tossing their wall-eyed heads.

He slowed as he came up to the camp. A small band of children was walking towards him, the older ones hand in hand with the younger, one of whom hung back wailing: 'Mam! Mam! No!'

'What's the matter with him?' asked Angus, drawing rein.

''e don't like school,' said one of the others. ''e don't like t'food.'

'You don't walk all the way, do you?' It was a good four miles, two of them down the green road.

'Miss Maythorpe gets us. Comes in the 'unt Land Rover and teks us to the bus.'

Even as he spoke there was the sound of an engine, grinding up the lane in low gear. In a few years they'd have to tarmac the blasted road, thought Angus, to accommodate the buses and police cars and social workers who wanted to get here.

'Wouldn't you rather live down in the village?' he asked the children.

A girl wiped her nose on the back of her hand. 'Nah. They'd never leave us alone. Bloody do-gooders.'

He laughed. Instead of riding to the wagons he turned and went with the children to meet Jean. She, squinting through the windscreen into the sun, saw his hair touched with gold. He sat straight and tall on his horse and around its legs clustered the shabby group of children. Her heart took up an erratic and panicky beat, and when she got out to pile the children into the back she was unnaturally brusque. 'Get in, Emmie, do! And stop your squawking. Fish is on Fridays, it's Wednesday today.'

Angus leaned down from his cob. 'Jean – can I talk to you?'

'No. I've these children to get to school.'

'I meant later. I thought we might go for a drive.'

'No, thanks.' She got back in her seat and rammed the gear lever into the wrong gate. There was a ghastly screeching sound and one of the children tried to get out.

'It's broke! We can't go if it's broke.'

'It isn't broke,' snapped Jean. 'Broken. I mean – it isn't. Sit down, all of you.'

'I'll pick you up,' said Angus. 'In an hour.'

She said nothing, wrenching the gear lever into the correct hole and hauling the big vehicle in a circle. Blades of new grass died under its wheels, and orchids, growing wild against the hedge. What was more important? thought Angus. Kids to school or wild orchids? Both, surely. There was no point in teaching children to live in a world where the orchids had gone.

He went quickly back to the stables and gave up his horse to the lad. They'd have to get rid of him soon, no doubt, now that the guests were gone. Back it all went, like pasture overtaken by thistles. There was a certain rich inevitability about it.

Jean was waiting for him at the bottom of the Maythorpe drive. She got in the car quickly. 'I don't want Dad to see,' she explained. 'He'd only get ideas.'

'You worry far too much about him.'

'That proves you're a Hellyn. You don't care about anyone.'

He grimaced. 'Actually, I think we're just rather bad at showing it.'

He drove up on to the moor, across two cattle grids, pulling off the road on to heather. The wind howled against the car, the only obstacle for miles. Even the sheep crouched down in the hollows, for the sun could do nothing against the cold breeze.

Angus said, 'I came up here to apologise.'

She sniffed. 'What for, exactly? Being ungrateful, being utterly foul, or dropping me when people said I wasn't the right sort?'

He felt himself colour. 'I didn't drop you. If you remember, you started this thing with Toby –'

'When you were getting yourself all set up in London. Don't pretend, Angus. You decided I wasn't the sort of wife you wanted.

437

Too vulgar. Dad started out from a terrace in Barnsley, and you don't get rid of that in one generation. All right, we're not your sort of people. That isn't something to get upset about. I admit I was hurt, but so what? You don't marry people because of what they feel. You do it because of what *you* feel.'

'You don't know what I feel,' said Angus.

Jean grinned. 'Pretty sick, I should think. Mara's done for you this time, hasn't she? And here you are, aristocrat with no prospects, falling back on good old Jean.'

He looked at her thoughtfully for a moment. Then he said, 'I'd be bloody upset if good old Jean wasn't there to fall back on. That's what I came to say. That I've missed you. When I had the good times I didn't find them nearly as good without you. And the bad times are lousy without someone you love to hang on to.'

She snorted, 'You don't love me! But right now there isn't anyone else to stand by you and you're feeling lonely. That's it, isn't it?'

'That's what I mean!' Angus reached across and put his arm around her shoulders. 'You stick by me through thick and thin. I've done a lot of growing up lately. And right now, when there isn't a single thing going my way, I realise I don't give a damn if I've got you. That's got to be love, hasn't it?'

Jean sniffed and looked out across the moor. 'It might be. I don't know if I'm bothered.'

'Oh, Jean, come on!' He leaned across and brushed her ear with his lips, and when she didn't resist he moved across to her cheek. All at once she turned to him and flung her arms around his neck. 'Oh, Angus, you've made me so damned miserable! I haven't been so sad in all my life. And I'm sorry about Toby, truly I am. It was just stupid.'

He didn't trust himself to speak about Toby. If he had ever wished anything in his life it was that Toby would disappear, die, evaporate like a bad dream in daylight. If he had never come to The Court they would have drifted away, all of them, instead of being held here. They were like tortoises tethered on pieces of string, legs and arms swimming but drawn back again and again to home. If there was no home, would they fare better? Or would they crawl away forever and be lost?

Chapter Forty-Four

Angus took Jean back to The Court for lunch with Lisa. The cook, Mrs Rogers, had handed in her notice and they were subject to the inexpert attention of one of the maids. So they ate a lacklustre salad in the small dining-room.

'We must all thank you for what you did for Drew,' Lisa said tightly. 'I'm sure Mara would wish that we did so.'

'Where is she?' asked Jean, uncomfortably. Although why Lisa should mind about Toby she didn't know. She hadn't wanted him. Perhaps it was just that Lisa knew what had happened, and somehow, when Jean met her eyes, she felt as if Lisa might have been there and seen for herself.

'Mara isn't very well,' said Lisa euphemistically.

'I'm not surprised,' said Jean, with too much enthusiasm. 'Did you see the papers this morning? They're brutal. Honestly, you'd think she trailed him down a dark alley and raped him! Everyone's working so hard to have him coming up smelling of roses, they don't give a damn what Mara smells of.'

Angus laughed but Lisa said nothing. Clearly Jean and her brother had made it up. Well, she never had thought that Jean was all that keen on Toby, which made it all the more despicable — she took a long breath through her nose. All at once she found herself wondering how much Reg Maythorpe was worth, and if he'd be prepared to use any of it to pay off Toby. These days her mind constantly juggled figures. She had even got up in the middle of the night to look at a cream jug which she thought might have been overlooked by some impoverished Hellyn when he was flogging off the silver. Sadly, it had not. The jug was plated, like very much else.

'Are you — um — getting married?' she asked nonchalantly.

'Steady on, Lisa! Jumping the gun a bit, aren't you?' Angus glanced from one girl to the other. Jean went very red.

'Oh, I'm sorry,' she said. 'But Angus has been so miserable since you quarrelled I thought you must be. And you were quite prepared to marry Toby, so you can't have all that much against it. I mean, there isn't any reason why you shouldn't – if you wanted, that is.'

'I think you might give me the chance to do my own talking, Lisa,' said Angus in a warning tone. 'Jean never was engaged to Toby, as a matter of fact.'

'Oh. Really?' Lisa allowed her voice to express patent disbelief.

'Yes, really,' snapped her brother. 'Anyway, Jean and I would have to think hard about marriage. After all, we're not exactly sound breeders, are we?'

'Good heavens, you talk as if you were horses. Or pigs,' said Jean shakily.

'No, just inbred aristocrats. I was thinking of Marcus.'

They were silent for a moment. Jean said, 'Drew's fine. A lovely baby.'

'Marcus was too,' said Lisa. 'Everyone said he was the nicest little boy.'

'But the rest of you turned out all right.' Jean looked at them both, pink with indignation. 'Talk about stupid! If you knew for certain something would pass on then OK, but you don't know. You can't. And if Angus doesn't have children, that's the end of the Hellyns. Isn't it?'

Angus nodded. 'But I'm not sure that we're all that important. I thought you disapproved of us.'

Jean crunched a piece of celery. 'Perhaps I do. But The Court's been here forever, and if the family doesn't take care of it no-one will. No-one else would bother. And someone should.'

Lisa looked down at her hands. Why did that someone always seem to be her? She was in limbo, waiting for Toby to find out that the guests had gone. He was going to yell for his money and she hadn't got it. Knowing him he'd take the house, the tapestries, the lot. It was what he intended in the beginning and the Hellyns were nearer the end than they knew.

'What's the matter?' asked Jean.

'What?'

'You made a face. I hope I haven't done something to upset you.'

Lisa passed a hand across her forehead. 'Now, why should you think that? I'm sure you needn't consider me when you decide to do things. I was thinking about the lake. I think we should pond, Angus.'

'Pond? Now? The water's freezing!'

'If we leave it too late the lilies flower,' coaxed Lisa. 'Why don't

we? It's bound to cheer Mara up. And Jean can come. Can't you?'
The thought of Jean arriving in designer pants to pond cheered her
immensely.

'But what do you do? When?'

'I thought tomorrow.' Lisa grinned, like a scheming elf. 'You'll
enjoy it, I promise.'

The next morning dawned pale and cloudless. The staff that remained
had been told to prepare for ponding, and there was an air of
suppressed excitement about the place. Curtiss got into his ponding
clothes, an ancient boiler suit covered with a thick leather apron.

Mara looked out of her bedroom window, watching Curtiss
command two young footmen carrying a stack of bamboo poles.
How it reminded her! Henry, Curtiss, in fact all the men wore those
boiler suits and aprons when she was young. It was left to the girls to
wade about in the water, and an air of lascivious adventure enveloped
the day. But to Mara it had all been innocent fun.

She would not help today. For one thing she hadn't the strength,
she felt drained of everything except lassitude. It was almost more
than she could do to pick Drew out of his cradle and dress him, every
button on his suit taking a major effort of will. If it wasn't for him she
wouldn't go on, she thought. There was nothing worse than loneliness, nothing worse than this dragging loss of self-respect. For almost
the first time she thought about what she had done, considered that
she might have done something else. But at the time, somehow, it had
all seemed inevitable. What she wanted she took, every thought
meant action, with never a pause for consequences or alternatives.
How naive she had been, how neglectful of herself. She had lived on
the high wire and, too late, discovered she should have had a safety
net.

Thank God she had Drew. He needed her and she could live for
him, wrapped up in that strange world that was The Court. Here, she
felt different somehow. Balanced. The house was her centre, her
refuge. When she walked down the long, dusty corridors she almost
felt that she could look over her shoulder and see the past, see the
Hellyns stretching back through the centuries. And before her, dimly
seen, were the Hellyns to come, who wouldn't judge her as she was
now judged. No, here she had her place, watching the present fade
into yesterday. Here she could try and face tomorrow.

She lay back on the bed, Drew kicking against her, gazing up at the
sunshine on the ceiling. A plaster nymph smirked down at her, saying
'I told you so,' echoing the world. She had been told and she hadn't
cared to know.

441

She threw out a hand and switched on the radio at the side of the bed. The pips sounded for nine o'clock. 'A statement has today been issued by Prince John of Denham,' began the plummy voice. Mara stayed quite still. She stayed still right until the very last word, until the newsreader was deep into accidents on the M25. Then her hands curled into fists, the nails digging in crescents into her palms.

She replayed the words in her head. When at last he had no choice he acknowledged Drew. Nothing to be grateful for in that, was there? And he rejected her. Well, she knew that too. And bleat as he might about an end to press harassment this would be just the beginning. Even the quality papers would feel obliged to publish a photograph of the bastard and his mother.

She picked him up and he chuckled, kicking his strong young legs. The nation's sympathy was at her disposal; she had only to appear pale, strained, with Drew in her arms, for everyone to know she had been misused. But by God, she would not endure pity, she would not let them see that Mara Hellyn was hurt, hurt to the core, hurt beyond everything. They would not see her blood.

The ponding began in earnest at half-past nine. To begin with long bamboo rakes were dragged across the surface of the water, reaching as far out as arms and handles would permit. The weed was heavy, and as soon as it had been pulled to the side helpers had to load it on to a trailer. If left for even a day it stank of rotting fish. After lunch they would use the booms to tackle floating islands of weed, steering them to the bank where they could be hacked into pieces and hauled away. Every now and then a frog leaped up in someone's face, or a trapped fish suddenly flapped, so the air was filled with squeals and shouts. Lisa shivered deliciously. Ponding was always the greatest fun.

A few minutes later Mara came down, with Drew in his carry-cot. She put the baby on a bench out of harm's way, pulled on a pair of gloves and took hold of one of the rakes.

'I thought you weren't going to help,' said Lisa, who had tried in vain to make her join in.

Mara smiled seraphically. 'Changed my mind. Beautiful day, isn't it?'

'Wonderful.'

Mara's height and long arms lent themselves to handling the rake. She leaned out from the bank, her hair impractically loose, guiding the tangles of weed this way and that. Years of practice had made all the Hellyns ponding experts; they knew just how much weed could be tackled in one go, how to cajole it into position, how to leave others

442

to the filthy job of chopping it up and carting it. One of the men commandeered the tractor, and another stood in the trailer neatly levelling the forkfuls flung up to him. It was much like harvest, with satisfaction every time the trailer filled. If only they could sell the darned stuff, thought Lisa.

Angus looked up from his rake to see Jean running towards them.

'Angus! Angus! Have you heard the news?'

'What on earth's happened?' He lent on his rake, watching Jean slow as the full aroma of ponding reached her.

'Phew! You do stink.'

'You should have come earlier, you don't notice when you're doing it. What's the crisis?'

'There's a statement about Mara. He acknowledges Drew and tells Mara to get lost. Does she know?'

Her voice had innate carrying ability. Mara looked up and smiled.

'Of course I know. Don't worry, I'm not upset.'

'You will be! There's two television vans blocking the lane.'

Mara shrugged and continued to wield her rake, long arms sweeping gracefully this way and that.

'You might at least show some morsel of concern,' yelled Angus.

'Brother dear, I'm sure you can panic enough for both of us,' she retorted.

He dropped his rake and stared across the lawn. Even at this distance he could see an unusual number of cars on the drive, and by the gate the tall roofs of two vans. People were hurtling towards them.

'Curtiss!' yelled Angus. 'Get on to the police. Mara, go into hiding.'

'Certainly not,' she said. 'If they want pictures, they can have them. The world can see me ponding.'

Lisa came back from a trip on the trailer. Her hands were dripping in green slime. 'What on earth's going on? Are they all photographers?'

'I suppose there's the odd journalist,' said Jean. 'Waiting to hear the immortal words "Get stuffed" coming from Mara's lips. What are we going to do?'

'Get rid of them!' declared Angus. He began to stride across the lawn towards the advancing hordes, shouting, 'Now see here! This is private land. I insist that you all leave immediately.'

The ones nearest had the grace to slow down and smile apologetically. Those on the flanks simply executed wide curves and approached the lake rather more obliquely, whilst the photographers, with the hunted expressions of men whose jobs depend on the day's labours, hung on to their mighty zoom lenses and began snapping.

443

One enterprising gentleman went so far as to barge up to Mara, kneel on the bank before her and take shot after shot of her face. Mara simply picked up her rake and dripped a large dollop of weed on to him.

Lisa lost her temper. 'Go away! Go away all of you!' she yelled. 'You're ruining our ponding.'

'How well do you know the prince?' demanded a girl with a notebook.

'Go away,' said Lisa, drawing herself up to her full insignificant height. 'Go away at once!'

A single policeman came striding over the grass, looking far too young and unsure of himself to do anything about the chaos of the situation. Several of the invaders had spotted the carrycot, and Lisa yelled: 'Mara, at least you can take Drew inside!'

'He doesn't mind,' said Mara nonchalantly. 'He's asleep.'

Angus was yelling at the policeman, to no real effect, and Lisa blinked away tears of impotent rage. How could Mara be so calm when she was inflicting this upon them? She had the sudden and vicious desire to push her sister head first into the water.

A very tall, burly figure was coming towards her. Unmistakably it was Toby, and why he had to come back now, in the midst of this, was beyond her. She turned her back, trying to pretend she hadn't seen. Everywhere lay weed and water, the banks of the lake were coated with mud, the staff were bemused and bewildered and they were suffering a Fleet Street invasion. It was total and unrelieved disaster.

'Hello, Lisa.'

She put her green hands behind her back. 'Hello.'

'What are you doing?'

'You mean — the lake? Oh, we're ponding. The weed you know. It gets out of hand.'

'You don't say.' He looked quizzically round at the confusion, his dark eyes unreadable. He was wearing his cream tropical suit, and looked expensive and out of place. His tiepin was a small nugget of gold.

'It isn't my fault,' she said in a low, trembling voice. 'You can't say anything because it has absolutely nothing to do with me!'

'I didn't say it was.'

'You didn't have to. I always know what you're thinking.'

He turned away and left her, and she reached out a hand to catch his sleeve, at the last moment realising that she would undoubtedly leave a green handprint on him. Unrestrained, he strolled over to Mara. 'Best to give them some pictures, don't you think? You and the baby, beautiful and smiling. Say a few words even.'

444

'What sort of words?' Mara looked at him cautiously under her long, golden lashes.

'Well – you had a brief affair. Unexpected pregnancy. He wanted you to have an abortion, but in all conscience you couldn't agree, though you knew it would be terribly hard alone. You never at any time appealed to him for support, but when the baby was born he appeared to have a change of heart. For the child's sake you hope he does accept his responsibilities but as for you, your only wish is that he leaves you alone.'

Mara considered. 'What a clever man you are,' she murmured. 'With one stroke of the pen, I become a heroine.'

'Gold plated. Go on, get changed into something glamorous. You can pose on the terrace, I'll get Lisa to set it up.'

As soon as Mara nodded Toby turned, put his hands on his hips and roared, 'All right, you lot! My name's Ledbetter and I'm in charge around here. Give your names to the butler and you can have interviews and photographs in one hour. One hour exactly. You can have coffee out here while you wait, and anyone trying to get shots before then will be evicted by the police. Now, get yourselves lined up, it's first come first served.'

Gradually order descended on the scene. Lisa stomped over to the trailer, thrusting handfuls of weed up on to it. Standing carefully aside, Toby said, 'I told Mara you'd set up the photocall.'

'I don't see why the hell I should! We're ponding. I like ponding. She's ruined my ponding day.'

He scanned the swathes of trailing weed. 'Couldn't you get a chemical or something?'

'I really have no idea. But I don't want a chemical. I want to pond, I decided to and I will.'

'After you've set up Mara. Lisa, she's got to look good, for her pride if nothing else. You don't want everyone thinking he's broken her heart.'

Lisa stood letting the weed drip from her hands. 'No. Because that would be true and we can't let people know the truth, can we? Let's keep on living a long, complicated lie.'

She went to her room and changed into a dress of white cotton. She put up her hair in a smooth knot, exposing the length of her fragile and fleshless neck. It made her look like a dancer, thin, strained, looking out warily at a world that demands perfection. Toby was on the terrace, waiting for her. He had assembled a chair, a screen and a flower arrangement, all of which Lisa dismissed. 'We'll have the pale screen please, from the morning room. And the flowers from my room, I'll redo them. Take the chair away, Curtiss. We'll have a

445

bench, so she can spread her skirt.'

'I thought the chair was more dignified,' said Toby.

'We'll have natural innocence and natural dignity, if you please,' snapped Lisa, and pushed him out of her way.

Curtiss hid a smile. If there was one thing never ceased to amuse him it was the way Mr Ledbetter allowed himself to be bossed around by Lady Eloise, and she half his height and quarter of the weight. And she was mighty dictatorial when he was around. Oh yes! No sooner did Mr Ledbetter appear on the horizon than she turned into a Sergeant Major, so she did.

Mara took an extra half-hour getting ready, and the pressmen became restive, as deadlines rushed upon them. At last, Lisa went to find her. She was sitting in front of her dressing table, doing nothing.

'What are you waiting for? You look marvellous. Come on, Mara!'

Mara turned a stiff face to her. 'I don't think I can. Not after everything. All those articles, they said I was a slut.'

'And now's your chance to show how wrong they were,' said Lisa forcefully. 'This is your guilty secret, you haven't got any others. None that they can prove, anyway.'

'But what will Jay think? He told me to keep quiet.'

Lisa picked up a brush and administered a last fierce swipe to her sister's shining hair. 'I bet he did! You're not to care what he thinks, you're not ever to care again. Promise? Promise Forever?'

It was an old pact, in which Lisa had always been too young to join. Amongst the children it had held the utmost rigour of solemnity. Mara took a deep breath. 'Promise Forever,' she said.

Suddenly, at two in the afternoon, everyone was gone. Dirty coffee cups and empty film wrappers lay everywhere, and half the chairs in the house were lined up on the terrace, covered in the footprints of photographers trying to get a good view. One diffident gentleman from a much-respected monthly magazine was found lurking in the morning room and was sent with one of the maids, who knew more history than anyone, on a tour of the house. Politeness forbade that he should ask indelicate questions and the resulting article was tedious in the extreme.

Lisa sat on the bench, so recently vacated by her sister, and gazed despondently at the lake. 'You never get a second chance at ponding,' she said dismally. 'Look, everyone's got other things to do.'

Toby said, 'I'll get a firm in. If you leave it like that it's going to stink.'

She flared at him. 'I don't want a firm! I want to do it properly, ourselves, the way it's always done! Why don't you ever understand that there isn't any point in doing something if you don't do it right?'

'Now you're being stupid.'

'But you always think that. And perhaps I am. We haven't any guests, you know, I sent them away.'

'Yes. That's why I came.'

Strands of hair blew around her face. 'I couldn't raise the money,' she said dolefully. 'So I suppose you'll take the house. I tried to stop you but all I'm good for is choosing wallpaper.'

Angus came out of the house. He was dressed again for ponding, in boilersuit and apron.

'You look like a butcher,' said Toby.

'And you look like a used car salesman. I take it you have no objection to ponding? You can't control every aspect of our lives.'

'I don't recall that I ever wanted to. I don't recall that I ever tried. But if it makes you happy to treat me like an ogre, Angus, please feel free. How's Jean by the way?'

'That has absolutely nothing to do with you.'

Toby put his hand across his heart. 'Oh, how shall I survive it! She's left me for a bankrupt.'

'Shut up, Toby,' said Lisa in a low voice. 'We agreed.'

'What the devil have you been agreeing? Lisa, what's going on?' Angus looked from one to the other, his face darkly flushed.

Lisa jumped up. 'It's nothing. We agreed he wouldn't be rude about Jean, though he's all sour grapes. And I think we should pond – you as well, Toby. I'll get Curtiss to find you a boilersuit.'

The three of them went down to the lake, in stolid silence. After a while Mara came out, and took up her rake again, pushing the weed this way and that. There was no-one to cart or drive the tractor, so they piled the weed into heaps and left it there, drying in the warm sun. Soon they had cleared all the bank, and the great central mass was left, enticingly green and inviting. There was something pleasurable about scything into the islands of weed. However tired you became, the next and the next mass urged you on.

Lisa pulled off her T-shirt. She had her bathing suit on underneath. 'Are you coming, Mara?' she called. 'We can push the boom.'

Mara nodded and unfastened her blouse. The two girls took up one of the long bamboo poles and dipped their toes in the water. Mara wore a tight blue suit, flashing with mermaid's scales; next to her sister she was a beautiful, golden Amazon. Lisa wore a suit she had bought in Rio, white with red stripes down the sides. Over the last months she had lost weight. When she held out her hands in involuntary rejection of the cold, the sunlight shone through the skin.

Toby stood and watched them. There was something almost

447

religious in the way they went into the water, as if repeating a ritual. They stepped in time, shuddering as the water touched warm skin, until at last they were down, their shoulders below the surface, swimming with the pole held in front of them.

They stayed near the shore, careful that one foot at least should rest on the muddy bottom. Mara, as the taller, swam out in an arc, taking the boom with her. She swam out and round, and the bamboo collected its first cut of weed. And then Lisa swam, bringing the boom with its burden close in to the shore. The men waded in the shallows, hauling it out with rakes and spades. As soon as it was gone the girls swam out again, to bring in more and still more again. The water grew dark and muddy. When either of them stood up their shivering bodies were coated with leaves and weed.

'They're getting tired,' said Toby at last. 'And Lisa's cold. We'll stop.'

Angus said, 'We never stop. Another hour and we can clear this end. The girls don't mind.'

'Look, I know you don't want to agree with me,' said Toby, 'but they're cold. They must stop.'

'And I say we go on.' Angus knew he was being ridiculous. He could blame Toby for many things, but it was Angus who first invited him to The Court, who gave him the right to involve himself in their lives. Even his affair with Jean would never have happened but for Angus.

Toby walked to the edge to call the girls out. He did what he wanted, whether anyone else agreed or not. Angus said, 'We'll change over. We'll go and swim and they can rake it out.'

Toby turned. 'All right. Yes, if you like.'

The men stripped down to their underpants. Toby was darkly tanned, the hair on his chest arrowing down to a badger stripe on his belly. Lisa watched, swimming steadily towards him with a boom full of weed. Her teeth were chattering. When she kicked her legs they felt stiff and unresponsive.

Once in the sun the girls began to dry off. Lisa rubbed her arms and legs, sending showers of leaves up into the air. Mara said, 'I do so love ponding. It's so disgusting.'

Lisa wondered if that was what she herself liked about it. Surely not. It was more the intense satisfaction of carving out great chunks of weed, the sense that nature was being tamed by united effort, by a combined Hellyn assault. Once, when she was little, Henry, Charlotte and all four children had dived into the water and heaved on a weed-laden boom, heaved until at last they got it to shore. What wonders they achieved on ponding days, and how happy it made them.

The men brought greater loads of weed than ever the girls could manage. Mara wielded her rake like a battle-axe, sweeping it here and there with an almost vengeful fury. Her sister cut and slashed and struggled. But they couldn't keep up. At last the men had to come out and help them, clearing away the ropes of weed that lay on the shore.

'We'll have one more sweep to clear this end,' said Angus finally.

Toby glanced at him. If Angus had such a burning need to be in charge, he ought to make sure he could afford it. But he let it pass.

'We'll help,' said Mara.

All four got into the water. Angus and Mara raced each other to the weed, but Lisa swam breast stroke and Toby kept beside her. 'You all right?' he asked.

She gave him a cool glance. 'Of course. Whyever not.'

'You look tired. In fact, you look exhausted.'

'Please don't concern yourself.'

But when they got hold of the boom and began pushing it towards the shore, Lisa suddenly sank completely. Toby reached out and hauled her to the surface, spluttering and coughing.

'What's the matter?' called Mara.

'Nothing. I'm fine,' called back Lisa, almost choking on slime. 'I swallowed some water.'

'Watch out, you'll have a fish down there,' shouted Angus. 'Push on you two, we're doing all the work.'

Lisa hung on and Toby pushed. When at last they reached the shore, Toby said. 'You girls go in. We can manage.'

Lisa nodded, too far gone even to protest. She walked away towards the house, her thin legs trembling.

Chapter Forty-Five

Ten minutes later, wearing a bathrobe borrowed from Curtiss, Toby went up to Lisa's room. No-one answered his knock and suddenly he imagined her lying dead inside. But when he barged in he saw her; sitting on the floor wrapped in a towel.

'What are you doing there?'

She looked balefully up at him. 'I'm raising the energy to get up and have a bath.'

'God, but you're a foolish girl! You don't eat and you don't rest. Come here, will you?'

He knelt down in front of her, taking the pins from her hair, peeling the towel from round her shoulders. He began to rub her with it, working on arms and legs until her skin was red and glowing. 'Now you can have a bath.' He went into the next room and turned on the taps, filling the tub with almost boiling water, throwing in half a bottle of bath oil.

He bent and picked her up. It wasn't difficult. She was featherlight, nothing but bones and hair and fierce, inner spirit. He carried her into the bathroom, still in her bathing suit, and gently lowered her into the steaming tub.

'I've never had a bath with my clothes on before,' she said.

Toby picked up the soap and began to create handfuls of lather. 'I'm not taking them off for you. We've been through all that and it didn't work.'

She let her hair trail in the water, feeling the blood vessels in her scalp expand and relax. 'It was my fault. I'm not a warm person, Toby.'

'Aren't you?' He picked up her arm and gently lathered it, working from fingers right to the dark hollow of her armpit. Her eyelids drifted up and down. 'Aren't you?' said Toby again.

He washed her, and petted her, and she lay there and let him. A delicious langour was overtaking her, warm and soft and sleepy. At last, when some part of her had decided that she would never ask him to stop, he lifted her out. The air was cold and unfriendly.

'I'm all right now. I'll get dressed,' she said quickly, and he put her down. She pulled the towel round herself.

'Why don't you go to bed? I'll bring you something up on a tray.'

She watched him warily. Such a big man. How could he, at one and the same time, hold her family to ransom and be capable of such gentle tenderness? 'You're not going to let us off the money are you?' she asked.

He looked at her. 'I see you still haven't told them.'

She shook her head, and then burst out, 'Well, how can I? There isn't anything they can do. Angus hasn't even got a job any more. And even if he had − Toby, I've had an idea.'

'And I've got a better one. Get into bed.'

'No, Toby, listen! I will work for you. I'll do up your clubs and things and pay you back out of my wages, or perhaps you needn't pay me at all. I haven't thought it out. But anyway − that's the idea.' She trailed off dispiritedly. He didn't look as if he was thrilled. 'Get into bed,' he said gently.

When he was gone Lisa dropped the towel on the floor, stripped off her bathing suit and ran shivering to find her nightdress. It was pale lilac cotton, when she felt more inclined to snuggle down in thick winceyette.

Toby brought up toast and eggs on a tray, with a pot of tea. Lisa's throat was hurting, and when she looked at the window the light stabbed her eyes. She picked at the food, every mouthful observed from start to finish.

'You're really knocked up, you know that?' said Toby.

'I think I've got a cold,' she said.

'I'm calling the doctor.'

He got up and went downstairs. Lisa pushed the tray aside, and laid her aching head on the pillow. She felt terrible suddenly. Toby was hard enough to cope with when she was well, but with her head banging and her throat raw flesh and this dreadful tight pain in her chest, she hadn't the strength.

In the evening she heard voices, but the evening went and the voices stayed, and when it was quiet it was evening again. The same day, the same hour? She had lost track. The pain in her chest was worse, much worse, and alternately she burned and shivered. Once she thought her mother was there, but when she reached out for her it was a man's hand. Toby's. She opened her eyes and saw him.

He said, 'You're real crook, you know. Pneumonia.'

451

'Hurts.' The air crackled in her chest.

'You and your bloody ponding.'

She smiled at him. He put his face down and kissed her forehead.

That night, when Angus and Mara settled down with a brandy after dinner, Toby joined them.

'Good heavens, we are honoured,' said Mara, swinging her legs over the arm of her chair. 'I thought you were keeping a vigil at Lisa's bedside.'

'Glad to see you're concerned,' said Toby thinly.

'Of course I'm concerned! But it doesn't do any good mooning over her. I should hate it, and I'm sure she does too. What with the doctor three times a day, Curtiss wearing the carpet thin bringing yet another bunch of flowers, and half the maids running up and down with bottles of mineral water and bowls of broth, I can hardly see her through the crowd.'

'Don't exaggerate,' said Angus. 'I thought she looked better today.'

Toby said, 'She is. She spoke to me.'

'I bet that's made your day.'

It wasn't entirely ironic. Mara watched him for a moment, then shut her book and sat up. 'All right, then. What do you want to talk about?'

Toby went across to the drinks tray and poured himself a scotch, adding a handful of ice.

'Do you have to adulterate single malt?' asked Angus.

Toby shrugged. 'If you want me to ask before I help myself to a drink, you're wasting your time. I pay the bills around here. You seem to find it very easy to forget that.'

'On the contrary. After all, we have you to remind us, which you do, don't you? Constantly.' Mara rested her head on one long, languid hand.

Drink in hand Toby positioned himself in the exact centre of the Persian rug. 'It's about money.'

'You've got it and we haven't. So what?' said Angus.

'So you owe me some. Rather a lot, as a matter of fact. Look, I discussed this with Lisa months ago and she didn't want you to know. God knows why. But I'm sick of watching you two use her, ignore her, put her last in any small piece of consideration you might be capable of.'

Mara looked patiently at Angus. 'Toby dear, Lisa doesn't have to do what she doesn't want. We're none of us making her stay here, or work, or anything. We are rather hard up. That does leave us

452

somewhat limited options, don't you think?'

'I am trying to tell you something rather important,' remarked Toby. 'Listen. You've fallen down on the contract, and brought the penalty clause into play. You owe me a fortune, but I'd settle for five hundred thousand. And you can't pay.'

'I don't remember any such clause,' said Angus quickly. 'We didn't discuss it!'

'Nonetheless it's in,' said Toby. 'Sorry, Angus, old boy. But you were so damned glad to be fished out of a hole you didn't care what you put your name to. Not a good idea, relying on generosity. There isn't enough of it about.'

'I see.' Angus looked almost resigned. 'But − why didn't Lisa want us told?'

'She said you hadn't the money. She wanted to see if there was any way it could be raised, and I'll say this for her, she's thorough. She's talked to everybody. Now it looks as if you'll have to sell The Court to me.'

At last, he had their full attention.

'You aren't serious!' Mara was white. 'Do say you're joking. This is our home. It's Drew's home. We've been here forever. The whole reason we got into this thing with you was because we didn't want to sell!'

'Couldn't sell, more like' said Angus. 'Toby, what would you want it for? If you ask me you're on some kind of ego trip here. You fancy yourself as Lord of the Manor, you think you can buy history! All right, you have it. Let it be a millstone round *your* neck. It's damn nigh throttled us!'

Suddenly Toby sat down. His face was grim, strained. 'I don't want the bloody place,' he said thickly. 'I don't even want the money. It's my fault Lisa's ill, she's worried herself half to death over it. She even offered to work for me as some kind of slave, trying to pay off the debt. And if you want it that much, you can damned well get on with it.'

Angus rubbed his cheek. 'I'd much rather not,' he said. The others looked at him. 'Well, why should I want to keep it?' he said defiantly. 'I don't like the place. I don't want to look after it. Marcus cares but I don't, and I won't waste my life taking care of something that I don't want.'

'It isn't a waste,' said Mara. 'You'd be making something. All the Hellyns made this, every one changing it, adding to it. You can't not want to be a part of that.'

'Yes I can,' said Angus. He got up and grinned rather sheepishly at Toby. 'I'm sorry to be so churlish when you've made such a grand

453

and noble gesture. As far as I'm concerned, you can do what you like with the place. It's got nothing to do with me.'

Mara said shrilly, 'And what about us? Me, Drew, Lisa? What about Father, he gave up his life to care for The Court.'

'Mara, that is absolute balls.'

Toby looked from one to the other. 'So what are you going to do, Angus? You haven't got any sort of career.'

Angus flushed a dark red. He hadn't looked so embarrassed since he was caught smoking aged eight. 'I'm working with Jean,' he said stiffly. 'We're doing a gypsy resettlement project. The Council's funding it, but of course we can't live on that. I'm hoping to stand for Parliament again. As a Democrat.'

'One of that lot?' shrieked Mara. 'What an absolute waste of time! And you'll never get in. Honestly, Angus, why don't you grow up? There is no point in ganging up with a bunch of well-meaning do-gooders who want the world to be civilised, the poor to be happy and the rich open-handed.'

'Sounds all right to me,' said Angus. He laughed. 'What a cynic you are. Perhaps if we all gang up, we'll get just that.'

'And perhaps you won't.'

'At least I'm going to try.' He turned on his heel and went out, leaving the door open. Toby went to shut it.

Mara got up and began walking restlessly round the room. She said, 'He doesn't understand. The Court's more important than any stupid ideas about changing the world. It's so special, you see. The ultimate sacrifice. Giving your life to make something so – so special.'

She spread wide her arms, encompassing not only the pretty room in which they stood, but the whole house, and the parkland, even the high, windy moors.

Toby said, 'Angus ought to learn to cope with reality. And you could do with a bit less dreaming. It's just a house, when all's said and done.'

She gave her most beautiful smile. 'I wish you'd stop trying to change us, Toby. More this, less that, do this, stop that. We are as we are. Idle and selfish and incompetent. And sometimes busy and philanthropic and capable. I know it's confusing, but there you are.'

She watched shadows passing across his big, strong face. 'What are you going to do?' she asked.

He stirred. 'About the house? I don't know.'

'I didn't mean that. Lisa. And you. I thought you were going to marry her and I did my best to discourage it, but you got in a muddle all by yourselves. I wonder why.'

'I bet you do! It isn't going to happen. If you must know we don't get on. Sexually.'

'Good God!' Mara looked completely taken aback. 'You're not impotent, are you?'

'No. No, I'm bloody not.' Toby got up and went to pour himself another drink. This time he left out the ice. There was an enormous relief in talking about it, letting light into the dark recesses of his mind. 'She doesn't like it,' he said harshly. 'I frighten her. I'm as gentle as I know how and still she lies there like a board. If I could live without it I would, because she's wonderful when she knows I'm not going to ask her, but there's no way I can. So — there's no way.'

'I see.' After a while she said, 'Actually, it does fit with her character rather. She's always tense, you know.'

Toby nodded. 'I just want her to — to learn to trust me! I'd never hurt her. Not at all. Not ever.'

'Poor you,' said Mara softly. 'Poor, poor you.'

Toby had never known what other men saw in Mara. Just then, when she was soft with sympathy and gentleness, he understood.

The next day Lisa was very much better. She sat up in bed wearing an ancient embroidered bed-jacket that someone had unearthed. Toby brought yet more hothouse flowers and sent maids running up and downstairs looking for vases. And he made her eat oysters, because they were nourishing.

'I wish you wouldn't make such a fuss,' she croaked, picking at the bedcover with skeleton fingers.

'I want to fuss you. By the way, I talked to Angus and Mara last night. I'm prepared to forget all about the debt.'

Her eyes were as big as saucers. 'You can't! It isn't fair.'

'I don't mind. And I'm sorry I bothered you about it. I was angry, I wanted to upset you.'

'Toby, that's ridiculous! You can't wave goodbye to all that money, you're not a charity. I won't let you. Have the house, do what you like with it. I'm sick and tired of the place.

Toby grinned. 'That's what Angus said. He doesn't want it either.'

'Doesn't he? Oh dear.'

She was so lovely sitting there, to him if no-one else. Some people had an eye for her charm, others saw nothing. It wasn't obvious.

Toby said, 'So you'll have to get a job after all.'

'I knew you'd see sense.'

'Not with me! Anywhere. You could get a job in London and go to all the parties.'

'I suppose I could.' She looked at him doubtfully. 'But I'm not all

455

that keen on parties. They almost always disappoint you.'

He sat watching her, and suddenly he said, 'We could try again, you know.'

Her thin hand dragged the sheet upwards. 'No, we couldn't! I wanted a job, that's all. We agreed it was all over.'

'I agreed nothing! And even if I did, I can take it back. Lisa, I want you to know – '

'And I don't want to know! It isn't any use and it doesn't do any good!' She put her hands over her ears.

A knock came on the door. It was the doctor. 'Are you all right, Lisa?' he said stiffly. 'I heard raised voices.'

'Did you?' She tried to laugh. 'That wasn't anything. A business discussion. Toby, if you wouldn't mind, the doctor wants to examine me.'

There was nothing to do but leave. He went downstairs, his mind full of confusion. Ought he to stay? Perhaps he should leave and be done with it, and this time mean to keep away. Without thinking he wandered into the library. When he saw Mara kneeling to sort through a shelf of books he turned to go out again, but she called out: 'Would you believe what there is in here? I swear these are some sort of High German. I don't think they've ever been read. We could put Micky Mouse in leather covers in here and no-one would notice.'

'Great intellectual tradition you Hellyns have,' said Toby sourly.

Mara sat back on her heels and looked at him. 'Do you want me to have a talk to her?' she asked.

He tried to grin. 'I can't. It's barbed, like treading on thistles. We can't say a word to each other that isn't misunderstood.'

Mara said, 'I will talk to her. She really can be most terribly prickly, but that isn't her, you know.'

'I know.' He picked up one of the books, and could understand none of it. Typical Hellyn muddle. He put it down again. 'Are you OK?'

For a moment her face was bleak. He saw the truth suddenly, the naked pain. It was courage alone that held her up, that got her through the days and the long, dark nights. Say what you like about the girl, about her morals or her manners or her ruthless use of charm, she had courage.

'The house helps,' said Mara suddenly. 'It isn't surprised. Compared with the murder and mayhem it's seen, what I've done isn't quite so terrible.'

'I didn't think you cared about scandal.'

'No.' She swallowed, and for a moment her eyes swam with tears. But she blinked them away. 'It takes something like this to show what

456

you do care about. I hate to be alone, you see. And of course I've got Drew, and I'm not, really. All the same —' She turned back to the books and dusted one, vigorously.

'You'll survive,' said Toby.

She cast him a look of scorn. 'Of course I will. I don't much want to but I suppose I bloody well will.'

He had to admire her. He had to laugh.

Chapter Forty-Six

Lisa slept for most of the afternoon and woke as the sun was going down. The room was full of shadows, soft purple and grey, and she had that sense of timelessness that comes from days spent in bed. The past hours were marked by nothing more than trays of food and dozes.

'Are you awake?' It was Mara, peering round the door. 'I came up before and you were sleeping.'

'I think I'm awake.' Lisa struggled up in the bed. 'I get stupid lying in bed all the time. My brain stops working.'

Mara perched on the end of the bed. She was wearing jeans and a T-shirt, both quite dirty. She watched her sister like a speculator looking for development potential. 'I've been talking to Toby,' she said. 'Poor man, you are tormenting him.'

Lisa shrugged. 'I don't think I am. I want him to give me a job.'

'You can't really expect it. Not when he's so much in love.'

Her sister blushed and looked away. Her hands plucked at the bedcover until Mara said, 'Lisa, what's the matter? He says it's bed.'

'Has Toby been talking to you? How dare he talk to you! That's my private business.'

'But is it that? Lisa? Surely you can tell me.'

Lisa said jerkily, 'I don't want to tell anybody. It seems so – unfeminine. Something to be ashamed of.' Her sister said nothing. And suddenly Lisa burst out: 'When he gets on top of me, I hate it! He wants it so much and he's so big and I know, I just know, that he could kill me if he wanted. I can't forget what he's like with other people. How tough he is. And that's so stupid because he isn't like that with me.'

'Everybody has more than one side to them, don't you think?'

Lisa nodded. 'I know. To begin with I didn't think he really loved me at all. But he does. He tries so hard. And – well, I can't respond.

458

Mara, I don't care if it's never marvellous, I don't want to feel the earth move, I just want it to be — loving. I want to be able to love him. To love him back.'

Her sister sprawled across the foot of the bed, one knee up. 'There are other men,' she said. 'It might be wonderful with someone else.'

'Yes.' Lisa sighed. 'I can't see me sleeping around until I finally get it right somehow.'

'Good God, neither can I!' Mara rolled on to her stomach and put her chin in her hands. 'It isn't all that hard. Not if you trust somebody.'

'But it's very hard to trust people. Anyone. It would almost be better with someone I didn't know. I hate him seeing me — like that.'

'When you were little, you didn't like people to see you cry,' said Mara. 'It's the same, isn't it?'

When her sister said nothing, she pushed herself up off the bed. 'You're making poor old Toby feel like a rapist. Why don't you go away together for a bit?'

Lisa burst out, 'I just wish it didn't have to happen! I wish we could be friends and never ever have to do it. It's disgusting and primitive and embarrassing.' She clutched her hands in her hair.

'And honest,' said Mara. 'Don't you think that's the trouble? When you make love properly, when you care for someone, you can't pretend. You have to be honest.'

When she had gone Lisa slipped down below the sheet again. She felt afraid. All the feelings that she had shut away, walling them off behind a screen of efficiency and cold, had to be brought out and looked at again. They had to be made to work, however creakily. She had to be made to work. Love was a simple commodity. The more you were given, the more there was to give away, and if all your life you had lived in the shadow of others, then you had very little love to call your own. The human warmth that Lisa possessed she kept safe and secure deep within her. But unless she learned, somehow, to let it out it wouldn't grow. And in the end it would wither away to dust.

Next morning Toby arrived with her breakfast. Lisa felt wretched, lank-haired and in need of a bath. Her nightdress was stained with cough mixture. 'I don't know why you didn't get someone else to bring that up,' she said testily. 'We have plenty of staff.'

'Yes.' Toby put the tray down and then sat on the bed. She wondered if she had a spot coming on her forehead. One of the things he liked most about her was her grooming and yet here she was, rumpled and sticky.

'Australia,' he said. 'Good time of year. I've been thinking about a club in Sydney.'

459

She raised her eyebrows, reached out and poured herself some coffee.

He said, 'I thought I'd book a flight at the end of the week.'

Her hand shook. 'Why not sooner? There's no point in hanging around once you've made a decision.' She managed a brittle smile.

'But I thought you might not be up to it.'

'Oh! You mean me to come. Do you?'

'Well, yes! Wasn't that what Mara — I thought you agreed.'

She nodded vigourously. 'Yes. Yes, I think I did. Seemed best — don't you think?'

'Yes.' He sounded doubtful. Then he got to his feet, rubbed his hands together heartily and said, 'Right then, that's settled! End of the week.'

Angus spent most of the morning talking to Reg Maythorpe's solicitor. Afterwards he felt glum, and to cheer himself up called to see Jean on the way home.

'How did it go?' she demanded the moment he appeared.

'Not too bad.'

'Don't be so laid back. Can he get Marcus out? That's what you wanted.'

Angus said, 'Actually — well, he convinced me there isn't a lot of point.'

Jean opened her eyes wide at him. Angus burst out, 'Look at it sensibly! He may not mean harm but he does it nonetheless. Whatever his motivation he took Mara's baby and almost caused it to die. What's more his medical records show violence towards Lisa, hallucinations, and at times total disregard for his own welfare. He needs to be institutionalised.'

'Not with mad axemen and rapists! An institution, yes, but not some hellish gaol!'

Angus said wearily, 'We discussed the alternatives. These places are graded. With luck he could end up in the country, somewhere quite pleasant. That's what we're trying to arrange.'

'Oh. Oh, I see. Well, that's all right then.'

Angus looked at her sardonically. Jean never spent long in discussion, she put something in a box and was done. 'But is it all right? When it comes to Marcus I always feel guilty. I feel as if I ought to be able to resolve something. Once and for all.'

Jean said, 'I do think that's stupid. You're doing what you can, and it isn't as if anyone made him ill. He just is. So there's no point in everyone being dismal about it.'

460

Angus put his arm around her. 'You really are terribly good for me.'

Jean grinned up at him. 'I know.'

Angus and Jean came to the airport. They insisted, despite all Toby could do to discourage them. Mara remained in purdah at The Court, for still the odd photographer camped out at the gate and no-one had any wish for Toby and Lisa's departure to be headline news. 'Sister of Royal Mistress in Airport Drama!' declaimed Angus as he loaded cases on a rickety trolley.

'Holiday Hideaway for Odd Couple,' giggled Jean unwisely.

'Put a sock in it' said Toby grimly.

'More than a sock,' added Lisa. 'How about an unexploded bomb?'

But Jean and Angus continued tormenting them. 'Whereabouts are you going?' asked Jean.

Toby said distractedly, 'I'm thinking about a club in Sydney. I need Lisa's help.'

'What an odd way of putting it,' said Angus, and Toby burst out: 'Will you two bugger off? Go and amuse yourselves somewhere else, we're not the cabaret.'

The pair tried to suppress their chuckles. 'I think we'll go,' said Angus. 'Though we did come to wave you off.'

'We'll manage,' said Toby.

'Yes. Goodbye,' said Lisa.

When they had gone, Lisa said, 'What do they find so funny?'

'I suppose it is a bit odd. Two people going off together when they hardly appear to be speaking.'

'We are speaking! Not very often, perhaps. But we are.'

'Yes.'

Silence fell. After a while Toby bought a *Financial Times* and read it while Lisa engrossed herself in a brochure about Australia. 'It says here that Australians are noted for their friendly and hospitable dispositions,' she declared.

'You don't say! As far as hospitality's concerned, I've got a beach house up country. I thought we might go there. I could practise being friendly.'

'It says that tourists should beware of spiders, snakes and jellyfish.'

'Too right! You'd better stick with me and my friendly hospitality.'

She laughed, for the first time that day.

They travelled first class, and despite the champagne and the pampering, the flight reduced Lisa to a husk. When at last they

461

landed Toby was impossible, demanding a doctor and refusing to let her stand up in the immigration queue. Feeling horribly conspicuous, Lisa found herself plonked in a wheelchair and whisked past officials to a large black limousine.

'Are we going to your house?' she asked feebly. Her head was throbbing and she wanted nothing so much as a bed. Any bed, so long as it was cool, flat and motionless.

'That's half the country away. We have to fly there. For tonight I've booked a hotel. Suite actually. One room each.'

She closed her eyes in all too obvious relief.

That night she fell asleep as if diving into a deep, black well. When at last she woke, lying for long minutes keeping her bones utterly still, there was the sound of rain on the window. Eventually she got up and went to look for Toby, finding him in the sitting-room working on some papers.

'Perhaps we should have stayed in England,' she said. 'It's horrible weather.'

He yawned and threw a bound report to the side. 'Isn't it just? We'll get off to the beach house when you feel better. No sense hanging around here. It's up north, there's bound to be some sunshine.'

She nodded and sat in a chair. The room was warm enough. She put her feet up on a stool. 'I feel terribly lazy,' she said. 'But I will work, I promise. Are those the designs for the club?'

'Yes. But you're not looking at them yet, you're having breakfast.'

He went to telephone room service and while he was distracted Lisa reached out and picked up the folder. The report had been prepared by a design consultant. There were photographs on the inside cover of interiors of which they were proud, and swatches of suggested materials attached at certain points. Lisa wrinkled her nose. 'What an awful lot of plastic,' she said disdainfully as Toby returned.

'Yeah.'

'And why is the place littered with fake wood? Don't you have real trees in Australia?'

He grinned. 'One or two. That's only a spec report, they're touting for the business.'

'In vain, I fear.' Lisa got up and went over to the window. Although it was raining there was none of the lowering cloud of an English winter. The hotel had given them the best suite, facing out across the harbour. Some yachts were beating up and down in the rain.

'I wish I felt better,' she said suddenly. 'I want to go out and look at everything.'

Toby came up behind her. 'Another time. Next time we come. I want to take you to my house and baby you.'

'Do you?' She looked anxiously over her shoulder at him and he put out his arms quite quickly and held her round the waist. 'Oh, Lisa! Lisa!' But try as she might she was stiff and unyielding. He held on, and she turned her head away, looking out at the great bridge arching across the bay. There was a knock at the door. Lisa's breakfast had come to save them.

The day passed awkwardly. Toby booked a flight for early the next morning, but Lisa couldn't pin much hope on sun and sand to put things right. There must be something fundamentally wrong with a woman who couldn't express love, she decided. Because she did love Toby. She cared for him with a blind, unreasoning devotion, the same helpless loyalty that a dog has to give. It was such an undignified emotion. She almost despised herself for feeling it.

In the late afternoon they began to relax. It was mutually understood that nothing would be attempted until they got to the beach house, and in the meantime they were free to enjoy each other's company. They dined at a small restaurant on lobster and scallops, and a man got up in the middle of the floor and recited poetry, and afterwards he played the flute. The candles on the tables burned low, and the light shone only on Toby's mouth and hands. He had a good mouth, thought Lisa, with finely drawn lips. He didn't show his teeth much when he smiled, but when he laughed he threw his head back and revealed rows of white ivory. He was a relentlessly healthy man.

'Tired?' he asked eventually.

She shook her head. 'Not really. This is such heaven. But I suppose we ought to go.'

'All right.' He got up and Lisa said, 'Haven't you forgotten to pay?'

He grinned. 'No. I own the place.'

'Oh.'

She looked round in embarrassment at the waiters and the manager, and saw that they were all looking at her. 'I wish I'd known,' she murmured to Toby. 'We must have seemed awfully familiar with each other.'

'That's why I didn't tell you.'

They went out into a starlit night. There was a taxi waiting, but Lisa stood looking up, at a southern moon. 'I love travelling with you,' she said suddenly. 'It's such an adventure.'

After a moment, Toby said, 'I think that's the nicest thing you've ever said to me.'

'Is it?' Lisa made a face. 'Then I must be very horrid to you. I'll try

463

and think of nicer things than that.'

The following day was cool and cloudy. There seemed nothing to prevent them going to the beach house and Toby booked a flight for eleven o'clock.

'It's not exactly an easy journey,' he explained apologetically.

'Three hour scheduled flight and then a couple of hours' driving. I could get a plane to do the last part and land on the beach, but the country's beautiful. You'll want to look around.'

'Yes. Yes, I shall.'

She dressed in dark brown trousers and white silk shirt, throwing an Aran sweater round her shoulders. Her illness had taken her down to skin and bone, but gradually the flesh was reappearing. Toby fed her at every opportunity, like a fledgling bird. At the airport they were ushered into the VIP lounge, to be treated to champagne, and Toby insisted on sandwiches. They were brought double quick. It seemed Toby was a celebrity here, one of Australia's success stories. When the sun broke through the clouds and momentarily dazzled them, he yelled for a steward and made him pull the blind. She turned her head away. Sometimes Toby was impossibly autocratic, almost like her grandfather.

When at last they made the plane, a small ten-seater, he said, 'I've hired a jeep. The road's rough as hell so it seemed best. But I'll get a car if you'd prefer.'

'If you ought to get a jeep, get a jeep,' said Lisa. 'Honestly, I wish you wouldn't behave as if I was difficult, or as if I might break.'

He glanced at her. She was the most difficult and fragile person he knew.

They landed a little late, circling above an airfield gleaming brilliant green in the sun. Horses grazed near brightly painted corrugated iron airport buildings, and a breeze was filling the windsocks and rustling the leaves of the trees. Lisa felt tense with excitement, and pushed her sweater into a bag. She wouldn't be needing it here.

The jeep was a dull brown and had no doors. It wasn't particularly old, but seemed to have worked hard during its life, with the odd dent here and there and a cracked glass on the speedometer.

'Haven't you got anything better?' demanded Toby of the hire-car man.

'It's the one you always have, Mr Ledbetter,' said the man quaveringly.

'If the lady wants something a bit more comfortable –'

'I think it looks fine,' said Lisa calmly. 'Toby, if we wait any longer we won't get there.'

As the luggage was loaded, he said, 'You don't notice these things

464

when you're by yourself. I let things go a bit at the beach house. Bound to be a bit rundown, now I think about it.'

'Sounds wonderful. Please Toby, will you stop worrying about me? I was brought up at The Court, remember? Mice in the bath and no heating. It takes an awful lot to make me uncomfortable.'

He grinned sheepishly and got behind the wheel. 'Have a good trip,' said the hire-car man. 'You want me to give you a check call tonight?'

'No thanks, we'll be OK,' said Toby. 'Buy yourself a beer.' He tossed some money across and the other man caught it.

They stopped off at a store and bought several boxes of food, loaded it up and started out of town. The roads were good to begin with, smooth and straight, running past homes set back amongst trees and paddocks. Soon the building gave way to open country, flat until the far distance. Only the odd windmill stood out, drawing water up for the stock. They turned off the tarmac road on to rough beaten earth, took a left fork and a right fork and then followed the finger of a weather-beaten signpost. There were no other cars. A bunch of cattle merged into the thornbushes, turning white faces to watch them go by.

'I didn't realise it was quite so out of the way,' said Lisa after a while. 'Are you sure there's a beach down here?'

'Positive. They're not allowed to move the sea. I built the house myself, there was just a shack when I bought it. And a jetty for sailing. There's a radio in case of trouble, we're not that cut off.'

She hadn't realised they would be quite so alone. It was already getting dark, with that sudden twilight that is so unlike England. She looked sideways at Toby's profile. A strong face, with jutting chin and high, wide forehead. His nose was too big, a bulbous statement in the centre of his face, so he was very far from good-looking. He turned the wheel with big, capable hands. As night fell her stomach began to twist itself into knots.

The road was full of potholes. 'I ought to get some of these filled in,' said Toby, and almost before the words were out they lurched into one. There was a shattering crash and the front of the car sagged, nose-down and despondent. 'Shit!' said Toby forcefully, and unbuckled his seat belt. He went round to the front of the car, bent to look underneath and swore again. Lisa got out and stood beside him. 'What is it?' she asked.

'Front axle. It's buggered, we can't move it an inch. And I told him not to bother with a check-call. Shit, shit, shit.'

'Is it far? Could we walk?'

'I could. Take most of the night though. It's over thirty miles. You

465

stay here and I'll get to the house and the radio. You'll get picked up by mid-morning.'

She looked around at the shadows, the gathering gloom. There weren't even doors on the jeep. 'I'll come with you. I'm not staying here.'

'You can't, you'll slow me up. There's nothing going to eat you.'

'I don't care, I'm not staying. Anyway, there isn't any hurry. It doesn't matter how long we take.'

He reached into the jeep and pulled out his jacket. 'You can use this as a blanket. Don't wander away from the car, you'll get lost.'

'I'm not staying.' She pulled on her jumper, arms flailing wildly. 'There, I'm ready.'

He loomed over her, full of menace. 'And suppose you collapse? You've never walked thirty miles in your life. I could end up with you half dead in the middle of nowhere. If I leave you out there and go for help you could fry in the day. People don't walk past every half hour, not out here!'

She looked up at him, her face a white blur in the gloom. 'But I want to come. It's something we should do together.'

Toby felt the iron weight of his own responsibility. He should have hurried, he should have asked for a check call, he should never have treated Lisa's life as lightly as he did his own. 'Just do as you're told,' he said fiercely. 'Just do it! Don't make things worse.'

He turned and began to walk, and behind him came the sound of Lisa's footsteps. When he looked she was padding in his wake, carrying his jacket. 'It's going to get cold,' she said. 'No point in leaving this behind.'

He came back and took the coat. This time she walked beside him, but in minutes he had paced ahead. She was quite unable to keep up. He stopped and waited for her to cross the yards between them.

'Lisa, it won't work!' he pleaded. 'Go back now. Please.'

It seemed to her so symbolic. He was capable, strong and whole, and she held him back. They didn't match, not in anything. They couldn't even walk together. She put a hand up to her eyes. 'I'm sorry. Now I am being difficult. None of this is going to work, is it? I think it's about time we stopped trying.'

'You've been ill. If you hadn't been ill — '

'And if I wasn't so small, or so stiff, or so downright frigid, then everything would be all right! But I am! Toby, don't you see, this is me, this always will be me! There's no point in hoping for something different.'

The night was like black cloth, they were wrapped in it, inches apart. Toby knew that it could all so easily come to an end. He said,

466

'You can't go back now anyway. You might not find the jeep.'

'Of course I will. You're being silly.'

'So why don't we hold hands.'

It was comforting, to slip her palm into his, to feel his huge hot hand. 'I don't want to be alone,' she said.

'No. Neither do I.'

They began to walk, and in the dark, before the stars or the moon came up, they blundered slowly along the track. He could have gone no faster. The first stars began to rise and they could see to pick their way around holes and boulders. Something crashed in the bushes and Lisa choked on a shriek.

'Kangaroo,' said Toby. 'You gave him a fright.'

She laughed and held tight to his hand. Its shape was becoming familiar to her, the seg at the base of his little finger, the unexplained gall on his thumb. When she brushed her own thumb through his fine finger hairs she felt a shiver of mysterious delight.

When the moon came up they walked more quickly, and Toby began to sing. Lisa joined in, and they sang 'Waltzing Matilda' out of deference to the country, and 'John Peel' out of deference to her. The temperature dropped. They walked hand in hand through a night made of silver, walking forever towards a far and faint horizon.

As midnight approached they rested often. Toby estimated that they had walked about fifteen miles, and though he was almost as fresh as when they began, Lisa was all too obviously wilting. They sang no more. Once she sat on a rock and asked, 'What will you do if I can't go on?'

He looked down at her. 'I'll carry you, my sweet. Don't worry, I won't leave you here.'

'You're too good to me. I don't know why you're so good.'

He touched her face. 'It's just because I love you. People do it all the time, it isn't so odd.'

She got up and they went on, and after a while she said, 'I want to say it too. It's very hard, it makes me blush at myself.'

Toby laughed. 'It's dark, there's no-one looking. I won't look.'

She held tight to his hand, that was coming to seem so friendly, so dependable. 'I – I love you. Quite a bit. I mean a lot. Toby, I think I love you as much as I ever loved anyone in all my life. More. The most. Actually.'

She heard him swallow. 'I wish you'd said that before,' he said finally. 'If you knew how miserable you've made me.'

'You didn't look miserable. All that fun and games with Jean Maythorpe.'

'Her! I tried bloody hard to like her and I couldn't. She's a potato,

467

nourishing and straightforward and useful. With no mystique. Not a grain. We bored each other rigid.'

Lisa said huffily, 'I don't believe you.'

And he said, 'You've got to. We're officially in love.'

Dawn found them with barely three miles to go. Lisa's shoes had collapsed and Toby stopped to look around for soft leaves to put inside. The light was pale, dusty pink, and lit the air before the ground. 'Wait a bit,' said Lisa. 'You can't see what you're doing.'

Toby yawned. 'Let's have a sleep. We're nearly there, we can waste an hour or so.'

She nodded. He scooped out a hollow in the sandy earth, and it was as dry as any bed. They lay down together, lying close for warmth. 'I hated sleeping next to you in Rio,' said Lisa dreamily. 'I kept thinking you'd wake up and strangle me. Wasn't that stupid?'

'Yes. I've never killed anybody.'

'But you could.'

He turned his head to look at her. 'Perhaps. I'm not so tough. Where you're concerned I'm not tough at all.'

The light was turning her hair to strands of oldest gold. 'I know that. I try to believe.'

He pulled himself up to kiss her. His head, coming down to hers, blotted out the sun, the day, everything. She found his hand and held on to it. This hand she knew, and she must learn to know each part of him, bit by bit. His tongue, filling her mouth, invading her. Half remembered fears of suffocation lurked at the edges of her mind. The kiss ended, and she opened her eyes. 'Again,' she whispered, and put her fingers into his hair to draw him down.

Gradually Toby realised she wanted him to go on. 'We can't do it here,' he whispered. 'It wouldn't work.'

'Why not?' she put her little hand into his shirt, tangling her fingers in his chest hair.

'Clothes. The ground's hard. It's almost broad bloody daylight!'

'But I want to. Honestly, Toby, I do.'

He sighed, like a man on the rack. 'Don't blame me if it's an absolute bloody disaster.' He began to pull off his jeans.

Lisa stood up and undressed slowly. There was no-one to see, and indeed nothing to see except scrub and bushes, with a light band across the horizon that might or might not be the ocean. The sky seemed to shelter them, holding them on the earth like insects under a cup. Never had she felt so tired. It was as if body and mind had lost all connection, although each functioned quite well. Her thoughts were clear as water, and yet her body, set free for once, felt soft and heavy with wanting.

468

Toby was watching her. She went to him and put her arms right round him, pressing herself against his naked skin. His penis was hard against her, and for the very first time she knew her own power, that she could do this to him. She looked up into his face and felt a surge of joy. Nothing was new, nothing was different, and yet everything was changed.

He was beyond gentleness. When they lay in the earth together they might have been animals, clinging and rolling and moaning. The dust got in her mouth, they licked grit from one another and Toby wiped his tongue on her hair. He held her hips and pushed up into her. She let out a long, low groan and opened her eyes.

They finished in sweat and saliva and sticky ropes of semen. Toby lay on his back in the earth. 'I was going to have flowers and the sea and champagne,' he murmured. 'I was going to be so clean you could operate on me.'

Lisa rolled her cheek against his huge barrel of a chest. 'It isn't supposed to be clinical. I feel very odd.'

'You're not ill, are you?'

'I don't think so. I think it's orgasmic langour. I did have an orgasm, didn't I?'

He began to laugh. 'You had it, don't ask me! I certainly did. I'm absolutely bloody knackered.'

'Poor you. Poor, poor you.' She leaned across and gently stroked his forehead.

So early in the morning the bushland air seemed thin and salty, easily warmed by the sun. They lay for a while until Toby pushed himself up. 'Time to get on. We don't want to boil on the last few miles.'

Lisa curled up, putting her hands over her eyes. 'Come back for me. I'm asleep.'

'Like hell I will! On your bike, madam, and how!'

She was stiff and lazy. She trailed after him like an old dog, getting further and further behind. Toby walked on, unable to contain his sudden, burgeoning energy. He stopped on a small rise and called out, 'Can you see it? Lisa, look, it's the sea.'

Wide, empty, sun-bleached space, edged with frothing waves. Toby's house was long and low, made of salt-stained wood that was weathering to silver. The light was so brilliant that it hurt. Lisa put up her hands and peered through her fingers. A strange place, frightening in its emptiness. Far away down the beach a black man was standing up to his ankles in water, casting a net.

'The Abos come here to fish sometimes,' said Toby. 'No-one else.'

'It's so lonely. How can you bear it here by yourself.'

He shrugged. 'I don't come very often. Odd thing, loneliness. Until I met you I didn't know I was alone.'

All at once she felt tearful, as if her heart would burst with strong emotion. If she was happy that was a small word for what she felt, on a day when the sun shone hot on a strange land and she knew herself loved. Other days would cover this, cloud it over with new and vivid memory, but she would never forget. Her life was changed, forever.

The house was large, cool, with sand drifted in at every door and window. Toby called up on the radio and arranged to have the car fixed and brought on. The Abo from the beach came by and gave them some fish, which was a mixed blessing since he came in and stayed while Lisa cooked it for breakfast, with a gas bottle that was breathing its last.

'You married?' asked the black man, grinning.

Toby said, 'No. Not officially. Not yet.'

Lisa glanced up. 'We're having the honeymoon first.'

Outside the waves hushed against the sand. The fish was soft, with marshmallow texture, and bones like fine wire. The Abo smelled of seaweed. 'Bloody good luck,' he said.

Chapter Forty-Seven

The first batch of afternoon visitors had arrived. Mara watched from upstairs as they parked and wandered towards the house, remarking on this or that. Several dozen people, she assumed motivated by vulgar curiosity, and for this they employed two pensioners from the village, one to take the money and one to do the tour.

She checked on Drew and went down. When they saw her an unnatural silence fell, but Mara was becoming used to it. People in the village who had known her all her life now watched as she walked down the street, although she didn't know what they hoped to see. Signs of heartbreak, perhaps. She was defiantly cheerful.

'Please don't mind me,' she declared, treating everyone to a brilliant smile. 'I'm joining the tour. I might learn something.'

'Certainly, Lady Mara.' The pensioner was flustered. He adjusted his tie and led off down the corridor, marching as first he had when posted to India as a captain during the war. Mara strode determinedly after him and the visitors straggled behind. It was ludicrous, she thought, dragging people around like this. What could they ever learn of The Court except a few, disjointed facts?

The pensioner began his talk, a brisk catalogue of furniture and events, entangled with garbled anecdote. Mara listened with half an ear, wondering if she could tactfully slip away. But they were reaching the tapestries, and in the gloom she could let her thoughts wander. When they were small they had all run round in here. Would Drew do that also? The tapestries might be gone by then. Alone in the great house, she and Drew would be like ghosts in a crumbling mausoleum, as much exhibits as the tapestries themselves.

The man droned in the background. 'Sewn by unknown hands, probably French. The rooms were constructed to accommodate the hangings, not the other way round.'

A man wandered off, peering up at the figures. 'What are they

471

about?' he asked of Mara, the pensioner, anyone. 'Do they mean anything?'

Mara shrugged. 'We've never known. Perhaps they're part of something larger, though it's hard to imagine what. To us – well, they're about life, really. Lust and love, happiness and laughter, grief and pain. They aren't scholarly. And people who try and analyse them lose the whole point.'

She went and stood looking up at the largest picture. It was a huge, tangled canvas, full of horses and dogs and people. Exuberance came from it, and a certain wild, pagan excess that had no place in a museum, or between the pages of a reference book. What were they doing conducting squads of people round in this way? It was like trying to force laughter back down your throat.

She walked away from the group, going quickly through halls and galleries, down passages and narrow stairs. The house seemed to whisper, the faces of her ancestors stared grimly from the walls. It was all going wrong, she thought. The Hellyns were going and nobody wanted what the house had to give. The Court's own family had turned against it, forgetting the past. Left like this, given without care to the dead hands of scholars, the house was dying.

Marcus sat looking at the window. The glass was thin, and thick bars spanned it from top to bottom. A blind drew down from the top and sometimes in the middle of the night it would come loose and roar upwards with a terrifying rattle. So he left it undrawn for the most part, although now and then one of the nurses would pull it down. They were officious, these people. When you entered one of these places you lost any vestige of free will that remained to you.

He had asked for Angus twice today. They said he had been yesterday, but Marcus couldn't remember. Perhaps he had. The days merged one into the other, except for sudden, unexpected intervals. Like today. And now he wished not to be aware, not to be conscious of the enormity of his fate. He did not need to know what place this was, that he was in it now, and forever.

But had he ever been free? In body, yes, but never in mind. Even as a child, before this, before anything, he didn't remember freedom. Rather an endless and wearying obligation, for he was the heir, and much was expected.

It should have been Angus, of course. He would have held the fort for a generation, without the imagination to do anything fundamental. When he was ten Marcus had planned to turn one of the galleries into a bowling alley one day. He laughed to himself. He should have done that, it would have been fun.

472

He felt sad, suddenly. His illness had robbed him of so much fun and nowadays people had a fit if he showed the slightest sign of amusement, assuming he was about to go bananas. Tonight he felt clear-headed, a brief, liquid interval between storms. He took a long, deep breath.

Silver moonlight was coming in at the window. The day had gone, somewhere. Night had crept up on him, and might almost be done for all he knew. So went the hours, the days, the nights, the weeks, and ultimately years and years and years. To the end. The end of time. The end of pain and hope and everything.

He went to the window, looking out into the moonlit garden. A place he had been in, he couldn't remember which, had concrete below his window, like a true prison, not this makeshift attempt at one. And how he loved to look out at the grass and the trees, on the good days. On bad days he drew the blind. And it rattled up, in the night, because of − what? The ghosts. The creatures. The beings that wanted him amongst them, wanted him out in the air, flying.

The bars were loose. He had loosened them bit by bit over weeks and no-one ever noticed. Strange how they thought madness made you stupid. You could always get some of what you wanted, even here. Tonight he would go out into the garden. He lifted the bars, one by one, and laid them carefully down on the floor. He pulled the chair across, stood on it and made himself ready. Moths rattled against the glass, as if they were calling him, raising soft and ghostly voices to call his name. He turned his head to hear them. 'Marcus! Marcus!' And he went out.

The message came in the very early morning. Perhaps they woke earlier in institutions, or perhaps the night staff did one last round before they went home to sleep. Someone had seen the window, or saw him on the ground, out there, in the thin dawn light.

To admit at once, that was the best policy they decided. Any delay had the relatives accusing you of cover-up, or worse. Please God this lot didn't take it into their heads to make a fuss. Amazing how often guilt at the missed visits, the relief of getting rid, was translated into furious accusations of murder or negligence. The brother seemed quiet, stunned. Asked if anyone else was involved. 'No sir, no-one,' they said. 'It was his illness, sir. The balance of his mind was disturbed. We never found him a difficult patient. In all his time with us he harmed no-one but himself.'

Chapter Forty-Eight

Angus drove mindlessly, covering miles to places he had no particular wish to see. After a while he came to the A1, and that wasn't a road you could tackle without proper thought. He did a U-turn on a bridge and headed back towards The Court.

He felt very odd. It was almost as if his head was disconnected from his body. His arms and legs functioned, driving the car, while in his mind a continuous film ran, of every day, every hour of Marcus's life. Of course it was never so complete, but to Angus it seemed to be. From his first breath to just last night, he had been half of something, and today he was all that was left. Marcus was gone, Marcus had ceased to matter; one of creation's little mistakes.

Despair threatened to overwhelm him. No-one could understand what it was to lose his twin, who had been lost to him for so long anyway. He wasn't even sorry, not in any ordinary sense, because Marcus was gone and was out of it. But the sorrow for what might have been, that was there; the clever, kind, imaginative boy who had begun so well and finished so tragically.

What was to happen now? Angus changed down a gear and sent the car hurtling round a bend. A woman with a pram retreated hastily back on to the pavement, but he barely noticed her. Just as he was getting his life together, getting free of The Court, free of everyone's expectations, he was shackled again. The Earl. Borne down by the weight of all those that had gone before, many of them just as reluctant, just as ill-suited as he was. He felt like the ham-fisted son of cobblers, forced to make dreadful shoes because that was his heritage, and no doubt siring children who couldn't make shoes either.

Thank goodness his children would have Jean as a mother. It must surely give them a head-start in the capability stakes. He felt soothed and momentarily lifted his foot from the accelerator.

474

The village had a speed limit sign embedded in the hedge. Angus slowed automatically, and then as his thoughts raced so did the car. The road was empty, it was early evening and not yet harvest. The tractors and trailers were parked up in fields and farmyards, not chugging noisily through the village. He saw no-one as he passed, except the pub dog, taking the evening air in refuge from crisps and beer. Coming out of the houses Angus took the bend in a wide swing, wider than he intended. The boy on the horse hardly had time to yell.

Angus stamped on the brake, skidded and careered across on to the grass. He turned off the engine and scrabbled for the door, seeming to take years to find the handle. But when at last he got out the horse was still struggling back to his feet. He was big, coarse, huge splashes of black looking like paint on his dirty white coat. He stood blowing down his nose, stamping his great feet and trembling.

'You done for me hoss, mister! You done for me hoss!'

One of the gypsy kids. If he tried Angus thought he might recognise him. 'Are you all right? I didn't see you at all.'

'You wouldna, going that fast.' The boy glowered at him. He had a bloody head where the gravel had raked him, and his jeans were torn. But they were probably torn anyway.

'The horse looks all right,' said Angus, catching hold of the string that served as a head collar.

'You done fer him. Won't win no trotting now. Worth a thousand pund that hoss were.'

'You little —' Angus stared in amazement at this miniature Fagin. He couldn't be more than ten. 'Get off with you,' he said weakly. 'I'll send a hamper round to the camp. A thousand pounds indeed.'

'Could've been more,' said the boy, and grinned.

Angus tossed him back on to the horse and watched them rattle off on their way. The gypsies amazed him. The boy had escaped death by inches and yet he was still out for what he could get. You had to admire the resilience they showed. They might be a thorn in the flesh, but at least they hung on, fighting a lost cause to the last barricade. Something had to be done for them.

He drove very slowly to The Court. To his surprise Reg's big Mercedes was parked outside and when he went in he found Jean there as well, having tea with Mara.

'We came as soon as we heard,' said Reg, embarrassedly wiping cake crumbs from his mouth. He knew he ought not to have stopped, not on a visit of condolence, but he couldn't resist. 'Tragedy about the earl. You'll feel it, try as you will to say it's for the best. Change your life, this will. Lot of responsibility coming your way.'

Angus passed a hand across his face. 'It was kind of you to come.'

475

Mara poured him a cup of tea, saying, 'I tried to get in touch with Lisa, but nobody seems to know where she is. Toby's office is trying to reach him, they've gone on some sort of walkabout in the bush.'

'There's got to be an inquest, the funeral won't be for a while,' said Angus distractedly. 'She can probably get home.'

Jean said, 'Sit down, Angus, do. It does no good exhausting yourself.'

But he took no notice. He walked around the room, and stopped at the French windows to look out across the lake. A flock of waterfowl were pecking at one of the mouldering lumps of weed, a relic of the ponding, dried iron-hard.

He turned to stare at the people in the room. 'I want to tell you what I've been thinking,' he said clearly. 'I don't want to live at The Court. I've got no wish to spend my life worrying about the wet rot and the dry rot, the gutters and the drains. I don't give a damn about visitors, whether they come or not. I'll not spend my life taking care of people looking for somewhere to go on a wet afternoon. It isn't important. The house isn't important.'

'I don't see that it matters what you think,' said Mara disinterestedly. 'You've got the job, like it or not.'

'Can't shirk that sort of responsibility,' said Reg, shifting in his chair.

'It's about time I lived my life for myself,' said Angus. 'Not for anyone else, except perhaps Jean, and I know she'll back me. I'll take my seat in the Lords, of course, as soon as possible. And we'll get on with the gypsy project, and see if we can't do something about homelessness, and the price of houses, and work in a rural community.'

'Oh, God!' said Mara. 'You're going to suggest we turn The Court into flats for the gypsies, I can see it coming.'

'Don't be facetious, Mara,' said Jean breathlessly. 'The Court can stew in its own juice as far as we're concerned.'

Reg spluttered: 'I never heard such a load of sentimental clap-trap in my life! This place is the earl's responsibility. Like it or not, my lad, you should shoulder the load. And I'm shocked at you, Jean, for encouraging him.'

'Sorry it upsets you, Reg,' said Angus mildly. 'But The Court is finished as far as the Hellyns are concerned. We can't afford to live in it, and that's that.'

'Well — if it's money —' began Reg, but Angus waved him silent.

'Save your breath, Reg. This place eats money. If the nation wants it, the nation can have it. If not, we put up the shutters and go.'

Mara's eyes blazed in a chalk-white face. 'I won't let you,' she said throatily.

'There isn't anyone can do a single thing to stop me.'

'And what about Drew? And your children, and their children, and all the Hellyns from now till the end of time? They won't have anything, not a single thing to be proud of. Not a great family any more, just a collection of faces, with a title tossed here and there, not meaning anything.'

'The house isn't important,' said Angus. 'The people matter more.'

'But the people go, they die and get forgotten. The house is always here. It's a monument — to us, to the centuries, to a thousand years of history. If it isn't important, then I don't know what is. It's like great books or great music, great anything! We're remembered by what we leave behind.'

'I'm sorry, Mara.'

Tears threatened, and she got up and ran out into the hall. Curtiss was ushering two callers into the library, his customary hiding place for visitors to whom the family might not be at home.

'Excuse me,' muttered Mara, turning away.

'Mara! Mara dear, it's me.'

Clare. And next to her, his grizzled moustache bristling, Samuel.

Mara swallowed, stretched her mouth in a smile and put out both her hands. 'Clare. Dear Clare. How did you hear so quickly?'

'Hear what?'

'Marcus is dead.'

She felt Clare's hand tense through her fine leather gloves. Her feathered hat bobbed. 'Samuel — ?' she looked at him imploringly.

'I'm sorry we had to come at such a time,' he said stiffly. 'We didn't know. We had to come and talk to you, Lady Mara.'

Mara let go of Clare and put her hands behind her back, like a naughty schoolgirl. 'I don't want to talk to you, Samuel,' she said. 'Clare's always welcome, but if you're going to yell at me I'd much rather you got back in your car and went home.'

'I only wish that were possible.'

They glared at each other.

It was clear that they meant to stay. In retaliation, Mara invoked all the power and grandeur of the house. She installed them in a room fitted out in red and gold, like the stateroom of some Chinese potentate. When they came down neither Mara nor Angus was anywhere to be seen, and they did not appear until dinner. Both the earl and his sister were in full evening dress. Samuel, in a lounge suit, had to go up and change.

'What is this about Clare?' Mara leaned one elbow on the fireplace, gorgeous in blue crêpe de chine.

477

Refusing to be upstaged despite her short dress, Clare said, 'You know I'm not supposed to tell you.' She lifted her eyebrows skywards, indicating Samuel.

'Well, you'd better. I don't want to be roused to violence at our own dinner table.'

'God forbid!' said Angus.

Clare said, 'Oh, it isn't that dreadful. It seems that Ferdinand of Havenheim would like you and Drew safely out of the country. He's suggested America. If he doesn't get his own way he's going to be a mule about Nato exercises, and you can imagine how that is ruffling the feathers in Whitehall.'

'It's that damned woman's idea!' flared Mara.

'Darling, without a doubt. But why not? A fresh start. You've never been, you'll love it.'

Angus said, 'I think it's a very good idea. You don't want to be here while the house is being fought over. Go on, Mara. For Drew's sake, get him out of here and into somewhere fresh.'

Mara laughed, shrilly. 'Did I tell you, Clare, that he means to shut up The Court? He's going to try and hand it over to the historic buildings people, and if they won't bite he's going to close it down. He'll flog the tapestries and we'll live in seamless luxury.'

'Good God,' said Clare.

'I haven't said a word about the tapestries,' said Angus. 'You don't have to paint the worst case, you know.'

'There isn't a better one. There just isn't.' She chewed the nail on her long, pale forefinger.

Samuel came back into the room and Clare got up with a bright smile. 'Dear Samuel, how much better you look. Are we to have fifteen courses at dinner, Mara? Everything's so wonderfully grand.'

'The cook's left, so the food's gone off,' said Mara disinterestedly. She no longer felt the urge to flatten Samuel with Hellyn pomp, not when her world was falling in pieces about her. She no longer even felt the need to pretend. She turned to Samuel. 'Why didn't Jay stand up for me? He knows I won't want to be shoved off to foreign parts.'

Samuel sipped at his sherry, casting a sideways look at Clare. She widened her eyes expressively.

He said, 'I don't think he dared say a word, my dear. I'll be honest with you. The princess has been very depressed, very unsettled. If the prince is out of sight for any length of time she's sure he's with you. It was felt best that temptation should be removed, visibly removed. You should be flattered. Clearly Princess Anna is none too sure that she has won.'

'She's won all right,' said Mara, in a strained, high voice. 'I

478

wouldn't have him back if you paid me. You can tell her that. You can tell *him* that. And if anyone should be packed off somewhere, it's them. They can bugger off back to Havenheim and leave me alone!'

'Bravo!' said Clare.

Mara gave a shaky laugh. 'But I thought you wanted me to go!'

Clare said, 'I think you should make a fresh start, yes, but not on their say-so. If they're so worried about their silly little kingdom they should go away and live in it, and not bother us with their politics.'

'My dear, you are inveterately naive,' said Samuel, with a smile.

They went through to dinner. Seated at the vast table, Angus at its head, Mara at the foot and their guests spaced out in the centre, the whole event should have been ridiculous. But somehow The Court was never that. The house lent dignity, and grace, and a sense of times long past to what was after all an odd occasion.

'You must have very mixed feelings,' said Samuel to Angus. 'Now that you're the earl.'

'Less now than ever,' said Angus. 'At least now I can do what I want with the house. We can move on. Ever since Father died the family's been lost in confusion.'

'At least we had the house,' said Mara. 'It held us together, you know. I think it cares about us.'

'Don't be so damned sentimental!'

Mara reached out to help herself from the dish Curtiss held suspended by her shoulder. 'You're just insensitive. Marcus had too much sensitivity and you haven't any at all. Your problem is you don't want to live on Jean Maythorpe's money, you want to sell the tapestries. And you justify that with a façade of new thought, when all you want is to be footloose and fancy-free. Thank you, Curtiss.' She replaced the spoons.

'If you sell the tapestries, there'll be a national outcry,' said Samuel.

'If the nation wants them they can damned well buy them!' snapped Angus. 'It isn't my responsibility! Good God, generations of Hellyns have wasted their lives here and I won't add my name to the list. I won't ask my children to do it.'

'I think they should have the option,' said Mara. 'You shouldn't be allowed to decide something so important.'

'Your children might not thank you for it,' added Clare. 'What a pity if The Court's long gone.'

Angus pushed back his chair and stood up. 'At least we could start something new. Frankly, I've had enough. You can't preach at me, Mara, don't you remember how it was? When you wanted us to sell the spoons so you could go to London? I don't give a damn about the

479

house, you can do what you damn well like with it, but the tapestries are up for sale. It's time someone in this family had the sense to cut free and get out!'

He stormed to the door and Mara leaped up to stop him, eyes brilliant in a ghastly face. 'Angus. Angus, you can't!'

'I can and I will!' He shook her off and flung open the door. She half fell, clutching at the handle, but he never glanced back.

She pulled herself slowly upright.

'I do believe he means it,' said Samuel.

'Yes. So do I.' Mara tried to laugh.

Clare said, 'But he can't. The tapestries are priceless. I never thought Angus would consider doing such a thing.'

'He mustn't,' said Mara dazedly. 'They belong here. They're part of the house.'

'They could always go to a museum,' remarked Samuel. 'The Victoria and Albert, perhaps.'

Mara's head came up. 'Take them away? Put them in some sterile room in London?' She picked up her wineglass and drained it to the last, heady drop. 'Over my dead body.'

Chapter Forty-Nine

Clare and Samuel stayed on, unhappy witnesses to the conflict that raged night and day. Angus was adamant, the tapestries were to be sold.

'Do you want me living off my wife's money all my life?' he demanded, waylaid on his way out to see Jean. 'I've heard enough about heritage and duty, and I'm damned if I'll inflict the same ghastly problems on the next generation. We're not just links in a chain, we're people, we've a right to be happy.'

'You'll have more than enough money,' snarled Mara. 'And you want to destroy something precious just so you can have a few shekels lying in the bank labeled "his" instead of "hers". It's despicable.'

Angus looked at her bleakly. 'You say that so easily, knowing full well that you and Drew won't starve. I've asked a valuer to call, an expert. He's coming tomorrow.'

That night she went to look at the tapestries. She stood shining a torch up at them, watching the colours come and go in the thin beam. Did they matter? Did anything matter? Was she wasting her time in needless fighting because it put off the moment when she must decide what she would do with her life?

A draught came from somewhere and stirred the hair on her neck, like someone breathing. She turned quickly. The house was full of ghosts, people said. It was easy to believe, here alone, in the dark, with the faces of long-dead people looking down at her from the walls. She rubbed her arms quickly, and made for the door. If you lived too long at The Court, in no time at all people said you were eccentric, and a few years on they called you batty instead. She should go away and forget about the house, the tapestries, everything. As Samuel said, she should go to America.

But, as she was about to go out, she turned and shone the torch again. The faces laughed at her, they cried, they leered and let out

481

great ugly yawns. The Court without its tapestries would be dead, dull, just another house that once had been great and was no more. It was unthinkable.

Because Clare and Samuel were downstairs she went to her bedroom to use the telephone. Before she dialled she glanced into Drew's cradle, and saw that he was sleeping with his arms flung out and his hands like starfish against the quilt. She trailed her finger across one palm and the hand momentarily closed up, then opened again, slowly. Love swelled her heart into a weight within her chest, as if all her emotion was centred on this one, small boy. She shook herself. It was pathetic to be so doting; pathetic and wrong. If it did children no good at all to be unloved, it did them just as much harm to be stifled by an excess of it.

She opened Lisa's office telephone book, appropriated since she left, and ran her finger down the entries, looking for an official number. At this time of night she had no expectation of reaching anyone. Her best hope was an answering machine, so she could go to bed secure in the knowledge that at least she had begun to resist Angus. There might be rules and regulations governing the sale of things like tapestries, the historic buildings people might be willing to purchase them if the alternative was to see them go. She lounged on the bed waiting for the click and whirr of machinery, and was taken aback when a voice said, 'Yes? Chandler here.'

'Good heavens,' said Mara. 'Are you asleep under your desk?'

'This happens to be my home,' said the Professor crisply. 'And I never go to bed before midnight.'

'What a terrible habit. Still, I suppose it's all that scholarly research you have to do. Best undertaken by lamplight I suppose. Do you know anything about textiles, by the way?'

'No, it isn't my field. Who are you, by the way?'

'Don't sound so suspicious! I'm not going to offend you by talking about men's underpants, or jockstraps or something. Unless you want to, of course.'

'Definitely not my field, I'm afraid. Look, I'm taking this in the hall and if you're going to get obscene I'd like to be comfortable. We scholars don't get much light relief.'

'Sorry to disappoint you,' said Mara. 'My name's Hellyn. Mara Hellyn. My sister has you down as the man I should talk to about the house. And as my brother's selling the tapestries, I thought − '

'He's WHAT?'

'I see that I've shocked you at last.'

'I should think you have. Has he a buyer? How much does he want?'

482

'The valuer's coming tomorrow. And I thought you should know because — '

'Thank God you told me. I'll be there first thing.'

The 'phone went dead. Mara looked at it and laughed.

The Professor's stylish if somewhat battered car rolled up at half-past eight the next day. Mara was breakfasting with Samuel while Clare set about her leisurely and complicated toilette. Curtiss showed the Professor into the breakfast room.

'How do you do?' said Mara, rising from the table with outstretched hand. 'I'm Mara Hellyn.'

He tossed back his forelock and shook her hand. 'Yes. I recognise you from the photographs.'

She grimaced, and Samuel, wiping crumbs from his moustache, said, 'That is water under the bridge. I'll thank you to remember it.'

The Professor paused in the act of pulling a notebook from the baggy pocket of his jacket. 'I don't think we can rewrite history, whatever the situation,' he remarked. 'And Lady Mara can hardly expect the world not to notice her. She's a very noticeable woman.'

'I'm going to start wearing a wig,' said Mara easily. 'Now, sit down and have some coffee. Angus is bringing his valuer this morning, and I'm hoping against hope that there's some law we can invoke to stop him selling the tapestries. Or at least stop them leaving the house. I don't care who owns them as long as they stay here.'

'I won't have coffee, thanks. I'll see the tapestries.'

'Will you indeed?' Samuel bridled. 'I doubt you have the right to come in here and do as you like. This is Lady Mara's home, not some sort of museum. You scholars forget yourselves. Think you can call the tune.'

'Oh, do be quiet, Samuel,' said Mara, putting her fingers to her forehead. 'What with Angus and you, and Drew awake at half-past five this morning, I don't care what he does so long as he does something. Anything. Come on Professor, do.'

She led the way along the corridors. 'I do know my way around,' he said crisply. 'Your sister was good enough to give me a very free hand.'

'Was she indeed?' Mara glanced sideways at him. 'You're much younger than I expected. Are you senior enough to be able to do anything about this, do you think?'

'I'm Head of the Commission. But I don't think God himself could stop your brother selling the tapestries if that's what he wants. We can stop him exporting them, of course. Or at least, some of them. Other than that, we'd have to launch an appeal.'

483

'Then launch one,' retorted Mara.

He looked at her quizzically, his hair falling into his eyes. But he said nothing.

When they stood in the shaded gallery, looking up at the walls, he said: 'You're amazingly autocratic. For the present day.'

Mara was silent. After a moment she said, 'I suppose I should apologise. You know, I ought to be a Catholic. Then I could go to confession and repent with incessant regularity. Nobody's said a good word about me in weeks.'

'I didn't say I minded that you were autocratic.'

'Isn't it a vice?'

'I don't think a woman like you can have vices. Only misjudgements and misdemeanours.'

She stepped back a little and looked at him. 'Lisa never said you were like this,' she murmured.

'I return the compliment. Now, let's look at these tapestries. As you know, it's –'

' – not your field,' supplied Mara.

' – but I've done some research since first I saw them. Three million should secure them, I think.'

'Will you write me a cheque?' enquired Mara. 'Or should we take cash.'

The Professor looked at her. 'We don't have that sort of money. And with so short a timescale I think you're probably going to have to let them go.'

Mara stared at him in furious disbelief. Why had he come if only to tell her that? All at once she turned on her heel, stormed to the window and threw back the shutters. 'We might as well have a proper look at them,' she declared. 'Who cares if the sun fades them now? They'll never be the same away from the house. No-one's ever going to build a room like this again. Is that why you came, to get a last look at something no-one else is ever going to see, Professor Chandler?'

The sun glinted on her golden hair. Beyond, on the hills, curlews were calling. 'They ought not to be kept in the dark,' said the Professor. 'Perhaps we could cover them individually, show them one by one. This room's magnificent in the sunlight.

'Oh, if we're talking about showing the house off properly, we haven't begun,' said Mara. 'We should have cooking in the kitchens and a man making armour and Elizabethan ladies sewing samplers in the hall. But we needn't worry about the tapestries, Professor. They're going to be gone.'

'Call me Hugo,' said the Professor.

Mara snorted.

484

She watched as he walked round the room, touching this and that hanging, wrestling with a window catch that had rusted solid. He was playing with her, she realised. Teasing for his own dubious ends.

'Where do you come from?' she asked suddenly.

He stopped and looked at her. 'Wales, originally. My father was a miner. But I went to Oxford.'

'Oh, the double first shines out all over you,' said Mara. 'So much arrogance.'

'Possibly.'

'Look,' she said. 'I always take my little boy for a walk in his pram around this time. I'll talk to you later.

He glanced across at her. 'No, no. I'll come. We can talk.'

Samuel was in the drawing room, telephoning, when they came down. As they passed the open door they heard him say, 'She's adamant. No budging her. One of the new breed of stubborn women, I'm afraid, listens to nothing and nobody.'

Mara made a face. 'You see,' she said, shifting Drew from one shoulder to the other. 'Unless I do as I'm told, everyone's furious.'

'Why don't you then?'

'Because everyone tells me different things! And besides, I'm extremely bad at doing what I should.' Briefly, she sparkled up at him, and then went quickly to the dog room where the old, high pram stood waiting for their outing.

They walked along the weedy gravel paths, letting the baby clap his hands at leaves and sparrows on the grass. 'We need time for an appeal,' said Hugo. 'Will your brother wait?'

She shrugged. 'I don't know. Possibly. But no-one would spend all that much money on us without wanting something back, would they?'

He glanced down at her. 'You said it earlier. We'd have to expand the concept, make the house work, staff it, act out history. Day trips for schoolchildren and so on. You'd have to accept a very different life here.'

She took in her breath, and almost choked on a sob. 'I'm sorry,' she said quickly, fishing for a handkerchief she couldn't find. 'I don't mean to be so stupid. It's just − life's been rather trying recently. I've been feeling somewhat beleaguered, but it's all my own fault.'

'Why do you say that?' He gave her his own, crumpled handkerchief.

'Well, if you live a wild life and have affairs and get pregnant, you can't say anyone made you do it, can you? You can't complain when people shut you out. That's what Angus is doing of course. Getting his own back. I didn't listen. I didn't take any notice when I made

485

things hard for him, and now he doesn't care if he makes things hard for me. My own fault. And Samuel's always hated me right from the first. Mind, I don't like him, he's a pompous twit.'

The man beside her turned to look down into her face. 'What do you want to happen? What do you want to do?'

Mara sighed. 'Oh, I don't know. Angus thinks I only care about The Court because I want to live here as we always did, but it's more than that. I want it to be there for the future. For always. Not just for Hellyns, and not just for anyone, but for people who can love and understand a house like this. To me, it's special.'

She held out the handkerchief, but instead of taking it he touched her hair. 'You should never go from this house,' he said. 'It suits you so well.'

'Will you keep me like the furniture, well dusted?' She made a face. 'I've got to go. Whatever happens, there's no place for me.'

'Were you always this sad?'

She stopped in the act of pushing the heavy pram. 'Good heavens, no. And if I'm sad I deserve to be. People have to take turns at being happy, and I kept my turn much too long. So now I have to sit out. It's not very easy when you're not used to it.'

They walked on round the front of the house. The lake was ruffled by a breeze, with little wavelets springing up on the surface. A car was drawing up. 'The valuer,' said Hugo. 'From Sotheby's. I recognise the car.'

'The vultures gather,' said Mara. 'I think we'd better try the appeal don't you? And put a funfair out here and an icecream parlour in the stables.'

'I was thinking more of jousting and an armoury. It doesn't have to be a public appeal, you know. You could organise one yourself. Surely a couple of million would pay your brother out. You could run the place, just as you wished. And live here, of course.'

'Is this entirely your field?' asked Mara quizzically. 'Reorganising smashed lives, so to speak?'

He reached out to put two fingers in the hollow of her throat. A pulse was beating there, quite rapidly.

Samuel, watching from the window, exploded. 'Clare! Clare, will you look at that! She's got the man pawing her already, he's only been here an hour!'

Clare barely looked up from the letter she was writing. 'Mara's liaisons are beyond me, Samuel darling. No doubt she's trying to persuade him to give her some money.'

'Not again! Good God, does the girl never learn.'

Mara invited Hugo Chandler for lunch, only to find that Angus had invited the Sotheby's man as well. They drank sherry while making polite conversation, until Hugo suddenly said, 'What will you settle for Lord Melville? Have you decided?'

Angus flushed. 'I don't think it's anyone's business but mine, actually. I've decided to sell and that's that.'

'But your sister might be interested in buying, you see,' went on Chandler. 'We must have a figure at which we could settle.'

'You're getting very proprietorial, sir,' snapped Samuel.

Hugo grinned, lightening his rather intense face. 'Lady Mara and I find ourselves on the same side, I feel. She has my full support in anything she does to prevent the tapestries leaving The Court.'

'That is kind,' said Angus nastily. 'I warn you, Mara's path is littered with broken hearts.'

The man from Sotheby's cleared his throat nervously. 'Wonderful tapestries,' he murmured. 'Quite exceptional. Such a pity to see them leave the house – '

'I asked you here to value them, not to preach,' said Angus coldly. 'What did you say? Three, perhaps four, million?'

'To the right purchaser.'

'You will of course take a reduced price if they stay in the house,' said Hugo.

Angus spluttered. 'There's no of course about it! I've had enough of this pussyfooting around. The tapestries are going and the future earls of Hellyn will live in a house built with the proceeds. As to this barrack, Mara can deal with it. For once in her life she can shoulder some responsibility.'

'Not an ideal custodian, I fear,' said Samuel, signalling to Curtiss for more sherry.

'On the contrary.' Hugo wandered to the fireplace and studied the carved pilasters. 'She's just what this house needs. Lady Mara is all beauty and all passion. The Court will be magnificent.'

They stared at him in stunned silence. Finally Clare said, 'Do you know this gentleman well, Mara?'

'Not at all,' she said. 'But it is so lovely to hear someone say nice things instead of reviling me for misbehaviour.'

'Of course you're reviled,' declared Chandler. 'You're out of your time! In a dull grey world you're colour and light. God forbid that you start living like all the rest. It would be a tragedy.'

Curtiss announced luncheon. As they walked through, Samuel muttered to Clare, 'What sort of people are they taking on nowadays? The man's obviously some sort of left-winger.'

'I don't think historians are politically aligned,' said Clare, furrowing her brow. 'I think he's merely making critical observations.'

'As far as that girl is concerned, they're not nearly critical enough!'

Over the soup, Mara said, 'Angus, I'm going to try to raise the money. Hugo thinks we could start a private appeal, with functions and perhaps membership of a Tapestry Trust. We'd get some government funding apparently, and we could hold a ball, and open the park. All you've got to do is agree not to sell on the open market.'

'What a brilliant idea,' said the Sotheby's man, unwisely. Angus withered him with a look.

'I take it you mean to cast me as the wicked earl?' he said thinly. 'I warn you Mara, I won't have you profiting at my expense. I can see that this is a good chance for you to rehabilitate yourself, getting your picture in the paper as saviour of the family heritage, but I'll not be the villain to your damsel in distress.'

'Hear, hear,' said Samuel.

'We'll say it's family necessity,' soothed Mara. 'And it is. We can't go on in penury so the money must be raised. It just so happens you're the only one that needs it right now.'

'Oh, for God's sake!' said Angus, tearing his bread roll viciously apart. 'All right, Mara! Two million, not a penny less.'

'She turned to Hugo. 'Can I get two million? Is that possible do you think?'

'My dear girl, it's nothing. You'll raise it in an instant. An Arab's pocket money.'

'How true. Angus, it's a deal.'

Samuel waved testily at Curtiss for a glass of wine, pulling the napkin from his collar. 'Is there any hope that you'll do any of this money-grubbing in America?' he demanded.

'More than likely,' said Hugo.

'If I do, it will be at my convenience, not yours,' said Mara coldly. Her long fingers, playing with the bread, scattered crumbs across the cloth. 'In any case, I shouldn't go anywhere until after the ball.'·

Long streamers had been let down from the beams of the Great Hall, and entwined in each were flowers. The garlands moved in the warm breeze of a September evening, sweet and fragrant. Mara stood with Hugo Chandler, listening to the distant chink of glasses being set out, the rattle of a thousand ice cubes into buckets.

'Do you like it?' she asked. 'My sister Lisa sent a plan. She was going to come, but she's pregnant and can't travel.'

'Your brother's coming though?' Hugo glanced down at her and Mara noticed his bowtie was crooked. Automatically she reached up to straighten it.

'He's going to make a speech. Do you know, Hugo, the last time we

488

had a ball here was the night my father died. And afterwards, everything changed.'

'Except you.'

She laughed and walked out into the garden, knowing he would follow. Her dress, of dark, burgundy satin, trailed across the grass. When she reached the trees, in the gathering dusk, she turned and looked back at the house.

Light blazed in every room, spilling out like liquid gold into the night. Above and beyond the yellow pools the bulk of the house loomed huge and black, daunting in its magnificence. 'I did change that night,' said Mara slowly. 'I began to change. I used not to care about anything except my father, and when he was gone I had to learn to care for – other things. Other people. Why have you never married, Hugo?'

'Waving his hand in mock grandeur, he said I was never prepared to sacrifice my independence for the minor convenience of regular sexual congress.' He stood behind her and put his arms around her waist, his hands flat against her belly. 'Obviously it was a wise decision. Neither of us has to apologise to anyone for our lusts.'

Mara leaned back against him. 'Honestly, Hugo, if you want me to sleep with you don't you think you'd better declare something a little less animal than lust?' The satin of her dress bunched in his hand as he pressed between her legs. His breath was hot on the bare skin of her shoulder.

'You won't catch me in your web,' he murmured. 'Your lovers never get away unscathed.' He half turned her, burying his face in the dark fold of her cleavage. Mara let out a low, throaty moan.

Cars were arriving, their headlights arcing into the sky. 'Someone will see,' said Mara, but Hugo pushed her against a tree. The bark bit into her shoulders, the whalebone of her dress dug into her breasts as he dragged them out. When he touched her nipple she experienced a sensation so sharp that she cried out, hanging her head back, mouth open with need.

She held up her dress so he could take off her underclothes. Her skirt crushed between them, she stood with her arms full of satin as he pushed into her. Every stroke was firm, decisive. When she opened her eyes she saw him staring down at her, holding on to the tree to steady himself. For weeks she had known they would come to this, but now she felt bewildered. She didn't know this man, and she did not understand him. Yet all at once she knew, without a doubt, that she was about to become pregnant.

Her pleasure turned cold. She had the feeling that she was hanging on to the spokes of a wheel, watching it grind inexorably on. Before she could think, the face above her convulsed in a rictus of satisfaction.

489

'What's the matter?' he asked, for she still stood there, her skirt held up.

'It's nothing – nothing.' She glanced quickly up at him. He was looking away, as if he had embarrassed himself.

'What would you do if I was pregnant?' she asked slowly. 'If you had made me pregnant?'

He paused for a second. Then he said, 'I feel the weight of ages on my shoulders. That question has been asked so often in these circumstances. One can imagine a cavewoman, or a queen's handmaiden, or even the queen herself. If, taking your pleasure, you have got me with child, what will you do? Let me see to your hair, it's full of twigs.' He reached up and shook her golden mane, in a controlled gesture of affection.

'I think you have. I think you did.'

'What?'

She turned away and straightened her skirt, brushing at the creases.

She began to walk quickly back to the house, and then to run, all the time aware of the seeds of panic, verging on hysteria. Angus caught her as she fell through the open French windows into the ballroom.

'Mara! People are arriving. What on earth have you been doing?'

'I went for a walk. I saw the cars, I had to run back. Angus, I'm so frightened. Is it going to be all right, do you think?'

'You! Frightened? There was never anyone braver than you.' Angus reached out and took a leaf from her hair. He was awkward suddenly. In all the last months he and Mara had let coolness develop into ice. Angus had abandoned the house absolutely, and with it his sister, as if one moment's weakness would have him back there, trapped again. Tonight, when she looked so ruffled and upset, his heart went out to her. Dear Mara. No-one was ever quite proof against her charm.

"I'm glad I came" he said gruffly.

Mara smiled at him. "So am I. But I knew you would in the end. You're too nice to leave anyone in the lurch, even me."

"Especially you." he struck his fist to his chest like a ham actor and they both laughed.

Angus said "Actually there was an announcement I wanted to make tonight."

"Your engagement" said Mara. She tapped his arm. "About time. Reg has been quite mournful, he was beginning to lose hope."

"Well, we had to sort ourselves out. A house, that sort of thing. But there was something else. Mara, 'I'm changing my Will. When I die the house will pass to you, and your descendants. The Earl won't have any claim at all."

490

She put her hand up to her mouth. "That isn't right. Angus, you know it isn't."

"But it's fair. If you save The Court it should be yours. Yours absolutely."

Shaking her head, Mara said "Angus no! Please don't! I'd love it for Drew, of course I would, but your sons should at least have the chance. I know you mean to be kind Angus, but I wish you wouldn't tempt me like this. Don't say anything tonight. Please."

"I've been thinking about it for ages, Mara. Jean's agreed."

"And I don't agree. You'll be grateful to me one day, when you've got a basketful of boys." She looked up at the great beams, draped once again with banners. "I love the old place, for itself and nothing more. I don't have to own it to want it to live."

Guests were drifting towards them, and brother and sister instinctively turned to do their duty, trained to it from birth. Angus reached out and squeezed Mara's hand and when she glanced at him, briefly, he saw her eyes brimming with tears.

At midnight she thought about Henry. All night she had danced and talked, smiled and danced again, and now, tired, she stood in the shadows and thought of her father. A man with his faults, she knew that now. She had seen her father through a child's eyes, and now she must look at him differently. But nothing could diminish her love for him. He was not the giant she had thought him but a man, with human frailty, whom she had loved. As she had loved Jay. It was past, that love. Past, gone — and never forgotten.

Hugo was coming towards her through the crowd. She waited, calmly, until he came up to her. "I wanted to talk to you" he said. "I meant to before."

"Did you? Look, if you really would rather avoid me, then do so. I won't get upset about it."

"I can't imagine ever wanting to avoid you. In fact, you rather fascinate me."

"Like a fine piece of china. Or is that not your field?"

"I've got some expertise in that direction." He stood, looking down at her, his eyes dark and intense. She thought, perhaps he did see her as nothing more than an object. A beautiful, admired artefact.

He said "I gather you had a premonition tonight."

Mara felt herself colour. "Something of the sort, yes. But I don't mean to entrap you. I'm more than capable of coping with these things on my own."

"What a bleak and unattractive prospect." He tossed his hair back untidily. He was always rather untidy, thought Mara. "You'd be

491

marrying beneath you, of course" he remarked. "In every sense except the intellectual."

For a moment she didn't understand him. Then she stepped back, saying haughtily "Please don't feel obliged to offer! The sacrifice would be quite dreadful. But I suppose you regard it as some sort of duty, bringing brains into the played-out bloodlines of the English aristocracy."

He grinned at her, with unnecessary confidence. "That's one way of looking at it I suppose. Genetics – "

" – isn't really my field" finished Mara.

The night felt unreal, and faintly shocking. She had forgotten about sex, the way it lured and intrigued. Engage the senses, and all too soon you must engage her heart, if not in love then in hate, and pain and bewilderment. Once again she had stepped into danger, blinded by her own need. Now she could almost wish herself back, with the act undone. But she wasn't a woman to live her life alone.

She leaned against the pillar, glancing up at him under her lashes. He excited her. A tall, spare man who might or might not love her; that she might, one day, know well enough to love. He might be good for her, both in bed and out. He might be good for Drew.

Life always surprised her, she thought suddenly, twisting and turning round bends and corners to bring her back on herself. And if she turned away now, what was she to do? The future had once seemed like a land of plenty, and she stepped into it with courage high. But lately she stood in a place of mists and shadows, where nothing was quite dependable, where only The Court stayed the same. She leaned her cheek against the marble of the pillar, letting the spirit of the house fill her with strength and constancy. Perhaps it was time to pick up her courage and go forth once again. Perhaps it was time to take another chance. Mara put her fingers to her lips and considered.